SUDDENLY LUCIUS
HAD SEIZED HER AND HELD HER...

"It was never my brother who made your pulse quicken, who appeared in your secret dreams. I am the one, my darling, *I* am the one—"

"Lucius! What are you saying?"

"I am saying what we've both known in our hearts every long miserable day and lonely night since the first time we saw each other. Since the day you came to our wagon so proper and ladylike with your pencil and ledgerbook—"

"Lucius, stop it!" She struggled to free herself, but he held her helpless. He pulled her closer, seeking her lips.

She turned her face away from him. "Let me go, Lucius!"

"I will never do that.... Even if it were certain death to do so, I would love you..."

JOURNEY TO QUIET WATERS

By William Lavender
from Jove

CHINABERRY
CHILDREN OF THE RIVER

WILLIAM LAVENDER

JOURNEY TO QUIET WATERS

VOLUME TWO OF
THE HARGRAVE JOURNAL

A JOVE BOOK

First Jove edition published June 1980

10   9   8   7   6   5   4   3   2

Printed in the United States of America

Jove books are published by Jove Publications, Inc.,
200 Madison Avenue, New York, NY 10016

Prologue

WHEN LUCIUS HARGRAVE was three months old his father held him aloft before an assembled multitude and said: "Thy name shall be Lucius, Bringer of Light, for thou hast brought light into our darkling world." It was unfortunate that the infant could not appreciate the tenderness of the moment, for it would never be equalled.

The circumstances of Lucius Hargrave's origins are these:

He was born on the last day of March 1816, in a tiny village called South Bar, on the Indiana shore of the Ohio River. He was the son of Oliver Hargrave, a self-styled itinerant preacher, and a buxom pink-cheeked girl named Sarah Gilpin who did not become Mrs. Hargrave until the day her baby's father saw him for the first time and gave him his name.

The Reverend Hargrave was thirty years old and a widower when he came to South Bar in 1815, bringing with him his six-year-old son Isaac from his first marriage. When he fled in the night two years later he left behind a grief-crazed young wife, his sons Isaac and Lucius, and three other lives in ruins, among them that of his second child by Sarah, a daughter yet unborn. The child Martha, whose fragile brain was damaged beyond hope in an accident during the nightmare hours of her father's fleeing, was born with the next rising of the sun, and existed for seven years in a world of infantile bliss before death closed her beautiful vacant eyes.

So Oliver Hargrave departed, and was never seen in South Bar again. His legacy to the town was a festering wound of bitterness, betrayal, and hatred, to endure through the next generation.

The boy Isaac grew up to be something of a local curiosity. If his father had seemed to some to be the devil incarnate, Isaac was a visitation from the angels. He was the model of most of the traditional virtues—thrift, modesty, sobriety, industriousness—and enjoyed the kind of prosperity that pious folk liked to think resulted therefrom. Sarah had raised him as her own; he called her Mama Sarah, and lavished upon her a filial devotion that few mothers could claim from their sons. When he was a teenaged boy Isaac went to work for a man named Cyrus Thacker, who owned the local woodyard, and this was followed as if by design by Cyrus's wooing and winning Sarah as his bride. Isaac soon became a full partner in the woodcutting business, and continued to live with Cyrus and Sarah, showing no inclination to marry and generate a family of his own. It was a cozy arrangement, the kind the townspeople admired. South Bar was proud of the Thackers and their adopted son Isaac. And it was a measure of Isaac's good standing in the community that people were willing to overlook the unfortunate fact that he was a son of Oliver Hargrave.

A good part of the Thackers' status derived from Sarah's being the daughter and only surviving child of the founder of South Bar. Samuel Gilpin had brought his family from Connecticut to the Ohio River Valley in 1800, at a time when it was the farthest outpost of westward expansion. As his seventy-fifth birthday approached nearly forty years later, old Samuel still lived, alone and a widower and fiercely independent, in the house he and his son George had built of split logs and rough-hewn planking when George was a teenager and Sarah was a baby. The sturdy old house had held life, and it had held death. Samuel's wife Matilda had died there; the drowned and lifeless body of Sarah's daughter Martha had lain within its protective walls; George's life had drained away there at the age of forty-nine, when he had chosen to return to South Bar after years of self-imposed exile. Samuel had in recent years spurned invitations from the Thackers to come and live with them. He meant to live in his

2

own house until the day of his death, and to die there.

All these facts about the Gilpins and Hargraves and Thackers were known and understood by the good people of South Bar, Indiana. What was not so well understood was the enigmatic character of Sarah's son Lucius.

When the Reverend Oliver Hargrave had held the infant up before the community's astonished eyes and given him his name it had been in a voice that rang deeply with genuine emotion. In that tremendous moment a shamed man had miraculously transformed humiliation into triumph. But Lucius, Bringer of Light, brought only torture to himself, implacable hostility to others, and perplexity to all. When he was sixteen he tore himself free from the quiet constricting place of his birth and flung himself upon the world, making his way down the Ohio and the Mississippi Rivers to become the apprentice and junior partner of a footloose gentleman named Albert Pettingill, the exact nature of whose business was never satisfactorily defined for the curious folk in South Bar.

Lucius had never been back. When he left he carried with him a raging hatred for those whose enmity he believed he had inherited with his name. And in a secret place in his heart he nursed a wistful love and longing for an imaginary father of shining-pure saintliness—a longing that would stay with him to the last day of his life.

In four years he had not lived in one place longer than three weeks. At twenty he abandoned his aimless life on the river and went off in a new direction, thinking to fight like a hot-eyed zealot in the war for Texas Independence. He was disenchanted with the adventure as soon as it began.

Lucius was a born wanderer, a searcher after something he yearned for constantly but could not recognize when he saw it. His cross was the disappearance of his father, and he bore it with a notable lack of stoicism. The absence of Oliver Hargrave made an aching void in his life, which he filled with a father of his own devising—a phantom figure wrought from dreams, scraps of information and misinformation, festering resentment, impassioned illusions. He kept a notebook, which he called his Journal, in which he tried to capture the image that had formed in his mind, piece by piece, beginning far back in childhood. He also set down strongly colored depictions of the significant events of his life, and the people who figured in them.

Gradually, as Lucius's writings aged and took on the look

of permanence, they seemed to him to become imbued with the aura of unquestioned Truth, even as they contradicted themselves. Somewhere in the gray recesses of his mind, reality fused smoothly with fantasy. The distinction between them had never held much interest for him.

Once, in a remote wilderness place, Lucius met a mystic, who saw him for what he was.

"Be your own man, Lucius," the mystic said. "Do not spend your life chasing after phantoms."

Lucius shook his head, and would not listen. He went on chasing after phantoms, for that was all he knew how to do.

Part One

(1)

IT WAS OCTOBER, but the white-hot sun refused to admit it. Relentlessly it beat down on the venerable old mission church of Nuestra Señora de Guadalupe and the cluster of smaller buildings and houses around it, turning them into whitewashed ovens. Over the parched and dusty roads the air danced and shimmered in the late-morning heat. It was the only thing that moved.

A mile or two southeast of town on the San Antonio Road (so called because it was the highway leading from the U.S. border to San Antonio) there was a squat little adobe house with a wooden plaque on the wall near the front door. The sign read: *Hargrave and Kenyon, Land Agents, Authorized Representatives of the Nacogdoches County Land Commission, Nacogdoches, Republic of Texas. Col. Ashton Hurley, Commissioner*. The chiseled letters of the sign stood out in bold relief, and supported a thick layer of dust.

Inside, the house was dark and gloomy. A small wooden table occupied the center of the tiny front room, and at the table, facing the front doorway, a young man sat idly manipulating a deck of playing cards. Lucius Hargrave was in his early twenties, tall and robust, with a shock of thick sandy hair, and hazel eyes that moved restlessly. On the floor in a

7

corner of the room a large orange-and-white cat lay curled, at once deeply asleep and ready for instant action, as only cats can be. And because Lucius liked to talk and there was no one else to talk to, he addressed the cat.

"Well, Mortimer, what have you got to say about this weather, hmm? I distinctly remember when we came here you assured me that September would be cool, and in October the rains would start. So here it is October, and look at it. Hell on earth. What have you got to say for yourself, eh?"

Mortimer stirred slightly, but was silent.

"You're a liar, that's what you are. But at least you don't try to deny it. That's what I like about you, Mort. You're the only honest liar I know. Besides me."

Mortimer yawned, shifted his position, and went back to sleep.

The dull clopping of horses' hooves sounded from outside, and Lucius glanced casually at the two men dismounting in front of the house, then went on shuffling his cards.

A soft-eyed boyish-looking young man stepped into the room and blinked. "Lucius! What are you doin'?"

Lucius held the cards out. "Pick a card, Brad."

The newcomer grimaced in annoyance. "Put those damned things away, Lucius, we've got a customuh." He turned back to the doorway and called: "Come on in, Mistuh Adkins. I want you to meet my partnuh, Mistuh Lucius Hargrave."

Adkins was about thirty-five, grimy and unshaven, dressed in ragged buckskins. He clumped heavily into the house and eyed Lucius warily.

Lucius barely glanced up. "Good morning, Mr. Adkins. What can we do for you?" He was picking up his cards and stacking them with loving care.

"You just go ahead and tell Lucius your problem, Mistuh Adkins," Brad said. "He'll help you if anybody in Texas can. Meanwhile I'll just put on a pot of coffee." He flashed a smile and disappeared through a doorway into the back of the house.

"Pull up a chair, Mr. Adkins," Lucius said.

The visitor sat down. Lucius went on fingering his cards, and waited. Adkins cleared his throat noisily, and Mortimer looked up in alarm.

"I got this here land scrip," Adkins said.

Lucius looked pained. "Don't tell me you bought some of those phony Texas land certificates!"

8

"No, sir, not a bit." Adkins was pulling some papers out of an inside pocket. "This here's genu-ine veteran's scrip, issued to me when I was mustered out o' Gen'l Houston's army after San Jacinto. Yo' partner Mr. Kenyon tol' me you an' him was veterans too, so you mus' know it's good."

Lucius reached for the papers and glanced through them. "Well, yes, it's valid, all right. A bit old, though. I see you were mustered out in July of 'thirty-six."

"What about it?"

"This is 1838. Two years is a mighty long time in Texas, Mr. Adkins."

Adkins's eyes narrowed. "I don't git you."

Lucius leaned back in his chair and gave his visitor a patient look. "Surely you're familiar with the glorious history of the Texas Republic so far? After independence the next logical step was admission to the United States. Any fool knows this big empty piece of real estate can't stand as a nation, it has to go with the U.S., or back to Mexico. But did our valiant leaders pump for statehood, and pump hard? Hell, no. They halfheartedly let it be known they'd consider it if somebody begged 'em, and when nobody begged 'em they acted insulted and grew surly, and now they're talking about backing away from the idea altogether. Y'see, General Houston's getting visions of grandeur now. He and his friends see themselves as molders of an empire—"

"Who gives a damn about Houston?" Adkins demanded. "He'll soon be out, anyhow."

"Yes, and who do you think's going to be the next President? That lunatic Lamar, that's who. We'll be wishing we had old drunken Sam back."

Adkins was growing restless. "What's all this got to do with my damn scrip, Mr. Hargrave?"

"What I'm trying to tell you is that while your scrip is perfectly good, it's not worth much. Why? Because Texas has no future. The Mexicans haven't forgotten the licking they took here. They'll be back with blood in their eye, and next time the Texans won't have a chance. Then neither your land claim nor mine, nor any other American's, will be worth the paper it's printed on. And that's because our heroic leaders are too damned busy getting rich on their private speculations to have time to worry about the country."

Adkins leaned forward, scowling. "Mr. Kenyon said you'd gimme a good deal on this here scrip."

Lucius smiled. "Mr. Kenyon's a Southern gentleman. He

likes to be pleasant to people. Sometimes I have to contradict him, because I think it's important to be honest, even if the truth is not always pleasant. All I can say is, I'll do the best I can for you, and it'll be as good as you can get anywhere."

Lucius picked up the papers and studied them further. "Let's see now . . . three hundred and twenty acres. Not good. Can't do much with a claim that small. Best I can offer you is sixty cents on the acre. Texas money."

"Oh, I got to have U.S. money. I'm headin' for th' States."

"In that case . . . thirty cents an acre."

Adkins growled his judgment of this. "Why, that's robbery. Plain, outright robbery."

Lucius laid the papers on the table. "Well then, take it on to New Orleans and unload it there. Frankly, my friend, I hope you do that, because I'd probably take a loss on the deal."

Adkins pulled on his lower lip for a while, deep in thought. "How much money is that, at thirty cents an acre?"

"Ninety-six dollars."

After another moment of indecision Adkins gave up. "All right. I'll take it."

The transaction was completed in a few minutes. Then Lucius stood up and held out his hand, smiling.

"Nice to do business with you, Mr. Adkins. And whenever you're in Texas, drop in and see us. After all, we're here to serve you. Any time."

When Brad Kenyon came back into the room, Lucius had his playing cards laid out in a game of solitaire.

"Coffee's almost ready," Brad said. "Couldn't Mistuh Adkins take the time?"

Lucius glanced up in annoyance. "Brad, your Southern manners are very charming, but for God's sake, will you stop offering refreshments to every vagabond who comes in here? We're running a land office, not an inn."

Brad sat down and gazed accusingly across the table at the cardplayer. "I heard what you told him, Lucius."

"And?"

"You know it's Colonel Hurley's policy to redeem the veterans' land scrip for no less than fifty cents an acre. That's what the government's selling it for in the States, and veterans ought to get at least that much—"

"Veterans, hell!" Lucius snorted. "Most of these so-called veterans got no closer to the fighting than you and I and

10

Hurley did, which was about two hundred miles, if you remember."

"It wasn't our fault the war was over before we got there."

"Hell, if every damned braggart who claims to be a veteran of San Jacinto had actually been there, Houston would have had a standing army of a million men. He could have conquered the world."

"That's got nothing to do with Mistuh Adkins' scrip."

"I *told* him to take it to New Orleans. With a little effort he could've gotten twice the price I paid. But he's too lazy. That's his problem, not ours."

"But Lucius—"

"Hey—how about that coffee?"

Brad went out to the kitchen, sighing heavily, and Lucius grinned after him and turned his attention back to his cards.

In the afternoon two horsemen—a white man leading, a black man trailing behind—came up the road from the direction of the U.S. border, and stopped in front of the little adobe house. The white man dismounted, handed his reins to his servant, and walked up to the front stoop. He was studying the sign on the wall when Lucius appeared in the doorway and boomed a hearty greeting.

"Good afternoon, friend."

"You the land office, eh?" said the stranger.

"That's right. Lucius Hargrave, at your service."

"My name's Shelton," the man said. He was middle-aged and well dressed, stiff and dignified in his manner. "I'm from Tennessee. Lookin' to emigrate to Texas."

Lucius seized the stranger's hand and pumped it vigorously. "Come in, come in. Welcome to the land of opportunity."

In the front room Lucius showed his guest to a chair and smiled apologetically as he took his seat behind the table.

"We're a little disorganized today. My partner's doing kitchen duty because our housekeeper didn't show up."

"He'p hard to find?" Shelton asked.

"Practically impossible. It's the price we have to pay for prosperity, I guess. I shouldn't complain."

"Won't bothuh me none. I'm bringin' my slaves with me." Mr. Shelton looked inquiringly at Lucius. "Anybody goin' to gimme trouble about that?"

"That's your business, Mr. Shelton. In Texas nobody sticks his nose in other people's business."

11

"Well, that's fine. Many Southernuhs in Texas?"

"Lots of 'em. More and more all the time. My partner's one. From Natchez. You Southerners know a good thing when you see it, and you're smart to be coming in now, because pretty soon there won't be a lick of prime land to be had."

Shelton's eyebrows went up. "That so? I heard there was plenty o' land in Texas. Land for th' askin'."

Lucius gave him an indulgent smile. "Plenty of land, yes. I was speaking of *prime* land."

"Hmmm." Shelton was thoughtful for a moment. "How's chances for annexation?"

Lucius leaned toward the visitor and assumed a low-voiced confidential tone. "Keep this under your hat, Mr. Shelton. It'll happen just as soon as old man Houston steps down and Beauregard Lamar becomes President. Lamar's a Southerner too, y'know, and he's got powerful friends in Washington. Yep, there'll be a brand-new state here in another year, and you smart Southerners'll be in charge."

"Well," Shelton mused. "That's mighty interestin'."

"Yes sirree. That's why I say you're making a smart move, because the men who grab the land early are going to be the land barons of the future. Now, how big a piece of property were you thinking of, Mr. Shelton?"

"How much can I get free? I understand they're givin' farmers headrights."

"Oh, you don't want to fool with *that*, my friend. No self-respecting farmer would waste his time with it. Nothing but sand and sagebrush. In the middle of Indian country too. No, quality goods carry a price. Isn't that the way the world is? What I can offer you is fine bottomland. Loamy soil, plenty of good water. At a price that can't be beat."

Shelton hesitated. "Uh, well, I wasn't figgerin' to buy jest yet—"

"Quite right. You should look around first. But you should buy your *claim*. Good claims are getting scarcer and scarcer every day."

Lucius had extracted some papers from the table drawer and was fingering them. "Now, I just happen to have here a real beauty. For three hundred and twenty acres in the lower Brazos River region. Choice, Mr. Shelton. Absolutely choice."

Lucius handed his client some papers, and Shelton scanned them, frowning.

"Three hunnerd an' twenty acres, y'say?"

"That's right. The perfect size."

"How much?"

"You're in luck, my friend. I can let you have it for a dollar fifty an acre, cash. That's U.S. money. Four hundred and eighty dollars. Best bargain you'll ever run across in your life."

Mr. Shelton was plainly dubious. "Sounds a mite steep to me."

"I come from southern Indiana, Mr. Shelton. I tell you, you could spit across the piece of farmland you could buy up there for four hundred and eighty dollars." Lucius held up a cautionary hand. "But look here, don't let me influence you. I'm just a government agent, not a salesman. Anyway, that claim came in here this morning, and I promise you it'll be gone by tomorrow."

Shelton rubbed his chin and ruminated. "Fo' hunnerd dolluhs is all I can part with right now, Mistuh Hargrave."

Lucius's smile was kindly. "Mr. Shelton, the minute I laid eyes on you I knew you were the type of settler we're looking for here in Texas. Good, solid, upstanding, salt of the earth. I'd like to see you take advantage of this opportunity, because you may never get another one like it. It's yours for four hundred."

While Lucius filled out the necessary papers Shelton studied him carefully.

"How do I know you're on the up-and-up, Mistuh Hargrave?"

Lucius gave the man an injured look. "You saw the sign outside, didn't you?"

"Well, yes—"

"You noticed it said 'Authorized Representatives of the County Land Commission,' right? Did you notice the name of the land commissioner? None other than Colonel Ashton Hurley."

Mr. Shelton's reaction to this information was a blank stare.

"Colonel Hurley and General Houston fought side by side at San Jacinto, Mr. Shelton. I know—it was my privilege to serve under Colonel Hurley. No finer man ever lived, Mr. Shelton. A Southerner too, by the way. If you can't trust men like that, who *can* you trust?"

Shelton was properly repentant. "Oh, well, I didn't mean to cast aspersions—"

"That's perfectly all right. I just wanted to set your mind at ease." A warm smile crinkled Lucius's handsome face. "After all, I'm here to serve you."

* * *

13

Brad returned to the room a little while later and found Lucius alone again, with his playing cards spread out on the table.

"Supper'll be ready in about twenty minutes, Lucius. That all right?"

"Fine, Brad, fine." Lucius pushed his cards away, leaned back in his chair, and stretched mightily. "I'll be ready for it, I'll tell you. It's been a damned hard day."

(2)

THE NEXT MORNING Colonel Hurley came. The colonel had a metallic look about him—his long flowing hair was prematurely silver and his narrow face a coppery tan; his hard eyes were the color of polished steel. He was a small man, almost comically diminutive atop a magnificent stallion. He wore a tailored frock coat, a large black hat, and a haughty expression. Within half a minute he had dismounted and secured his horse, stomped up to the front door of the house, paused for a brief scowl at the sign on the wall, and gone in without knocking.

Lucius was leaning back in his chair with his feet on the table, reading a small book. He glanced up and smiled.

"Well! Good morning, Ash. What brings you out before noon?"

Colonel Hurley took off his hat and looked around. "Wheah's Kenyon?"

"Gone to town for supplies. Our housekeeper's sick, and Brad's filling—"

"What's the meanin' o' that sign outside, Lucius?"

"What's the meaning of your question, Ash?"

"I couldn't believe it when somebody tol' me 'bout that

14

sign you got on the front o' yo' house. I absolutely couldn't believe it."

"What's the matter with it? Did I spell your name wrong?"

Colonel Hurley pulled up a chair and sat down, and his quick rough movements expressed anger. "You know damn well what our agreement is. You're supposed to handle only clients I send you. You're not supposed to take trade off the road, and you're damn well not supposed to advertise. 'Authorized Representatives,' indeed! What the hell you tryin' to do, ruin me?"

"Why, certainly not, Ash," Lucius said mildly. He closed his book and took his feet off the table. "Even though you're trying to starve us, we hold the highest loyalty to you."

"What do you mean, starve you? I do the best I can. When I get a suitable client for you I send him ovuh heah. But dammit, man, you're supposed to operate unduh covuh. I cain't afford to have my name and my office linked with you, I'll lose my damn commission."

"Business is bad, Ash, haven't you noticed? We haven't made a dime here in over a week."

"Business is goin' to be nonexistent soon if we're not careful. I jes' got word that gov'ment investigatuhs are comin' to have a look at my operation. Too many complaints about funny goin's on, and it's all youh doin'."

"That's fine," Lucius said casually. "We'll engage 'em in a little poker game and clean 'em out. Haven't had a good game in a long time."

Colonel Hurley leaned on the table and fixed Lucius with a ferocious glare. "How old are you, Hahgrave?"

Lucius was taken aback. "Why, let's see now . . . I'll be twenty-three my next birthday."

The colonel nodded grimly. "You're one o' them quick-maturin' boys. Always big for theah age. You prob'ly been impersonatin' a grown man since you was fifteen yeahs old."

Lucius shrugged modestly. "Sixteen."

"Well, you do it damn well, and you git away with it most o' the time. But once in a while your tendah yeahs show."

"That a fact?" Lucius said without interest. He began to leaf through his little book.

"Pay attention, Hahgrave, dammit. I'm talkin'!"

Lucius pushed the book aside. "I'm listening, Ash. Go ahead, lecture me."

"As you know, it was through mah family background and mah outstandin' military record that I was able to make

15

Pres'dent Houston's acquaintance, and secure the post of commissionuh—"

"The way I heard it, Ash, the thing old Sam liked about you was the fact that you're about the only other man in Texas who's as big a drunk as he is. And don't forget that wagonload of fine Kentucky whiskey you sent him last Christmas. *That* didn't hurt your standing one little bit."

Colonel Hurley endured the interruption with fuming impatience. "But as you also know, Pres'dent Houston's jes' dyin' to find an excuse to close down the land office till aftuh all the lands have been surveyed. And uncoverin' a little operation like yours would be all the evidence he'd need."

Lucius sighed. "All right, Ash. What do you want me to do?"

"First I want you to git that goddamn sign down, and burn it. Then I want you to git out o' heah. Lay low fo' a while. I'm goin' to tell them investigatuhs I've been doin' a little investigatin' on my own, and I'm goin' to lead 'em straight to this house. And if you know what's good fo' both of us, Lucius, you won't be heah."

"You mean you want me to *hide out*? Like a common thief?"

Colonel Hurley's chiseled features permitted a cold smile. "Theah are times, my boy, when even *un*common thieves have to hide out."

Lucius nodded. "Very well put." He opened the table drawer and brought out his deck of cards. "How about a little game?"

"No, thank you," the colonel said stiffly. "I nevuh play with professional gambluhs."

Lucius began to lay out a game of solitaire. "You didn't feel that way back in 'thirty-six. Remember that night in the little hotel in Natchitoches? You wiped out your losses and collected about forty-five hundred more that evening, as I recall. Best night you ever spent. You didn't mind playing with a professional when the professional was on your side, did you?"

Colonel Hurley looked faintly bored. "Ancient history," he sniffed.

"Yes, we were great friends in those days, weren't we, Ash? You had great plans, too. You were going to join the Texas rebels and get just close enough to the fighting to hear gunfire in the distance, then rush back to the States and proclaim

16

yourself a war hero. Maybe run for Congress. But something went wrong, didn't it, Ash? Texas heroes were common as dirt, and all you could get out of your hero pose was a minor appointment in the Texas Land Office. Promised to get me one, too—after all, you *were* a tiny bit indebted to me—but nothing ever came of it."

"I did the best I could," Colonel Hurley snapped. "I'm no miracle workuh."

"That you're not," Lucius readily agreed. "Nobody could accuse you of an excess of gratitude, either."

"What do you want from me, Hahgrave?" the colonel demanded. "I've provided you with this house and sent you business, and you've taken such liberties as to endanguh mah commission. I've introduced you to important people. You've offended them and embarrassed me with your acid sarcasm about all things Texan. I've given you every opportunity I could think of, and you've bungled 'em all. What the hell else do you want?"

Lucius's face was grim as he laid out his cards one by one. "Never mind, Ash. What I want, you ain't got to give."

Colonel Hurley got up abruptly and went to the door. When he stopped and looked back his haughty facial mask was securely back in place.

"Move out, Hahgrave. I want this house vacated within twenty-fo' hours. Keep out o' sight fo' a while. Get in touch with me in about a month."

Lucius grinned and gave the colonel a jaunty salute. "Whatever you say, boss-man. I'm here to serve you."

When Brad Kenyon returned from town at the end of the day, Lucius was sitting on the low stoop in front of the house enjoying the coolness of late afternoon. Mortimer the cat reclined in regal serenity beside him. Brad dismounted, tied his horse, and joined the company.

"Brought you some fish heads, Mort," he said, and chucked the cat under the chin.

The big tom gave the man a sleepy look and closed his eyes.

"What took you so long?" Lucius said.

"Ran into Colonel Hurley in town. He said he'd been out heah talkin' to you."

Lucius chuckled. "Uh-oh. He gave you the lecture too, eh?"

"Wasn't any surprise to me. I been tellin' you all along this was crazy. It couldn't last."

"Well, nothing's forever. It's been a nice little interlude."

"But what are we goin' to do now?"

Lucius reached behind him and extracted from a back pocket the little paperbound book he had been reading earlier. Idly he leafed through it.

"Persevere, Brad. Persevere."

Brad gave his partner a dark look. "You know, Lucius, theah's somethin' about you that bothuhs me a little. I have the feelin' that the longuh I know you the less I know what you're really thinkin'. Everything you say seems so . . . so *easy* fo' you."

Lucius looked blank. "Talking comes easy to me. Is that a sin?"

"You take this Texas thing, for instance. A fellow comes along who wants to sell his land; you tell him it's not worth much because the Mexicans are goin' to grab it all back. Somebody wants to *buy* land, you tell him it's deah, because annexation is just around the corner and things are rosy. And not long ago you were promotin' stock in some new investment company because Texas is goin' to stay independent and spread all the way to the Pacific Coast. Whatevuh happens to fit the occasion is what you—"

"Brad, my dear boy—" Lucius was making an effort to be patient—"any one of those theories could turn out to be the shining truth. Whichever way it goes, *some*body's going to get rich. It won't be me—all *I'm* doing is trying to earn a modest living. For *both* of us."

"I know, Lucius. And I appreciate it. I just keep thinkin' . . . well, I guess I just don't like this business we're in."

Lucius was silent for a moment, studying his book. "Funny you should say that. Because I think the time has come when, for the good of all parties concerned, we should separate our destinies from that of the Texas Republic."

Brad leaned forward, his eyes wide and eager. "You mean that, Lucius? Where'll we go? What'll we do?"

"Where? Back to the States. What?" Lucius shrugged. "I don't know. Got any ideas? Got any rich relatives who need young partners in some easy business?"

Brad thought about it. "My Uncle Amos has a big sugah plantation in Louisiana."

"Sounds like work," Lucius said with unmistakable distaste.

"Yes, but theah's money in it. Amos Whitehurst is one o' the richest men in that state."

Lucius closed his book and frowned. "Whitehurst," he murmured. "Does he have a daughter named Amanda?"

"Sure does. She's an actress, quite well known around New Orleans. Have you seen her?"

"Once or twice. An old friend of mine used to, uh, used to know her."

Brad laughed easily. "Well, yes. Amanda's had quite a few gentlemen friends."

Lucius's eye held a look of sly amusement. "So that's your cousin, eh?" He chuckled. "Funny world."

"Anyway, it's Amanda's sistuh *you'd* like. Her name's Arabella, and she's just about the prettiest thing you evuh saw. Maybe we'll go visit her when we get back."

Lucius heaved a longing sigh. "Ah, yes. To behold a beautiful woman again . . . what a joy that would be." He went back to reading in his book.

"What in the world is that you're readin', Lucius?" Brad demanded.

Lucius handed him the book. With an incredulous look on his face, Brad stared at the cover.

"*Confessions of a Reformed Drunkard*, by Millard Weedy," he read. "*The Intimate Revelations of a Life of Sordidness and Sin, as Seen from the Retrospect of Blessed Moral Redemption.* Good Lord, Lucius! Wheah'd you get this trash?"

"Peddler came by today, selling 'em. Fifty cents a copy. Says this fellow Weedy's making a fortune on his little literary gem."

With a disdainful shrug Brad tossed the literary gem aside. "Well, *you* certainly don't need it, you're already reformed. You haven't had three drinks in the two and a half yeahs we've been in Texas. I nevuh heard of anybody givin' up liquor the way you did."

"I had a bad experience once," Lucius said.

Brad waited for more, and got only silence. Lucius was gazing off into the orange-glowing sunset sky.

"What was it, Lucius? You never told me about any bad experience."

A faint smile touched Lucius's lips. "Brad, old friend, do you imagine I tell you *everything*?"

Brad adopted a complaining tone. "Well, that's just what I was talkin' about a minute ago, Lucius. The longuh I know you the more I realize how little I know. And why do you call me friend, then? How can I be youh friend if I don't know what's in youh mind?"

With a sigh Lucius relented slightly. "I've told you about my father, haven't I?"

"Only that he was a travelin' preachuh who went away when you were a baby and nevuh came back."

"He was much more than a preacher, Brad. He was one of the greatest men who ever lived in the Ohio River Valley. He had a kind of inborn nobility that set him apart. Next to him the average man was no more than a viper, crawling on the ground. And he was surrounded by vipers. They hated him. He didn't leave home voluntarily, they *drove* him away. His enemies hounded him into exile."

Brad hazarded a timid question. "How do you know he was so noble and great, if you never knew him?"

Lucius responded with a grimace of annoyance. "You might as well ask a holy man how he knows God if he's never seen Him. There are some things a man just *knows*. And that's *precisely* why I don't tell you things—you ask such idiotic questions!"

"All right, Lucius," Brad said meekly. "What about this bad experience?"

But Lucius was in an irritable mood now. "There is no point in this conversation," he snapped. "No point whatsoever."

"Come on, Lucius, please," Brad urged. "Confide in me."

Again, this time grudgingly and with reluctance, Lucius relented. "Remember the fortune-teller?"

Brad's face remained blank as he echoed, "The fortune-telluh . . . ?"

"When we were on our way to Texas. The brigade had camped near Fort Jessup, remember?"

"Oh yes. The crazy man who wore a turban and called himself some ridiculous name—"

"The High Priest of the Temple of Eternal Light."

"Somethin' like that, yes. What about him?"

"I was already drunk that night, before I went to see him. And the minute I stepped inside his wagon he pulled out several bottles of mescal and two glasses, and started pouring. I drank, and he poured, and I drank, and all the time he kept asking me questions about my family, my childhood, my entire history. I kept drinking and he kept pouring and asking questions, and I kept talking and talking and getting more and more drunk—it was strange. Before I knew it I was

20

blind-drunk, I was in a white fog, and the fortune-teller's voice was ringing inside my head. I must have passed out or something. The next thing I can remember is looking up at this crazy fortune-teller, and . . . looking straight into the face of my father. Don't ask me how I knew, I can't tell you. But I recognized my father as surely as if I'd seen him every day of my life." Lucius was quiet for a moment before going on. "Well, I got out of there as fast as I could and went back to camp—although for the life of me I can't remember how I got there. The next day we went into Texas. And that day I swore off drinking."

Again Lucius lapsed into silence, and again Brad waited breathlessly, frowning in confusion.

"What are you sayin', Lucius? Are you sayin' you think the fortune-telluh was youh father?"

Lucius was leaning forward, hands clasped tensely together and working against each other. "I don't know what I'm saying, Brad. Don't even know why I'm talking to you about this. I only know that whoever the man was, he was no stranger. He knew things about me and my family that no stranger could have known. There was something *there*, Brad, something tremendous—and I missed it. An opportunity that will probably never come again—to discover some scrap of information about my father—and I missed it. Lost it. Let it slip right through my fingers."

Grim-faced and eyes remote, Lucius was again staring off into the darkening twilight sky. He seemed no longer aware of the other man's presence.

Brad shook his head, hopelessly baffled, but eager to express sympathy—which he genuinely felt—and understanding, which eluded him. "That's sad, Lucius. And to think, I'm the one who suggested you go to visit the man." He placed a gentle hand on Lucius's shoulder. "You *are* a mystery, you know—keepin' somethin' like that bottled up inside you so long. How come you've nevuh talked about it?"

Lucius got to his feet, impatiently taking himself out of Brad's reach. "Because it doesn't concern you. And because it's past and done with, and can't be helped. I prefer to talk about things we can do something about. For instance, getting the hell out of here. How soon can you be ready to depart these miserable premises?"

"Anytime you say, Lucius. When do you want to go?"

"Early in the morning."

"I'm with you."

21

"Fine." Lucius rubbed his hands together; slowly he was returning to good spirits. "And in honor of the occasion, I thought we might have a little drink tonight."

"What about youh vow?"

Lucius shrugged. "Well, you know...things have a beginning and they have an ending. Life must go on."

He stepped past Brad on the steps and strode purposefully into the house.

Half an hour before sunup the lower part of the sky toward the east was a luminescent sheet of pearl gray, silhouetting the jagged line of piney woods that stood along the horizon. The world was quiet.

Lucius came out of the house and walked down to the road where Brad was sitting on his horse, waiting. On one side of Brad's mount a packmule stood, heavily laden, and on the other side, Lucius's horse, saddled and ready. Under his arm Lucius carried a battered old leather satchel. He went to the pack animal and carefully secured the satchel under a strap, giving it a gentle pat.

Brad watched him. "That ol' satchel's fallin' apart, Lucius. You ought to retire it from active service."

"It belonged to my father," Lucius said. "It'll outlast both of us, I guarantee you." He swung into his saddle.

There was a slight movement in the brush at the side of the road. Mortimer was stalking some small ground-dwelling creature.

"What about ol' Mort?" Brad wondered aloud.

"He can earn his own living," Lucius said. "He was doing it before we came, and he can do it again."

They sat for a moment looking at the little adobe house.

"Looks kind of lonesome all of a sudden, doesn't it?" Brad said. "Sort of sad and forlorn, as if it knew we were leaving. Y'know, I think I'll miss it just a little."

Lucius's eyes roamed idly over the silent landscape. "I'm still looking for the place I'd miss," he said.

Brad gave his friend a solemn look. "You're a mystery, Lucius."

"Let's go," Lucius said curtly. He pulled his horse around to face the east.

Mortimer crouched low and stared in mute disapproval as the horses went clopping off, disturbing the tranquility of early morning. Then, when the noise of the hoofbeats had

22

faded away and the world was quiet again, he went back to stalking his prey.

(3)

FROM THE JOURNAL of Lucius Hargrave:

Life begins with a flowering of confidence born of youth and vigor. It is a dangerous and transitory illusion. The flowers fade, vigor softens, confidence gives way before the realization that the world is stronger than the individual, and that it is in essence hostile.

I began keeping this Journal as a very young man with the intention of setting down a clear picture of my life and the forces that shape it, starting with my origins and moving forward by logical and orderly steps. A few years later I closed it in despair, overwhelmed by the feeling that I had lost my way. Logic and order were lacking. Instead of illumination there were shadows and darkness. The story was a mystery; I was an enigma to myself.

At sixteen I departed from southern Indiana, the place of my birth, spent four exciting years traveling on the Mississippi River, prospered, and grew into robust manhood. During this period I was under the tutelage of a man named Albert Pettingill, a worldly-wise gentleman of formidable sophistication. Mr. Pettingill blessed me with a thoroughly practical education in the ways of human commerce, and cursed me with extravagant tastes that were a burden to me for years, until I recognized their frivolous nature and discarded them. Eventually, too, I perceived the frivolous nature of Mr. Pettingill himself, and with sadness (for we had grown fond of each other) broke with him, and went my separate way. I had come to realize that, for all my early success, my life lacked the essential ingredient of meaning. In quest of that missing element I then spent two and a half years in the Republic of Texas, which period proved to be a tedious interlude, and quite as empty of meaning as anything that had gone before.

A major source of trouble for me, I eventually concluded, was my unfortunate affinity for weak companions. Following Albert Pettingill there was my young friend Brad Kenyon, from whom I had derived my ardor for the Texas venture. Brad was the most likeable man I had ever met, but a hopeless simpleton, a starry-eyed idealist who in thirty months in Texas never gained the slightest comprehension of the base and cynical forces of human avarice that motivated the struggle for that huge chunk of real estate. To Brad the Texas Revolution had been merely a group of sturdy farmers rising up to throw off the yoke of a despot. At first I, too, held that simplistic view, but not for long.

I looked around me and saw chaos and corruption. Unscrupulous land speculators were playing havoc with the value of both land and money under the very noses of the authorities, many of whom were enthusiastic speculators themselves. I could see that a few honest men in key places were desperately needed, and began to look for a way to be of help. It happened that my old military commander, Colonel Ashton Hurley (leader of a puny force with a mighty name—the Sons of the South Brigade of Volunteers for Texas), had managed to secure for himself a post in the Texas Land Office. He urged Brad Kenyon and me to join him, and we agreed, reasoning that, having risked our necks assisting at the birth of the Texas Republic, we should do what we could to help breathe life into it.

Following hard on the heels of this high-minded decision came disillusionment. It dawned upon me after a time that the very people for whose welfare we were so earnestly striving—the citizens of Texas—were distinctly less than grateful. In the eyes of the old settlers, we who had come from the States after 1835 were upstart newcomers, opportunists seeking to reap quick profits from the efforts of others. We were readily accused of engaging in what was then the most popular of Texas pastimes—illegal land speculation. No matter that the most prominent and respected Texans practiced it openly; we were the outsiders, so we were the guilty ones.

There have been times in my life when I have been pulled up short, with a sick feeling in the pit of my stomach, at yet another example of the immense capacity for ingratitude that can reside within the breasts of supposedly decent members of society. I have (and will always have) floating before my eyes the tragic figure of my father, the Reverend Oliver Hargrave, who, though he walked only in the narrow path of virtue, was driven from his home and family by enemies whose sole grievance was his selfless service to them. My father has been lost to me since I was a baby, lost somewhere in the far reaches of this continent or beyond. Yet he lives, I know it. And I know, too, that someday we will find each other.

Brad Kenyon and I left Texas in October, 1838, our destination his family home near Natchez, Mississippi, where we planned to rest and revive our flagging energies and resolve upon some new career. Though Brad was two years my senior (I was but twenty-two at the time) he had long since adopted me as his leader, and meekly deferred to me in important decisions. I dared not reveal to him my true feelings as we faced the long road back. I was sunk in a deep depression; life was bleak, the future a desolate wasteland.

Yet my sojourn in Texas had not been entirely useless. I had grown, I had suffered, I had attained maturity, and with it an expanded awareness of the true nature of my fellowman. Discouragement gradually fell away, confidence returned, and now and again I felt a twinge of that bold optimism that had coursed through my sinews when I was sixteen. Perhaps, after all, it was not unreasonable to dream of seizing the world by the throat and showing yourself its master.

At last I felt I was ready to write in my Journal again.

Part Two

(1)

Mr. Bradford Kenyon
Roland Hall
Natchez, Mississippi

Dearest Cousin Bradford,
    Oh, happy, happy days! You just can't imagine how thrilled I was to hear that you are back from that horrid old Texas, and are once again living like the gentleman you are! When Mama returned yesterday from her visit to Roland Hall and told us you were there, I literally shrieked with delight. I do not exaggerate one little bit, Bradford, I let out such a shriek that Crissy ran in to see what in the world was the matter. But that was nothing! When Mama went on to say that you were thinking of coming to Carolina Grove during the Christmas season, well! I just practically expired on the spot, from sheer ecstasy. Dear Uncle Ben went rushing off to get the smelling salts, thinking I was going to faint, as I often do when suffering from extreme happiness. Well! My

senses were reeling, I can tell you. I could barely stay on my feet.

Of course I sat right down first thing this morning to write this letter, in which I propose first to scold you most severely for never writing (why did you not let us know you were coming, you naughty boy?) and second, to inform you, sir, that if you value your dear cousin Arabella's love you will permit nothing on earth to prevent you from putting in an appearance here over Christmas. If you fail to do so I will never speak to you again, for such an injury would be quite unforgivable.

Now, then. Mama tells me you have a houseguest, a young Mr. Hargrave, who was with you in Texas. I must tell you Mama's description of him has me intrigued. He is not a Southerner, she says. Well, my heavens, that's not _his_ fault, is it? She says he is very charming in spite of a slight tendency toward boastfulness, and that he is just ever so handsome. Well! My dear cousin, you had better not fail to come to Carolina Grove, and you had better not fail to bring your Mr. Hargrave with you. You know how seldom I get a chance to meet an interesting man, or any man at all outside our stuffy plantation society.

Oh, Bradford, I am so everlastingly _bored_ with the sons of planters! Papa has them all convinced that in order to court me they must first court him, so they sit and listen while he drones on endlessly about this year's cane crop, and how he built the first sugar mill in Louisiana, and how the Whitehurst mill produces the finest sugar there is, and on and on, while I sit and play wistful nocturnes on the pianoforte. I could scream!

By the way, Amanda will be here at Christmastime with her current gentleman friend (this is the first time she has ever been so bold as to bring one of them _home_ with her!) and Adam will be here too (not with _his_ paramour, heaven forbid!) and with you here also, Bradford dear, and your nice Mr. Hargrave too— goodness me! You know how I love gaiety, and that will be the gayest holiday season ever!

So let me know at once what day and on what steamboat we may expect you. I shall be on pins and needles, counting the hours, and when the moment arrives I shall be at St. Charles Landing with bells on, to greet you with hugs and shower you with kisses! Oh, it's ever so exciting!

Till then, keep well, and give my love to Aunt Louisa and Uncle Robert.

Oh, and Uncle Ben says, "Tell Mr. Bradford to please come, and I will be his valet even if I have to neglect Mr. Amos!" Isn't that sweet?

Your most affectionate cousin,
Arabella

(2)

LUCIUS HARGRAVE and his friend Bradford Kenyon leaned on the deck railing of the steamboat and watched as the St. Charles Landing drifted slowly toward them across the flat brown sheet of river water.

Lucius was pondering. "Let me see if I've got it straight now. The parents are Amos and Adeline. Adeline's your father's sister. And the children are, in order, Amanda, Adam, and Arabella."

"Right."

"Everybody's name starts with an A. What kind of a game is that?"

"It's what you call Whitehurst whimsicality. Actually it's Uncle Amos's doing. They say as soon as he and Aunt Adeline were married he announced that all theah children would be given names beginnin' with A, and that furthermore he'd appreciate it if they'd all marry people whose names begin with A."

Lucius closed his eyes for a moment and held his forehead in his hand. "Now, to continue. Amos disapproves of all his children: Adam because he maintains a quadroon mistress in New Orleans, Amanda because she lives a sinful life as an actress, and Arabella because she's too fun-loving and

31

frivolous, and all of them because nobody shows any inclination to get married and provide him with grandchildren, who no doubt he'd insist have names beginning with—"

Brad's laughter drowned him out. "Now, Lucius, I'll admit the Whitehursts are rathuh quaint. But if you'll keep an open mind I think you'll find them amusing."

"Sounds like a delightful holiday coming up," Lucius said grimly.

The straight-line distance from the river landing to the main house of the plantation called Carolina Grove was less than one mile, but the winding dirt road made it closer to two. It meandered like a stream through fields of deep green velvet dotted with great oaks that stood silent and sepulchral under shrouds of hanging moss. It was a landscape of dreamlike beauty, silent, brooding, melancholy. Lucius gazed out over the scene from the creaking little carriage and felt himself falling under a spell.

"Reminds me of an illustration in one of my grandfather's old books," he said. "King Arthur and his knights ought to be out here, jousting."

When the carriage stopped at the front gate Lucius leaned forward to get a better look at the house, fifty yards away at the end of a double row of bay trees. It was a square two-story structure, brilliantly white against its setting of lush greenery, with broad verandas around the front and sides, above and below. There was an odd incongruity between the upper and lower levels, as if one house had been set down on top of another. The walls and columns of the ground floor were made of painted brick, while the upper section was entirely of wood. Along the second-story gallery slender colonettes supported the steep, shingled roof, contrasting strikingly with the heavy brick columns directly below them. Rows of tall double-shuttered French windows lined both upper and lower galleries, and in the middle of each row was a wide doorway, graced by a fan-shaped transom of colored glass.

"It's a castle," Lucius said, his voice soft with awe.

Brad Kenyon leaned over his shoulder and pointed. "And look theah, sittin' on the lower veranda. The king."

Big Amos Whitehurst, silver-haired, florid-faced, and hugebellied, sat on the veranda with both hands resting on the knob of a carved walking stick. With narrowed eyes he watched as the black driver opened the door of the carriage, and the two young men alighted.

Then Amos opened his mouth and bellowed in a thunderous voice: "Benjamin!"

Instantly a stout black man appeared in the central doorway.

"Yes, suh, Marse Amos?" He immediately caught sight of the carriage at the front gate, and his eyes opened wide.

"Oh, lawsy! Marse Bradfud's heah!" He hurried on short legs down the gravel walkway toward the carriage. Soon he returned, struggling under the weight of two large valises and chattering at the pair of young men who followed him.

"Lawsy, Marse Bradfud, Miss Arabella's gon' be mos' put out 'bout not meetin' you all. I b'lieve she jes' plain forgot. She's out to de west towuh, helpin' Marse Adam git settled. You gen'emen's gon' have de east towuh—"

"Benjamin!" Amos barked. "Get off with you!"

Ben exchanged an understanding smile with Brad Kenyon and went off down a side path with the luggage.

Amos held a fat and trembling hand out toward the visitors. "Come heah, Bradfud," he commanded.

Brad Kenyon stepped up onto the veranda, bowed, and shook the old man's hand. "It's a great pleasure to see you again, Uncle Amos. You're lookin' very—"

"I'm glad you decided to stop wastin' yo' time in Texas, Bradfud. What the hell you find to do with yo'self out theah fo' two goddam yeahs?"

"It's an interesting place, Uncle Amos. A whole new society in the process of—"

"Who's that with ya?" Amos snapped. He was looking past Brad toward the second young man.

Brad gestured to Lucius. "Uncle Amos, I'd like you to meet a deah friend of mine. Mistuh Lucius Hahgrave."

Lucius stepped forward and shook hands. "Honored to meet you, sir."

Amos frowned. "Wheah you from, Mistuh Hahgrave?"

"Indiana, sir. But I've traveled around so much I—"

"Any Ca'lina folks settled in that region?"

Lucius hesitated. "Uh, yes, I believe there's—"

"Best theah is, y'know. Ain' no bettuh stock anywheah than good ol' Ca'lina Anglo-Saxon. I come down heah in Eighteen-oh-nine 'cause I like warm weathuh yeah 'round.

33

Built this place and called it Ca'lina Grove, 'cause it's the only place in Louisiana pretty enough to remind me o' my native state."

Lucius started to ask a question. "Is that North or—"

"Paid fo'ty dolluhs an acre fo' this land, when land all around it was goin' fo' ten. I wanted th' best, an' I was willin' to pay fo' it."

Lucius tried again. "Is that North or South Carolina, sir?"

"Why, South, son, South!" Amos roared. "Nawth Ca'lina ain' nothin' to compare! When you say Ca'lina, that's *South* Ca'lina. You want to talk about *Nawth* Ca'lina, you got to specify *Nawth*. Try to remembuh that, son."

"Yes, sir. I'll remember." Lucius shot a pleading look at his companion.

"'Scuse us, Uncle Amos," Brad said. "We'll just go and see if we can find—"

"You know anything about th' sugar business, Mistuh Hahgrave?" Amos demanded.

"Uh, not really, sir. In Indiana we—"

"I built th' fust propuh sugah mill in Louisiana, Mistuh Hahgrave. Took me six months, and damn near broke my back. Since then I've had three othuhs built at fancy prices, an' wadn't a one of 'em half as good as th' one I built."

"I believe they're starting a bit of a sugar industry in Texas now," Lucius offered, and was startled by the explosive reaction from Amos.

"Sugah, hell! I wouldn't feed my hogs th' rotten stuff they turn out in Texas, son!"

"'Scuse me, Uncle Amos," Brad began again. "Are the othuhs all heah?"

Amos kept his eyes on Lucius. "You stick around a few days, son. Soon's my gout stops actin' up we'll go down to th' mill an' I'll show you how we make *real* sugah."

"I'd like that, sir."

Then Amos turned his pale watery blue eyes up to Brad. "Adam's heah," he said curtly. "Adam's gon' honuh us with three whole days of his time. He's gon' leave his nigger mistress in N'yawlins fo' three whole days, an' visit his mama an' daddy at Christmastime. Ain't that nice?"

Brad squirmed with embarrassment. "Really, Uncle Amos, I hahdly think—"

"Now Amanda, on th' othuh hand, my dahlin' Amanda can't make it home at all till next Thursday. She's a famous

34

actress, y'know. Her public demands performances every damn day till then, includin' Christmas day. Christmas day!"

Amos turned an indignant scowl on Lucius. "I ask you, Mistuh Hahgrave, do they have theatrical puhfawmances in Indiana on Christmas day?!"

Lucius was no longer listening. He was standing open-mouthed and transfixed, staring at an airy apparition floating toward him down the veranda.

"Ah, heah's Arabella!" Brad said with obvious relief.

She was a picture of dazzling brightness—white dress, whipped-cream skin, tumultuous sunny blonde hair, and lights dancing like jewels in her large blue eyes. She was about twenty years old, but her delicate face revealed nothing but childlike innocence.

"Bradfud! Dahlin'!" She flew into Brad's arms and gave him a quick kiss and a long hug.

"Arabella, how good to see you! My, you've grown up! Lovelier than evuh—"

"Oh, Bradfud, you sweet thing, you!" She held him at arm's length and beamed a radiant smile at him. "I'm *evuh* so happy you've come, I just *know* it's goin' to be the most joyful Christmas evuh, I just—"

The eyes had come to rest on Lucius. She disengaged herself from Brad and extended her hand toward the other man, her smile softening coyly.

"And this must be Mistuh Hahgrave."

While Brad spoke hasty introductions Lucius held a slender milk-white hand and gazed deeply into luminous blue eyes.

"I'm charmed," he murmured.

"My goodness gracious!" Arabella said breathlessly. "It's evuh so sweet of you to come, Mistuh Hahgrave. Mothuh told me what a delightful young man you—"

"Arabella!" Amos's walking cane slapped sharply on the veranda floor. "Wheah's yo' mothuh? Don't she know we got guests?!"

"I'm right heah, Amos," a soft voice said.

Adeline Whitehurst had emerged from the house. She was a small ashen-faced woman with pale gray eyes and a vague expression, and a strangely disembodied voice that seemed to float aimlessly in the air.

"So glad you-all could come, Bradfud deah," she said wispily. She gave her nephew a pecking kiss on the cheek and extended her hand to Lucius.

"And heah's Adam!" cried Brad, and rushed to greet a young man who had appeared from around a corner of the house.

Arabella was beaming at Lucius. "I do hope you and Bradfud can stay for a nice long visit, Mistuh Hahgrave. It'll be evuh so much fun!"

Lucius smiled noncommittally. "I hope we can. However, I do have certain business matters to attend to, and—"

Brad was tugging at Lucius's sleeve. "Lucius, I'd like you to meet my cousin Adam. Mistuh Whitehurst, Mistuh Hahgrave."

Adam was in his late twenties, of medium height and stocky build. His square jaw and rather angular head, capped with stiff brown hair parted in the middle, gave the impression of a woodcarving.

"Mistuh Hahgrave," he said in a flat voice, and bowed slightly. His face was stiff and unsmiling.

"A great pleasure, sir," Lucius responded.

"Adam's the business head in the family," Brad said to Lucius. "Anything you want to know about the import-export trade, just ask him."

"Bradfud exaggerates," Adam said unctuously. "My firm provides administrative assistance and warehouse facilities to the shipping industry. Purely routine."

"Sounds like very important work," Lucius allowed.

Adam let his expressionless eyes rest on Lucius for a moment before turning them to Adeline. "What time is dinnuh, Mothuh?"

"I thought about eight, deah. Will that be all right?"

"Fine. I'd like to spend a little time lookin' ovuh the household books with you, if I may."

Adeline looked faintly distressed. "Oh ... do we have to do it now?"

"I think it best to get chores out of the way before leisure begins, Mothuh."

Arabella had slipped between Brad and Lucius, taking each of them by the arm. "And I will show our guests to theah quartuhs," she said, smiling up at first one and then the other. "I'm sure you'll be evuh so cozy in the east tow—"

"Arabella," Adam said sharply. "I'd appreciate it if you'd join Mothuh and me. Aftuh all, a good portion of the household expenses centuhs on you."

Arabella's pretty mouth dropped open in outrage. "Why, Adam! I'll have you know I am *not* extravagant!"

36

Adam arched an eyebrow. "Theah is some difference of opinion on that subject, my deah little sistuh."

"Oh, Adam, you're evuh so rude! What about our guests?"

"Bradfud's been heah a million times. He can find his way to the east towuh without assistance. Come along now." Adam took his mother's arm and escorted her into the house.

Arabella followed, pouting. In the doorway she paused to give Lucius and Brad a sad little wave of her fingers before going inside.

Brad turned quickly to Amos. "If you'll excuse us, Uncle Amos, we'll go and get freshened up a bit. See you at dinnuh, all right?"

Amos gave no indication of having heard. He was sitting with his hands draped over the knob of his walking stick and his chin resting on his hands, watching the shadows of late afternoon lengthening among the bay trees in front of the house.

"Thu'ty goddam miles," he muttered.

Brad leaned down close. "What's that, Uncle Amos?"

"Thu'ty miles from heah to N'yawlins, an' th' only time he comes home is when he wants to check th' goddamn books. Thinks he owns th' place."

"Yes, well...see you at dinnuh, suh."

With a swift look at Lucius Brad moved quietly away, and Lucius followed, leaving the old man alone and mumbling under his breath.

After dark they gathered in an enormous high-ceilinged room for dinner, where Amos took his place at the head of a long table. To his left were Brad and Lucius. On the right sat Adam, and next to him, Arabella. At the opposite end of the table Adeline sat in isolation, with several empty places between her and the others. The long white tablecloth shone like new-fallen snow under the soft light from tiers of candles in a glittering crystal candelabrum in the center of the table, and fine chinaware and silver gleamed at the place settings. A pair of black women in starched white uniforms moved silently and smoothly around the table serving the first course, a huge chilled fruit salad.

Amos turned his myopic eyes on the young man at his left. "Well, Mistuh Hahgrave, I suppose you've had a tour of the house by now. How do you like it?"

"Oh, I think it's very—"

"It's Creole style, y'know. I came to Louisiana, I figgered

37

th' Creoles had been heah a long time, they ought to know how to build fo' th' climate. I didn't know then what lunatics most of 'em are. I hired me th' most famous Creole architect in th' state to do this house. Paid 'im a fo'tune, an' it was wuth it. He was crazy, but he was a genius. They got any houses like this in Indiana, Mistuh Hahgrave?"

"To tell the truth, sir, it's been so long—"

"Most Americans, they won't have nothin' to do with th' Creole style. They're damn fools. Shuah, the Creoles are crazy, but in one thing they know exactly what they're doin'. Tha's architecture. You know what th' Americans are buildin' around heah these days? Big ol' ugly plastuh-cast imitations of Greek temples. Disgustin'!"

Amos paused to attack his fruit salad, and Brad Kenyon hurriedly seized the opportunity. "Lucius and I were very much intrigued by the Mexican style of architecture in Texas, Uncle Amos."

"Good God!" Amos thundered. "Can you two speak of nothin' but Texas?!"

"But Uncle Amos, I think theah are things to be said fo'—"

"Looka heah, Bradfud, if you an' Mistuh Hahgrave are among them damn idiots pumpin' fo' statehood fo' Texas, I hope you'll jes' keep it to yo'selves, 'cause I don't want to heah it."

"I'm neithuh for it nor against it, Uncle Amos, but I think it's bound to happen, soonuh or latuh."

Amos turned belligerent eyes on Lucius. "Is that youh opinion, Mistuh Hahgrave?"

"I expect to see Texas revert back to Mexico in a few years," Lucius said, rushing to get the words out quickly.

Amos smiled. "You're a well-spoken man, Mistuh Hahgrave." He beamed at the others around the table. "Tha's what I like. A man who has intelligent opinions, and knows how to express 'em without ramblin' on and on and on—"

Adam suddenly laughed.

Amos scowled at him. "What's so damned amusin'?"

"Fahthuh, you know puhfectly well the only reason you're against statehood fo' Texas is because you're afraid of competition from the Texas sugah industry."

"Tha's a goddamn lie!" Amos growled.

"Amos, please!" Adeline pleaded from the other end of the table, and Arabella joined the protest.

"Really, it's evuh so borin' to heah nothin' but politics and business from mornin' till night. Can't we talk about somethin' pleasant?"

"Talk about any damn thing you like," Amos rumbled. "I ain't stoppin' ya."

A steaming roast goose had been placed before Amos. He picked up a great curved carving knife and went to work with a murderous frown on his face.

Arabella leaned forward, and her sparkling eyes flitted between Lucius and Brad. "Guess what I have planned for aftuh dinnuh?" she said excitedly. "Uncle Ben's goin' to set up lantuns in the east gahden, and we'll have a nice game of lawn bowlin'. Won't that be fun? I thought Mistuh Hahgrave and I would be pahtnuhs, Bradfud, and you and Adam—"

"Good heavens, Arabella," her brother murmured, "can't you evuh think of anything but playing games?"

"Well, I *surely* didn't think you'd object to a little game of lawn bowlin', Adam," Arabella said petulantly. "Aftuh all, it's not *expensive*."

Lucius heaved an inward sigh and looked wearily at the candelabrum shining in pristine silence before him.

(3)

THE SO-CALLED TOWERS were exactly that: twin hexagonal structures of whitewashed brick flanking the main house, and separated from it by some fifty yards. About thirty feet across, each rose two stories and nearly sixty feet to the peak of its steep pyramid-shaped roof, and was almost completely hidden by shrubbery and trees. Their identical interiors were starkly simple: a spacious sitting room below and a chamber for sleeping above, the two joined by a narrow staircase against the wall.

The morning sun streamed into an upper window of the east tower. Lucius Hargrave stood before the window, basking in the gentle warmth and surveying the beautifully landscaped grounds below. The only activity he observed was the flapping of pigeons, jostling each other under the eaves of the tower and in the branches of nearby trees. In the room behind him were two narrow beds along opposite walls, a dressing table near each, several chairs, and a huge wardrobe. On one of the beds Brad Kenyon sprawled on his back, hands under his head, watching Lucius.

"Well, how do you like Carolina Grove so far?" he asked.

"Impressive," Lucius pronounced without looking around.

"I'll say it's impressive. The Whitehursts are a lot richer than the Kenyons, you can tell that, can't you? You could just about put Roland Hall inside the main room of Carolina Grove."

Lucius remained silent.

"These towuhs are interesting too, don't you think?" Brad went on. "They're really called *garçonnières*—part of the Creole tradition. But the nigras can't manage a word like that, so they're just called towuhs."

"Hmmm," Lucius said. He went on looking out the window.

"And what do you think of the Whitehursts?" Brad persisted.

"Oh, uh...unusual. Very unusual."

"Isn't Uncle Amos a charactuh? I *told* you he was a charactuh, Lucius. Adam's a bit stiff, but he's a smaht man, and very decent, once you get to know him. Aunt Adeline you'd met before, of course. And how about Arabella, Lucius? Isn't she exquisite? I sweah, if I wasn't her fust cousin I do believe I'd come courtin' her myself."

Lucius turned and assumed a half-leaning, half-sitting position against the windowsill. He regarded the other man with a dark frown. "Brad, are we friends, or are we merely acquaintances, being polite to one another?"

Brad sat up and swung his legs over the side of the bed. "Why, we're friends, Lucius. I sincerely hope."

"Then let's be honest, shall we? The Whitehursts are insufferable bores."

Brad accepted the judgment meekly. "Oh. Sorry you feel that way."

"Your Aunt Adeline I'd gotten used to. That blank look on her face, as if she's not quite sure who the hell you are—that I can put up with. But the others—my God! Your Uncle Amos is an arrogant old despot, and he's got a great big talking machine inside of him that runs all day and all night, and there's no way to turn it off. Arabella's another talking machine, of a different sort. Who can listen to that infantile prattle of hers for longer than five minutes without wanting to stuff a rag in her mouth? And Adam! Words fail me. Adam's a reptile, pure and simple."

Brad sat with sagging shoulders, looking despondent. "I'm sorry, Lucius. It's all true, I know, you're absolutely right. I haven't seen these people in several yeahs, and I guess I'd just plain fo'gotten." He frowned, shaking his head. "Funny, though. You had me fooled. I could've sworn you'd taken a shine to Arabella."

"Just because we went for a stroll in the moonlight after the game of bowls last night? That was a desperation measure, my friend. *Anything* to get away from Adam and Amos a few minutes. But you noticed how Adam put a stop to it right quick, didn't you? Came and found us under the grape arbor, and spoke very sharply to Arabella about how she mustn't stay out in the night air because it gives her the sniffles. Good God!"

"Poor Arabella," Brad said sadly. "I do feel sorry for her. For several reasons. And I'll feel sorry for the poor fellow she marries."

"Amen!" Lucius agreed.

"Well . . ." Brad heaved a discouraged sigh. "Sorry to have gotten you involved heah. Hope you can stand it a few days. At least till Thursday. Amanda's comin' on Thursday, and—"

"I'm afraid that's impossible," Lucius said crisply. "I think we should beg off, and leave tomorrow."

"Oh, but you'll *like* Amanda, Lucius. She's different from the others, she's—"

Lucius was firmly shaking his head. "Brad, I've got to be in New Orleans by Thursday. I want to get back to Natchez, thank your parents for their hospitality, and be on my way."

Brad was aghast. "On youh way! I thought we were goin' to stay in Natchez fo' six months or so, and think about what to do next."

"Out of the question," Lucius snapped. He began to pace the floor, betraying an inner discomfort. "Must have been out of my mind when I suggested that. Can't sit *anywhere* for six months, Brad. Got to be moving. I wasted two and a half years in Texas, and I don't propose to waste another week."

41

"But I can't leave home yet, Lucius, I just got theah. My mothuh would be heartbroken if I left again so soon."

Lucius stopped pacing and gave his companion a steady look. "I know that, Brad. I understand perfectly."

"Oh, I see," Brad said quietly. "So I guess we'll soon be pahting company, then."

"Just for a while. Till I can ... get some new ideas going."

With another sigh Brad gave it up. "All right, Lucius. I'll make an excuse, and we'll leave tomorrow. No point in hangin' around heah, I suppose."

"Good. Thank you."

There came the sound of soft footfalls on the stairway, and a short knock on the door. "Enter!" Lucius called, obviously welcoming the interruption.

It was old Benjamin. "Mo'nin', gen'emens. Miss Arabella, she say would you-all join her fo' cakes an' *café au lait* in de gahden?"

"Tell her we'll be there in five minutes, Ben," Lucius said.

"Yes, suh."

"And, Ben, is Mr. Whitehurst up and about? Mr. Amos, that is?"

"Oh yes, suh, Marse Amos, he gits up wid de chickens. He fixin' to go down to de sugah mill."

"Would you mind asking him to wait a few minutes? I'd like to go with him."

Ben beamed approval of this. "Why, sho', Mistuh Lucius. He be glad to wait fo' you. Marse Amos, he *loves* to show off dat ol' sugah mill." Ben shuffled slowly back down the stairs.

Brad stared at Lucius in disbelief. "Lucius, you must be out of yo' mind—aftuh all that complainin' about what a talkative old bore Uncle Amos is! That sugah mill is the nastiest, stickiest, smelliest place on earth, and Uncle Amos'll have you climbin' around on yo' hands and knees peerin' into every nook and cranny of it. Even *I* wouldn't submit to that!"

Lucius stroked his chin thoughtfully and a cunning gleam came into his eye. "Ah'm a practical-minded man, Cud'n Bradfud," he drawled. "Fo' that reason theah's one thing about Ca'lina Grove that tickles mah curiosity."

"What's that?"

"Wheah the money comes from." For the first time that morning Lucius smiled.

(4)

IN LATE AFTERNOON of New Year's Eve, Arabella Whitehurst stood beside the big grand piano in the main hall of Carolina Grove, working on a flower arrangement. Her delicate young face was grave with concentration, and a small frown creased her brow. She hardly glanced at the butler Benjamin when he came into the room and approached her.

"'Scuse me, Miss Arabella."

Arabella kept her eyes on her work. "What is it, Ben?"

"Mistuh Lucius is heah, ma'am, and—"

"What?!" Arabella was all attention. "Lucius Hahgrave?!"

"Yes'm. Jes' got off de steamboat. He say—"

"Well, don't just stand theah, Ben, for heaven's sake—show him in!"

"Mistuh Lucius, he say he want to speak wid you in private, ma'am. He down by de bay trees. I tol' him to come in, but he say—"

Arabella had flown out of the room.

It was twilight, and the double row of bay trees created a tunnel of deep shadows along the front road. Arabella walked a short way and stopped.

"Lucius? Lucius, wheah are y—"

She gave a little gasp of fright when she suddenly found him at her side.

"Forgive me, Arabella," he murmured. "I didn't mean to startle you."

"Lucius, for heaven's sake, what's the meanin' of this strange behaviuh?"

43

"Again, forgive me. I seem to have a long list of things to ask forgiveness for."

"Well, I should think so! You and Bradfud both. Leavin' so abruptly last week, aftuh such a short stay—goodness, you gave us the impression you just didn't enjoy bein' heah."

"It was Brad who insisted on going back home immediately. Seems his mother has a strong hold on him. But I wanted to stay, you know I did. It broke my heart to say goodbye to you."

Arabella was partially mollified. "Well... now that you've come back, perhaps I can forgive you."

Lucius made bold to seize her hand. "My dear Arabella... when you so sweetly invited me to come back as soon as I could, I knew then that there was nothing on earth that could keep me away. Do you know I've thought about you every single day? Not an hour has gone by that I haven't—"

Arabella withdrew her hand and uttered a little laugh that was laced with a hint of impatience. "Goodness, Lucius, do stop talkin' so *solemnly*! It's New Yeah's Eve, dahlin'! Mean old Adam's gone back to New Orleans, so we don't have to contend with *him*. Amanda's heah now, with her gentleman friend, and guess what? He's just about the most *adorable* man I evuh saw. I'm shuah you two will like each othuh, and I just *know* it's goin' to be the nicest New Yeah's evuh!"

Suddenly grim-faced, Lucius stepped closer and spoke in a tone of hushed urgency that caused the girl to blink in surprise. "Arabella, regarding this gentleman friend of your sister's... there's something in the back of my mind, some stray memory, about someone who used to know her. It's nothing, really, just a vague suspicion... but, tell me—what is his name?"

"His name? Why, it's Albut Pettingill. But you'll meet him in just a few—"

She stopped abruptly and stared, and her surprise gave way to alarm. "What's the mattuh, Lucius, are you ill? You've grown deathly pale—"

"I might have known it," Lucius muttered. He turned away from the girl. "Yes, by God, I think I *did* know it, I just couldn't face up to it..."

Arabella was tugging at his sleeve. "Lucius, what *is* it?"

He turned back to her, composed and smiling. "Once more, my dear, forgive me. It's nothing, nothing at all. I'm looking forward to meeting this Mr. Pettingill. *And* Amanda."

44

Arabella took him by the arm and returned his smile as she pulled him along toward the house. "And do you know who's goin' to be the happiest one of all that you've come back? Papa! He hasn't left off for one second, talkin' about what a fine intelligent young man Mistuh Hahgrave is. Poor Papa, he so seldom gets a chance to show anybody the sugah mill, and when somebody actually takes an interest, why..."

Lucius stopped listening as they strolled toward the house. Benjamin had lit lamps in the front room, and through the open French windows Lucius could see a tall blond woman of about thirty, graceful, poised, beautifully statuesque. And with her, smilingly debonair, elegant in dress and manner, his wavy hair touched with just enough gray to convince any woman that the approach to forty is the age of perfection in masculine good looks—Albert Pettingill.

They were whispering together, their backs to the doorway, as Arabella and Lucius entered.

"Hel-loo-oo-oo!" Arabella trilled.

The couple turned. Pettingill glanced at Lucius without a hint of recognition, then turned his bland social smile on Arabella.

"Amanda, dahlin'," Arabella was saying to her sister, "I want you to meet my deah friend, Mistuh Lucius Hahgrave."

Amanda came up close to Lucius and gave him her hand, and her smile seemed to fill his entire field of vision. "I'm thrilled to meet you, Lucius." Her voice was husky and intimate. "Papa's been tellin' me how intelligent you are. Nobody told me how *beautiful* you are." Her eyes roamed over his broad-shouldered frame.

Lucius blinked. "Oh, well, I, uh..."

"And Lucius?" Arabella was firmly pulling him away. "I want you to meet Amanda's friend Mistuh Pettingill. Mistuh Pettingill, Mistuh Lucius Hahgrave."

Mr. Pettingill's smiling eyes remained for the moment on Arabella. "Now, now, Arabella, my dear. First names, remember? We promised."

"Oh yes, of course, Albut. Sorry."

Albert turned his smile on the other man. "So, Mr. Hargrave." He offered his hand. "Lucius, is it? May we be on a first-name basis too?"

Lucius was stony-faced as he shook hands. "Whatever you say."

"Splendid. I've been trying to achieve that small degree of informality with Arabella, here, for two days now."

45

Arabella's eyes shone with pleasure. "I won't forget again, Albut. Truly, I promise."

Lucius turned to Amanda. "It's a curious thing, Miss Whitehurst. I know I've seen you on stage many times, but it's only this instant I remember the very first time."

"Really? When was that?"

"Must be six or seven years ago. I can't recall the play, but I distinctly remember being dazzled by the beautiful Amanda Whitehurst and wondering if I could ever hope to meet anyone like that."

Amanda uttered a low throaty laugh. "Six or seven yeahs ago? You must have been most awfully young."

"I was. Very young and very foolish. I was keeping rather disreputable company in those days." Lucius glanced at Albert Pettingill, and found the older man observing him with what appeared to be secret amusement.

"And seems to me *your* name sounds familiar, Mr. Pettingill," Lucius said.

"Ah-ah-ah," Mr. Pettingill scolded, and waggled a finger. "It's Albert, remember?"

"Are you from New Orleans? You don't sound like a Southerner."

"To tell the truth, I follow a rather nomadic life," Mr. Pettingill said. "Up and down the river—hardly ever in one place longer than a day or two."

"That's too bad. I've been a wanderer myself, and I've just about come to the conclusion that a man can't expect to find real happiness until he's got a permanent home to house it in."

"Very prettily put," Amanda said.

"Albut works for a steamboat line, Lucius," Arabella said. "It's an evuh so important position. Has to do with freight rates, and things like that."

Lucius made an elaborate show of interest. "Oh, really? Sounds fascinating. I'd love to hear about it. *All* about it."

Albert made an even more elaborate show of modesty. "Oh, it's nothing, really. Rather dull, I'm afraid. Matter of fact, I agree with what you said about having a permanent home. When I'm in the company of such enchanting ladies as the Whitehurst sisters, I can easily imagine myself being serenely happy in a domestic life."

Arabella giggled. "Oh, you sweet thing, you!"

Amanda was getting restless. She glanced around the room. "Wheah the hell's Uncle Ben? We need some drinks around heah."

Lucius shot her an appreciative look.

"Oh, we haven't got time for drinks!" Arabella said. She skipped to Albert Pettingill's side and put her arm in his. "We're goin' to sing duets, and Albut's goin' to teach me how to harmonize, aren't you, Albut?"

Albert gave her a kindly smile. "Not only that, my dear, but it happens I've got a beautiful new song for you. A Scottish tune called 'Annie Laurie.'"

"Oh, lovely!" Arabella fairly squealed. "Teach it to me, please!" She pulled him away toward the piano.

Lucius and Amanda exchanged looks, and Lucius was seized with a sudden inspiration.

"Look here, why don't I go find Ben and see about those drinks?"

"Thank you, Lucius," Amanda murmured. "You're a love."

As Lucius turned to go, Arabella's milk white hands fluttered over the keyboard, and a delicate arpeggio rose like something shimmering in the air. Albert Pettingill cleared his throat noisily. A second later his rich baritone voice began to throb with thrilling vibrato.

"Wait, dahlin'," Amanda said, and hurried after Lucius. "I'll go with you."

At eight o'clock in the evening, Albert Pettingill was standing before a long mirror in the second-story room of the east tower. He was brushing his hair, and after each stroke he turned his handsome head from side to side, examining the result. Behind him Benjamin stood holding a dinner jacket, and waiting.

At last the gentleman seemed satisfied with his grooming. "How's that, Ben?"

Ben's answer was mechanical, automatic. "Fine, suh. You look jes' fine."

Mr. Pettingill put down the hairbrush and turned to gaze thoughtfully at the jacket in the servant's hands. "I wonder . . ." he mused. "Maybe I should wear the darker gray—"

His thoughts were interrupted by a knock at the door.

"Come in," Mr. Pettingill called.

Lucius Hargrave stepped into the room.

Mr. Pettingill beamed. "Ah, Lucius! How nice of you to stop by!"

"Thought we might have a little chat before the party begins," Lucius said.

"Fine, fine. Look here, maybe you can help us out. Ben and

47

I were just trying to decide whether this light gray jacket is formal enough for such a gala evening. What do you think?"

Lucius glanced without interest at the servant and the garment he held. "I'm afraid I'm not very good at that kind of thing."

Mr. Pettingill's discriminating eye drifted over the somewhat threadbare coat Lucius was wearing. "No, I suppose not," he murmured. "They do say life in Texas tends to atrophy one's sense of gracious living."

Ignoring Lucius's glower, he took the jacket from the servant. "That will do, Ben, thank you. Tell the Misses Whitehurst we'll join them in a few minutes."

"Yes, suh." Ben went out, and his footsteps slowly faded away as he descended the stairway to the lower floor.

Mr. Pettingill gestured his guest to a chair. "Sit down, Lucius."

Lucius took a chair and sat stiffly. Mr. Pettingill sat down on the edge of his bed, crossed his legs, and swung his foot languidly. He smiled.

"Splendid old fellow, Ben, don't you think? Can you imagine Mr. Whitehurst sending his personal valet out here to serve me? You can say what you like about these slaveholding Southerners, they certainly know how to make a guest comfortable."

Lucius's face was grim. "All right, Albert, let's talk. What the hell are you doing here?"

Albert expelled his breath in relief. "Thank God, Lucius! Finally we can behave normally toward one another. I hope you appreciate the fact that I've held back and allowed you to set the tone of our exchanges. I saw right away you wanted to play that little game of 'let's pretend we're strangers,' and I went along with you, didn't I? I'm really a very nice fellow, Lucius, I don't think you've ever fully apprecia—"

"Albert, what the hell are you doing here?" Lucius's tone was gruff and demanding.

Albert's expression was pure innocence. "Why, I imagine I'm doing approximately the same thing *you're* doing here."

"All *I'm* doing is paying a social call on some nice people who happen to be relatives of my friend Bradford Kenyon, of Natchez. You remember Brad, I imagine?"

"Of course I remember him. That's a little like asking an abandoned wife if she remembers the woman who came into her house and stole her husband away."

Lucius grimaced. "That's a thoroughly distasteful thing to say, Albert."

"Maybe, but it's apt. We were very close, Lucius. When I plucked you out of the Ohio River all those years ago you were an ignorant backwoods boy, begging for crumbs off my table. We were almost like father and son then. And when you grew older and more experienced and took on a little sophistication—having learned the things I taught you, that is—we were like brothers. Then one night we came down the river on a steamboat and you met Brad Kenyon, and the next morning you were gone. You walked away from me without even saying goodbye, without so much as a backward—"

"Excuse me, Albert." Lucius had taken a gold watch from his pocket and was consulting it. "It's getting late. Let's not waste time with all these tiresome biographical musings, eh? I learned all your old tricks quite well. What I'm interested in knowing is what you're up to right now."

Albert got up and walked to a window, and stood gazing toward the main house, where lamplight streamed from the tall French windows and lay in golden swaths across the darkened grounds.

"Tell me, Lucius, how much does your friend Brad Kenyon know about me?"

"You mean have I ever told him what you are? Certainly not. What am I, a gossip?"

"Good. Perfect."

Lucius was fuming with impatience. "Albert, for the last time, are you going to tell me what you're doing—"

"Can't you guess, my boy?" Albert had turned toward him, smiling.

"Surely you're not trying to get old Amos into a card game?"

Albert laughed. "Surely not. No, Lucius, I'm after much bigger game. Like you, I've grown tired of card tricks. Like you, I am now looking for a rich wife."

"Naturally," Lucius muttered. "I should have known."

"That's right. You certainly should have."

"Well..." Lucius's wry little smile was almost a grimace. "I suppose there's enough Whitehurst money for both of us. Maybe we can have a double wedding. Arabella and I, and you and Amanda. It'll be the social event of the year."

Albert came back across the room and sat down again.

49

"Lucius...do you have any idea what kind of woman Amanda is?"

"Well, she's an actress. What more can you say?"

"You can say she's totally dedicated to her independent life. She is utterly without morals, conventions, or scruples. She changes lovers about as often as she changes her undergarments, which is very often, indeed. She loves her life and she aims to keep it just the way it is. Now, I have no objections to her way of living, it suits me fine. I'd have married her years ago if she'd have had me. But she wouldn't, and she won't, and she never will. Amanda will never marry."

Lucius looked at the other man warily, eyes narrowed. "What's the point of all this?"

Albert rose, picked up his jacket, and began to put it on. "The point, Lucius, is that I don't plan to marry Amanda at all, for the very good reason that it's not possible. I plan to marry Arabella."

While Lucius sat mute, motionless, and pale, Albert crossed the room and opened the door.

"The party will be starting," he said. "Shall we go?"

Like a cat Lucius was on him, grasping him by the lapel and forcing him against the wall. "You will *not*!" he growled between clenched teeth, and his fierce eyes were inches from Albert's. "I will not permit it."

Albert glanced down at the hand gripping his jacket. "Please," he said mildly. "This is my best frock coat."

Lucius held on, and his jaw jutted in anger. "You remember me, Albert? I'm Lucius Hargrave, your old gambling partner. If you attempt to do this, I swear, I'll tell everything."

Albert remained unperturbed. "No you won't, Lucius."

"Why the hell won't I?"

"Because if you tell all about me you'll have to tell all about yourself too, won't you? Or if you don't, I will. Then we both lose. On the other hand, if we conduct an honest competition, like the gentlemen we are, one of us wins, the other cooperates by keeping silent, and is generously taken care of by his grateful partner. After all, Lucius, we're still partners as far as I'm concerned, all that Texas foolishness of yours notwithstanding." In the face of menacing belligerence, Albert smiled. "Now, that's a much more civilized approach, don't you agree?"

Lucius released his grip and stepped back. He bowed his head and grasped his temples between his fingers.

"Goddamn!" he mumbled. "I'll just be goddamned!"

"There," Albert said soothingly, "I knew you'd see it my way." Carefully he smoothed his jacket collar back into place, turned and descended the stairs.

When he reached the front door of the tower Lucius called him.

"Albert!"

Albert looked up. Lucius was at the top of the stairs, glaring down, the muscles of his jaw working furiously.

"Damn you to hell, Albert," he said in a hoarse whisper.

Albert seemed pleased. "Ah! That's my boy, Lucius! Just like old times!"

(5)

THE GREAT MAIN HALL of Carolina Grove glittered with the light of three hundred candles set in a dozen crystal sconces attached to the lofty walls, and in the arena thus formed a throng of guests produced a seething rush of sound—chatter, laughter, music, the rustle of taffeta skirts, the clinking of glasses. Adeline Whitehurst, looking regal in a long velvet gown, wandered slowly about dispensing glassy hostess-smiles in all directions. Occasionally she paused to issue whispered instructions to one or another of the several uniformed servants who moved silently through the crowd with trays of food and drink, their gleaming black faces fixed in concentration.

In one corner of the room a dozen people were gathered in a tight huddle around the grand piano. One of the guests was playing, while Albert Pettingill and Arabella Whitehurst stood close together rendering their duet version of "Annie Laurie." Albert's arm was loosely curved around Arabella's slender waist, and as their voices intertwined in harmony the girl's shining blue eyes smiled up into her partner's.

In an opposite corner of the room Amanda Whitehurst was the center of attention in another admiring group. She was telling anecdotes about life in the theater world, and her throaty voice would occasionally rise to a point of raucous laughter, bringing forth a corresponding burst of hilarity from her listeners. Amanda was wearing a tight-fitting gown of warm and vivid orange that did spectacular things for her magnificent hourglass figure. The contrast between her dress and Arabella's demure, lacy, ice blue gown was striking, even at a distance.

Around the outer edges of the group clustered about the piano, Lucius Hargrave prowled restlessly, clutching an iced drink close to his chest and peering between the heads of the people in front of him for an occasional glimpse of the singers. Once Arabella looked in his direction as she held a long trilling note, and Lucius leaned forward on tiptoe trying to catch her eye—but in vain; she returned her attention to her handsome partner. The eye Lucius caught instead was Albert Pettingill's. Albert winked at him. Lucius turned away, glowering.

In a little alcove that formed a relatively quiet haven from the noise of the party, Amos Whitehurst sat in company with an elderly couple. Amos's broad beam occupied an entire two-person settee. He was cradling a glass of dark-colored liquid in his hands, and was holding forth according to his custom.

"So I tol' this heah Creole architect, I says, 'Look heah, son, I aim to put this heah house to *use*, not jes' set it up fo' show. I want ten-inch cypress joists on fawty-inch centuhs unduh-neath them floahs, and don't tell me it's too expensive, 'cause *I'm* tellin' *you* cost is no object. I want them floahs solid, you heah me?'" He paused to take a long pull on his drink.

The prim little gray-haired lady sitting at Amos's left put a hand over her mouth, trying to hide a discreet yawn. The man at his right drained the last of his drink and stared glumly into the empty glass. Amos turned to him.

"Ain't it a shame what they're buildin' these days, Ed? Have you seen that piece o' trash th' Langleys are puttin' up ovuh theah on Bayou des Allemands? Greek Revival, they call it. Hell, it ain't nothin' but a mess o' white plastuh ovuh pine boards. Won't last thu'ty years. I can't unduhstand why people—"

"Excuse me a minute, Amos," Ed said suddenly, and held

up his empty glass. "I'm gon' go find me a refill." He got up and hurried away.

"Them damn nigguhs ain't doin' theah job," Amos growled, addressing the woman. "They ought to be bringin' fresh drinks around heah. Ain't it hahd to find decent house nigguhs, Millie? I sweah, sometimes I think ain't a one of 'em wuth theah keep."

"That suttenly is true," Millie agreed. She was getting restless. "Would you excuse me too, Amos? I want to go find Adeline and compliment her on the lovely floral decorations."

Amos was left alone. He stared into his drink and went on, undiscouraged, with his monologue.

"No, them nigguhs ain't no damn good. Ain't a one of 'em knows how to do anything right. And Arabella fixed th' flowers, not Adeline. Arabella's the only one 'round heah gives a dang 'bout Ca'lina Grove. Amanda don't. And Adam! Hell, he don't even come home but once a—"

Amos stopped suddenly as he became aware of someone standing over him. He looked up, and his broad face broke into a smile.

"Well, Mistuh Hahgrave! Why ain't you ovuh theah singin' and carryin' on with the othuh young folks?"

"I noticed you were alone, Mr. Whitehurst, so I thought—"

"Well, now, ain't that nice? Sit down, sit down."

By the time Lucius had taken a seat Amos had launched another monologue.

"You know, I was jes' tellin' Ed Appleton a minute ago, I says, 'Ed—'"

"Excuse me, Mr. Whitehurst. I'm sorry to interrupt you, but—" Lucius was leaning close to the other man, and his low voice carried a note of urgency.

"What's the mattuh, son?" Amos demanded. "You look like you ain't well. You had too much to drink?"

"Sir, there's something I want to tell you, and I beg you to listen carefully and keep what I say in strictest confidence. It's a delicate matter."

Amos leaned forward. "Go ahead, son. I'm listenin'." For once in his life he was.

"You're a rich man, Mr. Whitehurst. And there are human leeches in this world who would love to get their hands on your money, by fair means or foul."

"Go on, son. You ain't told me anything yet I don't already know."

53

"Sir, there is one of those leeches in this house tonight, hard at work."

Amusement crinkled old Amos's eyes. "Fo' heaven's sakes, only one? I thought theah was at least a dozen."

Lucius did not share the amusement. "You don't understand, sir. The man I'm speaking of is a master thief. Known from New Orleans to St. Louis as one of the best in his profession."

Amos had stopped being amused. "Who is he?"

People were passing nearby, laughing and chattering. Lucius glanced around uneasily, drew his chair close to Amos's, and dropped his voice lower still.

"Can't talk about it now, sir. I just came up from New Orleans today to warn you to be careful. I've got to get back to the city immediately."

"Tonight?!"

"This is not the proper time and place for such things, in any case. I'd like to return to Carolina Grove in a week or so, and discuss this with you in private. May I do that?"

"Well, whatevuh you say, son." Amos's attention was wandering. "Looka heah, will you do me a favuh?" He held up his glass. "Fetch me a fresh drink. Them dang nigguhs don't look aftuh me wuth nothin'."

"Be glad to, sir." Lucius took the glass and got up. "You take rum and coffee, don't you? Half and half. Plenty of ice."

Amos was pleased. "Tha's right. You're very observant." He put a hand on Lucius's sleeve to detain him. "You know wheah I git th' ice?"

"No, sir. I was wondering about that."

"Adam sends it up from N'yawlins. It's brought down heah on ships from th' Nawth. Adam bein' in th' shippin' business, y'see, he gits a special price. He keeps me supplied."

"That's very nice of him."

"No, it ain't. He jes' does little things like that to make up fo' nevuh comin' home."

Lucius went off to get the drink. When he returned, the chairs on either side of Amos were occupied, and Amos was deep into his standard narrative about how he had built the first successful sugar mill in Louisiana. Lucius went around behind the old man, handed him his drink, and bent down close to his ear.

"I'll see you soon, Mr. Whitehurst. And we'll have a long talk about that little matter I mentioned, all right?"

Amos showed no signs of comprehending the meaning of

Lucius's remarks. "Oh, shuah, son. Anytime you're in th' neighborhood, you come by. You're always welcome at Ca'lina Grove."

Lucius melted away in the crowd, and without a pause Amos turned back to his companions and went on with his story.

As the final minutes of the year 1838 ticked away, the excitement and the noise level rose together. A tall floor-standing clock in the central hallway became the center of attention as a crowd gathered around it and waited for the stroke of midnight. Benjamin stationed himself at the rear of the hall, holding aloft in one hand a large iron plate suspended on a chain, and in the other a heavy stick. When the hour struck there arose shouts from the gentlemen and shrieks from the ladies, accompanied by a fearful clatter from Benjamin. The doleful chiming of the old clock would have sounded oddly incongruous, could it have been heard.

An orgy of kissing began. Lovers clung together in long embraces weighted with meaning, then milled about to exchange more antiseptic kisses with friends, relatives, acquaintances, and strangers. Arabella Whitehurst announced her intention to kiss every gentleman in the house, and men gleefully lined up to receive her charming attentions. When she came to Albert Pettingill she aimed a little nearer to the lips than the standard middle-of-the-cheek location, and allowed the kiss to linger a split-second longer than usual. A moment later she came upon Albert again, standing expectantly in line.

"Why, Albut!" she breathed. "I've already kissed you!"

"I demand an encore," he murmured. He pulled her up close and kissed her full on the mouth.

She drew back, gasping. "Albut, really! That's evuh so impropuh!"

Her effort to sound indignant was unconvincing. She cast a sidelong smile at him as she moved away, and her cheeks were aflame.

Amanda took Albert by the arm and pulled him into a corner. She stood very close and gazed probingly into his eyes.

"Well, dahlin', how are things progressin'?"

"Splendidly, Amanda, just splendidly! It's a marvelous party."

"Well, just let me remind you of one little thing, heah?"

There were daggers concealed in Amanda's honey-soft voice. "You can play around all you like, but you're *not* goin' to get into my little sistuh's bed until that weddin' ring is on her finguh, do you unduhstand that *quite* cleahly?"

Albert looked both astonished and injured. "Why, Amanda, what are you talking about? I wouldn't dream of trying to take advantage of Arabella. She's a mere child, and I—"

"She is not a mere child, she's a twenty-year-old virgin who's just pantin' for love. But she is goin' to do it the propuh way, Albut. She is goin' to get married; she is goin' to have a lovely wedding; she is goin' to settle down and have lots of babies and make Mothuh and Daddy happy grandparents. They're dreadfully disappointed in both Adam and me, but they're not goin' to be disappointed in Arabella. I know, because I'm personally goin' to see to it."

Albert's hands had crept around Amanda's waist. He pulled her gently toward him, and his lips brushed her cheek.

"Darling, I agree with you wholeheartedly. But you know quite well my taste is for more mature women. And of all the mature women on earth the one who most excites my blood—" he was nibbling on Amanda's earlobe—"is you."

She pulled her head back and looked him in the eye. "You're a liar."

He kissed her on the lips. "Come to the east tower later, and I'll prove it to you."

"I'd be delighted." Something devilish gleamed in Amanda's eyes. "Unless I should happen to get confused and go to the west towuh instead."

Albert looked horrified. "You mean *Lucius*? Oh, you wouldn't like him, darling, he's much too crude. Not your type at all."

Amanda looked around suddenly, a faint frown on her brow. "By the way, wheah *is* he? I haven't seen him in an hour."

Albert gave a disinterested shrug. "I wouldn't be surprised if he were out in the bushes wrestling with one of the Negro wenches."

They broke apart quickly as Arabella descended upon them, bubbling with some new enthusiasm. "Oh, Albut, do let's sing 'Auld Lang Syne'! You too, Amanda, come *on* now, it's New Yeah's!"

She took her sister and Albert each by the hand and led them forcefully across the big room toward the piano.

"Oh, Albut. Amanda . . ." She beamed at first one and then the other, and her vivacious blue eyes danced with young joy. "Somehow I just have the feelin' that 1839 is goin' to be the very loveliest yeah of my life!"

"I do fervently hope so, my dear," Albert purred, and gave her hand a little secret squeeze.

(6)

AT ELEVEN O'CLOCK in the morning Arabella's young black maid entered her mistress's darkened bedroom, tiptoed across to one of the several pairs of latticed doors that led to the second-floor veranda, and opened them. The room was suddenly awash in a stream of sunlight. The maid approached the big four-poster bed and peered into mountains and valleys of billowing softness.

"Miss Arabella? I's 'leben o'clock, ma'am."

There was a slight stirring from the depths, a faint and tremulous sigh, and a slender arm rose like the neck of a languid swan, hovered for an instant, then drooped over the side of the bed. The maid moved away to open another set of French windows. When she turned back to the bed her young mistress was sitting up and rubbing her eyes.

"Mawnin', Miss Arabella," the maid said. "You ready fo' yo' bath now?"

Arabella pushed a mass of tousled blond hair back from her face, smoothed her lacy nightgown, and blinked at the morning light. She gazed out past the ornate veranda bannisters to the gleaming sunlit foliage of trees and flowering shrubs, and the little-girl eyes opened wide in wonder.

"Oh, Crissy, look!"

The maid looked out, saw nothing unusual, and frowned. "What, Miss Arabella?"

"It's the first day of 1839, Crissy! The whole world is bright and clean and sparklin' with newness! Isn't it exciting?"

Crissy's broad face was expressionless. "Yes'm," she said dully. "Sho' is."

Arabella pulled her knees up and hugged them tightly, and rocked with joy. "Oh, Crissy, wouldn't it be wonderful if a person could see the whole yeah ahead, and know all the nice things that are going to happen to them?"

Crissy was moving around the room, picking up various garments strewn on the floor. "Yes'm, sho' would. You want yo' bath now, Miss Arabella?"

"In a minute, Crissy. First I have to think about last night. Oh, it was a lovely pahty, Crissy, just evuh so! I just know it's a favorable omen for the new yeah!"

"Yes'm, I seed you an' Mistuh Pettingill in dere, just a'singin' fo' deah life." Crissy flashed a smile. "Dat sho' was purty."

"Oh, he's a delightful man, Crissy! Honestly, if I were the envious type, I'd be evuh so envious of Amanda. She meets such mahvelous men in New Awlins, and I have nothin' but dullards to keep me company out heah in the country."

"Seems lak Mistuh Hahgrave's a nice gen'eman," Crissy offered.

Arabella's shoulders moved with a little shrug. "Oh, he's nice enough. But evuh so earnest. Oh, I *do* get bored with earnest men, Crissy! I want wit and fun and gaiety."

"Did you read de lettuh I brung you?" Crissy asked.

Arabella gave her a blank look. "What lettuh, Crissy?"

"Last night Mistuh Lucius gi' me a lettuh fo' you. I lef' it right on yo' pillow when I turned down yo' bed."

"Good gracious, Crissy! When somebody gives you a lettuh to give me, fo' heaven's sake, *give* it to me!" She was rummaging angrily through her bedding.

"Heah it is, I found it," Crissy announced. She picked up something off the floor and handed it to her mistress.

Arabella snatched the letter and tore it open. "Really, Crissy, how utterly stupid of you!"

Looking hurt, Crissy moved away to the opposite side of the room. "I'll be gittin' yo' bath ready, Miss Arabella."

Arabella's wide eyes were already devouring the letter.

December 31st, 1838
11:30 P.M.

My dearest Arabella,
I sit alone in the west tower. From the big house

58

across the grounds the laughter and music of the party waft on the night breeze and reach my ears as a gentle murmuring. But it is not music to me, it is a hateful sound. For I had a beautiful dream about this night, and that dream now lies shattered at my feet. I am desolate.

Sweet Arabella, let me tell you about my dream. I had pictured us strolling on the upper veranda in the moonlight, with those same sounds of the party providing a serenade from belowstairs, gentle in the distance, enchanting our senses. We would come to a certain pair of latticed doors. You would pause, push a door ajar, and with an enticing smile say, "This is my bedroom, Lucius. Would you like a peek?"

I would peek; I would inhale the narcotic fragrance that hangs about that lovely chamber and peer into it as if gazing into paradise itself. Then with the ardor in my heart no longer containable I would clasp your hand and lead you to the edge of the veranda where the moonlight would play softly upon your hair, and there I would declare my undying love for you, my angelic Arabella, and ask you to be my wife.

Oh, I know this is entirely improper, not at all in keeping with the refined and stately traditions of courtship. We have but recently met, and have had only fleeting moments together. But I am a desperate man, Arabella, and time is of the essence. I beg you to forgive my haste, and consider my suit with the kindness that I know lies in your heart.

I must leave now. I am called away suddenly on a matter that demands my urgent attention—but, that aside, I can no longer bear to linger here and see you in the clutches of an evil scheming reprobate who smiles with false charm upon you, but who in reality is impelled by the most despicable of motives.

Please convey my regrets to your parents and your sister, my thanks for their warm hospitality, and my humblest apologies for this abrupt departure. It cannot be helped.

I pray heaven will watch over you until we meet again. I will return as soon as circumstances permit, and when I do I will ask you to walk with me beneath the ancient oaks and give me the answer that will lift me to rapturous happiness, or plunge me into a despair from which I may never recover. Until then, Arabella, I love

59

*you, I kiss you, I whisper your name with infinite
longing in my dreams.*

*Think of me tenderly, dear one. My life is in your
hands.*

Yours in undying devotion,
Lucius

When Crissy came back into the room Arabella was still sitting
in bed, gazing dreamily out into the morning sunshine. She
held Lucius's letter in a drooping hand. Crissy came close, her
eyes asparkle with curiosity.

"What he say, Miss Arabella?"

"He loves me," Arabella announced casually.

Crissy squealed. "Oh, I knew it, I jes' *knew* it!"

Arabella was busy recollecting. "You know, Crissy, I
thought theah was something funny about the pahty last night,
and now I know what it was. I hahdly saw Lucius all evening.
It's because he was called away suddenly on some kind of
urgent business. It's just evuh so mysterious."

"Gracious me, sho' is," Crissy agreed. "Come on now, Miss
Arabella, yo' bath watuh's gon' git all cold if you don't quit dat
dawdlin'."

Arabella started to slide out of bed. Halfway up she
stopped suddenly, a great frown darkening her delicate
features.

"Oh, bothuh, Crissy!"

"Wha's de mattuh, ma'am?"

"Do you know what this means?"

"What?"

A pretty little pout lay on Arabella's lips. "We won't have a
foursome for lawn bowlin' this aftuhnoon!"

"Awww!" Crissy said, in deepest sympathy.

(7)

The earth may be changeless from one aeon to the next, but the only constant feature of human existence is inconstancy. Change is an everlasting characteristic of life.

I felt like an intruder during my sojourn in Texas, and returned to the United States only to find myself no less homeless there, an alien among strangers in my own native land. Had my countrymen changed, or had I? Both, surely—and it was immediately clear to me that I must live with profound and painful change for a long time before I could ever hope to achieve any sense of a destination reached, or a respite from my wanderings.

The necessity for one important change appeared quickly with the realization that I had to rid myself of Bradford Kenyon. Brad was a man entirely without toughness and ambition. After our ill-fated Texas venture he wanted nothing more than to return to his family estate near Natchez, Mississippi, and spend the rest of his life riding to hounds in the morning, having tea and cakes with the ladies in the afternoon, and attending polite musicales in the magnolia-scented evenings. I watched him slipping easily back into the aimless ways of his people, and knew that soon I must shake his hand, wish him good luck, and, as I had done on several previous occasions, go my separate way. Another parting, another lump in the throat and a moistness in the eye—and life goes on.

My association with Brad having been unremittingly sterile, it was ironic that very near the end of it he did something that altered the very foundations of my destiny—

he introduced me to his relatives, the Whitehursts of Louisiana. We spent a few days around Christmastime at Carolina Grove, the Whitehurst plantation, and the experience was an astonishing revelation to me. Situated in St. Charles Parish some thirty miles upriver from New Orleans, Carolina Grove was a palatial estate, resplendent in gracious beauty and magnificent wealth. The Whitehursts themselves were a sad illustration of what I believe to be axiomatic about rich people: that they tend to be overwhelmed by the burden of their wealth, and end up serving it rather than being served by it. Still I was dazzled by the sharp mind of old Amos Whitehurst, a potentate of the Louisiana sugar industry, and in my layman's judgment an authentic genius. His wife Adeline was a colorless woman, but pleasant enough. The son of the family, Adam, I found coldly aloof and insufferably pompous. But I was thoroughly delighted by the younger daughter, Arabella, who possessed a combination of childlike charm and womanly loveliness that beggared description.

On my first visit I missed meeting the older sister, Amanda, and it was partly to remedy this deficiency that I felt myself drawn back to Carolina Grove a second time. There was something about Amanda that intrigued me. The name had brought to my memory's eye a vision of an actress, gorgeously gowned and bejewelled, parading her ample figure and meager talents before an enthusiastic and not very discriminating audience (mostly male) in the theatres of New Orleans. Amanda's reputation was legendary, not for her dramatic ability but for the prodigious number of lovers she had had—and one of them, I knew, had been my former associate, Albert Pettingill. Now I understood she had gone to the unusual length of bringing her current paramour home with her, and the thought that tantalized my mind was this: could it by any chance be that disreputable old adventurer himself? I considered it unlikely after so long a time—still, a hint of perverse curiosity impelled me to investigate. And it was a fateful decision.

To begin with, the intriguing unlikelihood turned out to be a horrible fact—Albert Pettingill not only still maintained his disreputable liaison with Amanda, but there he was at Carolina Grove, grinning at me. And hard on the heels of this unpleasant discovery came another, a realization that struck me with the force of a hurricane and left me stunned: I was in love with the angelic Arabella!

What a baffling mystery, love. By what exotic alchemy is a

strong man reduced to a mass of quivering jelly in the presence of a maid—or in her absence, by the mere thought of her? The deadly infection had crept into my veins with devastating swiftness; I had come to Carolina Grove for the first time just before Christmas, and by the dawn of the new year I was suddenly a mewling wretch, afflicted beyond hope of recovery.

Ah, Arabella—in those sunny blue eyes lurked a terrifying peril. Her innocence, so integral to her charm, barely concealed an enormous capacity for inflicting pain. She considered all men her playthings, baubles to be trifled with for amusement's sake. Her own emotions as yet unawakened, she had no conception of the dangerous surges of passion she could arouse in others. And yet, so enchanting were her pretty ways that I submitted to suffering willingly, and longed for more. Almost against my will I found myself forming the resolve that I must make Arabella Whitehurst my wife, or die of heartbreak.

But—life being the way it is—the moment this goal was set, malevolent forces rose up to threaten it. I had tried to avoid Albert Pettingill as much as possible—no need to renew that useless old relationship—but I soon perceived a fact that made my blood run cold. The shameless old philanderer had grown tired of Amanda, and was casting his seductive wiles upon my innocent Arabella! It was plain to see he cared not a whit for either lady; his only interest was in getting his greedy hands on the Whitehurst fortune.

It was no use warning Arabella—she would only scold me for spoiling her fun. I tried to call her father's attention to the danger, but old Amos was in a perpetual fog from the rum and coffee he insatiably craved, and could not quite grasp what I was trying to say. In desperation I fled; I could not bear to witness what was happening. I went to New Orleans, settled myself in modest quarters, and plunged into work, hoping thereby to wash all thoughts of Arabella Whitehurst from my mind. It was hopeless, of course—but I did have important work to do, and I undertook it with feverish determination.

Two tasks I had set for myself. One was to write a book.

In the course of my youthful years on the great river I had occasion to observe at close range and in considerable detail one of the most dreadful social evils that had ever afflicted America: my countrymen's insane passion for gambling. During my subsequent wanderings I had reflected deeply on this, and had concluded that sooner or later someone must expose the ghastly curse for what it is, or else it will eventually eat the nation's heart out. Someone must—why not Lucius Hargrave? I set to work, looking upon the undertaking as a painful but vitally important civic duty.

My other task was to renew and intensify that sacred quest that had impelled me since childhood, and which I was bound to follow to the last day of my life, if necessary. That was the search for my missing father.

(8)

ON A DAMP AFTERNOON in February, Arabella White-hurst was in the garden at Carolina Grove trimming the wisteria vines when Lucius Hargrave crept up behind her and slipped his hands over her eyes. Immediately Arabella smiled in the delight of game-playing.

"Who*evuh* can it be?" she breathed.

"One who adores you," Lucius whispered, then released her and stepped back, smiling.

"Albut!" She whirled on him, beaming with expectancy— but instantly her eyes reflected disappointment. "Oh, Lucius . . . what a surprise."

His smile turned to a scowl. "So. You're expecting Albert Pettingill."

"Why, yes, as a mattuh of fact I am."

"I see," Lucius said grimly.

"Really, Lucius, I wish you'd let me know when you're comin'." Arabella sounded a trifle annoyed.

"Well, don't worry, I'm not staying. I just stopped by to say hello, and to find out if you've been getting my letters."

"Oh yes, I shuahly have. You write beautifully, Lucius, I've come to enjoy youh lettuhs evuh so much."

"Then why have you never answered, Arabella? Not a

single line. Do you realize what a torture it is for me? I pour out my heart to you, over and over, and in return I receive nothing but silence. You are cruel, Arabella." His face was a picture of suffering. "*Why* are beautiful women so cruel?"

Arabella was conducting a minute examination of the leaves of the wisteria vine. "Oh deah, I do believe this vine is becoming infected."

Lucius took a step closer to her. "Arabella—will you do me the courtesy of answering my question?"

She went on studying the vine. "I've been punishing you, Lucius."

"But why?"

"For your horrid behavior New Yeah's Eve. Honestly! Leavin' without so much as a single word of goodbye! Is that considered good mannuhs in Indiana?"

"But I explained in my letters. Explained and explained, and begged your forgiveness. I just couldn't bear to see you giving your smiles to another man. Especially *that* man."

"Well, for *you* I have nothing but frowns," Arabella said, and gave him one. "Lucius, you're being utterly unreasonable. Albut Pettingill is a puhfect gentlemen. Whatevuh do you have against him?"

"For one thing, he's old enough to be your father."

Arabella laughed in scorn. "Oh, for heaven's sakes, that's just silly!"

"For another thing, he's a disreputable character. Probably has a shady past."

"What*evuh* do you mean by *that*?!"

"Think about it, Arabella. What do you really know about him? About his background, his character? What is his profession, exactly? Do you know?"

Arabella was flustered. "Why, of course I know. He does some, uh...some very important work with some steamboat line or othuh—"

"What kind of work?"

"Oh, some...administrative work or othuh. Really, Lucius, I don't see why I should be subjected to this kind of questioning. I know every bit as much about Albut as I know about *you*."

Lucius stepped closer still, and his voice went low. "About me you need know only this, my dearest: that I love you more than it is safe or sane to admit, and that I stand ready to lay my life and fortune at your feet, if only you'll say yes to my—"

Arabella laughed again, but this time with affectionate

65

gentleness. She laid a little white hand on Lucius's shoulder.

"You're sweet, Lucius, really you are. And I'm just evuh so honored by your proposal. But I'm simply not *ready* to think about marriage, I just—"

Lucius groaned.

"I'll promise you one thing, though," she went on. "When I *am* ready, I'll considuh youh suit just as seriously as anybody else's."

Lucius was not visibly comforted by this news. Arabella gave him one of her sweet smiles and a playful pat on the cheek.

"Come on now, let's go inside. Albut will be heah soon, and we'll have some lovely refreshments."

She took him by the hand, and as they strolled across the garden toward the house she shot him an appraising sidelong glance. "Do stop lookin' so grim, Lucius. Really, it's evuh so depressin'. You must try to be a little more *fun*."

Lucius looked grimmer than ever.

The sugar mill at Carolina Grove was almost a mile from the house, situated in a clearing beside a little bayou that wound sluggishly among huge moss-dripping trees and soggy cane fields. In midwinter the fields were empty stubble, awaiting the plowing and planting of spring. The mill was a long rectangular building of windowless brick walls rising to a height of five feet, above which a shingled roof was supported on short wooden posts that separated it from the walls by three feet of open space. In the shadowy interior two separate centers of work were in simultaneous operation. On a platform at one end of the building three massive cast-iron rollers as tall as a man were grinding, powered by a pair of mules plodding around a circular course and turning a winch-and-gear assembly. Teams of muscular black men, stripped to the waist and gleaming with sweat, fed stalks of cane between the first and second rollers, then pulled them out and fed them back through the second and third rollers in the opposite direction. The juices drained in a steady stream down to a vat below the platform.

At the other end of the building a gigantic copper pot sat atop an eight-foot-square brick oven in which a fire seethed and roared. A catwalk of heavy planking provided access to the pot, and from this platform several black men stirred a steaming brew with long wooden paddles.

Amos Whitehurst was standing on the sawdust-covered

floor near the furnace end of the building, conferring with his foreman, a burly bearded white man. The two stood close together and shouted to be heard over the din of roaring fire and screeching machinery.

Lucius Hargrave appeared in the doorway of the building and called to Amos. The big man turned and frowned at the interruption, but when recognition came his broad face brightened. He came hurrying to the door, grasped the visitor's hand, and shook it vigorously.

"Lucius, my boy! Glad to see you. Didn't know you were comin'."

"Happened to be passing by on my way north, sir, so I though I'd stop by and say hello."

Amos had taken Lucius's arm and was leading him away from the mill. "Le's go ovuh heah wheah we can talk."

They settled in wicker chairs in the shade of a tree a short distance away.

"Theah, tha's bettuh," Amos said. He sighed heavily and mopped his brow. His shirt was soaked with perspiration. "My Lawd, I don't know how many mo' yeahs I can go on workin' like this."

"I don't see how you do it, sir," Lucius said. "If it's that hot in the mill in February, what's it like in July?"

"The mill don't operate in the summuh, thank God. We'll be done with last year's crop by the end o' March, and won't staht cookin' ag'in till next fall."

"Well, I certainly admire your stamina, sir."

"You got it right, son. Tha's what it takes. Stamina."

"And brains," Lucius added.

Amos looked pleased. "How come you're down heah at the mill, son? How come you ain't up at th' house havin' cookies and chocolate with Arabella and her Mistuh What's-his-name?"

"Sir, I'll be perfectly frank to tell you, I find Mr. What's-his-name—Pettingill—a tedious bore. Nothing but small talk and simpering. I'd rather visit with you, if you don't mind."

Amos was even more pleased. "Well now, that's mighty nice of you."

"Because I've been thinking a lot about the mill operation, sir, and I'd like to make a—"

"Now you're bein' smaht, son. Ain't no bettuh business for a young fella like you to learn than this'n. And right heah's the place to learn it."

67

"I agree. And I have a few ideas to offer that I think might help your—"

"Quite a few young fellas come around wantin' to learn, but when they find out what hahd work it is, they disappeah fast."

"Oh, not me, sir," Lucius said earnestly. "I'm interested."

Amos smiled. "I b'lieve you are."

Lucius had taken a small notebook out of his pocket. He opened it and displayed for Amos's inspection a set of intricate diagrams.

"Would you like to hear my ideas, sir? I think you might find some of them worth considering."

"Why, suttenly, son. I'm all eahs."

Lucius pulled his chair closer to Amos and pointed to one of his sketches. "Well, to begin with, about the rollers. It seems to me they ought to be bigger and heavier . . ."

After a while the girl Crissy, Arabella's maid, came down the little dirt road from the house, saw Amos and Lucius sitting under the tree, and went toward them.

"'Scuse me. Mistuh Lucius, suh?"

Lucius looked up from his notebook. "Yes?"

"Miss Arabella, she say won't you come and jine her and Mistuh Pettingill? They gon' sing some songs."

"Give her my thanks, Crissy, and tell her I'm sorry to say I have absolutely no talent for music."

"Yas, suh." Crissy turned away and started unhurriedly back toward the house.

Lucius snapped his notebook shut and put it away. "I won't take up any more of your time, sir," he said to Amos. "What do you think of my ideas so far?"

Amos gave his answer with a pleasant smile. "Mostly harebrained, I'd say."

Lucius was crestfallen. "Oh."

"But interesting. Damned interesting. You prob'ly got a good point when you say the way to improve the operation is to enlahge it. I wouldn't be surprised if theah wasn't a good practical idea lurkin' somewheah unduhneath that notion." The old man reached out and clapped Lucius on the shoulder. "I like you, son. You got a damn good head on youh shoulduhs."

Lucius's smile was charmingly modest. "Thank you, sir. I appreciate that." He stood up. "And now I've got to be going."

"Wheah you off to now?" Amos demanded. "Seems like

you're forevuh rushin' off somewheah."

"I'm on my way to Indiana to see to my family's investments. We have vast holdings all through the state, you know, and I'm the only one with enough business sense to look after them."

As Amos squinted thoughtfully up at him Lucius suddenly became hesitant.

"And, sir, I, uh . . . I want to apologize for my behavior at the New Year's party, trying to warn you about people being after your money. I was insulting your intelligence, telling you things you already know."

Amos frowned, trying to recollect. "Oh, that. Why, tha's all right, son, I appreciate youh concern. I 'spect it was that Pettingill fella you had in mind, wasn't it?"

"Yes, sir. But of course you're aware of such things. It's poor innocent Arabella I'm worried about. It pains me to see her affections toyed with."

Lucius took a deep breath and made a solemn announcement. "I'm going to be completely honest with you, Mr. Whitehurst. I have a certain selfish interest in all this. The truth is, I'm deeply in love with Arabella. The first time I laid eyes on that girl I knew I'd never have another moment of peace in this world unless I could make her my wife. Of course—with your approval, sir. Only with your approval."

Amos studied Lucius's earnest face with a quizzical expression on his own. "Well, I'll be damned," he said softly.

The foreman had come out of the mill, and now called to his employer. "You bettuh come look at this yere batch o' syrup, Mistuh Whitehurst. I b'lieve mebbe it needs some mo' lime."

Lucius extended his hand. "Goodbye, sir. I hope we'll have a chance to talk again soon."

Moving very slowly, Amos got to his feet. "I sincerely hope so, son. Listen, you have a good trip to Indiana, y'heah? And in the meantime—" he pumped Lucius's hand and gave him a conspiratorial wink—"I'll put in a good word for ya."

Lucius walked the two miles back to the river landing without stopping at the house. It was late afternoon when he got there, and the sun slanted low across the water, burnishing the placid surface.

Lucius sat down on a wooden bench and waited. Without moving he watched two steamboats plow past, headed upstream. In half an hour, when a New Orleans-bound steamer came downriver, he stood up and hailed it, waving his arms.

(9)

AMANDA WHITEHURST, wrapped in a silken kimono, sat at her dressing table in the bedroom of her New Orleans apartment and looked at herself in a great gilt-framed mirror. She turned her head this way and that, and with professional detachment examined her features.

Roundness was Amanda's dominant physical characteristic, a trait reminiscent of her great-girthed father. Round brown eyes and full rounded lips complemented a round face—only a turned-up nose broke the pattern. The body tapered from a large round bosom to a tiny waist, then spread again to curvaceous hips.

Amanda put a finger to golden hair wrapped in a tight chignon, and sighed. "I'm not really beautiful, am I, Ella?"

Ella, standing behind her mistress, was a tired-looking middle-aged black woman in a maid's uniform. "No, ma'am. But you're purty."

"No I'm not." Amanda tilted her head and stared critically into her own eyes. "I'm not even pretty. What I have is...what would you call it? Animal vitality?"

Ella shrugged. "I reckon so, ma'am."

"Sort of an earthy, sexual magnetism?"

Ella shifted her weight from one foot to the other. "Yes'm."

"I guess you're right." Amanda sighed again. "I suppose that's why men find me so incredibly desirable."

"What gown you want to weah this evenin', ma'am?" Ella asked patiently.

Amanda considered the question. "Well, let's see. I'm dinin' with Mistuh Jenkins tonight, and he likes me in blue, so I guess I'll weah that—"

She was stopped by a knock at the door, sounding urgently from the outer room. "Now who can that be, Ella? It's too early for Mistuh Jenkins."

Ella was on her way to answer. In a moment she was back in the bedroom doorway.

"It's Mistuh Hahgrave, ma'am. Wants to know if he can speak wid you."

Amanda's hand flew to her cheek. "Lucius! Good heavens!"

"You want me to tell 'im to come back some othuh time, ma'am?"

Amanda glanced at her image in the mirror, and gave her coiffure a quick touch. "No," she said. "Show him in."

Lucius sat stiffly on a little settee near Amanda's dressing table and looked admiringly around the bedroom. It was a chamber of satin, soft candlelight, and brocaded opulence.

"Beautiful place you have here," the visitor remarked.

Amanda made a sad little gesture full of theatrical artifice. "Everybody says that. But it's not, really. It's a lonely place. The life of an actress is a lonely life, Lucius."

"Really?" Lucius was fidgeting nervously. "Well, anyway, I appreciate your letting me come in to see you like this."

"You have something on your mind," she said. "Tell me what it is."

Lucius cleared his throat. "Actually, it's about Arabella."

"Hmm. I bet I could've guessed that."

"I'm desperately in love with her, Amanda. I want to marry her."

"Yes, I've heard." She reached out and patted him on the knee. "I think it's puhfectly adorable, really I do."

"But I'm meeting with nothing but frustration. Arabella's a maddening woman—thinks of nothing but fun and games, morning, noon, and night. I write her letters, pouring my heart out. She's too busy having fun to reply. Time after time I go to see her. She's either getting ready for a party or recovering from one. I was up there last week, and what do I find? Arabella packing to go on a three-day steamboat excursion to Baton Rouge with a crowd of her fun-loving friends. Barely had time to say hello and goodbye. She's driving me out of my mind."

Amanda produced a soothing smile. "Oh, I wouldn't be too discouraged if I were you, Lucius. Arabella's a very popular girl, but I happen to know she's very fond of you."

71

Lucius was leaning forward, frowning. "Are you aware that one of her most ardent suitors is your friend Albert Pettingill?"

"Oh yes."

"But, good Lord, don't you . . . don't you *mind*?"

Amanda giggled. "Not in the least."

Lucius leaned back and huffed in exasperation. "Well, I'll be damned! Will I *ever* understand women?!"

Amanda's laughter pealed. "Oh, you mustn't feel that way, Lucius deah, because you see I'm not an ordinary woman at all—"

"Amanda, how much do you know about Pettingill?"

"I know he's a sweet, gentle, adorable man, who wants very much to marry comfortably, and I sincerely hope he can. I'd have married him myself a long time ago, if I could stand to think of being a married woman. He'll make some lucky girl a mahvelous husband."

"But not Arabella! He's old enough to be her father!"

"He's neahly forty, that's true. All the more reason I hope he'll succeed in settlin' down soon. He can't go on forevuh bein' a rivuhboat gambluh."

Amanda watched the look of astonishment rise in Lucius's face, and giggled again. "Oh yes, dahlin'. I know all about Albut's profession."

Lucius stared, aghast. "And you mean to say you'd be willing to see your little sister *marry* such a man?"

Amusement glinted in Amanda's brown eyes. "I also know that for a few profitable yeahs *you* were his pahtnuh."

Lucius gripped his forehead and groaned. "Oh God!"

Amanda was patting him on the knee again. "Lucius, honey, it doesn't mattuh. Arabella hasn't the faintest idea, and as for me, I don't care a fig—"

"There's a big difference between Albert and me," Lucius blurted. "I'm repentant. I've reformed. But Albert will never—"

"I told you, it doesn't mattuh. I think you're both puhfectly adorable men. Arabella couldn't go wrong, whichevuh one she chooses."

With a quick rustle of silk Amanda was sitting beside her visitor. The lower folds of her kimono draped open, revealing pretty knees. Lucius glanced at the pink flesh, stiffened, and looked away hurriedly.

"Lemme tell you how it is, dahlin'." Amanda's husky voice sounded close to Lucius's ear. "I've had many lovuhs, and I expect I'll have many more. Albut's one of my favorites. But you know what I told him when he decided to court Arabella? I said, 'Go right ahead, dahlin', if you can win her I'll turn you ovuh to her with all my blessin's. But then you'll keep youh hands off little Amanda, 'cause you can't have *both* the Whitehurst girls. *No* man's *that* deservin'.'"

Amanda was leaning close to Lucius, and her fingers were playing with a tuft of hair behind his ear. "Now, to *you*, I just have this to say. I think you're absolutely the most beautiful young man I've seen in yeahs. If you win my little sistuh I'll be truly happy for both of you, but if you lose . . . come back to see me, and maybe I'll give you a consolation prize."

Lucius gulped, and stared for a few tense seconds at Amanda's beguiling eyes floating before him. Then with a sudden lurch he was on his feet.

"It's a trick," he muttered. His narrowed eyes darted around the room. "You and Albert are in cahoots, trying to trap me. Trying to prove my love for Arabella is so weak I'd be willing to sacrifice it for a moment's pleasure. Well, let me tell you, you're sadly mistaken."

Amanda's face was frozen in astonishment as she stared up at him. "Why, Lucius, dahlin', whatevuh makes you think—"

"I'm not stupid, Amanda. It wouldn't surprise me if Albert were hiding right here in this room, ready to leap out the minute I've compromised myself."

For a moment longer Amanda's astonishment held, then dissolved into merriment. She put her hands to her cheeks as her laughter trilled forth.

Lucius glowered in righteous fury. "All right, damn you, laugh! You've never met a virtuous man before, have you? Naturally you think it's funny!"

"Oh, deah, deah . . . this is too much!" Amanda could barely contain her amusement. "Albert *spying* on you?! Really, Lucius, Albert would as soon walk down the street in his unduhdrawuhs as do a thing as vulguh as that! Besides, he's out of town, don't you know?"

"How the hell should *I* know?"

"Didn't Arabella mention it? He's her escort on the steamboat excursion."

"No she didn't," Lucius said in a weak voice. "She chattered on at some length about it, but somehow she never got around to mentioning *that* detail."

He sat down again, slumping, staring despondently at the floor. "I give up. I'm beaten."

73

Amanda gave him a playful nudge. "Oh, pshaw! You don't deserve a nice girl like Arabella if you give up *that* easily."

"I'm beaten, I tell you. She's going to marry Albert, and do you know why? Because his name starts with an A, that's why."

Amanda's laughter bubbled up again. "Don't be silly, Lucius. That was Papa's little whim, and he lost interest in it yeahs ago."

Lucius refused to be cheered. "Oh yes, she's going to do it, I know she is. And I might just as well start trying to find some other way to—" He stopped.

She watched him shrewdly, amusement still lurking in her eyes. "Were you about to say . . . some other way to make a living?"

His smile was disarmingly sheepish. "It's a great comfort to talk to you, Amanda. You're so very understanding. Will you have dinner with me tonight?"

"I already have a dinnuh date. In fact I ought to be gettin' dressed."

"But I want to talk to you some more. Can I see you soon? Please?" His hand crept over her knee.

"Not right away, dahlin'. On Monday I staht rehearsals for a new role. It's Lady Teazle, in *School for Scandal.* I'll be awful busy for quite a while. Anyway . . ." Gently she pushed his hand off her knee. "It's not consolation time *yet.*"

Lucius's face went dark. "You're just like all the rest. The same as Arabella. Teasing, toying, playing with men, laughing all the time. Cruel, malicious . . ."

Amanda pulled her kimono tightly around her. "If you'll excuse me, Lucius, I really must be getting dressed—"

"There's not an honest bone in your body, or in Arabella's." Lucius was on his feet again, and his eyes were hot with anger. "The only honest women I've met in Louisiana are the honest whores on Girod Street."

"Well, why don't you go theah, then?" Amanda's voice was icy.

"I am!" Lucius shouted. "That is exactly where I'm—"

"'Scuse me, Miss Amanda?" The maid Ella was standing in the doorway, and her voice brought instant silence. "Mistuh Jenkins is gon' be heah in a few minutes, and you ain't even stahted gettin' dressed."

"Goodnight, Lucius, deah," Amanda said sweetly. "Next time do send a note around and ask for an appointment, will

74

you? Then we won't have to cut our visit short—"

Before she could finish, Lucius had brushed past Ella in the doorway and stomped out of the apartment.

(10)

April 21st, 1839

Mr. Lucius Hargrave
c/o General Post Office
New Orleans, Lousiana

My dearest Lucius,

I hardly know how to begin writing this. I am sitting here in the garden on a beautiful Sunday afternoon, and I am so depressed I simply don't know how I can bear to go on living. Carolina Grove is so lovely this time of year, Lucius. The camellia trees and the roses and the wisteria vines are all literally bursting with blooms and fragrance, and the huge old century plants seem to grow an inch a day. Even the gloomy old oaks seem almost cheerful. Yet they give no solace to me. My heart is sorrowful, and can be comforted by none but you.

Why do you neglect me, Lucius? You have simply stopped coming to see me. Even your adorable letters, which were so precious to me, have ceased. What have I done to offend you, dearest one? Why do you suddenly spurn me, after all those declarations of undying love? You quite captured my heart, you know. Then as soon as you had me dependent upon you, you turned your back on me.

And why, pray? Is it because you thought I did not take you seriously enough? Is it because I have been too

75

gay and flighty when you wished to sit and converse about important matters? Is it because you thought I was seeing too much of Albert Pettingill? Oh, sweet Lucius, it is all true and I humbly beg your forgiveness! And yet deep down inside I have taken you very seriously indeed, and have wanted ever so much to sit and converse with you, but I have been afraid to, because you are so terribly intellectual. Papa says you are by far the most intelligent suitor I have ever had, and I quite agree with him.

And as for Albert Pettingill—well! Lucius, I should like you to know that I am utterly finished with that man, for I have discovered him to be nothing so upright as a man at all, but rather a horrid, loathsome toad! I can see you in my mind's eye, nodding your head wisely and saying, "I told you so." Yes, you were right, dear Lucius, ever so right. I should have listened to you. I know the error of my ways, and if you will give your poor repentant Arabella another chance I promise I will always listen to you, none but you, forever and ever!

Oh, Lucius, please come. I am so lonely, and so longing for the comforting touch of your strong and gentle hand. I shall send Uncle Ben to the river landing with this immediately, to be posted on the very first packet. And if you ever loved me, Lucius, if there was ever the tiniest bit of truth in all your beautiful declarations of devotion, you will fly to me. I must see you, I must tell you to your face how sorry I am that I ever seemed to be neglectful of your attentions. I must whisper in your ear how very much I love you.

Hurry, my darling. I expect to sit right here in the garden every day with my hands folded in my lap, receiving no other visitors, waiting only for you. If you don't come soon I shall lie down under my favorite camellia tree and quietly die.

> *All my love, and tenderest entreaties,*
> *Arabella*

Lucius arrived at Carolina Grove on Tuesday afternoon and found Arabella alone in the big main hall, listlessly picking out "Annie Laurie" on the piano with one finger. Ben ushered him in, and stood in the doorway watching as Lucius slipped up behind the girl and covered her eyes with his fingers.

76

"Lucius!" Arabella shrieked, twisting in her seat and clutching at him.

"Congratulations," Lucius said teasingly. "This time you guessed right."

Ben withdrew, chuckling.

Arabella was up and embracing Lucius, her eyes shining. "Oh, Lucius, dahlin', you've come, you've saved my life! Thank you evuh so much!"

"You knew I would, didn't you? You must have known I hadn't forsaken you; I only thought you'd forsaken me."

"Oh, nevuh, dahlin', nevuh, nevuh!" She put her head against his chest and hugged him fiercely.

He laid his hand on the blond tresses. "Funny you should say I saved your life. The truth is, your letter saved mine. I was just about gone in despair—"

"Oh, Lucius!" Her voice trembled as she turned a tearful face up to him. "To think I've made you suffuh—oh, it makes me feel wretched, just evuh so!"

"Well, never mind, sweetheart. It doesn't matter now."

"Then you're not angry with me?"

"Of course not. I'm just amazed at the sudden change. What happened?"

"Why, I just finally came to my senses, that's all."

Lucius eyed her suspiciously. "What about Albert?"

Arabella made a face. "Albut! Don't mention that name to me! He smiles and smiles, and lies and lies. It becomes boring aftuh a while, Lucius, it really does."

"Well, of course," Lucius said smugly. "I could have told you all that."

"Oh, I know, dahlin', I know. You're evuh so wise, and I'm ashamed it took me so long to see what you saw so easily. I'm just grateful my eyes are open at last, before I made some dreadful mistake."

"Ah, yes. Thank God for that."

"Oh, Lucius!" Arabella's eyes danced with some intense emotion as she stepped back and took his hands in hers. "Do you remembuh that very first lettuh you wrote to me, on New Yeah's Eve? I do. You said you wanted to walk with me unduh the oaks, and receive the answer that would lift you to rapturous happiness or plunge you into deep despair. You see how seriously I've taken you? I've got youh lettühs locked away in a secret place, and I've practically memorized every line of every one."

Her bright eyes darkened with a sudden solemnity.

"Theah's been a terrible misunduhstanding between us, Lucius, deah. It's all my fault, and now I want to make it up to you. I'd like to walk with you beneath the oaks today, and I hope you'll ask me that important question once more, because now I'm ready to give you my answer."

Lucius stared. He studied every detail of the girl's face, and saw a cunning little smile beginning to form at the corners of her mouth. He stepped close to her.

"Arabella..." he breathed. "Can it be?" Their lips were almost touching.

"It can be, dahlin'," she whispered. "If you still love me."

"Oh, Arabella, my sweet, my—" His lips were over hers, his arms winding around her slender waist.

Then with a little laugh she pulled back and slipped out of his embrace, and when she spoke her voice had a merry lilt.

"Shall we stroll among the oaks?"

She took him by the arm, smiled up into his eyes, and led him toward the French windows that opened onto the side veranda and the sunlit garden beyond.

In twenty minutes they returned from their walk, strolling with languid ease across the lawn, Lucius's arm snugly around Arabella's waist and holding her close to him. They went up onto the side veranda, but instead of entering the house they went toward an outside staircase leading to the gallery of the second floor. Arabella took Lucius's hand and led him up the stairs.

As they walked along the upper veranda, Lucius glanced curiously at one after another closed lattice door with a dark and silent room behind it. He stopped abruptly, frowning.

"Where *is* everybody, Arabella? Where are your parents?"

Arabella's cunning smile reappeared. "I was wonderin' when you'd notice. They're away for a few days, visitin' friends over near Bayou des Allemands."

Lucius's jaw dropped. "You mean you're...you're here *alone*?"

"That's why I wanted you to come this week, dahlin'. After all, I *am* a scheming female, you know. Or didn't you?"

Lucius blinked as he pondered this information.

Arabella giggled suddenly, and pulled on his arm. "Come along now. I have something to show you." She led him to the last of the double French doors that lined the veranda, and stopped.

"I'm still rememberin' that first lettuh of youhs, dahlin'.

Where you said you'd dreamed of strollin' along heah, and peekin' into my bedroom. Well, I'm goin' to do bettuh than you dream." Her face had gone solemn, and her eyes wide and luminous. "I'm goin' to let you come inside."

Lucius smiled weakly. "Well, that's very sweet of you, my dear, but—"

"Just give me one minute," she said. "When I'm ready, I'll call you." She pushed the door open and slipped inside and left him standing there.

He stepped across to the outer edge of the veranda, leaned on the bannister, and looked out over gardens that were glowing in the slant of late-afternoon sunlight. He was tight-lipped, and his fingers drummed fitfully on the railing.

Soon the soft sound of Arabella's voice drifted to him. "Lucius? You can come in now."

His fingers stopped drumming and gripped the railing for an instant before he moved away.

Inside he blinked and squinted, and peered into the recesses of the semidarkness.

"I'm ovuh heah, Lucius," he heard her say.

He moved to the center of the room, located her, and stopped in his tracks. The color drained from his face.

"Arabella, what . . . what are you—"

She was sitting on the edge of her bed, wearing a nightgown of gossamer transparency. The abundant blond hair had been loosened, and fell in wanton torrents over bare shoulders.

Lucius was stunned. "Good Lord, can I trust my eyes?!" He was moving slowly toward her.

"I want to prove my love for you, my dahlin'," She raised her slender arms toward him. "Come. Take me."

He was kneeling beside her, and her arms floated down to rest around his neck.

"It's puhfectly safe," she whispered. "Crissy has strict instructions not to let anybody come on the second floor unduh any circumstances. She can be trusted to do her job."

"Arabella, listen to me." His hands were clutching at her. "I feel a heavy responsibility. I know you must have always dreamed of being a bride of pure virginity, and I—"

"Of course I have, dahlin'. But as long as it's *you* . . ." She nuzzled his nose with hers.

"Arabella, I cannot let you abandon that ideal, not even for me. Because I have always preserved my own virtue in that same ideal."

79

Her eyes went wide. "Oh, Lucius! You mean you've nevuh, evuh—"

"No, darling. Never. When we enter our marriage chamber, I want us to enter in virginal innocence, like tender lambs, together."

"Oh, Lucius!" she wailed. "That's so sweet it makes me want to cry!"

"So you see I cannot allow this to happen, my angel. It would be far less than honorable." He was up and sitting beside her, his lips planting hungry little kisses on her cheeks and eyelids and mouth.

"But I *want* to, dahlin'. Would it be honorable to reject me?"

"I could never reject you, sweetheart, never. But somehow we must force ourselves to come to our senses!" His hands were beneath her flimsy garment, exploring the smooth and slender body.

"Do you like my nightgown, Lucius?" she whispered.

"I love it, my angel." He was trying to work it up and off. "But this is insanity—we must get hold of ourselves!"

"It's from my trousseau. I was saving it for—"

"Oh God, Arabella, stop me! I'm a miserable wretch, I must not *do* this!" His voice quivered in anguish as his lips devoured her throat and shoulders and his hand closed over a tiny breast.

Soon Arabella disengaged herself from his eager grasp, and with a deft movement drew off her nightgown and let it slide to the floor. Then she lifted her face to the ceiling, closed her eyes, and sighed in languorous contentment as her lover's hands and lips moved with ravishing ferocity over her tender nudity.

"Oh, Lucius," she murmured. "Dahlin', dahlin' Lucius. Let this aftuhnoon be our wedding night."

At dusk Benjamin moved through the great gloomy house, lighting lamps. Crissy followed along behind him and carefully adjusted each lamp after it was lit.

"Dey sho' done been upstairs a mighty long time," Ben said suddenly. "What you s'pose is goin' on?"

"Ain't none o' yo' bizniz what's goin' on," Crissy said in a flat voice.

Ben chuckled. "I'm in charge o' de house, Crissy, it's plenty o' my bizniz what's goin' on."

"You may be in charge o' de *rest* o' de house, Ben. But you ain't in charge o' *nothin'* in Miss Arabella's room, nothin' a-tall."

Ben threw back his head and cackled.

After a while Arabella came downstairs leading Lucius by the hand, found the servants in the front room, and went skipping toward them, her face flushed and glowing.

"Uncle Ben! Crissy! We want you all to be the first to know—Mistuh Lucius and I are goin' to be married!"

Crissy shrieked and clasped her mistress in her arms. "Oh, Miss Arabella! It's so wonduhful, I jes' cain't hahdly b'lieve it!"

The great gulf of color and station between them momentarily forgotten, Crissy and Arabella hugged each other like sisters, laughing and crying.

With a genial grin that in no way diminished his correct formality, Benjamin bowed to the prospective bridegroom. "My congratulations, Mistuh Lucius, suh. Can I fix you a drink, by way o' celebration?"

Lucius was watching his bride-to-be, who was already busy giving Crissy a complex set of instructions concerning the preparations for the wedding. He heaved a deep sigh and turned wistful eyes on the butler.

"Make it a stiff one, will you, Ben? I feel a little weak tonight."

(11)

July 14th, 1839

Mrs. Sarah Thacker
c/o Thacker and Hargrave, Associates
Number One Gilpin Street
South Bar, Indiana

Dear Mama,
    I am embarrassed to have to beg your forgiveness

81

yet again, after so many offenses, for my slovenliness in correspondence. Yet I do beg it, most humbly, and I know you will forgive again and love me still, for your heart is so warm and kind it cannot do otherwise. But let me tell you of the momentous events that have befallen me this past half-year, and you will find it easier to be patient with me.

As you know, I returned to the United States late last year (I assume you got my letter written just before my departure from Texas, which I posted the moment I set foot on American soil), and was of course going to come to see you just as soon as I had recovered from the grueling journey. But something intervened, Mama, something I believe you will understand and approve of—love.

Mama, your wayward son is now a married man—captured, tamed, and thoroughly domesticated. Unbelievable? I find it so as well. My wife is none other than Arabella Whitehurst, youngest daughter of the Whitehurst family of St. Charles Parish, Louisiana. I half expect you to gasp in astonishment, but that's silly of me; the name can mean nothing to you. It is hard for me to remember that there are people in remote parts of the country who have never heard of the Whitehursts, so great is their fame locally.

My father-in-law, Amos Whitehurst, was one of the pioneers of the sugar industry here, and is among the wealthiest men in the state. His plantation, called Carolina Grove, covers nearly fifty thousand acres of rich bottomland, and is worked by several hundred slaves. These hordes of black laborers are managed by hired white overseers—the Whitehursts themselves of course do not come in direct contact with them (I doubt that Arabella has ever actually seen them at work in the cane fields, except perhaps from a distance). Amos only concerns himself with his pride and joy, the sugar mill, the great machinery of which roars night and day during the autumn milling season, producing the heavy brown syrup that is almost worth its weight in gold. And now I am to be his partner.

My beautiful Arabella is a dream, Mama, you would adore her (you _will_ adore her, for I will certainly bring her to see you). Though only twenty years of age she is a gracious lady, full of wit and wisdom and maturity beyond her years—very much like you, in fact. I think that is one reason I love her so dearly.

But, Mama, here is the most exciting news of all. As I write this I glance from time to time at my angelic bride who is sitting quietly in the corner knitting tiny bootees for the child she is carrying. Think of it, Mama—I am going to be a father! Oh, how I pray it will be a son! Of course a daughter will find me a loving and devoted father too, but you know there can be no greater joy in this life for a man than to have a son. Please, Mama, join your prayers with mine in this.

I do apologize for not inviting you to the wedding. You must know how I longed to have you here, and Isaac too, of course. But our schedule was outrageously hectic. There simply wasn't time. Besides, I remember how much you dislike riding on steamboats. I'm sure you'll be understanding in this as you are in all things.

But I promise you, as soon as the baby is here and old enough to travel we will come for a nice long visit, and you will become acquainted with your new daughter-in-law and grandson. Meanwhile I send you love and kisses, and a big hug for good old Isaac, and one for Grandpa too, bless him—I hope he is still well and active. Oh, how I yearn to see the three of you!

Till that happy day,

Your devoted son,
Lucius

P. S. My respects to your husband.

August 7th, 1839

Mr. Lucius Hargrave
Carolina Grove Plantation
St. Charles Parish, Louisiana

My dear son,
Your letter has left us all completely stunned. I never received the letter you mention having written at the time of your return from Texas. In fact I have not heard one word from or about you since the one letter you wrote after arriving in Texas, in the summer of 1836. For three years I have not known where or how you

83

were, or whether you were alive or dead. So maybe you should not be too sure I will forgive again and love you still. Well, yes, of course I will always love you, because I am your mother. But forgiving becomes more and more difficult.

So there, I have scolded you. Now let me admit that your letter filled me with such joyousness that for several days I almost forgot how angry I am with you. (Almost, but not quite.) So you are married! I'm sure your Arabella is as lovely as you say she is. The very name summons up visions of loveliness. I might have wished it could have been an Indiana girl—but no matter.

And you are going to be a father—that is happy news indeed! I will gladly join you in prayer for your child, though not quite in the way you suggest. I will pray that he or she, boy or girl, is born in good health and will grow up to live a happy and useful life. Will that do?

It grieves me to know that your in-laws are slaveholders. Surely you're not suggesting that the pains they take to keep themselves physically removed from the field laborers in any way relieve them of moral responsibility? Anyway, don't feel bad about not inviting us to the wedding. I must say I think I would have felt horribly out of place there, such a plain homespun person as I among all those elegant Southern ladies in their finery.

And now maybe you will be amazed in turn to hear that Isaac will soon be a married man too! Yes, dear Isaac, who is thirty now and seemed destined for lifelong bachelorhood, is going to take a wife. She is a widow named Lucy Stovall. The Stovalls came here from Ohio several years ago and opened a dry goods store. When Mr. Stovall died suddenly not long afterward, Lucy sold the store but continued to live here. She is a nice person, and seems devoted to Isaac. They plan to live in Lucy's house, a cozy little cottage out at the west end of Jemison Road. Cyrus and I are both very happy for them, but there is one little thing that worries me. Lucy is close to forty, almost ten years older than Isaac. In her first marriage she had only one child, which died in infancy. I know Isaac has always dreamed of having children of his own, and now I fear he is headed for disappointment.

As for your grandfather, I am happy to say he is still spry and as determined as ever to remain independent, living all alone in his house. His orchard has mostly gone to seed because he is no longer able to care for it properly, but he pretends it's fine and refuses all offers of help. Except for puttering in that useless orchard the only thing that interests him is politics. He supported Mr. Harrison for president in 1836, and was furious when "Old Tippecanoe" lost. He is contemptuous of Mr. Van Buren, calling him "that prancing dandy who claims to be against slavery but doesn't lift a finger against it." Mr. Harrison won't do anymore either, Papa says. A plague on both their houses. His new hero is Mr. James Birney, a former slaveholder who has reformed and gained prominence in the Abolitionist movement. Papa expects Mr. Birney to be nominated for President by the new Liberty Party, and plans to go out next year and campaign for him. Considering that Papa will be seventy-five soon, I think that's quite remarkable, don't you?

Poor Papa, he is not very well liked in South Bar anymore. People regard him as a sour old grouch, and really, he has become an awful recluse. But he grinned from ear to ear when I read him your letter, and said to tell you he is tickled about having a great-grandson, and can't wait for you to come and bring your little family. It's been ages since I've seen Papa look so pleased about anything.

Cyrus sends his affectionate greetings too, and wants me to remind you that now that we have this huge house there is worlds of room for you and Arabella and the baby to come and stay as long as you like.

Lucius, it seems impossible to believe that after all these years you still insist on holding onto old grudges against a man who never felt for you anything but kindness and love. I'm not sure whether Cyrus failed to notice that same old tone of cold formality in your P. S., or whether he just decided to overlook it. I certainly noticed it, and was deeply hurt. Cyrus was no more responsible for those terrible events surrounding your father than you were, and you perfectly well know it. (Oh dear, I am scolding again. Forgive me.)

Your brother is standing here waiting impatiently for a chance to add a postscript, so I will close now. Give

Arabella a hug and a kiss for me and assure her that I
can't wait for us to have a chance to get to know each
other. Maybe now that you have a permanent residence
you will be able to correspond more regularly, and,
who knows, possibly even keep your promise to come
for a visit. I do wistfully hope so.

All my love, and congratulations to both of you,
Mama

P. S. Lucius you rascal! I am so excited about all this
good news I cant even sleep at night! Well it turns out
you beat me getting marryed but you didnt beat me by
much! I am sorry I didnt get to be your best man but I
wish you would come and be mine. Lucy and I have
planed our wedding for Saterday September 14th but if
you cant make it then we will change it to soot you.
Lucy is such a dear sweet person Lucius you will love
her just like I will love Arabella I know I will! I am
dyeing to meet her and Lucy is dyeing to meet booth of
you!

Well I dont want to bore you with to much of my
terrible writing Lucius. I have been drilling myself on
spelling and I think I am emproving a little. I am also
starting to work on puctuwation. I still don't care to
much for comas but I like exclemation points a lot!

Let me know if you can make it to our wedding.
Lucy and I will keep our fingers crosed.

Your loving brother,
Isaac

(12)

IN THE AFTERNOON of the second day after Christmas,
1839, old Amos Whitehurst sat slumped in his easy chair,
scowling at a tiny fire in the big fireplace at Carolina Grove.

Benjamin came into the room carrying a steaming cup on a tray, and bent over his master.

"Heah's yo' rum an' coffee, suh."

Without taking his eyes off the fireplace Amos reached for the cup and began to sip noisily. "What kind o' damn puny fiah you call that, Ben? Put some mo' wood on theah, I'm freezin'."

"Yes, suh." Ben went to work on the fire.

Adeline, sitting in a rocking chair with her lap full of yarn and knitting needles, offered an opinion. "I think it's quite comfortable in heah."

Nobody paid any attention.

In a minute Ben crossed the room to where Arabella was reclining on a couch amid piles of pillows. She was reading a letter, and on the floor beside her was a basketful of others. A quilt covering the lower part of her body trailed on the floor. Ben picked it up and tucked it under her feet.

"You comf'table, Miss Arabella? Can I git you anything?"

"Yes," Arabella sniffed. "You can get me a huge dose of castor oil. Maybe it'll make this pesky ol' baby come—"

"Arabella!" Adeline gave her daughter a horrified look. "It's not time for that baby yet. You must be patient."

Arabella frowned down at her swollen belly. "I'm sick of how awful I look," she said sullenly.

Ben scolded her. "Why, dat's nonsense, Miss Arabella. How's a mothuh carryin' a baby s'posed to look?"

"Tomorrow I'm goin' out ridin'," Arabella announced. "Maybe *that'll* speed things up."

Ben shook his head and walked away, muttering, "I ain't nevuh heard such foolish talk!" He went to the opposite end of the room where Lucius was sitting at a little writing table in a corner.

"Can I git you anything, Mistuh Lucius?"

"A whiskey and water, please, Ben. And plenty of ice."

"Ain't no mo' ice, Mistuh Lucius."

"Goddamn!" Lucius growled. "Didn't anybody tell Adam we're out of ice?"

"Yes, suh. I did. He say theah ain't been no shipments from up Nawth lately."

"Well, forget it then." Lucius huffed with anger. "Can't depend on that man for a damned thing!"

"Yes, suh," Ben said, and went out.

The four people in the room were quiet for a few minutes, each wrapped in private thoughts.

87

"Wheah's Amanda?" Amos demanded suddenly.

"Upstairs packing, deah," Adeline said. "She's taking the aftuhnoon packet back to New Awlins, you know."

"Oh, shuah. Couldn't expect her to stay home three whole days, could I?"

"Now, deah," Adeline said patiently. "She's stahting work on a new play next week. That always makes Amanda restless, you know."

"And she's between lovers again," Lucius offered from his corner. "That always makes Amanda restless too, you know."

"Don't be vulguh, Lucius," Arabella said with annoyance.

"Anyway, it's bettuh than Adam could do," Amos muttered. "He comes on Wednesday and leaves ag'in on Thursday. Twenty-foah hours is all he can stand."

"Adam's awfully busy, deah," Adeline said. "You know his work at the import company keeps him—"

"That ain't it," Amos snapped. "He can't stand more'n one night away from his goddamn nigger mistress on Rampart Street."

Lucius laughed.

"Really, Amos!" Adeline said indignantly. "I wish you wouldn't say such—"

"What are you laughin' at?" Amos hurled the question like a challenge toward the far end of the room.

Lucius was still chuckling. "You said something funny, Amos. It isn't often anything funny gets said around this gloomy old mausoleum."

"If you think it's so damn gloomy how come you nevuh stick yo' nose out of it? How come you nevuh go neah th' sugah mill, fo' instance?"

Lucius waved a hand at the papers on the table before him. "I have important work to do here."

"You got work to do at th' mill, too. You're s'posed to be a pahtnuh, ain't you? Goddamn, I work my ass off, and all you evuh do is—"

"Amos!" Adeline protested shrilly.

"What am I supposed to do there, Amos?" Lucius said. "I go down to the mill, I see things that need correcting, I make suggestions, and you pay no attention whatsoever. What do you expect of me?"

"I expect you to listen an' learn!" Amos bellowed. "I damn well don't expect you to be an expert right off—"

"Oh, stop it, you two, you're giving me a horrible headache!" Arabella cried.

Lucius had left his writing table and was standing in front of the fireplace. "You take my advice and build that second mill, Amos. You get it built in time for the cooking season next year and turn it over to me. And get all that acreage down below Little Bayou cleared and planted, because I guarantee you I'll not just double our sugar production, I'll triple it."

Amos sipped his rum and coffee and glared at his son-in-law. "You're a man of big talk, Lucius. Big talk and little action."

Then Amanda came in, followed by Ben carrying several valises. "Well, I'm off, everybody," she announced breezily. "Whoevuh wants a goodbye kiss, pucker up."

Lucius went back to his writing table and sat down.

"Don't go, Amanda," Arabella pleaded.

"I must, dahlin'. Millions of things to do." Amanda sat down on Arabella's couch and stroked her sister's brow. "You take care of youhself, heah? 'Cause I'm gettin' in the mood to be Aunt Amanda to a cute cuddly baby."

Arabella was in the mood to complain. "It's been evuh so dull around heah this Christmas. Not at all like it usually is."

"Nevuh mind, dahlin'. You're just depressed right now, but it'll pass. Aftuh the baby's born and you're spry again you come and stay a few days with me."

"Oh, that'd be evuh so lovely, Amanda. I'm so *bored* with Carolina Grove!"

Amanda kissed her sister, then went to her mother and father in turn, giving them both kisses and promises that she would see them again soon.

"Very likely," Amos grumbled. "We'll prob'ly see you ag'in next Christmas."

Amanda sauntered down to the other end of the room and stood next to Lucius's chair. "Well, goodbye, Papa-to-be."

Lucius was busy writing. After a moment he looked up and with profound formality, said, "Goodbye, Amanda. Very pleasant seeing you again. I wish you the best of luck in your forthcoming production."

Amanda giggled. "Well, how prettily said, dahlin'!" Playfully she ruffled his hair with her fingers, and when she spoke again her voice had dropped to a soft and intimate murmur. "And by the way, if you should happen to come to New Orleans, don't hesitate to call on me. You know wheah I live, I believe."

Lucius gave her a searching look. "Yes," he said quietly. "I know where you live."

Arabella was up on an elbow, frowning at them. "Hey, what are you two talkin' about?"

Amanda's merry laughter pealed as she walked rapidly back through the room. "Just flirting a little with my handsome brother-in-law, dahlin', nothin' important. G'bye, everybody!"

With a wave of her hand she went out, and Ben scurried after her, the valises banging against his knees.

Silence descended again on the big room. Soon old Amos began to snore softly, his massive gray head drooping on his chest, his half-finished drink clutched in his hand.

"Poor Amos," Adeline said. "Every yeah the sugah mill makes him more exhausted. I wonduh how long he can go on." She put her knitting aside and went to her husband, took the cup out of his hands, and coaxed him to his feet.

"Come along, deah. Time for a nice nap for you."

Amos opened his eyes wide and peered around the room. "Damned urgrateful young'uns." he muttered. "Work all my life to give 'em a nice home, and they'd rathuh take a beatin' than spend two days a yeah in it." He continued to grumble as Adeline led him out of the room.

Arabella had resumed examining her basket of correspondence, picking up letter after letter and glancing over it, then with a listless drooping of her hand letting it flutter to the floor.

"Oh deah." She sighed wistfully. "When am I *evuh* goin' to get all this Christmas mail answered, Lucius?"

Lucius was busy at his writing table. He did not look up. "I'm sure you'll have it done by next Christmas, sweetheart."

"Well, aren't you goin' to help me with it?"

"Why should I? They're your friends, not mine."

"Not entirely." Arabella picked up a letter. "This note from Brad Kenyon, for instance. It's obviously written to you. He's my cousin, but he's youh friend."

"He's a bore," Lucius said.

"And you're a cad," Arabella snapped.

"Arabella, I am *trying* to work," Lucius said with strained patience.

"Lucius, what in the world *is* it you're writing that's so important?"

Lucius turned in his chair to face his wife. "It is an attack on an insidious evil that afflicts our society. I'll be performing an enormous public service by exposing it."

"What evil?"

"For certain important reasons it must remain undisclosed for the time being."

"For what reasons?"

"They too must remain undisclosed for the time—"

"Ohhh!" Arabella slapped the side of the couch in exasperation. "I said it before and I'll say it again. You're a cad! A beastly cad!"

"And now may I have a little peace and quiet?" Lucius said. He turned back to his work, not seeing Arabella sticking her tongue out at him.

Then there was Crissy, bending solicitously over her mistress's couch. "Le's git you upstaihs now, Miss Arabella. Time fo' yo' aftuhnoon rest."

Arabella wailed. "Oh Lord, that's what I'm doin' *now*, Crissy! That's all I *evuh* do anymoah—rest, rest, rest!"

Crissy took hold of Arabella's shoulders and lifted. "Come on now, Miss, don' gi' me no trouble."

On her feet, Arabella clutched at her protruding belly and threw a furious look at Lucius. "Tomorrow, I sweah, I'm goin' ridin'!"

Lucius paid no attention. Arabella sighed and allowed Crissy to lead her away.

Lucius had half an hour of peace and quiet, then Benjamin returned from the river landing. He came into the room with several new letters in his hand, picked up the litter of mail that Arabella had left on the floor, and put it on a table. Then he turned toward Lucius.

"Mistuh Lucius, suh? Heah's some mo' mail, off the mawnin' packet. Shall I put it wid de rest?"

Lucius put down his pen and sighed in defeat. "Ben, how in God's name will I ever get a book written in this madhouse?"

Ben backed away a little. "'Scuse me, suh."

Lucius held out his hand. "Well, let me see 'em." Absently he began to glance through the half-dozen letters. "Look here, Ben, I want you to do something for me, will you?"

"Yes, suh?"

"I want you to—" Lucius stopped abruptly and stared at one of the letters. Then quickly he recovered his train of thought and went on. "I want you to fix up the east tower for me to use as a study. All I need is a table and chair and a lamp. But I've *got* to have some privacy."

Ben's frown spoke disapproval of the idea. "Suh, Mistuh Amos likes the towuhs to be kept available fo' guests."

Lucius gazed up at the butler with something close to a pleading look in his eyes. "Ben, in all this drafty old cavern of a house there is not one dark musty corner I can call my own. Even *you* have a little room to yourself, which is more than *I* have."

Ben mulled over this information. "By golly, you right, Mistuh Lucius. Nevuh thought about it dat way." He nodded. "I'll fix up de east towuh fo' you."

"Thanks. Now, tomorrow I'm going to New Orleans for a few days. Got some business to attend to. And when I get back next week—"

"You goin' away *now*, suh?" Ben's disapproving frown was there again. "Jes' when Miss Arabella's baby is 'bout to come?"

"That's nonsense, she's only eight months along. And when I get back I'd like to have the tower ready for me, all right?"

"It'll be ready, suh."

Lucius had placed one letter facedown on the table. He handed the others back to the butler. "You can put these with the rest of Miss Arabella's mail, Ben. And then I'd like that whiskey and water, please. Without the ice."

"Yes, suh."

As soon as he was alone Lucius ripped open the letter he had kept and hurriedly read it through.

December 1st, 1839

Miss Arabella Whitehurst
Carolina Grove Plantation
St. Charles Parish, Louisiana

My dearest Arabella,
As I write this a gentle snowfall is quietly at work beyond my window, blanketing the orchards and wooded hillsides here at my ancestral home in the Hudson River Valley of New York State. For several days there have been rumblings in the stormclouds hovering over the dark old Catskills to the west, and I thought surely Mr. Washington Irving's little mountain men were playing at bowls again. But now the temperature has dropped and the silent snow has taken charge.
Are you wondering why I am in such an unlikely place? It's really quite simple. Very soon after I last saw

you I received word that my grandmother here had died, and, as her sole living relative, I had fallen heir to her mouldy old estate. I hastened here intent on liquidating the property (for which I have no love), converting it into money, and hastening away again. Unfortunately there were complications, and I have been obliged to stay on a maddeningly long time. I'm afraid the tranquil life of a country squire is not for me. I miss my old haunts and my old friends—especially you, my lovely Arabella. How vividly I remember those duets we used to sing—how delectably your sweet voice blended with mine! Now the only music I hear is the occasional wailing of a wintry wind.

It has been so long, little one. I know I am committing an offense, addressing you as Miss White-hurst—by now you are surely Mrs. Lucius Hargrave. With great pleasure I send both of you my warmest good wishes for a long and happy life together. For Lucius, a brotherly embrace. We had a contest fair and square, and he won. And for you, dear Arabella, a tender kiss on your rose-petal cheek. Surely Lucius will not begrudge me that tiny crumb with which to nourish myself through the long empty years ahead.

Forgive me, my sweet girl, for flying from you so precipitately, as I did. The moment I saw it could not be for us, I thought it best to disappear quickly and completely. I hope you have taken that as I meant it—as an act of kindness toward you whose happiness I desire above all else, and whom I shall never cease to adore. The crowning tragedy of my life is that you are a luxury I could never afford.

> For always, your devoted
> Albert

Lucius stared at the letter for a full minute. Then he stuffed it into an inside pocket of his jacket, and by the time Ben came back into the room with the drink, he was again deeply immersed in his work.

(13)

EARLY THE NEXT EVENING Amanda's maid Ella cracked the door of her mistress's New Orleans apartment in response to a knock and squinted into the shadows of a foliage-draped courtyard. "Who's deah?" she demanded.

"It's Lucius Hargrave," the caller said. He took a small step forward into the light. "Will you tell Miss Amanda I'm here?"

Ella's black eyes were cold. "Is she 'spectin' you, suh? She didn't say nothin' to me 'bout it."

"We'll see," Lucius said coolly. "Just tell her I'm here, please."

Ella hesitated a long time before stepping back and opening the door. "Well, jes' have a seat in the parluh, suh. Miss Amanda ain't dressed yet."

Amanda herself was in the parlor, though, having emerged from her bedroom tying the belt of her silk kimono around her waist. She pushed her loose hair back and smiled at her visitor.

"It's all right, Ella, it's my brother-in-law, you see? A membuh of the family. Come on in, Lucius."

She went back into her bedroom, and Lucius followed. In the doorway he paused and gave Ella a wink before going in and closing the door behind him.

He pulled the little settee as close to Amanda's dressing table as he could get it, then sat down, languidly relaxed, and watched as she brushed her tumultuous golden hair. A bemused expression crept over his face.

"I got your message," he said.

She gave him a blank look. "Message?"

"What you said to me when you left Carolina Grove yesterday. Sounded like a message to me. Am I wrong?"

94

"Not necessarily." Amanda resumed brushing her hair. "Not necessarily right, eithuh."

"You said I shouldn't hesitate. And I agree, I think I've been hesitating much too long."

Amanda gave him a noncommittal smile.

"Do you have an engagement tonight?" he asked.

"As a matter of fact, I don't."

"Saturday night, and Amanda Whitehurst, the toast of New Orleans theater society, has nothing on her social calendar?"

She smiled again. "Strange, isn't it?"

A look of profound self-satisfaction spread over Lucius's face. "Now I'm sure of it. It was a message."

She put her hairbrush down, and was suddenly deadly serious. "Lucius—"

"Come over here, Amanda." He patted the space on the settee beside him.

She stayed where she was. "Lucius, theah's something I want to make cleah to you."

"Make it brief, too. I'm impatient."

"Yes, I was sending you a message at Carolina Grove. I was furiously sending you messages that whole last day. I was theah—wigglin' my hips in front of you every chance I got."

"I thought so."

"And do you know why?"

"Because I'm a devilishly handsome, irresistibly charming—"

"Listen to me, Lucius. I'm serious. You know it was strictly hands off between you and me as long as you were courtin' Arabella. And when you married her, that should have been the end of it for good."

"It was bound to be, Amanda. As natural as water flowing downhill."

"Ordinarily I wouldn't considuh makin' love to my sistuh's husband all that natural. *Ordinarily*, I wouldn't. But in this case it's all right."

Lucius chuckled and again patted the seat beside him. "So come over here, and let's begin."

"And the reason it's all right is because your marriage is no good."

Lucius's face went sober. "You figured that out, did you?"

"I just realized it the othuh day, watchin' you and Arabella togethuh. You dislike each othuh thoroughly, don't you?"

He looked at her a long time before replying. "You're very observant."

95

"I'm beginning to wonder why you wanted so badly to marry her. Could it be you were just another fortune-huntuh, like Albert?"

"Look here, people sometimes behave foolishly," he said with a touch of annoyance. "If they didn't there couldn't be any plays, and then you couldn't be an actress, and how would you like that? So don't worry about it."

"Oh, I don't worry about it. I just worry about the baby, that's all."

"Don't worry about the baby, either. My son is going to have the best of everything."

"What if it's a girl?"

"*She'll* have the best of everything, too. But it's going to be a boy." He leaned forward and looked at her pleadingly, as if hoping she would somehow confirm his statement. "I am going to have a son, Amanda."

She gave a shrug of indifference. "All right, if you say so."

"I may be a rotten husband, but I'm going to be a damn good father."

Amanda laughed softly. "I can't imagine you as a father. You're so like a little boy yourself." She reached out and fluffed his thick sandy hair with her fingertips. "So nice and cuddly..."

Lucius smiled, and his intense face softened into an appropriately boyish look. "So let's be done with all this boring conversation and get on with more important things, shall we?" His hand was on her leg, moving smoothly from knee to thigh.

She leaned toward him and nuzzled his nose with hers. "Ummm," she breathed, smiling with eyes closed.

There was a timid knock on the bedroom door. Lucius pulled back quickly, muttering a curse under his breath.

"Yes?" Amanda called.

The door opened and Ella appeared. "'Scuse me, Miss Amanda. Will you be needin' me any mo' this evenin'?"

Before Amanda could say anything Lucius got up and beamed a pleasant smile at the maid. "It's Saturday night, Ella. The free coloreds have their big voodoo dance in Congo Square on Saturday nights, don't they?"

Ella's eyes widened a little. "Yes, suh. Dat's right."

Lucius had taken out his wallet and extracted several bills. He handed them to the woman. "Here. You go along now, and have a good time. Miss Amanda won't be needing you again till tomorrow."

Ella glanced at her mistress, who gave her a quick nod. She crumpled the money in her fist and smiled shyly up at Lucius.

"Thank you, suh. Thank you very much." In an instant she was gone.

Lucius closed the door after her, and pushed a sliding lock into place. Then he returned to the settee, sat down, and crossed his legs. For a moment he and Amanda looked at each other, surrounded by a silence that tingled with hidden excitement.

"How kind you are," Amanda said. "How very generous." Her soft voice caressed Lucius's ear, but the little smile that played at the corners of her mouth was teasing.

Lucius's eyes drifted up and down the magnificent body, not quite visible but radiantly vivid beneath the silken kimono. "Well? Are you going to come over here now? Or am I going to come and get you?"

She stood up and moved languidly away from him across the room toward her big many-pillowed bed. Her hands toyed with the belt of her kimono, untying.

"You come and get me," she murmured.

He did.

The knocking at the outer door had been going on for some time before Amanda opened her eyes and frowned at the morning light. The sun's rays were filtering through the leaves of a trailing vine outside her window, making a busy pattern on the bedcovers. The knocking became louder and more insistent. Amanda pushed her hair out of her face and glanced at Lucius beside her. He was lying on his stomach in the billowy-soft bed, snoring gently.

"Wheah's that damned Ella?" Amanda mumbled under her breath. She rolled out of bed, snatched her kimono off the floor, and slipped it on as she hurried out of the room, closing the door softly behind her.

As the door closed, Lucius sniffed and snorted and turned on his side, and tried to ignore whatever it was that was disturbing him. It would not be ignored. Gradually he became aware that the sounds he was hearing were voices, male and female, high-pitched and unnaturally animated. Then words emerged from the muffled gibberish and fell into place to form sentences.

"Have you been to Adam's? Maybe *he'd* know." That was Amanda.

Then a man's voice—it was Benjamin from Carolina

97

Grove. "Yes'm, I done been deah. Mistuh Adam say he don' know wheah Mistuh Lucius is, say he ain't seen 'im."

Lucius raised his head and held himself breathlessly still, wide awake and listening.

"Well, did you tell him what happened?" Amanda asked.

"Yes'm, I tol' 'im. Didn't seem to make much diffunce. He say give Miss Arabella his best wishes."

Lucius was out of bed like a cat, reaching for his clothes.

"Well, I tell you what, Ben," Amanda was saying. "You go on back to Carolina Grove. I'll find Mistuh Lucius and give him the news, and he and I will come as fast as we can."

"Miss Arabella'll kill me if I come back 'thout findin' 'im," Ben said. "She was awful mad already 'bout him goin' off an' not bein' deah when de baby come."

"Nevuh mind, Ben, I can find him easier than you can. You go on back, and I'll—"

Lucius flung open the door and rushed into the room. Amanda closed her eyes, put a hand over her brow, and groaned. "Oh my God!"

"Mistuh *Lucius*!" Ben said. He was frozen in the center of the room, his eyes wide and staring.

"What about the baby?" Lucius barked. With both hands he grabbed the black man by the collar of his threadbare coat and almost lifted him off his feet. "What happened, goddamnit?! Tell me!"

Benjamin gulped several times. "Mistuh Lucius..." he croaked. "You let loose o' me, and I'll tell you what happened."

Lucius released him. Ben stepped back and straightened his clothing, and took his time recovering his dignity.

"It was mah intention to offuh you congratulations, suh. You are the fathuh of a fine baby boy."

Lucius stared, ashen-faced. Again he reached for Ben, but this time imploringly, touching him gently on the arm. "A boy, Ben? Did you say...a boy? A *son*?"

"Yes, suh. Ol' Aint Wilma was midwife, and a good 'un she is. She's brought hunnerds o' babies into de worl', and she say dis 'un's as fine as any she's evuh seen. He ain't big, but he yells good an' loud. Aint Wilma say dat's what's impawtant."

"A son..." Lucius breathed. He swayed; hastily he reached for the nearest chair and sat down heavily. He turned glistening eyes toward the woman.

"Did you hear that, Amanda? I have a son..." He could barely manage to get the words out.

Amanda had fixed a cold glare on Lucius. Now she stepped toward Ben, and her face was instantly lit by a sweet smile.

"Oh, Ben, do me a favuh, will you? Don't mention to Arabella that you found Mistuh Lucius heah. She might, uh, you know, get an entirely *wrong* idea. Mistuh Lucius just stopped by this morning, and we, uh, we were just havin' a little chat. It's so easy for things like that to be misunduh*stood*, you know?"

Lucius had recovered his wits and was on his feet again, smiling and slapping Benjamin on the shoulder. "Yes, uh, Ben... I want to thank you for coming all this way to bring me the news. Really good of you. I'd like to offer you a little, uh, little token of my, uh...."

He was groping in his pockets. "I seem to have left my wallet in my jacket pocket." He started for the bedroom. "Excuse me, I'll be right—"

"You cain't bribe me, Mistuh Lucius," Ben said quietly.

"Oh, no, no... I mean just a little thank-you token, just a little—"

"I don't want yo' money, suh." Ben's face was fixed in granite dignity as he looked from the man to the woman and back to the man. Both shrank from his penetrating gaze.

"But you-all don't have to worry none, I ain't gon' say nothin'. When I was jest a little biddy boy I already knew what my place in dis worl' was. It was to do my job de best I could, and not to see nothin', heah nothin', say nothin', nor think nothin'. Tha's the way I live, an' I git along real good with ever'body. 'Sides, I wouldn't nevuh say nothin' that'd hurt Miss Arabella. She may not be de brightest one, but she's my favorite of de Whitehurst chillun. Always was."

Ben pushed a decrepit old felt hat down on his head and walked to the front door. He paused there to look back at Lucius.

"An', by de way, suh, she's doin' jes' fine."

He went out and closed the door behind him.

The silence was overwhelming. Lucius sat down again, took a deep breath, and rocked slowly back and forth, staring into space. Amanda watched him for a few seconds. Then she pushed her hair back with an angry movement and began to pace the floor, very slowly.

"Well, congratulations, Papa. You shuah messed us up good."

He looked up at her blankly, uncomprehending. "What?"

"For God's sake, did you have to come busting out like a damn fool? I could have handled it puhfectly well, if you'd have only—"

Lucius was staring into space again, not listening.

Amanda made an explosive noise of exasperation, flounced into her bedroom, and slammed the door.

Lucius went on staring into the distance and rocking gently.

"I have a son," he whispered.

(14)

FROM THE JOURNAL of Lucius Hargrave:

How odd it is that the two supremely critical moments of our sojourn in this world—birth and death—must remain forever hidden from our knowledge; our senses are insufficiently developed to observe the first, and are obliterated by the second. Fortunately there are two other profoundly significant types of events in our lives that we are usually permitted to know fully—marriage, and the births of our children.

I find it difficult to trace the infinite degrees by which my marriage to Arabella Whitehurst grew from a distant dream to present reality; I can only tick off the milestones in chronological order. I met her; I was enraptured; I fell in love; I was alarmed by the threat to her innocence posed by the ruthless fortune-hunting Albert Pettingill; I won the admiration of her father and the affection of the other members of the family (except the cold fish Adam); I even won the support of the house servants, who, though they had no voice in such matters, had certain subtle ways of exerting influence. In short, it began to appear that I might suffer the ironic fate of winning almost everything except that which I sought—when suddenly my adored one fell into my arms as naturally as a ripe peach falling from a tree. Arabella consented to be my wife on an afternoon in April, 1839, and two weeks later we were married.

But my recollections of the Great Event are strangely deficient. I moved as if in a trance through the days of feverish preparation and through the wedding itself. They tell me that the big house at Carolina Grove was alive with swarms of guests, and that the ceremony was beautiful enough to bring tears to the eyes of the most hardened observers. I must accept all this as truth—I am in no position to dispute it.

For a honeymoon we spent two glorious weeks in that palace of luxury, the St. Charles Hotel in New Orleans, where we received an endless stream of well-wishers. Albert Pettingill was not among them, I was delighted to note; having been jilted by Arabella the moment she discovered his true nature, he had slunk away and disappeared like the sore loser he was.

Then back to Carolina Grove, where we found that the plantation carpenters had converted Arabella's room and an adjoining one into a private apartment for us. And I had hardly unpacked my bags before Amos was asking my advice on some technical matter concerning the sugar mill. I saw what was expected of me. I sighed good-naturedly and accepted my role as partner to my new father-in-law.

There was more than enough to do. Besides my duties on the plantation I was still carrying on the search for my father—nothing could distract me from that—and was busy on my book exposing the evils of riverboat gambling. And naturally my sweet young bride required vast quantities of attention. Yes, life was suddenly full. Almost overnight I had acquired a lovely wife, an established home, a career, and social position. The cup of good fortune was filled to the brim—and after some months, when in the marvelous course of time and nature my beloved wife grew large with child, I saw that soon would "my cup runneth over."

Alas, perfection is an unnatural phenomenon in this world, and can exist only as a fragile and transitory illusion. The birth of my son—what should have been the supreme moment of my life—was cruelly whisked past me the moment my back was turned.

It chanced that a few days after Christmas, 1839, I was called to New Orleans on a business matter. Arabella was in her eighth month of pregnancy and suffering from depression, and I hated to leave her—but the business was urgent, and I would be gone only a day or two. Of course my child was born in my absence. And of course I was looked upon with sanctimonious disapproval by everyone from my parents-in-law to the lowliest house servant for not being at my wife's side at the critical hour. I ignored the abuse; it was nothing compared to my joy when I came home and found my dear wife well on the way to recovery and my little son gurgling happily in his cradle.

Though premature, he was a splendid little fellow, his bright eyes already ashine with the fine qualities of character and intelligence that were gifts to him from his Hargrave and Gilpin ancestry.

One additional indignity: chiefly, I think, as a punishment to me, my in-laws had taken it upon themselves to have my child christened in my absence. He was given the name James Justin, after Amos's father, who had been a distinguished (so Amos claimed) barrister in South Carolina.

I endured this insult as I had learned to endure all such—without a murmur of complaint. The truth is I had no strong preference concerning names. It was a trivial thing, and trivial things could no longer bother me. My spirits were soaring again, my sense of well-being unassailable.

One day I carried my son Justin (that is what I had decided to call him, his mother preferring Jamie, which I found effeminate) in my arms among the majestic oaks of Carolina Grove, and suddenly I stopped in my tracks. My eyes swept over the broad green lawns of the spacious estate, then I looked down at the little boy who might someday inherit it all, and I sucked in my breath from sheer astonishment. Life was not only good, it was bursting with a harvest of blessings that less than a year before I could not have conceived of in my wildest fancies.

I wanted to cry out, Oh God in Heaven, how generous are thy gifts! I had never known a feeling of such humble gratitude, and simultaneously such a welling up of confidence and power. Surely there was no man on earth nor force in heaven or hell that could slight me ever again, do me harm, or ever wish me ill.

So I thought.

(15)

Mrs. Sarah Thacker
c/o Thacker and Hargrave, Associates
Number One Gilpin Street
South Bar, Indiana

Dear Mama,
   I'm sure you will be able to sense the pride with
which I write to inform you of the birth of my son,
James Justin, who came into this world on Saturday the
28th of December, 1839, at Carolina Grove. Though he
is an eight-months baby he is a fine fellow in every
respect, and is developing so fast that every day brings
new astonishment. I remember when I was a boy,
Mama, you once told me that my father had regarded
my own early birth as a good omen, referring to some
ancient legend or other that held prematurity a blessing.
Well, I know nothing of such things, but I can easily
believe it in Justin's case. My in-laws all think his beauty
and intelligence are Whitehurst legacies. I smile and say
nothing, but I know better. They are gifts, through me,
from his paternal grandparents. He has your eyes,
Mama, that strange sort of mixture of soft brown and
amber that I always thought contributed so much to
your beauty.
   But—back to earth. I am sorry to be so long in
responding to your last letter, and Isaac's. I don't mean
to make excuses, but I can assure you I have never
worked so hard in my life as I do now as co-master of a

great southern plantation. Let it never be said in my presence that the southern planter is a man of leisure!

Of course I am overjoyed to hear of Isaac's marriage, and sorrier than I can say that I couldn't be there. And Mama, I think it is unbecoming of you to be pessimistic about its chances for success. You should rather wish for its success with all your heart, and not admit a shadow of a reservation. Has it ever occurred to you that one of the reasons for Isaac's appallingly slow development as an independent man could be your excessive motherliness? (I can feel you bristling! Forgive me Mama, it is not my place to voice such a thought.)

Tell Grandpa for me that I am delighted he remains well and active. Surely, though, he can find better ways to spend his dwindling energies than on such an idiotic business as campaigning for an abolitionist candidate! The anti-slavery sentiments in the North are sheer nonsense, Mama. I assure you that the colored people at Carolina Grove are healthy and happy, and enjoy as much freedom as the poor simple souls could make use of. They are not on the abolitionists' side. Even they know that the destruction of the slave system would lay waste this land, and leave in ruins the lives of all people, black and white.

Arabella sends both you and Isaac a hug and a kiss, and joins me in a solemn promise that we will come to South Bar just as soon as Justin is old enough to travel safely. Then you will have the joy of clasping that handsome young fellow to your heart—which after all is a grandmother's right!

> *With much love, as always, your devoted son,*
> *Lucius*

P.S. Regards to Mr. Thacker. (Mama, do not waste your breath scolding me about my "old grudges." Cyrus and I took each other's measure many years ago. We know where we stand, and you can't change that, ever.)

LUCIUS reclined in a wicker chair on the foredeck of the

(16)

LUCIUS RECLINED in a wicker chair on the foredeck of the
steamboat *Orion* and with half-closed eyes watched the north
shoreline glide imperceptibly past as the ship climbed
upstream toward Louisville and Cincinnati. In the month of
May the wooded banks of the Ohio were spectacular with
foliage and fragrance, and La Belle Riviére glittered with the
dancing light of afternoon sunshine.

A large man in a rumpled blue serge suit came along the
deck and tipped his captain's hat at Lucius. "You wanted me
to remind you when we came to South Bar, Indiana, Mr.
Walker."

"Um-m-m. Yes."

"We'll be puttin' in there in a few minutes, to take on
wood."

"Thank you, Captain."

"Nice little town, South Bar. One o' the best woodin' places
on the river."

"So I've heard."

"You might want to step ashore for a bit, stretch your legs."

"I think not," Lucius said. He locked his hands comfortably
behind his head.

Twenty minutes later the woodloading operation was in
progress, accompanied by a cacophony of shouts from ship
and woodyard workers. Lucius got up and strolled in the
direction of the guardrail. He stopped just inside the shadows
formed by the overhang of the upper deck, leaned against a
post, and watched the work going on below. Soon his gaze
drifted up and across the water to come to rest on the
rambling stockade-like woodyard, and its tall sign facing the

105

river traffic: THACKER AND HARGRAVE, ASSOCIATES. WOOD PRODUCTS. Squarish block letters, the black paint beginning to peel a little around the edges. Somehow it all seemed smaller than Lucius remembered.

After a while the captain came and leaned on the guardrail near him. "Quite an operation down below, eh, Mr. Walker?"

Lucius was still studying the big stockade on the shore. "You say this is one of the best places on the river, Captain?"

"Sure is. Fine outfit, Thacker and Hargrave."

"Who are they?"

"Fella named Cyrus Thacker built the place way back when, then took his stepson in as his partner. Hargrave's the one really makes the business go. Not 'cause he's 'specially smart, but 'cause he's so well-liked. You go in there and Isaac Hargrave'll meet you at the door and take you into his office and serve you whiskey, or coffee, or a meal if you want it. Makes you feel like a goddamn king."

Lucius's eyes were scanning what was visible of the little tree-shaded town spread out on the gentle slope above and behind the woodyard. "I see a big house back up there," he said. It was a question disguised as a statement.

"That's the Thacker house," the captain said. "Finest house in town. I met Mrs. Thacker once, in the woodyard office. Mighty pretty lady she is. There's a juicy story they tell around here 'bout her. Seems when she was a young girl she got seduced by a travelin'—"

"I don't listen to small-town gossip, Captain," Lucius snapped.

The captain let go of the railing and stood up straight. "I'm goin' ashore to settle my bill now, Mr. Walker. Want to come along? Or don't you care for small-town socializin', either?"

Lucius let his eyes dwell on the quiet little river settlement a moment longer before answering.

"I have work to do," he said then, and abruptly walked away.

The captain watched him go, then with an uninterested shrug strolled off in the opposite direction.

(17)

IT WAS A TALL narrow two-story frame house, looking stiff
and formal behind a small yard of flower beds and neatly
trimmed shrubs.

Lucius rapped on one of the glass panels in the front door,
stepped back and waited. The middle-aged man who
appeared was ruddy-faced and flame-haired, stiffly erect of
bearing and formally attired in a morning coat.

"Yes, sir?"

Lucius appraised the man with a quick sweep of his eyes.
"Is this the residence of Dr. Thaddeus Ewing, of the
Methodist Episcopal organization?"

"It is."

"Will you announce me, please? I am Lucius Hargrave, of
Louisiana. I believe Dr. Ewing is expecting me."

The tall man chuckled as he opened the door wider and
extended his hand. "Consider yourself announced, Mr.
Hargrave. I am Dr. Ewing."

"I beg your pardon, sir," Lucius said hastily. "I suppose I
didn't expect a man of your eminence to be answering his own
door."

"Not only that, I do look like a butler, don't I?" Dr. Ewing
continued to chuckle as he led his visitor into a musty-smelling
book-lined parlor and motioned him to a chair. "Leastways,
all my friends say so. There was an English fellow visiting
Cincinnati last year. He told me if I ever got up against it I
ought to come to England. I'd not want for employment
there, he said. I'd be the perfect gentleman's gentleman."

Lucius slapped his knee and laughed heartily. "Most
amusing, sir."

107

"He was only joking, of course," Dr. Ewing went on. "All he meant was—"

"Uh, Dr. Ewing," Lucius said. "I'm deeply grateful to you for granting me an interview. And I'm going to try to take up just as little of your time as possible."

"Oh, don't worry about that, Mr. Hargrave. I've got plenty of time."

"Unfortunately, *I* am desperately short of it."

"Well, in that case, let's get down to business." Dr. Ewing brought forth from a vest pocket a pair of pince-nez glasses, which he mounted with great care on the bridge of his nose. Then he picked up a sheaf of papers on the table beside him.

"I have here all your correspondence, from your first inquiry, dated...let's see...October of last year, to your recent note telling me you were coming to Cincinnati. Quite a considerable amount of literature here." He hefted the stack of papers in his hands as if weighing it.

"I'm not complaining, mind. In fact I've been fascinated to read of the splendid achievements of your father. What a remarkable man. Oh, and I mustn't forget to thank you again for the generous contribution you made to the church. Most gratifying, Mr. Hargrave. The Lord will bless you for it."

Lucius nodded graciously. "I meant it as a kind of gesture to honor my father, Dr. Ewing. In recognition of the good work he has done for the church."

"Uh, yes, uh...to be sure." Dr. Ewing cleared his throat nervously and shuffled the papers in his hands.

"And that could be merely the first of a long series of contributions, Dr. Ewing," Lucius went on. "You see, I need help in the work I'm about to undertake, and I believe you're the man who can provide it."

"I don't see how, Mr. Hargrave. I'm only an elder in the Ohio Conference of the church—"

"But I know your reputation, sir. You've been described to me as the unofficial historian of the Methodist Church in America. If there's any man alive who can help me, it's you."

Dr. Ewing seemed to be growing uncomfortable. "Oh, I hardly think, sir—"

"Understand, I don't mean to insult you by offering to *buy* your services. But I'm a businessman, Dr. Ewing. Practical, hardheaded, down-to-earth. My gratitude is going to be considerable, and the only way I know to express that gratitude is with money."

The churchman was fidgeting. "Look here, Mr. Hargrave.

I had thought to go over this curious business of yours with you step by step, but... perhaps I'd best come right to the point, bluntly and honestly."

Lucius leaned forward, his face tense with expectancy. "By all means."

Dr. Ewing put down the letters and picked up a second stack of papers. "I have made extensive inquiries. As extensive as I could, that is, considering the limitations you placed on the task. And as far as I've been able to determine there is no record of any Reverend Oliver Hargrave in the history of the Methodist organization in the Ohio Valley."

The Minister paused for a reaction. There was none; his guest's face was an expressionless mask. Dr. Ewing continued.

"Of course I was severely hampered by the restrictions you placed on me. By your own admission, South Bar, Indiana is the only place on the river where the Reverend Hargrave was known to have spent any considerable time. And that is the one location you have proscribed from my investigations."

"But I *explained* all that!" Lucius's voice rasped with sudden agitation. "South Bar is where my father was finally cornered by his enemies, and ruined. In that place you could hear nothing but lies, not a word of truth. I was trying to avoid wasting your time."

Dr. Ewing eyed his visitor with scholarly patience. "It seems to me that a method of selective investigation such as you suggest could not possibly be aimed at the discovery of facts. It must be for some other purpose."

Lucius stiffened. "My purpose, sir, is to rescue my father's good name from slander, and restore it to its rightful place of honor."

Dr. Ewing studied his visitor a moment longer, then turned his attention to the papers he was holding. "There is one little thing here. An elder of our church, Reverend Jacob Nellis—a greatly respected resident of this city for many years, now deceased—left some notes on a special interest of his, which was the apprehending of, uh... shall we say... impostors."

Again there was a pause. Lucius waited.

"It's a serious problem for the church, always has been," Dr. Ewing went on. "This business of men going into isolated communities and posing as ordained ministers in order to gain... well, I don't know what. Prestige, or—"

Lucius made a noise of impatience. "What about this man Nellis?"

109

"He makes mention of someone whose name was . . . well, the Reverend's handwriting was not the best." Dr. Ewing offered a paper for Lucius's examination. "Here, look for yourself. Seems to be Hangrave, or Hargrove, or possibly Hargrave."

Lucius gave the paper a cursory glance and handed it back without comment.

"A very interesting coincidence, in any case," Dr. Ewing said. "Reverend Nellis is talking about someone who was unlawfully impersonating a Methodist minister in 1815 and 16. The place was South Bar, Indiana."

There was a long silence while Lucius gazed at his informant through narrowed eyes. Then he produced a sad philosophical smile.

"Ah, me, how difficult is communication between us mortal beings, eh, Dr. Ewing? We might as well be set on tiny islands in the sea, separated from one another by miles of open water."

Dr. Ewing was puzzled. "I'm afraid I don't quite—"

"Let me start again from the beginning." Lucius was now speaking in a crisply businesslike tone. "I am the owner of one of the great sugar plantations of Louisiana—but that is a mere avocation. By profession I am an author. At the moment I am in Cincinnati to confer with the people at C.S. Foster and Company about the publication of a book of mine. It's an exposé of the evils of gambling, and I firmly believe it will save many an American family from ruination."

"The Lord will bless you, sir," Dr. Ewing said solemnly.

"For my next book, I intend to turn away from evil and sing the praises of goodness. I will write a biography of my father, Oliver Hargrave."

In his turn Lucius waited for a reaction and received none. Dr. Ewing sat silent and stone-faced. Lucius continued.

"But I need help with that one. A collaborator. One whose name on the title page will lend authority—"

Dr. Ewing was shaking his head. "You're confusing me, Mr. Hargrave."

"I will write the book, sir. You will sign it as author. We will split the profits equally. It will be an inspirational book, full of all the ingredients of success. By hardly turning your hand you'll be rich."

Dr. Ewing rose and walked across the room. He stood for a moment before a window. Then with his hands clasped behind his back he turned toward his guest, and his face was stern with righteousness.

"It's quite impossible, sir. The facts are not known, and the evidence, such as it is, is far from inspirational."

"I can easily fill in the empty areas, working from what I know. All you have to do is—"

"You'll be writing fiction then, not biography. Biography must be based on facts."

"Damn facts!" Lucius was on his feet with a roar, his eyes blazing. "My father's life is not just a collection of dry lifeless facts! It holds something far more glorious than that, it holds Truth! Truth, sir, do you comprehend the word?! My book will capture the essence of the man, and reflect in some small way his noble qualities, his . . ."

Lucius' outburst was over as suddenly as it had begun. He stood drained of resolve, his eyes wandering as if in confusion.

"Excuse me," he mumbled.

Dr. Ewing took his visitor by the arm and led him toward the front door. "Mr. Hargrave, I wish you nothing but the best of luck in all your endeavors. Sorry I can't help you. But thanks for stopping by." He extended his hand.

Lucius gaped. "Are you turning me out?"

"I can't be of any service to you, Mr. Hargrave, so there's no point in—"

"Damn you." Lucius's eyes were aflame again, but his voice remained low. "Damn you for thinking that because you possess church credentials you are the sole arbiter of what's truth and what isn't. Damn you because you never knew my father and don't *want* to know him."

Dr. Ewing edged his visitor toward the open door. "If you don't mind, I have another appoint—"

"Damn you for being the perfect embodiment of all the jealous, sanctimonious, narrow-minded, vindictive—"

"Mr. Hargrave!"

"—Evil old bastards who make it their life's work to ruin great men. Evil, evil, evil! I *spit* on you!"

Dr. Ewing pushed the raging man out of the house and started to close the door. Lucius stopped it with his hand. They stared at each other, tense and rigid.

"Please," Lucius whispered. His eyes were full of pleading, all hostility faded. "Help me. I've got to find him."

"I am sorry for you, my friend," Dr. Ewing said gently. "If it's your desire to *find* your father, why, that's another matter,

111

and I wish you all success. But I must tell you, sir, you cannot *create* him."

A little smile softened Dr. Ewing's features. "Good day, Mr. Hargrave," he said, and closed the door.

(18)

November 15, 1840

Mr. Lucius Hargrave
Carolina Grove Plantation
St. Charles Parish, Louisiana

Dear Brother,
I supose I will have to break down and write you one of my terible letters, which I know cause you much distress, because I dont write very well, as you have pointed out to me many times before, but at least I think you will find my Punktuation somewhat improven. You remember, I use to have no use for comas, at all, but now I have descovered what useful little devils they can be, and I have come to like them a lot, but Lucy says my writing is still terible, she says I use to many comas, and not enough periods. Well, I am just hopeless, I guess. But, be that as it may.
To get on to the substence of my comunication, I want to tell you how happy I am, to be a married man at last. Lucius, my darling Lucy is just an angel, there is no better word to discribe her, she looks after me, she pampers me, and spoils me, and makes sure that I am properly dressed, when I go out, and sees that I eat properly, and, well, I cant think of all the ways she makes my life comftable. I am, what you would have to call, a lucky man. We celibrated our first aniversery in September, and are happly embarked on our second year of bliss. There is no adition to the family on the

way, as yet, that I know of, but, I feel sure, it is only a matter of time, for, you may be sure, I am not neglecting those plesant husbanly dutys so nesessary for that purpose, if you know what I mean! Oh, Lucy will scoll me for that last remark, which she will say is lude, but I think a little joke between brothers is permisable. But, to be serious now.

Lucius, I am worryed about Mama Sarah. In the first place, she is bitterly angry with you, because you said something in a letter, about her being bad for me, being to motherly, or something. Lucius, how could you be so foolish, I have never heard anything so rediculous in my life. She is also bitter because, she says, you have never had any intention of ever coming to see us, and you are just a lier. I cant believe that, and I tell Mama Sarah she is wrong, but she will not listen to me. Also, she has a hard time at home, these days. Cyrus likes to go home after a hard days work and have a good supper and a drink or two of whisky and doze away the evening in his faverite chair. He is not the greatest talker in the world, and I know Mama Sarah has been lonely since I got marryed and moved out, and it makes me feel bad to think about it. It is not for me to tell you what to do, dear brother, but I will just say, look into your heart, and listen to the voice of your consience.

How is Arabella, and your little Justin? Lots of times when I go to see Mama Sarah we just sit, and try to emagine them, and what they are like. Little Justin must be nearly a year old now, I can hardly believe it, oh, how I wish you would send us some news!

Grandpa Gilpin remains healthy and active, thank the Lord, and, in fact, is engaged in truging around the town of South Bar, urging one and all to vote for James Birney of the Liberty Party for president, next month. Mama Sarah is helping him, which I think is foolish, she should be trying to get him to stay home and take care of himself, and I say so even though I am in favor of the Liberty Party, to, because it is antislavery, and all.

Lucius, I am sad about you, but I will not give up, because I know that someday you will show us that your heart is in the right place.

Your Loving brother,
Isaac

113

(19)

Jacob Worthington, Attorney-at-Law
Number 5 Orchard Street
South Bar, Indiana

February 23rd, 1841

Mr. Lucius Hargrave
Carolina Grove Plantation
St. Charles Parish, Louisiana

Dear Mr. Hargrave,

Permit me a word of introduction. As the only licensed attorney in the vicinity of South Bar, Indiana, I have for the past several years enjoyed cordial business and personal association with the company of Thacker and Hargrave, Associates, with your mother, Mrs. Sarah Thacker, and with Mrs. Thacker's father, the distinguished Mr. Samuel Gilpin. I write this letter to you now at the request of Mrs. Thacker, and your brother, Mr. Isaac Hargrave, whom I have the honor to represent.

It is my sad duty to inform you that your grandfather, Mr. Gilpin, is now deceased, having passed away at about five o'clock in the afternoon of Thursday last, the 18th day of February, 1841. According to Mrs. Thacker her father's health had begun to fail shortly before Christmas, and since that time he had been living in the Thacker home, under Mrs. Thacker's care. Apparently death came peacefully, with no pain or distress. At the time of his passing Mr. Gilpin was 76 years and 6 months of age, so I think it is appropriate that we allow our grief to be tempered by the knowledge that he lived a long, abundant, and extraordinarily worthwhile life. Surely it is no exaggeration to say that there is not a riverfront urchin in South Bar who does not know that Samuel Gilpin was the town's founder and has always been its first citizen.

Funeral services were held on Sunday the 21st, conducted by the Reverend Millard Thomas of the local Methodist Church, and interment was at the River Road Cemetery. That old burial ground is not much used anymore, and regrettably has fallen into neglect, but since Mrs. Thacker's mother and brother are buried there (as well as a young daughter, I understand), it was her express wish that her father should rest among those loved ones.

Mrs. Thacker desires me to notify you that your grandfather left you a few remembrances in his will—nothing of great monetary value, but a few books and personal mementos, which I am sure you will treasure for the sentiments attached thereto. She would also appreciate your letting us know what your wishes are with regard to their disposal. She says she will be happy to store them for you if you wish, against the day when you might by chance pass this way.

In closing may I offer you my deepest condolences at the passing of your beloved grandfather. I had the pleasure of knowing him for only a year or two, but during that time I was continuously impressed by the quality of both his intellect and his sterling character. You must feel intensely proud of being descended from so fine a man.

It will be a great pleasure to hear from you, at your convenience.

I am, sir,

> Your most respectful servant,
> Jacob Worthington

(20)

FROM THE JOURNAL of Lucius Hargrave:

There are times when I am tempted to believe that some dark
force in nature has singled me out for a peculiarly fiendish
form of torment: no sooner does life seem to have reached a
plateau of stability and satisfaction than it promptly plunges
downhill.

Consider:

I who have always been devoted to my mother, have seen
her turn her back on me and shut me out of her life like an
unwanted foundling. She has never ceased resenting the fact
that at sixteen I was able to go forth into the world and find my
own way—and particularly galling for her was the stark
contrast to the behavior of my timid half-brother, Isaac.
Though only her stepson, he had attached himself to her like a
perpetual babe-in-arms, and was only won away by a wife
when he was thirty years old. From letters I received it was
quite clear that my mother hated the thought of that marriage,
and showed all the warmth of a glacier to the "other woman"
(I believe that is an accurate description of how she felt).

Still I had no idea of the depth of her bitterness toward me
until one day there came a stuffy letter from a lawyer in South
Bar, casually informing me that my dear old grandfather,
Samuel Gilpin, was dead. I was devastated. They tell me that
for the better part of a week I wandered alone by the river in a
kind of daze, mumbling to myself. That could well be true—I
have noticed that when I suffer an unusually painful blow I
have a strange tendency to lose all rational contact with the
passage of time. In this instance the pain was twofold: there
was the melancholy news itself, and there was the cruel

116

manner of its delivery—that my mother could be so spiteful as to leave it to some utter stranger to inform me in language cold and formal—dear God, surely I did not deserve that!

With tenderness and sorrow I remember that fine man, my grandfather Gilpin. Fine, and pathetic—an authentic hero of the early pioneering days in the Ohio Valley, he threw his life away at last in pursuit of an idiotic goal. At seventy-six, frail of body surely and apparently frail of mind as well, he went out into the teeth of winter to promote the cause of some amateur presidential candidate who had no hope of election. And my mother, whose intelligence I had always respected, encouraged him in this fatal foolishness! The pen trembles in my hand—I can write no more of this.

But these were not the worst of my trials. Much more grievous was the fact that the years-long search for my father had turned up not a trace. I had questioned thousands of people up and down the central river valleys. I had consulted everyone I could find who had any connection whatever with any branch of the Christian faith, including the highest officials of the national church organizations. I met not only with completely negative responses, but with open hostility— even, once, with the outrageous suggestion that my father might have been an impostor! Insult heaped upon the most callous indifference—how I bore it, I know not.

Moreover, my marriage, which I had thought to have been made in heaven, had begun to show its flawed construction. It was nobody's fault; my dear Arabella was simply not ready for adulthood. At twenty she was still a child, living only for pleasure, pleasure, and more pleasure. She saw marriage as another delightful game, like lawn bowling, and was prepared to devote herself to it about as much as to a pleasant afternoon of gamboling on the green. When the blessed state of motherhood shone down upon her a new word intruded in her vocabulary: responsibility—and odious it was to her taste. She turned on me, she blamed me for her morning sickness, for her temporary disfigurement, for the tedium of waiting, for the pain of birth, and the tiresome duties of caring for an infant, and most of all for the fact that it was not all fun. It did not escape my attention that when our lively little boy fell down and bruised himself he ran for comfort not to his mother, but to the always open arms of Crissy, the maid.

Still there were glimmers of light in all this darkness. First, my book, entitled "Confessions of a Reformed Gambler," was published in the summer of 1841, and became an instant success up and down the Mississippi and Ohio thoroughfares. To lend an air of authenticity to my material—as authentic it certainly was—I pretended to be the Reformed Gambler (using a nom-de-plume, of course). I cared not a whit for personal credit, nor expected gratitude for the incalculable service I was rendering my fellowman; the inner glow of satisfaction I felt was thanks enough.

But of infinitely greater importance to me was that supreme joy, solace, precious thing that is mine and will keep life forever worth living, despite all else. My son, Justin.

What a marvel he was as he approached his second birthday, scampering about the big house at Carolina Grove, the maker of mischief and the source of endless delight for everyone, master and servant alike. He was the king of all he surveyed, the ruler of the realm, the owner of all hearts. His grandparents were positively comical in their adoration of him, and the house Negroes would have been his willing slaves even if slavery had not existed in the land. He was naturally affectionate toward all, but when my boy spied me, his eyes would take on a special sparkle as he ran to greet me on little fat churning legs, arms outstretched, chortling in glee. Compared with that, what are the worst of misfortunes but flea bites on an elephant's back?

Justin knew me for his father and I knew him for my son, and as long as we had each other, nothing else mattered.

In such small pleasures lies the true sweetness of life.

(21)

FROM THE SOCIETY NOTES of the *Delta Observer*, a New Orleans newspaper:

Friday, December 10th, 1841

As the sugar processing season draws to a close and the festive mood of Christmas grows ever brighter, our theatres, restaurants, and hostelries are being enlivened by the presence of more and more distinguished gentlemen of the outlying provinces and their ladies, bent upon a well-earned holiday in the city, and respite from their labors.

Item: Checking into the St. Charles Hotel yesterday were Mr. and Mrs. Lucius Hargrave, of Carolina Grove Plantation, St. Charles Parish. Mrs. Hargrave is the daughter of Mr. and Mrs. Amos Whitehurst, of Carolina Grove. Mr. Whitehurst is one of the pioneers of the Louisiana sugar industry, and in recent years Mr. Hargrave has been assisting his father-in-law in the management of the plantation, said to be one of the largest in the state.

The Whitehurst name is well known in this city in other respects, as well. Mr. Adam Whitehurst, a brother of Mrs. Hargrave, is prominent in the import-export trade world of the Port of New Orleans and is one of the city's most eligible bachelors, while Miss Amanda Whitehurst, a sister, is celebrated as a dramatic actress of extraordinary beauty and talent, who has worked with many of the leading local theatrical companies. Miss Amanda has but recently returned to New Orleans from a tour of river cities with the Allen Blake Company, with which she appeared in the starring role of Lady Teazle in Sheridan's School for Scandal. From all reports her performances were met everywhere with enthusiastic acclaim.

Mr. Hargrave, originally from Indiana, is a gentleman of means in his own right. He is reputed to have extensive land holdings in his native state, as well as in the Republic of Texas.

Arabella lay motionless on the long couch in the sitting room of the hotel suite, an arm over her eyes. Once in a while she sighed softly; otherwise she displayed no sign of life.

There was a knock at the door.

After a few seconds Arabella called, "Sally, wheah are you? Go to the doah, for heaven's sake!"

A young black woman in a maid's uniform materialized and opened the door, and Amanda Whitehurst, draped in furs, came in, followed by her brother Adam, staunch and solid in a long black overcoat.

"Hello, dahlin'," Amanda called to her sister.

119

Arabella sat up and glared at the maid. "Well, don't just stand theah, Sally, take theah coats!"

"I'll keep mine on, thank you," Adam said. "I can only stay a minute."

The maid relieved Amanda of approximately ten pounds of furs and disappeared into another room. The guests seated themselves.

"Wheah's Crissy?" Amanda asked.

"At home takin' care of Jamie, which is all she's willin' to do anymore. Simply re*fused* to leave him. I have to get along with this dumb ol' hotel maid."

Amanda laughed. "Jamie's an angel, I don't blame Crissy. Anyway, cheer up, dahlin', you're supposed to be on a holiday. Did you see the nice piece about you in the *Observer* today?"

"About *me*?!" Arabella shrieked. "It's about Papa, and about Lucius, and about you, and about Adam, and about everybody in the world *except* me!"

"Oh, deah," Amanda murmured. "Our little sistuh's in a tempuh."

"Well, I have a right to be. I lead a wretched life!" Arabella said hotly.

"And whose fault is that?" Adam asked, directing his question to the ceiling.

"Don't start, Adam," Amanda said in a warning tone.

"Why don't eithuh of you think to ask wheah my adorable husband is?" Arabella demanded. "Is my maid more important than my husband?"

"That could be debated," Adam simpered.

"All right, I'll ask," Amanda said. "Wheah is he?"

"Downstairs in the Gentlemen's Dining Room. Can you *imagine* such a man? He brings me on a pleasure trip to the city, then spends his time in the Gentlemen's Dining Room and leaves *me* to twiddle my thumbs!"

"So," Adam said without interest. He crossed his legs and changed the subject. "How are Mothuh and Fathuh? What about this yeah's sugah crop?"

"Good heavens, don't ask *me* about the sugah crop!" Arabella snapped. "All I know is, Papa complains that Lucius talked him into expanding, and now won't shoulduh his share of the burden."

"I *knew* that would happen," Adam said grimly.

Arabella flounced to her feet. "Oh, *damn* the sugah crop! My life is ruined, and all you can talk about is business!"

120

"Dahlin', don't be angry with Brothuh, he can't help it," Amanda said. "In his veins flows the purest gold, and his brain is made up of millions of little dolluh signs, all linked togethuh."

"You're not funny, Amanda," Adam said with a peevish sniff. "If it weren't for me you'd have been out on the streets begging, long ago. Both of you."

Amanda stuck her tongue out at him.

Arabella sat down next to Amanda and reached for her sister's hand. "Amanda, you've got to help me."

"Yes, dahlin', I *want* to help you, and I'll begin by telling you that the first thing you ought to do is stop being such a virtuous long-suffering wife, and take youhself a lovuh."

Now Adam was up, quivering with righteous outrage. "Oh, good Lord, Amanda! *That's* no course of action to urge on a—"

Amanda made a show of exasperation. "This is woman talk, Adam, do you *mind*?!"

"Well, *I* don't want to heah it," Adam sniffed. He began to stroll around the room, idly examining the furnishings.

Amanda went on talking to Arabella, but in a more intimate undertone. "Now, dahlin', what I suggest is that you just suddenly kick ovuh the traces and give that big bad Lucius a dose of his own medicine. Why don't you come and stay with me for a while? Crissy's a wonderful Mammy, and you can leave Jamie with her indefinitely."

A little conspiratorial smile crossed Amanda's lips as her voice dropped almost to a whisper. "I happen to know several chahmin' young gentlemen who'd be just puhfect for you. Any one of them could make you fall in love with life again, ovuhnight."

From the far end of the room Adam offered a comment. "I've heard the St. Charles cost close to a million dolluhs to build, and I can believe it. Theah must be two thousand dolluhs' worth of interior decorating right heah in this room."

Amanda gave him an annoyed glance. "Adam, do take off that ovuhcoat, it mades me perspire just to look at you."

"Got to be going," Adam said, and strolled into the bedroom.

"Well, what do you say, dahlin'?" Amanda said to her sister. "You come and live with me awhile, and I'll guarantee you, you'll nevuh be satisfied with Carolina Grove again."

Arabella had grown thoughtful. "You really think I ought to be unfaithful to Lucius?"

"I think you should have been unfaithful ages ago."

"Do you think he's been unfaithful to me?"

Amanda threw her head back and laughed throatily. "My deah, I can promise you he has, countless times."

"How can you be so sure?"

"Dahlin'... you know I've had oodles of experience with men. I haven't met one in yeahs I couldn't read like an open book. And I nevuh saw one easier to read than ol' Lucius."

"So you think theah's another woman?"

"Not exactly anothuh *woman*. Othuh *women*. No other woman could stand very much of that arrogant, possessive, demanding, ovuhbearing—"

"Amanda!"

"I'm only repeating what you've said youhself, dahlin'," Amanda said innocently.

Adam emerged from the bedroom. "I've nevuh seen so much ovuhstuffed luxury in my life! Positively sinful."

His sisters ignored him.

"So, how about it, hmm?" Amanda was saying to Arabella. "You come stay with me, and I'll introduce you to some real gentlemen."

Arabella remained stubbornly glum. "It's not that easy, Amanda. It's evuh so much more serious than that."

"What do you mean, deah?"

The answer came in a piteous whimper. "I'm pregnant again."

Amanda groaned. "Oh Lord!"

"And I don't want it, Amanda. That's what you've got to do for me, first of all. Help me get rid of it. You must know the right people, don't you?"

"Oh, you bet I do, little sistuh." Amanda gave her a reassuring pat on the hand. "I know a voodoo woman who's an absolute wizard. She's fixed *me* up several times, and I'm none the worse."

"Amanda, you can't be serious!" Adam stood over her in towering indignation. "You'd take Arabella to a... a *voodoo woman*?!"

"Well, maybe you have a bettuh suggestion," Amanda said acidly. "Who does youh little quadroon whore on Rampart Street go to?"

Adam chose to ignore this. "Well, good Lord, I just... I just nevuh thought I'd see the day—"

"My God, what do you expect of me?!" Arabella screeched, eyes flashing. "You think I ought to go on breeding children I don't want for a husband who makes me miserable? I'm too young for that, I've got a whole life to live. I haven't even had any *fun* yet!"

"Well, you did *marry* the man, Arabella."

"I hate him! And you hate him too, you always have. Don't deny it."

"I will admit this—" Adam spoke with icy deliberation. "I curse the day Brad Kenyon brought that Yankee adventuruh to Carolina Grove."

"Nevuh mind, dahlin'," Amanda said soothingly. She put a protective arm around Arabella and pulled her into a motherly embrace. "We'll have you fixed up in no time."

"I've got to get back to the office," Adam snapped. "See you girls tomorrow." He started for the door.

"My God, it's nine o'clock at night!" Amanda bellowed. "Do you *live* at that damned office?"

Adam stood for a moment with the outer door open, looking back. "One day my esteemed brothuh-in-law will get his comeuppance," he announced. "And he'll get it from me."

"That's fine!" Arabella yelled at him. "And I'll thank you for it!"

Adam's eyes were pinpoints of flint as they rested on his younger sister. "I doubt that," he said coldly, and departed.

(22)

LUCIUS SAT SIPPING port wine in the magnificent, lofty-ceilinged, richly paneled Gentlemen's Dining Room of the St. Charles Hotel. He was alone, and he was in a tranquil mood. Between sips of wine he puffed on a large cigar and gazed absently off into a dense blue haze that was the product of his own and several dozen other cigars in the cavernous room. He did not look at the person who was suddenly standing at his elbow; he assumed it was the waiter.

"Nothing else, thank you," he murmured.

"Hello, Lucius."

It was a smoothly cultivated voice, and Lucius recognized it immediately.

"Good God!" He scowled up at the man. "Albert Pettingill!"

"Or Alfred Welles, if you prefer to remember your former colleague that way. And maybe I should call you Tom Walker, for old times' sake." Albert Pettingill pulled out a chair on the other side of the table and sat down. He beamed a huge smile across at Lucius. "How are you, old friend? May I join you?"

Lucius's face was expressionless as he turned up a spare wine glass and poured. "It appears you already have."

"Ah, thank you, thank you," Albert said, and sipped the wine with relish. "Ummm. Excellent. It does pay to frequent the better places, I always say. Of course I taught you that, didn't I? And you learned your lessons well, that's certain."

Lucius puffed on his cigar and studied his guest with narrowed eyes, and said nothing.

Albert glanced around at the palatial dining room. "But I must say, I prefer the St. Louis Hotel to this one. Much less ostentatious, much more refined. Do you know the St. Louis?"

"Certainly," Lucius said disinterestedly. "It represents the old French culture, of course, just as this represents the new American. Naturally you'd prefer the old. I prefer the new."

Albert chuckled. "Same old Lucius. Always looking ahead. There's nothing much of interest *behind* one, eh?"

He sipped his wine and beamed at the other man. "Ah, it's good to see you, Lucius. You're looking splendid, you really are. That's an exceedingly handsome suit you're wearing."

Lucius acknowledged the compliment by flicking an imaginary speck of dust off an embroidered cuff. "Sorry I can't say the same for you, Albert. You're looking a bit seedy. A bit haggard. Things not going well with you?"

Albert's easy smile contained a hint of discomfort. "The past couple of years have been rather sterile. But I've been through lean times before and bounced back, and I will again." He seemed determined to be cheerful.

"You look as though you could use a good meal," Lucius remarked dryly.

"Well, to tell the truth—silly of me—I've been in such a rush today I've hardly taken the time to eat a thing."

Lucius had snapped his fingers for the uniformed Negro

waiter. "Bring this gentleman one of your roast beef dinners, please."

"Yes, suh."

"And tell the chef to be generous. My friend here's been too busy to eat lately."

"Yes, suh." The waiter departed.

"Thank you, Lucius," Albert said softly. His cheerfulness had somewhat abated.

Lucius picked up the wine decanter and refilled both glasses. "Now tell me, Albert, where have you been for two and a half years? And why did you disappear just when Arabella and I were about to get married? I won her fair and square, didn't I? And as I recall our agreement, the loser was supposed to be gracious about it."

Albert looked sheepish. "Sorry. I suppose I did behave peculiarly. Oh, I know it started off as a friendly contest between us—sort of like one of our little card games in the old days—but I found myself feeling *sorry* for Arabella. She was so sweet, so innocent and trusting—and there she was, caught between a couple of cynical, scheming, fortune-hunting scoundrels." Embarrassment overcame him. "Can you imagine *me*, developing a conscience all of a sudden? I tell you, I began to fear for myself."

"So you ran away. Not very sporting of you."

"No, I didn't, really. Something came up. I had to go to New York State and take care of some family business, and—" Albert paused, frowning. "Didn't Arabella tell you? I wrote her a letter from there, explaining it all."

"She never mentioned it."

"Strange. I suppose it must have gone astray."

The waiter arrived with a cart of steaming dishes.

"Well, no matter," Lucius said casually. "Here's your dinner."

Albert was thoughtful as he watched the waiter set the food before him. "You know, that makes me feel a lot better. I was afraid Arabella was angry, and deliberately ignoring me."

"Eat your dinner before it gets cold," Lucius said. He leaned back and sipped his wine, and began to watch the traffic moving in and out of the dining room.

Albert spent several minutes concentrating on his food.

"So," he said finally. "How *is* the charming girl?"

"Arabella? Fine, fine."

"Give her my best, won't you? And I hear you have a little one now."

"We have a son, yes. He'll be two years old in a couple of weeks."

"Splendid! And how's my old flame, Amanda?"

"Insufferable."

"Oh? In what way?"

"She's demanding, she's possessive, she's egotistical beyond belief."

"Aren't those things permissible in celebrated actresses?"

"She's insulted because I refuse to be just another one of her lovers-on-call, waiting outside her boudoir door, panting like a puppydog for the chance to be next in her bed."

Albert laughed. "Ah, Lucius. Life is so full of lovely irony. I remember when you *were* a puppydog, wagging your little tail at the thought of such an enchanting creature as Amanda Whitehurst."

Lucious looked pained. "Never stop being superior, do you, Albert?"

Albert was seized with a new thought. "Oh, by the way, I picked up something interesting at a cigar counter not long ago." He reached into an inner coat pocket and brought forth a slender paperbound book, and scanned the cover.

"*Confessions of a Reformed Gambler*, by Thomas A. Walker." He put the book on the table in front of Lucius. "I was hoping I might have the author's autograph?"

"What makes you think *I'm* the author?"

"You're Tom Walker, aren't you? Always were, when we were partners. Why, I remember the first time you used that name. It was on the *Cincinnati Queen* coming into the landing right here in New Orleans. Tom Walker! How stupid, I remember thinking. How common. Then I thought—wait a minute, it's not stupid at all, it's clever. So common it's clever." Albert chuckled. "Besides, after reading two pages of this book I *knew* it was you; I recognized you in every line. Pompous, superior, stuffy, shining with pure and saintly virtue, and crusading—oh God, crusading to beat the band. Burning to save mankind from its own vices, after having spent some years getting rich off those same vices. That's Lucius, I said to myself. That's my boy."

"Thank you," Lucius said coldly.

"But I'm joking," Albert went on hastily. "Actually I'm impressed with the book, I think it's quite well written. You certainly exposed all our tricks, didn't you? Marvelous reading for all the good pious folk in the land. At fifty cents a copy, it must be making a fortune for you."

126

"Well, it's not all profit. I paid the cost of manufacture myself, and I'm acting as my own distributor. I've got about seventy-five dealers up and down the river, and not half a dozen of 'em are honest."

Albert made sympathetic noises. "Tsk, tsk, tsk! What's this world coming to?"

"But it's doing all right." Lucius picked up the book and idly leafed through it. "I'm making as much money exposing the profession as I ever made practicing it, and I'm working one-tenth as hard." He shot a quizzical look at Albert. "Sorry if it's put a damper on your activities, old boy."

"Come now, you don't really think it has, do you?" Albert's smile was disdainful. "People who gamble don't read that sort of thing, Lucius. The people who read it are the virtuous folk, and they don't need it. Anyway, I, uh . . . I haven't been very active lately."

"Which no doubt accounts for your rundown look."

"Having inherited my grandmother's farm in New York State, I've been trying to convert myself into a country gentleman. Thought maybe I'd get married and produce some heirs, and have the village parson and his wife in for tea on Sunday afternoons." Albert heaved a long sigh. "Don't know yet if I'll succeed, or if it'll drive me stark mad first. Truth is, I miss the old life. The excitement, the danger, the living by my wits. If I had a good partner I'd go back to it in a minute. Never had but one really first-rate partner, and he left me some years ago."

"That's too bad," Lucius said in a manner devoid of interest.

Albert's eyes went dreamy in reminiscence. "Ah, those were the good old days, eh, Lucius? Remember all the great times we had? The hustle and bustle of the steamboat landings? Looking over the crowds, picking out our pigeons? All the lively towns? The saloons, the restaurants, the hotels? The women? The sheer *fun* of it all? Remember, Lucius?"

Lucius sat silent, stolid, unresponsive.

Albert leaned across the table toward him. "How about it, old partner? Want to pick up where we left off? We were so good together, the best on the river. Two weeks of practice, and we'd be the best again."

Lucius had taken a pencil out of his coat pocket and was scribbling something on the inside of the book cover. When he finished he closed the book and laid it down again, and snapped his fingers for the waiter.

"Bring this gentleman some more wine, please. And anything else he cares to order. It's on my bill."

"Yes, suh." The waiter took the wine decanter and went off.

Albert was solemn-faced as he gazed at the younger man. "Come back, Lucius," he said softly. "I need you."

Very slowly Lucius shook his head. "*I* don't need *you*, Albert."

For a long moment they sat in silence looking at each other. Then Albert took a deep breath and lowered his eyes to his nearly empty plate.

"Well, thanks for the dinner," he said.

"My pleasure."

Albert was smiling again. "Funny. I just remembered the night I took you on as my apprentice. It was in New Madrid, Missouri, in 'thirty-two. Good Lord, that was almost ten years ago. You came barging into the hotel there where I was having dinner, and you were such a forlorn, ragged, half-starved, miserable-looking creature that I just couldn't help taking pity on you. I bought *your* dinner that night."

With a leisurely movement Lucius crushed out his cigar in the ashtray. Then he got to his feet, and stood looking down at Albert's still wavy, still thick, but now almost entirely gray hair.

"Now we're even," he said. He walked away, going toward the wide, arched doorways that led to the main lobby of the hotel.

Shortly the waiter returned to the table with a fresh decanter of port. "Shall I pour, suh?"

Albert sat staring at nothing across the room, his fingers drumming on the tablecloth. He made no answer.

The waiter refilled the gentleman's wineglass, put down the decanter, and withdrew.

After another minute had gone by, Albert noticed the book lying on the table. He looked at it with an air of mild surprise, as if he had forgotten it was there. Idly he picked it up and opened it. Lucius's bold disorderly scrawl filled the top half of the inside cover

New Orleans, December 10, 1841

To my old friend Albert—
  On whom my afffection, like the warmth of the sun,

will fall most pleasantly from the proper distance.
Thanks for being an important part of my past.

Lucius

Albert's durable smile reappeared. "That's my boy," he murmured.

He picked up his wineglass and emptied it in one gulp. Then he tucked the book under his arm, rose, and made his way quickly across the dining room in the direction opposite from that in which Lucius had gone, out of the brightly lit building and into a dank winter night.

(23)

May 1st, 1842

Mr. Lucius Hargrave
Carolina Grove Plantation
St. Charles Parish, Louisiana

Dear Brother,
I am writing this in secret. That is, I don't want Mama Sarah to know I am writing, because she says it is useless for us to write to you anymore, because you don't care anything about us. I know that is wrong, Lucius, but I am in very low spirets these days, and I am just tired of argueing with her about you.
I am no longer a marryed man, Lucius. It all hapened very sudenly, that is, suden for me, maybe Lucy had been thinking about it for a long time, I don't know. She ran off with a steamboat Captin. His name is Captin Milner, he is from Louisville, and I know the man well,

he has been one of our best custemers for years, in fact he has even been in our house as a gest. Well, around the first of March, one day I came home from work and found Lucy gone. She had left me a note, and she said she had gone with Capt. Milner, and she was sorry, and she hoped I wouldn't be to hurt, and all like that. I thought maybe she would come back as soon as she relized how foolish it was, and I was prepared to be forgiving, but she did not come back, and pretty soon I got a letter from her, telling me she couldnt be marryed to me anymore and we had to get a devorce. You know, they say Indiana is the easiest state of any to get a devorce in, my lawyer friend Jacob Worthington says marryed people come from all over the country to get a devorce here, it is so easy. Anyway, we are getting a devorce, and I have moved back home, that is, with Cyrus and Mama Sarah, and that is that.

I feel very bad about it, I tryed to be a good husband, but gess I just wasnt cut out to be one. Mama Sarah keeps telling me, never mind, Isaac, it is all for the best, Lucy wasn't good enough for you, anyway, but that is not true, she was a fine woman, and better than I deserved. Mama Sarah is just trying to make me feel better, and I apreciate it.

Well, I wanted to tell you, I have been doing a lot of thinking lately, and I have come to the cunclusion that maybe I aught to get away from South Bar for a wile. You always told me I should leave for good, and I don't believe that, but maybe I aught to get away for just a little wile. So I got the idea, why not go to Louisiana and see Lucius, and meet Arabella and my little nefew Justin? What do you say, Lucius, wouldnt it be great to be together once again, it has been ten years sence weve seen each other, ten years, think of that!

I cant do it right away, thogh. Cyrus and I are going to be buzier than ever this summer, we are expanding the mill again, and we are getting ready to bild us an iron boiler for steam power, and when that is done Thacker and Hargrave is going to be the bigest and best mill between Louisville and Evansville. But about September I'll be ready to do it.

I know you are a buzy man, Lucius, and don't have much time for writing, so if I don't here from you to the contrery, I will take it to mean it is all right for me to

130

come. Of corse if you can find the time to write it would
be helpfull to have some directions, but, if not, I can
inquire my way.

So I will just start makeing my plans. I feel better all
ready, Lucius. Now I cant wait for September to come.

Your loving brother,
Isaac

(24)

AMOS WHITEHURST sat in the merciful shade of his broad
front veranda and squinted through watery eyes at the heat
shimmering above the sun-baked grounds before the house.
In his right hand he clutched an iced drink, and in his left a
paper fan, which occasionally fluttered like one wing of a
dispirited butterfly.

Near the old man's feet on the floor of the veranda little
James Justin Hargrave sat playing with a set of wooden
blocks. He was building a tower. At the age of two and a half
the boy was not much interested in the principles of sound
construction; his aim was to see how tall a tower could
become before toppling to the floor in a delightful clatter.
Slowly and with breathless deliberation he placed one block
on top of another, and each time looked to see if his
grandfather was watching. From time to time Amos glanced
at the child, and his grizzled features would soften with a fond
smile. Then he would shift his eyes back to some vague point
in the sunny distance and resume his natural scowl.

"It ain't right," he mumbled. "It jes' ain't right." He drained
the last inch of dark liquid in his glass and shouted, "Ben? Uh,
Ben!"

The butler came out of the house and approached his master with a disapproving frown on his ebony face. "Now, don' ask fo' anothuh rum and coffee, Mistuh Amos, you done had enough."

"Jes' shut yo' mouth and fix it, Ben," Amos snapped, and held out the glass. "I got enough trouble without havin' to ahgue with *you* all the time."

"But Doctuh Patrick said you ain't s'posed to have but one rum and coffee a day, an' you s'posed to stay quiet, an'—"

"Patrick's a goddamn fool, an' so are you!" Amos bellowed. "I'm s'posed to stay quiet, like hell! Who's he think's gon' run this place while I stay quiet?!"

Ben gave up, took the glass, and went back into the house, shaking his head.

Justin's tower had exceeded all bounds of natural law. As its builder watched wide-eyed it teetered dangerously and came crashing down, its parts careening off in all directions. The boy looked up and found his grandfather's eyes on him. He pointed to the scattered blocks and smiled.

"Faw down," he explained, and pride shone in his face.

Amos shook with wheezing laughter, and the little boy laughed with him in a piping treble.

"Fall down?" Amos echoed, beaming. "Yes, it shuahly did, didn't it? James Justin, you're a mighty smaht young fella, yes you are. You gon' be talkin' a blue streak 'round heah, fo' we know it."

Elated, Justin scrambled to collect his blocks and prepared to start again.

"You gon' build anothuh towuh, James Justin?" Amos asked.

"Big towuh," Justin announced, and Amos cackled.

Ben brought a fresh drink, and Amos grinned up at the black man. "Ben, that James Justin's th' smahtest little snippet I evuh did see. Got mo' brains'n all th' rest of my family put togethuh."

Ben flashed a smile. "An' he's always busy at sump'm, ain't he? Work, work, work, all the time."

"Tha's right," Amos agreed. "He don' take much aftuh his daddy, does he?" Overcome with the humor of his remark, Amos leaned back and closed his eyes and enjoyed a good laugh. Ben departed without replying.

"Yes, suh, James Justin," the old man said. "You jes' go on buildin' with yo' blocks. When you grow up you gon' build lots bigguh things, yessuhree."

But the child had temporarily lost interest in his work. He came clutching at his grandfather's knee and reaching for the frosty glass.

"Dink," he said demandingly. "Dink."

"You want a drink, James Justin?" Amos chuckled. "Well, all right, then." He lifted the boy up onto his lap, but kept the glass just out of his reach. "You tell me who I am, an' I'll give you a drink."

Justin squirmed impatiently and reached for the glass.

"Say Grandpa," Amos commanded. "Come on, you can say it. Grandpa."

"Gan-pa," Justin said.

"Attaboy!" Chortling in glee, Amos held the glass to the child's lips.

After taking a small swallow Justin made a sour face and spat. The dark brown liquid dribbled down his shirt.

"P-too!" He pronounced his opinion of the drink, climbed down and went back to his blocks, and left his grandfather again shaking with laughter.

"Lawdy me, James Justin." The old man's face grew gentle and pensive as he watched the child at play. "I'm so thankful to have you heah. 'Cause, you know sump'm? You're th' only human bein' in this world I got to talk to, 'sides Ben. You're th' only membuh o' my family that's evuh heah, and tha's all right, 'cause you're th' only damn one o' th' lot's got a grain o' sense or a spahk o' decency, anyway."

The boy wasn't listening. He was busy designing an intricate new block structure. Amos's eyes drifted off again into the distance.

"I tell you sump'm, James Justin. I hope when you git to be an old man it won't happen to you like it happened to me. Heah I am, sixty-fo' yeahs old, my enuhgy gone, my health broke. Worked like a nigguh all my life to provide fo' this fam'ly, and what've I got to show fo' it? A wife that spends mo' time in her bruthuh's house up in Natchez than she does in her own. When she's heah she's so damn quiet I don't know she's alive. Up to my eahs in debt to my only son, an' you think he gives me any consideration 'cause I'm his fathuh? Hell, no. I'm jes' anothuh bad debt, fah as he's concerned. Y'know sump'm, James Justin? When I'm dead, yo' Uncle Adam's gon' be th' happiest man in th' state o' Louisiana, you wait an' see. And my daughtuhs. Good God! Yo' mama an' yo' Aunt

133

Amanda, James Justin—theah's two women that put togethuh ain't wuth a plug o' cheap chewin' tobacca. Lost Amanda yeahs ago, when she took it in her head to be an actress, an' tuhned herself into a goddamn whore in th' process. An' now Arabella. I feel mighty bad 'bout yo' mama, James Justin, 'cause it's pahtly my fault, what happened to her. She married one o' th' most wuthless human bein's that evuh crossed my threshold, and I encouraged her to do it. Mind now, James Justin, this ain't no reflection on you. But if yo' daddy was a black slave b'longed to me, I'd sell 'im fo' twenty dollahs and figguh it's good riddance."

Justin took no offense. He smiled up at his grandfather and went on with his construction while Amos continued his monologue.

"Yes, we were taken in, James Justin. I'm ashamed to admit it, but it's true. An' now look at yo' mama. Jes' *look* at 'er! Gone off to live with Amanda in N'Yawlins, an' you know what that means, don't you? Well, I ain't gon' tell you what it means, 'cause I don't want you to know that 'bout yo' mama, an' I hope to God you nevuh find out."

Amos drew a deep sighing breath and took a long pull on his drink. When he spoke again he was no longer addressing the child at his feet, but some unseen listener off in the heat-drenched distance.

"Theah ain't nothin' left. Nothin' a-tall. Th' well's run dry, an' th' last few drops are bittuh. Bittuh ..."

A man came up the long gravel path from the front gate—a white man, grimy with dirt and grease, his hard lean face dripping sweat under a straw hat. He stopped just far enough up onto the veranda steps to get out of the sun, took off his hat and wiped his brow with a sleeve, and waited to be recognized. Amos was slumped in his chair and staring glumly at the veranda floor, aware of nothing but his brooding thoughts. Justin, eyeing the stranger with some misgiving, left his blocks and wandered off toward the opposite end of the long veranda.

The man cleared his throat timidly. "Uh, Mistuh Amos?"

Amos started, and glared at the visitor as if he were an intruder. "What you want, Bailey?"

"I hate to bothuh you, suh, but we got a little problem down at th' mill."

Amos's scowl deepened. "Fo' God's sake, wha'sa mattuh now?"

"You know that firepan fo' th' new oven? I'm 'fraid it ain't gon' fit on th' foundation."

"What d'ya mean, it ain't gon' fit?"

"'Peahs to be 'bout six inches too big, Mistuh Amos. I b'lieve we gon' have to knock out th' brickwork, an'—"

"God Almighty!" Amos roared. "Can't you stupid bastards do anything right? Didn't nobody *measure* th' goddamn thing?!"

The hired man cringed before his employer's anger. "Yes, suh, Mistuh Lucius took th' measurements, you 'membuh? I went strictly by the figguhs he gimme—"

Amos was groaning. He had thrown down his fan and was grasping his forehead with a trembling hand. "My Lord in heaven! I might 'a' known that was th' trouble, I might 'a' *known* it!"

Bailey shifted his weight nervously from one foot to the other. "Well, like I say, Mistuh Amos, I don' want to bothuh you, I was jes' wonderin' when you think Mistuh Lucius might be back. It can wait a few days—"

"Like hell it can! Heah 'tis July already, damnit! Cookin' time's gon' be on us fo' you know it, and that new mill ain't even half done yet!"

"But, soon's Mistuh Lucius gits back—"

"Damn Mistuh Lucius! Ain't no tellin' wheah he is or when he's gon' honuh us with his presence ag'in, an' he ain't wuth a spit in th' wind, anyway. Ben!" Amos was on his feet, thundering for his servant. "Uh, Ben!"

Ben was there, frowning in open disapproval. "Mistuh Amos, what you carryin' on about?"

"Tell Jock to hitch up my buggy, I'm going' down to th' mill."

"In this heat? Mistuh Amos, you must be done gone clean out o' yo'—"

"Goddamn it, Ben, stop yo' jabberin' an' do as you're told, 'fo I blistuh yo' hide!"

Ben's patience was exhausted. He went off, scolding. "All right, next time Doctuh Patrick comes I'm gon' tell 'im how you been actin', I'm jes' gon' *tell* 'im!"

"You go on back, Bailey," Amos said to the mill foreman. "I'll be theah in a few minutes."

"Yes, suh." Bailey clapped his hat on his head and hurried away.

Amos started down the veranda steps, grunting as he shifted his bulk from each step to the next, and grumbling to

135

himself. "What they gon' do when I'm gone, I'd like to know. I'd jes' love to come back six months aftuh I'm gone, and see how they—"

A short distance along the front walkway he stopped with a sudden thought. He turned and called. "James Justin?"

The little boy came to the top of the porch steps.

Amos held out his hands invitingly. "Want to go fo' a buggy ride with Grandpa?"

"Buggy wide!" Justin squealed, and rushed to his grandfather's arms.

When they were almost to the front gate Crissy came out of the house. "Mistuh Amos! Wheah you goin' with that chile?"

With the boy nestled in the crook of his arm, Amos turned and glared at the black woman. "Who the hell you think you talkin' to, Crissy?"

Crissy hastily shifted to a pleading tone. "Come on, Mistuh Amos, it's Jamie's nap time. Don' go carryin' 'im off someplace."

Amos snorted his disgust. "Jamie! I'm sick an' tired o' hearin' that sissified name! Th' boy's name is James Justin, you heah? James Justin!"

"Yes, suh, Mistuh Amos." Crissy held out her arms. "Jes' bring 'im back heah, please?"

Amos hurled his reply in an angry shout. "An' I can damn well take my grandson fo' a buggy ride anytime I want to, y'understand?" He stalked away.

In half an hour the hired man Bailey was back. He came up onto the veranda and, seeing no one about, went to the open front door and knocked. Ben emerged from the shadowy depths of the house.

"Yes, suh, Mistuh Bailey?"

"I was jes' wonderin' if Mistuh Amos was gon' come down to th' mill, like he said."

Ben frowned. "Why, ain't he theah? He lef' heah twenty minutes ago."

"I ain't seen 'im."

Crissy had appeared behind Ben, and was staring over his shoulder at the white man.

"You didn't see nothin' of 'im on th' road?" Ben asked.

"Didn't come by th' road," Bailey said. "Come up th' back path."

Ben pondered for a moment. "He must 'a' had trouble with

136

th' buggy, or sump'm. He's had time to go down to th' mill and back, by now."

Crissy had come out of the house. She was standing on tiptoe, squinting in the sun as far as she could see down the narrow dirt road that skirted the edge of the cane fields on its way to the sugar mill, half a mile away.

"Jamie," she whispered, and clutched at her throat as if to catch and hold some quick-rising panic. "Jamie!"

"Wha's the mattuh with you, Crissy?" Ben demanded.

She gave him no answer. She darted down the steps and out to the front gate, flung it open, and ran down the road as fast as she could. Her large eyes were bright with anxiety born of a deep-seated mother instinct, and fixed straight ahead in the blazing July heat.

The men stared after her.

"Now, wha's got into that fool woman?" Ben muttered.

Then, as if stabbed with a silent answer to his question, he too ran, and Bailey was right behind him.

Crissy was halfway to the mill and fifty yards ahead of the men when she saw Amos's buggy. It was at the side of the road, partially obscured by the underbrush, and tilted at a perilously unnatural angle. The horse was standing still in its harness and nibbling placidly at the weeds at its feet. Crissy stopped, panting and drenched in perspiration, her hand again clutching at her throat. Her lips trembled. This time she screamed her fear at the top of her lungs.

"Jamie! Jamie!" With Ben and the other man still some distance behind her, she ran on.

One wheel of the buggy was off the roadway and into a small weed-filled ditch. Crissy clambered up onto the upper side of the vehicle and peered in. It was empty. She jumped down and made a quick search underneath, ran around to the other side, stepped with hardly a glance over the bulky form lying there, slipped and fell in the muddy ditch and struggled to her feet again, and ran back out onto the road, sobbing and whimpering.

The men had arrived at the buggy, but Crissy paid no further attention; her interest was not there. She went on down the road, walking slowly now, faint and stumbling from exhaustion and the heat, and calling, "Jamie! Jamie, wheah are you?"

Suddenly there he was, in the shade of a small roadside

tree. He had been sitting at the edge of the little ditch that bordered the roadway, and was in the process of building something with mud and sticks, but, hearing Crissy calling, had interrupted his work and climbed up to the road to meet her.

With a surge of new energy Crissy ran to him and swept him up in her arms "Oh, Jamie, Jamie, my baby! Thank de Lawd, my baby's all right!" Tears of relief rolled down her cheeks as she hugged him fiercely and pelted him with kisses.

The little boy was looking up the road where the buggy was, where the white man and the black man were crouched over the large inert thing lying partly under the vehicle and partly in the ditch. He frowned, and his little face twisted itself into a knot of concentration as he struggled with the intricacies of speech.

"Gan-pa," he said, and pointed toward the buggy. "Gan-pa . . . faw down."

(25)

THE WHITEHURST WOMEN were seated in the great main hall at Carolina Grove. Adeline sat near the dark fireplace in the big armchair that had been her husband's favorite. On a couch across from her sat her two daughters, Amanda and Arabella. The women were dressed in unrelieved black, and all looked unnaturally pale in their somber clothing. At the opposite end of the room, Lucius Hargrave, nattily dressed in a cream-colored business suit, quietly paced, moving from one French window to the next and pausing at each to stare thoughtfully out into the bright summer sunlight.

Adeline spoke, to no one in particular. "It was a lovely funeral. Everybody said so. One of the loveliest in yeahs." Her voice was barely more than a whisper.

"Yes, Mama," Amanda said.

"I'm shuah theah must have been at least three hundred people theah," Adeline went on. "Anna Dunlap told me she was quite positive Amos had many more people than her Clifton had last yeah—"

"Oh, Mama!" Arabella was suddenly animated by a spasm of annoyance. "Do we have to go *on* and *on* talkin' about funerals?"

Adeline looked hurt. She dabbed delicately at the corners of her eyes with a little lace handkerchief.

"You just don't know what it's like, Arabella. To lose the man who's been youh constant companion fo' thutty-five yeahs..." Adeline's voice slid alarmingly upward, and her chin trembled.

"Oh, Mama, don't staht *cryin'* ag'in!" Arabella moaned.

That was all Adeline needed. She turned her head to one side and shook with convulsive sobs. Immediately Amanda was up and bending over her, murmuring comfort. As soon as Adeline had recovered, Amanda returned to her seat and gave her sister a hard look.

"Dahlin', I think this would be a lot easiuh if we all just try to have a little patience."

"Patience, hell!" Lucius growled. He was now standing behind the couch where the two sisters sat. "I wonder if His High and Mighty Majesty King Adam the Great thinks I've got nothing better to do than stand around here all day, awaiting his pleasure?"

"Oh, do be still, Lucius!" Arabella snapped.

"They just got heah a few minutes ago," Amanda said. "Give 'em time to freshen up a bit, will you?"

Ben appeared at one of the French windows that opened onto the side veranda. "They comin' now," he said to the people inside.

"That's no way to announce royalty, Ben!" Lucius shouted at him. "Summon the trumpeters!"

Ben started to grin, thought better of it, and moved quickly away.

Adam Whitehurst was wearing a dark gray suit with a black armband, as was the elderly stoop-shouldered man with him. The two were chuckling discreetly over some private joke as they came along the veranda, but as they stepped into the main hall their faces went abruptly solemn. Adam led his

139

companion to where the women were seated.

"Waltuh, I b'lieve you know my mothuh, and my two sistuhs, Amanda and Arabella?"

"Oh yes, how do you do, Mrs. Whitehurst? My deepest sympathy to you, ma'am." The visitor spoke to Adeline in a voice of funereal profundity, and nodded to each of the younger women. "Ladies? My condolences on youh great loss."

Adam looked around and spotted Lucius, who had moved back to the far end of the room. "And ovuh heah, Walter—" He took the older man's arm and led him in that direction. "Ovuh heah's my brothuh-in-law. You remembuh my mentioning Lucius to you?"

"Oh yes," Walter said, and smiled mysteriously.

To Lucius, Adam said, "Mistuh Lucius Hahgrave, I'd like you to meet Mistuh Waltuh Simmons of New Awlins, ouah family attorney."

"How do y'do?" Lucius said curtly.

"I'm deeply honuhed to make youh acquaintance, suh," the other man said, and executed a stiff bow.

Adam turned his attention back to the women. "Sorry to have kept you all waiting. Waltuh wanted to go ovuh one or two last minute details with me and, uh . . . but nevuh mind that, let's get on with it, shall we?"

"By all means, let's," Lucius said sharply.

"Let's see now." Adam rubbed his hands together and looked around the room. "Waltuh, you sit right down heah." He conducted the attorney to a small table, and brought a chair to it. "You can spread youh papuhs out and, uh, proceed at youh pleasuah."

The attorney was carrying a thick black portfolio under his arm. He laid it on the table, opened it, and began to leaf through a sheaf of papers.

Adam stood by and beamed at his mother and sisters with uncharacteristic good spirits. "My, my," he breathed, "you all look positively lovely today. You know, I think it's a shame that women so seldom weah black except for such, uh, such solemn occasions as mourning, because it's really most becom—"

"Are we going to get on with this, or not?" Lucius barked. He was sitting on the piano stool a little distance away, waiting.

Adam smiled apologetically and turned to the attorney.

"Well, I b'lieve we're all ready, Waltuh."

Mr. Simmons was seated, holding some papers before him. He cleared his throat noisily and began.

"Deah friends, we are gathered heah today fo' the reading of the last will and testament of youh beloved fathuh and husband, Amos Whitehurst, deceased in the sixty-fouhth yeah of his life, on the seventh day of July, in the Yeah of Our Lord Eighteen hundred and fawty-two—"

"Excuse me a moment, Waltuh," Adam said quietly. He moved a few steps toward the wide doorway that led to the central hallway of the house. "Ben!"

The black man appeared.

"I heah whisperin' out theah in the hallway, Ben. The house nigras are eavesdropping, aren't they?"

Ben looked acutely uncomfortable. "I hope you'll 'scuse 'em, Mistuh Adam, suh. They be terrible worried 'bout wha's gon' happen to 'em, and—"

"They will know soon enough!" Adam said in a thunderous voice. "I will not tolerate eavesdropping, Ben. You send the nigras about theah business right now, you heah me?"

"Yes, suh, Mistuh Adam," Ben said meekly, and withdrew.

Adam turned a bland smile on the attorney. "Pahdon the interruption, Waltuh. You may proceed."

The lawyer cleared his throat again. "As I was saying, the last will and testament of Amos Whitehurst, etcet'ra. Now, the text of the main document reads as follows: 'New Orleans, Louisiana. February tenth, 1842. I, Amos Whitehurst, of Carolina Grove Plantation, St. Charles Parish, Louisiana, being in good health and in full possession of my mental faculties, do hearby voluntarily set down the following instructions—'"

"Excuse me, Mistuh Simmons." This time it was Adeline interrupting, in a soft and timid voice. "What was the date you said?"

"The tenth day of February of this yeah, ma'am."

"That must be a mistake. My husband's will was made yeahs ago."

"Yes, ma'am, it was. But this is a new statement from Mistuh Whitehurst, and as you'll see from the text—"

"I'll explain, Waltuh," Adam said. "Mama, you remembuh when I was heah last wintuh, and Papa went back to New Awlins with me for a day or two? I had suggested a few, uh, minuh changes in his will, in view of certain, uh, recent

141

developments, and Waltuh heah thought it best to, uh, simply prepauh a new document." Adam gave his mother a reassuring smile.

"I see," she said vaguely.

"Well, to continue," Simmons said, "the following instructions, which in sum are to be taken as my last will and testament, superseding all previous statements, the same being given by my own hand as attested to by the witnesses whose signatures appear—"

"Good God!" Lucius was up and advancing on Simmons with a mighty scowl, and the attorney's eyebrows went up in alarm.

"At this rate we'll be here far into the night. How would it be if you just skipped all that legalistic mumbo-jumbo and got right to the meat of the matter?"

Arabella shot a pained look at her husband. "Lucius, must you be so boorish?"

"Oh, but he's right, he's right," Adam said genially. He was still smiling. "We suttenly don't want to boah anybody, least of all a busy man like Lucius. Waltuh, why don't you just go directly to the ahticles? They're what everybody's primarily interested in, I b'lieve."

Amanda was staring up at her brother with a look of wonderment on her face. "What's come ovuh you, Adam?" she said quietly. "You're not youhself at all."

Adam gave her a smile but no answer.

Simmons had turned past two pages of the will, found a new place, and cleared his throat once more. "To continue," he said doggedly.

"First, let me explain that the instructions in this testament are arranged in ahticles, each of which deals with the late Mistuh Whitehurst's legacy to one of you. Cleah? Very well. Now—Article One: 'To my beloved wife Adeline I leave a lifetime stipend which I pray will be sufficient to keep her, if not in the luxury to which she is accustomed, at least in reasonable comfort. This stipend is to be provided to her in monthly installments from a fund set up for that purpose and administered by our son Adam, in accordance with procedures described in Article Four, below, and in Appendix B, attached hereto.'

"Article Two: 'To my daughter Amanda—'"

"Excuse me again, Mistuh Simmons." Adeline was leaning forward, searching the lawyer's face with a confused look on her own. "Is that all? I mean . . . is that all concerning me?"

142

"Yes, ma'am. That is the entirety of Article One."

Adeline turned stricken eyes to Adam. "But... I don't unduhstand..."

"Wait, Mama, let him finish," Adam said patiently. "It will all be puhfectly cleah."

"Article Two," Simmons said. "'To my daughter Amanda I leave the pride of our carriage house, the Parisian carriage. She has always admired that elegant vehicle, with its fine satin upholstery and velvet draperies, and, indeed, I believe it would be more fitting to the ostentatious life she has chosen to lead than it ever was to my own.'"

Amanda glanced at her sister, then at her mother. Both women's eyes were dazed, their faces tense with some mysterious anxiety. The attorney's voice droned on.

"Article Three: 'To my daughter Arabella I leave a valuable possession that has been hers since she was a child, and, God willing, will continue to serve her for many years to come—the faithful slave woman, Crissy. I make this bequest also in the interests of my grandson, James Justin Hargrave, in consideration of the deep bond of affection that exists between the child and his nursemaid. Should Arabella feel slighted by this bequest in comparison to her sister's, she is reminded that the current negotiable price for a woman of Crissy's qualities in the New Orleans market is ten to twelve hundred dollars, fully equal to the value of the French carriage.'

"Article Four—"

"Good heavens!" Arabella shrieked.

Lucius was up and advancing again, this time on Adam. "What the hell is this, some kind of demented joke?"

"Please," Adam said mildly. "You wanted to move this thing along, didn't you? Then stop interrupting, and let him finish."

Mr. Simmons gripped the papers with both hands, and plowed grimly on.

"Article Four: 'To my son Adam I bequeath burdensome duties, and, I trust, some slight reward as well. Upon him fall full executory responsibilities for the instructions contained herein, including the administering of the funds for the support of his mother, the resources for which shall be fifty percent of the moneys to be derived from the liquidation on the open market of my estate in St. Charles Parish, Louisiana, known as Carolina Grove—'"

There was a sharp gasp from Adeline. She had paled, and

143

was pressing a hand in horror against her cheek.

With his jaw set in determination, Mr. Simmons continued.

"'... and all appurtenances thereto, including all buildings, grounds, machinery, and implements, sugar refining facilities, and slaves, except the aforementioned French carriage and the woman Crissy, and any others whom Adam at his discretion shall exempt. The remaining fifty percent of such moneys shall fall to Adam as his inheritance. This liquidation is to be accomplished with all possible dispatch at the direction of the executor, Adam, who shall proceed under the authority vested in him by the provisions of Appendix A, attached below, and by the deeds to the aforementioned plantation and accompanying properties, which are transferred to his name and ownership on the date of my death, with the stipulation that he assume therewith complete obligations for all claims, indebtedness, liabilities, and mortgages pertaining thereto.'"

Simmons paused for a breath. "And that, ladies and gentlemen, concludes the articles."

A profound silence filled the room. Adeline sat as if thunderstruck, her lips moving soundlessly. The two younger women sat deathly still and stared at the attorney. Lucius stood at the other end of the room, his narrowed eyes fixed on Adam.

Simmons turned to the next page of the document. "Don't know if you all care to have me read these heah appendices or not," he said casually, scanning the page. "They're mostly jes' technical instructions, setting' forth the proceduahs by which—"

"That's enough," Lucius said. He came walking slowly up the room toward the man he had firmly identified as his chief adversary.

"This is your doing, Adam."

Adam was the picture of innocence surprised. "I beg youh pahdon, Lucius?"

"Explain it. Tell us how in hell you expect to get away with this outrageous piece of trickery. Good God, I've seen villainy in my day, but this is the ultimate—trying to perpetrate fraud and forgery on your own mother and sisters—"

Adam laughed indulgently. "Oh, well, Lucius, seeing that youh concern is not at all for youhself, but so unselfishly for othuhs, I'll be more than happy to explain to you exactly what all this means, and why."

144

"Well?" Lucius's jaw jutted belligerently. "We're listening."

"It means, quite simply, that my fathuh was bankrupt. Carolina Grove hasn't been a paying proposition for yeahs, because Papa was more interested in tearing down puhfectly good sugah mills and building bigguh ones than he was in running a profitable business. He borrowed from me till I wouldn't lend anymoah, then he borrowed from othuhs till his credit was gone. A few yeahs ago I thought I was beginning to get him unduh control, but then *you* came along, Lucius. You, who'd nevuh set foot on a plantation before in youh life, took ovuh the management of this one. And when *that* happened, my deah brothuh-in-law, I knew it was the beginning of the end."

Lucius was struggling to contain his rage. "You goddamned ignoramus, you don't know what the hell you're talking about! If you'd ever bothered to show your face around here, you'd have seen that I singlehandedly kept this place running for three whole years—"

"You ran it, all right. You ran it right into the ground."

Arabella was up and standing beside Lucius. "Oh, Adam! How could you be so cruel?" Her bright eyes bored accusingly into her brother.

Adam held out supplicating hands in defense. "Look heah, if any of you think I'm reaping riches while the rest of you are turned away with a pittance, you're very much mistaken. All I'm inheriting is fifty percent of a plantation that's so deep in debt I'll be lucky if I get out from unduh without *losing* money—"

"But it's evuh so unfair!" Arabella wailed. "Papa distinctly promised Lucius and me a large share of this place in return for Lucius becoming his pahtnuh. He gave us his solemn word, and he told us it was written in his will!"

Adam shrugged. "Papa was forevuh talking about rewriting his will." He took the papers out of the lawyer's hands and fingered them thoughtfully. "This is the only time he evuh got around to doing it."

"Well, I'll break the damn thing," Lucius muttered.

Adam gave him a blank look. "You'll do what, Lucius?"

"I said I'll break it. It's not valid, it was written under duress from you. It's as clear as daylight what happened. You got to Amos and poisoned his mind against me."

Adam pointed to the sheaf of papers in his hand. "You see

145

this, Lucius? This is not just my fathuh's last will and testament, it's his confession. In these pages he confesses his mistakes, which were many, but the worst one of all—and well he knew it—was trusting in his good-for-nothin' Yankee son-in-law."

Lucius took a small step toward Adam, his eyes narrowed to slits.

Walter Simmons was up, hastily retrieving the will from Adam's hands and confronting Lucius.

"Mistuh Hahgrave, it's youh privilege, of course, to challenge this document in any way you see fit. But I must tell you that in the state of Louisiana it's jes' mighty nigh impossible to break a man's will. Why, you'd have to show proof that Mistuh Whitehurst was clean out of his mind, not responsible for his actions—"

Lucius was not listening. He brushed the lawyer aside and stepped still closer to Adam.

"Now I understand why you were so strangely cheerful, coming in here today, Adam. You were really looking forward to this little scene, weren't you? Because you hate my guts. You've hated me from the first day I walked into this house."

"I've nevuh been pahtial to fawtune-huntuhs," Adam said stiffly.

"If that's what I was, why didn't you get rid of me to begin with, by telling me the true conditions?"

Adam's laugh was cold, without mirth. "Oh come now, Lucius! In the first place, you'd nevuh have believed me. And in the second place, who's to say we'd have been bettuh off with that vulture Albert Pettingill in the family? He was fawtune-hunting too, you know, and Arabella was all set to marry *him*, till he found out theah wasn't any fortune heah to hunt, and ran like a scared rabbit—"

"Adam, how *dare* you?!" Arabella shrieked.

Lucius stood as if staggered by a physical blow. Adam moved toward him, ignoring Arabella.

"Oh yes, Pettingill was a smaht man, I'll give him *that* much credit. Much, much smahtuh than *you'll* evuh be, Lucius. He took the trouble to do a little private investigating, and found out for himself. Then he dropped my little sistuh like a hot potato, nevuh showed his face again. Poah little Arabella. She was so thankful she had *you* to fall back on."

Lucius had turned to Arabella. Her face was wet with tears and contorted in anguish as she shrank from his gaze.

"No, Lucius, no . . ." she whispered. "Don't listen to him, it's not true."

"Oh yes, it *is* true," Lucius said quietly. "I know it's true, because all at once some troublesome questions are miraculously answered. Why did Albert abruptly withdraw from a contest he was obviously winning? Why did you suddenly stop adoring him, and develop an overnight passion for me? Oh yes, it all makes perfectly good sense now. Everything falls into place."

"Oh, Lucius, you're evuh so wrong," Arabella said whimperingly. "You ought to realize that Adam doesn't only hate you, he hates all of us. Are you goin' to take his spiteful word against mine? I'm youh lovin' wife—" Sobs choked off her words.

Lucius watched her for a moment, stone-faced. "I'm afraid I have no choice." His eyes drifted around the room. "He's the only member of the Whitehurst clan who has ever spoken the truth to me." He started for the door.

Arabella quickly recovered her voice. "Lucius, wheah are you goin'?"

"To catch the four o'clock packet north."

"And leave me heah, stranded and helpless?"

In the doorway he stopped and looked back at her. "Don't worry, I'll be in touch with you, my pet. We still have business to settle. Meanwhile I'm sure Amanda will continue to find suitable amusements for you."

"Oh, Lucius . . . you're evuh so cruel!"

He was gone, and once more the room was filled with a temporary silence. Then Adam heaved a soft sigh.

"Well, he was right about one thing. I *have* been looking forward to this little scene. It's just too bad Papa had to die before I could have my pleasuah."

For the first time Amanda stirred. She got up, smoothed her skirt, and strolled in Adam's direction.

"You rotten bastard," she murmured.

His innocent look reappeared. "Amanda, what can I—"

She had turned her back on him, and was talking to Arabella. "Well, I'm due back in the city this evenin', dahlin', so I'd bettuh be gettin' ready. Comin' with me?"

Arabella was puckered up, ready to cry. "Oh, Amanda, how could you even *think* of it?! Don't you realize I'm *penniless*?"

"All the more reason you mustn't neglect your gentlemen friends in New Orleans," Amanda said coolly. She put a

147

comforting arm around Arabella and led her out of the room.

Adeline was sitting as if in a trance, staring into space. Adam bent over her. "Are you all right, Mothuh?"

"What's to become of me?" she whispered.

There was no answer.

Lucius was a quarter of the way to the river landing, walking rapidly, when he heard a voice behind him.

"Mistuh Lucius, suh? Wait fo' me!" It was Ben.

Lucius waited until the black man came up to him, huffing and blowing from exertion. "Well, what is it?" he snapped impatiently.

"I was at de window, suh," Ben said. "I heard it all."

Lucius's eyes glinted with sardonic amusement. "Your new master doesn't approve of eavesdropping, Ben."

Ben's mood was too earnest to appreciate banter. "Mistuh Lucius? Take me wid you, suh."

"What the hell are you talking about, man? You're just like the rest of 'em, you've been against me from the beginning—"

"No, suh, that ain't so, Mistuh Lucius, I was nevuh against you, suh. One time I coulda tol' a bad thing about you, an' I nevuh said a word, you know I didn't. Now I need yo' help, suh. 'Cause Mistuh Adam's gon' sell me, shuah as this worl', he is."

"Well, that's his right. He's your master now."

"An' when he does, it's gon' kill me." Ben's voice trembled. "Please, Mistuh Lucius. Take me wid you."

"I have no use for a personal servant, Ben, it's not my style."

"Please, suh, I'll do anything—"

"I'm sorry. I can't help you." Lucius turned away and walked on.

Ben followed him. "Please, Mistuh Lucius. Please..."

Lucius walked another hundred yards, then paused to look back. Ben had dropped behind, finally coming to a stop in the middle of the road. He was looking after Lucius with mute misery written on his leathery face. Lucius scowled. For a few seconds he compressed his lips intensely, struggling with indecision. Then he gave the black man a quick beckoning wave.

"Well, come on, then, goddamnit!" he yelled. "Let's go!"

He went on toward the river, and Ben uttered a short high-pitched yelp of triumph as he ran to catch up.

(26)

Mr. Isaac Hargrave
Thacker and Hargrave, Associates
Number One Gilpin Street
South Bar, Indiana

Dear old chum,

I can't imagine what you meant, saying I don't correspond faithfully. I've always tried to be very conscientious about that. For instance, I arrived home toward the end of May from an extensive business trip north, found your letter awaiting me, and put it on my desk with every intention of sitting right down to answer it first thing the next morning. Is it my fault that on that very morning the first of a long series of crises developed at Carolina Grove that required my undivided attention for weeks?

When I married Arabella Whitehurst I must have unknowingly signed a contract agreeing to assume full responsibility for the management of that huge plantation, down to the most minute detail. My father-in-law was an authority on the sugar industry before I was born, yet from the first day I came here he was never again able to make the slightest decision without consulting me. And just let me be away for one day, and he'd be sure to do something foolish, making it necessary for me to do it over again when I returned. Ah, well, let us not speak ill-temperedly of the poor old

149

fellow. He died suddenly two weeks ago, God rest him. Drank himself to death on rum and coffee. Needless to say, that unfortunate event has increased the burden of my responsibilities tenfold.

But, to the purpose of my letter. First off, of course, you must put the thought of a visit to Carolina Grove quite out of your mind. The Whitehursts would neither like nor understand you, nor you them. You can't imagine the vast gulf that exists between those indolent, amoral, luxury-loving Southern aristocrats and us tough, honest hardworking Yankees. In fact, it has been in the back of my mind for some time that I am really not cut out for plantation life, and the recent outbreak of trials and tribulations has hardened that thought into a conviction that can no longer be denied. I am about to make a clean break. I am going to divest myself of my share in the inheritance, and return to Texas. True, I once had a taste of frontier life and thought I didn't like it, but I am older and more mature now, and I have come to realize that if a man hopes to rise above the commonplace in this world he must go toward the front, he must be in the advance guard of the human army. He must get to the treasure before the rabble arrives. In our American society that can only mean the frontier, wherever it may be.

What does all this have to do with you, old chum?

I am proposing that you sell out your share of Thacker and Hargrave, pull yourself up by the roots, and come with me. Now before you faint dead away from fright let me hasten to assure you that in Texas a man with your skills could not avoid becoming rich overnight. East Texas is magnificently endowed with virgin forest just waiting for somebody like you to turn it into lumber, and with the tremendous growth taking place there—well, you can easily see what kind of opportunity beckons you. Reach for it, Isaac. It would be the best and bravest thing you have ever done, and you need it desperately. It is absolutely shocking that at your age (I reckon you to be about 33 now, correct?) you are again living with my mother, at her beck and call. It is unnatural, Isaac. And your recent attempt to solve the mysteries of matrimony was a disastrous failure by your own admission. I am sorry to hear that sad story, but not surprised. Women are baffling creatures, and have confounded far more experienced men than you.

On the other hand it would be beneficial for each of us to have the other to rely upon for a while, as we seek to find our way. We both need new surroundings and new beginnings; and above all we need trustworthy alliances. And if I have learned a single thing in the ten years I have been on my own, it is that in all this wild and treacherous world there is nobody you can trust—absolutely nobody—except your own blood-brother.

I want you to give this proposal some serious and sober thought, old chum. It is clear by now that you don't have the gumption to tear yourself free from the apron strings of your dear "Mama Sarah." Someone must help you do it. And who better than I could perform that service for you? Get your courage together and form your resolve. This may be the best chance, possibly the only one, that will ever come your way.

Destroy this letter and say nothing to anybody, breathe not a word if you value my trust. One small exception could be your lawyer friend Mr. Worthington, who strikes me as an intelligent and interesting man. You might mention to him that I am likely to be in South Bar soon, and if so will certainly want to make his acquaintance. Impress upon him, however, that this information is in strictest confidence.

Do not write to me. I am no longer at Carolina Grove; I am now in St. Louis and will be God knows where else during the next month or two. When the time is ripe I will let you know, and then we will move quickly. That is the way things must be done—cleanly, quickly, and with no backward looks.

Await further word, old chum. Think about this, make your secret plans, keep silent, and bide your time.

> Yours in brotherly conspiracy,
> Lucius

(27)

FROM THE JOURNAL of Lucius Hargrave:

Here is a mystery that must forever defeat the wisest of oracles. What is it about the sight of his sister's husband that transforms an otherwise civilized man into a raging beast, exhaling the blistering fires of hatred? Is it jealousy born of some dark deep-seated incestuous desire? Who can say? My father's happiness was destroyed in part by the unreasoning hostility of his wife's brother, and as it happened to him, so it happened to me. The parallel is uncanny, and I can only stand in helpless and bewildered awe of it.

When I married Arabella Whitehurst I intended to embrace all the members of her family as my own, and to be embraced in return. It was a naive expectation. From the beginning Arabella's brother Adam fixed on me the cold reptilian eye of suspicion. Adam was an Important Personage among the Whitehursts, and his rare appearances at Carolina Grove were celebrated events. He was arrogant and domineering, and moreover possessed a strange hold over his parents. His opinions on all subjects were handed down as Law, and meekly accepted as such. I should have known that my marriage to the vapid weak-willed Arabella was doomed, for the force of this man's enmity was clearly set against me, and would not rest until ruin was brought down upon my luckless head. How he would have accomplished his goal without external aid can only be guessed at, since Providence inexplicably chose to intervene on his behalf, and my fate was settled.

Amos conveniently died. And it was only a day or two after the poor old man's funeral that his son stood in the middle of the main hall at Carolina Grove and proclaimed himself the new master there. At his elbow stood his hireling lawyer, grinning like a court jester, proud of the way he had set down the shameless usurpation in legal-sounding language. Then, in front of the family and a small army of eavesdropping house servants, Adam denounced me to my face, laid on me the blame for all the mismanagement of which Amos had been guilty for so long, and declared that I had married Arabella for no other purpose than the hope of inheriting a fortune. It was all preposterous—the last charge particularly so; I had enjoyed greater prosperity as a boy in my teens working on the steamboat lines than I had ever known as partner in the sugar plantation. Calmly I pointed this out. Adam laughed at me, and moved in for the kill. With his voice rising in triumph he announced that Arabella had married me only because her first choice, the contemptible Albert Pettingill, had cast her aside!

Surely now the audacious villain had overreached himself. I waited for my wife to throw the filthy lie in his face. She would not—or could not. She had already joined her sister Amanda in a life of debauchery in New Orleans, and clearly had no further interest in me, her child, her marriage, or her family home. I appealed to her, and the silence she gave me rang in my ears like the voice of doom.

I fled from that house as from a pit of vipers, and for a time wandered like a homeless waif, cursing the wanton cruelty of a world that could take from me the best I had to give, and offer me only bitter mockery in return. It was as if the Eternal Power had chosen to lead me on the thorny path my father had been forced to walk, to instill in me some glimmer of understanding of the sufferings he had endured.

Very well, then, so be it. Slowly my serenity of spirit returned. I knew there was one thing left for me to do in connection with that wretched place from which I had fled, one precious possession to be retrieved from the rubble and ruin of my destroyed marriage. That was Justin, my son.

With him I would pick up my life and go forward once more, and, true to my constant nature, never look back.

Part Three

(1)

THERE CAME to the little village of South Bar, Indiana, a golden day of Indian summer late in September, 1842. A soft breeze ruffled the surface of the Ohio River around the wharf of Thacker and Hargrave, Associates, the big woodyard that was the town's principal business establishment, then moved on up gravel-bedded Gilpin Street to scatter the first yellowed leaves of autumn across the broad lawn of the Thacker house, two hundred yards from the river. The Thacker place was the next property on Gilpin Street after the woodyard, separating that huge enclosure from the rest of the business part of town, farther on. The house was a square boxlike two-story structure of wood siding, painted white, with large dark green shutters accenting high windows. Though only six years old, it reposed far back from the street among slumbering old walnut trees as if it had been there for generations.

In midafternoon Sarah Thacker sat on the front porch with a small sewing basket in her lap. Sunlight slanted under the eaves and played gently on her tawny hair, which was drawn back into a bun behind her head.

The processes of nature had treated Sarah with kindness. As a young girl she had possessed a glowing pink-cheeked complexion that could have faded early, and a plump figure that had threatened to expand into matronly girth at any moment. The girth had not developed, her figure taking on a statuesque quality instead. The girlish complexion and the sunny hair remained undimmed, and the lively brown eyes were as bright as ever. As a girl she had been merely pretty; at forty-four she presented a picture of quiet beauty in perfect maturity.

She sat now demure and domestic with her attention fixed on the sewing work in her hands, and glanced up with a casual smile when her stepson Isaac Hargrave came up the front path and stopped at the bottom of the steps, frowning at her.

"Mama Sarah, what are you doin'?" he demanded.

At thirty-three, Isaac still retained a look of youthfulness in his open boyish face, but there were lines around his kindly eyes, and the wispy brown hair was receding from a sloping forehead. The approach to middle age was well under way.

Sarah looked up in surprise. "Why, I'm mending your shirts, dear. You asked me to, so I—"

"But not *today*, Mama Sarah! The *General Sloane* is due in half an hour!"

Sarah had to think for a moment before her face registered a flicker of comprehension. "Oh yes, the *General Sloane*. And you think Lucius is going to be on it, is that right?"

"I *know* he's goin' to be on it, and you might as well stop teasin', because I'm goin' to be right about Lucius, and you're goin' to be wrong."

"Really?"

"Yes, really. We've had two letters from him this month, sayin' he'd be on *that* boat on *this* day. And he will, don't you doubt it."

Sarah smiled and resumed her needlework.

Isaac watched her for a moment. "Will you come down to the wharf?"

She gave him no answer.

"He's your own son, Mama Sarah. Aren't you even goin' to come and *meet* him?"

She kept her eyes down. "In the first place, he's not coming. And in the second place, if he *does* come, it will be for some private purpose that has nothing to do with us. So don't ask me to waste my time standing around on that grubby old wharf."

With a snort of exasperation Isaac turned and started back for the front gate. Halfway there he stopped and looked back.

"When I bring him home will you at least try to be nice to him? Please?"

Sarah gave a little shrug. "I'll try. For your sake."

"Thanks." Shaking his head Isaac went off, mumbling to himself: "Stubborn... my *God*!"

After a while the blast of a whistle announced the arrival of a steamboat at the river landing, and a few minutes later the hum of wharf activity reached Sarah's ears. She put aside her sewing basket, got up and walked down to the front gate, and went out to the edge of the road and looked down toward the river, shading her eyes with her hand. She could see the steamboat sitting squat and heavy in the water like an oblong wooden tub. The name emblazoned on the superstructure was clearly visible: *General Sloane*.

Sarah stood in awkward uncertainty, looking up and down the street. A horsedrawn buggy went clopping by, and its passengers nodded and lifted their hats to Sarah. She smiled and waved back. When she looked again toward the river she saw two men emerge from around the corner of the woodyard fence and start up the street toward her, walking rapidly. One was Isaac. He was clutching his companion's arm and talking with the animation of high excitement. The other was a younger man, tall, athletically proportioned, sandy-haired, and so meticulously well-dressed as to be an oddity on the dusty small-town road.

Involuntarily Sarah took a step back toward the gate. Her hand flew to her face; nervous fingers wandered over her cheek and pulled at her lower lip. Her eyes darted this way and that, as if she were looking for a place to hide.

Then someone called to her. "Mama!"

The younger man was hurrying toward her, arms outstretched, his handsome face beaming.

Sarah closed her eyes. "Lucius..." she whispered. Then: "Lucius!"

She shouted his name at the top of her voice, and went running to meet him.

Lucius leaned back in a big armchair and inspected the spacious but simply furnished parlor of the Thacker house. Sarah sat on the edge of her chair across from him, her eyes devouring his face.

"Nice, Mama," Lucius said. "A very nice house."

159

Sarah made a little gesture touched with modesty. "Oh, it's a nice enough house. But it's so big—hard to get used to. I liked our old house."

Isaac, standing before the dark fireplace, scoffed. "Now, Mama Sarah, you know that old place was too small. Anyway, it was falling apart."

"I remember something you wrote me in a letter once, Mama," Lucius remarked. "Something Cyrus had said. You were the finest lady in South Bar, and you deserved the finest house. Something like that. I must say, I agree with him."

Sarah searched her son's face for the thousandth time. "Have you *seen* Cyrus?"

"Not yet. I didn't feel like going into the woodyard. As you know, it's a place I've never been particularly fond of." Seeing anxiety in Sarah's eyes, he smiled. "But don't worry. When he comes home I'll greet him the way I greeted Isaac. Like a long-lost brother."

"*Will* you, Lucius? I'm so glad."

"Oh sure. A sane man can carry a grudge only so long, after all."

Sarah's gaze drifted from Lucius's face down over his fine worsted woolen suit, to his shiny black boots, and back up again to his face. "It's so strange seeing you again, Lucius. You're so much the same ... yet so different. Here's your boy's face before me, just the way it was when you went away. But you're such a big fine gentleman now, I hardly know you. You're so ... so grown up—"

Lucius laughed, and Sarah broke off, smiling her embarrassment.

"Well, for me it's more than strange, Mama, it's absolutely miraculous. Do you know that in ten years you haven't changed a particle except to grow more beautiful?"

She lowered her eyes at that, blushing like a schoolgirl.

Soon a man came from the river landing, pushing a cart containing Lucius's luggage, and right behind him came Cyrus Thacker. Now in his late forties, Cyrus had grown gaunt and angular over the years; his dark hair was beginning to gray, and his extreme height had been tempered by a tendency to stoop-shoulderedness. As Isaac was leaving youthful years behind, Cyrus was advancing rapidly on old age.

While the baggage man deposited his load on the front

160

porch Cyrus went around him and stepped into the parlor, squinting in the subdued light.

"Sarah?"

"I'm here, Cyrus," she said from across the room.

"And so am I," Lucius said, rising from his chair and coming foward with hand extended. "How are you, Cyrus? It's good to see you." He grasped the other's hand and pumped it vigorously.

Cyrus's mouth worked in futility for several seconds. "Well, by God," he blurted finally. "By God, it *is* Lucius, ain't it? By God, I never would 'a' b'lieved it."

"That's not the way you said you'd greet him, Lucius," Isaac called out gleefully.

Lucius laughed and grabbed Cyrus in a playful bear hug. Cyyrus's jaw dropped in astonishment.

"By God, I never would 'a' b'lieved it," he said again.

Isaac went out to the porch to see to the baggage man. When he returned the others were seated, and Lucius and Cyrus were looking at each other with polite mechanical smiles.

"Well, you haven't changed a bit, Cyrus," Lucius was saying.

Cyrus chuckled a protest. "Oh, that ain't quite so, Lucius boy. My eyesight's beginnin' to weaken a bit. But you, now, *you're* the one who's changed. Here you are a fancy gentleman, and last time I saw you, you were a...a..."

"An insolent young whelp," Lucius offered with an esay laugh.

"Well, that's all forgotten now," Cyrus said hastily. "Anyway, I'm not surprised to see you like this. I always figgered you'd make good."

Lucius's eyebrows went up. "Did you now?"

"So, what brings you to an out-o'-the-way place like South Bar?" Cyrus went on.

Sarah immediately challenged the question. "What do you mean, Cyrus? This is his home, isn't it?"

"True, Mama." Lucius turned an amiable smile on her. "No matter where my wanderings take me, this will always be home."

Sarah beamed with pleasure and Cyrus gave Lucius a long searching look.

"Tell us about the Whitehursts," Sarah said then. "I know you've been writing to Isaac, but he's been terribly secretive about it for some strange reason. Is everything all right with you and Arabella?"

Lucius sighed. "Well, I guess there's nothing secret about it anymore. We've agreed to go our separate ways. We're getting a divorce."

Sarah gasped. "Oh, Lucius! How dreadful! First Isaac, and now you. How can you both be so unlucky?"

Lucius shook his head glumly. "I loved Arabella very much, and I tried, God knows I tried. But—"

"What about Justin?" Sarah asked.

"He's mine," Lucius said with a vehemence so sudden that Sarah was taken aback. "*I'm* getting the divorce, *I'm* the one who was wronged. And Arabella doesn't give a damn about the boy, anyway, so there's no argument there."

There was a short silence while Sarah stared at her son in mute horror, and he leaned foward and clasped his hands together, becoming reflective.

"I should have listened to you, Mama. I should never have married a Southern girl."

"I never said that," Sarah protested.

"No, but you implied it, and as usual you were right. Southerners are not just people who live a different kind of life in a different kind of place. They're an altogether different species."

Sarah was baffled. "But you described Arabella as such a sweet, gentle, affectionate girl. I don't understand—"

"Oh, it wasn't her fault. Not entirely. She was manipulated. My in-laws never got over resenting the fact that she married an outsider. One by one they worked on her, poisoning her mind against me. And they succeeded—oh, how they succeeded! I took Carolina Grove when it was on the verge of ruin and single-handedly brought it back to prosperity—but that didn't matter. I was an outsider, I could do nothing right."

"Why, that's perfectly shameful!" Sarah declared hotly.

"Well, I never asked for gratitude," Lucius went on. "I did hope for a little human decency, but apparently even that was too much to expect."

"Oh, you poor, *poor* boy!" Sarah's voice quivered in outrage and motherly sympathy.

"Thank you, Mama." Lucius's eyes were heavy with sorrow as he gazed into his mother's face. "After all these years, you're the only one I can turn to for understanding."

Cyrus cleared his throat noisily and got to his feet. "What time's supper, Sarah?"

With difficulty Sarah shifted her attention to her husband. "Oh . . . at six as usual, I suppose. Unless Lucius would prefer some different hour?"

"At Carolina Grove we hardly ever had supper before nine," Lucius said.

Cyrus gave a loud snort. "Good God! Them Southerners sure as hell *are* a different species. A working man could starve to death!"

"Cyrus!" Sarah hissed indignantly.

"But six will be fine," Lucius said mildly. "After all, I'm back in South Bar now. I'm home again."

He patted his mother's hand, and they smiled at each other like young lovers.

(2)

WHEN CYRUS CAME DOWNSTAIRS the next morning he found Sarah in the kitchen.

She presented her cheek to him for kissing, and said, "Morning, dear."

"Where's Isaac and Lucius?" he asked.

"Up and gone already."

"Where they off to so early?"

"Didn't say. Lucius said he had some business to take care of."

"Business? What the hell kind o' business has he got in South Bar?"

"I don't know, Cyrus. He didn't go into detail, and I didn't want to seem nosy. I expect they're just going around to visit some old friends, do a little reminiscing—"

"Didn't know Lucius ever had any friends around here."

Sarah slapped a plate of eggs on the kitchen table. "Sit down and eat your breakfast," she said curtly.

163

Cyrus sat down heavily and began to eat, while Sarah busied herself on the other side of the room.

"Kept me awake half the night with their jabberin', them two," Cyrus said. "Thought they'd never shut up."

Sarah paused in her work and gazed distantly past Cyrus out the window. "What a thing to complain about," she said pensively. "Lucius is home, and he and Isaac lay awake for hours chatting like a couple of dear old friends. It's absolutely perfect, a dream come true for me. And you complain."

Cyrus squirmed in his seat. "Well, I didn't mean it quite *that* way, Sarah." He studied his plate, pondering what he wanted to say. "You don't need to think I'm still harborin' bad feelin's about the boy. I ain't. He looks fine, and I'm glad to see 'im, and all that, but—"

"But what?" Impatience rang in Sarah's voice.

Cyrus lifted solemn eyes to her. "He's takin' you in, Sarah."

Sarah turned to him bristling, hands on hips. "Oh, I see. He's taking me in. Would you care to tell me exactly what he's taking me in *about*?"

"I don't have no idea what it is he's up to. But whatever it is, he'll have you doin' your part. He'll twist you around his little finger, just like he always did—"

"All right, Cyrus. Hurry up and finish your breakfast and get out of here. I want to get this place cleaned up." She turned her back on him.

He ate the rest of his breakfast in silence, and when he had finished he got up and went to stand beside his wife.

"We've been married sixteen years, Sarah."

"That's right." She was busy scrubbing a skillet, and would not look at him.

"I've tried to be a good husband, and I've never wanted anything but for you to be happy."

"I know, Cyrus."

"And I never had but one quarrel with Lucius. I know we used to fight about every little thing, but deep down I only had one quarrel with him. That was that he caused you pain."

"Well, that's all over and done with, so just forget about it. He's a fine young man now, and he's grown up to be an absolutely perfect gentleman. You said so yourself."

"That's so, yes. A perfect gentleman." Cyrus frowned, his mind trying to capture some elusive thought. "Somethin' bothers me, though."

"What *is* it?" Sarah's impatience was growing into exasperation.

164

"Somethin' about his looks—somethin' around his eyes—can't quite put my finger on it."

Sarah sighed wearily. Cyrus shook his head as if to throw off the bothersome thought, leaned forward, and kissed Sarah again on the cheek.

"Well, I'll be off, dear. See you this evenin'."

In the doorway he stopped suddenly and looked back. "Now I know what it is ," he said. "Yes, by golly, that's it. He's beginnin' to look like Oliver."

He went out, and Sarah stood motionless, staring at the empty doorway for a long moment before going back to her work.

Isaac and Lucius walked up Gilpin Street to the main part of town and watched the thoroughfare coming alive with the bustle of a new day's business.

"This town's growin', Lucius," Isaac said with obvious pride. "Can you tell?"

Lucius shrugged. "Don't see much difference."

"Just look over there, f'rinstance. We have our own hotel now, just like a big city."

Lucius looked across the road at a two-story clapboard building with a large overhanging sign. "Hmmm, yes, I see. The Indiana Hotel. Very impressive."

"Well, it's nothing like the big fancy hotels *you're* used to, I guess."

"That it isn't," Lucius agreed.

"But it's pretty nice for this part o' the country. I tell you, Lucius, someday South Bar's goin' to be the biggest town in southern Indiana. I figure in ten years it'll be as big as—"

"Isaac, old chum—" They had reached a corner, and Lucius put a hand on the other man's arm and pulled him to a stop. "Let's get back to what we were talking about last night, shall we? It's time you made a decision."

Isaac frowned at the ground. "It's hard, Lucius. Really hard."

"You've had two months to think about it. How long are you going to procrastinate?"

"I don't know." Isaac looked away as if he were admitting something shameful.

"Well, just remember one thing. This will probably be your last chance, ever. Either you break away with me now, or you'll go on being your Mama Sarah's little boy and Cyrus's flunky for the rest of your life, and that'll be that."

"I'm thinkin' about it, Lucius. Every day, every minute, I'm thinkin' about it. I want to do it, I really do. I think you and me bein' together would be the greatest thing in the world. But I'm . . . I'm just—"

"You're scared."

"I guess that's it. I'm scared."

They crossed the street and walked on.

"Look here," Lucius said patiently. "I'm going to do all the preparatory work. I have powerful friends in Texas—it'll be easy. I'll go down there this winter and arrange everything. All you'll have to do is make a deal with Cyrus about your half of the business here, and pack your bags. Then in the spring we'll go, and a year later you'll be running the biggest sawmill in the Republic of Texas."

Isaac's eyes shone. "Oh, Lord, it just sounds wonderful, Lucius."

"And, Isaac—" Lucius lowered his voice and winked. "Do you have any idea how passionate those beautiful dark-eyed Mexican señoritas can be?"

Isaac laughed, and his laughter was tight with embarrassment.

Lucius grabbed his arm. "So, is it settled?"

Isaac was frowning again. "I don't know, Lucius. I'll have to think about it awhile longer."

With a snort of disgust Lucius stopped and looked up and down the road. "Where's that damned lawyer of yours?" he growled.

Isaac pointed ahead. "See that little building on the other side of the mercantile store? That's Jacob's office."

"All right. See you a little later." Lucius walked away.

"Want me to come and introduce you?" Isaac called after him.

"I'll introduce myself," Lucius answered without looking back.

"Well!" said Jacob Worthington, attorney-at-law, beaming at his visitor across the tiny desk in his tiny office. "So this is the famous Mr. Lucius Hargrave!"

Worthington was a large man of perhaps thirty years of age, whose coal black hair brushed straight back gave him a youthful look—an effect that was cancelled by a tendency to paunchiness.

"Oh, I make no claim to fame, Mr. Worthington," the

visitor said with genteel modesty. "I *am* a man of means, however. I admit to that."

"Yes, Isaac was telling me. You have a sugar plantation in Louisiana, I hear."

"Not just a sugar plantation. The biggest and finest in the state."

"Ah!" Mr. Worthington's eyes gleamed.

"But, as often happens to men in my position, I have acquired certain, uh, delicate legal problems. I need a really good lawyer."

Worthington rubbed his hands together. "Well, I can tell you, you've come to exactly the right—"

"Not just a good lawyer. A resourceful one. An ingenious one. One who, if the situation requires, can interpret the fine points of the law with some degree of, shall we say . . . creative imagination?"

The lawyer had grown thoughtful. "Well, you being, as you say, Mr. Hargrave, a man of means, why—" He chuckled softly. "Many things are possible."

Lucius smiled. "By the way, I want to thank you for the beautiful letter you wrote me last year, at the time of my grandfather's death. Most gracious of you. I could tell right away you were a man of sensitivity."

Mr. Worthington tried to look humble. "Samuel Gilpin was a great man, Mr. Hargrave. If I can now be of service to his grandson, why, I'll deem it an honor."

"Well, I believe you can be."

"Good, good."

Lucius was studying the attorney carefully, through narrowed eyes. "By the way, can I depend upon you to hold every word that passes between us in strictest confidence?"

"Oh, absolutely, Mr. Hargrave. I couldn't practice law any other way."

"Then before I get to my principal business I'd like to put a very discreet question to you."

"Go right ahead."

Lucius leaned forward, resting his forearms on the edge of the desk. "What do you know about my brother Isaac?"

Worthington blinked. "Why . . . I know he's a fine man, one of the most respected men in this—"

"Let me be a little more specific. What is the gossip around South Bar concerning the relationship between Isaac and my mother?"

167

The lawyer's jaw dropped open. "Between Isaac and Mrs. Thacker?! What can you possibly mean by that?"

"Surely there must be talk. A thirty-three-year-old man who insists on living in perpetual intimacy with his stepmother, who's quite a good-looking woman and only a few years older than he is—"

"Mr. Hargrave! Really, I—" Worthington was momentarily struck speechless. He shuffled a few papers on his desk as he searched his mind for the appropriate response. "I can assure you, there is nothing like that, nothing whatever. Well, maybe a few people consider Isaac a little bit odd in some respects, but as to your mother, why...my heavens, she's the absolute model of respectable behavior—"

"I know that. I'm trying to find out what the gossip is."

"There is no gossip. Anybody who knows those two people at all knows very well that—"

"Oh, come now, Mr. Worthington! No gossip? There's gossip up and down the *river* about my mother. I've heard it myself, and I haven't been in this town for ten years."

"Old gossip, maybe. About certain aspects of her early years. About your father's doings, and such as that. But about her present life I've never heard a thing."

Lucius arched a skeptical eyebrow. "I wonder if you've got your ears open, Mr. Worthington. I can't believe the malicious small-town gossips would pass over a succulent opportunity like that."

Mr. Worthington was growing impatient. "My dear sir, I know all about small-town gossips. I've lived among them all my life, and as a lawyer I make it my business to keep my ears open. And about your mother and brother there is nothing. Not a word, not a murmur, not a whisper. Believe me."

With a smile Lucius leaned back and relaxed. "Well, I'll trouble you no longer with these foolish thoughts. Let's turn to my main business, then."

"Fine, let's do that," the lawyer said, and breathed a small sigh of relief.

At half past six Cyrus was sitting at the kitchen table, fuming. Sarah was puttering at the stove trying to look busy, though the supper had long since been ready.

"Well, you can't blame them for being late," she said defensively. "It's Lucius's first day in town. He's got a million people to say hello to."

Cyrus glared at her. "They ain't visitin' nobody. They're

168

sittin' in the bar at the Indiana Hotel, drinkin'."

"Don't see how you can know *that*."

"I know it because Lucius came to the woodyard this afternoon, clapped Isaac on the shoulder, and said, 'Let's go up to th' hotel, I'll buy you a drink.' And Isaac drops what he's doin', and away they go, like a couple o' carefree boys."

"Well, good. I'm glad."

"You're glad if Isaac starts neglectin' his work to sit in a bar all afternoon?"

"Oh, Cyrus, stop it! Once in ten years Isaac takes a few hours off because his brother's home, and—"

There were heavy footfalls on the front porch, and a burst of laughter.

"Here they are!" Sarah said triumphantly, and gave her husband a fierce look. "Now you be nice, you hear?"

The young men were flushed with alcohol, and exuberantly cheerful.

"Sorry we're late, Mama Sarah," Isaac said. "Lucius kept wantin' to have one more." A beatific grin was fixed on his face.

Lucius clapped Cyrus playfully on the shoulder. "Looks like I'm right back to my old delinquent ways, eh, Cyrus? Always late for supper!"

"Oh, that's all right," Cyrus mumbled.

"You two wash your hands before the food gets cold," Sarah commanded, and smiled as Isaac and Lucius raced each other to the washbasin on the back porch, giggling like small boys.

During the meal Lucius held forth, enumerating all the people he'd seen that day, how some had greeted him warmly, others had eyed him with suspicion, and some had not known him at all.

"Well, don't forget," Sarah said, "you were just a gawky sixteen-year-old when you went away. Nobody thought you'd ever amount to anything then."

"*I* did," Isaac proclaimed.

"But it was a productive day, anyway," Lucius continued. "I had a fine talk with Jacob Worthington this morning. Very clever man, Worthington. Much too clever to be wasting himself in a small place like this. And that, ladies and gentlemen, brings me to the announcement I wish to make."

He paused and looked around the table to make sure he had everybody's attention. "First off. Tomorrow I go up to

169

Louisville. And the next day I return, bringing with me that flower of Southern womanhood, my dearly beloved wife, Arabella."

There was a stunned silence.

"Arabella..." Sarah echoed breathlessly. "Here?"

"*And* Justin. At last you'll get to meet your grandson."

There was a dazed expression on Sarah's face. "I don't understand, Lucius. I thought it was all over between you and—"

"It is, it is. We're getting a divorce, as I said. And we're getting it right here in South Bar."

"Why, how's that possible?" Cyrus demanded. "You ain't legal residents."

Lucius grinned. "I told you, Jacob Worthington's a very clever man."

"Look here, Lucius." Cyrus's voice had gone hard. "Are you tryin' to pull somethin' fishy?"

Lucius gave him a blank look, as if unable to comprehend the question.

"Why, Cyrus, what a question!" Sarah said indignantly. "You know perfectly well Mr. Worthington's a fine lawyer, and a very respectable man. He wouldn't do anything 'fishy', as you put it."

"He's respectable as the next one, I reckon. But he *is* a lawyer."

"Oh, pooh!" With a disdainful toss of her head Sarah dismissed this notion and turned her attention back to Lucius. "But what's Arabella doing in Louisville, for heaven's sake?"

"Traveling with some friends. On her way to New York. She'll be meeting her sister Amanda there. They're on their way to Paris for the winter."

"My goodness, how exciting!" Sarah's eyes became distant and pensive. "What sophisticated people they must be. Cincinnati's as far from home as *I've* ever been. I'm sure I won't know what to say to Arabella, or how to behave."

"Don't worry, Mama," Lucius said casually. "Just be your own sweet self."

Sarah managed a weak smile. "Well, at least it'll be wonderful to have Justin here."

"Oh, you'll love him, he's a great little fellow," Lucius said. "Of course we will."

"And he'll love you too, both you and Isaac."

As if in afterthought Lucius glanced at the third member of the household. "And Cyrus, old friend, I don't want you to be

170

concerned about all this. I intend to keep this invasion of your home as brief as possible. Your tranquility will not be disturbed, I promise you."

Smiling genially, Lucius resumed eating, while Cyrus sat staring at him with an expression gone dark and grim.

(3)

WORD WAS OUT that Lucius Hargrave's beautiful Louisiana wife was coming. That she was from Louisiana was known and that she would be beautiful was not doubted; beyond that, considerable disagreement existed among the South Bar citizenry as to her nature—some picturing her as a lady of quality and refinement, others as a hussy. So at four o'clock on a certain afternoon when the steamboat from Louisville hove to at the South Bar landing, the wharf was strangely well-populated with people strolling about pretending to have business there, waiting to test their theories against direct evidence.

Isaac was there, with Cyrus's fancy carriage polished to perfection, and he stood beside it fidgety with excitement and squinting across the narrowing stretch of water as the ship inched in. He spotted Lucius at the railing, and beside him a young blond woman in a bright green dress. He waved, and stared at the woman. Lucius returned the wave. The woman returned the stare.

"Is that youh brothuh?" Arabella asked.

"Yep. That's Isaac."

Arabella wrinkled her pretty nose. "He's funny-lookin'."

Lucius chuckled.

"And he's starin' at me," Arabella complained.

"Everybody's staring at you, pet. In South Bar you're a phenomenon."

171

Arabella frowned as her eyes wandered over the little river-town landing. "It's evuh so small, isn't it?"

"It's not exactly New Orleans."

"How long will I have to stay heah, Lucius?"

"That depends entirely on how cooperative you are."

"Oh, I'll be evuh so cooperative, I promise."

"In that case you ought to be on your way again in a day or two."

"If I can *stand* it that long!"

"You can stand it. Just smile a lot, and do exactly as I tell you."

Arabella sighed. "All right, Lucius."

Once ashore Lucius took Arabella's arm and guided her toward Isaac and the carriage, ignoring the curious eyes on all sides. Crissy, carrying little Justin in her arms, followed along behind. Isaac came forward to meet them, grinning broadly, unable to wait for introductions.

"I'm sure glad to see you, Miss Arabella, ma'am. Hope you had a nice trip down. I got a carriage here to take you up to the house, and one o' my men'll bring your baggage along in a few minutes."

"Thank you, Mistuh Hahgrave," Arabella said primly. She eyed the muddy wharf plankings with distaste, and held her green velvet skirt up a few inches.

"And this must be Crissy," Isaac said cheerily, and tipped his hat to the maid.

"Yes, suh," Crissy said, smiling. "And dis heah's yo' nephew, suh."

Issac chucked the boy under the chin. "H'lo there, little fella. Can you say hello to your Uncle Isaac?"

Justin couldn't. He gave the stranger a wary look and buried his face in the maid's neck. Crissy laughed.

"Jes' give 'im time to git used to you, suh. He'll be fine."

At the carriage Isaac tried again. "Want to ride out front with me, Justin?"

Justin looked the carriage over, and his eyes brightened. "Buggy wide!" he exclaimed, and allowed his Uncle Isaac to take him from Crissy's arms.

When the carriage creaked to a stop in front of the house, Sarah came out to meet it, smoothing her dress and giving her hair a nervous last-minute pat.

Lucius leaped out and helped his wife down.

172

"Mama, this is Arabella," he said.

Sarah took the young woman in a light embrace. "It's so good to meet you, my dear."

Arabella presented a cheek to be kissed. "I do hope we're not imposin' on you too much, Mrs. Hahgrave."

"It's Thacker, sweetheart," Lucius mumbled. "Mrs. Thacker."

"Oh no, it's just plain Sarah, please!" Sarah said laughingly. "And you're not imposing a bit, you're more than welcome."

"So kind of you," Arabella said, and suddenly remembered to smile.

Sarah's eyes lit on the little boy in Isaac's arms. She went to him.

"Hello, Justin," she said softly.

The child stared at her with wide eyes.

"I'm your grandmother," Sarah said. "But I hope you'll just call me Mama Sarah, the way your Uncle Isaac does. Can you say Mama Sarah?"

Justin gave it a try. "Mama Say."

Sarah laughed, ruffled the boy's hair, and kissed him. Then she noticed the black woman standing beside the carriage.

"That's Crissy, Mama Sarah," Isaac said.

Sarah smiled and extended her hand. "How do you do, Crissy? Welcome to South Bar."

Arabella uttered a little gasp.

Crissy gulped, executed a clumsy curtsy, and shook Sarah's hand. "How do, ma'am. Thank you, ma'am."

Greatly pleased, Sarah beamed at the group. "Well, let's go in and have some refreshments, shall we?" She led the way.

Arabella sat stiffly in her chair and accepted a cup of tea from a tray Sarah had brought from the kitchen. "Thank you, Mrs. Thackuh. That looks lovely."

Sarah smiled at Crissy, who was standing beside Arabella's chair. "Will you have some tea, Crissy?"

Arabella closed her eyes and went rigid.

"Oh no, ma'am. Thank you, ma'am," Crissy mumbled.

"Are you sure you don't want to sit down? You must be terribly tired."

"No, ma'am. I'm fine."

Sarah turned to the men. "Tea, Lucius? Isaac?"

"None for me, thanks," Isaac said.

"I think I'll go out in the kitchen and see if I can find some whiskey," Lucius said, and left the room.

Sarah sat down and poured herself some tea, then looked at Justin, who was lying on the floor idly tracing the pattern in the carpet with his finger.

"And what can I get for Justin? A glass of milk?"

"Actually, I've always preferred to call him Jamie," Arabella said coldly.

"Oh, I'm sorry. Lucius seems to use Justin, mostly."

Arabella gave a little shrug. "Well, it doesn't mattuh. In a day or two it won't—" She checked herself and sipped her tea. Sarah stared at her.

Arabella glanced at the boy. "Really, the only thing he needs right now is a nap. Don't you think so, Crissy?"

"Yes'm, he sho' do. He's a tahd little boy."

"Isaac, will you show Crissy around upstairs, please?" Sarah said. "They'll have the rose room."

Isaac was up. "Sure, Mama Sarah."

Crissy swept the child up off the floor, cradled him in her arms, and followed Isaac up the stairs.

Sarah smiled at Arabella. "My husband asked me to give you his apologies for not being here. He had to go up to New Albany for a day or two, to see about some sawmill supplies. I expect you passed his steamboat on the way down."

Arabella wasn't listening. "Mrs. Thackuh, I don't mean to be critical, unduhstand, but . . . Crissy's really not accustomed to being invited to pahticipate in white people's social activities. It only makes her feel uncomfortable. You seem so kind, I'm shuah you don't want to make anyone uncomfortable."

"I should say not," Sarah agreed.

"Crissy is only heah to look aftuh my things, and to take care of Jamie. She's evuh so quiet, and she eats very little. She'll take her meals with youh servants, of course. That is, if they're black. If they're white, she'll take her meals aftuhwards."

"I don't have servants, Arabella," Sarah said evenly.

Arabella seemed unsure that she had heard correctly. "You . . . don't have servants?"

"No. Neither black nor white. So I hope you'll excuse my ignorance about these things."

"But . . . who does youh housework?"

"I do."

"Well, I declauh." Momentarily speechless, Arabella sipped her tea.

"I want you to feel at home here, Arabella," Sarah went on.

"And I'll try very hard to make your stay as pleasant as possible. Please be patient with me, though, if I don't treat Crissy just the way you'd consider proper. I've been deeply opposed to slavery all my life, and I just can't quite force myself to think of another human being as a . . . well, in that way."

"Oh, that's all right, Mrs. Thackuh," Arabella said easily. Her smile was working automatically now. "I'm shuah we'll manage just fine."

"But I certainly don't intend to inflict my views on you," Sarah said hastily. "Because I do want you to feel at ease here, and—"

"I wonduh wheah Lucius is," Arabella said, suddenly frowning in the direction of the kitchen.

At that moment he reappeared. "What's all this solemn discussion?" he asked.

Sarah was up immediately. "Oh, Lucius, why don't you take Arabella upstairs while I get supper started? Maybe she'd like to rest awhile, too."

"Yes, I would," Arabella said emphatically, and set her teacup down.

As she went up the stairs with Lucius she rolled her eyes at him with a look of deep suffering and moaned softly, "Oh, Lord! Two whole days of this?"

"Just keep smiling and stop complaining," he growled in her ear. He took her elbow and hurried her along.

Late that night when the house was quiet Sarah sat wrapped in her housecoat before her bedroom dressing table, brushing her hair. She was mildly startled when a soft knock sounded at her door.

"Come in."

Lucius entered. He pulled a chair close to his mother's dresser and sat down, smiling. "Well, Mama. At last we can have a little private chat."

"All right, Lucius. What shall we chat about?"

"I must say, I didn't think you were your usual pleasant self this evening. Awfully reserved. Aren't you feeling well?"

"I feel fine. But I have to admit, Arabella makes me tense. I can't seem to get on an easy footing with her."

"Oh, never mind Arabella. She'll be gone soon, and you'll never see her again."

"I'm sorry I won't be able to get to know her. And yet I guess it's just as well." Sarah had stopped brushing her hair, and was frowning at her image in the mirror. "I feel dreadful about that Crissy. There we were, all having supper in the dining room, and there *she* was, sitting out in the kitchen all by herself—"

Lucius snorted. "Oh, Mama, forget about it. That's their way of life. Crissy wouldn't want it any other way."

"She doesn't know any other way. She's been kept in ignorance."

"Let me tell you something, Mama. In the four years I lived at Carolina Grove I never saw Crissy unhappy but once, and that was the day she had to leave that house. The only servant they had who ever wanted to get away was their butler, fella called Ben. And that was only because after Amos died Ben was afraid of being owned by Amos's cold-blooded son Adam, and I can't blame him for that. Ol' Ben practically got down on his hands and knees and begged me to take him away."

"And did you?"

"I did. Not because I had any use for him. Because it struck me as being a good joke on Adam."

"What did you do with this Ben?"

"Took him to St. Louis and got him a job as a bootblack in a big hotel there. And I can promise you he's working twice as hard now as he ever worked at Carolina Grove."

"But I'll bet he's grateful to you, just the same."

"Yes, I think he is." Lucius chuckled. "And it *was* a good joke. I heard that bastard Adam worried himself sick trying to figure out what became of Ben. He put 'runaway slave' advertisements in every newspaper in the state."

Sarah suppressed a smile. "So there. You did a good deed. I'm just sorry you insist on pretending you did it for a bad reason."

"It wasn't a bad reason, it was a perfectly good reason." Lucius's voice was edged with annoyance. "Mama, I really wish you wouldn't moralize so much. It's not for housewives in Indiana to have lofty opinions about how people in Louisiana conduct their—"

"Well, that's just where you're wrong, Lucius." Sarah turned on him with a flash of vehemence. "This *is* one country, isn't it? Indiana housewives and Louisiana planters and St. Louis bootblacks have that in common, and they all ought to have an equal say in things—"

"Mama . . . !" Lucius smiled indulgently and patted his mother's hand. "May I change the subject, please?"

"Oh, I'm sorry," Sarah said archly. "My lofty opinions bore you, don't they?" She went back to brushing her hair.

Lucius took some folded papers out of his pocket and spread them on the dresser. "I told Cyrus the other day, and I tell you, too—I want this business with Arabella to trouble you just as little as possible. All I need from you is your signature on several of these pages. Here, and . . . here . . . and here."

He looked around the room. "You don't have pen and ink, do you? No. I'll just scoot across the hall and get it, and be right back."

When he returned Sarah was reading the papers and frowning.

"You don't need to bother wading through all that legal jargon, Mama. All it says is that Arabella and I are residents of Indiana, and—"

"Good heavens, Lucius, I think it says a lot more than that. It says you've been living here since last September!"

"Well, yes, you see . . . turns out there's some sort of silly rule about needing a year's residency before you can file for divorce, so—"

"Goodness, yes. I remember that now, from Isaac's divorce. But I can't sign a thing like this for *you*, Lucius. It isn't true."

"You don't understand, Mama, it's just a formality. Means nothing at all. Worthington has it all worked out. He has friends in Indianapolis, you see. All purely routine." He held the pen out to her. "Here, Mama. Just three signatures, and you'll be troubled no more."

She was staring at him. "Lucius, I really think I'd better wait till Cyrus comes back, and—"

"No!" Something hard surfaced in Lucius's eyes, and was immediately gone again. He leaned over his mother and spoke to her in a gentle voice. "Mama, you know how Cyrus is. Why get him all upset? I honestly think he meant it as a subtle insult, going off just when Arabella was due to come, but the truth is I couldn't be more pleased. He's the one person we don't need to have involved in this. It's a private family affair."

"Private family affair! Lucius, Cyrus is my husband! I need his advice—"

"And I'm your son. Would I do anything that would be in any way harmful to you? And Jacob Worthington's one of the most highly respected men in this town, I've discovered that in the few days I've been here. *You've* known him for years.

177

Isn't he perfectly trustworthy?"

Still Sarah resisted. "Why didn't you get your divorce in Louisiana? Wouldn't that have been the normal thing to do?"

"It would have, except for one fly in the ointment—Adam. Mama, there's no way I can explain to you what a devil that man is. He's tremendously powerful, and he hates me. Always has. Somehow he'd find a way to wreck the whole thing, out of pure spite."

Lucius pushed the papers closer to Sarah, and pointed. "Look here. Isaac signed as witness, you see? And you know what a stiff-necked moralist *he* is." Again he offered her the pen. "Come on, Mama. You've got to help me with this. Please. I'm desperate."

Sarah drew a deep breath, took the pen, and signed.

"Thank you, Mama. You're a real friend." In an instant Lucius had put the papers away and was giving Sarah a hug. "I remember when I was a boy I said it, and I say it still. You're the best friend I ever had." He kissed her on the forehead. "G'night, Mama."

From the doorway he smiled back at her. "Oh, and, uh...of course we'll just keep this to ourselves, all right? Nobody's business but ours." He threw her a little wave and was gone.

Sarah still held the pen. She kept turning it over in her hands and frowning at it, as if it were an alien object.

(4)

LUCIUS AND ARABELLA were out all afternoon the next day, not returning to the house until after nine o'clock in the evening.

When Arabella came in she stopped short and stared into the parlor, and Lucius paused behind her. Sarah and Crissy were sitting side by side on the sofa. The maid's head was bent low over an open book in her lap, and Sarah was leaning close to her, observing. Isaac and little Justin were sitting crosslegged on the floor, playing a game involving a number of small pieces of wood.

"Crissy!" Arabella hissed.

"Oh . . . yes'm!" Crissy closed the book and was on her feet, quivering.

"Oh, hello, you two," Sarah called out. "I didn't hear you come in."

Arabella advanced to the center of the room and stood looking around, thunderstruck. "What*evuh* is goin' on heah?!"

Crissy was speechless.

"I was just giving Crissy a reading lesson," Sarah said. "She's very good at it. She's learning the letters so quickly—"

"Just *look* at Jamie!" Arabella snapped. She was glaring at her servant. "Lying around on the floor! Disgusting!"

"The floor is perfectly clean," Sarah said with a tightening voice.

"That doesn't mattuh, it's cold and drafty down theah! And it's way past his bedtime. Crissy, what *can* you be thinking of?!"

Crissy hung her head in shame. "'Scuse me, ma'am. I didn't notice how late it was gittin'."

Cowering under her mistress's ferocious look, she picked up the little boy and ran from the room. Justin squealed his protests all the way up the stairs.

Sarah got up. Her face was grim.

"I'm sorry you're so constantly offended by our crude ways here, Arabella."

"Please don't go on apologizin' all the time, Mrs. Thackuh, it's really not necessary." Arabella waved an impatient hand. "I'm just a bit irritable tonight, I'm afraid. It's been a thoroughly exhaustin' day, and I'm evuh so ready for bed. If you-all will excuse me, I'll say goodnight." She swept past Lucius still standing in the doorway, without a glance, and went quickly up the stairs.

Lucius came into the parlor and sat down. Isaac remained sitting on the floor, glumly toying with the wooden pieces.

"Brought these from the woodyard for Justin," he said. "Carved 'em myself."

"That's nice," Lucius said.

"Have you had anything to eat, Lucius?" Sarah asked. "There're plenty of leftovers."

Lucius shook his head. "Arabella and I had dinner at the Indiana Hotel. She felt the need of an evening out, after spending all afternoon with that windy old bore, Jacob Worthington."

Sarah made a face. "I don't imagine she liked the hotel very much, either. It's not a very nice place."

Lucius smiled wryly. "She didn't."

Sarah had sat down again, and was staring at the book Crissy had dropped. "Crissy's such a bright person. And so nice. What a shameful waste!" She drew a long sigh. "If only I could *talk* to Arabella. If *only* she could learn to see things from another point of—"

"Mama." Lucius raised weary eyes to his mother. "Forget about it. Just . . . *forget* about it."

Isaac began to pick up the wooden pieces and put them in a box. "Speakin' of bright people, Justin's one o' the brightest *I* ever saw."

"Oh, he is, he's just a marvel," Sarah said, and smiled. But the smile faded quickly; her mind was still on the thing that troubled her. After a few minutes of idle chatting she said goodnight and went up to bed.

Isaac stretched out flat on his back, hands under his head, and studied the ceiling. "What makes Arabella so touchy?" he asked suddenly.

Lucius chuckled. "You're not used to women with temper, old chum. All you're used to is Mama."

"I guess I *am* spoiled," Isaac said thoughtfully. "That's one thing I'll hate if I go to Texas with you, Lucius. I'll miss Mama Sarah somethin' awful."

Lucius was looking at him with drooping eyes, as if half asleep. "If you knew what you were doing to her, you'd be so damned anxious to get out of here you'd be upstairs packing right this minute."

Isaac sat up like a shot. "What do you mean by that?"

Lucius yawned. "Oh, never mind." As he got unhurriedly to his feet he delivered a passable imitation of Arabella's deep-South drawl.

"If you-all will excuse me, I think I'll mosey on back up to the Indiana Ho-tel. Theah was a good-lookin' lady up theah givin' me very significant looks. I'm evuh so anxious to make her acquaintance." He gave Isaac a wink and started for the door.

Isaac scrambled up, followed him out of the house, and

180

stopped him at the bottom of the front steps. "Wait a minute, Lucius. I want to know what you meant by that remark. What am I doin' to Mama Sarah?"

Lucius turned a hard look on his brother. "How is it possible that you can live in a place like this all your life and not know what small-town gossips are capable of? They can destroy people's lives. You've *seen* lives destroyed, you ought to know that. And I wonder how it's possible you can be so damned unaware of the talk that's floating around about *you*."

"About *me*!"

"About you. And your dear Mama Sarah."

Isaac took a step backward. His jaw dropped open, and his voice became a tremulous whisper. "What are you talkin' about?"

Lucius stepped closer. "Isaac, I have come here because I'm not only your brother, I'm your friend. Possibly the only one you have. You're in trouble, old chum. You need help, and I'm offering it to you. For God's sake, man, come away!"

"Lucius, what are you . . . what are you . . . ?"

"I'm telling you that this town is buzzing with nasty gossip about you and Mama. They're calling Cyrus a fuzzy-minded old fool who doesn't know what goes on in his own house. The man who sleeps with Sarah Thacker, they say, is not her husband as often as it is her stepson, Isaac Har—"

"Oh *God*!" It was a half-cry, half-sob, choked off in Isaac's throat. He turned away, groping for a seat on the porch steps. "Oh God, I can't believe that! Where'd you hear such a thing?"

"Lots of places. At the hotel. Up and down Gilpin Street."

Isaac held his head in his hands, stared at the ground, and groaned. "Oh, Lucius, that's . . . that's terrible, I just can't believe—"

"I'm truly sorry to have to tell you that. But I think you ought to know."

"Yes. Oh yes, you're absolutely right, I had no idea." Isaac was shaking his head in dazed disbelief.

"But don't forget, you do have a way out. Of course Mama'll blame me, call me cruel and heartless for taking you away, and so on. But, just remember—it's not only your name that's being dragged in the mud. It's hers too."

Isaac had partially regained his composure. "Well . . . thanks for tellin' me."

Lucius reached down and patted his brother's shoulder. "Goodnight, old chum. I'd think about it long and hard, if I were you." Then he was off, sauntering up the road and whistling in the darkness.

Isaac sat unmoving for a long time before he got to his feet and went with dragging steps into the house.

(5)

AT NINE O'CLOCK in the morning Lucius knocked softly on Arabella's door and, without waiting for a response, opened it and looked in. Arabella was sitting on the edge of a chair, hands folded in her lap. She was wearing her green velvet traveling dress, and her luggage was arranged neatly at her feet.

"Good, you're all ready," Lucius said. "The driver's here to take your bags."

He pushed the door open and stood aside, and a man in a blue uniform stepped into the room. On the pocket of his shirt were embroidered the words *Indiana Hotel*. He nodded to Arabella and reached for the baggage. Arabella rose and moved back out of his way. As soon as he had gone she turned to Lucius, and for the first time noticed little Justin standing in the doorway, peering in.

She held out her arms to him. "Come heah, dahlin'."

He came ambling toward her, and she lifted him up and hugged him.

"My, my, such a big boy!" she cooed. "My Jamie's gettin' to be, oh, evuh so grown-up!"

Lucius was fidgeting. "Let's not dawdle too long, pet. The time is now."

"Wheah's youh mothuh?" Arabella demanded.

"Way out back, hanging out laundry. All's clear."

Arabella smiled at her child and nuzzled his cheek. "Can you give Mama a nice big hug and kiss, Jamie?"

182

The boy complied perfunctorily.

"Oh, that was sweet. Now will you promise Mama you'll be a good, good boy, always?"

Justin was getting impatient. "Wanna go buggy wide," he announced.

Lucius took him from Arabella, and held him playfully aloft. "No buggy ride for you today, young fella. You stay with Mama Sarah."

He was pleased enough with that idea. "Go see Mama Say," he urged.

A darkness came into Arabella's eyes. She moved to a window and stood staring out into the morning sunshine, her back to the man and boy.

"Take him away," she whispered.

And it was done.

Sarah and Crissy were at the far end of the big backyard, hanging out washing and chatting like neighbors.

"Why, dis ain't no washin' a-tall, Miss Sarah, ma'am," Crissy was saying. "You ought to see de washin' dey used to hang out at Ca'lina Grove. Two hunnerd yahds o' line, stretchin' all ovuh de place!"

"Oh no, please!" Sarah protested laughingly.

"Why, heah's Mistuh Lucius," Crissy said.

Lucius had come down from the house with Justin perched on his shoulder. Under a nearby walnut tree he swung the boy down with a great swoop through the air that made Justin squeal with pleasure.

"Good morning, Lucius," Sarah said. "Is Arabella up? Shall I come and fix you some breakfast?"

"Don't bother, Mama, we'll pick up something later. I'm taking Arabella for an outing today."

"Oh, how nice. Where to?"

"Thought we'd take a ride in the country. I rented a carriage from the hotel."

"Lucius, for heaven's sake! We've got *two* carriages right here, and you're welcome to either."

"Ah, but the hotel carriage has a uniformed driver." Lucius chuckled. "It's just the kind of thing that makes Arabella feel at home."

He glanced at Justin, who was scouring the yard collecting sticks and stones, intent on some building project. "Will you watch the young'un awhile, Mama?"

"Why, of course. Goodness, it's a pleasure to have him around."

"No need o' dat, Mistuh Lucius," Crissy said. "I'm heah, ain't I?"

"You're comin with us, Crissy."

She looked at him in quick surprise. "Suh?"

"Come along now," he said sharply. "The carriage is waiting."

"Yes, suh. 'Scuse me, Miss Sarah, ma'am." With a baffled look on her face Crissy went off toward the house.

Lucius smiled at his mother. "Thanks, Mama. See you a little later."

"You're welcome, Lucius." Her eyes were troubled as she watched him hurry away.

"You know the plan, Chester," Lucius called up to the carriage driver. "Take us up the Post Road to McNulty's Landing."

"Yes, sir."

Lucius climbed in and sat next to Arabella. Crissy sat facing them, and clutched at a side strap as the carriage lurched away.

They rode in silence awhile, watching the houses on either side fall away gradually to be replaced by open fields and an occasional patch of rust-colored autumn woods.

Then Lucius cast a sidelong glance at Arabella. "I hope you appreciate all this."

Arabella was gazing steadfastly out the window, and made no answer.

"Have you ever seen anything work so smoothly?" Lucius continued. "Nothing complicated, nothing sticky, just the way you wanted it. And please note that even though your steamboat is at this very moment hove to at South Bar, I am going to all this trouble to take you three miles up to the next landing, just so you can get aboard without having to be stared at. Now, isn't that considerate of me?"

Arabella went on looking out the window.

"And just think, pet. Tonight you'll be back in the arms of your new lover, and tomorrow on your way to New York and Paris . . . and a life of happiness."

Arabella gave him a look of cool detachment, and held her silence.

Crissy was staring at her mistress. "Miss Arabella, ma'am? Wha's gon' happen? Are we leavin'? Are we goin' away fo' good?"

"Yes, thank the Lord!" Arabella blurted. "We're goin' away for good."

Crissy's eyes widened in alarm. "But... what about Jamie?"

"He stays with me, Crissy," Lucius said briskly.

Crissy turned her attention to Lucius, and a trembling came into her voice. "But, Mistuh Lucius, I'm his mammy, suh. Ain't nobody knows how to take care of 'im but me—"

"Crissy!" Arabella snapped. "You are very much mistaken. You're not Jamie's mammy at all, you're my maid, so just hush up!"

Crissy ignored this, kept her eyes on the man.

"Please, Mistuh Lucius. Don't take 'im away from me."

"Oh, look here, Crissy." Lucius squirmed in acute discomfort. "You mustn't think we're deliberately trying to be cruel to you. This is painful for everybody concerned. You know, we're none of us completely in charge of what happens to us in this crazy life. Sometimes things just sort of ... go out of control, you see?" He had taken out his wallet, and was extracting some money. "But you've done a wonderful job with the boy, and I want you to know I'm deeply grateful to you. So, uh, please accept this as a small token of that gratitude." He extended to her several tightly folded bills.

She shook her head vehemently, refusing them.

"You can buy yourself something pretty in New York," he said gently, and dropped the money in her lap.

She shrank back from him, her eyes brimming with an anguish that threatened to explode at any moment.

"Crissy, you behave youself, you heah me?" Arabella said angrily. "This is difficult enough, without you making a nasty scene!"

Crissy paid no attention. "Please, Mistuh Lucius, suh. Lemme stay wid 'im. Lemme stay heah, please..."

Lucius's face went hard. "I'm sorry, Crissy, that's not possible."

He reached up and pounded on the carriage roof. "Stop here, Chester!" He called.

The carriage ground to a stop on the deserted country road, and in the sudden quiet the twitterings of roadside birds made a timid intrusion. Lucius turned to Arabella.

"Chester will stay with you till the boat arrives at McNulty's, and see you safely on. He's a good fellow, and he's already been paid, so you needn't bother about that."

"Thank you," Arabella said. She did not look at him.

Crissy had a hand over her mouth, and was quietly sobbing.

"Well, I guess that's about it," Lucius said. He reached out and patted the fragile hand of the woman at his side. "Goodbye, Arabella. And for whatever part was my fault, I'm sorry."

"Goodbye, Lucius." Arabella's voice was dull and lifeless. "Take good care of Jamie." She kept staring off across the fields.

Lucius got out of the carriage and closed the door. Immediately Crissy's grief-stricken face was framed in the window. The tears were in full flow now.

"I didn't git a chance to say g'bye to 'im, Mistuh Lucius," she whimpered.

"It's better that way, Crissy," he said cheerfully. "You know damned well a big tearful farewell scene wouldn't have made it any easier for anybody. Least of all Justin."

"But, Mistuh Lucius—"

"Drive on, Chester!" Lucius shouted, and began to walk back in the direction from which the carriage had come.

"Mistuh Lucius, wait!" Crissy came out of the carriage, staggering as the vehicle started off and stopped again.

"Crissy!" Arabella shrieked. "You get back in heah this instant!"

Crissy moved toward Lucius, arms outstretched in supplication. "Please, suh, don't take 'im away from me. Lemme stay wid my baby—"

Arabella had come in pursuit, and now delivered a solid blow with her open palm against the side of the woman's head. Crissy sank to her knees, cowering, covering her head with her hands.

"Get back in that carriage, you disobedient bitch!" With furiously flailing arms Arabella rained down blows on the kneeling figure.

Lucius started toward them.

"Stay away!" Arabella spat at him. "I can handle this. You just . . . *stay away*!" Her eyes burned with white-hot ferocity as they lay on Lucius for a final moment—then no more.

Summoning uncommon strength from some invisible source she grasped her maid by the wrist, dragged her to the carriage and almost pushed her up the boarding steps.

"All right, Chester, drive on!" She got in and slammed the door.

Lucius stood in the road and watched until the carriage was

186

out of sight. Then he turned and started walking slowly back toward South Bar. Once more the dewy-fresh morning air was quiet, atremble with the gentle sound of birdsong. Lucius's eyes wandered absently over the fields he passed. From time to time he heaved a long sigh, and took an aimless kick at a pebble.

At the lonely place where the carriage had stopped, nothing remained except Crissy's money, which lay in the dirt of the roadway.

(6)

FROM THE JOURNAL of Lucius Hargrave:

My return after an absence of ten years to my mother's hearth and the village of my birth in southern Indiana was both necessary and ardently desired, but in several ways it was one of the most trying experience of my life.

Time had been kind to my mother's pink-cheeked comeliness, but had worked ill with her nature. She had become one of those busybodies who are forever appointing themselves guardians of the national morality, and she looked upon me as corrupted by my years in the South and in need of enlightenment. As for her husband and my old enemy, Cyrus Thacker, he was unable to sustain a facade of courtesy for longer than an hour after my arrival before he began to slip back into his old ways of viewing everything I said or did with suspicion and carping criticism.

And Isaac—poor old Isaac—a year or so of marriage had done nothing for him. He was right back where he started, more timid and self-effacing than ever, cowering before Cyrus like the lowliest employee at the woodyard, and being treated by my mother like a small boy that must never be allowed to grow up. For him, I quickly realized, I had come just in time.

So I moved with swift efficiency toward my goals, for they were simple and clearly perceived: to disentangle myself from Arabella Whitehurst (I had long since ceased thinking of her as Arabella Hargrave); and to rescue my brother from the quicksand of nothingness in which he had become mired. Then I would lead him and my little boy down the great river and across the far horizon to a fulfilling life.

The business with Arabella was painful, but easy enough. It was a sad and awesome thing to behold the change that had come over her. The moment the protective finery of the Whitehurst wealth was stripped from her she stood revealed in her true nature—ruthless, cutting, hard as a grinding stone. Somehow she had persuaded herself that it was all my fault that her diabolical brother Adam had stripped us both of our rightful inheritance, and she wanted intensely to be rid of me. Well and good—for once our purposes were in harmony. Division of property was simplicity itself—we had only two possessions of value: a considerable sum of money I had accumulated as a crusading author; and our son Justin. Arabella wanted the money, I wanted the child. A cynic might say I bought my son. I would not deign to argue the point. It was right that I should have him; I took him: those are the facts, and the only ones that matter.

So in good time my former wife went on her way, a free woman, and here I must leave off relating her melancholy story, for I know nothing further of her, nor ever shall, I am certain. My kindest thoughts go with her, she of tender cruelty and treacherous innocence. May a merciful God send her a little protection.

My task concerning Isaac proved more difficult. He had built a stone wall around his mind, and was stubbornly resistant to my offers of help. But by dogged perseverence I at last succeeded in convincing him that his unnatural attachment to his beloved "Mama Sarah" was bringing ridicule down upon *her* head as well as his. Gradually the fetters fell away. He was ready to become a man.

It was all agreed, then: I would go to Texas that winter, make the necessary arrangements, and return in the spring to pick up Isaac and Justin and take them to their new home. How much I felt like a parent as I departed on this mission—not only to Justin but to Isaac, and, incredibly, to my mother as well. She sulked like a spoiled child, refusing to believe that what I was doing was best for all concerned, not least for herself. But my spirits were buoyant. I knew that in my own humble way I was carrying on the sort of good work to which my father had dedicated himself so many years before, and which he was doubtless still carrying on in some remote corner of the world. I knew, too, that someday my mother would understand, and forgive me.

(No, I did not know *that*. I only hoped it with all my heart.)

(7)

TOWARD DUSK on Tuesday, the twenty-eighth of February, 1843, a noisy and disorderly crowd of masked revelers assembled at the Place d'Armes in New Orleans. Soon it was moving like a giant, pulsating, elongated jellyfish up and down the streets of the city, picking up new members and growing noisier and more boisterous minute by minute. At the junction of Canal Street and St. Charles it was met by a ragged street band, an encounter that stimulated an outbreak of impromptu dancing on the broad boulevard, after which the conglomeration continued via Chartres Street back to the Place d'Armes to regroup and start again.

While the din of music and merrymaking was at its peak along St. Charles, Lucius Hargrave entered a dingy little tavern called Napoleon's, on Girod Street, and sat down at the otherwise deserted bar. His clothes were rumpled, and his face carried several days' growth of beard.

The man behind the counter greeted his solitary customer with a hearty geniality. "Well, if it ain't Lucius Hargrave! 'Allo, Lucius, m'boy, good to see ye!"

"Hello, Nappy," Lucius said. "Let me have a whiskey, will you?"

Napoleon was short, fat, and swarthy, with a face wider than it was long. He brought the drink, and gave his customer a critical inspection.

"Ye look like ye need one," he said.

Lucius gulped his drink and motioned for a refill. He glanced around the empty room.

"This place is about as lively as a tomb."

"Well, it's Mardi Gras time," Napoleon said. He jerked a thumb toward the street. "That's where my customers are. Followin' the maskers."

"And picking a few pockets?"

"Why not? It's the fancy society bastards that dress up in funny clothes and parade up and down the streets makin' fools o' themselves. Creoles and Americans both—don't make no difference as long as they're rich. They can do what they want. If us common folks in Girod Street tried somethin' like that we'd get ourselves arrested."

Lucius chuckled "Come on, Nappy! There hasn't been a policeman show his face on Girod Street in twenty years."

The proprietor was studying his customer. "Don't see ye in a long time, Lucius. Not since ye married the Whitehurst gal and got to be one o' them fancy society bastards yerself."

"Yes, but unfortunately not a rich one."

"Yeah, I read in the paper. The ol' man died and the plantation turned out to be bankrupt. Too bad."

"Don't you believe it, Nappy. It was worth a fortune. My wife's brother stole it all, every lick."

"What a damn shame. Where ye been in the meantime?"

"Oh, here and there. Back to Indiana to visit my mother. Back out to Texas to see what I can get going there. Got to relocate my brother from Indiana, and I think Texas might be the place."

"You got yerself to worry about. How come ye're lookin' out for yer brother?"

A sly smile touched Lucius's lips. "Because when he sells out his half of the family business he's going to have money. Lots of it."

Napoleon grinned his comprehension. "Aha!"

"But in the meantime, I'm up against it a bit." Lucius frowned into his empty whiskey glass. "Got to get a windfall soon."

Napoleon refilled Lucius's glass without being asked. "Tell ye what, Lucius, I got a room upstairs gonna be empty in a few days. Fella that's in it's movin' out. Jest as well, too. He's a queer one, even fer Girod Street. How'd ye like to set up a little card game up there?"

Lucius shook his head. "No, thanks."

"Ye could have the room and yer meals fer twenty-five percent o' yer earnings."

"That's all behind me, Nappy. I don't go backwards."

"What are ye goin' back to Texas for, then?"

Lucius had no answer for this. He studied his drink.

Napoleon shrugged. "All right. Soon's the queer dog upstairs moves out I'll let a couple o' whores move in. At least then I'll know what goes on up there."

"What's so damn mysterious about this fellow upstairs?"

"Jes' can't quite make 'im out. He's got his nigger man bringin' women in all the time. Not tramps, either, I'll tell ye. Some of 'em look like rich society ladies. Religion's his game, seems like. Calls 'imself Father Xavier. Don't know what his technique is. I reckon he tells the ladies the end is near, then beds 'em." Nappy wheezed with laughter. "Don't matter to me, though. He's quiet, and he pays his rent. That's all that counts."

Lucius finished his drink and got up. "What do I owe you, Nappy?"

"Not a thing, Lucius. You jes' think over what I said about settin' up a game, y'hear? You were one o' the best operators on the river, they say. Ain't no use lettin' talent like that go to waste."

"Well, thanks. I'll think about it."

As Lucius reached the front door it was opened from the outside, and a man came in. He was tall, angularly thin, dressed in a suit of somber black and wearing a stiff-brimmed hat. Long iron gray hair flowed from beneath the hat, and a ragged beard of the same color graced his lean hawklike face. He and Lucius stood quite still for several seconds, staring at each other.

Then the stranger touched a finger to his hatbrim. "Good evening," he said in a deep and sonorous voice, and walked past Lucius toward the rear of the tavern room.

"'Allo, there, Father Xavier!" Napoleon called out cheerily. "Thought maybe you'd be out there paradin' with the Mardi Gras folks this evenin'."

At the foot of a narrow wooden stairway at the back of the room, the bearded man paused and gave the bartender a cold look. "You cannot mean that, Monsieur Napoleon. I'd as soon join forces with the devil himself as fall in with ignorant street rabble, profaning the Lord's holy purpose with their vulgar

191

revelry. No, no. Unthinkable. I believe you jest with me, sir." Moving with solemn dignity he went slowly up the stairs and out of sight.

Napoleon grinned at Lucius. "See what I mean? Some queer character, eh?"

Lucius paid no attention. He had crossed the room to the foot of the rear stairs and was staring up toward the dark second-floor hallway with a transfixed look on his face.

Father Xavier opened the door of his room in response to a soft knock. He had removed his hat and coat and was holding a candle, and his thick gray hair shone in the dim light. He peered into the unlighted hallway.

"Yes?"

"Excuse me, sir," Lucius Hargrave said timidly. "I hope I'm not disturbing you. But when I saw you downstairs a moment ago I had a strong feeling that I...that we'd met before, somewhere."

"It's possible," Father Xavier said. "I have traveled far." He made a vague gesture. "But I don't know, I cannot tell. The ungodliness of the world has quite bewitched my mind, young man. Memory falls away from me..."

Lucius edged forward. "Sir, may I come in for a few minutes?"

"May you come in? Of course you may. Young man, I have received in this room the lost, the lonely, the bewildered, the wayward. Men and women, old and young, rich and poor. I like to think that some of them have gone away refreshed and comforted, perhaps even strengthened. Shall I not wish the same for you?"

He had led Lucius to the center of the room, and now beckoned him to one of several chairs grouped around a table. "Please sit down, sir."

"First let me introduce myself," Lucius said. He extended his hand. "My name is Lucius Hargrave."

The other man shook hands listlessly. "A pleasure, Mr. Hargrave. I am Father Xavier. That is, the poor sinners here on Girod Street like to call me that. They think of me as their confessor, though I'm not a Catholic priest, nor do I pretend to be. But I have spoken admiringly of St. Francis Xavier, and have expressed desire to be like him, to dedicate my life to the spreading of God's love to the farthest corners of the heathen world—and because of this they call me Xavier. It is an irreverent thing they do, but they mean no harm, and there's no denying I'm flattered by it."

He had placed the candle on the table and now he gestured again to a chair, and as soon as his visitor was seated, he took one himself.

"So, Mr. Hargrave. What brings you to this humble place?"

"I was just . . . passing through. Saying hello to Napoleon. An old acquaintance of mine."

"I see. A kindly man, Monsieur Napoleon. But a fool, I think. He likes to tease me, as you noticed. He pretends to believe that women who come to me for spiritual guidance are being used in some sinful way."

"Yes." Lucius nodded agreement. "He *is* something of a fool, as you say."

For the first time Father Xavier looked at his visitor with interest. "Well, now. May I offer you a drink? I have some excellent Spanish sherry—"

"Oh no. No thank you, sir. Liquor plays strange tricks on me, I have to be very careful."

"I see."

"I got hold of some bad stuff when I was in Texas some years ago. I've never quite recovered from the experience."

"What a pity. I spent some time in Texas myself, Mr—uh, what was the name again?"

"Hargrave, sir. Lucius Hargrave."

"Yes. Interesting place, Texas. But morally beyond hope, I thought. Did you not find it so?"

"Uh, yes, quite beyond hope."

"Most disappointing. I had thought to find in that new land some fresh clean fields in which to plant the seeds of spiritual verdure. To cultivate a few souls unsullied by the weeds of sin that contaminate our old society."

"A worthy undertaking."

"Alas. It could not be."

There were a number of books on the table at Father Xavier's elbow. He now picked one of them up and leafed idly through it.

"But I will continue my search for those clean fields, Mr. Hargrave. I have traveled far, and will travel much farther yet—"

"Father Xavier—" Lucius was leaning foward in his chair. "During your time in Texas, sir, did you by any chance ever happen to, uh, practice the trade of . . . fortune-telling?"

The question elicited a blank stare. "I beg your pardon?"

"Fortune-telling. Excuse me, sir, I don't mean to insult

193

you—the fortune-teller I'm thinking of was a remarkable man. I met him on the road to Texas, and he told me startling things about myself. And the first moment I saw you, sir, I had the uncanny feeling that . . . you were he."

Father Xavier smiled, and toyed with the book in his hands. "A strange thing, Mr. Hargrave. And yet the world is full of strange things, is it not?"

"Would it be possible, sir?"

"Who can say?" Father Xavier's eyes began to wander about the room. "I have been taken for many things—a saint, a devil, a seducer, a savior, a rogue. Why not a fortune-teller? It's been a long time since I was in Texas, and as I said, my memory falls away from me now."

Lucius persisted. "Try to remember, sir. It was only—let me see—seven years ago, at the time of the Texas Revolution. This man wore a long robe and a turban, and called himself the High Priest of the Temple of Eternal Light."

"A charlatan," Father Xavier said disdainfully.

"But he had much wisdom, sir. And the strangest thing was that he seemed to know me. He knew of my family, of my past—I was not a stranger to him."

"Trickery, Mr. Hargrave. I cannot imagine why you'd still be interested in this wandering scoundrel."

"Actually, sir, I'm trying to find my father."

Again the blank stare. Lucius pressed on.

"Are you a member of the Protestant ministry, sir?"

"Not officially, no."

"Have you ever been?"

"I told you, Mr. Hargrave, my memory is becoming feeble—"

"Have you ever traveled on the Ohio River, sir? Have you ever lived in Indiana?"

"I have traveled on all the great rivers, young man, and soon I will travel on the sea. But the lands through which I've journeyed are no longer visible to me; they are obscured by clouds in my poor faltering mind. I can think only of my continuing search for the clean fields."

"But, sir, if you'd just please try to re—"

"Mr. Hargrave, has it ever occurred to you that soon all the surface of the earth will have been discovered, all the clean fields inhabited by the ungodly, and that something very precious and beautiful will be gone from human experience?"

He held up the book for Lucius's inspection. "Look here. Lately I've been reading translations of medieval literature.

Rather remote, eh? But I'm fascinated by the mystical feeling of awe in the face of the unknown that illuminates these pages."

Lucius was becoming restless. "Sir, if I may direct this conversation back—"

"Listen, Mr. Hargrave, let me read you something. This is Ordonez de Montalvo. Early sixteenth century."

Father Xavier held the book at an angle to catch the candlelight, and read:

"Know ye that on the right hand of the Indies there is an island called California, very near the Terrestrial Paradise ..."

He lowered the book, and his gaunt face was shining. "Think of it, Mr. Hargrave. An island called California! Where? Why, on the right hand of the Indies, that's where. Very near the Terrestrial Paradise. Isn't that beautiful? Sheer enchantment. This is the stuff of which legend is made, Mr. Hargrave, and legend is one of the richest sources of beauty in the world."

He closed the book and laid it on the table. The light in his face was gone, replaced by a distant haunted look.

"But soon the clean fields will all be discovered. And no longer will man be privileged to deal in legend."

Father Xavier closed his eyes and gripped his temples between his long bony fingers. "Forgive me, Mr. Hargrave. My mind is feverish. It wanders. I must beg to be excused from further conversation."

Lucius rose. He leaned over the older man.

"May I come again, sir?"

"Come if you like. It is all the same to me."

"Then if you don't mind, I'll come again tomorrow. And I'll bring something to show you. Something I think you might recognize."

Father Xavier drew a weary sigh. "Leave me now, please." With his eyes still tightly closed he waved his visitor away.

After dark the Mardi Gras street revelers disbanded to reconvene in taverns, ballrooms, and theaters. Their celebration would continue until the stroke of midnight. In Napoleon's the bar seats were beginning to fill with a motley assortment of citizenry—rivermen, panderers, thieves, vagabonds, and several painted and spangled women.

Lucius Hargrave came down the back staircase and walked rapidly through the room toward the front door. He looked neither to the right nor the left.

"Hey, Lucius, what's yer hurry?" Napoleon called from behind the bar, and one of the women turned in her seat to appraise the handsome young man.

He was gone without a word.

Two blocks away at a corner of the unlighted street he stopped, suddenly aware of footsteps behind him. He looked back warily.

"Good evenin', sar," a voice said.

"What do you want?" Lucius demanded. "Do I know you?"

It was a black man, tall and muscular, dressed in a tunic of vivid purple. His well-shaped head was clean-shaven. His chocolate brown skin shone dully and his white teeth gleamed as he nodded repeatedly, and smiled.

"Dat I cannot say, sar, but I know you. You are Captain Hargrave, from de Texas Volunteers."

Lucius stared, openmouthed. "Hell, yes, I know you! You're the fortune-teller's servant!"

"I am de servant of Fa'der Xavier, sar."

"By God!" Lucius slammed a fist into an open palm. "Then I was right! Now I'm sure."

"You visit wid Fa'der Xavier, Captain, yes? You have a nice talk?"

"He *is* the fortune-teller, isn't he?"

"Did he tell you so, sar?"

"No, damn it, he told me nothing."

"Den I can tell you not'ing, sar."

"Well, then, damn your soul, why do you follow me?"

"I want to say, Captain, you must come again. Talk to Fa'der Xavier long time. He know many t'ings, sar. Mebbe he tell you t'ings, by n' by."

"Yes, I will, I'm coming again tomorrow."

"Good, Captain, good." The black man stepped back and was quickly lost in the darkness. "Goodnight, Captain, sar," the voice said.

Lucius stood there alone for a moment, then took a deep breath and walked rapidly on across the street.

Ash Wednesday. The beginning of Lent, and a deep unnatural quiet covered the city like an invisible shroud. The day was raw and cloudy, and a damp wind swept in off the great crescent of the Mississippi and moaned softly along the cobbled streets.

Just before noon Lucius Hargrave opened the door of Napoleon's Tavern and stepped inside. He found the place quiet again, and the proprietor standing behind the counter, idly drying a tray of freshly washed glasses with a ragged towel.

"Howdy, Lucius," the fat man called out.

"Hello, Nappy." Under his arm Lucius was carrying a tattered old leather satchel. He started across the room toward the staircase in the rear.

"Where ye goin', Lucius?" Napoleon said.

"Upstairs to see Father Xavier. Is he in?"

"Too late," Napoleon said. "He's gone."

Lucius was already up to the fourth step. He stopped and stared down at the man behind the bar.

"What do you mean, *gone*?" There was a tremor in his voice.

Napoleon spread his hands in a gesture of helplessness. "Gone, that's all. What's a better word than gone, I dunno. Departed, maybe? Vanished? Disappeared? Whatever you want to call it, the bastard's gone. When I got up this mornin', I found—"

Lucius had bounded on up the stairs.

Napoleon went on wiping the glasses as he listened to the bumping of doors being flung open on the upper floor, and the sounds of frantic searching. Soon Lucius came rushing back downstairs. He slammed the leather satchel down on the counter, reached across it, and grasped Napoleon by the shoulders.

"Where is he? Where'd he go? Tell me, man, *tell me*!" He was wild-eyed and bellowing.

"Goddamnit, I was *tryin'* to tell ye!" Napoleon squealed. "When I got up this mornin' I found this note—" He was fumbling in his shirt pocket.

Lucius snatched the piece of paper as soon as it appeared, opened it, and read aloud:

"'Dear Monsieur Napoleon: This is to inform you that I am vacating my lodgings. As you know, I had intended to depart these sinful shores in the near future, but, certain compelling circumstances having suddenly arisen, I find it necessary to leave immediately. Enclosed is my final payment of rent, and I trust you will accept along with it my deepest thanks for your kind hospitality...'"

Lucius's voice trailed off. He slumped, crumpled the note in one hand, and with the other grasped the edge of the bar as if for support. From a safe distance the proprietor watched him.

"Reckon he left in the middle of the night," Napoleon said. "Kinda hate to lose 'im, in a way. He was a queer one, but he was a good tenant."

Lucius was breathing in short rapid gulps, and staring at the floor. "Gone," he breathed. "For the second time, gone before I had a chance to . . ." He was unable to continue.

"I don't reckon ye're goin' to tell me what this is all about, are ye?" the bartender asked. He waited, got no response, then went on. "Whatever it is, it's mighty damn peculiar, I'll say that. The nigger came back fer a few minutes early this mornin', actin' real sneaky, like he didn't want anybody to know he was here. Said he wanted to leave a message fer Captain Hargrave. That's you, I reckon."

"A message!" Lucius was eagerly attentive. "What did he say?"

"Said tell Captain Hargrave that, yes, Father Xavier is the fortune-teller. Didn't dare tell you the man's *real* name, he said, but he could tell you his *own* name. It's Camus. And he remembers you from when you were a baby." Napoleon shrugged. "Whatever all *that* means."

His face aglow with a strange light, Lucius took a step toward the proprietor, who backed away apprehensively.

"What else?" Lucius demanded in a hoarse voice.

"Said tell you they're goin' to California, and the ship they're takin' is the *Bold Venture*. And said you ought to forgive the Father, 'cause he don't know what he's doin'.'"

"California," Lucius echoed distantly. "An island called California . . ."

He stood there for a moment longer, his eyes roaming wildly. Then he picked up the old satchel from the counter and headed for the door.

Napoleon yelled after him: "If ye think yer goin' down to the dock to find the *Bold Venture*, jes' forget about it. The nigger said it was sailin' at nine o'clock this mornin'.'"

Lucius was gone.

"Damn fool!" Napoleon growled, and went back to work.

(8)

THE FIRST WEEK in April. After a day of indecisive cloudiness over South Bar, Indiana, a soft spring rain began in the early evening, drifting down as silently as a snowfall.

Little Justin Hargrave lay curled in his grandmother's lap, his head on her bosom, his solemn brown eyes wide open. Sarah was sitting in a rocking chair, and she held the little boy close and rocked at a slow, steady, hypnotic pace. Across the room Cyrus was sprawled in a chair in front of the fireplace, dozing. Isaac was sitting at a table where an oil lamp burned. He was bent over a newspaper, squinting at the small print.

"It says here they're thinkin' about buildin' a railroad spur from here up to Corydon," Isaac announced. "Now, wouldn't *that* be sump'm?"

"Hah! Railroads!" Cyrus scoffed. "Railroads ain't goin' to amount to a hill o' beans. Rivers are the natural highways. Always were, and always will be."

"I don't know about that," Isaac said thoughtfully.

"Well, I do," Cyrus said with finality.

Sarah pressed her cheek against Justin's hair and watched Isaac as he read. "Isaac, I really think you ought to see about having spectacles made for yourself."

"No time for that, Mama Sarah. Lucius'll be here any day now, and we'll be off. But I expect I'll be able to get spectacles in Texas, if I need 'em."

Sarah sniffed. "I doubt that. Nothing in Texas but Indians and bandits and sagebrush."

Cyrus stirred in his chair, chuckling. "Might as well give up, Isaac. Sarah don't like the idea o' Texas, and she ain't never goin' to."

"That's not true," Sarah said innocently. "I have no objection whatever to Texas or any other place. If that's where Isaac wants to live, if he feels he'll be happier there than here,

199

why, he's a grown man, he can certainly make those decisions for himself."

"You know, Mama Sarah, Texas ain't that far away," Isaac said earnestly. "It's not as if I'd be goin' away forever. I'll come to visit at least once a year, and you'll come to visit us, too." He waited. "Won't you?"

"I don't know," Sarah said crossly. "You know I'm not much for traveling."

She pulled Justin closer to her and increased the tempo of her rocking. After a moment she looked down and discovered the boy gazing up at her, wide awake.

"Why, you rascal!" she said laughingly. "I thought you were fast asleep!"

Justin pointed toward the front windows. "It's rainin'," he said.

"Yes it is. But it's a nice soft rain. Good to sleep by."

"Don't like rain," Justin murmured.

"Mustn't say that, darling. Rain's important. Makes the crops grow and the flowers bloom."

Justin was thoughtful for a moment. "Where Kissy?"

"Crissy? Oh, she, uh...she had to go away, you remember? We've talked about it several times. She asked me to take care of you for a while."

"Oh." The boy seemed satisfied. He closed his eyes and snuggled down comfortably.

"Ain't that strange, Mama Sarah?" Isaac whispered. "He only asks for Crissy, never for—"

"Shhh!" Sarah shushed him. "Let's be quiet now, he's going to sleep."

In a few minutes she arose and, moving quietly and carefully, carried the child upstairs to bed. As she came out of the bedroom and pulled the door almost closed she heard movement on the lower floor, and voices, subdued but animated. She hurried back down the stairs and found the cause of the sudden noise.

Lucius had returned.

"Well, I meant to let you know, of course," he was saying to Isaac and Cyrus, "but I wasn't sure just how soon I could—"

Then he caught sight of his mother, and went smiling to meet her.

"Hello, Mama."

She took him in an embrace, then held him at arms' length and looked him over, sober-faced. "You're soaked, Lucius. Better get out of those wet things."

He laughed as he allowed her to peel off his jacket. "Oh, it's nothing. Just a little mist. How's my boy?"

"Fine. Lively as can be. Keeps me running all day, but I love it."

Lucius started up the stairs.

"Don't wake him, please," Sarah called after him. "He just this minute fell asleep."

"Got to see my boy," Lucius said, and went on.

He was back shortly, cradling the sleeping child in his arms.

"Oh, Lucius!" Sarah reproached him.

Lucius sat down next to Sarah, hugging the boy against his chest. "He's grown, Mama. He must be an inch taller and five pounds heavier."

"Well, it's been almost six months, after all," Sarah said dryly.

"That's right, by golly," Lucius said. "He's a three-year-old now."

A wistfulness came into Sarah's eyes. "We've gotten used to having him here. Haven't we, Cyrus?"

"Certainly have," Cyrus agreed. "Jes' like havin' one of our own." He got up and stretched. "Well, think I'll say g'night now. Long day today."

On his way out of the room he paused and gazed down at the child sleeping on Lucius's shoulder. He reached down and touched the soft sandy hair.

"Funny. He looks exactly like what I always thought little Sammy woulda looked like." Then he went shuffling out of the room and up the stairs.

Moments later, Sarah too excused herself. "I'm sure you two have important plans to talk over," she said. "So I'll say good night, too."

"You don't have to run off, Mama Sarah," Isaac protested. "There's nothing secret about our plans, is there, Lucius?"

"Oh, uh, certainly not."

Sarah leaned over Lucius and lifted the sleeping child out of his arms. "Got to get this little boy back in his warm bed," she said, and went out.

Isaac shook his head, falling into a somber mood. "Ain't it sad, Lucius? You know, Cyrus never got over their losin' little Sammy."

"I know."

"That was way back—let's see—must be fifteen years ago. Sometimes Cyrus jes' sits here and watches Justin, and smiles

201

and chuckles to himself, and at the same time looks like he's ready to cry."

They were silent for a moment. Then Lucius leaned forward and gazed intently at his brother.

"Isaac, old chum, are you ready to go?"

Isaac took a deep breath. "I'm ready, Lucius. I've made a settlement with Cyrus, and I've left the woodyard. I'm jes' sittin' here waitin' for you to give me the word."

Lucius smiled. "Let's see, today's Tuesday . . ." He stroked his chin. "The word is Thursday. Early Thursday morning we go."

Isaac's jaw tightened. "All right."

"What kind of settlement did you make?"

"We figger the business is worth thirty thousand dollars. And Cyrus says half of it's mine."

"Decent of him. Of course it's worth at least fifty thousand, but—"

"I think it's fair enough. Generous, in fact."

Lucius dismissed the subject with a disinterested shrug. "Well, what the hell, that's your affair. What about Mama?"

"She hasn't put up any argument at all. I'm really surprised. I know she's not happy about it, but she's keepin' very quiet."

"Good. This is turning out to be easier than I thought."

"And what have *you* been doin' all this time, Lucius? Is everything all set?"

Lucius beamed optimism. "Old chum, you don't know how lucky you are to be in the hands of a master organizer. For the last three weeks I've been in St. Louis, buying supplies, talking with travelers, learning all about the Western trails, arranging every little detail. All you've got to do is come along."

"I don't understand, Lucius. St. Louis? Is *that* the way to Texas?"

"It's one way. The important thing is, it's the way to . . . everywhere West."

Isaac was frowning. "What's *that* got to do with anything?"

Lucius got up and began a slow pacing of the floor.

"Look here, old chum." He spoke hesitantly, choosing his words with care. "We don't want to make the mistake of jumping at the first notion that enters our heads. We might wind up missing the main chance."

Isaac watched him warily, and kept silent.

"You know, there are exciting things going on in the far West. I was amazed when I was in St. Louis. That place is

202

literally crawling with settlers getting ready to strike out for Oregon. And California! My God, you wouldn't believe the things I heard about California! They say it's practically a paradise on earth, just waiting to be discovered. In other words, there are lots of places besides Texas. Lots of opportunities. We've just got to watch out we don't pick a lesser one, and let bigger ones go by."

Lucius had stopped in front of Isaac, and was smiling down at him. Isaac did not return the smile.

"So you haven't made any arrangements in Texas," he said.

"Oh sure, I've made arrangements, all right. All I'm saying is, they can be changed. *If* we should happen to hit upon a better idea."

With misery written on his own face Isaac stared up into Lucius's. "I swear, Lucius, you jus' keep my mind in a constant turmoil. I haven't had a minute's peace since you started all this—"

Lucius laughed and clapped the other man on the shoulder. "Trust me, old chum, trust me!" Then he leaned down and continued in a tone of hard urgency, "Look here, Isaac. This is the most important thing either of us has ever done. And, by God, we're going to do it right. If we find that Texas isn't the right place, then we'll change our course, that's all. Now, I know quite a few knowledgeable people who think that California is the empire of the future. When the Golden Age arrives that's where it'll hit, they say. And when it arrives, don't you think the Hargrave brothers ought to be there to welcome it?"

Isaac was staring off into space.

"Just trust me," Lucius said gently.

"It's too late to turn back now," Isaac said bleakly.

"That's the spirit!" Lucius declared with enthusiasm. "Oh, and by the way, we won't mention any of this to Cyrus or Mama, all right? It's only speculation, after all, nothing definite. And if Mama's already used to the Texas idea, why, let's just leave it that way for the time being."

Isaac seemed to be in a mild trance. "Whatever you say, Lucius."

Lucius took hold of Isaac's shoulder and gave it a playful shake. "Come on. Let's go up to the hotel and have a few drinks, and—"

"No, Lucius." Isaac got to his feet. "It's raining out. Let's go lie in our beds and talk, like we used to. And you can tell me all about what you found out in St. Louis.

About California and all."

Lucius smiled into his brother's eyes. "Be glad to, old chum."

(9)

WEDNESDAY DAWNED CLEAR and fragrant after a night of gentle rain.

Cyrus came downstairs later than usual, found Sarah in the kitchen, and gave her a hurried peck on the cheek. "Jes' give me some coffee, Sarah. Got to rush. Overslept this mornin'."

"Sit down and eat your breakfast," Sarah said. "That woodyard won't fall down if you're twenty minutes late."

"Oh, well . . . all right." Cyrus sat down at the kitchen table.

Sarah served up two plates of scrambled eggs and poured two cups of coffee, then took a seat opposite her husband. They ate in silence for a few minutes.

"Them two were talkin' till all hours again last night," Cyrus said finally. "Did you hear 'em?"

"Yes, I heard."

"Sounded like they were plottin' somethin' fierce. Could you make out what they were sayin'?"

"I don't like to eavesdrop, Cyrus."

"Wish they'd do their plottin' in the daytime," Cyrus grumbled.

Sarah gave him a long look. "Don't worry. They'll be gone before you know it, and this house'll be quiet as a tomb."

"Well, if they're goin', I wish they'd hurry up and *go*," Cyrus declared. "This is hard on you. Hard on everybody."

"It'll be over soon," Sarah said. She stared into her coffee cup.

When Cyrus came home for his noonday meal he found the house deserted, and a note from Sarah on the kitchen table.

Dear Cyrus—

We are all off on frivolous diversions today. Isaac has taken his young nephew fishing at Sanford's Cove—you should have seen Justin jumping up and down for joy when Isaac suggested it! And Lucius has invited me to go for a ride in the country. Wasn't that nice? Food is on the stove.

Love,
Sarah

Cyrus stood scowling at the note. "What th' devil's he up to now?" he muttered.

They drove a short distance down Gilpin Street, then Lucius pulled the horse left and guided the buggy along quiet tree-shaded Old River Road.

"I thought you'd come this way," Sarah said. "But there's nothing to see at our old house. Cyrus uses it for a storage shed now. It's all boarded up."

Half a mile down the road Lucius reined to a stop and sat for a moment looking at a dismal and delapidated ruin. After a moment he gave the horse a little slap and went on.

"You're right," he said grimly. "Nothing to see."

A minute later he stopped again, in front of another house. Several small children were playing in the yard.

"Who's living in Grandpa's house?" Lucius demanded.

"A family named Caldwell. He works at the mercantile store."

Lucius frowned his disapproval. "Nobody ought to be living in Grandpa's house. It's historical, it ought to be preserved."

"Oh, it will be, Lucius. The Caldwells are taking very good care of it, and they're not permitted to change anything."

"They're strangers. They'll change it just by living in it."

"Oh pooh!" Sarah gently scoffed at him. "A house is made to be lived in."

Lucius gave her a sharp look. "You didn't feel that way about your *own* house."

"Yes I did, Lucius. But I had a choice to make. I could cling to the relics of the past, or I could get on with living in the present. I chose the second course, and I've never regretted it."

205

With a grimace of annoyance Lucius gave the horse another slap on the rump, and started off again.

"One more stop to make," he said as they reached the outskirts of town.

"I know," Sarah answered. "The cemetery."

They wandered through the old weed-grown graveyard, glancing in idle curiosity at the markers. Toward the rear of the grounds they stopped before a large headstone engraved with the single word GILPIN. Beneath it were a pair of smaller stones, side by side.

Lucius bent over one and examined the time-worn inscription. "It says here that Grandma Matilda died on October sixteenth, 1825. Strange. I was nine years old then, but I hardly remember her at all."

He moved to the second marker, and read the inscription aloud: "'Samuel Gilpin. Born June eleventh, 1764. Died February eighteenth, 1841. Founder of South Bar, Indiana.'"

Lucius turned an indignant frown on his mother. "Good Lord, Mama! Is that all? Grandpa was an important man. Is that the only written record of his life—'Founder of South Bar, Indiana'?!"

"Even that's more than he wanted, Lucius. Papa said that people who knew him didn't have to be told who he was, and people who didn't wouldn't care." She continued, as they stood together over Samuel Gilpin's grave, "He spoke of you often his last few years. He wanted so much to see you again. But in the final weeks, when his mind was going, he talked only of Oliver."

"He had faith in my father, didn't he?"

"He had faith, all right. He never gave up on Oliver, not to his last hour. It was the one great piece of foolishness of his life."

"Foolishness?" Lucius's voice had gone suddenly hard. "I don't think it was foolish at all."

Sarah turned away from him, but Lucius kept on, "I'm sorry I never really appreciated Grandpa, and I'm sorry I didn't see him again. But I promise him this—I'll keep his faith alive, as long as *I'm* alive."

Sarah closed her eyes in resignation. "All right, Lucius." She made a little gesture in another direction. "Your Uncle George is over here. Do you have a kind word for *him*?"

"No. No words at all. I hated him, but I don't anymore."

"Well, I'm glad of that. It's pointless to hate a dead man."

Lucius drew a deep breath. "Now I want to visit my sister," he said.

In a back corner of the cemetery he knelt beside a heavy oaken marker and ran the tips of his fingers over its deeply chiseled text. And as his fingers traced the words he spoke them softly, like a reverent recitation.

"'Martha/Beloved daughter of Oliver and Sarah Hargrave/Born April 28, 1817/Died July 10, 1824/One of God's gentlest creatures,/She will make heaven a happier place.'"

He looked up at his mother. "Mama, will you do me a favor, please? Let me have a minute here by myself? I won't be long."

She nodded without hesitation, and left him. He watched until she was a good distance away. Then he huddled close to the old oak slab and spoke in a voice barely above a whisper.

"I just came by to say hello, Martha. I haven't been here in a long time, I know. Now I'm leaving again, and this time I won't ever be back. But, uh . . . I wanted you to know I haven't forgotten you, and I never will. And, uh . . ." He picked idly at some weeds at his feet, and groped for words. "I wanted to tell you, if I ever have a daughter I'm going to name her Martha."

He glanced in his mother's direction. She had moved farther off, and was apparently busy inspecting other graves. Almost furtively Lucius drew something small and limp and fragile from his coat pocket and placed it carefully in the center of the little patch of sunken earth.

In a few seconds he was back at Sarah's side, taking her arm and saying, "Let's go."

They were halfway home before either spoke.

Then Lucius glanced at his mother and said, "I'm glad we had this little time together, Mama."

"So am I, Lucius. Because you're ready to go now, aren't you?"

"Yes. All ready, now."

"When?"

"Tomorrow morning. We're catching the eight o'clock steamboat."

"I see." Sarah stared rigidly ahead. After a moment she spoke again.

"You left something at Martha's grave. Would you tell me what? Or would you rather I didn't ask?"

"Oh, that's all right. I brought her something she used to like a lot."

"What's that?"

"Clover blossoms." Lucius smiled. "Kind of wilted, I'm afraid. But I guess she won't mind."

They rode the rest of the way home in silence.

(10)

TWO HOURS BEFORE DAWN, when the house lay in deep silence, Sarah sat before the glow of an oil lamp burning on the dressing table in her bedroom. She was fully dressed, and she was writing a letter.

The door opened softly and Cyrus came in. "The carriage is ready, Sarah," he said in a whisper.

"Thank you, Cyrus."

He came and stood beside her. "It's cloudin' up outside. It'll be rainin' again by mornin'."

Sarah went on writing. Cyrus looked down at her with a solemn expression on his gaunt face.

"You real sure you want to do it like this, Sarah?"

"Absolutely sure." She glanced up and gave him a firm smile. "Sit down a minute, I'm almost done."

Looking stiff and uncomfortable, Cyrus sat down on the side of the bed and waited.

Thursday, April 6th, 1843

My dear sons, Isaac and Lucius—
First I will address you, Isaac, and since you have always called me Mama, I do not hesitate to call you Son. But something strange has come between us, that I know. It makes you turn your eyes away from me when I look at you, and when I give you an affectionate hug or

kiss, it makes you stiffen and grow uncomfortable. You may not be aware of it, and I'm sure you can't realize how you hurt me, because you have never deliberately hurt anyone in your life, and never will. Whatever it is, it cannot touch my love for you, which is like a great old rock, warmed by the sun, and unmovable. I will just remember you from our happier times, and go on loving you as I always have. Remember us whose hearts go with you, and come back again. Meanwhile I will embrace you in my dreams as much as I want, and you will not turn away from me.

And Lucius. I will always cherish that private hour yesterday afternoon when we were together one last time, just the two of us. We have become strangers, haven't we? Yet there are things we share. Memories of old times, of your grandparents, of Martha—even of your father. And last evening was pleasant and tranquil and full of gentleness, and for that I am grateful, for I believe in my innermost being that it is the last remembrance I will have of you. Those things you told us of your Texas homestead, of how easy a journey it is, and how we will all visit each other frequently—they were all told out of kindness, but they do not deceive me. I know you are going to California, to the far Pacific shore, and that there will be no visiting across a distance so vast that it is the very peril of life to face it. And because I want to spare you the unpleasantness of having to watch me fight my tears during a leave-taking, I am leaving before you. Cyrus is taking me to Corydon, where I will spend a few days with my old friends Robert and Cordelia Morrow, and your Aunt Emily. By the time you are up we will be miles away. You will find plenty of food in the pantry. Eat what you want and take anything you can use on your journey. Close the door securely when you leave, and don't worry about the house. Cyrus has arranged for a man from the woodyard to stop by later and see to it.

Forgive me, dear sons, I don't mean to play tricks on you. I really believe this is the best way, surely the least painful one. I was never very much inclined toward heroism.

Give little Justin a kiss for me once in a while, Lucius. Don't let him forget. Make him remember his mother, and make him remember his beloved Crissy. And, *please, make him remember me.*

Cyrus and I wish for all three of you good health, good fortune, and happiness. My love, my prayers, and my constant thoughts go with you, and will remain with you as long as I live.

Goodbye,
Mama

Sarah placed the open letter precisely in the center of the dressing table. Then she arose and turned to her husband. On her face was a glow of serenity that came from resolution formed and crisis passed.

"I'm ready now, Cyrus," she whispered.

Cyrus was already on his feet. He went to the dresser and with a deft movement doused the lamp. Then he took his wife's hand and led her tiptoeing in the darkness along the upper hallway, down the stairs and out of the house.

(11)

FROM THE JOURNAL of Lucius Hargrave:

Once, as a very young man, I lay beneath the stars on a hillside in western Louisiana and thought that I had come to the watershed of my life. I was not only young, but exceedingly foolish; there was nothing there but a meandering path of transition. The real turning point came seven years later, and it came with a chance encounter.

I had spent some time renewing old acquaintances in Texas, and had acquired an option on some choice land. Then I returned to the States to await the coming of spring, when I could fetch my little family from Indiana and transport it to its new home. And it was then, in New Orleans, that the encounter occurred.

Mardi Gras time it was, and the streets of the city rang with

210

celebration and merriment. I sought refuge in a quiet out-of-the-way inn, and there struck up a conversation with a dignified gentleman in clerical garb. Father Xavier he was called, a strikingly handsome man whom I judged to be in his late fifties. I don't know when—perhaps once before in my life, not more—I have been so impressed by the power of a man's intellect, or moved by the purity of his character. Eager to develop this new acquaintance into a lasting friendship, I returned to the inn the next day—and found my new friend gone. The proprietor gave me a message that had been left for me by Father Xavier's black manservant, and it was this good man's message that changed the course of my life. He informed me that his master was embarking on a voyage that very day. The ship: the *Bold Venture*. Destination: California. And in an enigmatic way he further informed me that the true identity of his master was the Reverend Oliver Hargrave.

My feelings at that moment must be imagined; they cannot be described. Suffice to say that I was rendered speechless by the several aspects of the realization that struck my mind with cataclysmic force: that I had the day before looked directly into the eyes of my father, and had spoken with him; that the black man had been Camus, faithful servant to the Reverend Hargrave, and that his message to me was a sincere effort to help me in my lifelong quest; and finally, that the Reverend was the victim of a mental disorder that clouded his thoughts and destroyed all memory of the past (how else to explain the fact that though I had pointedly revealed my identity to him, it had elicited no hint of recognition?). Clearly the cruel sufferings that had been heaped upon his poor defenseless head in times gone by had done their work. His mind had taken refuge in a kind of gentle madness.

The next several weeks were feverish ones for me as I plunged into a kind of madness of my own, poring over dusty tomes in libraries, consulting with eminent physicians, trying to discover every scrap of information in existence concerning that most mysterious of subjects—the workings of the human mentality. Especially fascinating to me was that strange affliction characterized by the loss of the function of memory. Though it has been observed for hundreds of years, there seems to be no proper name for the malady. In seventeenth-century English writings there occurs the word *amnestia*, meaning oblivion, or total forgetfulness. American sources usually attribute the condition to witchcraft or some such nonsense, and dismiss it. Ignorance abounds; nobody knows anything. Discouraged—and yet in a sense heartened—I discontinued the useless investigation and returned to my normal affairs.

Back in South Bar I proposed to Isaac that we reconsider our plans to go to Texas, and think of California instead. I told him (quite truthfully) that I had heard wondrous tales of the marvelous opportunities awaiting enterprising settlers in that slumbering Mexican province, and he, always willing to trust me, readily agreed. It was all settled, then, and it remained only for my mother to make our leave-taking painful.

Poor Mama. All my life she had resented my spirit of independence, which she fancied to be neglect of her. But in the end it was she who deserted me. On the morning of our departure we arose to find her gone, and a letter of farewell on her dressing table. She had conscripted Cyrus to take her to the home of relatives, a day's journey away. Little Justin sensed that something was wrong, and wandered about whimpering for "Mama Say" as piteously as he had cried before for his "Kissy." O God! Why must the follies of men and women visit suffering upon the heads of innocent children! I swept the boy off his feet and told him we were going for a ride on a big steamboat, and his eyes danced for joy. He loved all machines of transportation, land or water, and any hurt of his could be instantly healed by taking him for a ride.

The Ohio River looked cold and somber that morning as the steamer pulled away from the South Bar landing, and Isaac's mood matched the scene perfectly. He watched the big, black, weathered letters that spelled out THACKER AND HARGRAVE, ASSOCIATES, WOOD PRODUCTS, disappear in a gray mist as we moved downriver. In his hand he clutched his Mama Sarah's farewell letter, and from time to time brushed away a tear.

But for Justin and me it was suddenly a beautiful day. We turned our eyes toward the bow of the ship, my little son and I, and it seemed to me there was a great beacon in the West, shining just for us. Surely, I thought, all the dark things were behind us now—our future would be drenched in light. I hugged my boy and ruffled his hair, and our voices rang together in laughter. What a joy it was to feel that at last my life had been set in its true direction!

I knew where my father had gone. My purpose was but to follow.

Part Four

(1)

IN THE EARLY 1840's the western edge of the nation was at the place where the Kansas River empties into the Missouri. Here, some four hundred miles upstream from St. Louis, the towns of Independence and Westport were hives of commerce, catering to the needs of tradesmen, trappers, and emigrants. Westward lay the great prairie ocean, and beyond that, the tremendous Rocky Mountains, and beyond those, lands so remote as to seem hardly more than the names of fantasy—Oregon and California.

Up along the south bank of the Kansas the trails began. For the first twenty miles the tough prairie grass was worn flat under the wheels of wagons and the hooves of horses, mules, and cattle, for this was a highway serving two streams of traffic. Then there came a fork. The old Santa Fe Trail veered southwestward, carrying trade to and from the dominions of Mexico. Another road continued on, soon to cross the Kansas and head northwestward to the Platte, there to begin a long climb toward the crest of the continent. It was known by several names that would in time be reduced to one: the Oregon Trail.

Not far from the fork was a campground called Elm Grove, a name more euphonious than accurate, there being only two scraggly old elms there, amid thickets of dogwood. But it was an ideal camping place, affording good forage for animals, plenty of water, and shelter from the almost constant wind. Here, and at other places like it, the emigrants assembled to form traveling companies. They were brave people, and daring, but they were also mostly reasonable, and they were afraid of the unknown. They sought safety in numbers; they sought guidance from that rare traveler who had been on the trails before; and because they were human beings, they sought companionship, protection from loneliness in the face of the long windswept distances ahead.

At Elm Grove on a Sunday afternoon in the middle of May, 1843, a group of seventeen wagons was gathered in an irregular semicircle facing the river. There was a quietness about the camp. A few men, some bearded, all weatherbeaten and squint-eyed, were standing in isolated knots and conversing in low voices. Their comments were brief, separated by lengthy silence. They were watching, while pretending not to watch, the only person in sight who was busy. It was a woman. She was perhaps thirty, perhaps slightly younger, with warmly beautiful lovely features. Shining auburn hair was pulled back over her ears from a middle part and tied behind her head. She was carrying an accountant's book under one arm and a small basket on the other, and she had just left one wagon and gone to the next. She knocked on the boarding beside the rear entrance. The canvas cover was pulled aside, and a male voice bade her enter. She stepped up onto the high stoop and went in.

"Good afternoon, gentlemen," the woman said gravely.

There were two men and a small boy in the cramped and untidy wagon.

"Good afternoon, ma'am," one of the men said. Smilingly he gestured the visitor to a seat, which was the top of a wooden chest. "Welcome to our little house on wheels. Hope you'll excuse the messiness."

"Oh, that's all right." The woman gathered up her long skirt and sat down. "We surely can't expect to be perfect housekeepers in wagons, can we?"

She looked toward the front of the wagon, where the second man, younger than the first, lolled as if half asleep on a narrow bunk. On the floor beside the bunk the little boy was sitting. He was staring at the woman with wide eyes.

216

When she noticed him she smiled, and in a warm voice said, "Well, hello there. What's your name?"

"Justin," the boy said in a shy, barely audible voice.

"And what's *your* name?" the man on the bunk said curtly.

The woman looked startled. "Oh, excuse me. I'm Catherine Shannon. My husband and I and our two children are in wagon number eleven. Mr. Endicott asked me if I'd act as official record-keeper, and I consented. I'm doing two things right now—taking a census of the company, and collecting votes for the election."

She opened her account book and balanced it on her knees. "Now, let's see. This is the Hargrave wagon, is that correct? Number fourteen?"

"Yes, ma'am, number fourteen," the older man said.

"And if you don't mind, I'd prefer we were known as the Hargraves rather than 'wagon number fourteen,'" said the other man. "I think names are vastly superior to numbers for identifying people."

The woman agreed readily. "You're quite right, Mr. Hargrave. The numbering system is only for the purpose of keeping track of how *many* we are, so that if anyone should turn up missing, we can—"

"I withdraw my objection, madam," the man on the bunk said with exaggerated courtliness. "You sound as if you know exactly what you're doing."

Mrs. Shannon stared at him for a few seconds before turning her attention back to her book. When she spoke again her voice was briskly official.

"Now, then. Which of you is Lucius Hargrave, candidate for the position of party leader? That's you, I take it?"

She addressed her question to the older man, who shook his head and nodded toward the man on the bunk.

"No, ma'am, that's him. My name's Isaac. We're brothers."

"Oh." The woman seemed faintly disappointed. She made a notation in her book and went on to the next question. "How many are in this wagon, please?"

"Just us two," Isaac said. "And Justin. He's Lucius's boy."

"I see." The information was written down.

"I guess you're wonderin' about Justin's mother," Isaac said. "Well, y'see Lucius was married before. So was I, for that matter. But we're divorced now, and—"

"Has *that* information been called for?" Lucius snapped.

"It certainly has not," the census-taker said firmly, and closed her book. "If you'll give me your votes for the election,

217

gentlemen, I'll trouble you no further."

"Oh, no trouble, ma'am, it's a pleasure," Isaac said hastily, and handed her two folded scraps of paper. "And I suppose you can guess who *we* voted for," he added with a grin.

She was not amused. "That's no business of mine, Mr. Hargrave." She put the pieces of paper in her basket and got up to leave.

As she climbed out of the wagon she glanced again at the little boy, and in a voice gone suddenly soft and warm, said, "G'bye, Justin."

He gave her a timid smile.

Isaac glowered at his brother. "I can't understand you, Lucius. What do you have to be so rude for?"

"She's a snooper, that's why. She's spying for the Endicott bunch."

"Aw, that's ridiculous! The Shannons are from Pennsylvania, they're not part o' that Missouri crowd at all."

"Then why did Endicott pick *her* to collect the votes?"

"Because she's an educated person, good at keepin' records and all. She's a schoolteacher, and—"

"Ha! She's a busybody." Lucius sat up and pointed a finger at Isaac. "And I'll tell you what else she is. She's a trouble-maker."

Isaac was astonished. "Why, for heaven's sake?"

"Because she's a woman. Women have no business on these Western trails. This is dangerous business. It's man's work."

"Lucius, how in the world do you expect places like Oregon and California to get populated, if men don't take women with 'em?"

Lucius answered by changing the subject. "I don't know how you expect us even to *get* to California, broke as we are."

Isaac groaned. "Oh Lord, are you goin' to start *that* again? I explained it to you a dozen times. Cyrus didn't have the money. Where was he goin' to lay his hands on fifteen thousand dollars all of a sudden? I took the two thousand he could scrape up, and he's goin' to send the rest on later, after we're—"

"Damnit, why didn't you tell me that at the time?"

"Because you'd make trouble, and I didn't want that." Isaac had a look of misery on his face. "You know how I hate trouble, Lucius."

"I know you're a coward, old chum," Lucius said grimly. "Always were, and always will be."

Justin was up and hanging on Lucius's knee. "Papa? We goin' to California?"

"Maybe so, Justin," Lucius muttered. "Maybe not."

"When we goin', Papa?"

Lucius put a hand on the boy's sandy hair. "When Mr. Walter Endicott, who's arranged a phony election to appoint himself party leader, tells us he's ready."

"Now, Lucius," Isaac said patiently. "We got no reason to think there's anything crooked about this—"

Lucius was up suddenly, lurching toward the rear exit. "I'm going for a walk," he growled.

Catherine Shannon stepped up onto the wooden crate that had been set in the center of the camp area, carefully avoiding the flock of eager masculine hands that had been extended to assist her. The people gathered round, silent and expectant. Though there were several women scattered within it, the assembly was predominantly male.

"Ladies and gentlemen," Catherine began, making an earnest attempt to enlarge her small voice, "I have made the rounds and have completed the census of our present company. I have also collected and tabulated the votes for the election of party leader, and since you're all probably more curious about the second item than about the first, I'll begin with that."

As she unfolded a sheet of paper her audience moved in a little closer.

"There are in the company twenty-nine males twenty-one years of age or older, which, as we agreed upon earlier, are the members eligible to vote. The results are as follows. Mr. Endicott, seventeen votes. Mr. Kendricks—"

Her voice was drowned out by a lusty cheer arising from one side of the gathering.

A number of people turned to a stout, grizzled, gray-haired man and clapped him exuberantly on the back and shoulder. He nodded to his supporters and smiled broadly, acknowledging victory.

As soon as she could be heard again Catherine continued, "Mr. Kendricks, seven votes. Mr. McNabb, three votes. And Mr. Hargrave, two votes. That is clearly a majority for Mr. Endicott. If there are no challenges, I hereby declare that Mr. Walter Endicott has been elected party—"

"There *is* a challenge." The statement was uttered in a low tone from the back of the crowd, but it brought instant

219

silence. Lucius Hargrave elbowed his way to the speaker's platform, his eyes fixed on Catherine Shannon.

"What is your challenge, Mr. Hargrave?" she asked in a tight voice.

"It's plain to see that the Endicotts and their friends and relatives from Missouri voted in a bloc. All right, that's their privilege. I'm just wondering how many votes they have among them."

"Eight, sir, eight." Walter Endicott supplied the answer. He came forward and stood before the challenger. "Three Endicotts, two Morrells, two Champions, one Towler. What makes you curious about that?"

"I'm curious because that's not a majority. You got a little outside help."

"So I did. Anything wrong with that?"

Lucius hesitated. "Who gave you the authority to appoint the official vote-counter? And why did you appoint Mrs. Shannon?"

A silent tension began to rise among the onlookers. Catherine Shannon glanced around wildly, as if longing to escape from her exposed position.

"I didn't 'appoint' her, Mr. Hargrave." Walter Endicott's voice remained steady and calm. "She offered, and everybody seemed to think it was a fine idea."

"I'm also wondering who her husband voted for."

Tension grew, and the silence around the two men deepened.

Then Endicott smiled, and glanced at a tall blond man standing near the wall. "Well, I couldn't answer that. Why don't you ask *him*?"

The blond man stepped forward. He was about forty, powerfully built, with pale watery blue eyes and short-cropped hair that curled tightly around his head. He scowled down at Lucius from his slightly superior height, and his jaw jutted belligerently.

"I'm Morgan Shannon, Mr. Hargrave. What's your theory? You thinkin' maybe my wife manipulated the vote count in favor of the candidate of my choice?"

"It's a possibility," Lucius allowed.

The tall man's face came a little closer.

"Well, let me tell you about my wife, Mr. Hargrave. She took on the job of countin' the votes because she's a schoolteacher, and she just loves to write things down and add 'em up. Makes her feel important. But she doesn't know, and

220

wouldn't give a damn, who I voted for."

Lucius arched a skeptical eyebrow. "That so?"

"Yes, that's so. Y'see—not that it's any of your business—I voted for John McNabb, and he didn't do much better'n you did. So if Mrs. Shannon was tryin' to favor my candidate, she didn't do a very good job of it, did she?"

A ripple of laughter moved through the crowd, and tension was relaxed on all faces except three—Lucius and Morgan Shannon continued to glare at each other, while Catherine Shannon stared tight-lipped at the piece of paper in her hand.

Abruptly Lucius lost interest in the confrontation, and turned back to Walter Endicott.

"Well, Mr. Party Leader, I have only one further question. When do we get moving out of this godforsaken place?"

"Soon's we collect some more wagons. Seventeen ain't near enough."

"Enough for what? Do we need a whole damned army?"

"We're only twenty-nine able-bodied men. We need at least fifty for safety."

Lucius looked around him. "A fine group," he said, contempt dripping from his voice. "I see nothing in these faces but fear and timidity. I wonder if there's a man here who's ready for the thing he's undertaking."

"What you see in our faces ain't fear, Mr. Hargrave," Walter Endicott said patiently. "It's just reasonable prudence."

"And that's a damn sight better than cocky ignorance," Morgan Shannon muttered. Again he drew a scattering of appreciative laughter.

Lucius took a deep breath and looked up at the woman standing rigid with discomfort on the wooden crate. "My apologies to you, Mrs. Shannon. I didn't realize the kind of handicap you've been working under."

With a cold glance at the woman's husband, Lucius turned away, forced a path through the crowd, and departed.

"You may proceed with the census report, Mrs. Shannon," Walter Endicott said.

Catherine Shannon's thoughtful eyes were following the man who was walking away from the assembly.

"Oh...yes, of course." With difficulty she pulled her attention back to her paper.

(2)

PRUDENCE WAS INDEED a virtue that Walter Endicott held in high value. Several others besides the younger Hargrave brother pressed for immediate departure, but the new party leader would not hear of it. "We must wait for more members," he declared, and wait they did. Taciturnity was another trait that Walter Endicott regarded as a useful virtue. He did not say it, lest his thoughts engender anxiety among the others, and an erosion of confidence in their elected leader—but in truth he waited and hoped for something more than mere additional bodies. He prayed for the appearance of what he knew this party perilously lacked—someone who possessed knowledge of and experience on the distant Western trails.

During the next day a few more wagons arrived to join the party. Walter Endicott scanned the new faces, briefly questioned the menfolk, and bade them all welcome—but what he was looking for was not among them. Late in the afternoon another wagon arrived. It was much smaller than the tall, lumbering vehicle that was the typical emigrant's wagon, and was drawn by a team of strong young mules rather than the more common oxen. It was occupied by one man, who made his camp at some distance from the others and displayed no interest whatever in his neighbors.

After a little while Endicott walked across the intervening space and approached the latecomer, and within a few minutes dared to feel that maybe—just maybe—his secret prayer was answered.

Baptiste Bourdeau was a French-Canadian, and a great handsome giant of a man about forty years of age. He was fussing with his mules' harness, and he paid no attention to his caller. After waiting in vain to be acknowledged, Endicott cleared his throat and spoke.

"Afternoon. My name's Endicott, and I'm the leader o' that party camped over yonder."

The stranger gave him a cursory glance and a slight nod. "Baptiste Bourdeau, at your service," he said, and went on with what he was doing.

Endicott stepped a little closer. "Well now, Baptist, you don't look to me like a man who's makin' his first trip across. Am I right?"

The other man grimaced. "Bap*teeste*, Bap*teeste*," he corrected with strained patience. "I am not a Baptist, Monsieur." Then, noticing the look of consternation on his visitor's face, he threw back his massive head and laughed heartily. "But I excuse you. I am used to the funny way you Americans talk."

Endicott stuck grimly to his subject. "You been on the trails before, I take it?"

"Been across eight times," Bourdeau said pleasantly. "Eight times in ten years. Fort Hall to St. Louis, delivering furs. Getting a little tired of it, tell you the truth." His own accent was a curious mixture of French, American Frontier, and Indian.

Endicott was encouraged. "Well, then, Baptiste—" this time he made a clumsy but careful effort to pronounce the name right— "we wouldn't mind havin' you act as our guide, if you'd be interested. That is, if we can afford you."

Baptiste produced a disdainful shrug. "Wouldn't take the job for money. You can travel along with me if you like, but I won't be tied down by no business arrangement."

"Fine," Endicott said eagerly. "We got twenty-two wagons now, countin' yours. How many you think we need before it's safe to go?"

The Canadian paused and pretended to give this serious thought. "I figure the ideal number is one. Any more than that just makes trouble." He spoke in a solemn tone, but the merry glint in his eye betrayed a teasing mood.

Endicott was taken aback, and took a moment to recover. "Well, uh . . . when d'ya think we can start, then?"

The reply was brisk and unhesitating. "I'm leaving at first light in the morning. Anybody who wants to come with me can." Baptiste turned his back on the other man and resumed

223

his work, and it was clear that he regarded the subject of little interest, and the conversation closed.

When Endicott returned to his own camp he was met by a small knot of men who had been watching his interview with the solitary stranger from a distance. He stopped before them and delivered an announcement in a gruff authoritarian tone.

"Fella over there by the name o' Baptiste Bourdeau, knows the trails like the back of his hand. He's goin' to be our guide. We discussed the matter of when to leave, and agreed we'd go tomorrow morning. So have your wagons ready to move out at sunup."

When he heard a soft derisive chuckle in the group, he knew where it had come from even before he shot a fierce-eyed glare at Lucius Hargrave.

(3)

CATHERINE SHANNON—*The Diary of her Family's Journey with the Endicott Party of Emigrants to Oregon/ California, 1843:*

Monday, May 15th

It is very late. Morgan and the children are fast asleep, and so should I be, too, for at dawn tomorrow the great journey begins. Abby and Byron were so excited tonight they could hardly bear to close their eyes, so anxious were they for morning to come. Poor dears, they think it is going to be nothing but a grand lark. I am as excited as they, although I know there are dangers awaiting us, too, and unimaginable hardships. But I do not speak of such things. I pray their optimism will

*prove truer than my apprehensiveness. As for Morgan,
he cares not for danger, nor for hardship, nor for what
anyone else is thinking, so all is well in his mind. He
sleeps the sleep of the untroubled.*

*I am not in the habit of keeping a diary, and do not
intend to become addicted to that pastime. But
tomorrow begins what will likely be the greatest
adventure of my mostly unadventurous life, and I do
believe I will be glad years hence if I take the trouble to
record my impressions of it as best I can.*

*This is called the Endicott Party because a gentle-
man named Walter Endicott has been elected leader,
and I am referring to its destination as Oregon/
California because some of us are bound for the one
place, some for the other. There is endless quarreling
among the men over the question of which is the
preferred destination. In truth there is endless quarreling over everything imaginable, be it important or
trivial.*

*One of the most quarrelsome of our members, it
pains me to have to say, is my Morgan. His robust Irish
temper is at a constant simmer, ready to boil over at any
moment. Another is a man named Lucius Hargrave,
who is headed for California with his older brother,
Isaac. Both the brothers are divorced men, it seems (the
one named Lucius has an adorable little boy), and I
suppose they are trying to forget their unhappy
marriages by seeking to start afresh in a new land. (How
fortunate are the males of the species, who can thus run
away from their failures! Where is the woman who can
enjoy such a privilege?)*

*The Hargrave brothers are so unalike that it is hard to
believe they are related. Isaac is the friendliest, gentlest,
most sweet-natured man I've ever met, while Lucius
seems to look upon all the members of the human race
as his aggregate enemy. He scowls, he glares, he eyes
everyone with undisguised suspicion. He is insanely
restless, as if driven by some fiery demon that will give
him no peace.*

*For some strange reason this man Lucius Hargrave
disturbs me deeply. I could predict with certainty that
such a one and my Morgan would immediately
clash—and so they did. Mr. Hargrave was one of the
unsuccessful candidates for the position of party leader,*

and his defeat so stung him that he was moved to cast
the most offensive aspersions on everyone concerned,
even me, who had innocently counted the votes and
announced the results. Then Morgan came to my
defense—so I thought. But instead of defending me, he
contented himself by suggesting that I was quite
incapable of caring who won the election, anyway! I
should be angry with him, but, poor man, he is so
insensitive he honestly doesn't know when he is
insulting me or heaping mortification upon my head.
Ah, well, such has been my lot since I was a bride of
nineteen. I should be used to it by now, after ten years.
But for all our sakes I just hope that Morgan and this
Lucius Hargrave will have the good sense to keep well
apart from one another.

So tomorrow we start. Mr. Endicott has been putting
off our departure, hoping for the arrival of more
members. Around noon today four more wagons joined
us, bringing the total to twenty-one. Still not enough,
Mr. Endicott said, and the younger Mr. Hargrave
cursed at the delay. This afternoon another wagon
arrived containing a man traveling alone. Evidently he
prefers it that way, for he took pains to make his camp
at a good distance from ours. However, Mr. Endicott
went to talk to him, and came back shortly with the
news that the man, whose name is Baptiste Bourdeau, is
vastly experienced at traveling the trails, and that he
had consented to act as our guide. Mr. Bourdeau is
French-Canadian, it seems, and is what is generally
known as a voyageur, one of those professional
travelers who deal mainly in the fur trade.

Mr. Endicott's last bit of news created considerable
excitement among us: after conferring with Mr.
Bourdeau on the question, he said, he had concluded
that we will get under way tomorrow morning.

So it is settled. In a few hours we start, and instead of
going to sleep as I should I am sitting here madly
scribbling, because, like the children, I'm almost too
excited to close my eyes. It is funny now to think how
fiercely I resisted the idea of picking up and going to
Oregon—but Morgan always has his way, of course,
and now that we are really doing it I think I'm more
enthusiastic about it than he.

As official census-taker I should mention that the

Endicott party in its final form numbers 59: 39 men, 9 women, 11 children and young people under twenty-one. The oldest member is Mrs. Irene Steelman, aged seventy-four. The youngest (and liveliest) is three-year-old Justin Hargrave.

I must stop this now and force myself to sleep, because it's up at 4 o'clock in the morning for all of us. I think, dear diary, that my future entries here will become somewhat infrequent. There will be neither time nor energy for such frivolity, I fear.

Farewell, then, restfulness and ease. I know not when I shall ever make your pleasant acquaintance again.

(4)

THE FIRST DAY was a good one. Under clear skies and a playful breeze the caravan crawled up and down undulating swells of earth, fording creeks in the bottoms, and on the crests flaunting its fresh white wagon covers like sails on a rolling sea. Spirits were soaring, and excitement rang in shouts and laughter and the camaraderie of high adventure.

The evening camp was made near a stand of cottonwoods lining one of the small streams that flowed northward into the Kansas. After dark a central campfire became a focal point for an evening of socializing and entertainment, and amateur talent blossomed. There were carnival songs that titillated not with their musical quality but with the rough ribaldry of the words. There were dancing and gymnastics, the strumming of banjos and guitars, and the throb of makeshift percussion instruments. Then came a more orderly musical program, when Catherine Shannon organized a chorus and conducted, with schoolteacherish authority, as twenty-odd untrained but ardent voices lifted folk songs to the night sky. Standing in the front row and singing loudest of all, his eyes fixed in rapt fascination on the conductor, was Isaac Hargrave.

Two men were absent from the scene of festivity. One was Baptiste Bourdeau. He sat with his back resting against a wheel of his wagon and sipped a dark fluid from a tin cup. When he heard a footfall near him he looked up curiously into the face of the second non-socializer.

"May I join you?" Lucius Hargrave asked politely.

Baptiste gestured toward a coffeepot near the coals of his tiny fire. "Take a cup there, and pour yourself some coffee."

"Thanks." Lucius followed the instructions, then sat down.

Baptiste grinned when he saw his guest take a sip and immediately grimace.

"What the matter? You don't like?"

"It's fine," Lucius said hastily. "Delicious."

"I mix it with ground acorns. Gives it nourishment."

"Good idea," Lucius mumbled. He gave the liquid in his cup a dubious look.

"Learned it from the Indians," Baptiste said. "Lots of things got nourishment that white men don't ever think of eating."

"You have a lot of Indian friends, do you?"

"I got Indian friends. My wife's part Shoshone, from up near Fort Hall. Good woman, too. Shoshone are good Indians. Best there is."

"That's interesting." Lucius moved a little closer. "Look, Baptiste, I don't know whether you know me or not. My name's—"

"I know you. Lucius Hargrave. You got a brother named Isaac and a little boy named Justin."

"That's right."

"Fine little fellow, Justin. I see 'im running round, making friends all over the place."

Lucius smiled fondly. "Yes. He has that gift, hasn't he?"

"Your brother's busy trying to make a friend, too."

Lucius's eyebrows went up. "How so?"

"He's got a fire in his heart for Mrs. Shannon."

"Oh. You've noticed that, have you?"

"I got eyes, Lucius. I agreed to be guide for this party, and already I'm looking for signs o' trouble. There's lots o' problems with an emigrant party—bad food, bad water, no forage for the animals, sickness, wagons breaking down, thieving Indians—but the worst trouble of all is women."

228

A grim look came over Lucius's face. "I knew it," he muttered.

"Not women." Baptiste corrected himself. "Men fighting over women. Soon's the fighting breaks out, I'm quitting."

"Well, you don't have to worry about Isaac," Lucius said. "He's harmless. He wouldn't fight with anybody over anything."

Baptiste was plainly skeptical. "When a man starts admiring another man's wife, Lucius, that's trouble getting ready to happen."

Lucius dismissed the notion with a chuckle. "There *are* some arguments going on, though. That's what I wanted to ask you about."

"Such as what?"

"The question of mules versus oxen, for instance. Endicott says oxen are best, I say mules, and I notice *you* have mules."

"That don't necessarily make you right. Mules are faster, but harder to take care of. Oxen are slow but sure, and they can find something to eat in a place where a mule would starve. Mules are best for experts, oxen are best for amateurs."

"Oh." Lucius seemed momentarily crestfallen. "Then there's the question of how many hours a day we should travel. I say we should go from dawn to dark, cover as much ground as possible. Endicott wants to rest for two hours in the early afternoon, and not travel at all on Sundays. Seems to me that's a waste of time."

"Well, it depends. Stopping to rest is a fine idea if you can afford it, and taking a day off once a week is nice even if you ain't religious, which I ain't. But—the important thing is to cover the ground. The worst mistake a party can make is to dawdle. That can be fatal."

"I agree," Lucius declared knowingly.

"What else?" Baptiste was warming to the discussion.

"Well, the question of Oregon versus California. Some swear by the one, some by the other. What's your opinion?"

"Depends on what you're after. Now, me, I travel to and from Oregon because that's where my business is. I take furs from the trappers down to the buyers in St. Louis."

Baptiste gave his listener a tap on the knee. "They talk about the famous explorers. Lewis, Clark, Zeb Pike, and all them. But they're nothing but Johnny-come-latelies. The real explorers, the people who laid out the trails in the first place, were the fur trappers, and they got most of their information from the Indians."

"I see."

"You take this fellow Fremont. Lieutenant John Charles Fremont, U.S. Army Topographical Engineers. Went out last year an' found out the easiest way across the Rockies is up over South Pass. Big discovery! Trappers have been using that route for thirty years. Now Fremont's a hero. An' what qualified him to be an explorer? His wife's the daughter of a U.S. senator, that's what."

"That's the way of the world, isn't it?" Lucius said musingly.

"Now Fremont's in Westport, busy outfitting his second expedition. This year, he says, he aims to find the best route to California. Hell, why don't he just ask us traders, *we'd* tell 'im. But he don't want to *know* it, he just wants to *discover* it. Fame's what he's after, not knowledge."

Lucius gave a sympathetic nod. "I know that arrogant military type. Sounds just like my old commanding officer in the Texas Volunteers."

He took a large gulp of the thick brown coffee-acorn brew, and shuddered faintly. "Now about this California-Oregon argument—"

"That ain't nothing to argue about," Baptiste said impatiently. "You can't go wrong. Good land for the taking, either place. You got to deal with the religious orders whichever way you go. California's in the hands of the Mexican Catholics, and Oregon's being taken over by your Protestant missionaries. Fellow named Marcus Whitman's leading a big pack of faithful to Oregon this year. Several thousand, I understand. Biggest party that's ever been on the trail." Baptiste chuckled. "Pity the poor Indians. They're going to be Christians whether they like it or not."

Lucius was pondering. "But, Oregon or California ... there comes a place where the trail divides, doesn't it? And people have to make a decision?"

"That's right. Soon after Fort Hall."

"Endicott and his gang are all for Oregon, and I know he's going to persuade most everybody that way. There won't be many of us for California."

"Probably not."

Lucius leaned toward the other man. "Baptiste ... I want you to lead us to California. We'll hire you, and pay you well."

230

"Why don't you just take the easy solution and go to Oregon with the rest of 'em?"

"California's my destination. Right now it's about the only thing in the world I'm absolutely sure about."

Baptiste smiled. "I like you, Lucius. You got determination."

"Will you do it, Baptiste?"

"You know what else I like about you? You're the first American I've met who pronounces my name right."

"I lived in New Orleans for years. I know quite a bit of French."

"That's good. I know very little, myself."

"Join forces with me, Baptiste. Let's be partners." Lucius held out his hand.

In his turn Baptiste became thoughtful. "I don't commit myself to be nobody's partner, Lucius. But I'll be your friend." He shook hands.

"Will you lead us to California?" Lucius persisted.

Baptiste laughed as he reached for the coffeepot and poured more brew for himself and his guest. "I tell you something, Lucius. I got a little house at Fort Hall. Nothing but a hut, but it's home. And my little wife's sitting there waiting for me. Her name's Mali, and she's the sweetest little lady in the world. That little hut's *my* destination. And that's the one thing in the world *I'm* sure about."

They were silent for a while, sipping their brew. The sounds of laughter and music around the main campfire a hundred yards away were reaching a peak. Lucius glanced in that direction, then turned a quizzical look on his companion.

"Tell me one more thing, Baptiste. The other day you said the ideal number in a party is one, and I don't doubt a man of your experience could travel fastest by himself. So how come you agreed to encumber yourself with this rabble?"

"How come? 'Cause I'm soft-hearted." Baptiste leaned his head back against the spokes of the wagon wheel and smiled gently. "You hear that celebrating over there? They're happy, they're having fun. They think they're on a holiday. They're fools, Lucius. They don't know that one-quarter of 'em won't make it across. They'll wind up in shallow graves on the plains, and their bodies'll be dug up and eaten by wolves."

Silence descended again, as Lucius stared solemnly into the dying coals of the little fire. Baptiste watched him.

"It ain't no holiday, Lucius. But you stick close to me, you

231

an' your brother and your little boy. I'll look after you."

"Thanks." Lucius reached into some secret place and brought forth a flask. "You like good whiskey, Baptiste? Thought maybe we could have a little drink together. Celebrate our partnership."

Baptiste's hearty laugh rang out. "Ah, Lucius my friend! You're a determined fellow, all right. I predict you'll become a rich man in California."

He emptied his coffee cup on the ground and held it out for whiskey.

(5)

CATHERINE SHANNON'S Diary:

Saturday, May 20th

This afternoon we reached the place where the crossing of the Kansas River will be made, and since tomorrow is the Sabbath, Mr. Endicott says we will rest here and cross on Monday. After five days we have covered a little over eighty miles, and everyone seems pleased with our progress so far. Everyone except the younger Mr. Hargrave. He is bound for California, and appears to be determined to reach his destination by next week at the latest.

He is really quite a handsome man, and some of the others say he is extremely well-spoken when he is not angry about something, which is seldom, it seems. How regrettable it is that such an attractive young man should be cursed with such an unfortunate disposition. He has never spoken another word to me since our encounter at the time of the election, and he needn't ever. I find his brother Mr. Isaac quite pleasant and sociable, on the other hand, and am perfectly content to leave it at that.

* * *

Little Justin Hargrave ran yelping with excitement across the field near the wagon camp, followed by another boy somewhat older than he, who in turn was followed by a pigtailed girl slightly older still. Lucius stood next to the Hargrave wagon, watching. There was a deep scowl on his face, and when Justin came near, his father shouted at him.

"Justin! Do you have to make such an infernal racket?"

The boy could spare but the briefest moment. "Byron chasin' me, Papa!" he yelled. "And Abby chasin' Byron!" Then he was off again, with the other children close at his heels.

Isaac came up to the wagon, carrying a bag of wet clothing. "Whew! Quite a walk from the river." He began to pull out wet garments and drape them over a rope stretched between the wagon and a small tree. "Washin' and dryin', washin' and dryin'," he sighed. "I'm beginnin' to appreciate how hard women work."

Lucius was still watching the children racing across the field. "Can't control that boy," he grumbled. "He's absolutely running wild."

"Leave him alone," Isaac said. "You ought to be glad he's found some playmates. Nice ones too. Those are the Shannon children, Abby and Byron."

"Oh my God! You mean Justin's taken up with the schoolmarm too?"

"Catherine Shannon's just about the nicest lady you could ever hope to meet, Lucius. Her husband's not very sociable, but Catherine's real friendly. I've been talkin' to her quite a bit."

"Catherine, eh? It's not Mrs. Shannon anymore, now it's Catherine. I guess she *is* pretty friendly."

Isaac looked pained. "Now, what does *that* mean? You know, it wouldn't hurt you a bit if you'd try to be a little more—"

Lucius snorted loudly and stalked away.

Catherine Shannon was sitting on a small canvas stool, reading. She glanced up when she sensed someone near her, and her eyes widened in surprise.

"Oh—Mr. Hargrave! Good afternoon."

Lucius gave her a stiff little bow. "I saw your husband down by the river, so I thought I'd stop by. I wanted to say a few words in private, if you'll permit."

"Oh, of course." Catherine looked around as if in

233

confusion. "I'm sorry I can't offer you a comfortable chair—"

"That's all right, I can only stay a minute." Lucius glanced at the book in the woman's hand. "You read a lot?"

"As much as I have time for." She offered the book for Lucius's inspection. "This is *The Adventures of Captain Bonneville*, by Washington Irving. I try to read whatever I can find about the West. After all, I suppose I'm going to be living there."

Lucius inspected the book absently. "Mrs. Shannon, I wanted to say first—I hope my little boy Justin hasn't been making a pest of himself."

"Oh, good heavens no, Mr. Hargrave! He's the most delightful child. *So* bright! My children both adore him, and so do I."

"He's very noisy, I'm afraid. And it *is* Sunday, after all."

Catherine laughed gently. "Oh pshaw! I can't believe the Lord objects to the sound of children at play, on Sunday or any other day."

Lucius leafed idly through the book, frowning. "Then, I, uh . . . I wanted to say, in regard to my brother Isaac . . . I hope *he* hasn't been bothering you."

Catherine gazed at her visitor with grave eyes. "Not in the least. Your brother and I have become quite good friends. And I'm glad, because I think we need all the friends we can get. Don't you?"

Lucius studied the book for a moment longer, then handed it back. "Well, fine. That's all I wanted to know."

"Would you like to borrow this book, Mr. Hargrave? You're welcome to."

"I have no time for it, thank you," Lucius said bluntly. "Good afternoon, Mrs. Shannon."

He repeated his bow and abruptly departed, and Catherine sat looking after him with a mystified look on her face.

CATHERINE SHANNON'S Diary:

Monday, May 22nd

Today we were ferried across the Kansas, our first traversing of a major stream, and Mr. Bourdeau warns us that we must not expect all crossings to be as easy as this one. The ferry, consisting of two rickety-looking rafts, is operated by a pair of very ancient Indians with whom Mr. Bourdeau conversed for well over an hour before an agreement was finally reached and their services contracted for. The price was 100 lbs. of flour, 50 lbs. of bacon, and a jug of whiskey. Everybody contributed.

All these complex negotiations took up a great part of the day, but despite that we managed to get about ten miles beyond the river before camping for the night, so our progress remains good.

Friday, May 26th

We are moving into country somewhat more arid than we have seen before, and are beginning to be troubled by a lack of both wood and good water. Mr. Bourdeau laughs and tells us this is nothing compared to what we'll face later. On Wednesday we forded a good-sized river called the Vermillion, and now move northwestward. According to Mr. Bourdeau we will soon face a larger stream, called the Big Blue. I don't know which I most dread—the rivers, or the arid and treeless distances between.

We have been averaging about 12 miles a day this week. Mr. Bourdeau says that after the Big Blue we will not face another major crossing until we reach the South Platte. In that stretch, he says, we must move along faster.

I cannot quite decide how I feel about Mr. Bourdeau. He is a rough, unlettered man, and a tiny bit frightening, but at the same time he seems to carry about him an air of tremendous strength of character, which is comforting. Morgan doesn't like him at all, but then Morgan doesn't like very many people. I find it curious that Mr. Bourdeau has apparently chosen for his boon companion none other than Mr. Lucius Hargrave.

I also continue to be baffled by Mr. Hargrave. Underneath that forbidding exterior I do seem to detect some good qualities, but he is a deeply troubled man, and would be impossible to get to know, I fear.

Tuesday, May 30th

Last night we arrived at the banks of the Big Blue, and, it being a formidable stream, Mr. Bourdeau says we will

235

have to construct rafts and float our wagons and animals across.

The children love this idea, but I must confess I do not. Little Justin Hargrave, who spends more time at our wagon than he does at his own, is wildly excited about it, and says we are going to build a steamboat. He is such a joy, that child, and yet such a sadness. Sometimes I notice him looking at me with big solemn eyes, as if longing for the mother that is so tragically missing from his life. Or if not that one, then some other, no matter who. My heart aches for him.

The elderly Mrs. Steelman lies sick tonight. Our medical officer, Doc Lund (who is a nice man but unfortunately no real physician), is looking after her. We all hope she will be better tomorrow.

Wednesday, May 31st

The men have worked all day constructing rafts under Mr. Bourdeau's direction. First a pair of cottonwood trees are felled, and their trunks stripped and hollowed out to form what are called "dugouts." These are placed parallel to each other ten feet apart and secured by a framework, and suddenly a primitive raft exists. The work is nearly done, and the plan is that we will cross tomorrow.

Mrs. Steelman is worse. She has a raging fever and is babbling out of her head, thinks she is back in her old home in Ohio. We pray for her.

The crossing of the Big Blue was delayed a few hours, for in the night the sick woman died. A shallow grave was dug on a hillside overlooking the river, and there the company gathered and looked with mute sympathy on the son and daughter-in-law of the deceased, and listened while several brief eulogies were spoken. Then John McNabb from Illinois, elderly himself and possessed of a voice as solemn as doom, held a Bible in his hands and intoned: "The Lord giveth, and the Lord taketh away," and a crude coffin fashioned of freshly hewn cottonwood was lowered into the ground.

Lucius Hargrave, standing toward the rear with Baptiste Bourdeau, leaned toward his companion and whispered, "The grave's awful shallow, isn't it?"

"Don't make no difference," Baptiste murmured. "The

wolves'll get her, no matter what."

Lucius scanned the hillside, bright with spring greenery and splashed with wildflowers, then looked over his shoulder at the long empty horizon to the west. A soft wind moaned across the distance. Lucius shuddered.

That night Catherine Shannon recorded the name of Irene Steelman, aged 74, from Ohio, as the first fatality of the Endicott Party of Emigrants to Oregon/California, 1843.

(6)

CATHERINE SHANNON'S Diary:

Saturday, June 3rd

Until now the weather has been uncommonly benign. Day after day Mr. Bourdeau has studied the sky and sniffed at the air, and said, "Where are the storms?" Late this afternoon his question was answered. A towering black menace arose before us, and gusts of chill wind tore at the canvas flaps of our wagons. Then a darkness almost as dense as night enveloped us, and down came a hellish torrent that lashed at us with violence and fury. Worse than the rain were the thunderbolts, crackling and crashing so close as to cause grown men to turn pale, women to tremble, and children to wail in terror.

And afterward Mr. Bourdeau laughs and says, "That was nothing. Wait till you see a bad storm. A man can't survive no matter what he does. If he stands up the lightning gets him, and if he lies down he drowns."

I am beginning to like Mr. Bourdeau. He is extremely handsome, with dark curly hair streaked with gray and a face so perfect I can imagine it carved in marble by

237

Michelangelo. He is a cheerful man, and his jests make hardships easier to bear, but he can also be very commanding. Tonight he informed us that we are moving too slowly, and tomorrow we will not lay by, even though it be Sunday. There was an outcry of protest, whereupon Mr. Bourdeau said, with an air of imperturbable calm, "Tomorrow I'm going on. You can come or stay, as you like."

No more was said. It is perfectly certain that tomorrow we go on.

Wednesday, June 7th

Today we saw our first genuine wild Indians. We have seen numerous Indians, of course, but mostly domesticated varieties, often dressed up like a white man and aping his ways. Our visitors today were proud fierce-eyed warriors, handsome and hideous in their warpaint and headdresses and mounted bareback on their horses. They came filing past our wagons during our midday rest period, gazed silently at us as we did at them, and went on their way.

"Pawnees," Mr. Bourdeau said. "We're in Pawnee country now. You see them funny-looking things dangling at their horses' flanks?"

We had, and had wondered about them.

"Scalps," Mr. Bourdeau informed us.

I felt a cold chill, and I do not believe I was the only one who did.

"They're probably on their way to wipe out some Arapaho village," Mr. Bourdeau said pleasantly.

"But why should they do that?" I cried in horror, and I suppose I must have sounded a bit foolish, for Mr. Bourdeau laughed.

"Because the Arapahos probably wiped out one of their villages last month," he said. He went on to explain more about the redmen.

"They're brave and powerful people, and their warriors are among the finest fighting men in the world. If they had the gumption and good sense to band together, they could stop the white man in his tracks. But they can't and they won't. Too busy fighting among themselves."

Mr. Bourdeau assured us that the danger from Indian

238

attack is grossly exaggerated. "The western Indians won't turn mean till it dawns on 'em that the white man intends to take over the whole damn continent. By the time they figure that out, it'll be too late."

Despite his assurances I know I shall sleep less soundly from now on, and will pray that our nighttime sentries remain alert.

Saturday, June 10th

Another storm this afternoon, the fourth in a week. We had just stopped for the day and were preparing camp when it descended upon us with the most amazing suddenness, and the children came tumbling into the wagon just as the first large drops began to fall. With them came Justin Hargrave. As Byron snuggled against me on one side little Justin did the same on the other, as easily and casually as if he were my own.

"Send him off," Morgan grumbled. "He's got no business being here."

I hadn't the heart to do it. Then there was Justin's father out in the rain looking for him, and I knew I had been foolish. I called to Mr. Hargrave and explained that the boy was with us and safe. And the glowering look he gave me fairly made me blanch! How could such a fierce man have such a sweet child?

We have been traveling along a stream called the Little Blue, and making better progress, so Mr. Bourdeau is somewhat mollified. He says that tomorrow we can lay by, not so much in deference to the Sabbath as to the fact that a number of wagons are in dire need of repairs. Morgan and several others plan to saddle horses in the afternoon and go looking for buffalo, and I think I shall take the children for a ramble along a pretty little creek that's close by here. The earth is radiant with lupin, verbena, wild indigo, and larkspur, and along the streams grow sweetbriar and honeysuckle. I regret that we can so seldom pause to enjoy nature's beauty.

Abigail Shannon wanted to grow up to be a schoolteacher like her mother, and at seven she was ready to begin. She sat on a grassy knoll beneath a little tree and called her class to order. Her class consisted of her brother, Byron, just past five, and

Justin Hargrave, three and a half.

Abby held up a wooden disc on which was printed the capital letter A. "All right, Byron first," she said. "What's this, Byron?"

"A," Byron said.

Abby held up another disc. "Justin's turn. What's this, Justin?"

"B," Justin chirped.

"Very good," Abby held up the next disc. "Byron?"

The larger boy jammed his chin into his palm and squinted and frowned, and thought mightily. His classmate watched him out of the corner of his eye.

"C," Justin whispered.

"C!" Byron shouted.

"No fair, Justin," the pigtailed teacher scolded. "He's got to learn to do it by himself."

Catherine came down out of the wagon and smiled at the open-air class. "Shall we go for a walk to the creek, children?"

There was a chorus of hurrahs as teacher and pupils scrambled up, lessons forgotten.

"Put away the letters, Abby, we mustn't lose them," Catherine told the girl.

"Can Justin come with us, Mama?" Byron asked.

Catherine glanced at the smallest child and found him looking at her wide-eyed and expectant. She hesitated.

"Well, I'd be happy for him to come, but . . . I have the feeling his father disapproves of his spending so much time with us."

Abby bent over the little boy and gave him urgent instructions. "Justin, run ask your father if you can go to the creek with us."

Justin flew. In less than a minute he came back across the camping area, trailed by his Uncle Isaac.

"Afternoon, ma'am," Isaac said to Catherine. "Nice day, isn't it?"

"It is indeed, Mr. Hargrave. And we were wondering if Justin's father would permit him to come with us to the creek."

"Well, Lucius is off somewhere with Baptiste. But I say it's all right.

"That's fine, then. Thank you. We won't be gone too long."

Isaac was gazing earnestly at the woman. "You, uh . . . goin' alone, ma'am?"

240

"Well...the children and I. Would you like to come with us?"

Isaac's face lit up with a bright smile. "Oh, why, thank you, ma'am. I think that'd be real pleasant. If you think it'd be all right."

"Why shouldn't it be all right?" There was a trace of defiance in Catherine's voice.

They sat in the sunshine on a small outcropping of rock and watched the barefoot children splash in the shallow water of a willow-shaded brook.

"Justin's such a nice child," Catherine said pensively.

Isaac nodded agreement. "I couldn't think any more of him if he was my own."

"I remember you told me his mother was from Louisiana. What kind of person was she?"

"Can't say. Never really knew her very well. She was a real fancy lady, but I guess she wasn't a very good mother. Mighty pretty, though. Almost as pretty as you." Having delivered this opinion, Isaac blushed violently.

"Thank you, sir," Catherine said easily, and became immediately thoughtful again. "Your brother—he's a strange sort of man, I think."

"Oh no, he's not. People just don't seem to understand Lucius very well. But he's a fine fellow, really. And very smart. A lot smarter than me."

"So he's the smart one in the family?"

"He sure is."

"Well, you're the nice one."

Isaac giggled like a small boy, and blushed again.

Morgan Shannon was standing over them before they were aware of his presence.

"Catherine, what are you doing?" he said sharply.

Isaac scrambled to his feet.

"Oh, Morgan, back so soon?" Catherine said. "Did you find any buffalo?"

"What are you doing?" he repeated grimly.

Catherine stared up at her husband. "Why, I'm conversing with Mr. Hargrave while the children play at the creek."

"I see. Very cozy."

Catherine got up. "What do you mean *cozy*?" She spoke softly though her eyes blazed.

Isaac tried to interject a soothing tone. "Oh, we were just

241

havin' a neighborly chat, Morgan. Didn't think there was any harm in—"

"There's nothing wrong with neighborliness, Mr. Hargrave. In camp. But when a married woman goes off on a long private walk with a man who's not her husband, that's something else altogether."

Isaac became abjectly humble. "Well, please don't blame your wife, it's my fault. She was bringin' the children down here to play, and I just sort of invited myself to come along—"

"That's not true," Catherine said vehemently. Her eyes were fixed on Morgan. "It was *my* idea."

Isaac squirmed with discomfort. "Well, I, uh, I guess I'll get back to camp. Shall I take Justin with me, ma'am?"

"Let him play, Mr. Hargrave," Catherine said. "I'll send him home later."

"Yes, ma'am." With a quick nod in Morgan's direction Isaac hurried away.

Catherine's stiff-backed stance radiated anger. "That was the rudest thing I've ever seen you do," she said. Her voice was husky and shaking.

"Catherine—" Morgan searched for words. "This is a very peculiar kind of society we're living in right now. All these people cramped together day after day after day, nothing but boredom to look forward to for months—"

"Exactly!" Catherine snapped. "But I'm to be censured because I have a little innocent conversation with a perfect gentleman while you go off chasing buffalo!"

"I think you don't understand the problem, Catherine."

"Apparently I don't."

"You've got to bear in mind that a lot of these men—the Hargrave brothers, for instance—have no access to women at all. And it's going to be that way for a long time. That's not a natural condition. It's not healthy. It can drive a man to thoughts and actions he wouldn't ordinarily—"

"Oh, Morgan, don't be vile!" With an exasperated toss of her head Catherine turned away from him.

He stepped closer to her, and stared for a moment at her shining mane of auburn hair. "I'm a proud man, Catherine. One of the things I'm proud of is the fact that the most beautiful woman I've ever known is my wife. But I also know that other men look at her with desire. And I think, under these conditions, you ought to keep yourself more aloof."

She turned and gave him a hard look. "You're a proud man,

you say? You're a *jealous* man, Morgan."

"Yes. I am that too."

"You hardly ever look at me with desire yourself. I wonder why you're so concerned that somebody else might."

He glowered at her, grim-faced, and made no answer. She shrugged and turned away from him again, and picked idly at a flowering bush nearby.

"Did you find any buffalo?" she asked.

"Not a damned trace," he said angrily.

"Mr. Bourdeau said you wouldn't, didn't he?"

"He was guessing. That didn't make it a fact."

"I don't know why you insist on disbelieving what Mr. Bourdeau says. He hasn't been wrong about a single thing yet."

"He's an arrogant ass. And he spends too damn much time with that other arrogant ass, the younger Hargrave. Those two sit around half the night every night, drinking and talking. My God, what do they find to talk about?"

"About how desirable I am, maybe," Catherine suggested in sly innocence.

Morgan's eyes flashed dangerously. "That's not funny, Catherine!"

"Morgan, I should think you'd be grateful that it's a harmless lamb like Isaac Hargrave who comes around to visit me, rather than his brother."

"What?"

"Mr. Isaac could visit a married lady every day for a year, and nothing would happen. But if Mr. *Lucius* ever looked at her with interest, her husband would have ample cause to worry."

Morgan stared at his wife in openmouthed astonishment.

"Worry about what, Mama?" Abby asked. She had come up from the creek.

"Nothing, darling. I was just making a little joke with your father. But I forgot, your father doesn't like jokes."

"Abby, go fetch Byron and tell the Hargrave boy to run along home now," Morgan commanded.

"Aw, Papa!" Abby protested.

"It's getting late," Morgan said curtly. "Go on, Abby, do as I tell you."

With a little pout on her face Abby turned and started back to the creek.

Catherine sighed. "Well, I guess that's enough pleasure for one week," she murmured.

* * *

Late in the night another storm threatened. Thunder rumbled across the black sky, and lightning etched the landscape in unreal illumination.

Justin Hargrave tossed in his sleep, came awake, and sat up, whimpering. Instantly he felt a comforting hand on his shoulder.

"Don't be afraid, Justin," Lucius said gently. "Nothing will hurt you. Come lie next to me, and go back to sleep."

Justin snuggled against the man's body for warmth and comfort.

Soon the storm threat abated. The lightning flashed less frequently, and the thunder drifted off toward some distant place. But Justin continued to lie awake, staring into the darkness.

"Papa?" he whispered.

"Hmm?"

"Can I go and live with Abby and Byron?"

"What?!"

"I wanna live with Abby and Byron."

"What on earth do you want to do *that* for?"

Justin took several seconds to formulate a thoughtful answer. "'Cause they have a nice mama."

Lucius snorted. "That's plain foolishness, Justin. You have a nice father and a nice uncle, so be satisfied."

Justin was quiet for a moment. Then: "Papa?"

"Yes?"

"When we get to California, will I have a mama?"

"Well, I...I don't know, I suppose you will. Someday, probably."

There was another short silence.

"Papa?"

"Shhh. Go to sleep now, no more talking. You'll disturb Uncle Isaac. He's dreaming sweet dreams, and that's what you and I ought to be doing."

The boy snuggled down and closed his eyes. Lucius put an arm around him and pulled him closer.

"We'll drift off to dreamland now," Lucius whispered. "We'll all sleep peacefully, and dream of a beautiful lady named Catherine..."

(7)

CATHERINE SHANNON'S Diary:

Tuesday, June 13th

We have now left the Little Blue, and, following a northwest course, have struck out for the Platte, two days' journey away. Around us now is a desolate country in which there is virtually no water except stagnant pools, covered with slime. Mr. Bourdeau and Doc Lund both warn us that such water is to be avoided, or if it must be used, it should first be boiled. I was careful to fill all our available containers before leaving the Little Blue, but I'm afraid many of our members neglected to take that precaution.

Thursday, June 15th

Today we arrived at the Platte River, and from here our course turns directly west. Mr. Bourdeau tells us we are now about 320 miles from Elm Grove, which in 30 days of travel amounts to an average of slightly less than 11 miles a day. Our guide is displeased, and says that rate must be vastly improved.

The early French explorers called this river the Platte (meaning flat), and indeed it does seem to spread out all over the countryside, "a mile wide and an inch deep," as it has been so aptly described.

Last night there was an Indian raid on our camp, and several horses were stolen. Mr. Bryce and Mr. Amberson, who were on guard duty, reported they heard strange noises among the animals, went to investigate, and discovered the intruders at work. Our men fired their weapons, but apparently made no hits. (Secretly I was glad of this, but don't dare voice such an unpopular attitude.)

Mr. Bourdeau says that when we judge the redmen we should not forget that they have only a dim idea of private property. The words "mine" and "thine" do not exist in their language. Mr. Bourdeau's tolerant remarks are greeted with scorn by our men. Mr. Endicott has ordered our nighttime watched doubled, and I fear our party begins to resemble some sort of grim military establishment.

Monday, June 19th

Today we passed the Forks of the Platte, and, since the trail follows the North Platte, it will be necessary to ford the south branch. This, Mr. Bourdeau says, is best done another 35 miles upstream.

The weather has turned intensely hot. For some days the sun has blazed down unmercifully, without obstruction of clouds, and those who were complaining of the storms a week or two ago are now praying for their return.

We see buffalo frequently now, and almost every day a hunting party leaves the wagon train to go in quest of fresh meat. They are not expert in that sort of hunting, and seldom succeed—except when Mr. Bourdeau goes along.

As I gaze day after day over this immense prairie around us I cannot help but liken it in my mind to the ocean, which I saw once as a child. Great wide swells roll away to the horizon, and the grassy surface lies sometimes in dead calm, sometimes tossing like waves under the wind. Off in the distance there is often a dark slow-moving mass of shaggy buffalo, like nothing so much as a school of whales, lolling and blowing in the water. And to complete the picture, gulls flap and soar here a thousand miles from the real ocean, as though they too are taken in by the similarity.

Then I think of us feeble human beings crawling like insects across this awful expanse. Our creaky wagons are nowhere near as worthy of this voyage as the little

246

ships of Christopher Columbus were worthy of his. It makes one wonder. Are we all mad?

I am sorry to say there is an outbreak of sickness in the camp tonight. Mr. Cameron, Mr. McNabb, and Mr. Ives all lie abed with fever. Another awful dread looms before us, one we hardly dare speak of.

A small knot of men stood at the muddy edge of the river and inspected the turgid current. The far side was several hundred yards away, and visible only as the place where the prairie grass began again, as if growing out of the water.

"Good," Baptiste Bourdeau said. "Water's not too high. We can roll across."

"The wagons can roll across *that?*" Walter Endicott said incredulously.

"Sure. Ain't no more'n three feet in the deepest part, and a firm sandy bottom. We'll take all the animals across except an eight-yoke team of mules, then pull the wagons over one at a time. Easy."

Morgan Shannon measured the distance across the South Fork of the Platte with a dubious eye. "Don't look any better here than it did two days back. How come we had to come way up here to cross?"

"Because it *is* better, whether you think so or not," Baptiste said casually. He pointed to the muddy ground. "See them ruts? Wagons have crossed here before, and they'll cross here again. Why? Because it's the best place."

Another man spoke up. "Three feet deep, y'say? That's still enough water to soak the insides of our wagons."

"Your wagons ought to be caulked," Baptiste said. "If you got any caulking, use it. If not, tack buffalo robes under the wagons and around the sides."

"What if we ain't got no caulkin', nor buffalo robes neither?"

Baptiste shrugged. "Then you ought not to be here."

A stout man in his middle fifties confronted the guide. "We need some layover time, Bourdeau. We got sick people in this party."

"We ain't got time to wait around for sick people to die or get well, Doc. They can do either one on the road just as well as in camp."

"But, damnit, man, they need rest. Old Mr. Ives especially, and Ed Cameron ain't much better." Doc Lund lowered his voice slightly. "Can't be sure, but I think it might be cholera."

247

There was a sudden stillness.

"Well, keep 'em isolated as best you can," Baptiste said. "But we got to keep movin'."

Doc Lund appealed to the nominal leader of the group. "What do *you* say, Walt?"

Walter Endicott sighed and gave his answer in a resigned voice. "I reckon we keep movin'."

Baptiste had already started to walk away without waiting to hear.

CATHERINE SHANNON'S Diary:

Saturday, June 24th

I have not written in this diary for several terrible days, but must force myself to do so now, if I am to continue keeping it.

At sunset today we stood at the edge of the plateau that lies between the river forks, and looked down upon the North Platte, shining far below us. At our feet was a steep canyon that drops three hundred feet to the river, and at the bottom of which is a little paradise of greenery—a grassy meadow decorated with wildflowers, and lovely little brooks gurgling among the first trees we have seen in what seems like weeks. It was a sight that should have brought cheers from all of us, but despondency now hangs over this company like a dark cloud, and will not be dispelled.

It began with the death of Mr. Ives on the day we forded the South Fork. He was a quiet man who kept much to himself, and I felt that he was suddenly gone from us before we knew him. He was given a burial of most un-Christian dispatch, at the insistence of Mr. Bourdeau. Our guide is becoming quite ruthless in his determination to brook no delay—though in the end I suppose we shall see he was right, as usual.

Then during the business of fording the South Platte, the wagon of the Haverhill family was capsized, much of their cargo lost, and Mr. Haverhill severely injured. It was a dreadful accident, made more dreadful by the fact that it was unnecessary, Mr. Haverhill having deliberately disregarded Mr. Bourdeau's warnings against riding inside the wagons during the crossing.

The next day we were twice confronted by the

248

specter of death. By morning Mr. Haverhill had succumbed to his injuries, and around noon Mr. Cameron died after lying for three days in the grip of what Doc Lunk believes may have been cholera. Again the quick funerals, with sheet-wrapped corpses dropped into shallow graves and covered, then left in their eternal solitude. It is almost too horrible to contemplate.

And the sickness grows. Mr. McNabb is somewhat better, but the elder Mr. Judson is down, as is Mr. Endicott's sixteen-year-old nephew Johnny Towler, and pretty Ellen Ayers, also very young, and but recently married.

Terror walks in our midst, and we are helpless.

Tomorrow we make the difficult and dangerous descent to the bottom of the canyon, to enjoy a brief respite from our trials in the cool greenery of the oasis, a place Mr. Bourdeau calls Ash Hollow. Pray heaven we may regain some of our strength there for the trials that still lie ahead.

(8)

ON SUNDAY MORNING they buried Ellen Ayers on the windswept heights above the river. Her young husband Frank stood silent and vacant-eyed with his father and mother while the simple eulogy was spoken. Walter Endicott conducted the ceremony, haltingly and mumbling, since the man who usually took that duty, John McNabb, himself lay fighting for life. Ellen Ayers had been a timid soft-spoken young woman, afraid of the journey from Kentucky that had been thrust upon her, but willingly trusting in those with whom her destiny was bound up. She was twenty years old when she died, a bride of four months, and two months pregnant. Frank Ayers waited until the service was over and the others had gone, then bowed his head and wept until his father took him by the arm and led him away.

Most of the day was then spent in the torturous descent to Ash Hollow, an operation involving a makeshift windlass from which spliced lengths of rope were fed out two hundred yards to lower each wagon foot by grinding foot down the steep canyon chute to the haven below. By late afternoon the job was finished. The animals were pastured in the meadow, and the people drank deeply of the cool clear brook and collapsed in exhaustion and gratitude under the trees.

Yet there was one task more. Wiley Judson of Tennessee was dead. He was a widower in his fifties, traveling with his two grown sons, both unmarried. The company had no further stamina for funerals, so Walter Endicott appointed a burial detail of four men—Alvin Champion, Boyd Kendricks, Thomas Steelman, and Isaac Hargrave—who took their spades and their shrouded burden and went at dusk with the two grieving Judson brothers to a remote area of the canyon, and were back in half an hour, tight-lipped, silent and bone-weary.

That night a company meeting was called. Men whose faces were drawn and haggard stared at each other like strangers across the flickering light of the campfire while Walter Endicott began the proceedings.

"I know you're all tired, an' would a lot rather be takin' your rest than standin' here, but I think it's time we took stock of our situation. We've had some hard luck, an' I've been hearin' some rumblin' and grumblin' like maybe you ain't satisfied with me bein' leader. Well, I want to say I'm willin' to step down th' minute th' majority of you says so. This here's a democratic organization, an' I'd like to keep it that way. So if there's anybody wants to put forth a motion for another election, I'll second it. Do I hear a motion?"

Endicott scanned the circle of listeners and found them all silent. His eyes came to rest on Lucius Hargrave.

"Lucius? Thought maybe I'd hear it from you."

Lucius shrugged. "Not me, Walt. Not interested."

"Well now, that's kind o' surprisin'.'"

"Shall I tell you why?"

"All right, tell me why."

"Because it doesn't make a damn bit of difference who we call party leader. That's just a game we're playing. We all know who the real leader of this party is, don't we? It's

Baptiste Bourdeau. Because he's the only one who knows where the hell we are and where the hell we're going. So why don't we all admit that, and stop playing these silly games?"

Endicott listened to this with thoughtful attention. "Well, move for a new election, then. Place Bourdeau's name in nomination. If he's elected I'll step down cheerfully."

"And I'd do it cheerfully," Lucius said. "But Baptiste won't."

All eyes turned toward the big Canadian. He was standing with arms folded, smoking a pipe, and gazing tranquilly into the fire.

"That so, Bourdeau?" Endicott said.

"It sure is."

"Why?"

"Because I don't want to get tangled up with this party."

"You're already tangled up with it, seems to me."

"No I ain't. I didn't come asking to be your guide, you asked me. You offered to pay me, and I said no. I want to be able to ride away from you anytime I feel like it. And the way things are going I'll feel like it before long."

"Go ahead," said a surly voice from the crowd, and attention was immediately riveted on Morgan Shannon. "We were on our way before you came along, and we can damned well go on without you."

With barely a glance at Shannon, Baptiste continued his conversation with Endicott. "*That's* what you better take a vote on. Let these people decide once and for all if they want me to guide 'em or not. If it's no, I'll be on my way before sunup tomorrow. If it's yes, I'll go along with you just as long as you agree to do things my way, and not a day longer."

"Fair enough," Walter Endicott said, and addressed the group at large. "Everybody in favor o' Mr. Bourdeau here continuin' on as our guide and, uh, unofficial leader . . . say aye."

There was a lusty chorus of ayes, led by Lucius Hargrave.

"Everybody against, say no."

Morgan Shannon and two or three others said no.

"It ain't even close," Endicott said. He gave Baptiste a solemn nod, and in it was a clear relinquishing of authority. "It's all yours, Bourdeau."

Baptiste knocked the ashes out of his pipe. "In that case I got a few words to say." He stepped to the front of the assembly and turned toward it, a grim look on his face.

"This party is in pretty bad shape, and it's going to get

251

worse before it gets better. We've covered about four hundred and sixty-five miles in forty days. That's less than twelve miles a day average, and that ain't near good enough. Now we got the sickness. There've been deaths, and there'll be more, you might as well get used to the idea. Now, what we're going to do is, we're going to take a couple of wagons and turn them into sick quarters, keep the sick people separate. And there ain't going to be no more delays, for sick people or dead ones. The burial details will have to do their work quick, then ride like hell to catch up."

"Uh, Baptiste—" It was Everett Towler, Walter Endicott's brother-in-law. "My boy Johnny's pretty bad off tonight. I was hopin' we could stay here a day or two, where it's cool, and plenty o' water—"

"We'll stay through tomorrow, Mr. Towler. One day. And we'll wish Johnny well, same as we do everybody. But Tuesday we go on, no matter what."

"Seems to me you're holdin' human life mighty cheap," Morgan Shannon blurted.

This time Baptiste turned to face him squarely. "Mr. Shannon, you got a pretty wife and two pretty children. I reckon you'd like to keep 'em healthy, wouldn't you? Well, the sooner you get 'em to high altitude the better chance they got to get away from this sickness. And even then, if we don't speed it up they'll be stranded in the mountains for the winter, and how'd you like that?"

For an answer Morgan could produce only a stony stare. Baptiste turned back to the assembly.

"Men, you got about a hundred and fifty more miles to Fort Laramie, and then you'll barely be a third o' the way. Then it's almost six hundred miles on to Fort Hall, and from there over eight hundred more to the Willamette Valley. If you ain't to Fort Hall by late August you won't make it through the mountains before snowfall. And if you don't do that, there won't be nobody left to take care o' the burials, or complain about a hard-hearted guide, or anything else."

A deep uneasy silence followed.

"All right," Walter Endicott said finally. "Anybody got anything else to say?"

There was no response. One man coughed nervously, and another kicked at a pebble at his feet.

"Well, I guess that's all, then," Endicott said. "Meetin' adjourned."

* * *

As the crowd dispersed, Lucius put a hand on Baptiste's shoulder. "Come on over to the wagon for a drink."

Baptiste was both astonished and delighted. "You mean you still got whiskey?"

Lucius held up two fingers. "One last nip. Then from here on it's dry weather."

They stopped abruptly in the near-darkness, finding someone in their path. It was Catherine Shannon.

"Good evening, gentlemen," she said gravely. "How are you feeling, Mr. Hargrave? Well, I hope?"

"Quite well, thank you."

"And Mr. Isaac, and Justin? I haven't seen either of them in a day or two."

"They're fine. In view of the sickness, we're trying to discourage too much social contact."

"Yes. You're right, I'm sure." She shifted her attention to the guide. "I heard what my husband said to you, Mr. Bourdeau. And what you said to him. I just want you to know I understand what you're trying to do for us, and I appreciate it deeply. I do hope you'll stay with this party. We need you. Be patient with us, please?"

Baptiste gave her a gallant little bow. "If everybody was as nice as you, madame, there would be no need for patience."

"I do hope, one day—" Catherine's hands were twisting at each other, and her eyes wandered vaguely— "in the future, when we're all settled somewhere in a normal life, we can meet again, and remember the terrible times we went through together and . . . and be friends."

The men exchanged silent looks.

"We join you in that hope, ma'am," Lucius said quietly.

"Well . . . good night, gentlemen." She turned away and was immediately lost in the shadows.

Lucius and Baptiste walked on.

"This is a bad thing for somebody like her," Baptiste said thoughtfully. "She's a beautiful lady. She wants a genteel life."

"And *I*," Lucius murmured. "I want a beautiful lady."

Baptiste chuckled. "Don't worry, you'll find one in California. A gorgeous Spanish señorita. Dark-eyed, hot-blooded—and rich." He gave Lucius a playful nudge in the ribs.

Lucius did not respond in kind. "It's a long way to California," he said. There was a bleakness in his voice.

(9)

Sunday, July 2nd

This past week has been a continuing nightmare. The sickness continues to hound us. Four more deaths in as many days. With dull mechanical fingers I record the names and numbers in my book, and let it go at that. My senses are completely numbed. The worst one was Johnny Towler, the second day out of Ash Hollow. He was a strong lad, so young and vigorous and full of life. I will never forget how he entertained us with marvelous feats of gymnastics, those first evenings by the campfire so long ago, when we were carefree. He fought the dark demon for five valiant days and nights before being conquered.

So we have lost ten, and our original number of 59 has been reduced to 49. It seems heartless, almost inhuman, that we go on each time as if nothing had happened, but what else can we do? Everywhere I look I see faces twisted with grief, and I can think of nothing to say. My thoughts are with my own. I keep looking at Morgan and Abby and Byron, and if one of them so much as sighs my heart stops, for fear the sickness has struck. With what is left of my attention I watch little Justin Hargrave, for whom I have developed an affection that I could not dare admit openly.

Dear Lord, forgive me. I have become selfish, I can't help it. No matter what else happens, spare us, I beg you. Spare the ones I love.

Well—I must force myself to think of other things.

For some days we have been passing spectacular rock formations that stand like giant sentinels guarding the river. One such, which Mr. Bourdeau says is called Chimney Rock, is an unbelievable needle-like spire rising several hundred feet into the air. It was in our sight for two whole days. How unfortunate it is that the horrors benumbing our minds make it impossible for us to give the scenic marvels around us their due appreciation.

Wednesday, July 5th

Praise be, we have gone three days without a death! Mr. McNabb was the first to be stricken and then recover, and now he is joined by several others. Can it be that the scourge has run its course? Mr. Bourdeau is optimistic. He has been saying all along that our best defense against the sickness lies in gaining higher elevation, and it is true, we have been climbing constantly and are now experiencing clear bracing daytime air and chilly nights. We hope and pray the horror is over.

Tonight we camp on the banks of the little Laramie River. Several miles farther on is the fort of the same name. We stop here rather than going closer, Mr. Bourdeau says, because the plain surrounding the fort is teeming with Sioux, who camp there during the spring and summer. Indeed we have been seeing a goodly number of Sioux the past few days. Mr. Bourdeau tells us they are the mightiest and most feared of warriors, and they certainly look it. Their lodges around the fort number in the hundreds, according to our informative guide, and the prevailing mood is carnival, day and night. We would not be harmed if we camped near them, Mr. Bourdeau says, but neither would we know a moment's peace.

(Goodness, I must have used the expression "Mr. Bourdeau says" a thousand times in this diary! But, truly, he is the fountainhead of all our knowledge. I cannot imagine how any of us could have survived thus far without the cool imperturbable competence of Baptiste Bourdeau.)

Tomorrow we will visit Fort Laramie, purchase such

255

supplies as may be available, and do a little discreet peeking at the Indians.

Thursday, July 6th

The visit to Fort Laramie was an experience I shall never forget.

First, the Indians. There appeared to be thousands, a veritable city of conical-shaped lodges dotting the plain around the fort. These structures are quite large, about twenty feet tall it seems, made of a framework of poles fastened near the top and covered with buffalo hides. At first I was thoroughly frightened, but when I saw women stirring cooking pots and children laughing and playing for all the world like our own, I stopped feeling frightened and started feeling foolish instead.

I think the character of the Western Indians has been grossly misrepresented. Though they do indeed appear stern and fearsome in their headdresses and warpaint, when they are taking their leisure they seem relaxed and sociable, even fun-loving. The young people are much given to games, music, and dancing, and the older men to endless sitting around puffing on long-stemmed pipes.

(Mr. Bourdeau tells us he once listened to a group of Sioux chieftains meditating upon the question: what are the most valuable things in life? After solemn and lengthy deliberations the warriors completed their list: first, whiskey; second, tobacco; third, horses; fourth, guns; and fifth, women. Our menfolk were of course hugely amused by this story, which Mr. Bourdeau swears is true.)

The Sioux women are quite beautiful, with copper-toned complexions and perfect evenness of features. Dress is impressive, of men and women alike. Their blouses and pantaloons and moccasins are all made of the finest soft buckskin, decorated with colored beads. All in all an exceptionally handsome people.

Viola Kendricks and I were the only women to accompany the twenty or so men from our company who went to the fort, and soon we two had broken away and were strolling about as comfortably as if we were back in our familiar hometowns.

Laramie is really not so much a fort as a trading post,

256

the principal one of the American Fur Company. It is a large square enclosure of high walls made of sun-dried brick called adobe. Around the perimeter on the inside are trading rooms, repair shops, offices, and living quarters. The courtyard is as crowded with humanity as any marketplace, since the fort gates are left open during the daylight hours and the Indians are permitted to enter and wander about freely, which they do in great numbers.

There are other emigrants here, too, many of whom are camped near us, and some of them are talking about turning around and going back home, having become too discouraged by the hardships of the journey to continue. I hope their discouragement won't infect the more dispirited members of our own party.

Then there are a number of other traders, men like our Mr. Bourdeau, most of whom are obviously old friends of his. I saw him greeting a pair of them with shouts and backslaps, and introducing them to his constant companion, Lucius Hargrave. A little later Viola Kendricks and I noticed this foursome sitting at a table in a little earthen-floored shed that appeared to serve as a tavern. They were partaking of some no doubt highly potent beverage out of a jug, and were becoming quite boisterous in their goodfellowship. Mr. Bourdeau called to us to come and join them—a joking invitation he clearly did not expect us to accept—and Mr. Hargrave, well along in inebriation, smiled at me and winked. I'm afraid I blushed like a schoolgirl. Then there were Morgan and Boyd Kendricks come to fetch us, scolding us for wandering into an area not meant for ladies, and leading us away like naughty children.

Ah, me. Sometimes I marvel at the injustice of the world. A man is allowed to deviate freely from the standards of dignified conduct and still retain the status of gentleman, but to be a lady a woman must be fully qualified for sainthood at all times.

Finally, back to camp, very tired, but exhilarated after the most diverting two hours we have spent since leaving Missouri. When we got there we found all the children of our company with Mr. Isaac Hargrave. He was seated on the ground surrounded by seven or eight young listeners, including his nephew Justin and our two, and he was keeping them all enthralled with some

257

long tale about the days of his early childhood, when he used to accompany his father, a traveling minister, up and down the Ohio River on a keelboat.

He is a dear man, Mr. Isaac. A bit awkward in some ways, perhaps, and certainly not handsome, but so kind and generous and considerate that it is wondrous to behold. Some of our male members (including Morgan, I am ashamed to say) consider him less than manly, laugh at him behind his back, and call him Aunt Nellie. Little do they know that there is many a woman in this world who would count herself blessed to have one so gentle and sweet-natured for a husband.

Well, now the holiday is over. At dawn tomorrow we face the trail again, and the long grueling days, each one so much like the one before that it would be impossible to keep track of them were it not for my diary.

But we are replenished. We have our second wind, and the sickness seems to have left us as mysteriously as it came. For the first time since we embarked on this journey I am beginning to feel a faint stirring of confidence.

(10)

Fort Laramie, Indian Territory
July 6th, 1843

Dear Mama Sarah,

I just have one piece of paper and a few minites time to write this, because there are some people at this place who I have met who are going back to "the States" as they say, so I asked them would they carry a letter back for me, and they said they would, so I must hurry and get it writen because they are moving out in a little wile.

I hope you will be glad to here that we are all three well, because I know that you have not herd a word since we left Misouri way back in early May, which seems like a million years ago now. But we are doing fine. Oh there has been a little sickness amung the company we are traveling with, but nothing serious, so dont let it wory you even the tinyest bit.

I hope you are well, and Cyrus to, I want you to know I miss you very much. And I want to say agin I dont hold it aganst you the way you left without saying goodby to us, because I know exackly how you must have felt and all, and I dont blame you at all because I know its not because you dont love us. Lucius was resentfull but I have talked to him about it sevral times and now I think he understands and isnt resentfull any more.

You mustnt think anything about it because Lucius isnt writing anything on this letter, you see, he has gone to Fort Laramie today and so isnt here and I must hand this to the people without delay. Lucius is going to by a sadle horse at the fort, it is a big trading post, you see, Lucius thinks he needs a horse, really it is Baptiste Bourdeaus idea. Baptiste is a french man trader from Canada who is our gide, he says we are fools to be without sadle horses, so Lucius is going to by one. Baptiste and Lucius are good frends and Lucius does whatever Baptiste says do and maybe that is a good thing, to, because Baptiste is a good man and a very smart one.

Once agin I want to asure Cyrus that he is not to wory about the finantial agreement we made. When we get to California and all setled and I need a little extra money I will let Cyrus know and he can maybe send a little. But if I dont need it I wont ask for it and we can let it go at that, I would a lot rather feel like I still have a little part of Thacker and Hargrave, Associates than to have any amount of money, anyway.

You will be glad to know that Justin is not only helthy and happy but is the most popular person in this company, he is the yungest member and everybody sort of thinks of him as a pet. There is one lady in particuler who has just about adopted him, he is good frends with her children, you see, and she treets him like

259

one of her own. Her name is Catherine Shannon and she
is just about the most sweet and good and beutiful lady I
have ever seen, besides you. I wonder if Lucius and I
will ever find anybody that good to marry. It is a
lonesome life, Mama Sarah.

I must close now. I will write agin as soon as I have
another chance to send a letter. We all love you and miss
you, and hope it will not be to long before we can be
together agin, somehow.

Justin has been saving up some very special kisses to
send you, and here they are. X X X X X X X X

Your fathful son,
Isaac

(11)

FROM THE JOURNAL of Lucius Hargrave:

The long view is the only merciful one. Someday that period
of the great overland journey, the supreme physical trial of
my life, will have receded into the past and my mind will wash
over with forgetfulness the dirt, the discomfort, the stifling
heat and numbing cold, the monotony of plain food badly
cooked, the thousand subtle stresses between strangers living
too close (but at the same time suffering the ache of
loneliness). Most of all there was the almost unbearable
tedium of days following days into some awful infinity, and as
I contemplated the far-off western horizon I wondered if its
marching ranges of mountains beyond silent mountains
would ever end. Eventually all those memories will fade, and
the wild cry of pain crashing against the inside of my skull will
be reduced to a whimper.

Then at last the beauty will be remembered: the vast miraculous plains, ageless as the sea; the curved and shining rivers; the flower fields ringed with dark green forest; the sparkle of sun on water across a windy distance and on snowfields clinging to a jagged cluster of peaks fifty miles away; and the incredible sky, sometimes dark and glowering in storm-fury, sometimes blinding in bright blueness, always there and close enough to touch.

It was an adventure in sheer madness, that is undeniable, and how any of us survived remains a mystery. We were a motley collection of humanity from a wide assortment of places, some homespun farmers and their families, but mostly men who either had no families or had left them behind for a variety of reasons, admirable or otherwise—all outrageously ignorant, utterly unprepared for the rigors that lay before us, trusting blindly in some kindly Providence to protect us from our own recklessness. Among the most pathetic of all were the Hargrave brothers—one a blissful innocent who at thirty-four had hardly ever been fifty miles from home, the other wordly-wise at twenty-seven and ordinarily well endowed with bravado, but who was soon staring moodily into the endless western distance and feeling an unnerving dread. It was I who had instigated the undertaking, and now I held in my hands the very lives of my brother and my little son.

I might have admitted defeat and turned back after a week had it not been for one solitary individual among us. Baptiste Bourdeau was a fur trader, a seasoned expert in Western travel, and a genuinely free-minded man unhampered by the clutter of civilized life. We recognized each other as brothers-in-spirit, and soon, seeing that it was the one hope of success for our ragged little band, I persuaded my fellow travelers to acknowledge him as our guide and leader (to replace an incompetent who should never have held the post in the first place).

So we toiled westward, enduring hardships that most of us had never before dreamed of, having neither the time nor the strength to mourn those poor souls left behind one by one in lonely graves in the wasteland. Lying exhausted but sleepless in our bunks at night, we listened to the wind and the howling of wolves somewhere in the distance, and wondered where our own graves would be dug.

Though torturously long, the trail was as direct as it could be, adhering unwaveringly to the one immutable principle that governed it: water is life. It followed the rivers, and the places of greatest danger were those points where a switch had to be made, where one life-giving stream had to be abandoned and the next reached for across sun-scorched desolation. We faced these trials fearfully, but with hope and determination breathed into our tormented bodies by our calm and confident guide, Baptiste Bourdeau.

But beyond the external ordeal I was confronted with a private complication of a totally unexpected nature: both my brother and my son proceeded to fall madly in love. The object of their yearnings was a woman named Catherine Shannon, a young schoolteacher from Pennsylvania who was going to Oregon with her husband and two children. My own poor motherless child could be excused for this folly, but Isaac's behavior appalled me. He spent every available moment with this married woman, shamelessly seeking her out and regaling her at length with the story of his life and the entire history of his family. Meanwhile her husband, Morgan, a surly Irishman with a naturally belligerent disposition, became increasingly ill-tempered as whisperings began about his beautiful wife and that sly fellow, Isaac Hargrave.

She *was* a beautiful woman—secretly I acknowledged it, knowing that in her presence my own pulse quickened dangerously. But I also had the good sense to know that under the circumstances such feelings were a deadly menace, and I prudently avoided her as much as possible. Earnestly I counseled Isaac to follow my example, but in his simplemindedness he was unable to see my point.

All I could do was pray that somehow disaster might be avoided, and that eventually we would reach our destination alive—and as we left the sickly lowlands behind at last and crept doggedly up the stupendous slope of the Rockies toward the Continental Divide, it began to seem like a reasonable hope. At our backs lay the old lands and the failed past; ahead lay the new world of the Pacific shore, and the glorious future. For the first time in many weeks I dared to admit a faint stirring of optimism again in my breast.

Had I listened to the voice of the mountain wind I might have heard the whispering of a wondrous tale—a tale I can never really tell—of strange events lying in wait for us that were to bring profound and permanent changes to the lives of the three adventurous Hargraves, father, son, and brother. But had I heard such whisperings I could only have bowed my head in helplessness, and gone on.

We are all the slaves of Blind Chance, and can never break our shackles.

(12)

CATHERINE SHANNON'S Diary:

Saturday, July 22nd

The scenery is becoming quite spectacular as we climb slowly higher and higher into the mountains. Tonight we camp close by an enormous mass of stone that is called Rock Independence, supposedly so named because it was discovered on the Fourth of July, sometime during the 1820's. It is a third of a mile long and well over a hundred feet high, and its sides are mutilated by numerous man-made inscriptions, some apparently very old. A few of the more immature members of the party insisted on adding their names to the permanent collection, and one or two saw fit to add vulgarities as well. Most distasteful.

Our numbers have fluctuated somewhat, and so, unfortunately, has the quality of our society. Having lost a number of members at Fort Laramie when the widow Haverhill and her children and the Amberson family decided to join a party going back to the States, we have since gained several others, all unattached males. One of them, a man named Otis Bruner, is decidedly roughneck in character, and spends much time looking at us few women and grinning most lewdly. I tell myself I must try to get used to things like that. I will probably be one of the rare women in a predominantly male society for years to come. As for the strength of our company, it now stands at 44, and I fervently hope it will be reduced no more.

This morning we said goodbye forever to the Platte River, and will now proceed up along a smaller stream called the Sweetwater. Ahead of us is a great stone gap called Devil's Gate, and beyond that we will begin our approach to South Pass, the crest of the Rocky Mountains and of the continent as well.

It is a world of grandeur, and a most inspiring prospect.

Friday, July 28th

This is the fourth day in a row that we have been forced to encamp with less than ten miles covered. Our progress has been disappointing, and Mr. Bourdeau frets and frets about it. There have been foul weather, wagon breakdowns, and the effects of long-range exhaustion affecting everybody. Morgan has not felt chipper for several days. Now there is some kind of sickness among our cattle, which Mr. Bourdeau believes is due to their drinking from the ponds of brackish alkali water that abound in this region. He and Doc Lund warn us that human beings can easily contract this sickness through infected cows, and are recommending that we discontinue the consumption of milk and butter for the time being. My Morgan is one of those grumbling at this, saying that he has no intention of obeying such an idiotic order. It is not an order, I tell him, it is a suggestion offered for our own good. It's plain d—d nonsense, he roars. This in spite of the fact that he is at that very moment complaining of a stomachache. Oh, what a stubborn man!

We camp under threatening skies tonight, surrounded by fantastic rock formations and deep chasms, a landscape more suggestive of some imaginary other-world than of our own familiar earth. It is quite cold—understandably so, since according to Mr. Bourdeau we are near seven thousand feet elevation.

Thursday, August 3rd

Two more oxen dead this morning, and another cow, the second this week. Our Blackie still holds her own,

264

thank heavens, although she's not looking too spry.

Morgan still not feeling well, though he only snaps at me if I inquire, so I can do nothing for him.

This afternoon, after so many delays, we stood at last on the summit of the Rocky Mountain range. Scenically South Pass is a disappointment, being nothing but a gently rounded hilltop that is unpleasantly windy and bare of all vegetation except scraggly brush. But Mr. Bourdeau, seated on horseback, waved his arm dramatically toward the panorama to the west and shouted: "There, my friends! Feast your eyes on Oregon!" A few of us gave a foolish cheer, as if our destination had been reached, whereupon our mischievous guide laughed and reminded us that the wilderness country called Oregon is a vast domain, and that the fertile Pacific valleys are still a thousand miles off. Chastened and subdued, we journeyed on.

On Sunday, August 6th, the party halted for noon rest on the banks of a shallow stream meandering through rolling open country that was dusty-dry and dull gray with scrub growth. There was no shade, no protection from the blazing sun except the interiors of the wagons. People went about the preparation of their noontime meal in listless preoccupation. Baptiste Bourdeau and Lucius Hargrave walked a short distance up along the stream. Justin went with them, walking barefoot in the ankle-deep water and inspecting every clump of weeds along the bank.

"Careful, Justin," Lucius called absently. It was an automatic instruction, empty of specific meaning.

"I'm lookin' for snakes, Papa," Justin announced.

"Never mind snakes. You have no use for snakes, and they have no use for you."

A few of the other men were also walking along the stream, and in a few minutes they drifted together to form a loose group. Baptiste squatted at the edge of the creek and tested the current with his fingers.

"Pretty good water level for the Little Sandy," he said. "That means the Big Sandy's up, too. That's good. We'll need as much as we can carry."

"How come?" Walter Endicott said. "Thought we were gettin' out o' dry country."

"We are, except for the stretch just ahead. From here we go straight west to the Green River. It's good level ground, but

265

for forty miles of it, beyond the Big Sandy, there's no water at all. Not a drop. We'll load up all we can carry and run for it. Two days at twenty miles a day will get us across to the Green."

Endicott gave a loud snort. "Hell, we can't make twenty miles in no one day, let alone two days in a row."

"We can, and we will. We'll travel at night if we have to."

Endicott was scowling. "I can't figger you out, Bourdeau. It's my understandin' the trail follows this here crick down to th' Green River, then up th' other side o' th' valley to Bridger's place, then north an' west to pick up th' Bear."

"That's the long way around. Why go a hundred and seventy-five miles way south and way north again when you can hit the Bear River in a hundred miles straight west?"

"Because there's water the long way, that's why."

"We can carry enough water for two days. And we can stash some forage for the animals, enough to get 'em across."

"You're a damn fool, Bourdeau." Endicott's voice was rasping in anger. "I've let you run this company because I recognize that you have th' experience. But, hell, you're used to travelin' alone. For families it jes' don't make sense to leave th' water an' travel across desert."

Baptiste was still squatting by the stream, chewing on a weed and watching little Justin Hargrave splashing in the shallow water.

"I saw a fish, Baptiste!" the boy called, and Baptiste chuckled.

"Goddamnit, Bourdeau!" Endicott was growling. "Did you hear a damn word I said?"

Baptiste stood up and turned his cool gray eyes on the other man. "Hear you, Walter? I been hearing you ever since I joined up with this party."

Endicott's anger was rising fast. "Well, goddamn you—"

"And I want *you* to hear *me* again, just one more time," Baptiste went on. "I told you before I was going to ride away from this party as soon as I got sick of the arguments, and I'm sick of 'em now. I'm going on the cutoff. Anybody wants to come with me is welcome. Everybody else can do as they damn please."

Baptiste went back to watching the little boy wading in the stream.

Walter Endicott glared at the back of the guide's head. "Well, I think maybe—"

"Wait a minute," another man said. "Somebody's comin'."

There were three men on horseback moving down the trail from the east. Seeing the cluster of men beside the stream a short distance from the wagons, the horsemen turned off the trail and approached. The lead rider, a huge blond man with a rugged and weatherbeaten face, touched his fingers to the brim of his hat.

"How do, gen'lemen."

"How do," Walter Endicott responded warily.

"Mind if our horses borry a little o' that water?"

"Help yourself," Endicott said.

The blond man's companions were Indians, stone-faced and silent, dressed in white man's clothing but with headbands holding their long black hair in place. While the three horses stretched their necks and lapped noisily at the water, the riders and the men on the ground studied each other. At length the big blond man let his gaze rest on Baptiste Bourdeau. He gave an almost imperceptible nod.

"How do, Baptiste."

Baptiste curtly returned the nod. "How do, Kit."

"You gen'lemen travelin' alone?" Walt Endicott asked.

The blond man chuckled softly. "Not hardly. Couldn't if we wanted to. The dad-blame trail's so full o' people—I ain't never seen it like this before."

"*We* ain't seen so many people," Endicott remarked.

"They're comin' up behind you. The Whitman party for Oregon'll be by in a day or two. Missionaries, y'know. Takin' settlers down to the Walla Walla. Must be close to a thousand people. Beats anything I ever saw. Two or three other companies comin' up, besides."

"Which party you gen'lemen with?" Endicott inquired.

"None o' them civilian parties, thank the Lord. We're scouts for Lieutenant Fremont, Yew-nited States Army. He'll be by in a couple o' days, too."

"That so? Which way you fellows goin'? Down by Bridger's, or 'cross the cutoff?"

"Down by Bridger's, o' course. We got no use for no cutoff."

"I see. Well, well." Endicott glanced significantly at Baptiste. The big Canadian was filling his pipe and paying no attention to the conversation.

After a few minutes of idle chatting the leader of the horsemen touched his hat once more, bade the emigrants good luck, and pulled his horse away. His two silent companions followed.

Endicott immediately faced Baptiste again. "Who *was* that fella?"

"Name's Carson," Baptiste said. "Christopher Carson. Calls himself Kit."

"Friend o' yours?"

"Wouldn't hardly say 'friend.' We respect each other, we don't necessarily like each other."

"He know his stuff?"

"He's the second best Mountain Man in the West." Sly amusement glinted in Baptiste's eye. "After me."

Walt Endicott looked around at the other men, and made a quick decision. "Well, tell you what, Bourdeau. Maybe we'll take another vote in this party. Whether we go on with you, or follow th' main trail."

Baptiste flashed a pleasant smile. "Go right ahead."

"Like that fella Carson said, there'll be plenty o' people comin' along. Safety in numbers, y'know?"

"Right." Still smiling, Baptiste turned away, and shouted at Justin Hargrave wading in the creek a short distance upstream.

"Hey, Justin, you catch us a nice fat fish for supper, eh?"

Later in the afternoon Walt Endicott called a company meeting. It was attended by all the men except Franklin Bryce and Morgan Shannon, who lay ill in their wagons. They were therefore represented by their wives. The meeting lasted half an hour, and when Catherine Shannon returned to her wagon she found her husband tossing on his bunk and fuming with impatience.

"What took so long?" he grumbled.

"Oh, it was just a discussion about which way we should go from here. Mr. Endicott wants to follow the regular trail, which dips pretty far south, and Mr. Bourdeau wants to take a shortcut straight west, to save time." Catherine touched her fingers to her husband's cheek. "I think your fever's down. That's good." She dipped a cloth in a pail of water, squeezed it out, and applied it to the sick man's forehead. He brushed it aside.

"Tell me what happened," he demanded. "Who won?"

Catherine hesitated a moment before answering. "Most of the people voted with Mr. Endicott."

"Good! That'll teach that smart-aleck Bourdeau a lesson. Majority rules in America, by God!"

"Well, it's not that simple, Morgan."

"What?"

"It looks as if the party's splitting up here. The ones who voted with Mr. Bourdeau have decided to go with him, because, after all, he *is* the only one among us with any real experience."

"Hah!" Morgan scoffed. "The Frenchman's so-called experience hasn't done a damn thing for us so far except to cause trouble." He looked at his wife with sudden suspicion. "So who's going with him? You didn't do anything foolish, did you?"

"Who's going with him? Well, let's see. The Hargraves, and the Kendrickses, and the Bryces, and Mr. Bruner. And us."

"What?!"

"Yes, Morgan. I voted with Mr. Bourdeau."

His face crimson with anger, Morgan struggled to raise himself on an elbow. "God*damnit,* Catherine!"

"Please, Morgan, don't excite yourself."

"You can't *do* that!"

"Yes I can. I did."

"Well, by God, it'll be *un*done! I'll call Endicott and tell him to disregard your vote. You're an addle-brained female who can't be trusted to make a—"

"Stop it, Morgan." Gently and firmly she pushed him back down on the bunk. "You're a sick man, you should try to keep yourself calm."

He twisted and squirmed in his anger. "I don't give a damn how sick I am! I by God haven't stopped making the decisions for this fam—"

"Morgan, listen to me." Catherine spoke with sudden severity. "We are in the middle of wilderness, over a thousand miles from home. And except for you and the children, I'm among strangers, do you realize that?"

"Is that my fault? You've never been good at making friends, you know that."

"Neither have you."

"But I don't *care,* you see? You *do* care, and you still don't make friends. You know what your trouble is, Catherine? You're too damned educated. You scare people off."

Catherine studied her hands in her lap. "Well . . . it's not true that I'm *entirely* without friends. I've made two. Viola Kendricks and . . Isaac Hargrave."

Morgan laughed painfully, and the laugh contained both

269

mirth and ridicule. "Wonderful! Two of the nicest ladies you'd ever want to meet. Viola Kendricks and Aunt Nellie Hargrave."

When he looked at Catherine again he saw something in her face that made him stop short and lose all sense of amusement. He stared at her, and some half-formed unspoken thought flashed invisibly between them.

"Yes, I see." He was quiet now. "You have to think about the possibility that I might not survive."

Her face twisted in an impatient grimace. "Oh, that's ridiculous! Why, you're as strong as a bear. You only have a touch of indigestion, for heaven's sake. I'm just thinking—" Her sudden flow of confidence began to falter again. "Well, I'd just like to stay with the few friends I have, that's all." She turned pleading eyes on him. "Please, Morgan, just this once—let me have my way?"

For a long moment he looked at her steadily as if he'd never seen her before. "You've been a good wife, Catherine. I'm afraid I haven't been a very good husband."

She shook her head, smiling. "Oh, Morgan, don't talk silly!"

He sighed and closed his eyes. "May I have the cloth, please?"

With a gentle touch and a solemn look on her face Catherine applied the wet cloth to her husband's burning brow.

(13)

CATHERINE SHANNON'S Diary:

Monday, August 7th

It is very late when we camp these evenings, and I barely have the strength to write a few lines. We pause

270

here in the middle of the most awful wasteland, with very little forage for the animals, and hardly any water at all. The poor beasts will be lowing in distress all night, and no one will rest. There is little time for rest in any case, for we must start again in four hours.

We are only six wagons now, the others having chosen to go on the longer main trail, while a few of us follow Mr. Bourdeau on what he calls the Green River cutoff. Our little band looks pitifully puny of a sudden, and we seem to draw closer together, for comfort.

But there is no comfort for the Shannons. Morgan's fever is worse, and he is complaining of severe pains. I try to keep a cheerful face for the children's sake, but inside a cold terror grips me. Hideous thoughts clamor to enter my mind, and I dare not admit them.

Isaac Hargrave is at our wagon every chance he gets, inquiring if there is anything he can do, and if nothing is asked for, he finds some way to be of help just the same. I thank Heavens for such a good friend. And, strange to say, Morgan has suddenly lost his animosity toward Isaac, greets him with a wan smile. That seems to me a minor miracle, and I am thankful for that, too.

Wednesday, August 9th

Normally I write in the evening, but it was past midnight when we camped last night, and utter weariness compelled me to wait until morning to record our progress. And progress there was, indeed. We reached the Green River at last, and, praise be to merciful Providence, Morgan seems much improved this morning. He is sitting up and has eaten a nice bowl of porridge for breakfast, and even seems a bit cheerful, to our great delight. And, to top it off, it is a lovely day.

Reaching this river was a tremendous blessing. The animals smelled the water two miles off last night, and heedless of all our efforts to control them, nearly wrecked our wagons in their pell-mell rush toward it. It is a fine stream, clear and cold and swift-running, and several hundred feet wide, but shallow and with a firm pebbly bottom, so that fording will be easy. It is lined with tender willows and succulent grasses for the animals, and here and there beautiful stands of poplar

271

and oak and sycamore. One could almost wish this spot were our final destination.

And good news today from Mr. Bourdeau. He says we can lay over here for twenty-four hours to rest from the last two arduous days. He and Lucius Hargrave left on horseback early this morning on a hunting expedition. Our guide declares there are fine antelope in this region, and some fresh meat would do us all good.

Generally I am enjoying a sweet mood of optimism this morning. Dare I believe that the worst of our trials are now behind us, and that our fortunes will be rising from here on? Yes, I do, I <u>will</u> believe it, with all my heart.

The hunters returned to camp near the end of the long summer dusk, two hours after the sun had dropped out of sight behind the far-off range to the west. Baptiste rode in front, a rifle slung over his shoulder, a satisfied look on his face, and the carcass of an antelope draped over his horse's rump. When he drew within sight of the camp he pulled his horse to a stop and Lucius came up beside him. The camp was strangely quiet. A few people could be seen moving listlessly around two or three small campfires scattered among the wagons.

"A day of rest didn't do 'em any good," Lucius said. "Everybody's still dog-tired."

Baptiste shook his head. "You wait. Somebody's going to want to lay over another day. And the answer's going to be no."

Boyd Kendricks came walking out to meet them. He was a heavyset man of about forty, with a shock of coal black hair and a wide face that was at this moment tight-lipped and grim. The men on horseback watched him approach, and unconsciously tightened the grip on their horses' reins as they waited.

"We've had another death," Kendricks said.

"Who?" Baptiste and Lucius said together in quick alarm.

"Morgan Shannon."

There was a moment of intense stillness before Kendricks continued.

"Around noon he began to have terrible stomach pains. Doublin' up and groanin' somethin' awful. Mrs. Shannon was frantic, cryin' for help, and naturally we tried our best to . . . to do whatever we could, but we're none of us doctors. There

272

wasn't anything we could do, really..." Kendricks spoke haltingly, frowning as if trying to think of a way to add meaningful detail to his story. "By two o'clock he was dead," he concluded abruptly.

The stillness deepened.

"Well, I'm damned," Baptiste mumbled vaguely. He glanced at Lucius, and saw that his companion was staring fixedly toward the camp.

"It couldn't 'a' been cholera," Boyd Kendricks said. "The symptoms weren't nothin' like what all those other people had, back down there on the Platte."

"It was alkali poisoning," Baptiste said. There was biting anger in his voice. "I warned 'em and warned 'em, but some people wouldn't listen. Some people have never listened, not to a damn thing. And Morgan Shannon was the worst of the lot."

Boyd Kendricks was skeptical. "But how could it be alkali poisoning? The alkali pools were way back yonder—"

"Don't matter," Baptiste snapped. "Sometimes it's quick, sometimes slow. No telling how it's going to work."

Kendricks sighed. "Well, anyway, the poor fellow's buried, and that's that." He glanced up at Lucius. "Your brother Isaac's lookin' after the widow and the children. Poor Mrs. Shannon, she's got this strange blank look on her face, like she can't quite get it through her head what—"

He stopped in surprise. Lucius had swung himself down off his horse, and was thrusting the reins into Kendricks's hands.

"Take my horse in, will you, Boyd? There's something I've got to do." Lucius started walking rapidly toward the wagons.

"Wait a minute, Lucius," Baptiste called to him.

Lucius kept going.

Isaac was stirring something in a pot suspended over a tiny fire near the Shannon wagon. Close by, the two Shannon children and Justin were sitting side by side, crosslegged on the ground, gazing into the fire with wide solemn eyes.

"Now Papa can't ever go to Oregon," Abby said wistfully.

"I don't want to go to Oregon, neither," Byron muttered. "I want to go back home."

"Try not to feel that way, Byron," Isaac said gently. "Try to remember what your father wanted for you. He wanted to find a new place in the world where you could grow up to have better opportunities than you'd have in the old place.

You've got to try and be strong, and carry on the way he would've wanted you to."

The boy made no effort to follow all this. He rested his chin in his palm and stared gloomily into the fire. "I want to go home," he said again.

"Mr. Bryce was sick, and he got better," Abby said fretfully. "And Mr. McNabb was sick once, and he got better. Why couldn't Papa get better? Why did *he* have to die?"

"Nobody can answer that, Abby," Isaac said. "Some people have good fortune, some have bad. Nobody can say why. You have to be glad Mr. Bryce and Mr. McNabb got better. It wouldn't help your father if they died too."

Abby conceded the point with a sigh. "I'm glad they got better." She looked up and saw several stars sparkling freshly in the sky as darkness came on. "I don't want anybody to die anymore, ever."

"My grandpa died," Justin offered helpfully. "He was riding in the buggy, and he fell out and died." He was looking at Abby as if hoping this information would cheer her up.

She gave him a sad smile.

Nobody saw Lucius until he was upon them.

"Come here, Justin," he said sternly, and the little boy started in surprise.

"Oh God, Lucius!" Isaac exclaimed. "I'm glad you're back!"

Lucius ignored him. His eyes were fixed on Justin. "Come here, I said."

Justin came around the campfire and stood before Lucius, who leaned down close and gave him instructions in a crisp undertone.

"Go to our wagon and stay there. I'll be along in a minute."

"I wanna stay here," Justin protested. "I'm goin' to have supper with Abby and By—"

Lucius seized the boy by the arm and half-lifted him off the ground. "I said go to our wagon and stay there. Don't argue with me. Go!" He gave Justin a sharp slap on the seat and sent him off whimpering in astonishment and outrage.

"What was that all about?" Isaac demanded.

Now Lucius turned to face his brother, and his words were ground out in anger. "What makes you think you have the right to risk my son's life?"

Isaac gaped. "Lucius, the lady in that wagon there lost her

husband today, and these children lost their father. I'm only trying to—"

"You're trying to infect Justin with the same sickness, that's what you're trying to do."

"*Somebody's* got to look after these poor fatherless children, for God's sake!"

"There are other *women* in this company, damnit—besides a number of able-bodied men. Why do *you* have to do it?"

Isaac stiffened, and a look of defiance came into his face. "Catherine Shannon and I have been good friends ever since we started on this trip. Now she's in trouble and needs help, and I'm goin' to help her. I'm doin' it because I'd consider it indecent not to."

"Oh, I see. Very noble. And a touch romantic too, I'd say. You sure didn't waste any time taking over, did you?"

"That's a mean thing to say, Lucius," Isaac snapped. "People have an obligation to help one another in times of trouble, and it's got nothing to do with—"

"You're excused from whatever obligation you feel here, Isaac," Catherine said. She had emerged from the wagon and was standing unsteadily beside it. She was red-eyed and pale, and stray wisps of hair fell across her drawn and haggard face.

Quickly Isaac moved to her side. "I'm sorry, Catherine. Pay no attention to Lucius, he doesn't know what he's sayin'."

"No, pay no attention to me," Lucius said grimly. "I'm just a nervous father, trying to protect his child."

"I understand your concern perfectly, Mr. Hargrave." Catherine spoke softly and carefully, making a firm effort to maintain calm. "I'd feel the same way in your place, I'm sure."

"Oh, that's ridiculous!" Isaac blurted. "Morgan died of alkali poisoning. That's what Baptiste called it right from the start, and we know that isn't contagious."

"We don't know a damned thing about what he died of," Lucius said. "Baptiste is a fine guide, but he's not a physician, and neither is anybody else around here." He brushed past Isaac to move close to Catherine. "Mrs. Shannon, I fully sympathize with you in your tragic loss, and I extend to you my sincere condolences. But beyond that, I must say I think our first responsibility is toward our own."

"And I agree with you completely," Catherine said without hesitation. "I think you're not only right to keep Justin away, I think you should take Isaac away too."

Lucius turned to Isaac with a look of satisfaction. "Did you hear that? Come on, Isaac."

"I will not!" Isaac shot back hotly.

"You're not going to be any help to Mrs. Shannon or anybody else if you take sick and die too."

"I'm not listening to you, Lucius."

"All right, be a fool, then."

"I'll be whatever I choose to be!" Isaac roared. He advanced on Lucius, who blinked in surprise and stepped back.

"All my life I've looked up to you, Lucius. And you've looked down on me. But I've never minded that. I've always thought it was right that I should listen to you, and let you tell me how the world is, and what to do and what not to do, because you're smarter than me, I've always known that."

Lucius took hold of his brother's arm and tried to speak soothingly. "Aw, come on, old chum, don't get all—"

Isaac shook him off. "But that's all over now, Lucius. You're not tellin' me what to do anymore, do you hear that? Not anymore, Lucius!" His voice rang with a fine passion.

Catherine touched his sleeve. "Isaac, please—"

He shook her off as readily as he had shaken off the man. "Don't interfere, Catherine. This is between Lucius and me."

"But I don't want to be the cause of bad blood between brothers. I—"

"Catherine—" Isaac had seized her hand. "I offered you something, and you accepted."

"It was a mistake." She tried to evade his eyes.

"No, it was not a mistake. It was the first time in my life I ever felt strong, and forceful."

Isaac looked at his brother. "You ought to know this, Lucius. When it happened . . . when it was all over . . . I offered Catherine my devoted service as her protector, for as long as she needs me. She accepted. I gave her my promise, and as long as there's a breath in my body, I'm goin' to keep that promise."

"Protector," Lucius said wonderingly. "Are you Sir Lancelot? Are we back in the age of chivalry and knighthood? What does *protector* mean?"

Isaac had no trouble with this question. "It means whatever Catherine wishes it to mean. Now or in the future. I am at her service."

"I see." Lucius looked from Isaac to Catherine, and seemed momentarily deprived of speech. "Well," he said finally, "I wish you both good luck, and congratulations on your new-found . . . whatever it is. Protectorship." He turned abruptly and walked away.

Catherine stood close to Isaac, clung to his arm, and leaned her head against his shoulder. He smiled down at her and laid a gentle hand on her hair.

"Don't worry," he whispered.

Then he turned to Abby and Byron, who were still sitting on the ground, huddled close together in quiet fright.

"Go and wash your hands, children," he said to them. "I'll give you your supper now."

CATHERINE SHANNON'S Diary:

Wednesday, August 9th

I write this very late at night, by the light of a tiny candle. It is the second entry under this date. This morning, an unfathomable age ago, I penned some silly lines babbling with optimism, little dreaming that this day would be the most terrible of my life.

Morgan is dead. He took a sudden and mysterious turn for the worse around noon, writhed in agony for two hours, and was gone. He is gone, just like that. I can state the fact as simply and calmly as if I were recording a bit of trivia, knowing full well those awful hours will haunt me as long as I live.

Doubts torment my mind now. To sleep is out of the question. Something there is in my conscience that keeps accusing me with hard questions. Why did I allow Morgan to persuade me to this foolhardy venture of going to Oregon? He was not the wisest of men, but certainly one of the most headstrong. Should I not have tried harder to provide some of the practical wisdom he lacked? Should I not have asserted my own thoughts and will more forcefully? Was I a good enough wife to him? Surely I can claim I was a dutiful one, constant and faithful. But is faithfulness and attendance to duty all a man needs in a wife? Did I love him enough? Oh, dear God. Did I love him at all? Heaven forgive me, I shrink from answering that question, even to myself.

I feel overwhelmed by misery. I cannot see that life holds anything further for me but emptiness. Were it not for the children I could cheerfully walk away from this hateful wagon and lose myself in the wilderness.

But no, there is one other thread connecting me with life. Isaac Hargrave. He has declared himself my protector, is apparently devoted to me and the children, and at this moment sleeps on the ground beside my wagon, wrapped in a buffalo robe. I believe he fancies himself to be in love with me, and this has caused a painful rift between Isaac and his strange brother Lucius, who seems to look upon me as some kind of—what? Threat? It is all too mystifying.

But I must think of Isaac. Am I being unfair to him, allowing him to expose himself to possible danger while trying to protect us? Allowing him to imagine there might eventually be more between us than I would wish to have? Or maybe I flatter myself. Maybe I run the risk of becoming too dependent upon a man who might soon find a newly made widow and two small children a tiresome burden, and yearn to be rid of us. I am helpless; I know not what to do.

Tomorrow morning we move on, and so I must leave my poor Morgan behind in a lonely grave that I will likely never see again. Isaac went to Mr. Bourdeau and asked that we lay over one more day, for my sake. Mr. Bourdeau said no, there was no good in it. I must believe he was right.

Abby and Byron cried themselves to sleep tonight. They are more frightened than sad, because they only vaguely comprehend what has happened to them. They have no father now, and their mother is weak and irresolute and far from home. Heaven protect their poor innocent souls.

I cannot bear to contemplate tomorrow, still less the future. And I have no further interest in this diary. It is stupid to keep a diary, anyway. I will put it away now, and never write in it again.

(14)

LATE SUNDAY AFTERNOON the wagons entered a beautiful east-west-running valley sheltered by high stony ridges to the north and south, and laced by shallow brooks that wandered through glittering stands of aspen. Here camp was made, the wagons dispersing loosely around a little meadow enclosed by walls of dense trees and bordered by one of the streams.

They had been delayed by storms—a deluge had struck during the night Friday and continued with brief respites through Saturday, sinking their wagon wheels in thick sticky mud. Now the weather was benign again, and the Milky Way gleamed across the early evening sky.

Baptiste Bourdeau was calculating the company's progress. He sat on the ground and thought aloud, while several other men gathered in a loose circle around a campfire listened.

"Let's see, now. If we don't get rained on no more we can make it to the Bear River junction in a day and a half. That'll be Tuesday. The middle of August already. Then it's eight or ten more days to Fort Hall."

"What about after that?" Frank Bryce asked.

"Well, after that you got another four, five days to the Raft River, where the folks going to California turn off. Then there's another seven hundred miles or so, whichever way you're heading. But that ain't my worry. After Fort Hall you're on your own."

Baptiste looked around the group and saw a few glum and worried faces. "But you won't have no trouble finding new guides at Fort Hall. The place is running over with 'em. And soon's we hit the main trail again at Bear River we'll have that

279

big gang of missionaries coming up on us. Plenty of company from there on. Least, for the Oregon folks."

"What about us California folks?" Boyd Kendricks wanted to know.

"Don't worry, Boyd," Lucius Hargrave said. "We'll talk him into taking us on to California."

Baptiste chuckled, put his head back, and gazed pensively into the fire. "My friends, there's a little woman at Fort Hall named Mali. She's got long silky black hair and a voice as soft as a running brook and eyes like a six-month-old fawn. And when I get to where she is it'll take an act of God to make me leave again right soon." A dreamy smile softened the guide's weathered face.

The heavyset squint-eyed man named Otis Bruner was shaking with laughter. "Well, boys, now we know why ol' Baptiste here's been crackin' the whip over our heads all the way, yellin', 'Faster, faster!' He's got 'im a little Indian whore at Fort Hall!"

Nobody laughed at Bruner's observation except Bruner himself.

"She is not a little Indian whore," Baptiste said. "She is my wife."

Something in the sound of the big Canadian's quiet steely voice choked Bruner's laughter off in his throat.

"What'sa matter, you got no sense o' humor?" he grumbled. "I think it's damned *funny* th' way you been beatin' hell out o' this here party, jes' because you got an itch in your pants to git to your little squaw—"

"Shut up, Otis." This came from Lucius Hargrave, sitting next to Bruner.

"And what'sa matter with *you?*" Bruner turned on Lucius. "You got no sense o' humor, neither. I reckon you're jealous o' your brother, ain't ya? *He* didn't settle for nothin' second-rate, that's sure. He went for th' high-class stuff. That there Isaac, man alive! He's what I call a swift-workin' man!"

At that moment Isaac walked into the light of the campfire. "Good evenin', gentlemen," he said with solemn formality.

Cursory greetings came back to him from several members of the group, not including Lucius.

"Hey, Isaac, we were jes' talkin' about what a swift worker you are!" Otis Bruner called gleefully.

Isaac ignored this, and looked directly at his brother. "Evenin', Lucius."

"H'lo, Isaac," Lucius said softly.

Isaac turned to the guide. "Baptiste, uh . . . Mrs. Shannon would like to speak with you for a minute."

Baptiste scowled. "What about? If it's about laying over, she might just as well—" And then he saw that Catherine was standing there, waiting to be acknowledged. He got to his feet.

"I hope I'm not interrupting anything, Mr. Bourdeau," she said.

"Not at all, madame." He looked around quickly. "Let me see if I can find you a seat."

"No, no, please don't bother. I only want to ask you something. It won't take long." Catherine glanced with vague uneasiness at the circle of curious male faces around her, and her hands fluttered nervously. "You see, my little boy is feverish tonight. And I'm so afraid . . . I thought maybe—"

"*Mon Dieu!*" Baptiste breathed. "You have had your share of misfortune, have you not, madame?"

His sympathetic response gave her a momentary strengthening of resolve. "Mr. Bourdeau, I know how you feel about delay. I know you have never permitted it for a sick *man*, but I thought perhaps . . . for a sick child . . ."

Baptiste was already shaking his head. He spoke with a mixture of weariness and patience. "I am so sorry, Mrs. Shannon. But the principle is the same. It would be foolish. It is no help for the child, and it imperils everyone else. There is nothing to do but go on."

"But . . . just one day? Would it make so much—"

"Madame, I speak the truth to you. If it was *my* son, I'd go on. Sometimes there's a doctor at Fort Hall."

"But that's a long way. By then he'll be well, or he'll be—" She stopped abruptly and bit her lower lip.

Baptiste shrugged. "Madame, I can only repeat—if it was my own son, I'd go on as fast as I could."

Catherine gave him a hard look. "My husband never trusted you, Mr. Bourdeau."

"I am aware of that, madame."

"We used to have some rather heated arguments. He found fault with you constantly, and I just as constantly defended you."

"I thank you for that."

"You may save your thanks, because now I'm sorry I did it. I think you are a cruel man, Mr. Bourdeau." Catherine wheeled and walked rapidly away, head high in defiance and eyes fixed rigidly ahead.

Baptiste watched her go and sighed, and was immediately confronted by Isaac, his face flushed in anger.

"One day is all she asked. One day wouldn't make any difference."

"That's right, one day *wouldn't* make any difference," Baptiste said. "So why *waste* a day?" Then his features relaxed into an easy grin. "Ah, Isaac, my friend, you are being foolish. You got love in your heart now, and it's clouding your mind."

Otis Bruner began to chuckle.

"You're right," Isaac said firmly. "I *do* have love in my heart, I admit it. But I'd rather be made foolish by love than be a cold, hard-hearted, unfeeling—"

Otis Bruner slapped his thigh and cackled.

"Isaac!" Lucius said sharply. "Stop making an ass of yourself."

Isaac kept his eyes on Baptiste. "If Mrs. Shannon and I laid over here a day or two, how hard would it be to get back on the main trail?"

"Oh Lord!" Lucius groaned.

"I wouldn't recommend that," Baptiste said gravely.

"I'm not askin' for your recommendations. I'm askin' you to tell me how to pick up the trail again."

"Don't tell him," Lucius said under his breath to Baptiste.

"You keep out o' this, Lucius," Isaac snapped. "I'm a grown man, I can make my own decisions."

Otis Bruner doubled up with laughter.

"Shut up, Bruner!" Lucius barked.

Baptiste addressed Isaac, ignoring the interruptions. "Well, if you insist on it, it's easy enough. You just stick to this valley straight west, and go up through the pass at the far end of it. From there you can see the Bear River ten miles ahead. The main trail follows the Bear, and there'll be plenty of traffic along there—"

"Cut it out, Baptiste," Lucius said. "For God's sake, don't encourage him."

"Thank you very much," Isaac said to Baptiste. He glanced briefly around at others, said a crisp "Good night," and with great dignity departed.

Otis Bruner leaped to his feet and shouted after him, "Hey, Isaac! When you're whisperin' sweet nothin's in 'er ear tonight, give 'er a little kiss and a pat on th' fanny for me, will y—"

His words were cut off by a heavy hand that came down on his shoulder and spun him around. He staggered, then stared, astonished, into a pair of hard gray eyes.

"I'm tired of listening to you," Lucius Hargrave said between clenched teeth.

A murderous look came onto Bruner's grizzled face. "You keep your hands off me, young fella. Nobody puts their hands on me like that."

Lucius took a small step closer. "If you want to go on traveling with this party you'll drop the subject of Isaac and Mrs. Shannon right now and for good, you understand that?"

Bruner studied Lucius's face for a moment as if not quite sure of what he had heard. "You're talkin' dangerous, young fella. You ain't goin' to tell me what I can talk about and what I can't. Anyway, everybody knows they're sleepin' together, it ain't no—"

"Whatever they're doing, it's none of your goddamn business. You say another word about it and I'll push it right back down your throat."

Bruner's hand moved to his belt. His fingers began to caress the carved bone handle of a hunting knife. Without removing his eyes from Lucius he called to Baptiste, "Hey, Bourdeau, you better call off your sassy young flunky here, if you don't want 'im to git his gizzard cut out."

Baptiste walked leisurely up to the antagonists, placed a finger on each man's chest, and gently pushed them apart. Then he addressed Bruner in a tone incongruously cool and casual.

"You do what he says, Otis. You drop that subject, or get out of this party."

Bruner blinked several times, rubbed his chin, and adjusted his hat. "Didn't mean no harm," he said finally. He threw a last sullen look around the campfire circle. "None o' you boys got no sense o' humor."

He stomped off into the darkness, muttering to himself.

In the silence that followed, Lucius pulled out a handkerchief and carefully wiped away beads of perspiration standing on his brow.

"Thanks," he mumbled in Baptiste's direction.

Baptiste gave his friend a weary look, and turned away. "Why did I ever let myself get tangled up with these children?" he asked the night sky, and resumed his seat.

(15)

BATTERIES OF SUNBEAMS slanted through the quivering foliage of the aspen grove, splashing a half-dozen different shades of green on the forest floor in patches of light and shadow. Gradually the nighttime mists rose, swirling, creeping away into invisible crevices of the earth.

By custom the time of departure was one hour after sunrise. So it was that after the breakfast fires had been made and extinguished, and the oxen and mules yoked and harnessed, five of the six wagons in the camp were drawn up and ready. But around the sixth, parked at some distance from the others, there were no signs of activity.

Lucius Hargrave approached this wagon cautiously, stopped and listened, detected soft movement inside, and after a slight hesitation knocked gently at the rear entrance.

The flap was pulled back and Catherine Shannon said, "Good morning, Mr. Hargrave."

"Morning, ma'am. How's the little boy?"

The reply was careful and guarded. "I think he's better, but I can't be sure."

"Baptiste tells me he was just here. Said he thought the little fellow looks pretty good. Thought he could travel just fine."

"Yes, that's what he said." A trace of disdain entered Catherine's voice. "Of course, as you've pointed out yourself, Mr. Bourdeau is no physician."

Lucius frowned. "So. I take it you're laying over, then."

"Yes. It's my inclination to, and Isaac seems quite determined about it."

"Strange. I never thought determination was one of his characteristics."

"Maybe you've never really known him very well."

Lucius was not inclined to pursue this line of thought. "Where *is* he?"

"Byron expressed a yearning for fresh berries this morning, so Isaac and Abby have gone walking along the creek to see if they can find some."

Lucius gazed earnestly up into the woman's face. "Uh, Mrs. Shannon, could I speak with you for a minute, please? Outside?"

Catherine blinked, appearing surprised, then uncertain. "Just a minute," she said finally. She disappeared briefly, then came back and allowed Lucius to take her arm and help her down to the ground.

They stood side by side, she watching him while he swallowed hard and fidgeted, searching for words.

"Mrs. Shannon, I, uh...I want to apologize for my behavior toward you the other day. That...that *bad* day. I feel rotten about it. I beg your forgiveness."

"That's all right. Think no more about it." Her manner was cool and formal.

"With your very natural concern for your own child, I thought maybe, if you reflected on it, you might understand how I felt about Justin. He's all I've got, you see."

"Oh, I *do* understand. I said so then, and I assure you, I meant it."

Lucius shifted his weight from one foot to the other. "Mrs. Shannon, I want you to know, uh..."

"Oh, Lucius." She smiled, and her formality suddenly dissolved into something warm and easy and relaxed. "How long are we going to go on with this Mr. Hargrave-Mrs. Shannon business? You know, I have a feeling my destination is now California, too. If we survive all this, there's no reason we shouldn't be friends, is there?"

"Oh, certainly not." Lucius was momentarily flustered. "Well, I just wanted to say, uh..." He rubbed his chin and frowned, trying to collect his thoughts. "What did I want to say? Well, for one thing, I think you're right about Isaac and me. I've never really known him too well. I've always thought of him as a simple fellow who never quite knew what was going on. Now it's hard for me to get used to the idea that I, uh..." Speech came with greater and greater difficulty. "Well, for the first time in my life...I'm jealous of him."

She stared at him. He grabbed her hand, and the words suddenly came pouring out.

"Catherine, you've got to know this. If Isaac hadn't moved in front of me so damned fast, I would have gladly—"

Then the moment was shattered. Catherine pulled her hand free and stepped back as Abby came running toward her, proudly displaying a little pail of blackberries.

"Mama, look what we found!"

"Umm, that's wonderful, darling!" Catherine exclaimed. "Come on, let's go see if Byron will have some." She glanced at her visitor, and her cool veneer was securely back in place. "Will you excuse us a minute, Lucius?"

When Isaac came up from the creek he found Lucius standing alone near the Shannon wagon, waiting for him. The brothers eyed each other warily.

"Mornin', Lucius," Isaac began.

"So you're staying over here," Lucius said grimly.

"That's right."

"How long?"

"Depends on how Byron does. At least one day, maybe two."

"You're a fool, you know. Baptiste says the boy isn't that sick."

"Lucius, let me see if I can explain it to you. Catherine will always have it in the back of her mind that Morgan might have lived if he'd had the chance to get enough rest. Maybe she's wrong. But now she's sort of dependent on me, and Byron's sick, and . . . well, by God, this time she's goin' to have it her way."

Lucius said nothing. The dark look on his face expressed his opinion clearly.

"It'll be all right, Lucius," Isaac went on. "We'll catch up in a day or two, or if not, wait for us at Fort Hall, will you? We won't be too long."

Lucius was fuming. "Biggest mistake I ever made, bringing you with me. You ought to be back in South Bar where your Mama Sarah could look after you."

Isaac's smile was calm and oddly self-assured. "You always said I ought to grow up and be a man, Lucius. Well, I'm bein' a man now, and, you know somethin'? You were dead right. It's a great feelin'. Best feelin' I ever had in my life."

"You'll kill yourself."

"If I do, I'll die happy."

Lucius made an explosive noise of exasperation. "All right, good luck to you. When I write to Mama and tell her I left you somewhere in the wilderness tending to somebody's sick child, she'll be pleased and proud." He started to walk away.

"Well then, stay with us," Isaac called. "Then you won't have to write that letter."

Lucius paused and looked back. "No, thanks, old chum. This is *your* show. For once in your life you got the jump on me."

Then he went off, and Isaac stood there looking after him with a baffled expression on his face.

When he was halfway back to the other wagons Catherine caught up with him.

"Wait a minute, Lucius."

He stopped and turned to her. Now it was she who was hesitant, and choosing her words cautiously.

"I wanted to tell you...it's not true what they're saying about Isaac and me. If it were I'd be proud to admit it, not ashamed. But it's not true. He's never touched me."

"Nobody's saying anything about you," Lucius said mumblingly.

"Yes, they are. Mr. Bruner was saying quite a lot last night. I heard him. I also heard the way you defended us. That gave me a warm feeling, Lucius. I'll always be grateful to you for that."

He shrugged. "It was nothing."

"Oh, you're wrong. It was very much something." She stepped closer to him and her voice became softer. "And I'm sorry we were interrupted a minute ago. I think you were about to say something important when Abby came running up."

He shook his head and avoided her eyes. "No. Not really."

She stepped back. "Well. Goodbye, then. See you in a few days." She was trying hard to sound cheerful.

Now he dared to look at her, and the look was stern and frowning. "Don't dawdle here, Catherine. One day, no more. Either Byron will be better by then, in which case your point is proven, or he won't be, in which case you'll know it's useless to waste any more time."

"All right, Lucius. Don't worry about us."

"I *will* worry."

She smiled. "Give Justin a kiss for me," she said, and turned away quickly, walking with rapid strides back toward her wagon.

He watched her for a moment. Then, his face clouded and

grim, he went on to the place in the center of the meadow where the other wagons were lined up ready to go.

(16)

THE BEAR RIVER: a shallow stream flowing rapidly over a rough and rocky bed, about fifty yards wide. Its valley was a pleasant land of lush grasses spangled with the deep blue blossoms of flax, its banks lined with wide-spreading cottonwood, small willows, stands of aspen, thickets of hawthorn and wild strawberries. As darkness fell on Tuesday the fifteenth of August, the east side of the northerly-flowing river was decorated with a long chain of yellow-glowing campfires, because this was the main trail again, and now was the time when the westward traffic of settlers and traders and explorers and adventurers reached its peak.

Lucius Hargrave sat on a rock outcropping on a hillside and stared down at the line of fires strung out like jewels in the dusky smoke-filled river valley. Atop a jutting boulder behind him, bathed in an orange glow of sunset, stood little Justin, his feet wide apart.

"Looka me, Papa!" the boy shouted, "I'm on top o' the mountain!"

Lucius gave back one of his automatic cautionary responses. "Careful, Justin. You'll fall and break your neck."

Lucius was brooding; his thoughts were far off. Soon he turned his eyes away from the campfires and watched Baptiste Bourdeau coming up the hill toward him. Baptiste wiped his brow, which was sweating from the climb, and sat down on another rock a few feet from Lucius. Lucius kept watching him, waiting.

"I was just talking to some advance members of the Oregon missionary group," Baptiste said finally. "They tell me their leader, this fellow Marcus Whitman, ain't just your ordinary run-of-the-mill missionary. He's a doctor. A real one. He'll be by here tomorrow, probably."

Lucius cradled his forehead in the palm of his hand and stared at the ground.

"Oh Lord! And those foolish people with the sick child are twenty-five miles behind us!"

"Looka me, Unca Baptiste!" cried Justin, perched on another daring eminence.

Baptiste chuckled and waved to him.

"Why did I go off and leave them there?" Lucius muttered.

"Well, Isaac's a grown man, Lucius," Baptiste said. "He told us so himself."

"The hell he is. He's just like Justin. Another child to look after."

"Don't worry. They'll be along by tomorrow evening, sure."

"We won't still be here then. Unless we wait for 'em."

Baptiste was shaking his head. "If I wasn't willing to wait back there, why should I be willing to wait here?"

Lucius drew a deep breath. "Well then, I guess this is where we part company, old friend."

An uneasy look came over Baptiste's face. "You going to wait?"

"I'm going back to get 'em."

"Going *back*? Don't be a damn fool, Lucius!"

"Too late to tell me that. I was a damn fool for bringing that crazy brother of mine with me in the first place. Now I've got to look after him. It's my responsibility, and I can't escape it."

Silence descended. For a time Baptiste watched the little boy playing among the rocks on the hillside above them. Then he shifted his position and frowned down at the campfires along the river. Finally he reached a reluctant decision. He got up and went to Lucius and sat down next to him.

"All right, tell you what we'll do. In the morning we'll ask the Kendricksses to take Justin in and wait here with our wagons. The rest of 'em can go on with some of these other parties or wait for the Endicott crowd. Then we'll go back along the trail on horseback. And I'll bet you five dollars we'll meet Isaac and Mrs. Shannon before we've gone two miles."

Lucius's eyes were shining with excitement and new hope. "You mean you'll go with me?"

"What the hell else can I do?" Baptiste growled. He made a

face that was half-grin and half-grimace. "*All* you Hargraves are children. *Some*body's got to look after you."

It was four o'clock Wednesday afternoon and they had gone back to within a few miles of the place where they had left Isaac and the Shannons before they came upon the wagon. It was on the side of a gentle slope, its back wheels planted in the inches-deep water of a tiny rock-strewn brook. Its front wheel on the uphill side jutted at a grotesque near-horizontal slant, and that corner of the chassis dipped almost to the ground.

"Goddamn!" Baptiste breathed. "A broken axle."

No one was in sight. Several of the oxen were grazing untethered on the grassy hillside.

"Morgan's saddle horse is gone," Baptiste said. "So's the cow. They must've abandoned the wagon."

"I don't like the looks of it," Lucius muttered. "Don't like it at all." He swung out of his saddle, handed the reins to Baptiste, and approached the disabled wagon.

"Hello! Anybody there?"

No answer.

Lucius glanced back at Baptiste as if hoping for a hint as to what to do next. At that moment, his eyes caught a flicker of movement in the shade of a small clump of trees a short distance away on the downhill slope. Abby Shannon had emerged from the shadows and was standing there blinking in the sun.

"Abby!" Lucius rushed toward her. "Where is everybody! What's happened?"

"I must've fallen asleep," Abby mumbled.

Then Baptiste was there too. The two men leaned over her, and Abby looked from one to the other with vague eyes.

Lucius knelt before her. "What happened, Abby? Tell me."

"Did my mama find you?" she said.

Lucius and Baptiste exchanged a quick look. The girl saw it, and her face immediately twisted in alarm.

"Didn't you meet her? She went to catch up with you. She left early this morning on Papa's horse. She said Byron and I must stay here and take care of Uncle Isaac as best we can till you come and—"

"Take care of *Isaac*? What do you mean? Where is he?"

Abby began to cry softly. Lucius took her by the arms and held her in a fierce grip.

"Abby, tell me! Where's Isaac, and where's Byron?"

With a brave effort the girl kept her emotions in check long enough to force out an answer. "Byron's all better. He's asleep down there under the tree. Uncle Isaac's in the wagon, sick. And Mama..." Control slipped away, tears gushed, and she ended in a piteous wail. "Mama's lost!"

Lucius was up and running toward the wagon.

Baptiste laid a gentle hand on the shoulder of the grief-stricken child, leaned down close to her, and murmured, "Do not worry, Abby. We will find your mama. Everything will be all right."

Abby stood sobbing, inconsolable.

Isaac lay on his back on one of the wagon's narrow bunks. His mouth hung open, his eyes drooped half-closed, his haggard face gleamed with perspiration. He started violently when Lucius touched his brow.

"Catherine..." he whispered. His eyes roamed vacantly over the canvas roof above him. "Catherine, are you there?"

"It's me, old chum. Lucius. I've come to get you."

Isaac turned toward the sound of the voice, but his eyes remained unfocused. "Where's Catherine? Where am I? What's happened?" His voice was a lifeless croak, and his hand clutched feebly at Lucius's clothing as he tried to raise himself.

"Just be calm, old chum. Everything's all right."

Isaac fell back in exhaustion and groaned, "Water..."

Baptiste had come in, stooping awkwardly under the low canvas ceiling. He watched while Lucius dipped water out of a bucket on the floor, lifted the stricken man's head, and held the cup to his parched and ashen lips. Isaac grasped at the cup with a trembling hand and gulped. Immediately his face contorted; his body twisted in a violent spasm; he retched, gasped for air, and lay back in helpless misery as the water he had tried to drink dripped from his chin and dribbled uselessly onto the bedcovers.

His eyes bright with anxiety, Lucius looked to Baptiste. "What can we do?"

Baptiste was already busy, loosening the rope fastenings of the wagon cover. "First thing we do is pull the canvas up, get some air in here." This done, he turned to Lucius and issued a crisp order: "Now get out of here and go see about the children, and let me have a look at the patient."

291

Gratefully Lucius relinquished his position and climbed out of the wagon.

Ten minutes later Baptiste came out carrying the water bucket. Lucius was sitting on a low rock a short distance away with the two children huddled close beside him. As soon as Baptiste appeared Lucius got up and moved to meet him, his eyes searching the other man's face.

"Well?"

Baptiste called to Abby and Bryon, "Children, come." He held out the bucket to them. "Fill this with fresh water for me, please."

Eager to be of help, the children scrambled to obey.

"Well, what do you think?" Lucius persisted. "Is it bad?"

Baptiste's expression was somber. "I think so, Lucius. Pretty bad."

Lucius's initial reaction was anger. "Damn!" He slammed a fist into an open palm. "What is it? The same thing that got Morgan?"

"No, alkali poisoning brings stomach pain, and he evidently hasn't got that. He's burning hot, can't keep anything down, and his mind is wandering. I'm afraid it's what they call trail fever."

"What causes it?"

"Spoiled food, maybe. Or bad water. Maybe just general exhaustion." Baptiste shrugged. "Nobody really knows."

"Is it . . . is it fatal?"

"It can be, if it lasts long enough. What can happen is, the victim just dies of thirst."

Lucius's anger gave way to despair. He sat down again on the rock, rested his head on his forearms and stared at the ground between his feet. "Oh Lord, Lord, why did I do it? He should never have left South Bar. Why did I take him away . . . ?"

He was unaware of the children returning, laboring under the load of the bucket sloshing fresh water over its brim.

"Thank you, children," Baptiste said cheerfully. Then, to Lucius, in a commanding voice: "Come, Lucius, no time for moping. We got things to do."

Lucius looked up, vacant-eyed. "Things to do?"

"Of course! We'll give the sick man a bath now—that'll help the fever a little. Then we got to hurry and round up the oxen before they wander off too far. Then we get after that broken axle. If we're lucky we can get it fixed before dark."

"Then what?"

"Soon as it's light tomorrow we move the hell out."

"What about—" Lucius shot an uneasy glance at Abby and Byron. "What about Catherine?"

"We'll find her. Maybe tomorrow, maybe the next day. But we'll find her."

Lucius scowled his distrust of Baptiste's optimism. "What makes you so damned sure?"

"I got a feeling." Baptiste smiled at the children and gave Lucius a hearty slap on the shoulder. "Come on now, let's get to work."

With a weary sigh Lucius pulled himself to his feet. "Thank God you're here, Baptiste."

At sundown the next day they made camp on a small patch of flatland beneath a towering monolithic stone wall. They had reached a point where the east-west valley began to narrow and climb toward its western terminus. All day they had traveled, wanting to hurry but feeling compelled to move slowly to spare the sufferings of the sick man in the wagon. And all day their eyes had roamed ceaselessly, searching the desolate solitude for some trace of Catherine. In vain.

In the evening Lucius prepared a simple supper of cornmeal cakes and dried antelope meat over a tiny fire, and later, as darkness fell, constructed for the children a little lean-to shelter of buffalo robes beneath a tree. After talking quietly to them for a while he left them in their pallets and walked a little way up to the base of the cliff, and sat down amid a jumble of rocks. Soon Baptiste emerged from the parked wagon and came up to join him. He sat down and took out his pipe and began to fill it from a small pouch. For a few minutes the two men sat without speaking, watching a full moon climb out of a distant range of mountains and bathe the valley in a cold and misty light.

"He's not any better, is he?" Lucius said finally.

Baptiste gave a little shrug. "Hard to tell, for sure. Mind's still wandering. That's not good. Tried to eat a bite, but couldn't swallow it. Took a sip of water, though, and I think he might have kept a few drops. *That's* good."

Lucius was staring at the wagon, lost in despondency. "He's dying, I know it. And it's all my fault."

"He ain't dead yet, Lucius. Don't make any rash predictions."

"I've seen a few deaths the past couple of months. I've seen that crazy wild look in people's eyes. It always turns out the same way."

"I've seen a few more than you have, I'll wager. And I can tell you it *don't* always turn out the same. There just ain't no way to know for sure."

They were quiet again for a while.

"The children all right?" Baptiste asked.

"They're feeling a little better, after I told 'em a pack of lies."

"You told 'em a pack of lies?"

"I told 'em Baptiste knows everything. Baptiste is never wrong. And Baptiste says we're going to find their mother."

Baptiste chuckled and puffed calmly on his pipe.

Lucius huffed with annoyance. "Goddamnit, why don't you stop kidding us? You know damned well we're not going to find her in all this—" He waved his arm in a wide arc. "This trackless wilderness."

"Wilderness, yes. But not trackless. Come here, let me show you something." Baptiste got to his feet, and Lucius sprang up and came quickly to his side.

"Look at that." Baptiste used the stem of his pipe to point back across the miles they had covered that day. The narrow valley lay clearly visible in the moon light, a dark green line winding between gleaming granite cliffs on either side.

"There are only two ways to go—east or west. And since Mrs. Shannon wanted to overtake us, naturally she came west. She didn't go climbing over the cliffs to the north or south, she came *this* way."

"Then why the hell haven't we come across her?"

"Because there is one place where it is possible to make a wrong turn. And she evidently made it."

"Where's that?"

"Right here."

"What?"

"Look yonder." Baptiste pointed up toward the western end of the valley, where the granite cliffs closed in to form a canyon. "There goes the trail, up that way. Now look over there."

The pipestem-pointer swung southward, and following it, Lucius saw a hundred-yard-wide break in the sheer canyon walls, half a mile away.

"There's what you might call a fork," Baptiste said. "Well, *I* wouldn't call it a fork, but when I got to thinking about where she could have gone, it came to me that maybe somebody inexperienced might figure the trail went that way instead."

"*Goddamnit*, Baptiste!" Lucius was clutching at his companion's arm. "That's the answer, isn't it? She went that way—she must've!"

"It's the only place she could have gone."

"Where would it take her?"

"Twenty or thirty miles to a dead end, walled in by mountains. Sooner or later she'd have to stop."

"So all we've got to do is go after her."

"Right."

Lucius glanced at the wagon, and his face clouded. "What about Isaac?"

Baptiste had a plan ready. "Only one way to do it. Tomorrow one of us takes the wagon with Isaac and the children on down to Bear River. Maybe we'll be lucky and find a doctor there. The other will go on horseback to look for Mrs. Shannon."

For a moment the two men stared intently into each other's eyes.

"You take the wagon," Lucius said. "I'll go after Mrs. Shannon."

A slow smile spread over Baptiste's face. "I figured that'd be your choice."

Lucius's earnestness was unruffled. "Will you wait for us at Bear River?"

Baptiste drew a long resigned breath. "Way back yonder when I first joined the Endicott party I made the mistake of saying I'd be your friend. There've been times when I've kicked myself for it. But I said it, and by God, I'll stick to it even if it kills me."

Lucius grasped the big Canadian's hand, and when he spoke his voice shook. "I want you to know I appreciate that, Baptiste, and I swear I'll—"

With a grunt of embarrassment Baptiste pulled himself free.

"Come on, let's get some sleep," he mumbled, and walked away.

(17)

HE HAD RIDDEN almost ten hours with hardly a pause for rest. Now it was late in the afternoon and soon the little wooded canyon would be deep in the shadows of the mountain massif to the west. All day he had followed the shallow brook in the center of the canyon floor, his eyes roving constantly, searching, and had seen no sign of her. And as his horse emerged from a willow thicket and gained the top of a slight rise, bringing into view yet another vista of virgin emptiness, he sagged back in his saddle and felt something hard and chilling grip his throat. Reluctantly he began to mull over the question of what gentle and considerate phrases he might use to impart to Abby and Byron the news that their mother was indeed lost, beyond all hope of finding.

As he rode on he thought: What's to be done with those poor parentless children? Surely there'll be some kind-hearted family that will take them in. The Kendrickses, probably. They're good, decent—

Then he saw her. His eyes had fallen upon a patch of light color in the midst of dark green shade beside the brook, and lay on it idly for several seconds before recognition registered. In the shock of surprise he pulled his horse to an abrupt stop. Then cautiously he rode on, his heart pounding.

She was lying on her back in the grass beneath a cottonwood tree. Her arms were flung out above her head, her auburn hair was loose and spread on the ground. Her eyes were closed and her face was as calm as death, and as pale.

Ten yards from the still form Lucius stopped again, and stared. Is she asleep or dead? he thought wildly. In a trembling voice he called, "Catherine?"

She opened her eyes, turned her head to one side and looked at him. He saw no recognition in her eyes.

He dismounted and walked toward her. "Catherine, are you all right?"

She sat up then, pushed her hair back, and looked around with an expression of dazed confusion.

"The wagon's broken," she said. "And poor Isaac's sick. And where are my children?" Her voice rose quivering in panic.

"Everything's all right, Catherine, don't be alarmed." He was kneeling beside her. "Thank God I've found you." He put a hand to her brow and looked at her closely. "Are you feeling all right?"

She stared at him with eyes gone blank. "Where am I? What day is it?"

"It's Friday, and you're twenty miles off the trail. You took a wrong turn."

"Yes. A wrong turn. I thought so, when I couldn't find the trail anymore."

She looked around, eyes unfocused, attempting to remember. "I tried to turn back, but then it got dark, and I . . . I thought I would die then."

"Well, you didn't. You're safe now." He took her hands and rubbed them vigorously one after the other. "Good Lord, you're cold! You must be half starved."

She watched him, gazing into his face as if at a stranger while he worked on her hands. "How did you find me?"

"Never mind. I found you, that's all that matters." He looked around with a sudden thought. "Where's your horse?"

"Gone. Ran away. I tethered him when night came, but then I thought, if I die, he'll die too. So I let him loose. And in the morning he was gone."

"Hmm. That'll make a problem going back. My old nag's about done for."

"I'm sorry."

"But we'll manage." He was abruptly cheerful. "And I've got plenty of supplies. Buffalo robes for shelter, and lots of food. I'll have you feeling fit in no time. Can you get up now?"

She allowed him to help her to her feet, but then stopped him with a hand on his arm. "Where are my children, Lucius? And what about Isaac?"

"The children are fine. We fixed the wagon, and Baptiste has taken everybody on down to the main trail at the Bear River. He'll wait for us there."

"Lucius—" Her eyes were stricken with sharp fear. "You're not telling me about Isaac."

297

He looked away, eyes darkened with pain, and hesitated a moment before replying, "Yesterday his mind began to wander. He thought he was back in Indiana, kept calling for his Mama Sarah. He was much closer to her than I ever was . . ." His voice broke; he swallowed hard and went on with an effort. "When I left him this morning he didn't know me. He couldn't speak or hold his head up. In his eyes was that certain look that told me what I didn't want to know. We'll never see him again. I'm sure of it."

Catherine had covered her face with her hands and was silently weeping.

He reached out and touched her on the arm. "Catherine—"

With a movement of spasmodic violence she pulled away and turned her back on him. "Go away! Leave me here and let me die too."

"No, Catherine, you're very important to m—"

"You should hate me, hate me! I caused his death, I'm completely to blame!"

With gentle hands that were yet firm with authority he pulled her around to face him and drew her close. She gave in, put her head against his chest, and tears flowed freely.

"There now," he murmured, and stroked her hair. "You mustn't feel guilty for things that can't be helped. We're all leading perilous lives. Some survive, some don't. Those who don't would not have the rest of us falter, they'd want us to carry on as best we can."

He held her until the weeping subsided and she was quiet. Still she remained huddled in his arms.

"I didn't want to leave him," she said after a while. "I thought even then I might never see him again. But when the wagon broke down he insisted that I go and try to find you. The last thing he said to me . . . he grasped my hand and looked at me quite intensely, and he said, 'Catherine, before you go, I want you to know I love you. You're the best reason I have for wanting to go on living. And if I could only know you love me too, I could beat this thing, I really think I could.' So I told him I did. No reservations, no doubts, I just said it. 'I do love you, Isaac, I love you with all my heart. *Please* go on living.'"

Lucius spoke soothingly into her ear. "That was generous of you. A beautiful thing to say."

She looked up at him, frowning, and started to protest. "Oh, I wasn't trying to deceive him, I really meant—"

Suddenly he seized her by the shoulders and held her with

a ferocity that made her gasp. "It was charity, Catherine. A sweet lie, told in kindness. Because it was never Isaac who made your pulse quicken, who appeared in your secret dreams. I am the one, my darling, *I* am the one—"

"Lucius! What are you saying?!"

"I am saying what we've both known in our hearts every long miserable day and lonely night since the first time we saw each other. Since the day you came to our wagon so proper and ladylike with your pencil and ledger book—"

"Lucius, stop it!" She struggled to free herself, but he held her helpless and his words poured over her like a torrent unleashed.

"I loved you then, and I've loved you ever since. I adored you with a passion so powerful it was a terror in my heart—"

"How can that be? You were always so cold, so aloof—"

"It was desperation, Catherine. I was horrified at the thought of being in love with a woman I had no hope of ever possessing. But now it's different. We're together at last, and I must have you. I *will* have you..." He pulled her closer, seeking her lips.

She turned her face away from him. "Let me go, Lucius!"

"I will never do that."

"I'm a cursed woman, and I bring down a curse on every man who comes near me. With my poor husband but a few days dead, I half-promise myself to another. And now yet another—"

"You didn't love Morgan Shannon. Any fool could see that."

Catherine's jaw dropped in horror and astonishment.

"And that was no promise to Isaac. It was comfort and solace to a dying man."

She groaned in her anguish. "Oh, leave me, Lucius, I beg you. I'm cursed, I strew death in my path."

He would not let her escape. "Even if I believed that, I wouldn't let you go. I could not. Even if it were certain death to do so, I would love you—"

He reached her lips at last, held her close and felt her rigid body go slowly limp against him, and dared to believe that she was his.

The thin mountain air was chilling after nightfall, and the cold light of the moon peeping into the corners of their lean-to of buffalo robes was stark illumination devoid of comfort.

They lay side by side, fully dressed, listening to the soft

299

mysterious sounds of the wilderness, and to each other's breathing. He reached out and touched her cheek; his hand moved caressingly down over the curve of her neck to her shoulder. With a subtle pressure he pulled her toward him.

"Lucius, I—" Even in a whisper her voice was tight and strained. "We must not, Lucius."

He was silent, but continued to pull her closer.

"Try to understand, Lucius, I just . . . I can't get Isaac's face out of my mind. And behind his face there is Morgan's. I am haunted by terrible things . . ."

The whisper had become a piteous whimpering.

He brought her to him then, and held her trembling in his arms. "Sleep awhile," he murmured, and stroked her hair with infinite gentleness. "Soon you will dream good dreams, the nightmares will all be gone, and you will know that life is for the living. The dead cannot interfere, nor do they wish to. We are the living, Catherine. Life is for us."

The trembling ceased. He held her like a child until she was asleep.

In some remote and secret hour she stirred, drifting in a dreamlike state halfway between darkness and light, and felt hot breath on her throat. Strong gentle hands were on her body, caressing, searching, pushing her clothing down and away, and a voice almost disembodied in softness was crooning somewhere near, saying something she could not understand but making a sound that drugged her senses. Then suddenly she sucked in her breath from the delicious icy freedom of nudity, and twisted her head this way and that in a frenzy to find the source of the hypnotic voice. Words began to emerge from the crooning sound.

"Darling Catherine . . . my beautiful love . . . this night may be all we are ever to have. Love me, Catherine. We are alone on the earth . . ."

She found his lips then, covered them eagerly with her own, and with a long deep surrendering sigh, stopped all speech.

Outside their little shelter there was the brook, gurgling its mindless little song over insensible stones through the night; a little farther away a lonely whispering of wind in treetops; far off, high on a mountain ledge, the cry of a wild animal. Nothing more.

(18)

IT WAS SUNDAY AFTERNOON when Baptiste found them. He was on his horse and leading a packmule, and he reined up and waited while they came trudging in his direction across a broad stretch of meadow. They were struggling under the weight of saddlebags and other provisions, their eyes downcast, their faces drawn with exhaustion. Catherine, in the lead, saw Baptiste first. She stopped in her tracks, dropped her load, and waved at him with both arms flailing.

"Mr. Bourdeau! Look, Lucius, it's Mr. Bourdeau!"

Then they were running toward him, hand in hand, like two eager children.

"Baptiste!" Lucius gasped, panting. "Thank God!"

Baptiste scowled down at him. "Where the hell are your horses?"

"Catherine's ran off. Mine turned up his heels last night and became food for the vultures."

"*Mon Dieu!* Don't you know the most important thing in the world is to take care of your horses?"

"Excuse me, Mr. Bourdeau." Catherine spoke with tight-lipped determination. "There *are* more important things in the world than horses. What about my children? And what about Isaac? Is he ..."

Lucius stepped to her side and took her hand again as they tensed themselves, waiting for the worst.

"Everybody's doing fine," Baptiste said. His tone was so casual that his listeners stood frozen, not sure they had heard correctly.

"That fellow Isaac," Baptiste went on, "he can sure fool you. He's tough—a lot tougher than he looks. A little weak

301

still, of course, but coming along very nicely."

It was Catherine who reacted first, and the reaction came with the impact of a physical force. "Lucius, did you hear that?!" Excitedly she clutched at him. "He's alive! He's pulling through!"

For Lucius comprehension was slower in coming. He stood slack-jawed and stunned, turning dazed eyes from Baptiste to Catherine and back again. Finally, to Baptiste, in a hoarse voice: "Are you *sure*?"

Baptiste grimaced at the question. "Of course I'm sure. Do you think I go about telling wild tales?"

Catherine was transfigured with radiance. "Lucius... oh, Lucius, isn't it wonderful? A positive miracle, a gift from heaven!" She flung her arms around his neck and clung to him in an ecstatic embrace.

Lucius blinked rapidly several times, his mind in turmoil. "My *God*!" he said breathlessly. "It's absolutely incredible! I could have sworn—"

Acceptance came at last. A broad smile wreathed his face. He held Catherine close to him and laughed, and in a sudden burst of exuberance spun her around, lifting her off her feet, and her joyous laughter mingled with his and rang through the silent spaces of the wilderness. And Baptiste watched, his face soberly thoughtful.

At length Catherine broke away from Lucius and turned shining eyes up to the man on horseback. "Tell us more, Mr. Bourdeau, give us the details!"

"We were lucky," he said. "When we got down to the Bear River junction Friday night, I found the missionary fellow there—Marcus Whitman. *Doctor* Whitman he is, and I reckon he's a good one. He gave our patient a strong purge, and some evil-smelling red medicine that he told me the name of but I couldn't pronounce, and that was that. Next morning Isaac's fever was way down, and by afternoon he was taking nourishment and beginning to worry about *you* two."

Catherine closed her eyes and murmured in a prayerful, half-choking voice, "Oh, thank God... thank God!"

"Thank God..." Lucius echoed in a distant voice. He turned partly away from the others, his gaze drifting off toward some remote mountain peak. "I have never been on speaking terms with God—don't expect to be now. But if He is there, and will hear me, I will say: Thank you, God, thank you... and forgive me if... at any moment in the past two days and nights I have been—" he struggled with the task of putting into words something that had to be pulled up from the darkest depths of his being— "if I have been glad to benefit from the sufferings of my brother..."

His speech became a whisper and trailed off, and during a moment of profound silence he stood with his head bowed and face buried in his hands.

Suddenly he turned, sensing that a mysterious change had taken place around him. He looked quickly at Catherine and saw that the joy that had shone in her face moments before had vanished, and she was staring at him with a kind of horrified wonder.

"Lucius..." Her voice was hushed. "You told me he was dying. You made me believe it."

He was stricken; his jaw dropped open in astonishment and protest. "But *I* believed it, Catherine. I believed it beyond the slightest doubt, you know I did." They stood with their eyes locked together in a silence of thundering intensity from which Baptiste and all else was excluded.

Lucius took a step toward her. "Good Lord, Catherine, do you think I was *lying* to you?"

She had begun to tremble as she went on staring at him, and her answer was agonizingly slow in coming. "I don't know... I may never know."

He seized her by the arms. "Catherine, surely you don't mean you—"

"No, don't!" She pulled herself free, her eyes flashing with a strange light he had not seen before. "Just... don't touch me now. I've got to think." She moved away from him.

Baptiste swung down off his horse. "Excuse me. I hate to interrupt this interesting conversation, but there's something else I want to bring up." His voice was quiet, but its sharp tone of impatience commanded attention.

"The Kendrickses are waiting for us at the Bear River with Isaac and the children. The others have gone on. Even the other members of the Endicott party have passed by and gone on. We are late. We have wasted a full week on this nonsense. I ought to be at Fort Hall right now, enjoying the comforts of home in the arms of my little wife. Instead I am a hundred and fifty miles away, wandering around in the mountains rounding up lost people. Now I want you both to try not to waste another minute of my time, because you've wasted enough of it already. You can settle your private quarrel later. In private."

Catherine was instantly contrite. "I'm sorry, Mr. Bourdeau.

It was all my fault, and I do earnestly beg your—"

"No, it is not your fault, Mrs. Shannon." The big man's manner was gentler now. "It was a foolish thing you did—you should have stayed with your wagon. But never mind, you are not experienced in these things, you did the best you could. The important thing is, you are safe. Everybody has survived, and for that we are all humbly grateful."

He handed her his horse's reins. "Here, you can ride my horse." Then, to Lucius, as he untied the mule's reins: "Come on now, let's get your things packed up and get going." He led the pack animal off toward the spot where the walkers had dropped their belongings.

Lucius waited until the other man was out of earshot, then stepped close to Catherine and spoke in a voice that was pleading, and drained of strength. "Catherine . . . what are we to do?"

"What are we to do, Lucius?" She kept her eyes resolutely away from his. "Why, we are to go back and take up our lives again, as if nothing had happened."

For a moment he was caught in the grip of paralysis. "But . . . what about *us*? What about what *happened* to us? We can't go back to being the same people, we are *not* the same, we are changed forever. We loved each other, Catherine. We belong together now."

Still she would not look at him. "It was an interlude, Lucius. A dream, not attached to the real world."

"That's not *true*!" His voice rose in desperation. "That *was* the real world, for the first time, for both of us, and all the *rest* is a dream—"

"Lucius, listen to me." She had whirled on him, and in her eyes he saw a steel-hard resolve that made him feel again the cold touch of despair. "I am promised to the best and kindest man I have ever known. I'm not quite sure how it came to be, and maybe it's all a horrible mistake—I don't know. But I am promised, and if he lives and still wants me, I will keep my promise."

"But Catherine, you—" Lucius's face contorted in torment as he groped for words. "You *can't* mean that, you know damned well you've never—"

"Come on, Lucius, let's get busy here!" It was Baptiste, shouting from a distance.

For a moment longer Lucius held his gaze on Catherine's face, searching desperately for a last lingering sign to give him hope.

"I mean it, Lucius," she said. "I'm sorry." She reached out and touched him gently on the arm, and the sad look she gave him contained a faint trace of tenderness—which was gone in an instant. "But that's the way it has to be." She turned her back on him.

Head bowed and ashen-faced, his eyes dimming in defeat and vacant misery, he went stumbling blindly off across the meadow to where Baptiste was waiting.

(19)

CATHERINE SHANNON'S Diary:

Fort Hall, Oregon Country
Tuesday, August 29th, 1843

My last entry here was three weeks ago, the day of Morgan's death. I made a resolve then never to write in this book again, but the days since that awful time have been the most momentous, terrifying, soul-searching days of my life, and now I feel compelled at least to record the bare fact that I have survived, and that the world will apparently go on turning.

Of those days I can say only that both my little Byron and my dearest friend, Isaac Hargrave, have passed through the Valley of the Shadow and have been spared; that I have been lost in the wilderness and have known how it feels to face the expectation of death alone; that I was found by Lucius Hargrave and we two were in turn rescued and delivered like little lambs to this haven of rest and safety by that most indomitable of men, Baptiste Bourdeau, the savior of us all. Perhaps some day, if I live to be very old, I will have the courage to relate to some trusted and sympathetic listener all that has transpired. But not now. Not here. Let us leave the shadowy depths behind.

This place is a big quadrangular structure of adobe and timber, situated on the banks of a river known as Lewis' Fork of the Columbia, sometimes called the Snake. Like Fort Laramie, it is not so much a fort as an outpost of trade and commerce. It is owned by the British Hudson's Bay Company, and is under the command of a certain Captain Grant. He is a handsome officer of affable manners who has made us feel welcome, but who has gone to some pains to assure us that this entire Oregon country is decidedly a British possession, and that unless we emigrants are ready to become British subjects we will be better advised to turn toward California. All this has no effect on my friends the Hargraves and the Kendrickses, whose destination was California all along. As for me and the children, we will go along with our friends. Apparently Oregon was never meant for us, any more than it was for poor Morgan, may his soul be at peace.

Mr. Bourdeau's wife is a pretty, shy, delicate young woman of mixed French-Canadian and Shoshone Indian blood whose name (as nearly as I can render it in writing) is Mali-Kuma, meaning something like "the quiet one." She lavishes an infinite store of affection upon her husband, and it is easy to see why he was so eager to get home. They occupy quarters in an out-of-the-way corner of the fort (a privilege Mr. Bourdeau receives as partial payment for his services to the company), and have kindly taken us all in for a day of rest before we go on. The apartment is small and simple—two rooms only, buffalo skins over dirt floors and walls of logs and clay—but the hospitality is genuine, and we all feel surprisingly comfortable. Though Mali has almost no English, she manages to convey through smiles and soft looks a feeling of warmth and friendliness. Ah, me, but for the goodness of strangers I fear we should all have perished long before now.

There is a man here named Caleb Greenwood, a very old and grizzled half-breed, who is urging all travelers to accept him as guide and claims he will lead them to a place called New Helvetia, in the valley of the

Sacramento River in California. This, we are told, is a fortified post established and operated by a Swiss gentleman named John Sutter, and if we will permit ourselves to be escorted there we will find pleasant employment and a prosperous life under the generous protection of this great man. So Mr. Greenwood says. He himself is a murderous-looking individual, but is known and respected by many, including Mr. Bourdeau. I believe we'll be traveling with him, for both Isaac and Mr. Kendricks are listening to his blandishments with eager ears. But not Lucius. He keeps strangely to himself, talks to few, listens to nobody. Oh, how he troubles me.

As I sit writing these lines and enjoying a rare moment of quiet I cannot but reflect upon the incredible turns my life has taken, and the breathtaking speed with which it has all happened. A few weeks ago I was Morgan Shannon's wife and never dreamed of being otherwise. Now I am a widow, have had experiences that are wildly inconsistent with my comfortable old notions of what is right and what is wrong, what is moral and immoral, and now find myself promised to a man I have known barely more than three months. Have I sinned? I'm not sure; I no longer feel confident to make such judgments, about myself or anyone else. It is an intensely unpleasant feeling, a sensation of being cut loose from one's moral moorings, and drifting helplessly. But I am resigned. What I have been through has taught me to accept life on any terms, and be grateful for it.

Lucius was collecting his belongings from the Hargrave wagon while his brother Isaac sat on a bunk watching him.

"One more thing," Lucius said. He pulled a heavy trunk away from a forward corner, opened it, and extracted from its recesses an ancient scarred and tattered leather satchel. He smiled at Isaac.

"That's it. You can take all the rest."

Isaac was frowning mightily. "Lucius, are you *sure* you want to do this?"

"Absolutely."

"But what are you going to *do* here all winter?"

"Plenty. In the fall I'm going hunting with Baptiste while Justin stays with Mali and learns some crafts and a bit of

Shoshone language. Then we'll cure the meat, dry the hides, and spend the winter making clothes. Haven't you noticed those beautiful buckskin shirts and breeches the Bourdeaus wear?"

"*You* don't know how to do that kind o' thing!"

"I'm going to learn, old chum. A man isn't alive if he's not learning." He smiled and gently stroked the leather satchel as if it were a living thing.

Sadness clouded Isaac's face. "It just won't seem right, goin' on without you."

"I'll be along in the spring. Baptiste says we'll start as soon as the snow melts. You'll hardly be settled in before we're there."

"Maybe we could get Mr. Greenwood to wait a day or two, if you want to think about it a little longer."

Lucius laughed. "Wait? It's the end of August, old chum, be realistic. You heard what Greenwood said. He's going to drive you lickety-split down the Mary's River and across the desert till your wagons fall apart. Then he's going to load you on the horses and mules and drive you over the mountains. You've got a long way to go before winter hits, and Greenwood's not going to let you rest, not one minute."

Isaac sagged on the bunk and hung his head. "Well then, I guess tomorrow morning it's goodbye again."

"Not goodbye, old chum. It's 'I'll see you in the spring.'"

"I wanted you to be my best man."

Lucius's face went dark. "You really think she's going to marry you."

"Of course she is, Lucius. We love each other, and she's given me her promise. Oh, I'm not going to press the subject, not till we get to California. It doesn't seem decent, you know? Everything's happened so awfully fast for her."

Lucius began to examine the frayed corners of the old satchel. "Oh, well... when and if the time comes, I'm sure you'll be able to find a suitable best man."

"But it ought to be *you*, Lucius."

Lucius exploded in sudden anger. "Damnit, you can't always have everything exactly the way you want it. For God's sake, don't be childish *all* your life!"

Clutching his satchel and his bag of belongings, he climbed out of the wagon and stalked away.

In two weeks of sales-talking old Caleb Greenwood had recruited a dozen or so wagons of emigrants for California, including several who were remnants of the old Endicott party. And at dawn on Thursday, the thirty-first of August, the caravan was drawn up on the open field before Fort Hall, ready to depart on the final leg of a journey that had begun in May twelve hundred miles back on the Kansas River, a time and place so remote now in the minds of the weary travelers as to be almost beyond remembering.

Lucius Hargrave and Baptiste Bourdeau were there to say goodbye, and slender doe-eyed Mali Bourdeau, holding a sleepy Justin Hargrave in her arms. Justin was hugged and kissed first by his Uncle Isaac, then by Catherine Shannon, then by his friend Abby Shannon, and by the time he waved goodbye to his other friend Byron the full solemnity of the occasion had dawned on him.

"Wanna go to California too," he whimpered, and Mali hugged him close.

Later, when Baptiste came to where Catherine was standing beside her wagon, she smiled and gave him her hand. "There's no way I can thank you for all you've done, Baptiste. You've saved our lives not just once, but many times. You know you'll always be welcome at my house, wherever it may be. Always."

"Thank you, madame. I'll accept that kindness when I see you in the spring."

After Baptiste had moved on Isaac came to Catherine's side and spoke to her in a low voice. "I'll walk on back with Baptiste so you can have a chance to speak with Lucius alone, all right?"

She reacted in alarm. "Oh no, Isaac, I don't think that's a good idea."

"Why not? Maybe he'll drop a hint to you about *why* he's so damned determined to separate himself from us."

"But, really, I don't think—"

"Here he comes," Isaac said under his breath, and hurried away.

Lucius walked up to her and took the hand she offered and gazed at her without speaking.

"Goodbye, Lucius," she said. "I'm really distressed that you've decided not to come with us, but...I suppose you know what's best for yourself. Anyway, we'll look forward to seeing you in the spring."

"We haven't spoken to each other in an age," he said. He was still holding her hand.

She uttered a nervous little laugh and pulled her hand back.

309

"Why, what do you mean? I think we've been very polite and civilized."

"Oh yes. Very polite. Perfectly civilized. Please and thank you. Good morning. Excuse me. How are you? But we haven't *talked* to each other."

"Just now we...we don't really have anything to talk about."

"Don't we? We don't have precious knowledge we can never share with anybody else in the world? Of two beautiful days, just you and I and the wilderness? Of lying in the grass together, beneath the trees, of two wonderful nights in each other's arms—"

"Lucius, *stop* it!" she hissed, and turned her eyes away from him.

"Oh, I know, it was just an interlude, detached from reality. I must put it out of my mind."

"Yes. That is exactly what you must do."

"I can't."

"You *must*. Because it was insanity, Lucius. Utterly irresponsible, selfish, sinful, unthinking . . . and besides that—" something hard came into her voice— "I can't get it out of my mind that you may have deceived me."

"I see." He was glowering now. "For a brief time I thought there was love between us, and that love contains trust. Evidently I was wrong. There was neither."

"Love or not, trust or suspicion...I don't know anymore." She made a weary little gesture. "Whatever it was, it's gone now, and can never be brought back."

There was a growing clamor of activity at the head of the wagon train, and suddenly the gravelly voice of old Caleb Greenwood whooped out the signal that it was time to move out. People scurried to their places amid shouts and last-minute farewells.

"Goodbye, Lucius," Catherine said. Her voice was almost a whisper, barely audible above the din. "We have no cause for complaint, you and I. We took more than we deserved, you know, and we have not been punished for it. I consider us both very lucky people."

Then Isaac was beside him, holding Abby and Byron by the hands, and the children, animated with excitement, chattered at Lucius in shrill voices: "G'bye, Uncle Lucius . . . g'bye . . . bring Justin soon, all right? We'll be waiting for him . . ."

"Goodbye, children," he mumbled at them. "Have a good

310

trip. Take care of your mother." His eyes were still on Catherine, who had already climbed onto the driver's seat of her wagon.

Isaac clapped him on the shoulder. "Well, we're off, Lucius. Baptiste tells me he expects to have you and Justin at Mr. Sutter's place by the middle of April at the latest. Now don't dawdle, you hear? We'll be very anxious..."

The lead wagons were moving out.

Lucius stood watching until the procession had moved far down the rolling slopes toward the river, turned southwestward, and was almost out of sight. The field was quiet. The sun was far up, the sky bright blue, and tall cumulus clouds floated serenely above the great wilderness far to the north.

Lucius took a deep breath. "Nice day for traveling," he said to himself.

There was a slight tug at his pants leg, and he looked down into Justin's sad little face.

"Papa? Why don't we go to California?"

"We will, Justin, we will. We're going in the spring. Very soon."

"Will I see Abby and Byron again?"

"Of course you will. They said they'd be waiting for you."

"And Aunt Catherine, and Uncle Isaac too?"

"Yes, of course. We'll all be together again." Lucius lifted the child in his arms and held him close. "But mostly it's going to be you and me, Justin. Just you and me together. We're going to stick together always, come what may. Let's promise each other that, all right?"

Justin was comforted. "All right, Papa."

At the gates of the fort a hundred yards away Baptiste cupped his hands and called, "Hey, Lucius! Come on. We got things to do."

Lucius threw a quick glance to the southwest. The wagon train was almost gone, a line of infinitesimal dots crawling on the distant horizon. He smiled at Justin, ruffled the boy's hair playfully and kissed him on the cheek, and carried him bouncing on his shoulder toward the fort.

(20)

FROM THE JOURNAL of Lucius Hargrave:

I have always been afflicted with a strange predilection for
weak companions, and never has this peculiarity caused me
more anguish than in the case of my dear, lovable,
exasperating half-brother, Isaac. Out of compassion and
kindness I undertook to rescue him from his monastic
existence in South Bar, succeeded at the cost of turning my
mother against me—and soon discovered that the entire
operation had been a ghastly mistake. At the age of thirty-four
Isaac was still a child, unequipped to deal with the harsh
realities of the world.

He never understood the dangers involved in our journey
West. When Indian braves appeared, menacing in their
warpaint and scowling with murderous thoughts no white
man could fathom, the rest of us quietly reached for our guns
and kept them at the ready. Not Isaac. He walked among the
savages smiling and unafraid, offering his hand in friendship.
More than once he had to be extricated from a difficult
situation and lectured on his foolhardiness. He would not
learn. Whenever a member of the party became ill Isaac was
the first to volunteer his services in caring for the sick or, if
need be, in burying the dead, with no thought for his own
safety. I believe it was his pathetic way of saying, "Look here,
I am a man, let me participate in these important grown-up
matters."

I have mentioned how he dismayed me on our journey by
falling in love with one of our fellow travelers. No one could
deny that Catherine Shannon was a beautiful and gifted
woman, and under favorable circumstances any man might

fall in love with her. But Isaac cared not for circumstances. Since he had no dishonorable intentions (seducing any woman—let alone a married one—was not a thing he could have conceived of) he saw nothing wrong in following Mrs. Shannon around like a devoted puppy. This was trouble enough while Morgan Shannon was there to glare ferociously at any man who glanced in his wife's direction. Trouble became a crisis when Morgan fell ill, and then, as swiftly as the crash of a thunderbolt, died. True to his nature—heedless of the danger of infection, unconcerned that his behavior was imperiling not only his own life but the lives of others—Isaac unhesitatingly appointed himself guardian of the widow and her two children.

What happened in the weeks thereafter is the tale I cannot tell. It is Isaac's and Catherine's story, not mine, and they spin it the way they choose. Indeed, they later developed a rosy romanticized myth to enchant the children with, about how they found their true love in the face of danger along the great Western trail. It is as good a myth as ever I heard, and serves its purpose well. I will content myself with saying merely that Isaac succeeded in catching the fever and lay for days on the brink of death, that Catherine managed to get herself lost in the wilderness, and that at some peril to ourselves Baptiste Bourdeau and I were able to rescue them both and lead them finally to safety at Fort Hall.

There, in the comfortable little home of Baptiste and his charming wife, I knew I had had enough. While Isaac and Catherine and her children went on to California with another party I accepted the Bourdeaus' invitation to stay with them over the winter. Justin and I spent six months there, learning the ways of the woodsman and the crafts and language of the Shoshone, one of the most engaging of American native peoples. It was the happiest time of our lives. Then in the spring we departed on horseback, following Baptiste and leading several packmules, on the final leg of our long journey. And Justin, who had cried bitterly at parting with the others the previous August, now cried just as bitterly at having to leave his "Aunt Mali." My heart suffered with him. But for the very young, grief dissipates quickly before the dazzlement of new adventure; by the second day he was singing Shoshone chants at the top of his lungs and babbling excitedly about going to California.

We entered the Valley of the Sacramento from the north in mid-April, 1844, almost exactly one year from that day in the distant past when we had departed from faraway South Bar, Indiana. And as I looked upon the tremendous open grassland surrounding us, mostly uninhabited, virtually treeless, and so strangely unlike the landscape of my youth, I was struck by the thought that I was now permanently separated from every scene of my entire past life, and from almost every familiar face. Suddenly I found myself longing to be reunited with that brother to whom I had said goodbye with some relief a few months earlier. And every night I hugged my little son close to me in sleep, listened to his gentle breathing, and felt sure that henceforth his life and mine would be more closely intertwined than ever.

Part Five

(1)

THERE WAS a primitive ferry across the American River at a point about two miles upstream from the place where the westward-flowing current widened and slowed and lost its force in a sea of tule grass, and joined its waters with the Sacramento. On the south bank of the American, some hundred yards up a little slope from the ferry landing, Isaac Hargrave was working. He was stripped to the waist and his thin bony frame gleamed with sweat as he repeatedly lifted an axe and brought it expertly down on a short section of log. He was splitting shingles. Around him, in a hundred-foot-square area covered with a soft carpet of wood chips and bark, several other men were working with whipsaws, laboriously converting logs into rough lumber.

Isaac paused to rest. He straightened, grimaced as he clutched at his aching back muscles, and wiped his brow with a large kerchief. He was about to take a fresh grip on the axe handle when he glanced toward the river and saw that the ferry barge was just being poled in to the landing. There were three passengers on the ferry—two men and a small boy—and several horses and packmules. Isaac froze for a few seconds while he studied the group. Then he flung his axe down and raced toward the river with an exultant shout, and the men around him paused in their work and stared after him in dumb astonishment.

As soon as Lucius stepped off the barge Isaac grasped his hand and shook it with a force that caused the younger man to grimace.

"Lucius, you sly ol' fox you, sneakin' up on me like this! But thank the Lord you're here! This is wonderful, just wonderful..."

Then Justin ran up to him, and Isaac opened his arms and shouted, "Justin, you rascal!" and lifted the boy off his feet and twirled him around and around, making him squeal.

Finally Isaac turned to Baptiste and greeted him with beaming pleasure. "You didn't have any trouble finding me, I hope?"

"Not a bit. All the natives around here seem to know you. Told us just where you were." Baptiste was chuckling. "They kept saying, '*Señor* 'Argrave *es hombre bueno. Muy bueno.*'"

Lucius waited patiently until Isaac turned back to him. Then with studied casualness he asked, "So, how's Catherine?"

"Fine, fine. Everybody's fine." Isaac was grinning, waiting for the next question.

"You, uh... you married?'

"Congratulate me, Lucius. I'm not only a married man, but the happiest one in the world."

Congratulations came instead from Baptiste, who laughed heartily and shook Isaac's hand all over again while Lucius stood silent and blank-faced.

"Yes, congratulations, by all means," Lucius mumbled finally.

"We were married in October, just a few days after we got here," Isaac said. "Everybody at Sutter's Fort turned out for it, just like we were their dearest friends instead of perfect strangers. Captain Sutter gave the bride away, Lucius, can you imagine that? Quite an honor, I tell you, because Captain Sutter's a very busy man."

"Well, that's... very nice," Lucius said vaguely.

"But let's not waste time standing around *here*," Isaac said impatiently. "Let me get my shirt on, and we'll go on up to the house. Catherine's goin' to be tickled to see you."

They went along a trail in a southeastward direction away from the river, Baptiste and Justin coming along behind with the animals while Isaac and Lucius walked on ahead. Isaac chattered continuously.

"Lord, I'm glad you're here, Lucius! Baptiste said we could

318

expect you by the middle of April and here it is the twenty-fourth, so naturally we were beginnin' to get anxious. But now that you're here we can relax and breathe easy at last, thank the Lord. Oh my, Catherine's goin' to be tickled! She's just been pinin' away for Justin. So have Abby and Byron. You're goin' to be surprised when you see our house, Lucius. It's not fancy, but it sure is cozy."

They came to a fork in the trail, and as Isaac took the left branch he pointed uphill to the right. "There's Sutter's Fort up there. You can just barely see it from here."

Lucius craned his neck and got a glimpse of the upper reaches of a typical high-walled fortification standing on a rise of open ground.

"Captain Sutter's a fine man," Isaac went on. "We were ready to drop in our tracks by the time we finally got here, but his hospitality saved us. He was happy as could be when he found out I'm experienced in lumbering, and right off asked me to take charge of that kind of work for 'im. I swear, Lucius, I really do believe I'm the luckiest fellow anywhere. I've got a job, I've got a home, I've got the sweetest lady in the world for a wife, and two beautiful children that I love as much as I would my own. And that's not all. Pretty soon there'll be a third one."

Lucius stopped dead still on the path.

Isaac was grinning proudly. "Yep. Catherine's expectin' sometime next month."

He chuckled as he saw Lucius's dumbfounded reaction, took his brother by the arm, and pulled him on. "Oh, it's not mine, Lucius. I know that, and everybody else does too. It's what Catherine calls . . . let me see, how does she put it? The final stamp Morgan Shannon put on the world before he departed from it."

"Very pretty," Lucius muttered.

"But that's all right with me. We'll have children of our own eventually, I know we will. But Abby and Byron are just like my own flesh and blood, and I'm goin' to feel the same way about this new baby too." He clapped Lucius on the shoulder. "I tell you, Lucius, I'm the luckiest man alive. I really mean that."

Lucius kept his eyes straight ahead and said nothing.

Abby saw them first, as she emerged from the squat little log-and-adobe house that was half-hidden between two venerable pepper trees, and she gave an excited cry that

319

brought Byron on the run across the yard and Catherine wide-eyed to the doorway. It was the beginning of several minutes of joyous babble.

Justin rushed at Catherine, shouting, "Aunt Catherine, Aunt Catherine!"

She stooped to give him a hug and examined him from head to toe with shining eyes. "Just *look* at you, Justin! You've grown so strong and tall!"

"My name is *Tu-gu-tsi-yu-qui-na*," Justin announced proudly. "That means Little Eagle."

Catherine laughed and hugged him again. "Oh, my fine little eagle!"

Abby and Byron had fallen upon Justin and were pulling him away with wild shouts, demanding his attention. Catherine turned to the others: first to Baptiste, shaking hands and graciously accepting a kiss on the cheek, then to Lucius, with whom she exchanged the same greetings with no perceptible change of manner.

Lucius's smile was blandly polite as he murmured, "Nice to see you, Catherine. You're looking lovely." He kept his eyes averted from her swollen figure.

"I'm awfully glad you're here at last," she said, addressing Baptiste and Lucius equally. "Isaac and I have been watching and waiting for days."

Isaac was hovering at her elbow. "Let's go inside, dear," he urged. "You shouldn't be on your feet too long."

Catherine gave him an indulgent pat on the cheek. "I'm terribly spoiled, you see," she said smilingly to the others. "Isaac pampers me outrageously."

They sat on simple homemade chairs in the front room of the low-ceilinged little house.

"How'd you come, over the Sierras?" Isaac wanted to know.

"When you travel with Baptiste you don't go over the Sierras," Lucius said, "you go around 'em."

"I quarrel with the California guides," Baptiste said. "Why turn south from the upper Snake and go across the worst desert and highest mountains when you can go on down the Snake to Fort Boise, turn southwest, follow the Malheur and the Pit to the Sacramento, and straight down the valley? Easy."

Isaac was prepared to argue the point. "Caleb Greenwood said the shortest way was down the Mary's River and across the Sierras. And he said you can't take wagons down the Snake, the terrain's too rough."

"Did you take wagons over the mountains?"

"Well, no, we had to leave 'em, but that was just for the final push. Anyway, Captain Sutter says there'll be a road over the mountains in a few years, and wagons'll be able to roll right across."

"Oh yes, maybe in some future time there will be roads everywhere." Baptiste shook his head over this melancholy prospect. "I hope I won't live to see the day."

Isaac shifted his attention to his brother. "I wrote to Mama Sarah as soon as we got here, Lucius. Told her all about Catherine and me. Told her we'd write again as soon as you arrived."

"Yes, well...I'm sure you'll take care of it."

"You know the mail has to go down to the coast, wait for the first ship going to Boston, and be taken around the Horn. Have to figure on at least five months, then at least five or six more for an answer. Terrible!"

"Boston ships put in often?"

"Once in a while. Nothing regular."

"How about ships from New Orleans?"

"Uh...I don't know about that."

"What are the main ports?"

"The one we use is Yerba Buena, on the San Francisco Bay. Fine harbor, but not much of a town. A few shanty buildings only. Monterey's really the main port, and the capital too. Beautiful place, they say. Then farther south there are places called Santa Barbara, San Pedro, San Diego, one or two others. None of 'em very big. Why do you ask?"

"Oh, just curious." Lucius had stretched out on a homemade cot made of a network of rope stretched across a wooden frame and covered with a hide. Idly he studied the open beams of the ceiling.

Catherine glanced at him. "It's a nice house, isn't it, Lucius? Isaac built it with his own hands. I'm so proud of him!"

Isaac protested, "Now, dear, you know everybody at the fort pitched in to help." To the two men he added, "You'd be surprised what a magical effect a civilized woman has in a place like this. Especially a beautiful one like Catherine."

"Ah, yes," Baptiste said, chuckling.

Lucius remained silent.

"I had nothing to do with it," Catherine said firmly. "It's because Isaac is an experienced sawmill operator. When

321

Captain Sutter found out about that, well, nothing was too good for us."

Isaac picked up on this new subject. "They're sure in bad shape for lumber around here. Trouble is, there's no timber available. There aren't any forests in this valley, for heaven's sake. We're draggin' logs cross-country by ox team from the foothills, forty miles away. Naturally, we got to do better'n that. Captain Sutter thinks maybe we could set up a mill up the river someplace, and jus' float the lumber down to the fort. I said I wasn't sure about that—might take more time and manpower than it's worth—but I told him I'd look into it."

Lucius sat up. "You mean you intend to work for this fellow Sutter permanently?"

"Oh, I don't know about permanently, Lucius. But for the time being it's the ideal arrangement. He's got what we need, and we can—"

"What's he got that you need?"

"A settlement. Other people like ourselves. Do you realize that Captain Sutter's is the only place in California that Americans can come to and be sure to find employment and shelter? All the rest of it's either Indian country or Spanish ranchos."

"You keep calling him 'Captain.' What's he captain of?"

"Used to be a captain in the French Army, he says. But not just an ordinary captain, a captain in the Swiss Guards. That's something special, I guess."

"Um-hmm. Another one of those military dandies." Lucius was rubbing his chin in thought. "But he's got quite a little power base here, apparently. How'd he come by it? The land, I mean."

"Got a land grant years ago, from the Mexican governor in Monterey."

"Can't other people do that too?"

"Well, it's not that easy. The *Californios* are already complainin' to the government about so many Americans comin' in uninvited. Uh, *Californios*—that's the Spanish-blooded people of California. They don't like to be called Mexicans. Anyway, even if you *can* wheedle a land grant, there's a stiff price to pay. You have to become a Mexican citizen, and you have to be Catholic. That's too high a price for me. I can't change my nationality and my religion just to get a free piece of land. I'd rather work at an honest job, save my money, and wait for the day when I can *buy* myself some land."

322

Lucius made a wry face. "I thought we were coming to California to find some exciting new opportunities. All *you* seem to be looking for is another South Bar, Indiana—"

"Lucius," Catherine broke in crisply, "Isaac is a decent hard-working man, not an adventurer. When he came here he took on the responsibilities of a wife and family, and when he looked around to see what he could do he made his decision with those responsibilities in mind. I think he's made an excellent beginning."

Lucius stared at her. "I stand corrected," he murmured almost inaudibly.

Isaac crossed the room and sat down next to him. "I was countin' on you to join me, Lucius. For a while, at least, till you've had a chance to look around for yourself. I've told Captain Sutter you were comin', and he's real anxious to meet you. He asked me what you could do, and, uh . . ."

Lucius smiled at Isaac's faltering. "Pretty tough question, eh?"

"I told him you'd work with me on the lumberin' operations."

"Oh God!" Lucius groaned, and clasped his forehead and stared at the floor.

"Just for a while, Lucius. And you can stay right here with us. Justin can move in with Byron, and there's a spare room in back big enough for you and Baptiste too, if he can stay."

Baptiste smiled and shook his head. "No, thank you. I go up to the fort for a day or two to visit some people I know, then down to Yerba Buena to take care of some business at the Hudson's Bay Company office there, then back home."

"Well then, you and Justin can move right in," Isaac said to Lucius, and put a hand on his brother's shoulder. "We'll be a big happy fam—"

"You know, Isaac, I was thinking," Catherine said suddenly. "For a man like Lucius, unencumbered with a wife, I expect it'd be better to stay at the fort than with a houseful of noisy children. There are quite comfortable quarters there, Lucius."

Lucius nodded and said, "Whatever you say, ma'am," in a way that made Catherine look at him sharply.

Isaac started to argue. "Aw, you wouldn't like it at the fort, Lucius. It's kind of . . . well, military-like."

"It'll be fine," Lucius said curtly.

"Well, at least he'll stay here tonight," Isaac said.

"Oh, of course," Catherine agreed. "And of course you'll

323

leave Justin here with us, Lucius. Please. He needs home life and a family. And we all love him so much."

"Fine, then, it's all settled," Isaac said cheerfully, and clapped Lucius on the shoulder again. "*Lord,* I'm glad you're here!"

After supper Isaac and Lucius walked Baptiste up to Sutter's Fort. Then, because the spring evening was balmy, they strolled back by a roundabout way and watched the last light fade on the placid gray waters of the river. And Isaac took a sidelong look at Lucius and became reflective.

"I know I've said it several times, Lucius, but I've got to say it once more. I'm a very lucky man. And it's not just the wonderful family and the house and the job, and all that. There's somethin' else, and it's high time I admitted it."

"What's that?"

"You."

A startled look came into Lucius's face, and disappeared immediately. He picked up a stone and plopped it into the river and watched the ripples spread in a quivering circle.

"I mean it, Lucius." Isaac went on. "I've been telling Catherine all along, I owe everything to you. If you hadn't dragged me away from South Bar I would've stayed there forever, plodding away with no point to my life at all. My God, Lucius! Do you realize, if you hadn't made me come with you, I'd never have met Catherine!"

"Hmmm," Lucius said. He picked up another rock and threw it far out into the middle of the stream.

They came to a rise in the path from which the house could be seen in a little hollow slightly below them, tucked cozily between its pair of pepper-tree guardians and radiating squares of warm lamplight through its windows. There Isaac took hold of Lucius's arm and pulled him to a stop.

"You know what we've got here, Lucius?"

Lucius sighed. "What have we got here, old chum?"

"We've got the same kind of situation that Grandpa Gilpin had when he settled in Indiana way back in 1800. We're pioneers, Lucius. Almost half a century later and twenty-five hundred miles farther west, we're following in Grandpa Gilpin's footsteps." Isaac's eyes were shining. "Doesn't that give you a kind of ... kind of tingly feeling?"

Lucius took a moment to consider the question. "No," he said finally.

"Aw, come on, Lucius! Grandpa Gilpin was a very wise man, and he always used to tell us we ought to learn all the history we could, because if we had some idea of where we came from we'd be better able to figure out where we are and where we're goin'. Now for the first time in my life I'm beginnin' to get a notion of what he was talkin' about. Maybe I *am* just workin' at kind of an insignificant job here, but I keep havin' the feelin' that in my own small way I'm helpin' to make history." Isaac grinned, sheepish over his sudden burst of speechmaking.

Lucius was studying him with a preoccupied look. "Tell me something, old chum. How far is it to Monterey?"

"Oh, 'bout a hundred miles, maybe a little more." Isaac blinked in sudden alarm. "Hey, don't tell me you're goin' to go rushin' off like a darn fool, lookin' for some kind o' golden opportunity. There's plenty of opportunity right here."

He was clutching his brother's arm again. "Stay with us, Lucius. We need you."

Lucius frowned as he gazed down at the little house in the hollow below them. "I'll stay . . . for a while."

"How long? If you'll stay through the summer, at least, we can get a lot done."

"I can promise only this much—I will stay until Catherine's baby is born."

Isaac was not entirely satisfied. "Well . . . Catherine'll be pleased about *that*, anyway."

"I wonder," Lucius said. He spoke softly, as if to himself.

(2)

IT WAS ISAAC'S favorite joke to refer to the woodcutting area on the south bank of the American River as Thacker and Hargrave, Associates, Western Branch. The primitive little facility bore no resemblance to the fine well-equipped establishment back in Indiana, but Isaac had developed affection for it, and a strong professional pride. Some dozen men were his crew—one or two Americans, but mostly Mexicans or Indians or a mixture—and he directed them with a kindly gentleness that did not obstruct his firm authority; he got the job done.

For several weeks after his arrival Lucius worked as a member of a detachment of men engaged in the enormous task of cutting timber in the Sierra's forested foothills and transporting it by ox teams, foot by grinding foot, forty miles to the sawpit at New Helvetia for conversion into desperately needed lumber. It was brutal work, straining bodies and tempers to the utmost. Lucius quarreled frequently with the other men; they complained to Isaac upon returning to the home camp; Isaac lectured Lucius repeatedly and patiently on the necessity of maintaining harmonious relations. Lucius fumed and grumbled and accepted his brother's better judgment grudgingly.

He spent little time at Isaac's and Catherine's house. When he was not away in the mountains he came every afternoon for a brief visit with Justin—or Little Eagle, as the boy insisted on being called—and during these visits became popular with the Shannon children as well, playing games and telling stories and conferring solemnly with Little Eagle on the matter of inventing colorful Shoshone names for Abby and Byron, to their delight. But he exchanged nothing more than polite greetings with Catherine and adamantly refused invitations to stay for dinner, accepting only on an occasional Sunday.

On Saturday the eighteenth of May, Baptiste Bourdeau returned to New Helvetia from a three-week trip to Yerba Buena. He was greeted warmly and invited to join a Sunday dinner gathering at the Hargraves' house the next day.

Sunday was bright and beautiful, and at the noontime dinner table Baptiste remarked that there were fat salmon running in the river, and proposed an afternoon fishing expedition. Lucius seconded the motion, and the children shouted their approval. Isaac would not go, he said. He would see the fishing party off but return to stay with Catherine. After all, her baby was due almost anytime.

So about two o'clock the men and children went off to the river, and Catherine took a book and settled herself in a chair. In a little while, hearing someone come into the house, she looked up to greet Isaac—and uttered a little gasp of surprise.

"I'm sorry," Lucius said. "Did I startle you?"

"Oh, not at all, I . . . I was expecting Isaac, that's all."

326

"I told him I'd stay with you so he could go fishing."

"Oh . . . I see." Catherine's fingers played nervously with the edges of the book's pages.

Lucius took a chair and brought it close to hers and sat down. "What's that you're reading?"

"Oh, it's, uh . . . it's called *Two Years Before the Mast*, by a man named Richard Henry Dana. Describes life in California. Listen to this." Catherine raised the book and read a passage aloud:

"The Californians are an idle, thriftless people, and can make nothing for themselves. The country abounds in grapes, yet they buy bad wine made in Boston and brought round by us, at an immense price, and retail it among themselves . . ."

She lowered the book. "Sounds rather arrogant, doesn't he? Typical Yankee superiority."

"I expect he's right, though," Lucius said. "I'd like to borrow that book sometime."

She gave him a gently reproachful look. "The last time I offered to lend you a book I was thoroughly rebuffed."

"Yes." Lucius sighed. "I've made a few dumb mistakes in my life, Catherine. Letting good ol' Isaac get ahead of me with you is by all odds the dumbest."

She looked unsure of what to say. "Well . . . thanks for offering to stay with me. Though of course I don't need it. I'm perfectly all right."

"Oh, it's no sacrifice," Lucius said airily. "The truth is, I consider fishing the world's dullest occupation. Duller even than sawing timber. But Isaac was dying to go, excited as the children. I insisted he go instead of me, told him I'd be happy to sit with you. He expressed some doubt as to my competence. Said if you had the slightest pain I should run to the fort and fetch Señora Sanchez, the weaver's wife. I told him not to worry, I was quite capable of looking after you for a couple of hours. After all, I looked after you for two whole days once. Of course, I didn't mention that *last* item."

Catherine had fixed him with a hard stare. "Why not? He knows about it. He knows I got lost and you came and found me, and then Baptiste came and rescued both of us. He knows all that."

"Does he now?" Lucius's eyebrows went up. "Does he know . . . *all* that?"

She made no answer, and her eyes fell away from him.

327

"I'll tell you something I've discovered about what Isaac knows and doesn't know," Lucius went on. "It's very curious. He has only the haziest idea of *when* all that happened. He remembers that after Morgan died he began to take care of you and the children, then Byron got sick, then *he* got sick, then you went to find us, and pretty soon he was with Baptiste, and then with the Kendrickses, and a doctor was treating him, and finally we were all together again and on our way to Fort Hall. But he has no conception of the time span involved. No notion at all about *dates*."

Catherine kept her eyes on her open book. "That's understandable, isn't it? He was a very sick man."

"Yes. And that's the answer to the riddle that had me baffled for a good long while. Why it is that Isaac is able to accept the rather fantastic arithmetic involved."

She closed her book and set it aside now, and looked steadily at Lucius. "What arithmetic?"

"You know damned well what arithmetic, Mrs. Hargrave. Morgan got sick way back in the latter part of July, before we ever crossed South Pass. He was sick for a good three weeks before he died."

"And?"

"And here it is the latter part of May. If that's Morgan Shannon's child you're carrying, you've been carrying it for at least ten months."

She had stiffened and turned deathly pale, but her eyes did not falter from his. "What of it? That's not an unheard-of biological phenomenon."

"Give me no learned discourses on biological phenomena, dear lady." Without warning he slipped off his chair and knelt beside hers and grasped her wrist with an intensity that made her cringe. "You know as well as I do that it's my child you're carrying—"

"Lucius, hush!" She tried to pull away from him, but he held her fast and brought his burning eyes closer to hers.

"Admit it, Catherine. *It's my . . . child.*"

Defiance blazed in her eyes. "I will *not* admit it! I would die before I'd admit any such thing!"

There was a moment of bristling silence while they strained against each other.

"Let me go," she whispered.

He released her and rose, breathing heavily. "Look at me, Catherine."

She refused. "Go away," she said. "Leave me alone."

"I have something to say to you, and I want you to consider it well. If you mean to deny forever the fact that we once loved each other, then do it, that's your privilege. But, Catherine... listen to me, Catherine, hear this. If it's a son ..."

She looked up at him with the quickness of sudden fear.

"If it's a son... I will claim him for my own."

She stared, transfixed. "I don't believe you," she breathed. "Only a devil could be capable of that."

"Man or devil, I will do it," he said, speaking now in deadly calm. "I swear."

After a moment she got to her feet. "Please excuse me. I'm going to lie down now." She swayed, and put a hand on the chair to steady herself. Lucius moved toward her. "Don't!" she said fiercely. "Don't come near me." Moving with careful deliberation she crossed the room to her bedroom, and closed the door softly behind her.

In half an hour Isaac returned home and found Lucius sitting alone in the front room reading Richard Henry Dana.

"Back so soon?" Lucius asked.

Isaac looked around quickly. "Where's Catherine?"

"Don't get panicky, old chum. She's taking a nap."

Isaac tiptoed to a chair. "I begged off the fishing trip," he said in a whisper. "Hated to leave Baptiste alone with that tribe of young Indians, but he said he could manage all right."

"Worried about Catherine? No need to, she's fine."

Isaac drew a long sigh. "It's not only that. I've gotten to the point where I just can't enjoy anything unless she's with me. She means so much to me, Lucius, I just can't tell you. She's... I don't know ... she's my whole life."

Lucius gazed at his brother for a long thoughtful moment. Then he put the book down and got to his feet.

"I'll see you tomorrow, old chum." He moved toward the front door.

"Aren't you goin' to wait for the fishermen to get back? They'll probably have some nice fat salmon, and we can all have supper togeth—"

"No, thanks." Lucius's manner had suddenly gone gruff. "I've got things to do."

"But wait a minute, Lucius, you don't have to go rushin' off like—"

Lucius was already gone.

(3)

LATE IN THE NIGHT of Saturday the twenty-fifth, Catherine's pains began. Isaac shook Abby awake, then leaped on the horse that he kept permanently saddled for this purpose and rode the mile to the fort like a latter-day Paul Revere with a lantern held high over his head, and by his shouts and pounding on the gate brought the sentries running with rifles and drawn sabers. The officer of the guard listened to Isaac's excited babble, then sent soldiers off to summon Lucius Hargrave, Baptiste Bourdeau, and Señora Sanchez.

Maria Sanchez was the middle-aged wife of the Spanish weaver at the fort, and in the absence of a physician she was heavily depended upon for her skills as nurse and midwife. She accompanied the men to Isaac's house, examined the expectant mother, and asked that a cot be moved into the room for herself.

"Eet weel be some time yet, *señor*," she informed the distraught husband.

Nine-year-old Abby hovered about, sleepy-eyed but wanting to help.

"Go back to bed, Abby," Isaac told her. "I'll call you when somethin' happens."

"Will Mama be all right?" Abby asked fearfully.

"Of course she will, everything's goin' to be fine." Isaac's trembling voice and hand-wringing manner lent little weight to his words.

For two hours the men waited in the front room. Baptiste stretched his huge six-foot-four-inch frame on the hide-covered cot and dozed; Lucius slouched in a chair, staring intently at the wall opposite; Isaac was up and down, sitting awhile, then walking restlessly around, now and then opening the bedroom door a cautious crack and peeking in, walking around some more, sitting down again.

"Calm yourself, old friend," Baptiste said to him.

"I can't," Isaac groaned. "This waiting is terrible, terrible! It takes so *long* to have a baby!"

"Not so long," Lucius murmured absently. "Only nine months. In some rare cases, I'm told, ten."

Baptiste gave him a sharp look. Isaac went on pacing, paying no attention.

As dawn broke a small group of people came down the path from the fort and knocked softly at Isaac's door, seeking news. Isaac admitted them.

"Nothing yet," he told them. "We've heard some stirrings in there, and Catherine's cried out once or twice, but that's all."

People stood awkwardly near the front door since there were not enough seats in the little front room. Baptiste got up from the cot and leaned over Lucius's chair and whispered, "Come on. Let's go for a walk."

They went down a little path that led to the nearest point on the river, where Isaac had built a small dock and kept a pair of skiffs. The sun was not yet above the high eastern horizon; the river lay cold and gleaming darkly. Baptiste sat down on a little wooden bench at the edge of the dock and pulled his buckskin jacket close against the early morning chill. Lucius walked a short way along the banks of the stream, collecting pebbles. Then he returned to the dock and stood spinning the stones one by one over the water in a flat trajectory that made them skip several times before sinking.

"Used to do this when I was a boy," he said over his shoulder to Baptiste. "Used to stand on the shore of the Ohio River and skip rocks across the water and wave to steamboats going by, and think of all the far places of the world I would go to someday, and all the wonderful things I would do."

Baptiste watched him with narrowed eyes. "Lucius," he said finally, "come over here and sit down."

Lucius willingly abandoned his game. He came across the dock and slumped down next to Baptiste, and stared across the river.

"Something's bothering you," Baptiste said. "Why don't you tell me about it?"

Lucius gave him a quick frowning look. "I don't know

what you're talking about." He went back to staring across the river.

Baptiste sighed. "My friend, I should have left for home two weeks ago. But I've been putting it off because I could see you were heading for trouble. You've been acting very strange, staring off into the distance all the time, not listening to what anybody says to you, thinking about something big but not talking about it. Now you better start talking about it, because time's running out."

"Time's running out . . ." Lucius echoed in a murmur of half-disbelief.

"That's right. Catherine's finally having her baby."

Almost eagerly Lucius turned to the other man. "You *know* what's on my mind, don't you?"

"I can guess." A hint of wry amusement glinted in Baptiste's eyes. "I may be uneducated, but I'm not blind, and I'm not stupid."

Lucius's lips were tightly compressed as if trying to hold back some intense pressure. "It's my baby, Baptiste," he blurted.

"You're sure about that?"

"Of course I'm sure! I've calculated it again and again, counted the weeks, the days, the very hours. It's *my baby.*" Elbows on knees, his hands clutching each other, Lucius gazed miserably down at the dock plankings. "And what am I to do?"

Baptiste seemed mildly surprised at the question. "Do? Why, nothing. Why should you *do* anything?"

"Baptiste . . . you don't seem to understand. It wasn't just an escapade. For those two days we were together I loved Catherine intensely, and she loved me. But now she denies it, she wants to forget it ever happened."

"Of course she wants to forget it. It was a terrible mistake, and people like to forget their mistakes if they can. She thought Isaac was dead and she was alone again in the world. But he was very much alive, and she was promised to him. Let me ask you this, Lucius—if she had turned her back on Isaac then and declared herself for you instead . . . how much respect would you have for her today?"

Lucius could find no answer. He remained silent. Baptiste put a fatherly hand on his shoulder.

"Don't be a romantic fool, my friend. It *was* an escapade, that's all you can ever call it. Isaac is Catherine's husband, they love each other dearly, and *he* will be the father of the new

332

baby. And *you* will go about your business and keep your mouth shut."

Lucius threw off Baptiste's hand with an angry movement and got up. "I didn't ask for your advice," he snapped.

Baptiste stood also, and his face was stonelike. "Yes you did. But even if you hadn't, you're getting it just the same."

Lucius strode across the little dock and turned to face Baptiste again with eyes now flashing a wild and dangerous light. "It's my own fault I lost Catherine, and I'm prepared to accept that. But I have sworn before God, if the child is a son, I will claim him as my own."

Baptiste came forward slowly, eyes fixed on Lucius with a stern implacable calm. "You will not," he said. His voice was steel-hard but soft as a whisper.

"What do you mean, I will not?" Lucius raged. "Who are you to tell me what—"

"If you do, I will break your head and throw you in the river."

Lucius's jaw muscles worked in spasms for several seconds while fury and some more rational instinct struggled for dominance within him. The rational force prevailed. He turned away, moved half-stumbling back to the bench, and sat down.

The conversation was over.

Baptiste had strolled up along the riverbank and was a short distance away when the voice of Abby Shannon rang shrilly through the still morning air.

"Uncle Lucius!"

Lucius was slumped on the bench at the dock. He sprang to his feet and stood openmouthed and frozen as the girl flew down the slope toward him.

"Uncle Lucius, the baby's born! The baby's born!"

Lucius was jolted when she rushed into his arms. Baptiste had come running, and now Abby turned from one man to the other, her face shining, words pouring forth in an uncontrollable torrent.

"Oh, Uncle Lucius, the baby's born, and everything's fine, and Uncle Isaac sent me to tell you both to come quickly, and, oh, it happened so *fast*, just a few minutes ago, and Mama's all right and everything, and . . . oh, isn't it wonderful?!"

Abby threw her arms around Lucius again, and hugged him as hard as she could.

Lucius grasped the girl by the shoulders and, with his own

face pale and tight-lipped, peered down into hers. "Abby, calm down a minute, will you? Just tell us . . . is it a boy or a girl?"

"Oh, it's a girl, Uncle Lucius! I've got a new baby sister!"

Lucius closed his eyes and pulled Abby to him and held her in a tight embrace. "That's nice, Abby," he said in a half-choking voice. "Very, very nice . . ."

When he opened his eyes again he saw that Baptiste was looking intently at him.

"Give thanks to the Lord, Lucius," Baptiste said in solemn deliberateness. "He did not choose to call your bluff."

"Nor yours," Lucius whispered.

The two friends grinned at each other.

(4)

CATHERINE OPENED HER EYES and tried to focus on the high window in the wall opposite her bed. A patch of sky there provided the only light in the semidark room. Then sounds of soft movement near her roiled the milky blank surface of her mind and brought her back to wakefulness.

"What time is it?" she whispered.

"It's five o'clock, sweetheart. Sunday afternoon. How are you feeling?" It was Isaac, leaning over her.

"I'm not sure." She started to shift her position, stopped with a quick grimace of pain, and lay still.

"There are people here waiting to see you," Isaac said. "I'll let Lucius and Baptiste come in first, but I told 'em they can only stay a minute, they mustn't tire you."

"Where's my baby?" Catherine said suddenly.

"Señora Sanchez is takin' care of her, don't worry. She's feedin' her goat's milk. Says you can probably start nursin' her by tomorrow."

"And are the other children all right?"

Isaac chuckled. "Of course they are. They're excited as can

334

be about the baby, they think they've got a new playmate."

Catherine managed a weak smile and closed her eyes.

"Well, I'll let your visitors come in now," Isaac said.

After a moment Catherine opened her eyes again and found Baptiste smiling down at her.

"My congratulations, madame. You have a beautiful baby. And why not? The baby has a beautiful mother."

She smiled back and gave him her hand. "Baptiste . . . good old friend!"

"Unfortunately I must follow up my congratulations with a sad adieu. I am going home now. I leave early in the morning. I have been away too long."

"Yes, I know. Your dear Mali misses you. You'll give her our love, won't you?" She took his large hand in both of her own and squeezed it. "Thank you for being so kind, Baptiste. Such a good man, such a *good* friend. We'll never forget you."

"Goodbye, madame. I wish you all happiness. You deserve it."

He gave her a little bow, kissed her hand, and stole away.

Then Lucius was there. They gazed at each other without speaking for a tense moment. His eyes were curious, searching her face; hers were guarded but calm. He pulled up a little stool and sat down next to her bed.

"Thought you might be amused to hear that Abby and Byron and Justin have been holding tribal councils all afternoon, trying to decide on an appropriate Shoshone name for the new baby. After much weighty deliberation they finally settled on *Ta-vu-tu-tzi-yu*. Roughly speaking it means . . . Morning Child."

Catherine smiled. "That's beautiful," she murmured. "I'll bet it was Justin's idea."

There was a short silence. Lucius took a deep breath and began again.

"There are just one or two little things I want to say, Catherine, and I'll say them quickly and go. First I want you to know that I'm sorry about the things I said to you. The silly threat I made. I've been half out of my mind with anger ever since last August over having lost you—through carelessness or the perversity of fate, or whatever it was—and now this . . . I had to lash out at somebody, make war on the world. It was crazy, and I didn't mean it. I promise you I'll never again mention those two lost days out there in the mountains. And I'll love the little girl just the way I love Abby and Byron, like a good uncle."

Catherine brushed at her glistening eyes and spoke in a shaky whisper: "Thank you, Lucius."

"Then I want to tell you that I too will be saying adieu now. The time has come for me to move on."

"Must you?"

"Yes. I came to California in search of something. I'm not going to find it at Sutter's Fort."

"Isaac will be sad." After a moment's hesitation she added, "So will I."

"We've talked about it. He doesn't exactly understand, but then he's used to that with me. Anyway, I think we've both known all along we'd wind up going our separate ways. We're much too unlike to stay on the same path for long."

"Unlike," Catherine echoed. "That you surely are."

"So . . . tomorrow morning Baptiste and I will go down to the river together. We'll say goodbye, and he'll head north for home. And I'll hop on Sutter's launch. It's going to Yerba Buena, and I'm going with it."

Catherine's eyes were searching his face intently. "Lucius? What about Justin? Will you leave him with us? At least until you've settled somewhere? It's not good for him to be dragged hither and yon, and he's so happy here with us. Please?"

"Isaac said the same thing. It's very generous of you. Fact is, I agree, and I was hoping you'd offer. I was a little hesitant about asking—"

"Oh no, you mustn't be. We *want* him with us, he's like a member of the family. Oh, that's wonderful, Lucius, thank you!" Her face was radiant.

"One last thing. Isaac tells me you don't yet have any particular name in mind for the little girl. Other than Morning Child, that is."

Catherine permitted herself a little laugh and tried to ignore the quick shaft of pain that came with it. "Yes, I suppose we'd better think of something a bit more practical than that, hadn't we?"

"I'd like to make a request. Name her Martha, please."

"Why Martha?"

"I had a sister named Martha. She died when she was seven. I always thought if I ever—well, I mean, I think it would be nice to have another Martha in the family."

Catherine was studying Lucius with a distant look of wonderment in her eyes. "You're a strange one, Lucius. Such a baffling mixture of hard and soft, cold and warm . . ."

336

The bedroom door opened and Isaac popped his head in. "'Scuse me, sweetheart. Captain Sutter's here, wants to pay his respects."

The new visitor strode right in. He was of medium height, about forty, with a fringe of dark curly hair beneath an enormous bald cranium, and long sideburns down his cheeks. He wore a well-trimmed mustache and a tiny patch of whiskers, a black tie, a long frock coat, gleamingly polished boots, and a regal air.

"My dear Mrs. Hargrave, I want to say—" His piercing eyes caught sight of Lucius. "Good afternoon, sir. Mind if I butt in?" He did not wait for a reply.

"I want to say, madame, first, congratulations to the birth of your child. I have looked at her and am pleased to note that she is a fine healthy specimen."

"Thank you, Captain," Catherine said demurely.

"It is good that she is a female. We need more women in California. Of course we need more people altogether, but we cannot hope to build an enduring society without women, now can we?"

Catherine responded with a weak smile, and Captain Sutter chuckled and rubbed his hands together and continued, "No, I should say not. And now that your husband is no longer, shall we say, preoccupied, I imagine he'll be getting ready to undertake that search for new lumbering sites for us. There's a desperate need, you know."

He turned to Isaac and laid a hand on his shoulder. "We expect great things from your husband, Mrs. Hargrave. He has exactly the sort of skills we value. And as I am positive of the glorious future of New Helvetia, so I am equally certain that your husband has a vitally important role to play in it. So do we all. That is why, madame, I say to you . . ."

Lucius heard no more. He had quietly slipped out of the room.

As darkness fell all visitors were gone and the house was quiet, and Abby and Byron sat at the kitchen table watching while Isaac ladled soup from a kettle and set a bowl before each of them.

"Potato soup," Isaac announced. "Very good, if I do say so."

"Why doesn't Little Eagle come to supper?" Byron wanted to know.

"He and your Uncle Lucius are just having a little private

goodbye talk. He'll be here in a minute."

Abby toyed distractedly with her soup. "Why is Uncle Lucius going away? Doesn't he like us anymore?"

"Of course he likes us, Abby. But he wants to go and make a life for himself someplace else. It's...well, it's just something he wants to do."

Justin came into the house and took his place at the table, and Isaac served him a bowl of soup.

Abby watched him. "Did you say goodbye to your father, Justin?"

"Um-hmm," Justin said casually, and began to eat.

"What did he say to you?"

"He said I should be a good boy and mind Uncle Isaac and Aunt Catherine."

Byron giggled. Justin eyed the other boy and responded with a giggle of his own.

Abby frowned. "But weren't you sad, Justin? Didn't you want to go with him?"

Justin was plainly surprised by the question. "No, *I* don't want to go anywhere. I have to stay here and help take care of Morning Child."

He took a huge spoonful of soup, and some of it dribbled down his chin, causing Byron to laugh. Justin grinned, a glint of sly mischief in his eye.

"Here, here, boys, behave yourselves," Isaac said patiently.

(5)

FROM THE JOURNAL of Lucius Hargrave:

As long as I can remember I have been fascinated by beginnings and endings. I like to study my life as it unfolds and say to myself: "Here ended this period, here began the next." It is not always easy. Sometimes the signposts are false, the real ones disguised and difficult to recognize. The shift of my life to California, for example, did not conclude with the completion of the physical journey, but with another event that came a full month later.

During that time I lived in the fortified establishment of

one John Sutter, in the valley of the Sacramento. I did this because I found on arriving there that my foolish brother Isaac had made good his impetuous determination to marry the widow Shannon, and was working for Sutter—stripped to the waist and sweating like a field hand, sawing lumber, trying to earn a living not only for the family Morgan Shannon had left behind, but for the dead man's third and last child, about to be born. Clearly he needed help, and clearly it was I who must provide it. So I moved into Sutter's and spent a month performing the kind of slave labor I had fled from South Bar, Indiana, twelve years before to escape.

Captain Sutter's place was a big adobe-walled citadel commanding the countryside south of the American River and east of the Sacramento. It was quite new—barely completed—but grim and somber in appearance, as if it had already withstood assaults and sieges. A gruesome Indian scalp—a souvenir left by one of its residents—dangled charmingly at the gate. The good captain himself called the place New Helvetia. Everybody else called it Sutter's Fort. I called it purgatory, a hellhole festering with the unwashed bodies of rogues, thieves, adventurers, deserters from English and American sailing ships, Mexicans, Indians, and half-breeds of every description, all milling about among pigs, horses, goats, dogs, and chickens. There were a few slovenly women about—half of them legitimate wives, the other half Indian concubines of the commander. Indeed, Sutter not only played the role of military commander to the hilt, but seemed to think of himself as a king, and his little patch of fortified ground as a kingdom. He was a complex man, generous to a fault but ruthless in his exploitation of others; charming and cultivated in manner and an excellent host, but a hopeless drunk and a shameless braggart, affecting a fictitious military title and forever telling equally fictitious tales of his past glories. I was careful to keep my distance from him, and when I left that place after one month (with no regrets) I was as much a stranger as the day I arrived.

But when a man lives through a period that affects him profoundly, even if the memories are as painful as old battle scars, there is a touch of sadness when it all comes to an end. That feeling enveloped me on a quiet Sunday afternoon, the 26th of May, 1844. At dawn that morning Catherine's baby had been born, a pretty, chubby, gurgling baby girl whose big soft brown eyes oddly reminded me of my mother. And it was this happy event that made me see that something had come to an end for me. An ordeal was finished, and my new life in this strange place called California was about to begin—for good or ill. The journey West had been a torturous crossing of a vast and awesome distance, and, I felt sure now, a crossing of no possible return.

I looked around me and saw Justin sitting crosslegged on the ground with his two friends Abby and Byron, the three of them happily concocting a Shoshone name for the new baby. I was about to do something that would tear my heart out—to leave my son behind there for a while, for his own safety and well-being—and I let my eyes feast on that pleasant scene, hoping it would make the pain of parting a little easier. I saw Isaac beaming with pride as if he were the father of the newborn child himself, and before the day was out he was deep in earnest conference with Captain Sutter about their plans for expanding the fort's lumbering operations. Poor old chum. Independence for him was still a long way off. Yet plainly he was happy and, miraculously, already securely rooted in a land in which I was still a stranger. He had no further need of me, and my own private purposes called. Once more, as had so often happened in my life, it was time to move on.

Early the next morning I stood on the banks of the Sacramento River and said a final goodbye—this to my friend Baptiste, who had stayed in California for a while after bringing Justin and me there, and was now anxious to get home again. That too was a painful parting. Baptiste Bourdeau was the finest man it had ever been my privilege to know—as stalwart as a block of granite and as incorruptible, yet with a marvelous gentleness about him, and an inborn nobility that put to shame the crude posturings of ordinary men. I was proud to call him friend, and I knew that my life would be sadly diminished by his departure from it.

Then I turned my eyes westward one last time, toward the place where the Pacific Ocean lay fog-shrouded on the edge of the continent. Whatever was in store for me in this alien land, I was ready for it. The central purpose of all this wild adventuring—the search for my lost and wandering father—had sometimes faded from my mind under the stress of the ordeal for days and weeks at a time, yet it never failed to return with an obsessive intensity. It was my cross. I had to pick it up again and carry it forward to wherever our ultimate destiny lay.

Part Six

(1)

JASPER HAWKES was an innkeeper and proud of it, and Jasper was fond of saying that his establishment was the first public house in Yerba Buena. This was an exaggeration but not far from the truth. His inn was called the Hawk's Nest, and sported a free-swinging wooden sign in front bearing a crude illustration of a hawk in resplendent flight. Jasper wanted his place to resemble the cozy country inns of his native England. It did not. It was a charmless two-story box, and resembled nothing except the fifteen or twenty other equally inelegant buildings in the vicinity. Jasper was apologetic about the inn's grubby appearance, which he laid partly to the fact that it was built of timbers salvaged from derelict vessels in the bay, and partly to something about the chill foggy air constantly rolling in off the ocean and across the bare sandy hills, which made any building, however new, look dilapidated a week after it was built.

The waterfront along the Yerba Buena cove was a muddy shore uncluttered with any such man-made refinement as a wharf. Still, sailors regarded it as one of the finest natural harbors in the world, an opinion Jasper Hawkes frequently cited in support of his belief that the dismal place had a bright future. There were no streets in the settlement; houses and other buildings were dotted almost randomly in the proximity

343

of a rough square formed by the bay on the east, two parallel trails leading away from it, and a third trail, running north and south, which community boosters like Jasper called the San Jose Highway. This was indeed the road to Pueblo de San José and points south, though the term *highway* described nothing more than a pair of ruts in the dirt just wide enough to accommodate the *caretta*—the Spanish oxcart, the only vehicle that most native Californians had ever seen.

The Hawk's Nest was situated on the San Jose Highway a little more than half a mile south of the square and about the same distance from the bay. Its comforts were primitive; it depended largely on the casual tavern trade that came almost exclusively from sailors off the occasional ships anchoring in the cove—mostly Americans, some British, now and again visitors from other nations. Seldom did native *Californios* appear. That is why Jasper Hawkes was surprised one crisp October morning when he looked out and saw a splendidly dressed Spanish gentleman on horseback stopping by the sign of the hawk.

Then he looked closer, recognized the horseman, and surprise turned to astonishment. "Good Lord!" he said under his breath. "Old Don Lorenzo 'imself."

Don Lorenzo Valadez did not ordinarily travel unattended. Don Lorenzo was seventy-four years old, somewhat frail, and extremely rich, and for all these reasons he hardly ever ventured forth at all. When he did he was usually accompanied by an escort of six or eight servants. But today he was alone. On his beautiful palomino he was an erect and commanding figure dressed in black, with purple satin trimmings on his jacket and trousers, a scarlet velvet waistband, and great brass buttons glinting in the sun. When he dismounted his slight build and five feet four inches of height sharply diminished the imposing effect, but when he walked toward the entrance to the inn he moved with such lordly dignity that two young Mexican boys seated on the steps of the front gallery got up and scurried away.

Jasper Hawkes held the door open. Don Lorenzo stepped inside, removed his hat, and bowed.

"*Buenos dias, señor.* I am Don Lorenzo Valadez, from Rancho Las Sombras."

Jasper indulged in a bit of bowing and scraping. "Yes, yes, I know you, Don Lorenzo. Well, good Lord! *Everybody* knows Don Lorenzo Valadez, I'd say. Jasper 'Awkes, at your

344

service, *señor*. This is a great honor. Step right this way, I've saved a special table just for you." This was a little joke; at nine o'clock in the morning the place was deserted.

Don Lorenzo did not acknowledge the humor. With a solemn gravity he bowed again, accepted the designated seat at a corner table in the tavern room, and studied the proprietor. Jasper Hawkes was as slightly built as his visitor, but a head taller. Thinning, wispy hair and a pinched and weathered face made him look older than his forty-odd years. He rubbed his hands together and smiled, eager to please.

"Well, what is your pleasure, *señor*? *Aguardiente*?"

Don Lorenzo's handsome gray head bobbed gently. "*Muy bien, gracias.*"

The innkeeper hurried off and returned in a moment with a bottle and a glass. There were two silver coins on the table.

"*One* dollar, Don Lorenzo, that's all," Jasper said.

"If you please, *señor*. I have further need of your assistance."

"Aha!" Jasper cheerfully swept up the money and stuffed it into his pocket. "What shall it be, *señor*?"

Don Lorenzo reached inside his jacket and brought forth a small piece of paper, neatly folded. "I have here a . . . how you say . . . *anuncio*."

"Advertisement," Jasper offered.

"*Sí*. It was brought to my attention . . ." Don Lorenzo opened the paper, squinted at the black print, and read aloud:

"*Delivery of mail and light freight. Quick, safe, and efficient. Bi-weekly from Monterey to Sonoma via Branciforte, San Jose, Yerba Buena, and points between. The Hargrave Mail and Express Company, Lucius Hargrave, President. In Yerba Buena contact J. Hawkes, agent, the Hawk's Nest, San Jose Highway.*"

With a jerk of his thumb Jasper pointed to himself. "That's me. Jasper 'Awkes, agent. At your service."

"And this Señor Hargrave," Don Lorenzo said. "Where can he be found, please?"

"Right 'ere. 'E 'as an office upstairs, and 'e's there this very minute."

"Ah." Don Lorenzo started to rise.

"No, no, keep your seat, *señor*," Jasper said hurriedly. "I'll get 'im. Lucius'd wring my neck if I made a client like you climb the stairs."

"*Gracias*," Don Lorenzo murmured. He poured an inch of liquor and swirled it delicately in his glass.

Jasper knocked softly on a door at the back end of the second-floor hallway, waited a few seconds, and knocked again, louder. The door was opened by a woman. Her age might have been guessed as the middle thirties; her well-molded features suggested a once-extraordinary attractiveness that had been eroded by hard use. She finished tying a flimsy housecoat around her statuesque figure, pushed a wealth of light brown hair back from her face, and blinked sleepily at Jasper.

"Lucius up?" Jasper snapped.

"No, he's asleep," the woman mumbled, and added with a touch of annoyance, "So was I."

"Well, get 'im up, 'e's got a customer."

"Christ, Jasper, he didn't get in till past midnight, he's knocked out—"

"I said get 'im up, goddamnit. It's old man Valadez."

The woman looked blank. "Who's that?"

"Who's that!" Jasper snorted. "Just the biggest damn landowner in Santa Clara Valley, that's all. Maybe in California. An' 'e's one o' the ringleaders in this 'ere rebellion movement against the gov'nor. What d'ya mean, who's that!"

The woman made a sour face. "Christ, Jasper, d'ya have to get mixed up in these damn Mexican political plots all the time?"

"Don't worry about it, Delia. Just get Lucius up, and keep out o' sight."

"Don't I even get a look at this Don What's-his-name?"

Jasper stepped closer to the woman and spoke in a harsh undertone. "I said *get Lucius up*. And keep your sweet little arse out o' sight."

Delia moved her open-palmed hands with affectionate self-admiration up and down her broad curvaceous hips, and a sly look came into her face. "It's sweet, all right, Jasper honey, and well you know it. But it ain't little."

She giggled as Jasper stalked away, muttering and shaking his head.

Don Lorenzo sipped his liquor and watched a tall strapping young *Americano* come striding across the room, stop before him, and bow.

"Señor Valadez? Lucius Hargrave, sir. How may I serve you?"

Don Lorenzo was on his feet offering his hand. "It is a great

346

honor, Señor Hargrave. Won't you sit down and have a drink with me? Perhaps Señor Hawkes will bring another glass."

The proprietor, hovering in the background, hastened to do this, then retired, and the two men sat down.

Don Lorenzo poured a generous portion into Lucius's glass and lifted his own. "A toast, *señor*. To your countrymen. To *Americanos* everywhere, and especially those who have chosen to make California their home."

After they had set their glasses down Lucius said, "I'm a bit surprised to hear Americans toasted by an upper-class *Californio*. I thought you people generally resented us."

"It is not safe to make such generalizations, *señor*. I, for one, am a warm admirer of your country. Your great revolutionary heroes—General Washington and the others— splendid men. We could use a few such in California."

Lucius's fingers drummed softly on the tabletop. "You wanted to talk to me about something, sir?"

"Yes. I have mail to be delivered. I understand you are in that business?"

"That's right."

"Yes. Well, you see, this is not ordinary mail. It is a . . . how you would say . . . delicate matter. For it to fall into the wrong hands would be . . . embarrassing."

"Well, you've come to the right place. I have two men traveling with me. Ex-sailors—tough customers. Both completely reliable, well-armed, and expert shots. Nobody trifles with us. We have a one-hundred-percent successful delivery rate."

"Yes, I see. *Muy bien*." Don Lorenzo remained hesitant still. "But now, you see, I must ask you—forgive me, *señor*, this is *muy indelicado*—I must know something about your, uh . . . *filosofia politica*—"

"How I stand on the California political intrigues?"

"Yes, yes. *Exactamente*."

"I stand completely neutral, because it is nothing to me whether California is ruled by a governor appointed from Mexico City or a native *Californio*. I'm just an outsider, trying to make a living."

"You are mistaken, *señor*. It matters much to you. Much, much . . ." Don Lorenzo's arm swept the air to indicate a vast amount.

"How so?"

"The Mexican governor Micheltorina is your enemy. He is the enemy of all *Americanos*."

347

Lucius raised a cynical eyebrow. "I see. But the native sons all look upon me as their blood brother, I suppose?"

Don Lorenzo's smile contained cunning and mystery. "Some do, *señor*. Some do not. It would be well for you to learn the difference." Don Lorenzo leaned back, relaxed and genial. "I assure you, *I* am among those who do."

"Thank you, that's nice to hear. Now about this mail of yours—"

"I understand you have applied to Micheltorina for a land grant," Don Lorenzo said abruptly.

Lucius blinked in surprise. "How'd you know *that*?"

The mysterious smile was there again. "I have friends everywhere, *señor*. Have you received any encouragement as yet?"

"Well, yes, I think you'd call it encouraging. Every time I'm in Monterey I stop by the governor's office to inquire—"

"Has he *seen* you?"

"Uh...no. But his secretary assures me the governor is favorably disposed. I brought in my witnesses, paid my twenty-six-dollar fee, took the oath of allegiance and swore my intention to embrace the Catholic faith. Everything's in order. Soon as my year is up—that'll be next June—I should be a California *Don*, just like you." Lucius beamed.

But now Don Lorenzo was grimly unsmiling. "Do you really believe that?"

"Why shouldn't I?" Lucius said testily.

"If everything is going so smoothly, why did you make such an unpleasant scene in the office of the governor's secretary last week? Angry shouting and pounding on the table?"

Lucius sat astonished for an instant before a sheepish grin stole over his face. "You *do* have friends everywhere, don't you?" Then, cheerfulness abruptly gone, he slumped despondently. "All right. You already know everything, why should I try to deceive you? Micheltorina's a lying, two-faced bastard. He took my money with no intention of ever approving my petition. I know that now."

Don Lorenzo spoke soothingly. "Well, do not judge him too harshly. The poor man is no longer in control of what happens. Console yourself with the knowledge that long before next June he will be gone, and your petition will be worthless anyway."

Lucius stroked his chin and pondered this. "You think so, eh?"

348

"*Por cierto*. You see, for years we *Californios* have been too busy quarreling among ourselves to fight off Mexican rule. But no more." Don Lorenzo leaned forward again, and his voice dropped to a near whisper. "For now we band together, north and south, against the common foe. And for Micheltorina that can mean only one thing—he will soon be a whipped dog, on his way back to Mexico, and with him will go the last feeble remains of Mexican rule in California."

Lucius was unimpressed. "Oh yes, I've heard about these California revolutions. One a year, regular. Nobody ever gets hurt. Because California's just a province of Mexico, after all. The same culture, the same Spanish heritage—"

Don Lorenzo uttered a hard little laugh. "How long have you been in California, Señor Hargrave?"

"About six months."

The old man refilled Lucius's glass and his own. "I've been here forty-four years. I came in 1800, as a soldier in the service of the Spanish crown, and I loved it so much I decided to stay forever. For twenty-five years it was a beautiful life, *señor*. Here was paradise on earth. We had brought the good things of Spain with us, and left the bad behind. But then came the Mexican Revolution, and our paradise was destroyed. The *Mexicanos* fought Spain for their independence and won, and when they went their separate way they took California with them. *Their* doing, not ours. Since then we Spanish of California have been without a country. For make no mistake, *señor*—I am no *Mexicano*. I was born a Spaniard, I have lived a *Californio*, and when I die I will die a ..." Don Lorenzo smiled and sipped his liquor. "Well, we shall see."

"All right," Lucius said casually. "Now you're after independence from Mexico. That's fine, I wish you luck."

Don Lorenzo sipped his liquor very slowly while he studied Lucius's face over the rim of the glass. "Will you join us, *amigo*?"

Lucius chuckled. "I just said I wish you luck."

"Will you deliver the mail for me?"

"Oh, of course, that's different. That's business."

Don Lorenzo reached inside his jacket again and produced a thick packet of papers, tightly sealed, and handed it across the table.

Lucius studied a neatly printed address, and read aloud: "*Don Francisco Avila. Casa Avila, Ciudad de Los Angeles.*" He scowled. "Los Angeles! Good Lord, that's way out of my territory."

"I understand that," Don Lorenzo said readily. "I can promise you that your remuneration will be generous, to compensate for the inconvenience."

"How generous?"

"Let us say ... a hundred dollars?"

"It's a damn long way to Los Angeles."

"A hundred and fifty dollars?'

"And there's danger involved."

"You will have the privilege of serving a noble cause, *amigo*."

Lucius greeted this observation with a loud snort. "My friend, I spent two years in Texas at the time of the revolution there, and I can tell you, I've had my fill of noble causes. I'm interested in personal causes. My own."

"Very well. Consider this. When we achieve our goal—and doubt it not, we *will* achieve it—you will be one of us. Then you will have your reward, whatever you fancy. You will need but to ask."

"A land grant?"

A little grimace on Don Lorenzo's face registered disdain. "A trifle."

Lucius tapped the packet of papers on the table and became thoughtful. "How long do I have?"

"Those papers should be in Don Francisco's hands before the first of November."

Lucius nodded. "They'll be there." He slipped the packet inside his shirt.

Don Lorenzo raised his glass once more, and this time his smile was triumphantly bright. "Another toast, *señor*. To the everlasting friendship between *Americanos* and *Californios*. And to a glorious future for both."

Jasper Hawkes, secretly watching from behind the bar counter at the other side of the room, saw money pass from Don Lorenzo to Lucius and the two men rise and shake hands. Jasper was there instantly, smiling and rubbing his hands together.

"Can I bring you anything else, gentlemen? Something to eat, maybe?"

"No, *gracias*," Don Lorenzo said. "I must be on my way." He looked at Lucius. "You have your instructions, *señor*. Is everything understood?"

"Perfectly," Lucius said with military crispness.

"And when you return you will come to see me at Rancho

Las Sombras and collect the balance of your pay. Can you find your way there?"

"Oh yes, I've passed by it a number of times."

"My house will be yours, *amigo*. You will find us not lacking in hospitality, I promise you." The old Don gave the other men stiff little bows.

"*Señores? Buenos dias.*" With immense unhurried dignity he turned and walked across the room and out into the morning sunlight.

Lucius burst into the upstairs bedroom, flung open a tall wardrobe chest, pulled out a canvas bag and began to toss assorted articles of clothing into it.

Delia Walsh came in, leaned against the doorway and watched him.

"Are you goin' away again, Lucius? Christ, you just *got* here!"

Lucius was too busy to look up. "Got to go, sweetheart. Got a very important assignment. A revolution's cooking, and I'm smack in the middle of it."

"Revolution, hell. These Mexican revolutions never amount to a damned thing but a lot of parading up and down and hollering."

"Go away, Delia, I haven't got time for you now."

Delia began to pout. "Why are you so mean to me? I'm lonely when you're not here, Lucius."

"You've got plenty of company."

"Humph! Jasper and the Mexican hired hands who don't speak English."

"And twenty or thirty sailors off every ship that comes in the harbor."

Delia's pout turned to indignation. "Listen, I'll have you know I was a whaling captain's wife, and after that the wife of the wealthiest merchant in Honolulu, and I think you ought to—"

"Wife of the first," Lucius said with a wink. "Mistress of the second."

"Whatever. You ought to know that common sailors are not proper company for me."

Lucius had finished packing. He closed his bag and went to Delia, and took her by the shoulders. "Listen, I'm sorry about your situation here. Your talent's mostly going to waste, that's certain. But be patient, better days are coming. For instance, do you know what's happened this morning?"

"No," Delia said sullenly.

"Your friend Lucius made a very valuable connection. What I've been looking for and waiting for all these months. I'm on my way, Delia, honey. And when I get to be what you call a Prominent Man in California, d'you think I'm going to forget my old friends?"

"Probably."

"Don't you believe it! I never forget a good friend, and you're one of the best. Jasper too."

"Really, Lucius?"

"Absolutely. Cheer up now. See you soon."

He kissed her quickly, picked up his bag and was off, leaping down the stairs at the end of the hall two at a time. She followed him to the top of the stairs and stood there with a forlorn look on her face, listening to the sound of his footsteps fading away.

(2)

THE LANDS of Rancho Las Sombras sprawled for miles in an irregular oblong shape along the base of the mountains that formed the eastern boundary of the valley of Santa Clara—sixty thousand acres, grass-covered flatlands and the tawny hills above them, splashed with the olive green of oaks and bisected by shallow rock-strewn arroyos where flourished sycamore, willow, and cottonwood. Partway up one of the hillsides, on a little wooded plateau, was the house. It was constructed of the traditional California adobe, thick-walled and dazzling white beneath a low red-tile roof, two hundred feet square, its size a mark of distinction. Around it a number of giant gnarled live oaks stood guard, spreading their heavy evergreen branches over great sixty-foot circles of perpetual shade, so that at any time of day in any season, at least part of the house was in the shadows—*las sombras*.

Toward noon on a warm spring day Lucius Hargrave pulled his horse to a stop at the long hitching rail beneath one of the trees, took off his hat and mopped his brow with a kerchief, and scanned the premises for signs of life. The place was eerily quiet. Lucius dismounted and tied his horse, and was walking up to the house when he noticed an ancient wrinkled Indian woman standing near the entranceway watching him. He approached her, smiling.

"*Buenos dias,*" he said cheerily.

She nodded. "*Buenos dias, señor.*"

"Am I at Rancho Las Sombras?"

"*Si, señor.*"

"Is Don Lorenzo at home?"

"No, *señor.* He is gone away."

Lucius scowled in annoyance. "Gone away? Where? When will he be back?"

The woman shrugged. "Gone away, *señor.*"

"Well, is anybody else at home?"

"Come back later, *señor.* Don Lorenzo gone away now."

"Damn!" Lucius muttered. He had jammed his hat back on his head and turned away when he heard a soft feminine voice.

"Who is it, Rosalia?"

He stopped and stared. A young woman had emerged from the dark interior of the house and was coming toward him.

His hat came whipping off again. "Good morning, *señorita.* My name is Lucius Hargrave, and I was wondering—"

"Ah, Señor Hargrave!" The woman's face was momentarily lit by a kind of recognition as she extended her hand to him. "I am Dolores Valadez. Welcome to Las Sombras."

She was striking for several reasons: she was extraordinarily tall, her intense black eyes only an inch or two below the level of Lucius's; she was dressed in a full-length skirt of black trimmed in several colors of gay pastel, and a white blouse bordered with lace—a costume of peasant-like simplicity that did not detract, Lucius noticed, from the same regal bearing he had seen in Don Lorenzo; her face was serene, the delicate features molded in classical beauty, easily illuminated by smiles but in repose oddly grave; lustrous dark hair, parted in the middle and tied in back with a ribbon, fell almost to her waist; her voice was a vibrant contralto, incongruously deep for one so slender and supple.

Lucius continued to stare for a few seconds before he caught himself, took the young woman's hand and bowed stiffly. "Well, I'm delighted, *señorita*...or should I say *señora?*"

The solemn face brightened for an instant with a smile that quickly disappeared. "*Señorita* is correct. I am Don Lorenzo's...what do you call it?...daughter of his brother."

"Niece."

"Niece, yes. Excuse me...my English is not so perfect."

"Oh, I disagree, I think it's *quite* perfect," Lucius murmured. He was still holding her hand. "Absolutely enchanting."

Dolores carefully retrieved her hand and gestured toward the house. "Please come in, Señor Hargrave. My uncle has gone to another part of the *rancho*, but I will send after him."

Lucius made a polite protest. "Oh, don't bother, I wouldn't want to cause inconvenience—"

"No, no, *señor*, it is not inconvenience. Uncle Lorenzo has been waiting and waiting for you to come. It will take not so very long. Meanwhile, I will do my best to—" Dolores paused to search for the appropriate word— "entertain you."

"With such a lovely hostess," Lucius said gallantly, "I will require very little entertaining." He watched for Dolores's teasingly short-lived smile, but her face remained grave and full of dignity as she gestured toward the house again and repeated her invitation.

"Come in, please. Our house is yours."

Don Lorenzo arrived home late in the afternoon and found his niece and Lucius Hargrave seated in wicker chairs at a table beneath one of the small flowering trees that graced the spacious enclosed patio at the center of the house.

"Ah, Señor Hargrave! Welcome, *amigo*, welcome!" The diminutive old man shook the hand of his guest warmly and at length, and smiled up into the taller man's face. "I am sorry I was not here to greet you when you arrived. Has my little *muchacha* seen to your comforts?"

"She has indeed. I have had an excellent meal, a siesta, and several hours of most delightful conversation."

Both men beamed down at Dolores.

"It has been a pleasure for me as well," she murmured demurely.

"*Bueno, bueno!*" Don Lorenzo said with enthusiasm. He gestured Lucius back to his seat and took a chair himself.

"I was beginning to think you had not taken my invitation seriously, *amigo*."

"I sent you a letter, Don Lorenzo—"

"Yes, I received it. You said you were staying in the south for a while. But here it is May . . . it has been a long time."

"I must apologize," Lucius said. "I was detained longer than I had thought. Certain personal affairs to be attended to—"

"Yes. You were making inquiries at all the seaports concerning a certain ship, I understand. Apparently waiting for some friend or other to arrive in California by sea, eh?"

For a moment Lucius was silent, blank-faced. "I almost forgot. You have friends everywhere, don't you?"

Don Lorenzo laughed easily. "Not wishing to be . . . how you say . . . snooping, I want you to know I am ready to help you in any way I can, should you wish to confide in me."

"Kind of you," Lucius said dryly.

"I also wish to say I have excellent reports about you from our friends in the south. You delivered the mail at Casa Avila on the thirtieth of October, and you made a most favorable impression on the brothers Pico. So favorable they offered you a military commission."

"Which of course I declined, with thanks."

"And well you did, *amigo*. It would not have been wise for you to associate yourself too closely with the southern faction. They are honorable men, but—"

It was Lucius's turn to laugh. "Oh, I see. Now that the so-called revolution is over, Micheltorina gone and California back in the hands of the *Californios,* it is time for the northerners and southerners to start bickering among themselves again."

Don Lorenzo smiled his mysterious little smile. Then he turned to Dolores and changed the subject.

"So, tell me what I have missed, *muchacha*. What have you two talked about?"

"Oh, many things, Uncle Lorenzo. I am afraid I have been a . . . what you call it? . . . chatterbox."

"No, I'm the guilty one," Lucius said smilingly. "I have regaled Dolores with the entire story of my life, from my boyhood days on the Ohio River right up to the present moment. I've been worse than a chatterbox, I've been a windbag and a braggart."

"Oh no, Lucio!" Dolores breathed. "It is a fascinating story, and most moving."

355

"Oho, so it is *Lucio*, eh?" Don Lorenzo's thin little body quivered with chuckles.

Dolores turned her wide eyes on him. "Do you know, Uncle, Señor Lucio has a little son? He is living with the family of Lucio's brother, near Sutter's Fort."

Don Lorenzo's face was stricken with dismay as he looked at Lucius. "*Dios mío!* I did not know you had been married, *señor*. What has become of your wife?"

Lucius's face was darkly brooding as he stared down at the patio paving. "Dead. Cut down in the full bloom of young womanhood. God rest her soul."

"God rest her soul." Don Lorenzo echoed solemnly, and crossed himself. His expression reflected more relief than sorrow.

"As for my son Justin, he's the joy of my heart," Lucius went on. "This nomadic life I lead is torture for me because I can't have the boy with me."

"There is no doubt about it," Don Lorenzo declared. "You should get married again as soon as possible."

Lucius smiled and turned the conversation in another direction. "I haven't done *all* the talking this afternoon, Don Lorenzo. I've done a bit of listening too, and I'm happy to say I'm now fairly familiar with the history of the Valadez family."

"Indeed? I trust my *muchacha* did not give away *all* the family secrets."

"I know that you have been a widower for ten years, that your two sons and three daughters are all married and scattered up and down California on *ranchos* of their own. I know that your brother, Dolores's father, died when she was a child, and since her mother's death a few years ago she has lived here with you."

"Yes," Don Lorenzo said pensively. "The years bring us happiness through the love of our dear ones. Then, little by little, it is all taken away." A trace of sadness lay on his old face as he looked around the quiet courtyard. "It is too bad, don't you think? This big house—home for just the two of us..."

Lucius hastened to change the subject again.

"I mentioned to Dolores that I was surprised at how well you both speak English, and she told me you had a tutor, an Englishman, and that he was also your children's tutor, and hers too."

This only served to reinforce Don Lorenzo's sadness. "That is true. Don Roberto Holmes was a fine gentleman and a man

356

of learning. He too has been taken from us by the passage of time." He sighed. "Ah, I am an old man, *amigo*. I have seen much."

"And you will see much more still, Uncle," Dolores said gently.

Lucius had also fallen into the pensive mood. "You told me you came to California in 1800, Don Lorenzo. That intrigues me, because it was the same year that my grandfather went west from Connecticut and built his house in the wilderness of the Ohio Valley. It seems to me that you and he, worlds apart and unknown to each other, were like partners, each helping to bring civilization to a great new continent."

"Oh, that is a beautiful thought, Lucio!" Dolores exclaimed. "Don't you think so, Uncle?"

Don Lorenzo's old eyes were misty as he gazed at the young American. "Señor Lucio... *amigo*... I hope you will stay with us for a long time."

"Oh yes, please do!" Dolores seconded fervently.

Lucius nodded. "I thank you, my friends. There is peacefulness here at Las Sombras. Quiet, tranquility... things I have had too little of." He looked at Dolores and saw that her dark eyes were wide and shining as they lay on him.

"There is no place on earth I would rather be," he said.

A good part of the front quarter of the house was taken up by the *sala*—the main room—in which the exposed ceiling beams, dark brown with age, contrasted with the creamy color of the adobe-and-plaster walls. In the evening, Lucius strolled there with Dolores at his side and listened while the young woman described some of her favorite things.

"This is handcarved cherrywood, from Spain." Dolores lovingly fingered the dark red scrolls of a huge cabinet, five feet in width and taller than Lucius. "Uncle Lorenzo and my father brought many fine pieces from the old country. This is one of the finest."

"Magnificent," Lucius agreed.

"The floor tiles are from Spain also." Dolores indicated a stretch of floor visible at the edges of the carpets, where a bold mosaic pattern of charcoal gray and burnt orange caught the eye. "The design is taken from the work of fifteenth-century artisans."

Lucius pronounced them beautiful.

"The carpets are Oriental, of course."

"Of course," Lucius said.

They paused by a massive eight-foot-long table on which a pair of large pottery vases held plants whose shining green leaves cascaded over the sides like fountains frozen and motionless.

"This table is another cherrywood piece," Dolores said. "It is about two hundred years old."

"Remarkable," Lucius declared.

"And here is my favorite thing, Lucio." Dolores stood in a corner of the room beside a square piano. "Uncle Lorenzo had it brought around the Horn years ago, when his daughters were growing up. It is one of the few in California." Idly she brushed the keys with her fingertips. "But nobody can play it. There is no teacher."

Lucius gazed dreamily at the silent instrument. "My wife used to play a little," he murmured.

Dolores turned to a huge gilt-framed oil painting, dominating the wall at the end of the room. "These are my grandparents, Don Ygnacio and Doña Concepcion. Valadez. Uncle Lorenzo had this brought from Spain when he was still a young man." She spent a moment studying the two flat expressionless faces that gazed with empty eyes out from a featureless landscape of dark blue. "They are lovely, don't you think? Of course I never knew them."

She looked at Lucius and saw that his eyes were on her rather than the picture. She smiled her quick fleeting smile. "Am I tiring you, Lucio?"

"Oh no, not at all. But I'm so entranced by the beauty of my guide that I find it hard to pay attention to anything else."

Dolores colored and put a hand to her cheek. "Oh dear! You are a bold one!"

Lucius pretended to be appalled at himself. "Forgive me. I didn't mean—"

"Shall we go and sit with Uncle Lorenzo? I think he will be lonely."

Dolores led the way back to the opposite end of the long room, where Don Lorenzo was sitting in a tall chair of elaborately carved scrolls and richly brocaded upholstery. He was asleep, his gray head drooping on his chest.

Dolores leaned over him and whispered, "Uncle?"

The old man snapped awake with a snort and looked around wildly. "*Josefa? Eres tu, Josefa?*"

"There, there, Uncle. It is Dolores."

The wild-eyed look was gone as swiftly as it had come. "*Si, si, muchacha.* Help me up, please." He leaned on his niece's arm for support, and when he was on his feet he turned to Lucius with a smile.

"You will excuse me, Lucio? These late hours are not for one of my age. I am sure you young people can entertain yourselves without the assistance of a sleepy old man." He clapped his hands sharply. "Pablo!"

A young Indian servant appeared immediately and soundlessly, and hovered at his master's side. In an undertone Don Lorenzo issued some rapid instructions in Spanish to the young man. Then he gave little bows to Dolores and to Lucius, murmured, "*Buenas noches, niños míos,*" received their good nights, and went out, leaning on Pablo's arm.

"Poor Uncle Lorenzo," Dolores said to Lucius when they were alone. "Sometimes he dreams of Tía Josefa. His wife."

"What is *niños míos?*" Lucius asked.

Dolores's lips twitched with embarrassment. "My children. Uncle Lorenzo thinks of all unmarried people, of whatever age, as children."

Cautiously Lucius moved a little closer to her. "Dolores...now that we're alone...may I tell you how I think of you?"

Dolores looked faintly uneasy. "Shall we sit down?" She took the big chair her uncle had just vacated.

Lucius pulled a smaller chair close to hers, sat down and leaned toward her. "I think of you as a solitary flower blooming on a hillside, lonely, wistful, and—"

He stopped short; someone had come into the room. The old Indian woman, Rosalia, hobbled to a chair that stood against the wall halfway down the length of the room, and sat down. She folded her hands in her lap and stared impassively at the opposite wall, not looking once in the young people's direction.

"You were saying, Lucio?" Dolores prompted gently.

Lucius leaned closer. "Do we have to have *her?*" he whispered.

"Rosalia? Oh, that is all right. She is my companion, my...what you call it...guardian."

"Chaperone."

"Chaperone, yes."

"Wonderful!" Lucius muttered. "That's just wonderful!"

"Do not pay her attention, Lucio. She understands very little English."

A strange wild look had risen in Lucius's eyes. "If I kissed you, would she understand *that?*"

Dolores recoiled. "Oh, *Lucio!*"

Without further warning he took her by the arms, lifted her out of the chair and kissed her fiercely, while she stood wide-eyed and paralyzed in his grasp. At length the paralysis wore off; she broke away from him and stepped back, trembling and gasping and clutching at her chair for support.

Old Rosalia was on her feet, glaring murderously at Lucius.

He laughed. "Well, Rosalia, how do you like that? Pretty forceful, eh? That's the way the *Americano* courts a lady. No beating about the bush, wasting time with endless polite conversation—"

"If you will excuse me, *señor*," Dolores said in a small voice, "I think I too will bid you good night. Pablo will show you to your room and provide you with whatever you need."

Lucius was suddenly seized with remorse. "Forgive me, Dolores, I . . . I don't know what came over me. That wasn't like me at all, I swear . . ." He reached for her hand, but she moved back quickly, avoiding his touch.

"Come, Rosalia," she called. "Good night, Señor Hargrave. Sleep well."

She swept out of the room, and Rosalia followed, giving the *Americano* one last indignant scowl before she disappeared.

Lucius was sprawled in the big chair, staring into the dark fireplace, when the Indian servant Pablo bent over him.

"Excuse, *señor*. You like to go to your room now?"

Lucius turned his eyes up to the young Indian's lean face, and studied it with some interest. "What is your tribe, Pablo?"

"The Costanoans, *señor*. My people are fishermen around the bay."

"You like being a servant better than being a fisherman?"

Pablo's small shrug was noncommittal. "My people do not live good, *señor*. My father was taken into the Mission of San Jose and taught the ways of the Padres, but he did not like that. He ran away and went to work for Don Lorenzo. That was a long time ago. He is dead now. But I follow his footsteps."

"So you're happy here, are you?"

The little shrug came again. "What means 'happy,' *señor?* Don Lorenzo is a good kind man. I am content."

Lucius continued to gaze thoughtfully up into the servant's face. "Pablo, Señorita Dolores said you would provide me with whatever I needed."

"Sí, señor?"

"Do you happen to have a pound or two of self-control you could let me have?"

Pablo replied in perfect solemnity, "No, señor. I am sorry."

"Well then, damnit, is there any whiskey in this house?"

"Whiskey, señor? No. Wine, rum, aguardiente. No whiskey."

Lucius heaved a long sigh of resignation and got slowly to his feet. "All right, Pablo," he said bleakly. "Lead me to my cell."

(3)

IN THE MORNING Don Lorenzo was sitting at a table set for breakfast on the patio. Sunlight filtered through the flowering trees and made a soft arabesque pattern on the white tablecloth. Don Lorenzo was waiting. Soon Lucius emerged from the house and came toward him, and the old man smiled and waved a greeting.

"Ah, good morning, Lucio! Come, sit down. I wait breakfast for you."

Lucius took a seat. "It's so quiet here, I'm afraid I overslept."

"Not at all, amigo. At Las Sombras everybody moves at his own pace. Even the servants." Don Lorenzo was in exuberant spirits.

A pair of Indian women appeared from the kitchen, bearing platters of eggs, ham, venison, jars of preserves, a large pot of coffee, and a basket of hot oven-baked bread. Plates were served, the servants dismissed, and a blessing mumbled over the food by Don Lorenzo. They began to eat.

Lucius's eyes roamed along the shadowy corredors—the covered verandas along the walls of the house, surrounding the patio. "Is, uh . . . Dolores sleeping late?" he asked casually.

Don Lorenzo laughed. "Ah no, never. She puts us all to shame with her industriousness. Up at dawn, a quick breakfast, off to the chapel for prayers, then on to the Indian village."

"The Indian village?"

"We have a large Indian population on the *rancho*. The *vaqueros* who tend the cattle, the various workers, the household servants—most are Indians. But they need daily care. There are the sick, the aged, the mothers with small children—it is a burdensome responsibility. Dolores sees to it all. She is an angel."

"Yes," Lucius agreed. "That is my impression of her."

Don Lorenzo smiled. They ate in silence for a while, and Lucius began to frown, pondering something.

"Don Lorenzo... has Dolores, uh... said anything to you about me?"

"Yes. She said you were a charming gentleman and delightful company, and she is glad you are here. Poor child. She leads a lonely life, as you can see."

"Nothing else? Nothing... in the nature of complaint?"

"Why, no." Shrewdly Don Lorenzo examined Lucius's troubled face. "What are you thinking of?"

"I find her an extremely attractive young lady, Don Lorenzo. I'm afraid I became somewhat impetuous last night. A bit too forward for her taste."

"Oh. You mean the kiss?"

Lucius looked shamefaced. "I was hoping she wouldn't tell you. I'm embarrassed."

"She didn't. Her woman did. Old Rosalia is a shameless, uh... what you call it?... tattler. But I pay no attention to her."

"Nevertheless, I'm afraid Dolores was offended."

"Oh, I think not. I understand in your country, Lucio, such incidents are not considered matters of life and death. As you know, I am a great admirer of things American, and I am trying to educate my niece in this. She is not so forward-looking as I yet, but she is coming along, coming along."

Lucius was only partially reassured. "Still, I feel terrible about it. I hope she won't—"

Don Lorenzo's laugh cut him off. "Nonsense, *amigo*, it was nothing! Come, come, eat your breakfast. We have a busy day ahead of us. I want to show you the *rancho*."

They rode for hours over green and brown lands stretching to all horizons and strewn with the dark shapes of cattle that crawled like insects over the grassy carpet. In certain fields dense beige masses of sheep grazed under the drowsy eyes of herdsmen. They encountered *vaqueros*, the cowboys of the *rancho*, who galloped at dashing speed across the ranges with no perceptible cause for haste, and, in passing, swept off their broad-brimmed hats to their master Don Lorenzo. At noon they broke bread and cheese and drank goat's milk out of leather flasks with these swarthy and genial men, and Don Lorenzo conversed with them in Spanish. In the afternoon they turned their horses up a winding trail and arrived at a hilltop commanding a windblown and sunlit panorama. From there Don Lorenzo swept his arm toward the landscape below, and his smile was full of quiet pride.

"Sixty thousand acres, Lucio. Twelve thousand cattle, seventy-five hundred sheep. All the finest breeding stock."

"Amazing," Lucius allowed. He remembered the tour of the *sala* that he had received from Dolores. "And how many horses?"

"Droves." Don Lorenzo shrugged. "In California nobody counts horses."

Far below them at the bottom of the hill were two scenes of teeming industry. Don Lorenzo pointed to one, where a number of workmen were trodding barefoot in ankle-deep mud contained in a twenty-foot circular depression in the ground. "They are making adobe brick, the one building material we have in abundance. The formula is fixed by tradition—clay, grass, milk, and blood."

"Blood?!"

"The blood of cattle. It is a powerful binding agent. Now look over there." Don Lorenzo pointed to a place where several great black iron kettles were steaming over fires in the open space between a pair of thatch-roofed sheds.

"Tallowmaking," Don Lorenzo explained. "When cattle are slaughtered the hides are cleaned and dried and the fat boiled down to tallow. The hides are taken by Boston ships, in trade. The tallow goes to South America for candlemaking. The blood is collected for use in the adobe, and the choice cuts of meat are dried and preserved for food. The rest is discarded."

"Most impressive," Lucius said.

Don Lorenzo sighed. "I'm afraid not, *amigo*. For here you see the full extent of industry in California. In this respect, as in others, there is much we can learn from the *Americanos*."

The tour was completed. They turned their horses homeward.

In the evening they sat in the dining room that adjoined the *sala*, and dawdled long by candlelight over a supper of native beans called *frijoles*—baked in a spicy stew of peppers and onions and garnished with cheese and boiled eggs—*tortillas*, fruit, and huge quantities of a heavy dark red wine. Dolores spoke animatedly about her day's activities, exhilarated by the fact that a sick Indian child she had been tending was at last beginning to recover. Afterwards they moved into the *sala*, where at Don Lorenzo's urging Dolores brought out a guitar, strummed softly, and sang old Spanish songs in a throaty contralto. Lucius watched the girl's face intently, a dreamy look in his eyes.

"Beautiful," he murmured when she had finished. "Reminds me of my dear late wife. She used to sing so beautifully..."

Pensively Dolores strummed a few chords. "I hope you will bring your little boy here soon, Lucio. I would so like to know him."

"Oh, I will, I will. Justin would love it here. He would love *you*."

Soon Dolores got up and put away her guitar. "Will you forgive me if I say good night now? I must be up early in the morning, to see about the sick child."

"Of course, *muchacha*," Don Lorenzo said.

Lucius was on his feet, protesting. "So soon? We've hardly had a chance to talk."

She offered him her hand. "I am sure you and Uncle Lorenzo have business to discuss, Lucio. We will meet again tomorrow. Good night." With a whirl of her long skirt she was gone.

Lucius sat down and stared glumly at the floor. "No doubt about it, I've offended her. She's avoiding me now."

"No, no, Lucio, you are wrong," Don Lorenzo said smilingly. "I asked her to leave us alone this evening. We *do* have business to discuss, do we not?"

Lucius looked up with sudden interest. "Well, yes, now that you mention it. There's the second half of my fee for the trip south. Then there's that little matter of a land grant for me. Or have you forgotten?"

Don Lorenzo smiled his enigmatic smile and said, "I forget nothing, Lucio. Let us dispense with the small matters first."

He pulled from a pocket a slender paper-wrapped package tied with a string, and handed it to Lucius. "Here is the remainder of your fee, plus a little, uh...what you call, bonus."

Lucius took the package and stuffed it into a pocket without a glance. "Thank you. But what's the bonus for?"

"For doing an excellent job. For incurring a certain amount of risk. And because it was a very important message you delivered."

"Oh?" Lucius grinned. "If I'd known that I'd have charged a bit more."

"Very important, indeed," Don Lorenzo went on. "It was my friend Mariano Vallejo's assessment of the forces we could bring to bear, as compared to those of Micheltorina's. It was nothing less than the word that put the revolution in motion. You are aware of who General Vallejo is, I imagine?"

"Oh yes. The big man in Sonoma. But, you know, these California revolutions confuse me. I don't understand why Vallejo, who was once the military commandant of the Mexican government in California, is on *your* side."

"Because, like me, he is a man of the world, not a *Mexicano*."

"And I don't understand why John Sutter brought his motley troops in to support Micheltorina, when he knows damn well the Mexicans would like to kick him out of California."

"Because he is heavily indebted to Micheltorina for certain generosities. And because, I regret to say, he is a fool. And, by the way, Lucio—that brother of yours who lives near Sutter's place—I hope he wasn't—"

"A member of Sutter's troops? Impossible." Lucius laughed. "If you knew Isaac you'd know how comical that idea is."

"*Bueno*. I am relieved to hear it."

"But, damn it all, I don't understand why, after risking your necks to get rid of Mexican rule, you and your friends are willing to let Pío Pico take over the governorship."

"That's his right, as head of the *junta*—"

"But he's setting up shop in the south, for God's sake! Are you northerners going to sit back and let him move the government from Monterey to Los Angeles?"

Don Lorenzo laughed, and clapped his hands sharply. Pablo materialized; Don Lorenzo whispered something in Spanish to the servant, who padded away.

365

"Pablo told me you had asked for whiskey last night, Lucio. It happens that I have a small private supply, which I bring out for special occasions only. I believe this may be one."

Pablo brought a bottle and two glasses and set them on a table at Don Lorenzo's elbow, and disappeared again. The host poured, then handed a glass to Lucius.

"To your good health, *amigo*."

"And to yours." Lucius sipped with deep appreciation.

Don Lorenzo set his glass down and crossed his spindly legs. "I must explain something to you, Lucio. For me, and for a few others like my friend Vallejo, there is a long view that everyone does not see. The first step was the ouster of the *Mexicanos*. After that, the northerners and the southerners begin their rivalry again, their squabbling among themselves. That is good, that is as we expected. The truth is, the *Californios* are no more inclined to rule effectively than the *Mexicanos* were. All is chaos. *Now* the stage is set for the final flowering of our plan."

Lucius was frowning. "I'm not following you too well."

"The flowering, Lucio, is that California becomes a part of the United States."

Lucius was quiet for a moment while he thought about this, then rejected it. "Excuse me, Don Lorenzo, but it seems to me that's pure fantasy. Look at the geographical isolation. Two thousand miles of mountains and desert and wilderness between here and the United States. Nobody can know what that means who hasn't been over it. I have. I know."

"A trifle, Lucio. Roads will be built, distances will shrink. Do you know that your new American *presidente* has said he intends to bring into the Union not only Texas, but California as well, and all the lands between? There is a man of vision, your Señor Polk. He will not be denied, because his vision is in perfect harmony with the natural flow of history."

"Well, maybe." Lucius shrugged. "I won't argue the point. I've never had much of a head for politics—"

"Ah, but you must develop one, *amigo*. Politics governs your life whether you like it or not. You are young, intelligent, energetic—and California is a lump of raw clay waiting to be shaped by the hands of men like you. Do not fail to seize your opportunity, Lucio."

Lucius was toying with his now empty whiskey glass with open impatience. "How can I seize any kind of opportunity when I don't have so much as a place to hang my hat? You

366

know damn well that in California a man without land is a nobody. My petition for a grant from Micheltorina turned out to be worthless, as you said it would, and as far as I can see I'm no better off with Pico in power. He hates Americans. Oh sure, he was plenty willing to accept help from us, but now he's not going to give us a damn thing but the back of his hand."

Don Lorenzo smiled his approval while he refilled Lucius's glass. "You are right about Pico, your perceptions are most accurate. And you are right about the importance of becoming a landowner. It is absolutely essential, so that when the day comes that the *Americanos* take charge, you will be in a position of influence, of power—"

"But how, damnit, *how?*"

"You could easily have your land, Lucio. You could have it from me."

There was a short pause while Lucius sipped his whiskey and eyed his host warily. "On what basis? I'm not following you again."

Don Lorenzo leaned forward and fixed Lucius with an intense look. "Lucio, it is very clear to me that our interests—yours and mine—lie along the same path. It is the wish closest to my heart to secure for my family an *alianza*—how you say, an alliance—with the *Americanos*, who I am convinced will soon be the ruling class in this land. And for you, it could only be beneficial to be connected with a name like Valadez. It is one of the venerable old names of California. There is prestige in it, and a tradition of great respect."

The old Don settled back in his chair, and an impish smile sparkled in his eye. "Now, Lucio, as to the little matter of your having stolen a kiss from Dolores last night—I hope you realize that you gravely violated the child's virtue, and placed a stain on the honor of our family. There is only one way a *caballero*—a gentleman—can make restitution for such an offense. I trust you will prove to be a true *caballero*. I took you for one the first moment I saw you, and you know, I pride myself on my judgment of human nature."

Lucius had put his glass down and, with hands tightly clasped, was staring in rapt attention at the older man. "I think I'm beginning to follow you."

Don Lorenzo's smile turned bland and genial. "Of course it is understood that Dolores will receive a generous *dote* upon her marriage. That is, uh, what you call, dowry. Five or six

367

square leagues of prime land, and a good supply of cattle."

"Very generous."

"Well, you know, my niece is as dear to me as any of my own children. She is a Valadez, after all, and so shall her husband be, in a sense. It would be unthinkable for him to be without land and position."

There was a longer silence now as Lucius thoughtfully sipped his drink.

"What is this, Don Lorenzo?" he said abruptly. "What are we doing here, arranging Dolores's life while she sleeps?"

"She is my ward, Lucio. And she is a dutiful and obedient girl."

"Oh, come now!" Lucius scoffed. "So obedient she'll marry some passing stranger just because you wish it for political reasons?"

Don Lorenzo chuckled. "No, of course not. I think perhaps, Lucio, you do not realize how very fond Dolores is of you. I had harbored a small secret hope for something like this in the back of my mind, but I must say, it is exceeding my wildest dreams thus far. Do you know what Dolores calls you when she speaks to me about you? *El hombre de oro.* The golden man."

Lucius spent another long moment in silence, pondering. Then he finished the last drop of his whiskey and set the glass on the table. "I think I'll say good night now, Don Lorenzo. I want to think about all this a bit." His eyes were roving. "There are several things I have to think about."

Don Lorenzo was studying his guest with shrewd attention. "Secret matters cloud your mind, Lucio, I can see that. As I have said, I am ready to assist you in any way I can. You have but to confide in me."

"No, no, thank you. There are some things I have to work out for myself. In any case . . ." Lucius's voice trailed off. He sat on the edge of his chair, his hands clasped tensely together, his eyes still roaming over the spacious room. He appeared to be hovering on the brink of a momentous decision.

"Maybe I'll get up early in the morning so I can see Dolores before she leaves the house," he said suddenly. "Not that I'm going to press my suit yet. I just want to get to know her a little better."

A hint of amusement glinted in Don Lorenzo's eyes. "Very wise. Before a man commits himself in matters of the heart he should take a close look at the lady in the clear light of morning. And I am sure you will not be disappointed."

"No possibility of *that*," Lucius agreed. There was something else on his mind, but he was hesitant to speak of it. "But, uh ... I've noticed that it's not very easy to, uh ... talk to Dolores alone around here—"

Don Lorenzo was chuckling. "Depend upon it, Lucio, I will stay mostly out of sight from now on. *And*, I promise you ... so will Rosalia." He rose and clapped his hands for his manservant, who appeared in an instant. "Pablo, Don Lucio wishes to retire now. See to his comfort, please."

"*Sí, señor.*"

Lucius got to his feet and extended his hand. "Good night, Don Lorenzo. Thank you for everything. And, uh ... wish me luck, will you?"

The old man's smile was at its warmest as he clasped Lucius's hand and held it for a moment between his own. "You have no need for luck, *amigo mío*, you have everything else in your favor. Everything. Your success is certain."

Looking faintly dazed, Lucius turned away and followed Pablo out of the room.

The master of the house was sitting placidly in his big chair by the dark fireplace when Pablo returned a few minutes later. The servant picked up the bottle and glasses, and hesitated when he noticed that Don Lorenzo's whiskey remained virtually untouched.

He offered the glass. "You want this, *señor*?"

Don Lorenzo made a sour face. "No, no, take it away, it is abominable stuff." Then, as Pablo started to move away he had an abrupt change of mind. "No, wait. Give it to me."

He swirled the liquid in the glass, sniffed it, sipped a little, and sighed. "One must remember this is the *Americanos'* taste in drink. And one must accommodate oneself to the ways of the *Americano*, eh, Pablo?"

The servant shrugged, and padded away.

(4)

LUCIUS STAYED ON as a houseguest at Rancho Las Sombras for several weeks, during which time he and Dolores were together almost constantly through the long daylight hours while Don Lorenzo was away attending to his far-reaching estate. Rosalia stayed obediently out of sight— but just barely. And in the cool evenings the old Don and his niece and their guest lingered for hours over leisurely suppers on the *patio*, and enjoyed music and gentle conversation in the *sala*. It was a charmed life, and Lucius tore himself away at last with a great show of reluctance, pleading that urgent matters demanded his attention elsewhere, and yielding easily to Dolores's heartfelt entreaties that he promise to return as soon as possible. He was as good as his word; he was back by mid-June for another two-week stay, then off once more, to return yet again at the end of July. This time there was no further talk of leaving.

And one day early in August, in the presence of Don Lorenzo and a cluster of house servants that had been assembled in the *sala*, he took the lovely Dolores in his arms, gazed for a moment at her parted lips, and kissed her tenderly. And all the watching eyes—even those of the grim old Rosalia—gleamed with quiet approval, for Don Lorenzo had just announced that the couple would soon be married, and that this handsome young *Americano*, Señor Lucio, was now to be regarded as a member of the family.

On an afternoon of shimmering heat and blazing skies the betrothed pair went riding on splendid horses across the rolling *rancho* lands. Dolores wore a wide-brimmed bonnet to protect her pearl-delicate skin, and was dressed in an airily flowing dress of lacy white—a costume someone of another culture might have regarded as more appropriate to the pouring of afternoon tea than horseback riding—but she perched sidesaddle on her mount with consummate grace and effortless ease, and pretended not to notice that her partner's handling of his own lively steed was labored and clumsy by comparison.

At length, when they had come to a stop on a grassy hilltop several miles from the house, she took pity on him and asked, "Would you rather go back now, Lucio? Perhaps you are not comfortable with your horse."

"No, no, it's fine. Let's go on." His enthusiasm seemed forced.

"You are not so experienced in riding, eh?"

His protest was vigorous. "Of course I'm experienced! I rode a horse practically all the way from Fort Laramie to the Sacramento Valley. I *ought* to be experienced. But this fellow, he's uh . . ." He gave his horse a pat on the neck. "He's a bit wild."

"Nonsense, Lucio, he's as gentle as a lamb."

"On the contrary, my dear, he's waiting for a chance to bolt. I'm holding him back so as not to alarm *your* horse."

A hint of secret amusement glinted for an instant in the girl's dark and solemn eyes. "Want to race?"

He was appalled. "Good Lord, no!"

She pointed toward another gently sloping hillside in the sunny distance ahead, where the meandering course of a tiny stream was delineated by a strand of twisted cottonwood trees. "Race you to the arroyo there," she said, and seeing the distasteful look on his face, added coaxingly, "Go on. I'll give you a . . . what you call it?"

"Head start?"

"Sí, head start."

After another moment of hesitation he chuckled indulgently, as if humoring a whimsical child. "Oh, all right. If it amuses you."

Then, his jaw set firmly in determination, he spurred his horse to a gallop. Within thirty seconds he felt a stab of consternation and amazement as she sped past him and, almost lost amid the throbbing of horses' hooves, a peal of merry musical laughter rang out. A few seconds later he gave it up and pulled back to a leisurely canter, knowing that he was not only beaten but hopelessly outclassed.

She was waiting for him in the shade of a big cottonwood, with her horse drinking from the shallow stream nearby. Her skirt was spread neatly out on the grass as she reclined there, cool and demure as a summer nymph, and when he had dismounted and come to stand beside her, looking down with a great stern frown, she rewarded him with a softly ingratiating smile.

"Come to me, Lucio," she murmured.

He was annoyed, and determined to lecture first. "You should *not* do that, Dolores. It is foolish, utterly reckless. You'll fall and be killed one day."

She looked instantly hurt. "Ah, Lucio, do not scold me, you will make me very unhappy." She lifted her arms to him pleadingly. "Come."

He came down over her, resting on an elbow, and gave her a searching look. "You surprise me sometimes, you know?"

"Kiss me now, to show you are not angry with me," she commanded gently, and without waiting for him to do it, she slid her arms around his neck and brought his mouth down on hers.

Ardor rose in him immediately; he pulled her up hard against him, and his kiss became hungrily demanding. At last she pushed him back, whispering, "That will do, Lucio. I am convinced."

He studied her face for a moment close up, and his own features crinkled with wry amusement. "Well, aren't you going to thank me for letting you win the race? Gallant of me, wasn't it?"

She remained serious, declining to banter.

"Ah, my golden man. You need not pretend to accomplishments you do not have, for my benefit. My admiration for you is already too great. If it grows any more it will burst."

Now, with a solemnity of expression matching hers, he looked deeply into her eyes. "It is I who should be overwhelmed with admiration, my sweet, and I am, do not doubt it. You are lovely beyond description, and what is more, full of delightful little surprises. I promise you—we will be happy together."

"I know that, Lucio. I am sure of it." A hint of sly furtiveness touched her face. "Shall I tell you a little secret?"

"Do."

"Everybody is congratulating Uncle Lorenzo on our betrothal. They all think he arranged it. But the truth of it is—"

"I will tell you the truth of it," he blurted, interrupting her. "Your Uncle Lorenzo only wishes he'd had the opportunity to arrange it. Fact is, I hadn't been here more than two or three days before I knew you were the only woman in the world for me—"

"No, no, Lucio, you too are wrong. The real truth is that it was *I* who decided it."

He chuckled. "You?"

"Yes. The morning after that first night you spent at Las Sombras—you remember, when you kissed me and upset poor Rosalia?—the next morning I said to Uncle Lorenzo, 'Uncle, I wish to inform you that I intend to marry Señor Lucio. Please see to the necessary details.'"

Lucius rolled over on his back and laughed in hearty delight. "Oh, good Lord, Dolores! Here I've been thinking you were the most serious, solemn person I'd ever met—but it turns out you've got a sly sense of humor that nobody knows about." He came up on his elbow again, grinning at her. "By heaven, you're devilishly amusing!" The grin faded abruptly. "And devilishly desirable," he added, and reached for her.

With a lightning movement she eluded his grasp and was on her feet, and the look she turned on him was a baffling mixture of playfulness and mystery. "Do you think I am joking, Lucio?"

"Well, naturally, I—" He blinked, confused. "That is, I guess I'm not sure." Chuckling again, he held out his hand to her. "Come back, tell me more."

But all lightheartedness was suddenly gone from her mood; she looked down on him now with a lofty and regal hauteur. "Time to go home now. We mustn't stay out too long."

"Not yet." His extended hand tried to coax her back. "Come give me another kiss or two, and . . . maybe another surprise."

She shook her head. Her face was again composed in its customary serene solemnity as she retrieved her bonnet from a low-hanging branch and put it on again. "It is not proper, Lucio. Not here. There will be time for that after we are married."

With mingled amusement and annoyance he watched her go to her horse and swing herself with marvelous dexterity back up into the saddle.

Patiently she waited for him. "Coming?"

In a moment he had remounted and had reined in beside her, ready to go. "How long will it take me to know you thoroughly?" he mused.

Her sly smile reappeared faintly for a moment, and was

373

gone again. "I hope, my Lucio...forever and ever." She
turned her horse toward home.

Lucius gazed after her in profound wonderment, and
followed.

(5)

THE WEDDING WAS SET for Thursday, September
eighteenth, and as the long parched California summer drew
to a close, a fever of excited activity at Las Sombras rose
toward its climax. During the week preceding the ceremony
the huge house began to fill, as the sons and daughters of Don
Lorenzo arrived with their families and retinues of servants,
and the long *corredors*, usually silent and empty, rang with
conversation, laughter, and the shrill voices of children. Fires
roared day and night in the mammoth brick ovens in the
kitchen, tended by Indian women who worked at preparing
mountains of food. The entire *rancho* hummed with
animation and industry, for a wedding in the house of a
Spanish grandee was not merely a wedding; it was a festival,
to be announced far and wide by the *vaqueros*, who galloped
up and down the countryside proclaiming the news.
Invitations were unknown; the announcement itself was an
invitation, and would be gleefully accepted by highborn and
lowly alike, native or foreigner, friend or stranger.

Under the hoary old oaks in the field next to the house, an
open-air pavilion was constructed, decorated with bunting
and banners and gaily colored streamers, and furnished with a
dozen ten-foot-long tables for the feasting, these arranged in a
square enclosing a bare area to be given over to that other
pleasure fully as important as the feast—dancing. Over all a
canvas top was erected in case of unfriendly weather, though
no such thing was expected, for this was the season of crisp

coolness amid warm sunshine, cloudless skies, and foliage turning brown not from the approach of winter but from the long, long absence of rain. Besides, this was a time of celebration, and celebrations permitted no mood but optimism.

The day before the nuptials Don Lorenzo gathered his clan together in the pavilion for a portrait to commemorate this final wedding over which he expected to preside. The artist, who had been sent for and brought from Monterey, was renowned. Señor Pepe he called himself, a stout man of mercurial movement and imperious manner, who arranged his subjects with painstaking care for the hasty charcoal sketch from which he would later produce a painting.

Seated in the center, hands in his lap, stiff and wooden-faced and dwarfed by the mass of humanity around him, was the diminutive patriarch, Don Lorenzo. Flanking him on either side were the bride and groom: Dolores radiant in a long white dress that gave a small hint of how she would look in her wedding gown; Lucius Hargrave appearing every inch the prosperous young Don in his Spanish-style suit. Standing next to these three principals were the leading members of the supporting cast, the three daughters and two sons of Don Lorenzo, positioned by Señor Pepe according to age: Doña Teresa de la Rio; Don Alfredo Valadez; Doña Margarita Cortina; Doña Carlota Bolanos; and Don Rafael Valadez. These five surviving members of a brood of nine produced by Lorenzo and Josefa Valadez ranged in age from Teresa's forty to Rafael's twenty-seven. Radiating outward from this nucleus were the spouses of Don Lorenzo's children, then their offspring, one or two of whom had spouses and offspring of their own. Four generations. Thirty-seven people Thirty-six *Castillianos* and one *Americano*.

Señor Pepe grimaced and perspired and worked as rapidly as he could, for he knew his subjects would become impatient and restless very soon, and he wanted this to be a good piece of work—perhaps, he told himself, the masterpiece he had never before quite succeeded in achieving.

Late in the afternoon Lucius's meager family representation arrived—Isaac, Catherine, and Justin. They came in a little caravan of horses and packmules, and were led by a pair of Don Lorenzo's young *vaqueros*, sent to escort them. Lucius came bounding out of the house to meet them, bringing Dolores by the hand and beaming welcome. Within a few seconds he had greeted Isaac with a vigorous handshake and Catherine with a discreet kiss on the cheek, and had brought Dolores forward to be presented to them. Dolores gave Isaac her hand and then was briefly embraced by Catherine, amid murmured courtesies, subdued and dignified. Lucius was bubbling with good humor.

"Just think how lucky you are, my dear," he said to Dolores, his eyes twinkling. "These are the only in-laws you have to contend with."

Dolores's smile was uncertain; she did not comprehend that a little joke had been made. "I am so happy you are here," she said with immense gravity, and bowed to Isaac and Catherine. "You are my brother and my sister, and our house is yours."

Justin was sitting atop a packmule, staring with wide eyes at the grownups. Lucius went to him, grasped him at the waist, and smiled up into his face.

"Well, here's my boy! How are you, Justin?"

"H'lo, Papa." It was barely more than a whisper.

"Are you as glad to see me as I am to see you? Come on, give your papa a big hug, eh?"

Obediently Justin leaned forward and put his arms around Lucius's neck, and Lucius swept him off the mule, holding him in a great bear hug and chuckling.

"Ah, that's my good boy! You've gotten so big, Justin!" He looked closely into the boy's face. "Let's see, how old are you now?"

"Five," Justin said, and quickly added, "almost six."

"That's right, by jimbo!" Lucius exclaimed. "You've got a birthday coming up in a couple of months, haven't you? Well, we'll have to see about that."

He went to Dolores, still holding the boy in his arms. "Justin, I want you to meet the beautiful lady who's going to be your new stepmother. I don't know what you'll call her. Maybe you'll give her an Indian name."

Dolores put her cheek gently against Justin's and held it there for a brief moment. "Hello, Justin. Maybe you will like to call me Tía Dolores, yes? *Tía* means 'Aunt.'"

Justin gave her a weak smile. For the present he was content to call her nothing at all.

Lucius put the boy down and turned to Isaac and Catherine. "Where are the other children?"

"We left them with the Kendrickses," Isaac said. "You remember the Kendrickses, from the Endicott party? They're livin' a little ways up the river from us."

"The Endicott party," Lucius said, suddenly pensive. "Good Lord, that all seems like ancient history."

"There's quite a few Americans settling in the Sacramento Valley now, Lucius. Must be two hundred of 'em came in last spring. Pretty soon California'll be as American as—" He checked himself, and aimed a sheepish grin at Dolores. "'Scuse me, ma'am. I guess I ought not to say that."

"That is perfectly all right, Señor Isaac," Dolores said. "My Uncle Lorenzo is one who believes that the coming of *Americanos* to California is a good thing. He is a wise man, I think. I trust his beliefs."

"Too bad you didn't bring your children, though," Lucius said, looking directly at Catherine. "I'd have loved to see them again. Especially little Martha."

Catherine gave him a long look before replying. "It just seemed like too hard a trip for a sixteen-month-old baby, Lucius. We're hoping you and Dolores will come and visit *us* soon. Next spring we'll be building a new house, and there'll be plenty of room."

"That's right, we're goin' to have our own place," Isaac announced proudly. "Goin' to build us a sawmill on some property we're buyin' from Captain Sutter. Fine timberland, up in the foothills—"

"You're *buying* land?" Lucius said, scowling.

"Oh, it's a bargain, Lucius. Wait'll you see it, I think you'll agree."

Lucius was plainly skeptical. "I hope you know what you're doing, old chum—but I doubt it."

Justin was tugging on Catherine's skirt and asking her something in a whisper. Catherine leaned down to hear his question, then looked toward Dolores.

"Justin wants to know if there are any other children here."

"Oh yes. Many."

"Justin," Lucius said, "when you want to ask Dolores something you can speak to her directly. She speaks perfectly good English. There's no need for an interpreter."

Justin stared at his father, blank-faced.

"That is all right," Dolores said softly. "We will become friends very soon." She smiled at the boy and held out her hand to him. "Come, Justin. I will take you to meet all my little cousins." To Isaac and Catherine she said, "Come in, please. Our house is yours." She led the way, holding Justin by the hand.

377

"I'll just show them around the grounds a bit first," Lucius called after her. "We'll be in in a minute."

They strolled slowly, Lucius walking between Isaac and Catherine.

"Now don't forget, you two," Lucius said in a low voice. "I'm a widower, not divorced. These people are very straitlaced Catholics, you know. We don't want any, uh...unpleasantness."

Isaac and Catherine exchanged an uneasy look.

"I just hope the subject doesn't come up," Catherine said. "I'm not fond of telling lies."

Lucius gave her a quizzical sidelong glance. "Catherine, you know very well there comes a time in everybody's life when a little white lie is the kindest possible solution to a problem. Think about it, now. Don't you agree?"

Color rose in Catherine's cheeks. "You needn't worry," she said curtly. "We won't give your secret away."

Lucius chuckled and took them each by the elbow. "Well, let's go in. Now that Dolores has met her in-laws, it's time for you to meet mine. I warn you, this may take a while. The Valadez clan is half the population of California." He paused for another quick chuckle, then continued, "Dolores will have to make the introductions, of course. For the life of me I can't remember all these people's names."

Beaming a big smile, he moved toward the house, where Don Lorenzo was standing in his doorway waiting to meet the new guests.

The ritual would consist of two distinct parts: the marriage ceremony, which would consume less than an hour, and the days-long marathon of celebrating to follow. The first part would take place in the *rancho*'s tiny chapel, half-hidden by vines in a secluded spot a short distance from the house. It would be conducted by Padre Mendoza, an eminent priest from San José, and would be witnessed by only a select few. The second part, the celebration, would encompass the house and the adjacent pavilion, and would be open to all.

Horses were important in this society. They were not only essential to daily activities, but symbolically significant in all ceremonies. It was said of the Spanish-Californian that he was born and raised on horseback, married on horseback, grew old on horseback, and, if he was lucky, died there. Don Lorenzo had inspected horses for days before selecting two well-trained specimens for a privileged service, and several Indian seamstresses had spent countless hours decorating flank aprons with strips of bright silk, embroidery of gold and silver thread, and tassels and tiny bells sewn on the hems.

Then it was the day. People began to arrive early in the morning, coming by oxcart and on horseback, and by eleven o'clock the pavilion was teeming. The ceremony was scheduled for high noon. At a quarter to twelve the crowd gathered in front of the house, where the two horses, magnificently adorned under silver-studded saddles and the gorgeous aprons that covered their flanks almost to the ground, had been led to the front door. A ripple of rising expectancy flowed through the throng of onlookers as the prancing steeds tossed their manes and awaited their riders. When it was almost noon a hush settled over the spectators. All eyes were fixed on the darkness beyond the open doorway through which the bride would momentarily appear. There was some small delay; the crowd grew restless with pent-up excitement; people edged in a bit closer, necks craning. Adults lifted children onto their shoulders for a better view.

Suddenly there was a rolling murmur of *oohs* and *ahs* from fifty throats in unison—the bride had appeared, a cascading brilliance of pure white from head to toe except for the blue-black sheen of her hair and her liquid dark eyes, large with awe and exhilaration and wonder. She was on the arm of the man who had been designated future godfather—Alfredo Valadez, her uncle's elder son. Don Alfredo was a large man with a broad and infectious smile that he now tried hard to keep under control on this solemn occasion. He was dressed in a suit of gleaming black, decorated with brass buttons and stripes of silken scarlet on the trouser legs and jacket sleeves.

After the bride and her escort came the groom and the godmother, Doña Francisca, wife of Alfredo. The bridegroom was a vision of splendor in his own right. His suit was the color of dark red wine, embroidered with intricate patterns of black and green, and the green appeared again in his broad silken waistband. His brass buttons glinted in the sunlight and the white lace of his shirtfront was as immaculate as new-fallen snow. Doña Francisca's gown was a vivid marine blue. She was a short dumpy middle-aged woman with darting eyes and a timid expression, and attracted the least attention of the foursome.

In accordance with long-established tradition the ritual

proceeded: the godfather mounted one of the horses, then took the bride on the pillion behind him as she was helped up by attendants; similarly the groom took the godmother on his horse; the procession then moved off in curious silence toward the chapel, where Don Lorenzo and the Padre were waiting. The horses, which were led by attendants on foot, seemed to sense the auspiciousness of the proceedings—they walked with a slow and weighty dignity that barely produced a whisper of tinkling from the little bells on their aprons, and the people following had no trouble keeping up the pace.

In the dim candlelit interior of the little chapel there was room for only a few witnesses: Don Lorenzo, his sons and daughters and their spouses, and Isaac and Catherine Hargrave. All others remained outside.

The ceremony was subdued and profoundly solemn. The bride and groom knelt before the altar; there was prayer, and the Padre offered up supplications for a holy blessing to fall upon their union, which was likened to that of Christ and the Church; the text of the ceremony was intoned; the vows were taken; the Sacrament was given and received; the bride and groom were encircled by a long silken scarf that was tied around their shoulders in a symbolic knot; there was more prayer; the couple were then bade rise as man and wife; the husband planted a kiss of the most exquisite tenderness on the trembling lips of his bride, and her eyes glistened with joy and wonder; there was heard a gentle sound of weeping in the darkened chamber, and for the first time the Padre's severe face was softened by a small smile. It was finished.

Outside the horses were mounted again, but for the return trip the partners were reversed. The husband took his new wife on his own horse, and the procession wound its way back past the pavilion beneath the oaks to the house. By this time more guests had arrived, and the pavilion was filled with a milling throng of festively dressed people. They closed in around the wedding procession as it returned, and followed it to the house, and the hush of expectancy rose once more. Solemnity was not yet discarded—though there were now smiles and winks and furtive looks that foretold an imminent eruption of merriment.

The bride and groom had gone into the house by the time Don Lorenzo and the priest arrived. Padre Mendoza had adopted geniality as his mood now, smiling and nodding this way and that to the people. When Don Lorenzo reached his doorway he stepped up onto a little stool and turned to survey the crowd. He waited. The hush was reduced to a total breathless silence.

Then Don Lorenzo clapped his hands once, sharply, and shouted, "*Comenzamos con la música!*" Let the music begin.

It was the signal that triggered an explosive release of energy. A great shout rose and was echoed and reechoed, and from somewhere in the gathering, guitars and violins made a miraculous appearance. Strings began to vibrate under the attack of bows and fingers. People ran toward the pavilion trailing laughter and squeals of anticipation of the pleasure to come. The disorderly sounds from the musical instruments gradually coalesced into form and melody and pulsing rhythm, and brightly colored skirts began to twirl in the sunlight and shadow.

The ritual continued. The wedding was over; the celebration began.

(6)

THERE WERE TWO PARTIES going on: one in the enclosed patio of the big house for the family and special guests, another in the outdoor pavilion for the general public. The outside party was bigger, noisier, livelier. The patio party was lively enough, though the music and dancing there reflected a shade more decorum. The quality of the feasting was the same inside and out. The tables were laden with platters of *tortillas* and *tamales,* stacks of beefsteaks charred over open firepits, steaming pots of *frijoles* and *guisado de carne*—a stew made from chunks of beef in a thick broth of tomatoes, peppers, onions, and a complex mixture of herbs and spices—piles of piping hot *batatas* or sweet potatoes, baskets of bread, bowls of grapes, olives, pears and melons, vessels of steaming chocolate, bottles and bottles of wine and the heavily sweet liqueur called *aguardiente*. Supplies were depleted, replenished, and depleted again in a never-ending process.

Among the celebrants at the patio party the least skilled and most enthusiastic dancer was the bridegroom. To the vital rhythms of the fandango he twirled and stamped his feet with an abandon that made his male in-laws smile forbearingly and the females giggle behind their hands. Dolores favored the more sedate dances. When the waltz began Lucius took his bride to the center of the floor, and then his crude efforts seemed to take on some of the disciplined grace of his partner. Together they achieved a harmony of movement that caused other dancers to draw back to give them room, and watch with whispered words of admiration.

They smiled into each others' eyes as they glided over the stone floor.

"You dance superbly, love," he said. "Almost as well as you ride a horse."

Her nod was serenely gracious. "And you, *amado mío*—now that you are dancing with *me*—you dance beautifully, too."

He chuckled. "Did you see me doing the fandango with your little cousin, Estella What's-her-name? Quite a sight, wasn't it?"

"Estella de la Rio," Dolores said. "She is Doña Teresa's daughter. And yes, indeed, I saw you. And I think, at the end, you kissed her in a way that was perhaps . . . not entirely cousinly."

He threw back his head and laughed outright. "Well, she's quite a fetching young wench—can you blame me?"

She looked at him gravely without answering.

"You know I have eyes only for my beautiful bride," he said in a voice suddenly gone intimate and husky. "You know that, don't you?"

"Shall I tell you another little secret, Lucio?"

"Please do!" His eyes sparkled with renewed amusement.

"Your bride is going to be a jealous wife."

"Oh God, no!" His face contorted clownishly in mock

dismay. "I wish you'd told me that before I married you!"

She declined to participate in his merriment, and again he turned serious. "You won't really be a jealous wife, will you? You'll never have cause to be, you know."

She relented, and her face was softened by one of her rare smiles. "Ah, no, I was only joking, *amado*."

"There, you see? I *knew* you had a sense of humor!"

But she had already gone solemn again. "I am going to try very hard to be a perfect wife—and a perfect wife could never be a jealous one."

Visibly pleased, he pulled her closer as they danced, and whispered in her ear, "I adore you madly, my angel. And if these damned people will ever go home and leave us alone, I'll show you *how* madly."

And the people around them, unaware of having been damned, watched the handsome young couple and beamed their approval.

Between dances Lucius and his bride sat at one of the tables that ringed the patio, to have a bite to eat and a little rest. At rare intervals they found a moment alone, held hands, and with long looks sent each other silent messages of ardor. In one such moment Isaac came and found them.

"I've just been out to the pavilion," he reported, taking a seat. "There must be two hundred people out there, all singin' and dancin' and eatin' and drinkin'. I've never seen anything like it."

Lucius smiled. "Weddings were never like this in Indiana, eh, old chum?"

"You should 'a' been there a little while ago," Isaac went on. "Catherine was dancin' with one o' the *vaqueros*."

"Good Lord!" Lucius groaned, and his smile turned to a scowl.

"Oh, they were good, Lucius, you should 'a' seen 'em. Everybody was clappin'."

"Isaac, go out and explain to your wife that she ought not to be out there carrying on like that, it's not appropriate. Bring her in here where she belongs—"

"Oh no, Lucio, you are wrong," Dolores said earnestly. "All those people out there are our friends, even the *vaqueros*. They are here to honor us. Come, let us go and greet them and bid them welcome."

Lucius looked pained. "Is that necessary?"

"Yes, it is." Dolores was up, taking Lucius's hand and pulling him to his feet. "You are Don Lucio now, a member of the family Valadez. You have obligations."

Isaac was grinning up at his brother. "That's right, Lucius. You're a big man now."

With a resigned sigh Don Lucio followed his wife out to perform the duties of his station.

Justin Hargrave, who preferred to be known as Little Eagle, was trying to organize a band of Shoshone warriors among his new Spanish cousins. He and half a dozen black-eyed children ranging in age from three to eight or nine were sitting in a circle on the floor of an empty room that had been set aside for a play area. Little Eagle was having no success, for it was evening, fatigue was setting in, and there was a formidable language barrier. Young eyelids drooped. One by one the littlest warriors were taken away by their mothers to be put to bed, and the bigger ones wandered off. Little Eagle was left alone. Then Lucius and Dolores were there, side by side, looking fondly down at him.

"Hello, Justin," Dolores said. "Do you want to go to sleep now? Come, I will take you." She held out her hand to him.

"My name is Little Eagle," Justin said. He made no move to get up.

"Never mind that, Justin," Lucius said. "It's time for bed now. No more games."

"Aunt Catherine puts me to bed," the boy said.

"Justin, listen to me. Dolores is my wife now, you see, and therefore your new mother. She's a very kind, sweet lady, and loves you very much, and I'm sure you'll feel the same way about her once you get to know her."

Dolores was kneeling beside the boy now. "Would you like me to tell you a story before you go to sleep, Justin? I know some beautiful old Spanish folk tales. I think you'd like them."

Justin picked at the toe of his shoe, keeping his eyes turned away from the adults. "Aunt Catherine reads me American stories out of a book. I like American stories better than Spanish stories."

"Justin, you're being rude!" Lucius snapped.

"Do not scold him, Lucio," Dolores said softly.

"But, good Lord, changes do occur in people's lives, and they have to adjust to them, children as well as grownups. He might as well start now—"

"Excuse me, please," Catherine said. She had come quietly into the room. "I was just looking for Justin. It's his bedtime."

384

Dolores stood up and stared at the other woman in tense silence.

Catherine looked from Dolores to Lucius, and her manner became apologetic. "I don't mean to butt in, but... it's a difficult thing for a little boy..."

"Yes, you are right," Dolores said crisply. "A very difficult thing." She smiled down at Justin and said, "Good night, Little Eagle," and went out quickly.

For an awkward moment Lucius held Catherine's level gaze. "Well, I'll leave it to you, then," he said finally. "Apparently you don't need any help."

He reached down and ruffled Justin's hair. "Good night, son."

Then he was gone, and Catherine and the little boy looked at each other in silent understanding.

The bacchanalia progressed through the first night at a fever pitch. In the pavilion the crowd swelled to a teeming multitude of merrymakers, and the dozen big whale-oil lamps that gave illumination to the scene sent up blue-gray streams of smoke that would drift away among the oaks and on down the valley for miles before morning. The fields and the roadside near the house were a mass of *carretas*, and horses were tethered at every tree and post.

Within the house the festivities slowed—guests went off from time to time for naps—but the central collective purpose was not forgotten: that by the company's tireless vigilance the newlyweds would be prevented from enjoying more than a snatched moment together, and that only under watchful eyes. It was a test of fortitude and patience under adversity, to last for three days and three nights. Successfully passed, it would prove the young husband and wife capable of withstanding any trial that life could devise.

Once, long after midnight, Dolores stole away, crept into her bedroom, sank down on her big canopied bed, and lay still with closed eyes. There was a furtive sound in the darkness; someone had followed her.

"Who is it?" she whispered.

Lucius bent over her, pulling her into an eager embrace.

"Oh, Lucio," she murmured, and slid her arms around him. "My golden man."

He kissed her hungrily, exploring her face and neck with

385

his lips. "At this moment, my darling, I am not so much a golden man as an angry one."

"Why are you angry, *amado mío*?"

"I want these people to go home. I want to be alone with my wife."

"We must be patient, Lucio. It is an old custom—"

"It's a stupid custom. Uncivilized. To hell with it."

He pulled her closer and pressed his mouth on hers, and her body writhed and trembled under his demanding hands.

"Ah, soon, my Lucio," she whispered then. "Soon I will be yours—"

The door was suddenly flung open, and the room was invaded by glaring light and a babble of gleeful voices and half a dozen grinning faces. The leader of the invaders was Ricardo Cortina, husband of Don Lorenzo's daughter Margarita. He was about thirty-five, short and chubby, his round face dominated by a huge squared-off mustache.

"Aha!" he cried, and his black eyes gleamed in merriment. "We have arrived just in time to save our little cousin from the evil clutches of this *gringo*!" He went through the motions of drawing an imaginary sword, and, thrusting it into Lucius's midriff, shouted, "Now, *gringo*, you die!"

Shrieks of laughter filled the room as hands clutched at Lucius and pulled him to his feet, while others reached for the bride. Dolores smiled at the roistering with stoic tranquility. Grim-faced, Lucius shot her a dark and desperate look before being hustled out of the room.

The morning hours of Friday were relatively quiet as the marathon sank to a low ebb. Vigilance over the bride and groom relaxed to the point of permitting them a few hours sleep—though assuredly not together; Lucius lolled in a hammock in a far corner of the patio while Dolores's bedroom door was guarded by sharp-eyed sentries. A little past noon Lucius was dumped unceremoniously out of his hammock and Dolores brought blinking out of her room, and the music began again.

The old patriarch Don Lorenzo had established himself in his favorite chair in the *sala*. There he sat watching the festivities on the patio, smiling as he received the compliments and congratulations of everyone who passed by. Isaac and Catherine Hargrave came to wish him a good afternoon, and he greeted them with warm enthusiasm.

"Ah, *señor, señora*. Come sit down, talk with me awhile. I

have not had the pleasure of making your acquaintance properly." He beamed at them as they seated themselves.

"You are in the employ of *Señor* Sutter, I understand," he said to Isaac.

"Yes, sir, but not for long. Only till I pay off my debt. I'm buying some land from him, y'see. Goin' to build me a sawmill."

Lucius had come in, munching a pear, and had pulled up a chair and joined the little group. "I wouldn't worry too much about a debt to Sutter if I were you," he said to Isaac. "They say he never pays his own debts."

"Well, I can't operate that way, Lucius. Still, I'll be just as glad not to be workin' for him anymore."

"Why is that, *señor?*" Don Lorenzo wanted to know.

"Oh, just professional disagreement. He wanted me to build a sawmill up in the mountains and float the lumber down the American River to the fort. I went up the river and looked around, and saw it wasn't possible. That river's too wild to float lumber down. But Sutter's determined to do it, so . . . we decided to part company."

"There are other reasons too," Catherine said. "Why don't you tell them the other reasons, dear?"

Isaac became hesitant. "Well . . . he's just not the kind of man I can respect. He keeps Indian slaves, and he keeps some of their women as, uh . . . uh . . ."

"Concubines," Catherine finished for him.

Lucius chuckled softly, and Don Lorenzo smiled his mysterious little smile.

"Do not be too hasty in applying your American standards of morality to California, *amigo*," Don Lorenzo said to Isaac. "Someday you may do so, but not yet. It is a different world—"

"Excuse me, sir, but I don't see that," Isaac said earnestly. "I think morality is morality, anywhere—"

"Don't get all worked up, old chum," Lucius said warningly.

Don Lorenzo went on smiling.

In the patio the musicians began to play a waltz, and Catherine seized upon it as a way to change the subject.

"I do love the music," she said. "And I love Las Sombras, Don Lorenzo. It is so very beautiful."

"You are most kind, *señora*." The old man appraised Catherine with the admiring eyes of a connoisseur, and was suddenly moved by an impetuous thought. "It is not often that

387

I feel the urge to dance at my age, *señora*, but I would be most honored to have a dance with you."

"Thank you, sir, I'd love to." Catherine was on her feet without hesitation, taking Don Lorenzo's arm.

When they were alone Isaac turned to Lucius. "I've been wanting a chance to talk to you, Lucius—"

Lucius emitted a hollow laugh. "Old chum, I haven't had a chance to kiss my wife, let alone talk to anybody."

"I've had a couple of letters from Mama Sarah. Thought you might like to read 'em."

"Addressed to both of us?"

"Well, no. Addressed to me. *I'm* the one who's been writing to her."

"Then I don't want to read 'em. Just give me a quick summary."

"Lucius, are you goin' to carry that grudge the rest of your life?"

"I can carry it as long as she can."

"But it's so silly, so—"

"What's the news from South Bar?" Lucius snapped.

"Well, she says they're both fine, but Cyrus has had a hard time keepin' the sawmill runnin' smoothly without me there. Seems like it's gettin' harder and harder to find good help."

"Oh Lord!" Lucius groaned. "She's just trying to make you feel bad about leaving. She'll keep that up forever, you know. Might as well get used to it."

There was a worried look on Isaac's face. "I'm not sure we did a smart thing, comin' to California. Oh, I'll never regret it, come what may, because that's the way I met Catherine. But I'm afraid there's goin' to be trouble. You know what a government man told Sutter not long ago? He said they're about to put out an order excluding Americans from California, and that Sutter should turn back immigrants from now on."

Lucius was smiling tranquilly. "Isaac, old chum, nobody in California pays any attention to what the government says, not even the natives."

"You know what else I heard? Fremont's on his way back, and this time he's got fighting men, and cannon. I tell you, I'm afraid there's goin' to be trouble."

"That's ridiculous. Fremont's a surveyor, not a combat man." Lucius tapped Isaac on the knee. "You see that ol

388

gentleman out there waltzing with your wife? Tell *him* that wild rumor, he might believe it. He thinks the United States is going to take over California pretty soon, and the natives'll go wild with joy. I think he's wrong on both counts. I think what we early birds have to do is wait. Just keep quiet and wait. As soon as there are enough of us here to make a significant force, we'll organize. And I'll be one of the organizers, because, after all, I'm one of the landed gentry, right?"

Isaac was lost. "Organize for what?"

Lucius leaned closer, and his voice went low. "To set up an independent nation."

"Oh my God, Lucius!" Isaac recoiled, eyes bright with alarm. "That sounds...I don't know, that sounds... *dangerous*!"

Lucius laughed. "Don't worry, old chum. Leave it to me, everything's going to be fine." He got to his feet. "Excuse me, will you? I just saw Dolores going out to the pavilion. I think I'll follow her, maybe I can steal a kiss behind an oak tree."

He went off and left Isaac rubbing his chin and staring at the tile floor, looking more worried than ever.

The second night Justin permitted Dolores to tuck him into bed, and listened politely while she told him an old Spanish tale about a wise and gentlemanly pig named *Padre Porko* who was uncommonly good at helping people solve their problems.

During the telling Catherine came into the room and sat down quietly at the foot of the bed, listening. When it was finished she smiled at Justin and said, "That's a lovely story. Don't you think so, Justin?"

"It's all right," Justin allowed.

Dolores smoothed his covers, her small hands moving with a feathery touch. "Well, good night, Little Eagle. Sweet dreams." She kissed him on the forehead.

"G'night," Justin mumbled.

Dolores got up and looked inquiringly at Catherine.

"I'll stay for a minute, if you don't mind," Catherine said.

A hard look came into Dolores's eyes. "It is quite late, *señora*. I'm sure Justin is very tired."

A subtle tension filled the room.

"Just for a minute," Catherine said quietly. "If you don't mind."

Dolores's nod was curt. "Of course." She went out, closing

389

the door softly behind her.

Instantly Justin was sitting up, eager eyes on Catherine.

"Have you talked to my papa yet?"

"Not yet, darling. I've been waiting for just the right moment. But it's very hard, with so many people in the house."

Justin was frowning. "I don't want to stay here. I don't like Dolores."

"Oh, Justin, don't say that. She likes *you* very much."

"I don't know what to call her."

"She suggested Tía Dolores. What's wrong with that?"

"I don't like it."

Catherine sighed. "Well, you have to call her *something*, whether you stay here or not."

Justin went on frowning. "I don't want to stay here."

Catherine patted his hand. "Well, we'll see. Whatever happens, you mustn't be sullen, you understand? That's not fair to anybody concerned." She kissed him and settled him back in bed. "Go to sleep now."

When she reached the door he called to her, "Will you talk to Papa soon?"

"As soon as possible, darling. I'll do the best I can." She blew him another kiss before she went out, and gave him a smile that was meant to be reassuring.

On Friday night the celebration regained its full vigor, and soared to new heights of revelry. The weather had turned chilly, so a great bonfire had been built near the pavilion, adding to the festive mood.

Catherine walked among the spectators around the dance area, found Isaac, and stood beside him watching the dancers at their tireless recreation. A throbbing fandango was in progress, and Isaac was plainly enjoying the spectacle.

"Just look at Lucius and that Mexican girl!" he said to his wife. "Aren't they a pair? I never knew Lucius could dance."

"If you'll look closely, you'll see he can't," Catherine said irritably. "Besides, he's drunk."

"Well, it's his wedding celebration, why shouldn't he enjoy it?"

With a toss of her head Catherine turned away. Isaac followed her.

"Somethin' wrong, sweetheart?"

Catherine struggled briefly for composure. "Isaac, I really think we ought to leave soon. Tomorrow, maybe. I don't like to be away from the children so long, and . . . well, I think I've had quite enough of all this."

"All right, if you want to. But have you talked to Lucius yet? About Justin, I mean?"

"That's the trouble. I haven't been able to catch him alone for an instant."

"I had a little talk with him this afternoon, while you were dancin' with Don Lorenzo. But I didn't bring it up. I thought it'd be better if you did it."

The music had come to an ear-shattering end amid a burst of shouts and applause, and the dancers milled about waiting to begin again.

Isaac had an idea. "Tell you what. I'll go over and suggest to Lucius that he invite you to dance. That way you'll have a chance to—"

"No!" Catherine shot at him. "I will not dance with him, and I will not talk to him while he's drunk."

"But, sweetheart, if you want to leave tomorrow, there's not much time—"

"Don't worry, I'll find a way," she said, and walked rapidly back toward the house.

At a certain moment, in a remote corner of one of the shadowy *corredors*, Catherine and Dolores encountered each other.

Catherine smiled a greeting. "Good evening, Dolores."

Dolores was coldly formal. "Excuse me, *señora*. Have you seen Lucio?"

"Oh yes . . . he's out in the pavilion I believe, dancing."

"*Gracias*." Dolores started to move on.

Catherine put a hand on her arm to stop her. "Dolores . . . forgive me."

Dolores arched an eyebrow. "I beg your pardon, *señora*?"

"Please, call me Catherine. I want very much to be friends with you. And I think I owe you an apology concerning—" she forced herself to say it— "concerning Justin."

Dolores stood silent, waiting.

"I know how you must feel," Catherine went on. "And I want to ask you to try to imagine how *I* feel. For all practical purposes I have been his mother since he was three years old. Not a very long time, perhaps—less than three years—yet, for a little boy it's an eternity. We've grown to love each other

391

very much, you see, and . . . it will be very hard for me to give him up."

"I am sorry, *señora*," Dolores said, though her manner remained unyielding. "But I am a passionate woman. I may not give that impression, but I am. I am passionate in my love for Lucio, and I am passionate in my desire that *everything*, good or bad, that is part of him, shall be mine. It is a fault to love too well, I know, and I shall try to fight against it—yet I am afraid it is in my nature."

Catherine was subdued. "Yes. I understand, and I don't blame you—I'm sure I'd feel the same. I think Lucius is a lucky man to have won your love."

There was a moment of silence between them, during which the subtle hostility in Dolores's manner dissolved and drained away.

"But no, *señora*—excuse me, Catherine—it is I who should ask forgiveness. I have not fully appreciated how painful this is for you. And I *am* sorry." She grasped Catherine's hand. "Please don't think that because I am Justin's stepmother now, you have to give him up. He is a wonderful little boy, and I know he will find room in his heart for both of us."

Catherine was moved. "Thank you, Dolores, thank you. I do so hope you will always feel that way." She squeezed the younger woman's hand, accepted her in a warm embrace, and tried to blink away a rising dampness in her eyes.

In the morning a chill gray mist hung over the ground, turning the great oaks into monstrous black specters. The bonfire was out, and the festival was again at a low ebb.

In the house Lucius sat alone at a little table in one corner of the *sala*. Squinting though bloodshot eyes he watched the young Indian, Pablo, pour steaming black coffee into a cup.

"Ah, thank you, Pablo. You're a good fellow."

"Anything else, *señor*?"

"Yes. Clear this damned place out, will you? Send all these people home."

It was not in Pablo's nature to joke. "I am sorry, *señor*. I cannot do that."

Lucius grimaced and waved the servant away, then slumped in his chair with eyes nearly closed and sipped his coffee. He was only dimly aware of someone sitting down opposite him.

"Good morning, Lucius," Catherine said.

"Mmm," Lucius grunted. "Want some coffee?"

"No, thank you, I've had breakfast."

"Mmm." Lucius buried his nose in his coffee cup.

"Is Dolores awake?"

"Up at the crack of dawn, gone to the chapel. Going to confession, she calls it." Lucius set his cup down and scowled at it. "Here's this innocent child who's never in her life done anything more wicked than snitching a pinch of sugar out of the pantry when she was a little girl, but she has to spend twenty minutes a day confessing! Confessing what? It's a confounded mystery!"

Tight-lipped, Catherine looked at the unkempt man across the table. "Lucius, I want to talk to you about something."

"Fine. I want to talk to you too." He looked directly at her for the first time. "How are you, Catherine? How are things with you?"

"Oh, fine, Lucius. I've started a little school at home. Two hours every afternoon, and I love it. Children come from the fort, and from the Indian settlements—from all around. Some grownups too. And can you guess who my star pupil is?"

"Little Eagle?"

"Exactly. He has such a good mind, Lucius, I'm just amazed. And, you know, it's terribly important for a child to get a good foundation in reading and writing at an early age."

Absently Lucius rocked his coffee cup and stared down into the dark fluid. "What do you think of Dolores?"

"She's lovely, Lucius. I'm very happy for you."

"And the others?"

Catherine laughed softly. "Don Lorenzo's an absolute delight. So charming... and something of a flirt too, did you know?"

"And the others?" Lucius persisted.

"Well, I... it's difficult to get an impression under these conditions. But they all seem quite nice. I *have* struck up a pleasant acquaintance with Margarita Cortina. We've been comparing notes on our children."

"Which one is she?"

"Don Lorenzo's second daughter. The lady with the narrow face and large eyes. Good heavens, Lucius, these people are your family now, don't you even *know* them?!"

"To tell you the truth, I don't know one from the other."

"Why, that's absurd! How can you say such a thing?!"

Lucius went back to staring into his coffee cup. "I'm in a tough spot here, Catherine. Oh, I suppose you think I'm a very lucky fellow, marrying a beautiful girl whose family is one of the wealthiest in California—pretty damned lucky, eh? Not so, my dear. I've got nothing but trouble ahead, I can see it very clearly. Besides Dolores, Don Lorenzo's the only one who thinks it's nice to have an *Americano* in the clan. All the rest think it's a disgrace to their fine Castilian blood—"

"Oh, I don't believe that, Lucius!" Catherine's voice crackled with impatience. "Would they be celebrating for three days over something they considered a disgrace?"

"They do what Don Lorenzo tells 'em to. But they avoid me like a leper, don't you see that?"

"No I don't. I think you're being very silly."

Lucius shrugged and gave up the argument. "Anyway, it's a tough spot to be in. Dolores and I have never had more than five minutes alone together at any one sitting. We hardly know each other. We need some time together now, time free of . . . well, other complications."

Lucius put his cup down and faced Catherine squarely. "What I'm trying to get around to is . . . I think I'd better ask you and Isaac to keep Justin awhile longer. Just a few months or so, till we've had a chance to get through this, uh . . . this adjustment period."

"Oh yes, of *course*, Lucius, I understand completely!" There was an eagerness in Catherine's voice, and a little flutter of inner excitement. "And you know Justin can stay on with us, just as long as you like. We absolutely adore him, and—" She checked her runaway enthusiasm and went on more calmly. "Besides, as I said, I'd very much like to have him go on with his schooling. It would be a shame to interrupt it just when he's getting such a good start."

"Fine, then, it's all settled. Now what was it *you* wanted to talk about?"

"Oh, uh . . . nothing, really. I just wanted to say I think we'll be leaving today. I hope you don't mind. We have a long way to go."

"Yes, I understand."

"And I hope Dolores won't be angry about our taking Justin back with us."

"Never mind Dolores. I'll handle her."

"Do you think Don Lorenzo will be offended? I mean, it's not very polite to leave before the party's over."

Lucius's reaction was a loud snort. "I'll be very frank with you, my dear. If this party doesn't end today, *I'm* leaving. I'll go and spend a day or two with a couple of old friends in

Yerba Buena, and to hell with it—"

"*Buenos dias,*" said Don Lorenzo.

Catherine and Lucius were startled; neither had noticed his approach. Catherine was the first to recover.

"Oh, good morning, Don Lorenzo. Will you join us?"

"No, *gracias, señora.* I must go and see to things outdoors." He smiled down at Lucius. "And how are you this morning, *Señor* Bridegroom?"

"Tired," Lucius answered.

"I must apologize for surprising you just now. I did not mean to eavesdrop."

Lucius squirmed. "Oh well...I was just joking a little—"

"Do not be embarrassed. Deep down in my heart I agree with you. I'm afraid many of our old customs are more quaint than sensible. The *Americanos* will sweep them all away in due time, I imagine."

Catherine protested politely. "Oh, I hope not, sir. I think your customs—most of them—are quite charming."

"Very kind of you, *señora.*" Don Lorenzo gave the bridegroom a fatherly pat on the shoulder. "Have a little patience, Lucio," he murmured, and moved away.

"Excuse me too, please, Lucius?" Catherine said hastily, rising. "I want to tell Isaac what we've decided."

Lucius watched her until she had left the room. Then he sighed, slumped in his chair, and stared moodily into his coffee cup.

Around noon Isaac and Catherine and Justin rode away from Rancho Las Sombras, again with two of Don Lorenzo's *vaqueros* as escort. Lucius had a horse saddled and rode a short distance with them. The sunlight of early autumn lay dazzlingly bright on the land, on golden harvest-ripe cornfields, hillsides, and pastures. The young *rancho* horsemen, frisky as their mounts, whooped and waved their hats and galloped on ahead. Justin watched them go, and bounced up and down in high glee on his perch atop the packmule.

"Papa!" he called to Lucius. "When I get big I'm goin' to be a *vaquero,* and make my horse run *fast!*"

Lucius smiled at him. "You keep doing well in your studies with Aunt Catherine, and you'll grow up to be a man who *employs* them."

"No, I'm goin' to *be* one!" Justin shouted. He bounced up and down harder, and let out a whoop that was a passable imitation of the *vaquero's* yell.

They came to a little inches-deep stream where their escorts were pulled up waiting for them, and there they brought their horses to a halt.

"Well, I'll have to leave you here," Lucius said. He maneuvered his horse next to the packmule, and put a gentle hand on Justin's shoulder. "Goodbye, son."

"G'bye, Papa." The boy gave him a little hug and a quick kiss on the cheek.

"I'm sorry we didn't get a chance to be with each other very much, with all those people around, and so much confusion...but we'll make up for it one of these days, I promise you."

"All right, Papa."

"You go on being a good boy, will you? Make me proud of you."

"I will, Papa." Justin's attention was on the *vaqueros'* horses, which were tossing their manes and splashing in the shallow stream.

"Goodbye, then. I'll see you soon." Lucius kissed the boy, gave the tousled sand-colored hair a final ruffle, and pulled his horse away.

Justin placed an expert slap on the mule's rump and moved off toward the *vaqueros*. He did not look at Lucius again.

"Now you and Dolores come visit us in the spring, Lucius," Isaac urged. "After all, we're your family too. And we'll want you to see our new place."

"Yes, do, by all means," Catherine seconded with cool politeness.

"Oh yes, we'll be coming," Lucius said absently. His eyes were beyond them, following Justin.

Isaac moved his horse alongside his wife's and took her hand. "Well, ready to go home, sweetheart?"

"Ummm, yes!" A blissful smile spread over Catherine's face. "It'll be *so* nice to be back in our own little house again." She leaned forward and kissed him on the cheek.

Lucius frowned. "It's getting late," he said curtly. "Better be on your way."

At the top of a little rise fifty yards from the place of parting, Lucius pulled his horse to a stop again and looked back. The travelers were another fifty yards on the other side of the little creek now. One of the young *vaqueros* had put his huge sombrero on Justin's head, and across the distance the little boy's delighted laughter rang out clear and pealing. For a few seconds Lucius watched, stone-faced, his eyes brooding and somber. Then with an almost angry movement he pulled on the reins and spurred the animal toward home.

In the afternoon, a little more than forty-eight hours after he had clapped his hands and said, "Let the music begin," Don Lorenzo silenced it. All the guests, inside and out, were summoned to the pavilion, where the aged host stood on a chair and informed the multitude that the festival was at an end. The bride was a girl of delicate constitution, he explained. The strain was telling on her. He thanked them all for coming and bade them have a pleasant journey home. There were sympathetic murmurings, a few mutterings of protest. Soon the pavilion grounds were a scene of milling disorder as people prepared to depart.

The bride and bridegroom stood for a long time in front of the house receiving farewell salutations from the throngs of pavilion guests, then went into the house and spent a longer time accepting the parting good wishes of tearfully affectionate cousins.

The three-day trial of fortitude and patience was deemed by unspoken agreement to have been successfully passed after two days and four hours.

When night came Las Sombras lay serene and quiet. Where the outdoor pavilion had been there was a bare space beneath the brooding oaks, suspended in stillness and solitude. Within the big house the silence was tomblike. Throughout all the dark rooms and deserted *corredors* one lamp burned—on the piano in the *sala*.

Lucius sat alone on the piano bench studying the yellowed ivory keys. He put his hand on the keyboard, and tentatively struck a note. The old out-of-tune instrument twanged a sour nasal sound. Lucius cocked his head and listened as the note died away. He struck another, and another, and began to grope clumsily for a tune.

Then through the long room Dolores came floating like a weightless vision in a gown of exquisite lace and silk, her dark lustrous hair loose and streaming down her back. Lucius glanced up at her, smiled vacantly, and went on searching the keyboard. Dolores sat down next to him.

"What's that melody, Lucio?"

"It's called 'Annie Laurie.' Somebody I once knew used to play it."

"It's pretty." She watched his probing fingers for a moment, then her eyes drifted up to his face. "Wasn't it nice of Uncle Lorenzo to go home with Alfredo and his family? He only did it so we could have the house to ourselves."

"Very nice," Lucius mumbled.

"And the servants are all gone to the village. We're all alone, Lucio."

"Yes. I know." Lucius stopped playing, closed the piano lid, and sat staring despondently at its dark red mahogany grain.

A small hand crept onto his shoulder. "What is the matter, *amado mío*? Is something wrong?"

He drew a deep sigh. "From time to time, my dear, you have delighted me with little secrets about yourself. Now maybe it's time I told *you* one or two. Maybe it's long *past* time."

"No, *amado*, it is not neces—"

"I'm no good for you, Dolores," he blurted.

Her eyes widened in horror. "Lucio, how can you say that?!"

"All my life I've been a rootless vagabond. I've never been really close to anybody, and every single person who's ever tried to be close to me has been hurt. Now it's your turn."

"Ah, no, Lucio, I do not believe that."

"Yes, it's true. I've lived a worthless life. I've been a gambler and a liar, and a drunken, whoring—"

"Lucio, stop it!" Dolores pressed her palms against her ears. "I do not want to hear it, I will not listen!"

He seized her wrists and pulled her hands down. "Damnit, don't you want to *know* about me?" he almost shouted.

"No, no, I only want to know you are my husband and I am your wife, and we love each other!"

He released her and looked away. "Shall I tell you who used to play 'Annie Laurie'?"

"No. It does not matter."

"My first wife. Her name was Arabella, and she was very beautiful."

Dolores maintained a stubborn silence.

Lucius gave her a hard look. "Shall I tell you about Arabella?"

"No. I do not want to hear about her."

"Why not? It's an interesting story."

"No, no. Please. I am afraid of what you might say."

"What do you think I might say?" His tone had become demanding.

"I think—" Dolores faltered, and her eyes fell away from his. "I think you will tell me she lives, and that you are a divorced man."

He stared at her, thunderstruck. "How did you guess *that*?! How did you—"

"I did not guess anything, and I do not want to know—"

"But you found out, somehow you found out! And you must tell me *how*!"

Her reply was halting and hesitant. "I have had a feeling...there have been times when people have asked about her, and...you've always avoided answering. And people have said things like...how sad it is that Justin lost his mother...and each time, I have seen some strange uncomfortable look on your face, or on the face of your brother, or Señora Catherine. So I thought...maybe that is the reason."

"Dolores, I—" Lucius swallowed hard, and his voice had gone weak and tremulous. "I don't quite know how to explain, I—"

"It is not necessary, Lucio," she said gently. She was calm now, and sure of herself. "What you did in the past has nothing to do with us. Whatever happened, I know you were not in the wrong. And you could not be expected to live according to the teachings of our Church, because it was not *your* Church *then*, was it? Besides...if I must choose between the rules of the Church and what I feel in my own heart...God forgive me, I will choose what is in my heart."

Tears brimmed in her eyes, but she blinked them away defiantly. "Yes, I know you have lived an adventurous life, *amado*. And I have lived a quiet and secluded one. But I will *not* allow myself to be a jealous wife, I promise. I will not question your past. I will trust you in all things. You will tell me what I need to know and you will not tell me what I do not need to know, and it will be good. We will be happy."

He stared at her, his face lit by a kind of enchantment. "I've heard it said that a worthless man can be redeemed by the love of a good woman. And, by God, I...I believe it must be true." A surge of some unfamiliar emotion hampered his speech as his eyes burned into hers. "I'll *try* to be a good husband, Dolores. I *swear* I will." His lips touched hers, found them moist and willing, and ground against them in quick-rising eagerness.

Then, with a rush of movement that made her gasp, he was on his feet and sweeping her up in his arms, cradling her like a child. Her arms wound around his neck and her soft hair fell billowing over his shoulder as he carried her through the silent house to her bedroom, kicked open the door, made his way in the darkness and laid his precious burden on the bed.

Still she clung to him, murmuring and cooing like a dove as his lips fed on her throat and shoulders and his hands fought past silk to find silken flesh.

"Oh, my Lucio, my husband, my love, my golden man . . ."

In the *sala* the little lamp sitting on the piano burned all night.

(7)

FROM THE JOURNAL of Lucius Hargrave:

My first year in California was so filled with dazzling new impressions that the days reeled by in a blur, events tumbled upon events, and time was meaningless. It did not begin auspiciously; when I left Sutter's Fort in the spring of 1844 my spirits were so low that I could scarcely force myself to go on. But go on I must, and I did so, though my heart was torn with grief because the rootless life I faced for a time compelled me to leave my son Justin behind at my brother's house—where he was loved and welcome, to be sure, but this did not lessen my longing for his company, nor his for mine.

Yet in a brief while I had made a new friend, and taken the first steps in establishing myself in the pastoral land of the *Californios*. The friend was an Englishman named Jasper Hawkes, who operated a small and primitive hotel in the miserable little wind-swept village of Yerba Buena, on the peninsula to the west of the Bay of San Francisco. And it was

Jasper who suggested to me a means of livelihood. The people of California had no postal system of any kind other than the friends and acquaintances who might happen to be traveling, and they were eager to pay handsomely for a professional service. I provided that service by setting up the Hargrave Mail and Express Company, using Jasper Hawkes's little hostelry as headquarters. Soon I was prospering—and enmeshed in political intrigue.

In Mexican California a "revolution" took place every few years, usually consisting of nothing more than rebellious growls from a few disgruntled citizens, followed by shouts of defiance from the current "despot" who would nevertheless promptly resign, whereupon a new government would be installed and a great fiesta held to celebrate the glorious new day, and everybody would go home friends. The utter *peacefulness* of the operation was a marvel, unique in the annals of human warfare.

But the revolution of 1844-45 seemed to me to contain some merit; the *Californios* were struggling to wrest independence from a Mexican government that had shown them not oppression but neglect. Remembering how I had helped the Texans to win their freedom from Mexico some years before, I threw my support behind the rebels, who were soon victorious. I did this with no thought of reward—and was stunned when blessings immediately began to rain down upon my head. One of the leaders of the new regime, an elderly aristocrat of Spanish birth named Lorenzo Valadez, not only clasped me to his bosom in friendship, but urged me to make his vast *rancho* in the Santa Clara Valley my home. And at this idyllic retreat, beneath the protective spread of ancient oaks, love came into my life.

Dolores was the orphaned niece of my host, twenty years of age, innocent as the dew of morning, and a living portrait of all that was gracious and beautiful in the womanhood of old Castile, the homeland of her ancestors. In a dizzyingly short time we had pledged our troths to one another, and my senses reeled at the incredible good fortune that had befallen me.

Yet my mind remained clouded. Thus far my efforts to find my father's trail in California had met only with dismal failure. I prowled the seacoast, searching every human habitation where a ship might conceivably have put in at any time in the remote or recent past. Not a soul anywhere had ever heard of a man of God such as I described, or of a ship called the *Bold Venture*. Desperately I racked my brain.

Could it be that I had misunderstood the ship's name, passed to me by the black man Camus in New Orleans? Impossible. I had verified it that same day at the docks. Unfortunately I had neglected to ascertain the vessel's ownership—a foolish oversight for which I now cursed myself. Doggedly I pressed on, collecting the names of every commercial maritime company I could, and writing letters of inquiry. But the great Atlantic ports were five to six months away; it would be a year before I could expect replies. Weary and heartsick, I disbanded the Hargrave Mail and Express Company and retreated to that haven of rest called Rancho Las Sombras, and into the waiting arms of the lovely lady Dolores.

We were married in September, 1845, and as we stood in the midst of an orgy of joyous celebration I thought of my boyhood days in Indiana, and of how I used to dream of someday finding my destiny in some fabled far-off place, little imagining how distant those far-off places could be. With sadness I thought of my mother, who had bitterly rejected me on the eve of my departure on my life's greatest adventure. Would her heart relent now? Would she wish to stand beside me and rejoice with that barefoot boy who once threw stones into the Ohio River and dreamed, and who had now become a landed Don of California?

So love engulfed me in its tender embrace, and with my beautiful bride I entered into the most blissful existence I had ever known. Perfect happiness was ours—serene, sensuous, all-consuming. And yet—perhaps *perfect* is too strong a word. There were minor blemishes. The world had surely not changed; it was as perverse as ever.

An early point of contention centered on Justin. I wanted the boy with me, yet I saw that to separate him from his beloved Aunt Catherine at that time would seriously have disrupted his basic education. Dolores seemed to accept my judgment at first, but was soon reproaching me as a negligent father, and urging that Justin be brought to Las Sombras forthwith. I was ready to acquiesce—Lord knows how my heart ached for my little son—but then the dark clouds of war loomed again in sunny California skies, rendering all travel unsafe.

By January of 1846 the redoubtable John Charles Fremont, now Captain, U.S. Topographical Engineers, had appeared in our peaceful land, and his arrival marked the beginning of a year of treachery, turmoil and strife that imperiled the safety of all, and set the old Spanish and the new American cultures on a course of mutual distrust that would last for—it is not for me to know how long. Fremont was a character afflicted with delusions of Napoleonic grandeur, and his avowed mission of geographical surveying was a sham concealing cynical warlike purposes. Soon he was parading his little army all over the Santa Clara Valley, rattling his sabers and frightening the local citizenry out of its wits. Then abruptly he wheeled about and marched north—for Oregon, it was said—and some of us breathed a little easier, hoping we had seen the last of this absurd mountebank.

Don Lorenzo watched all this agitation in great glee. He predicted that the American flag would soon fly over California, and was ready to stand up and cheer the minute it happened. And with a naiveté oddly incongruous with his years he was convinced that when the Americans took over California they would turn to men like him to lend respectability to the new society. After all, had he not already established his credentials by admitting an American to his family? It vexed my mind how I could protect this gentle but foolish old man from the disappointment he was surely devising for himself.

I had other vexations with Don Lorenzo. He had promised Dolores and me a choice section of land as a wedding present, and I was eager to receive it and begin building a home of our own. But the old man procrastinated endlessly, maddeningly, concocting a thousand excuses for delay. The truth was that he doted on Dolores, dreaded the thought of being left alone at Las Sombras, and secretly wanted to keep us there permanently. His pathetic plight touched my heart and kept me silent—though at a cost in private anguish.

Meanwhile I tried to find ways of making contributions to the workings of the *rancho*, much as I had once done at Carolina Grove. Why do we send our hides to Boston to be made into shoes and shipped back to us at exorbitant prices? I asked. Why not develop a tanning industry and manufacture our own leather goods? Don Lorenzo—he who had always complained about lack of industry in California—smiled and shook his head. That must all wait until the *Americanos* arrive in force, he declared—the Indians are untrainable in such complex disciplines.

My next suggestion met with more favorable response. Several times a year the stacks of dried hides and blocks of hardened tallow were taken to Yerba Buena for trading to the floating markets, the merchant ships. With our lumbering oxcarts it was a two-day journey to the port, after which trading might take weeks. Don Lorenzo hated these expeditions, and when I offered to assume this duty upon myself he was overjoyed to accept. I too was gratified, for it not only gave me a way to be useful, but afforded opportunities for me to visit my old friends Jasper Hawkes and Delia Walsh. Jasper I have spoken of, but perhaps I have neglected to mention Delia, a remarkable lady who, having been widowed some years before, had displayed a rare degree of business acumen as a partner of Jasper's at the hotel. Two admirable people, and good friends, both.

And there was another reason I welcomed the prospect of spending more time in the otherwise desolate hamlet of Yerba Buena. I could prowl the waterfront for days, talking to seafaring men. I could probe every nook and hovel, seek out men of every possible variety from captains to common sailors to skulking deserters, and engage them in conversation about ships and the sea and the sailing life. It would be no pleasure. I would be insulted, abused, rejected, put upon, used for free meals and drink, and bored with endless streams of garrulous bragging and rambling nonsense.

But sooner or later I would find a man who had some knowledge of a ship called the *Bold Venture.*

(8)

IN JUNE OF 1846 Jasper Hawkes completed construction of a new wing on his public house in Yerba Buena and, along with the enlarging operation, put up a fancy new sign out front. It read:

The Hawk's Nest
*Hotel * Bar * Cafe * Gaming Room*
Attractive Hostess to Serve You
All Nationalities Welcome

On the reverse side of the sign the same information appeared in Spanish, along with the additional inducement: *Se Habla Español.*

On a night when fog lay in a blanket of dense gray silence over the sandy hills there were few patrons of any nationality in the Hawk's Nest. In the front room that was the combination bar and cafe three men were having a meal at a table in one corner. They were Americans, bearded and rough-hewn, and they gave the operation of eating their entire attention, with none to spare for nonessentials like conversation. Near them a doorway opened onto the gaming room, wherein several occupants sat around a table applying another variety of concentration to a game of cards. In both rooms silence reigned.

Behind the counter along the rear wall of the bar-cafe Jasper Hawkes sat on a stool and surveyed his dominion. A few feet away Delia leaned against the counter and picked idly at her nails.

"Goddamn bloody cemetery!" Jasper muttered under his breath. He eyed the woman. "Why don't you see if you can drum up a bit o' business for yourself?"

Delia glared at him. "With these bums?! I wouldn't waste my—"

"Shhh!" Jasper hissed at her. The men at the corner table had glanced up curiously at the sound of Delia's loud voice.

Delia moved closer to Hawkes and spoke in an angry undertone. "Look here, Jasper, you know very well I'm a high-class woman. And I joined up with you because you told me you meant to run a high-class establishment—"

"I do the best I can, goddamnit. The 'igh-class clientele just don't come."

"Of course they don't, because there ain't none here."

"Sure there are. Plenty o' rich *Mexicanos* on big *ranchos* 'round the bay. But they don't come to Yerba Buena."

"Hell, no, why should they? To see a bunch o' sand dunes?"

Jasper gave the woman a crooked smile. "To see you."

"Jesus, they don't even know I'm here!" Delia's voice was booming again.

Jasper glanced nervously at the diners in the corner, and sighed. "It's all this bloody scare talk about war that's ruinin' our business. People are afraid to stick their noses out. The *gringos* think the greasers are gettin' ready to throw 'em out o' California, and the greasers think the *gringos* are gettin' ready to take over. Everybody's scared to death."

Delia uttered a disgusted snort. "And in the meantime, we starve."

Jasper brought forth a bottle of *aguardiente* from beneath the counter and handed it to Delia. "Here. Take this in to the blokes in the gamin' room."

"They ain't even finished the bottle they got."

"You tell 'em to drink up. They want to play cards 'ere, they'll bloody well patronize the bar, that's 'ow *that* goes."

Delia took the bottle and sauntered toward the gaming room. One of the diners in the corner stopped eating, his jaw frozen in mid-bite as his eyes followed the fluid swinging of the woman's hips. As she came close he grinned up at her and said in a low voice, "Howdy, sugar."

Delia gave him a cold look and a haughty toss of her head, and went on. The other two men glanced at their friend and snickered.

Jasper brought out another bottle and poured himself a drink. He had just raised the glass to his lips when the front door swung open and two men entered. One of them was Lucius Hargrave. His companion was a small man, shriveled and elderly, with a grizzled weatherbeaten face.

"Whiskey, Jasper," Lucius called out, and steered the older man toward a table at the end of the room opposite the three diners.

Jasper brought a bottle and two glasses and set them on the table. "Whiskey's in mighty short supply, Lucius, don't you know? Wouldn't *aguardiente* do?"

"Ned here likes whiskey, Jasper. And slap a beefsteak on the fire, will you? Ned's a mite hungry." Lucius smiled at his companion, and turned his smile on Jasper. "By the way . . . Jasper Hawkes, say hello to Ned Holloway."

"How do?" Ned Holloway piped.

Jasper gave him a grudging nod.

"Ned's off the *Orient Star*," Lucius said. "Just into the cove this afternoon."

Jasper's eyebrows went up. "Oh? Would've been mighty nice if you'd 'a' thought to bring some o' the other officers along too."

Lucius laughed. "Oh, they were a stuffy bunch, Jasper, you wouldn't like 'em. Ned here's not an officer, he's a cabin boy."

Ned was grinning. Jasper's face was stony as he looked from Lucius to the ancient cabin boy and back again to Lucius.

"Put the steak on, Jasper, like a good fellow?" Lucius said, and Jasper went off, shaking his head and muttering to himself.

Delia returned, spied Lucius at the table at the far end of the room, then rejoined Jasper behind the counter, her eyes wide with curiosity.

"Who's the old geezer with Lucius?"

"You want to know who the old geezer is?" Jasper grumbled. "I'll tell you who he is. He's a bloody cabin boy off a merchantman."

"What?!"

"I tell you straight, sometimes I wonder about Lucius. 'E loaned me the money to fix up the place—you'd think 'e'd be 'alfway interested in 'elpin' it along. So a ship drops anchor in the cove, and o' course Lucius is right there, the self-appointed greeter. And does he bring us the officers, 'oo might spend a dollar or two? Oh no. 'E brings us a goddamned cabin boy, and feeds 'im beefsteak and whiskey on the 'ouse!"

Delia rolled her eyes toward the ceiling. "The Lord moves in mysterious ways, Jasper, honey. And so does our boy Lucius."

In less than half an hour Ned Holloway had put away a large steak and one-third of the bottle of whiskey, and was dozing peacefully in his chair.

"How about a room for the night, my friend?" Lucius asked him. "Comfortable bed, nice and quiet. You can sleep like a log."

Ned chuckled, sleepy-eyed. "Y'know th' one thing I ain't never got used to in forty years at sea, Mr. Hargrave? Bunks. Them danged narrow little bunks. I do love a big bed, where I can stretch out."

"Well, you've got one, Ned."

Lucius summoned Delia with a wave of his hand. "Fix up the room next to mine for Ned here, will you, sweetheart? He's staying the night with us."

Delia shot a dark look at old Ned, who was dozing again. "Tell 'im it's four dollars," she snapped. "In advance."

"Just put it on my bill," Lucius said breezily. He reached

407

over and gently shook the sleeping man's shoulder. "Come on, Ned. Time for beddy-bye."

As soon as he was alone Lucius poured himself another drink and settled back in his chair. Immediately Jasper was standing over him.

Lucius smiled. "Sit down, Jasper. Have a drink."

Jasper sat down, glowering. "Lucius, what th' 'ell's goin' on? You think we're runnin' a charity 'ome 'ere?"

"Don't worry about it. Knock ten dollars off the five hundred you owe me."

"All right, I will. But what I can't figure is, how come some old broken-down cabin boy gets the royal treatment?"

"He's a colorful character. I like colorful characters."

"Come on! There's more to it than that."

"He's had a marvelously interesting past, old Ned has. Did you know that in the course of his long career he's shipped on no less than eleven different vessels? And did you know that one of those was a brig called the *Bold Venture*?"

Jasper's mouth fell open. "Good Lord! The bloody ship you been pesterin' people about all this time, tryin' to find out what became of it. What's that all about, Lucius?"

"I like to collect sea lore. It's a pastime of mine."

Jasper grimaced with impatience. "You're puttin' me on, goddamnit. What makes you so bloody mysterious?"

Lucius ignored this. His thoughts were moving on. "Trouble is, y'see, old Ned's a bit senile now, and his memory's awful weak. I have to pick information out of him a little at a time. *That's* the reason for the royal treatment."

Jasper gave a snort of exasperation and shook his head. "I give up on you, Lucius, I absolutely give up!" He went off, leaving Lucius chuckling quietly and sipping his whiskey.

Two of the three men at the other end of the room left their table, settled their bill with Jasper behind the counter, and wandered into the gaming room. The third—the one who made an unsuccessful attempt to catch Delia's attention—remained seated. He was looking down the length of the room toward Lucius.

After a few minutes he got up and strolled to the other man's table.

"Well, if it ain't Lucius Hargrave, as I live and breathe." His low voice contained no genuine surprise.

408

Lucius looked up, and stared.

The man grinned. "How are you, Lucius old boy?" He was swarthy, heavyset, grizzled, with narrow-set eyes and a mat of thick black hair.

"My God!" Lucius breathed. "Otis Bruner."

Otis Bruner chuckled. "Well, so you remember your old trail buddy. Now that's mighty flatterin'. Mind if I sit down?"

With a noticeable lack of enthusiasm Lucius indicated a chair, and the other man sat down immediately. Lucius sipped his whiskey and waited.

Otis was grinning again. "Well! Mighty small world, ain't it? I was by Sutter's Fort not long ago. Who do I run into but yer brother Isaac."

"That so?"

"And, by gum! Turns out he *married* that sassy little red-headed Mrs. Shannon. Now ain't that sump'm? I asked 'im about you—I'm not one to forget ol' friends, y'know, not me. Well, you coulda knocked me over with a feather when I found out you'd married a greaser gal. That's jes' the damnedest thing I ever heard of!" Otis shook with chuckles, and his grin grew broader.

Lucius sat stone-faced, fingering his whiskey glass. "So...what're you up to, Otis?"

"Got me a little ranch up the Sacramento, 'bout a hunnerd miles north o' Sutter's. Not doin' bad a-tall, not a-tall. Kind o' busy with somethin' else right now, though."

"Oh? What's that?"

Otis was not yet ready to come to the point. "I was up to the Valadez ranch th' other day, lookin' fer you. Isaac told me that's where you live. Met your missus. Very nice little gal. Damned good-lookin', fer a greaser." The grin took on a touch of lewdness. "And you didn't waste no time, I notice. She's about six months along with a baby, ain't she?"

Lucius nodded.

"Her Uncle Lorenzo's a friendly ol' gent. He tol' me I could find you here. 'Nother fella there, ol' Lorenzo's son-in-law, Ricardo sump'm-or-other—not so damned friendly. Kept wantin' to know what I wanted to see you about. Finally told 'im it was none of his business."

"What *do* you want to see me about?" Lucius asked quietly.

Otis's grin disappeared abruptly. He leaned forward, forearms on the table.

"Big things are brewin', Lucius. The American settlers in the Sacramento Valley are up in arms. We're tired o' bein' treated like dirt in California. The greasers don't want us to own land, or conduct business, or have any religion but the Roman Church—they'd dearly love to throw us all out if they could. Well, we've had a bellyful of it. Now we're cookin' up a little surprise for 'em."

Otis glanced around to make sure he wasn't being overheard, then pulled his chair around a little closer to Lucius.

"We're gettin' ready to take over," he said in a near-whisper.

Otis waited; Lucius gazed at him in stolid silence. Otis went on.

"We need numbers, o' course, so we're contactin' all the Americans we can find. Even people like you. Hell, jes' 'cause you married a greaser gal ain't no reason you can't join in. An I sure don't aim to bear you no grudge over that little run-in we once had about yer brother an' Mrs. Shannon. That was jes' horseplay, didn't mean nothin'." The genial grin reappeared.

Lucius's expression remained stony. "In my humble opinion, Otis, there's no way California can be claimed for the United States. The geography just doesn't—"

"Oh no, no, you don't git th' picture, Lucius, boy. We ain't claimin' nothin' fer th' U.S. We aim to set up an independent country. Then someday, if Uncle Sam wants to negotiate with us, fine, we'll talk business. But *we'll* do th' talkin', not the greasers."

Lucius's face had gone ashen. "You're out of your mind," he said in a voice weak with disbelief. "Absolutely out of your—"

"I'll be goddamned!" Otis blurted. "I got that same kind of an answer from yer sappy brother Isaac, but I expected it from *him*. I figured *you* was more of a man than that."

Lucius was squirming. "The point is, damnit, your timing's all wrong. It's insane, way too soon. Don't you think *I'm* in a position to watch the situation, to know when the time is ripe—"

Harsh laughter cut him off. Otis tapped Lucius's whiskey bottle and winked.

"Maybe you been hittin' this stuff too hard, Lucius, boy. You may be *watchin'*, but you ain't *seein'* much. We're movin', my friend, and we're movin' now. You want to join in, you

410

can. You want to wait, you'll be left out in th' cold."

For a moment Lucius sat silent and grim-faced. "Exactly what is the plan?"

Otis shook his head. "I don't know if I can trust you."

Lucius shrugged. "Well, if you can't tell a man what he's being recruited for, you can't expect to do much recruiting, can you?" He forced a little smile. "You think I talk about things like this with my in-laws? Don't be foolish. I never talk, I just listen. What's the plan?"

Otis looked around again, then moved his chair a few inches closer still. "We mean to move into Sonoma next week, take General Vallejo prisoner, and raise our own flag."

"Good Lord!" Lucius rolled his eyes toward the ceiling. "That makes no sense at all! Why Vallejo? He has no power, no troops, nothing. He's not even your enemy, for God's sake. He's like Lorenzo Valadez, just a peaceable fellow who goes around talking about how much he likes Americans—"

"That ain't th' point."

"Well, goddamnit, what *is* the point?"

"He's the symbol, Lucius. The symbol o' th' Mexican empire." Otis tapped Lucius knowingly on the arm. "When you're dealin' with th' greasers, my friend, you don't deal in logic. You deal in symbols."

"Oh, I see." There was a trace of ridicule in Lucius's manner. "Pretty fancy language, Otis. Logic...symbols...where'd you pick up words like that?"

Otis looked smugly cunning. "Never you mind. I got 'em from somebody who knows a lot more'n me an' you both."

"Oh! Pardon me." Lucius laughed, and the ridicule was out in the open.

Otis's swarthy face came closer, and his voice went hard. "Well, are you with us or not? Are you goin' to be a part of th' new regime, or would you rather sit it out, like yer brother? Wind up bein' one o' the peasants, along with th' rest o' th' greasers?"

Lucius slumped in his chair and stared at his glass. After a moment he looked across the room and caught Delia's eye. She was leaning on the bar watching him. He raised a hand and beckoned to her, and she came hurrying to the table.

"Delia, honey, bring a glass for my friend Otis, here, will you? We've got some serious talking to do."

Otis grinned, glanced up, and winked at Delia.

(9)

BY NOON THE NEXT DAY the fog had lifted, and the sand hills of Yerba Buena lay baking under bright skies. At four o'clock the Hawk's Nest was deserted except for one occupant of the cafe: Lucius Hargrave, who sat at his usual table at one end of the room. He was writing, and papers were spread on the table before him.

Someone stepped up to the front of the building and knocked timidly on the wall beside the open door.

"Come in!" Lucius called. In a moment he glanced up from his papers to see a well-dressed Spaniard standing in the doorway, looking at him.

"You don't have to knock, *señor*, this is a public house. Come right in. The waitress stepped out for a minute, but she'll be right back." Lucius went on with his writing.

The newcomer took off his huge sombrero and came slowly across the room toward Lucius. "*Buenas tardes*, Lucio," he said hesitantly, and his big square mustache twitched.

"Afternoon," Lucius said absently.

Then he looked up with a start of surprise and squinted at the man. "Well, for heaven's sake! Didn't recognize you at first." He was on his feet, smiling and extending his hand. "How are you, Alfredo?"

The visitor shook hands. "I am well, *gracias*. I am not Alfredo, however, I am Ricardo. Ricardo Cortina."

Lucius laughed easily. "Oh, of course, of course—silly of me. Sit down, Ricardo."

"*Gracias*." Ricardo took a seat. "I will not detain you long. I see you are very busy."

Lucius smiled as he gathered his papers and folded them

412

carefully. "Ah, yes, a million things to do. But I'm glad to see you anyway—always happy to see a relative. How are Doña Teresa and the children?"

Ricardo hesitated before replying. "Lucio... Teresa is Don Lorenzo's eldest daughter. She is married to Miguel de la Rio. My wife is Margarita, Don Lorenzo's *second* daughter."

Lucius sighed and fingered his papers. "You'll have to forgive me, Ricardo. I'm afraid I've been working too hard. What with the *rancho* business, and certain rather complex personal affairs... there seems to be no end to it. But enough of that." He smiled again suddenly, despondency abandoned. "What brings you to Yerba Buena?"

Ricardo clasped his hands together and twiddled his thumbs. "I have come from Las Sombras, Lucio. Margarita and I were there for a few days' visit. By the way, there was a man who came looking for you. A *Señor* Bruner—"

"Yes, he found me."

"He seemed very, uh... what you say?... agitated. I hope it was nothing serious?"

"Depends on your point of view," Lucius said.

"Oh?" Ricardo waited for more information. It was not forthcoming.

"Well, anyway... Don Lorenzo and Dolores are very worried about you, Lucio."

"Worried? What for?"

"Don Lorenzo tells me you are hardly ever at home these days."

"Really? Did he also tell you that when I'm away from home I'm usually tending to *his* business, and bailing *him* out of trouble?"

"Well, I—"

"Right now, for instance, I'm in the process of trading our spring supply of hides and tallow."

"But it's been almost a month—"

"Oh sure, Don Lorenzo used to trade with the first scow that came along, on whatever terms he could get. I wait for a quality ship, and I bargain for the best possible terms."

"Yes, but—"

"And did you hear what I was doing in April? Your father-in-law went to Monterey with General Vallejo, and didn't come home when expected. I had to go looking for him. You know what I found him doing? Making speeches saying that California ought to seek annexation to the United States. If I hadn't dragged the old boy home he would've gotten his

413

head busted. He's worried about *me*? *You* better be worried about *him*."

Ricardo nodded, looking gravely concerned. "That is true, Lucio. To be frank, most of us in the family do not share Don Lorenzo's enthusiasm for *Americanos*—uh, except, of course, we all hold *you* in the highest esteem."

He smiled hastily; Lucius responded with a glower.

"But I must admit, my heart goes out to poor little Dolores. She feels like a neglected wife, and with the baby so far along...it seems a shame..."

Lucius's fingers were drumming impatiently on the tabletop. "Look here, Ricardo, take them both a message for me, will you?"

"Of course."

"Tell them that while they sit around accusing me of neglectfulness I am working desperately to prevent their comfortable little world from crashing down around their heads."

Ricardo was puzzled. "I don't think I understa—"

"Why is it you people never seem to know what's going on in your own country? Too damn busy singing, feasting, and dancing, I expect. There's a revolution on, Ricardo. A *real* one this time. The Americans are planning to march on Sonoma next week, and I can tell you, they mean to make trouble."

"What?! *Dios mío*, Lucio!" Ricardo was half out of his seat, eyes aflame.

"You don't need to tell Don Lorenzo *this*, but I'll tell *you*—he was on their arrest list. But not anymore. He's got nothing to worry about if he'll just stay home and keep his mouth shut. And you know who fixed it for him?" Lucius jerked a thumb at his own chest. "The neglectful one. The one they're mad at because he refuses to sit around gathering dust at Las Sombras."

Ricardo sat stunned. "Lucio...what does it mean? What shall we do?"

"Go home. Do nothing. Wait till you hear from me."

"Oh, but Lucio, you must be very careful!"

"Listen, this is nothing new to me, I was in Texas when it happened there—it's the same old story. Only this time I'm going to get my share of—"

There was a movement behind them, and they both looked up, startled. Delia was standing there smiling at Ricardo, a hand resting familiarly on Lucius's shoulder.

414

"Well, who's *this*?"

Ricardo was on his feet, bowing. "Ricardo Cortina at your service, *señora*. I am a son-in-law of Don Lorenzo Valadez."

"Ohhh, I'm so *thrilled* to meet you!" Delia gushed, and held out her hand to him. "My name's Delia, and I was just saying to Lucius the other day, I *wish* he'd bring some of his distinguished in-laws around to see us!"

Lucius was up, stuffing his papers into his pocket. Delia turned to him, a coquettish glint in her eye.

"What are you goin' to get your share of, Lucius, honey?"

He gave her a sharp look. "It's not nice to eavesdrop, Delia."

Delia giggled. "I bet there's never been *anything* you didn't get your share of."

Lucius ignored this and spoke to his companion. "If you'll excuse me, Ricardo . . . there are letters here I've got to post on the ship that's leaving the harbor tonight. Then I've got to confer with the hide-and-tallow agent. And then I've got to get ready to make a little trip over to Sonoma and see about that little business I mentioned. Ah, me, there's never enough time."

"Oh no, Lucio!" Ricardo's eyes clouded with alarm. "You're not going to have anything to do with that . . . that—"

"On the contrary. I'm going to put a damper on it."

"But you will be careful, won't you?"

"Tell my dear wife and her fussy old uncle not to worry. And, Ricardo . . . tell them to trust me for once."

Lucius started for the front door. Halfway there he stopped and looked back, his eyes narrowed thoughtfully as they moved from Delia to Ricardo and back again.

"Uh, Delia . . . why don't you take care of Ricardo, hmm? Show him how hospitable Americans can be. He's a fine fellow, he deserves the best of everything." A sly smile flitted around Lucius's lips. "And I do mean the best of *everything*."

Delia giggled again, and turned a beaming smile on Ricardo. "Why, I'd be more than *delighted* to!" She faced him squarely, standing very close, and put her hands on his shoulders. "Now, you just sit right down and make yourself comfortable, Ricardo, honey. I'm goin' to get us a bottle of wine, and then I want you to tell me *all* about yourself, all right?" She gave him a playful pinch on the cheek.

Ricardo looked around the room, and saw that Lucius was already gone. He looked at Delia—at her smiling eyes, at her

415

moist red lips, and fleetingly at the cleavage of her fine bosom. His big mustache twitched.

"With pleasure, *señora*," he murmured.

He sat down and prepared to stay awhile.

(10)

OTIS BRUNER had never before held a position of authority, but now he was known as Lieutenant Bruner, and on Monday afternoon, June fifteenth, 1846, he found himself temporarily in charge of the insurgents' headquarters at the village of Sonoma. The lieutenant did not take his responsibility lightly. Though he had no uniform, he did have a piece of blue cloth tied around his arm to signify his rank, and his every move, every glance from his eye, was heavy with a sense of command.

The headquarters was the front room of a building that afforded a good view of the tiny village square and the house on the far side of it, a long rambling adobe that was by far the largest house in the village. At the moment there were perhaps a dozen men in the big high-ceilinged headquarters room. Most were immersed in some form of idleness: a few were playing cards, others lounging or sleeping in sturdy rope-strung chairs or cots. But idleness did not suit Lieutenant Bruner. He sat behind a desk at one end of the room, restlessly shuffling through papers, scanning one occasionally, stacking them neatly on the desk and then shuffling through them again. Once in a while he would get up and go to the front door and squint out into the bright afternoon sunlight. There was a kind of unnatural solitude about the town; the only people in sight were four sentries—two leaning against opposite ends of the long front veranda of the big house across the way, and two others listlessly patrolling the empty plaza. Lieutenant Bruner would survey this scene with a mighty scowl for a minute, then return to his desk and fuss with his papers again.

After a while one of the sentries came across the sun-baked road to the headquarters building, stepped inside, and approached the desk of the officer-in-charge. "Sir, there's a fella outside—"

"Take off yer hat when you come inside, Corporal," Lieutenant Bruner snapped.

The young sentry hastily swept his hat off.

"You men gonna have to start learnin' some manners, goddamnit," Burner said in a loud voice meant for the entire room. "Some, what you call, protocol, for Christ's sake. We're settin' up a whole dang gov'ment, y'know."

"Yes, sir," the sentry said, and began again. "Sir, there's a fella outside wants to see you. Name's Hargrave. Says he's a friend o' yours."

Otis Bruner grinned. "Bring the son of a bitch in here."

Lucius came toward the lieutenant's desk with his hand extended. "Well, Otis. Good to see you again. How are things?"

"Fine, Lucius. Couldn't be better." Otis shook hands without stirring from his chair. "Take a seat."

Lucius sat down. He glanced toward the idlers at the other end of the room. Several men were eyeing him with casual curiosity, but most displayed no interest.

"Came as soon as I could," he said. "I tell you, it's not easy to get across the bay. Nothing to be had but a few native skiffs—most of 'em rotten—and the owners rob you blind to row you across."

Otis nodded sympathetically. "Yeah, it's tough."

"That was the main problem I had when I was running my mail business. You know, Otis, I think that's one of the first things we ought to do something about in the, uh, new regime. Improved transportation."

Otis nodded again. "You're absolutely right."

Lucius glanced around the room once more. "Where are all your troops? Not here yet?"

"Oh, yeah, they been here an' gone, most of 'em. Back to Sutter's Fort. We had about forty altogether."

Lucius blinked. "*Forty*? So the action's postponed, I take it. Just as well, you're damn sure not going to take California with forty men."

Otis was grinning again. "We done took it, Lucius, boy. It's all over and done with."

Lucius's jaw dropped. "What?"

Bruner began to chuckle. "Oh, you should'a' been here, Lucius. Funniest damn revolution you ever saw. Want me to tell ya about it?"

A flush of anger had risen in Lucius's face. "Goddamnit, you told me it was set for this week. Here it is Monday, and I'm here. What do you mean, it's over and done with?"

"I didn't know it was goin' to go that fast. Didn't know it was goin' to be that *easy*. What happened was, a few of us set up camp just outside o' town Saturday, to wait for Merritt and the rest of 'em—"

"Who's Merritt?" Lucius snapped. "I don't know any Merritt."

"He came in over the trail last summer. One tough customer, Merritt. Can knock a man down with a shot o' tobacco juice. Anyway, Merritt -and the others come in Saturday night and decide to make the move right off, no delay. We closed in on Vallejo's house before dawn Sunday mornin'. There weren't no guards around or anything. Merritt bangs on the door, and some greaser houseboy opens it, and Merritt and several others jes' walk right in, nothin' to it. The rest of us waited outside. Well, we waited, and we waited, and we waited. Then we elected a couple other fellas to go in and find out what was takin' so long. Then we waited some more. Pretty soon the sun was up and people were out on the street and starin' at us and wonderin' what them damn gringos were doin' hangin' around in Vallejo's courtyard. Finally we sent in somebody else—fella by the name of William Ide—to find out what the hell was goin' on. You know Ide?"

"No," Lucius growled. He was showing little interest in the story.

Otis went on, plainly enjoying it. "So, what d'ya think? Before long Ide comes out and says our men and Vallejo and two or three of Vallejo's friends and relatives were sittin' around the table samplin' Vallejo's fine brandy and havin' the best ol' time you ever did see!" Otis could barely get the words out between chuckles.

Lucius rolled his eyes wearily upward. "Good God! A bunch of clowns!"

"Well, that was the end o' the party. Ide bein' a teetotaler, y'see, he made 'em put the liquor away, and sat right down and concluded the business."

Lucius arched an eyebrow. "And the conclusion was?"

"Vallejo's bein' conducted to Sutter's Fort under arrest. So's his brother Salvador, and his military aide, fella named Prudon, and his brother-in-law, Jacob Leese." Otis paused for a moment's reflection. "Don't know what to make of a fella like Leese. Here's a Yankee merchant, comes to California and marries a rich greaser gal, then forgets all about his own kind."

He shook his head sadly, then looked quickly at Lucius. "'Course, *you're* married to a greaser gal too, ain't ya? But, naturally, you're too smart to git confused about whose side you're on."

Otis stopped and rubbed his chin and eyed his visitor carefully, as if his attention were caught by a sudden new thought. "Or *are* ya? Since you didn't show up till the party was over, maybe you ain't much interested—"

"Goddamnit, Otis, I got here as soon as I could—"

"You should'a' come with me the night I was talkin' to ya in Yerba Buena."

"I had business to attend to. I can't just drop everything the minute you snap your fingers!"

"That won't hold much water with our big man. He wants people who are dedicated."

"And your big man's Sutter, I suppose. The Baron of the Sacramento, they call him. *He's* the instigator of all this—I might have known it."

Otis emitted a disdainful snort. "Hell, no, he ain't. Sutter's nobody. We got a damn sight bigger man than *that* behind us."

Lucius frowned. "Who?"

"Captain John Charles Fremont, United States Army."

Lucius sat stunned and silent. "Thought he'd gone to Oregon," he said finally, in a weak voice.

"Yeah, so did a lot of other people. But he didn't, he came back. He came around and gave us a good talkin'-to, and he said, 'Now look here, boys, there ain't no reason under the sun why you should put up with the treatment you've been gittin' from the damn greasers. Rise up. Let 'em know you're men, not sheep, and you ain't gonna be pushed around. And if you bite off more'n you can chew,' he says, 'why, don't worry about it. I'll be right behind you, and I'll see you don't git hurt.'"

"So," Lucius muttered, "*that's* where you got all your fancy talk about symbolism and such."

Otis's dark eyes were suddenly fierce with pride. "You figgered we were clowns, eh, Lucius, thinkin' we could take California with forty men? We ain't clowns, Lucius, boy. We got our forty, plus another couple o' hunnerd ready to grab their rifles the minute shootin' starts, *plus* Fremont's whole dang battalion, jes' itchin' fer a fight. Fact is, outside o' Leese and a few old timers like 'im, I don't know of but two Americans in California who ain't a hunnerd percent behind us. That's you and yer prissy brother Isaac."

There was a wry and disdainful look on Lucius's face as he stared out the window behind Bruner's desk. "And they say Fremont's commission is in the Corps of Engineers. What a joke!" He shot an accusing scowl at the lieutenant. "Strange that you didn't see fit to mention his involvement in this when you came to see me in Yerba Buena."

"Well . . . didn't figger I oughta tell you *all* our secrets." Otis grinned cunningly. "You might'a' lost interest right then an' there."

Lucius sat staring intently at the other man, his thoughts churning. "Look here, Otis, I'd like to—" He stopped abruptly and looked around the quiet room. The card game had ceased, sleepers were awake, loungers up and sitting on the edge of their chairs, all openly listening to the conversation between the stranger and their commanding officer.

Lucius stood up. "Lieutenant Bruner. May I have permission to address your men? I'll be quite brief."

The lieutenant took three seconds to rub his chin and consider the request. "All right, go ahead. We believe in freedom of speech."

Lucius took a position in the center of the room and gazed solemnly at the collection of silent faces around him.

"Gentlemen, as I understand it, you are mainly settlers in the Sacramento Valley. You came to California to build yourselves a home and a productive life in a new land. Fine. I did the same thing several years ago. Most of you are newcomers compared to me. Well, if you'll permit me to give you the benefit of my greater experience, I'd like to inform you that right now you're being made plain damn fools of."

There was a stirring among the listeners, and an exchange of dark and wary glances. Lucius noted this, and continued, "I thought this was going to be a gathering of mature, sober responsible citizens, come together to protest the wrongs they've suffered, and to demand redress. Yes, and to take matters into their own hands *if* necessary, at the proper time

420

and in the proper way. Instead I find you're being manipulated by a bunch of—" he glanced defiantly at Otis Bruner before saying it—"irresponsible clowns, who have done everything at the wrong time and in the wrong way, and who are destroying any chance we may have had of setting up a legitimate nation in California—"

There were more stirrings, and with them a muttering of belligerent dissent that threatened to drown out the speaker's words. Lucius raised his voice and went on, "Listen to me, gentlemen. I'm a veteran of the Texas Revolution, I know whereof I speak. The Texans did it right. They waited till they were strong enough to carry it through themselves, without having to seek help from some scheming opportunist in an American army uniform—"

"Careful, Lucius," Lieutenant Bruner said. He was looking relaxed and genial in his chair, but his voice carried a hard edge. "We tolerate free speech only jes' so far, and no farther."

"Oh, I don't blame you, Otis," Lucius said, and turned again to the others. "Lieutenant Bruner's not trying to fool you, men, he's one of the ones being fooled, just like you. But it's not too late to correct your mistake. What we have to do is—"

The mutterings were growing louder and more hostile, and Lucius raised his voice still more.

"Gentlemen, hear me out. Look at me. My name is Lucius Hargrave. It's men like *me* you should be looking to for leadership. I've already established myself, I've married into a prominent California family, I've got wealth and connections and influence—"

"Aw, go on back to your greaser wife!" somebody shouted.

Lucius ignored it. "Listen to reason, men. Maybe we can correct this thing before it's too late."

"So what are we supposed to do?" somebody else demanded.

"We've got to ride straight to Fremont and tell him to keep his goddamn nose out of *our* business. Then we've got to demand that General Vallejo and his friends be released immediately, with apologies."

"Why the hell should we do *that*?" came a voice from the rear.

"Because these people aren't our enemies, damnit. You can't mount a revolution if you're too stupid to know who your enemies are!"

"Aw right, big expert, who *are* our enemies?" It was more a

421

jeer than a question, coming out of an ominously rising buzz of anger.

With a darting glance Lucius found the owner of the jeering voice, pointed a finger at him, and shouted, "I'll tell you who they are, my friend. They're crazy little power-mad Napoleons like John Charles Fremont!"

There was a sudden burst of energy released in the room—strangely quiet, but with explosive force. Several men were on their feet, faces grim with fury, thrusting toward Lucius. And as movement began, sound arose again—snarls and shouts and curses, a hubbub of angry voices, some attacking the speaker, a few defending. Somebody shoved Lucius from behind. He staggered, whirled, and swung at his assailant. Another man stopped the blow by grabbing his arm, and simultaneously somebody else seized him on the other side.

From his chair Lieutenant Bruner watched, chuckling. Then he took a deep breath and bellowed, "All right, that's enough!" His powerful voice ricocheted off the high beamed ceiling, and as the echoes died out the room was left in stillness.

Lucius brushed himself off and glared at the men around him—dangerous adversaries an instant before, now suddenly looking awkward and shamefaced. Two of the outside sentries had rushed into the room, and stood clutching their rifles in the doorway, tense with apprehension.

Very slowly Lieutenant Bruner raised his bulk out of his chair and moved with studied nonchalance to the center of the room, planting himself before Lucius.

"Time's up, Lucius, boy. That's enough free speech for one day."

Lucius's eyes roamed around the circle of silent men. "You don't believe me, do you. You don't see that Fremont's just using you for his own purpose. When he's through California'll be run from Washington, *he'll* be a big hero, and *you'll* be right back where you started—on the outside, looking in."

Lieutenant Bruner took him by the arm. The lieutenant was smiling, but his words came ominously low and threatening.

"Say another word, and I'll put you in irons."

Lucius looked around the company once more. Some of the eyes he met were sympathetic; there were those to whom his words had made sense, and he knew it—but they kept silent. He took a deep breath and looked at Bruner.

"All right if I just say good afternoon?"

"Fine." Otis gave him a genial pat on the shoulder. "And when you git home, be sure and give that cute little greaser wife o' yours a kiss fer me, will ya?" He winked, and from the listeners came a few soft snickers.

Lucius started for the exit, and the men silently moved back to make way for him. In the doorway he stopped between the two sentries and looked up and across the way to the piece of frazzled cloth draped on the flagpole beside the Vallejo house.

"What do you call that funny-looking flag?" he asked.

"That," announced the lieutenant with ponderous dignity, "is the Bear Flag. The official banner of the Bear Flag Republic of California."

Then the stiff-necked Lieutenant Bruner reverted to the grinning Otis. "Better git used to it, Lucius, boy. You're gonna be livin' under it from now on."

"A bear, eh?" Lucius studied the flag for a moment, then shrugged lightly. "Looks more like a pig to me," he said, and walked out.

(11)

IN THE EARLY MORNING of Friday, September twenty-fifth, 1846, Dolores's baby was born. It was a hard birth, but presided over with quiet competence by the godmother, Francisca Valadez, and the old servant woman Rosalia. Afterward Doña Francisca went into the *sala*, where a dozen members of the family sat waiting in stoic patience, and one paced restlessly up and down, eyes fixed on the floor. Lucius stopped his pacing and watched, his face grim with suspense, as Francisca came across the room toward him. Her smile signaled good news.

"All is well, Lucio. Your wife is resting nicely. And you have a beautiful baby daughter." The little woman stood on tiptoe to kiss Lucius on the cheek.

The room came alive, and tension was abruptly released and transformed into movement and delighted laughter. People gathered around the new father, showered him with backslaps, handshakes, and kisses. He gazed blankly at one after another of them as if not certain of what was happening.

Toward the end of the day the excitement had died down—most of the people had gone. Remaining were only Margarita and Ricardo Cortina and the godparents, Alfredo and Francisca Valadez. They sat in the patio with Don Lorenzo and Lucius, enjoying the golden late-afternoon sunlight. The new addition to the family had been thoroughly inspected and extravagantly admired, and temporarily exhausted as a topic of discussion. Conversation was now at a low ebb.

Alfredo exchanged quiet remarks in Spanish with his brother-in-law Ricardo.

"If you please," Don Lorenzo said. "English is the language of this household."

"Oh, of course, Papa," Alfredo said hastily. He shot an apologetic look toward Lucius. "Sorry, Lucio. Sometimes we forget."

Lucius was staring into a glass of wine and paying nobody any attention.

"Perhaps someday Lucio will honor us by learning a little Spanish," Alfredo murmured slyly.

"That is not the point, Alfredo," Don Lorenzo snapped. "I remind you to speak English because California will soon be a part of the United States, and—"

"That is by no means certain, Papa." Alfredo dared to voice a polite dissent. "We are at war, but who knows what the outcome will be?"

Don Lorenzo snorted. "Do not be foolish. Our people cannot wage war against the United States. A sparrow cannot defy an eagle. There is no need of it, in any case."

"I hope there will be no fighting *here*," Margarita said plaintively, her large eyes larger than normal with uneasiness.

"I think it unlikely, my dear," Ricardo said, stroking his square mustache. "The *Americanos* have occupied all the towns, and our valiant General Castro and Governor Pico have fled to Mexico. There is no one left to fight."

"For shame, Ricardo!" Alfredo said. "They have only gone

to seek support. They will be back, do not doubt it. In the meantime our forces are gathering in the south. They will show their strength at the right moment, and when they do, Fremont's *bandidos* and the *piratas* in our harbors will wish they had never laid eyes on California."

Once more Alfredo gave his American cousin an apologetic glance. "No offense, Lucio."

Lucius looked up in mild curiosity. "For what?"

"For calling your countrymen *bandidos*."

Lucius gave a disinterested shrug and sipped his wine.

"Ah, Lucio!" Francisca said laughingly. "We are terrible, talking about nothing but politics and war, when all you can think about is your sweet little baby girl, eh?" She reached out and patted him on the arm.

"You have not told us what her name will be, Lucio," Margarita said.

"Oh, uh...I don't know, we haven't decided yet."

"But, Lucio, it must be done without delay," Alfredo said urgently.

Lucius gave him a cold look. "Who says?"

"It is our custom to baptize babies as soon as possible, just in case, uh...well, for safety's sake, you know? Francisca and I were hoping to take the little one to San Jose tomorrow, for Padre Mendoza to—"

"Good Lord! Take an infant on a twenty-mile horseback ride?! Can't you bring the priest here?"

"Padre Mendoza is old, Lucio, and much overworked. Do not worry, we will take good care. It is an old custom, after all. The important thing is to get the child baptized."

Lucius stretched in his chair and gazed off across the housetop. "We didn't have any customs like that back in Indiana where I was born. My mother told me I wasn't baptized till I was three months old."

"How terrible, Lucio!" Margarita exclaimed. "Just think, if you had died—"

Lucius chuckled.

Alfredo stared at him, solemn-faced. "I am disappointed in you, Lucio. You pretended to accept our Church, but it is quite clear that you are a man without religious convictions, and—"

"Oh, Alfredo, shame on you!" It was Ricardo coming to Lucius's defense. "It is not for any of us to feel morally superior to others. Who is without fault, after all? We must be tolerant of one another's, uh...frailties." He looked to Lucius

425

for support. "Is it not so, Lucio?"

Lucius's eyes glinted with amusement. "Exactly right, Ricardo. We understand each other perfectly, don't we?"

He drained his wineglass and got to his feet. "If you'll all excuse me, I think I'll go for a walk." He gave Ricardo a quick pat on the shoulder as he walked away.

The others sat for a few minutes in thoughtful silence.

"A strange man, Lucio," Alfredo said finally.

"A troubled man," Francisca said. "There is something on his mind..."

"Well, we must try to be understanding," Don Lorenzo said patiently. "Yes, Lucio is a troubled man, but all *Americanos* are troubled, are they not? They are restless men who cannot enjoy a moment's repose. They are driven by huge appetites they do not quite know how to define, much less satisfy. Ah, but they are men of talent, great talent. We must try to guide them in the right way. We must treat them gently, like children."

There was silence again.

Alfredo sighed. "I wonder if they will treat *us* gently."

Night had fallen, and Dolores lay quiet in the darkness. From time to time she stirred, moaned softly, and was still again. Then there was the yellow glow of lamplight in the room, and the movement of large silent shadows over the walls and ceiling. Dolores opened her eyes.

"Who is it?"

"It's Lucius, my dear." He had pulled a chair to her bedside, and was leaning over close to her.

"Oh, Lucio..." Her hand came out from beneath the covers, searched for his and clasped it. "I've been waiting and waiting for you..."

"I've looked in several times, sweetheart. You were asleep."

"Oh, Lucio, my husband," she murmured. "Are you happy?"

"As happy as a man should be."

"Have you seen our little girl? Is she not beautiful, Lucio?"

"Very beautiful. Almost as beautiful as her mother. Yes, I've held her in my arms, I've talked to her, and I believe we've become quite good friends."

"What did you talk to her about?"

"Well, I told her that when she grows up we're going to have to take care to find a proper husband for her. Just any

426

passing vagabond won't do, I said. It's got to be a man of such surpassing quality that—well, I don't know, we may never find him. She may have to go through life a spinster."

Dolores giggled a little. "Ah, Lucio, you are funny!"

Lucius's expression gave no hint of humor. He held Dolores's hand and with brooding eyes examined her face. "How can I tell her not to marry a passing vagabond? Her mother did."

"Oh no, Lucio! You are my golden man, and I love you very much." She was reaching for him.

He leaned down and took her embrace, then looked searchingly into her eyes. "Sometimes I wish you weren't so good, my angel."

"Lucio! Don't you want me to be good?"

"Yes, but not so good that you make me feel unworthy."

"Ah, no, *amado,* you can never be unworthy." She suddenly brightened as her hand moved caressingly over his face. "Lucio, we must name our child! Alfredo wants to take her to the priest tomorrow."

"Yes, I know." Lucius leaned back in his chair, his mood abruptly changed.

"Do you have anything in mind?" Dolores asked.

"For a boy I had thought of John. A plain, sturdy name, full of strength and character. I had planned to name Justin that, you know, till my high-handed Louisiana in-laws took it upon themselves to name him on their own. But for a girl . . . I don't know. Whatever you think."

"But Justin was a nice name, anyway." Dolores's thoughts had been tugged in another direction by the mention of Justin. "Lucio, can't we bring him to live with us now? I think it's so sad that he—"

"Yes, all right, dear, we'll see about it. Let's get this name business settled, shall we? I'm tired of being reminded of it every ten minutes."

"Well, if it would please you . . . I had thought of Elena. That was my mother's name."

Lucius gave it perfunctory thought. "Elena Hargrave. That's fine. That'll do nicely."

"But perhaps you would like *your* mother's name. Sarah, isn't it? Perhaps that would—"

"Enough, Dolores, let it be." Irritation touched the edges of Lucius's voice. "I said Elena will be fine." He got to his feet. "I think you'd better try to sleep some more now."

"Do not be impatient with me, *amado,*" she said gravely. "I

427

am so happy, I want you to be happy too."

He leaned down and kissed her, and she slid her arms around his neck and pulled him closer for a second kiss, longer and more intense. Again he looked probingly into the dark solemn eyes.

"Dolores," he murmured. "Dolores, Lady of Sorrows. They certainly named *you* well. Even when you say 'I am happy' there is something melancholy about it, some sadness..."

"That is because I know that even happiness brings pain, for after happiness is over there is nothing."

"That's not according to your religion, my sweet."

"Sometimes there are private feelings that must be kept apart from the teachings of religion. I believe that happiness is a little flower that blossoms for a very short while and never comes again. That is why I want us to nourish ours as long as we can."

With a tender touch he tucked the covers around her chin. "Good night, little mother." One more kiss, lightly on the forehead, then a last thoughtful look. "Tomorrow when I talk to Elena again I will tell her how we must both strive very hard to be your equal."

Her eyes followed him until he had gone out and softly closed the door.

There was quick movement in the *corredor* outside the *sala*, and voices low and urgent. The Indian servant Pablo, holding a lantern, was talking to Ricardo Cortina. When Ricardo caught sight of Lucius he came hurrying toward him.

"Lucio, there are several men at the front of the house. Pablo went out to see what they want. He says they want to talk to you."

"One of them is called Sergeant Bruner," Pablo said to Lucius. "He says he knows you from the time of the Bear Flag."

"Otis," Lucius muttered. "What the hell does *he* want?" He took the lantern from Pablo and strode forward toward the front entranceway.

"Be careful, Lucio," Ricardo called after him. "Pablo says they are armed."

Lucius went on, paying no heed.

Margarita appeared at her husband's side. "What does it mean, Ricardo? Are they soldiers?"

"I do not know. This Bruner fellow—he was the one who

was here last summer, looking for Lucio. I did not like the looks of him."

"Oh, *Dios mío*! What does he want now, in the middle of the night?"

"Let us hope it is nothing more than a social call."

"Poor Lucio. It must be difficult for him, torn between loyalty to his countrymen and loyalty to his family."

Ricardo shook his head. "Do not believe it, my dear. Lucio has only one loyalty. To Lucio."

"Ricardo, that is unkind!" Margarita said reproachfully. "And only this afternoon you were leaping to his defense!"

"Do not mistake me, *amada*, Lucio and I are the best of friends. There is a bond between us." Ignoring his wife's questioning look, Ricardo took her elbow and led her back into the *sala*.

There were six or eight men sitting quietly on horseback, their faces mostly hidden in the darkness and by the hats pulled down close to their eyes. Lucius held his lantern high and singled out the leader before he spoke.

"What the hell are you doing here, Otis?" he demanded.

Otis Bruner touched his fingers to his hatbrim and flashed his familiar grin. "Howdy, Lucius. Just passin' by, thought we'd say hello."

"They call you *Sergeant* Bruner now, do they? Last time I heard it was Lieutenant. You're not making a hell of a lot of progress, are you?"

Otis indulged in a small chuckle. "Oh, that Bear Flag business was jest a lark. We called ourselves any old title we felt like—didn't mean nothin'. But this is the real thing, Lucius, boy. You are now lookin' at Sergeant Otis Bruner of the California Battalion of Mounted Riflemen. This ain't no lark we're on *this* time, my friend. This here's the United States Army."

One of the other men interjected, "Uh, I b'lieve we're navy, Sergeant Bruner."

"The hell we are!" Otis snapped. "Major Fremont's our commander, ain't he? Fremont's army."

"Yeah, but Major Fremont answers to Commodore Stockton, and the Commodore's navy, so I b'lieve that makes us—"

"Well, army, navy—what's the difference?" Otis growled, and waved the other man silent. "The point is, we're United States troops."

Lucius was grimly shaking his head. "So now it's *Major* Fremont. Whatever the hell's going on, it's working out fine for *him*, isn't it? Every time I hear about him he's a notch higher."

"Things are gonna work out fine for all of us, Lucius. That is, all of us who're participatin'. 'Course, far as *shirkers* are concerned, I can't answer for what'll happen to *them*." Otis fixed an ominous look on Lucius.

Impatience broke through Lucius's tightly controlled manner. "What is it you want, Otis? It's getting late, and it's damned cold out here. Get to the point."

"Yeah, it *is* cold. If you had any manners you'd invite us in."

"You're right, I would. But I haven't, so get to the point."

"*Two* points, Lucius, boy. First, I want to tell you we're here to do you a favor. You should'a' joined up with us at Sonoma, but since you didn't, we're willin' to give you a second chance. Fremont wants volunteers. He wants anybody he can git, but in partic'lar he wants people who've been here a while and know their way around. Now, since you used to run a mail delivery service, we figgered you'd be a real good—"

Lucius stopped him with a sharp question. "How old are you, Otis?"

Otis blinked in surprise. "Why, I'm thirty-seven. Why?"

"Amazing. I'm thirty, and when I hear you going on about Fremont this and Fremont that, I feel like an old man listening to the babble of a child."

Otis was not amused. "We're takin' California for the United States, goddamnit. If you think that's child's play, you ain't got good sense—"

"You're not taking California for the United States, you're taking it for Fremont. He'll get all the credit, and you'll get your ass shot off."

A heavy scowl came over Otis's face, while angry looks were exchanged among his companions. "All right, suit yerself. But later on, when you're grovelin' fer crumbs, don't say you didn't have plenty o' chances to sit at th' table with th' first-class folks."

Then he abruptly relaxed, his good humor restored. "Now, point number two. We want horses. Fremont says we're to round up all th' horses we can, not so much 'cause we need 'em, but to keep 'em out o' reach o' th' greasers."

"Our horses *are* out of reach of the greasers," Lucius said. "And you can tell Fremont they're out of *his* reach too."

Otis grinned broadly as derisive laughter erupted among the horsemen.

"You're a funny man, Lucius. I git a big kick out o' you, damned if I don't." Otis pulled out a piece of paper, unfolded it and held it out to Lucius. "Here's a requisition fer two hunnerd prime saddle horses from th' Valadez *rancho*. We figgered we'd take thirty or forty now, and come back later fer more. Ol' man Valadez can redeem this fer cash from th' federal gov'ment later on, after th' fightin's over. *If* he behaves himself."

Lucius made no move to take the paper. "We've got no horses for you, Otis."

Otis waved the paper at him. "You might as well accept this. We'll take th' horses anyway."

Anger burned on Lucius's face. "In that case, stop calling yourselves U.S. troops. You're nothing but a band of robbers."

One of Otis's companions leaned close to him and muttered, "Le's go, Otis. We're wastin' our time with this lunatic bastard."

Lucius took a few steps back toward the house and turned again. "Tell you what, Otis. My advice to you is to turn around right now and get the hell off this *rancho*. I'll give you half an hour, that ought to be plenty of time. Then I'm going to call the *vaqueros* together and tell 'em to get their guns oiled up, there are horse thieves roaming around."

Muttering rose from the horsemen, and from them came a snarl: "Shoot the son of a bitch, Otis."

"You men just remember one thing," Lucius barked at them. "Fremont's a topographical engineer, not a combat officer. If he leads you into trouble, if the Californians get the upper hand, you'll wish you were on good terms with me. I'll be one of the few people in California who can save you."

The mutterings subsided into an uneasy silence.

"All right, let's go, men," Otis Bruner said quietly. He stuffed the paper back in his pocket and pulled his horse around in preparation to move out, then paused to give Lucius one last scowling look.

"I wish you luck, Lucius, boy. You're goin' to need it."

With a brief thunder of hoofbeats the horsemen were gone.

When Lucius returned to the house he found the others gathered in a huddle in the doorway, peering out.

"What is happening, Lucio?" Ricardo asked, his voice tight with anxiety. "Will there be trouble, do you think?"

431

"Not unless you consider a few raids on our stables trouble."

"Oh, *Dios mío!*" Margarita breathed in horror.

Don Lorenzo sighed with philosophical resignation. "Well, after all, it *is* war. If we suffer no greater damage than that, we must count ourselves fortunate."

"Lucio, do you think they would ever dare come into the *house?*" Francisca asked.

Lucius looked around at the cluster of worried faces, and smiled. "Rest easy, friends. I believe I can personally guarantee your safety."

"Oh, Lucio!" Margarita said, her large eyes shining. "We are so lucky you are with us!"

"True," Lucius murmured. "True."

They all drew back to make room as he walked with calm dignity into the house.

(12)

Monday, April 5th, 1847

Mr. Lucius Hargrave
Rancho Las Sombras

Dear Lucius,

I was at Sutter's on Saturday to pick up some supplies, and found your letter waiting for me. Lucius, what great news, that you and Dolores are coming to visit! I rushed right home to tell Catherine and the children, so excited I could hardly contain myself. The only trouble is that the 2nd of May is a long time off and it will be hard to wait. In the meantime we won't talk about anything else. Even little Martha seems to be caught up in the spirit of the thing, chattering and laughing the livelong day. Wait till you see her, Lucius, you'll be amazed. You know she will be three next month, and such a beautiful child I think I've never seen. I can say that without embarrassment, of course, since she isn't mine. (She is mine, though, as you will see. I am Papa and she is Papa's little girl.) Catherine says we all spoil her rotten, I especially.

Lucius, you would not be able to find our new place very readily without some help, and I would not trust in asking directions at New Helvetia. It is about forty miles from there, not on the river, and the road is pretty bad. So I will plan to be at Sutter's on Saturday the 1st, to meet you and escort you myself.

It's going to be wonderful to see you both. We are sorry you are not planning to bring little Elena with you, but you are right, of course. At seven months she is still a bit too young for that.

I will have this brought to you by Ygnacio, my mill foreman. I can hardly afford to spare him for several days, but I want to be sure you receive this. We sure need an organized mail service in California, Lucius. Too bad you gave up that business. Now that the war is over and California belongs to the United States, you'd think the American authorities would do something about it.

Well, I am rambling, it seems. I will see you on the 2nd of May. Till then, keep well. Our love to Dolores and the baby, and fond greetings to Don Lorenzo.

> *Your brother,*
> *Isaac*

P. S. Maybe you will notice a slight improvement in my writing, Lucius. Well, don't forget I am married to a beautiful schoolteacher, and guess who her best student is? (Not the smartest, that's Justin, I mean the hardest working.) I am. I write a page every night, and Catherine corrects it for me. She corrected this letter, too, and I'm proud to say she only found three small mistakes. Lucius, will you agree that I'm a very lucky fellow?

Abby Shannon was twelve, bright-eyed and pigtailed, and beginning to show signs of a prettiness that she kept nearly

433

concealed behind a tomboyish manner. She perched on the porch railing of a rustic pineboard house and squinted up at her ten-year-old brother crouched in the fork of a tree in the front yard.

"See anything, Byron?" she called.

"Nothin' yet," Byron reported.

"Come down and let me look," Abby said.

Catherine came out of the house and frowned at her daughter. "Abby, don't you dare climb up in that tree in your new dress."

Abby looked disgusted. "Mama, why can't girls wear pants, same as boys?"

"Because they'd look ridiculous, that's why." Catherine looked up at the boy in the tree. "And you be careful, Byron, I don't want you getting all dirty, either."

"Where's Justin, Mama?" Abby asked.

"Playing school with Martha. Trying to teach her the ABC's."

"She's too little for that," Abby said, and exchanged a knowing adult smile with her mother.

"I know, dear, but they enjoy it. Especially Justin."

Catherine walked down to the gate in the wooden stake fence that enclosed the yard, and looked down the hillside path as far as she could see.

"Nothin' yet, Mama," Byron called to her. "I'll tell you when I see 'em comin'."

Catherine came back to the porch and stood beside Abby. The girl studied her mother's face.

"Mama, why are you so nervous?"

"What do you mean, Abby? I'm not nervous."

"Yes you are. You haven't been still a minute this whole day."

"Well, my goodness, there's a lot to do when company's coming."

"I know what's the matter," Abby said. "You're afraid Uncle Lucius might take Justin away."

Catherine compressed her lips and looked away quickly.

"Isn't that it, Mama?"

"Yes. I *am* afraid. Terribly afraid."

"Oh, he won't, Mama," Abby said reassuringly. "It just wouldn't be right, because Justin's so used to living with us, and—"

"Here they come!" Byron shouted from his lookout perch.

434

Abby slipped off the porch railing and stood very close to her mother. "Don't worry, Mama. We just won't *let* him take Justin, that's all—"

"It's not for us to decide, Abby. He *is* Justin's father, you know." Catherine had regained her composure. "Come on, let's go and meet them." She took the girl's hand, and they together they walked down to the front gate.

Greetings were a flurry of smiles and laughter and embraces and animated talk that lasted for several minutes, after which Isaac took the horses off to the barn while Catherine led the visitors into the house. Later, when Isaac came in, he found Lucius and the women seated in the front room, Abby and Byron sprawled on the floor, and the little girl Martha clutching at her mother's skirt and staring wide-eyed at the strangers.

"It's Aunt Dolores and Uncle Lucius, darling," Catherine said to the child. "Will you give them each a kiss?"

The answer was plainly no. Martha retreated and stood half-hiding behind her mother's chair. Then she caught sight of Isaac, and her big brown eyes danced.

"Papa, Papa!" she squealed, and ran to him, and Isaac laughed as he swept her up in his arms.

Lucius watched this demonstration briefly, then looked away. "Where's Justin?" he asked abruptly.

There was a moment of silence. Catherine looked inquiringly toward her older children seated on the floor. "Do you know where Justin is, children?"

"*I* don't," Abby said.

"I think he went down toward the sawmill," Byron said.

"Good heavens, why would he do that?" Catherine said vaguely.

Isaac spoke more forcefully. "Go fetch him, Byron, please. Tell him his father and Aunt Dolores are here."

Byron got up and started for the door.

Little Martha squirmed in Isaac's arms. "Go see Justin!" she demanded. Isaac put her down, and she went running off after Byron.

Isaac took a chair, and smiled at Lucius and Dolores. "That child's absolutely devoted to Justin. Never saw anything like it. Follows him around like a puppy, morning, noon, and night. Don't know what she'd do without him."

Another silence rose to fill the room. Catherine looked at

the guests and opened a new subject.

"I hope Las Sombras came through the war without too much trouble?"

"Nothing serious," Lucius said. "Horse thievery, mostly. First one side, then the other. We got the impression the war was a contest to see who could steal the most horses."

"We were lucky," Dolores declared. "Some families we know had their houses broken into and plundered. Frightful!"

"You were lucky, indeed," Catherine agreed.

"I still don't think it was right, what the Americans did," Isaac said. He spoke directly to Dolores. "I'm ashamed to look your relatives in the face, knowing the Americans stole their country right out from under 'em."

"Do not feel that way, Señor Isaac," Dolores murmured soothingly. "My Uncle Lorenzo says it was the inevitable course of history."

"Yes, it's pretty much the way Don Lorenzo predicted," Lucius said. "He's been telling us all along that California was bound to go to the United States sooner or later. That's why he took pains to form an alliance with the Americans early."

"What do you mean, Lucio?" Dolores asked wonderingly. "How did Uncle Lorenzo . . . as you say . . . form an alliance?"

Lucius looked at her in surprise. "Why, through *me*, sweetheart. Why do you suppose Las Sombras came through all that with nothing worse than the theft of a few horses?"

She stared at him. "But I did not know that Uncle Lorenzo—or you—thought of our marriage as a . . . a political alliance."

"No, no, my angel, I didn't mean it quite like *that*, you see, I—" With an indulgent smile he reached out and patted her on the arm. "It was a careless choice of words. Strike it out of your mind."

"Well, here's Justin," Isaac said, and attention shifted abruptly.

The boy stood in the doorway, and his face was grave, unsmiling.

Lucius got to his feet. "Hello, son."

Justin came across the room and held out his hand to Lucius. "H'lo, Papa."

They shook hands with gentlemanly formality.

"Oh, now, we can do better than that!" Lucius laughed. He went down on his knees and took the boy in a hug that was accepted with expressionless passivity.

Lucius sat down again and watched while Justin ex-

436

changed greetings with Dolores, solemn and formal. Then he patted a chair beside his own. "Come sit down, Justin. Let's have a good talk."

Justin took the chair and sat patiently while Lucius and Dolores commented on how much he'd grown. Byron had come in again with Martha in tow, and the little girl scampered across the room to Justin and clutched at his knee.

"Sit with you, Justin," she pleaded, and he helped her up to sit beside him. "Well, Justin," Lucius said, "I hear you're still doing well in your studies. Aunt Catherine's star pupil."

A spark of life touched Justin's face for the first time. "Oh yes, I like school, Papa," he said eagerly. "And did you know that Aunt Catherine just got a big boxful of books she sent for from Boston?"

"No. Really?"

"Yes. Some are schoolbooks, and some are storybooks, and some are grownup books—all kinds of things. And I'm gonna read all of 'em."

"My, my. That sounds like an ambitious undertaking for a seven-year-old."

"Well...I guess it'll take me a while."

Lucius looked quickly at Catherine. She held his gaze for an instant, then dropped her eyes.

Little Martha suddenly sat up straight and spoke directly to Lucius. "Justin tells me ABC's," she piped.

"Oh, does he?"

"And Justin draws pictures for me."

"Really? I'd like to see one."

Martha scrambled down and went churning away, and was back in a few seconds with a large sheet of paper covered with a crude drawing of a house with a number of matchstick figures around it. Below the picture was a legend scrawled in a childish hand. Martha thrust the paper into Lucius's lap, then stood with her hand on his knee, helping him scrutinize it.

Lucius looked over the picture. "Very nice," he commented, "very nice indeed." Secretly his eyes strayed to the child beside him, examined the chubby hand on his knee, the mass of curly honey-colored hair, the round little face, the intense dark brown eyes.

Martha pointed to the words at the bottom of the picture. "Read that," she commanded.

"All right. It says, 'This is our family and the house where we live. Ponderosa Hill, California. Signed Justin Hargrave also Little Eagle. For Martha Hargrave also Morning Child.'"

The little girl smiled up at Lucius, grasped the picture and took it to Dolores.

"She's pretty smart," Justin said to Lucius, sounding like one of the adults discussing the children. "I like to teach her things. Pretty soon I'll have her saying her ABC's all the way through."

Lucius looked broodingly from the boy to the little girl, and said nothing.

Conversation at supper was given over mostly to the children. Abby told of her keen interest in animals; she owned a lamb, a calf, and a flock of chickens. Byron was praised as Isaac's sturdy helper at the new sawmill—still a sadly primitive operation, Isaac admitted, but they had big plans—and he was becoming expert in matters of forestry and lumber. Justin's interest lay in books.

"Maybe I'll be a writer when I grow up," he announced.

"Last time I heard you were going to be a *vaquero*," Lucius said teasingly.

"Oh, that was a long time ago," Justin said.

Martha talked softly to herself, played with her food, and smiled at everybody.

Later in the evening, after the children were in bed, the adults gathered again in the front room.

"Well, now for *our* news," Lucius said, settling back in his chair. "As you know, Dolores was supposed to receive a gift of land at our marriage, but we were never able to settle on a suitable location. Well, lately we've been riding over some very beautiful property, and, uh ... I think we've found it at last."

"Wonderful!" Isaac exclaimed, and Catherine echoed his reaction.

"Let us acknowledge our benefactor, Lucio," Dolores prompted.

"By all means. We have Dolores's cousin Ricardo to thank for it. It was his property, you see—he made it available to us through some sort of exchange agreement with Don Lorenzo. Damned decent of him."

"Sure was," Isaac agreed fervently. "He's a fine fellow."

"He is indeed." Lucius smiled. "Matter of fact, Ricardo and I enjoy a pretty close friendship. We, uh ... we understand each other."

He chuckled when he noticed a puzzled look on Dolores's

face, and gave her one of his indulgent pats on the arm. "Anyway, by the end of the year we ought to be living in our own home. Just in time for our second baby."

There was a moment of silence, followed by an outpouring of congratulations.

"You're sure gettin' ahead of me in the baby department, Lucius," Isaac said wistfully. "We're not doin' very well."

"We're doing just fine," Catherine said stiffly.

"Sure you are, you've got a houseful of young 'uns already," Lucius said to Isaac. "But we'll be taking Justin off your hands now. I've imposed on you much too long, I think. It's time he was where he belongs. With us."

He looked around quickly, sensing the strange tension that had risen in the room. "Well...you agree, don't you?"

Catherine stared at her hands in her lap and was silent.

"I guess you're right, Lucius," Isaac said with a sigh. "But it'll break our hearts to see him go, you know. He's just like one of our own. It's...." He glanced at Catherine as if hoping for help. It was not forthcoming.

"It's goin' to hurt," he finished lamely.

"It hurts *us* to be without him," Dolores countered.

"You should think of his education," Catherine said in a brisk schoolteacherish tone.

"You could go on saying that till he was twenty-one years old," Lucius said quietly.

"Yes, I could. And I probably will." Catherine fixed on Lucius a hard look of determination. "He's not an ordinary child, Lucius. If he were his education would be adequate right now. He can already read and write as well as half the adult population of California, of whatever race. But his mind is something...I don't know...it's something very special."

"Catherine, I know that." Lucius spoke with calm patience. "And believe me, I'll be forever grateful for what you've done for him. But he's *my* son. And I want him with me."

"It is not right, Catherine," Dolores said timidly. "Father and son should be—"

"No, it is certainly *not* right." Catherine's voice quivered like a taut bowstring. "It is not right to leave a child in other people's care until the sinews of his heart and theirs are so completely intertwined that—"

"Catherine, don't," Isaac pleaded, and reached for her hand.

She avoided him, her eyes remaining on Lucius. "Oh, I'm not just talking for myself, or Isaac. Abby and Byron love him

439

more dearly than any brother. They'll be shattered to lose him. And Martha. Have you seen those two together, Lucius? Have you *seen* them?"

The question echoed in silence.

"I think," Dolores began carefully, "we should not talk about this anymore tonight. I am very tired. If you will excuse me I would like to go to bed now."

Catherine went to her, and took both her hands as she arose.

"I'm sorry, Dolores. Forgive me. I . . . I've been talking like a silly fool."

Dolores's smile was sad and gentle. "No, no, my sister, do not apologize, you have a right to speak what is in your heart. I know what is there. I have known for a long time."

"I'll show you to your room," Catherine said. She put her arm around Dolores and led her out.

Isaac and Lucius sat in gloomy silence, not looking at each other. Lucius was slumped in his chair.

"Why is life so goddamned complicated?" he asked.

He was muttering to himself, expecting no answer, and got none.

(13)

IN THE MORNING Lucius and Isaac were up early and off to the sawmill, a fifty-yard-square compound enclosed by a rail fence, a quarter of a mile from the house. Nearby a small mountain stream gurgled past a jumble of rocks gray with age and green with lichen, on its way to the sun-baked valley twenty miles away. The air was sharp, and pungent with the aroma of mixed oak and pine forest at an elevation where the heat-loving valley oaks began to give way to the tall cone-bearers. Overhead a populace of birds twittered unseen, and underfoot lay a foot-thick carpet of pine needles and oak-leaf mold, the product of winters and summers beyond reckoning.

The mill was nothing more than several gaping sawpits under shed roofs, where six or eight brown-skinned, bare-backed workmen operated long whipsaws, grinding their steady patient way through pine logs dripping with resin and the sweet smell of new wood. Lucius sat on the rail fence while Isaac made his rounds, giving the day's instructions to his mixed Mexican and Indian crew.

When he finally rejoined Lucius, Isaac flashed a sheepish grin. "Well, this is it, Lucius. The new improved Thacker and Hargrave, Associates, Western Branch. Still doesn't look much like the original, does it?"

"Can't understand why you settled way up here in the first place," Lucius said.

"Look over yonder, Lucius." Isaac swept his arm in an arc toward towering rust-brown columns. "See those big ponderosa? There's enough prime lumber in one o' those to build a small house. And a little farther up the slope there's sugar pine. Clear wood, straight and strong. The finest. I settled here 'cause this is where the lumber is."

"But no people. No customers."

"Sure there are. You don't realize how fast the valley's fillin' up, Lucius. Every Friday my men load up two thousand board feet on wagons and head down toward Sutter's Fort. Before they get halfway there they've sold every stick they've got. We're makin' a livin', all right. And you know what? I've got a steam boiler ordered from Boston. Ought to be here by August. I'm goin' to set up a steam-powered saw, somethin' like what we had in South Bar. *Then* you'll see some production!"

"And you're independent of Sutter at last?"

"Almost. He's got somebody else lumberin' for him now. Fella named Marshall. Seems to think he can build a mill up on the American River and float the lumber down, like Sutter wants. I don't think they can do it, but that's all right, I wish 'em luck. I'm just glad to be on my own."

Lucius shrugged. "Well . . . as long as you're happy."

"I am." Isaac gazed contentedly around his little dominion. "Except for missin' Mama Sarah so much, I think my life's just about perfect."

"Good Lord!" Lucius groaned. "You're not weaned *yet*?"

"Oh, it's all right. We correspond. She always wants to

441

know about you—how you're doin, and all. I try to keep her informed."

"Good for you."

"You still haven't written to her, have you?"

"She hasn't written to me, either."

Isaac grimaced in exasperation. "I'd like to take the two of you and butt your heads together. I've never *seen* such stubborn foolishness!"

Lucius slipped down off the rail fence and clapped Isaac on the shoulder. "See you a little later, old chum. I'm going for a walk."

He went off along the creek at a brisk pace, leaving Isaac glowering after him.

In the afternoon Lucius and Dolores were guests in Catherine's reading class, held in a large sunny room at the rear of the house. Besides Abby and Byron and Justin there were a dozen or so others in the class, ranging from five or six years of age to nearly grown—mostly children of Isaac's sawmill employees. In deference to the special guests Justin was called on first; it was clearly something that had been arranged beforehand. At a nod from Catherine the boy stood up and faced the class, clutching a large book firmly in both hands.

"We're starting a new story today," he announced. "It's called 'Little Annie's Ramble,' and it's from *Twice-Told Tales*, by Nathaniel Hawthorne."

He cleared his throat, lifted the book higher, and tried hard to make his thin little voice sound large and authoritative as he read:

"Ding-dong! Ding-dong! Ding-dong!

The town-crier has rung his bell at a distant corner, and little Annie stands on her father's doorsteps trying to hear what the man with the loud voice is talking about. Let me listen too. Oh, he is telling the people that an elephant and a lion and a royal tiger and a horse with horns, and other strange beasts from . . ."

Justin paused, frowning in perplexity at the next word. Catherine's soft voice prompted: "Foreign."

". . . from foreign countries, have come to town and will receive all visitors who choose to wait upon them. Perhaps little Annie would like to go?"

Justin read an entire page, was helped past a difficult word once or twice more, and went back to his seat with a long warm look of approval from Catherine. Just before he sat down he glanced covertly at Lucius at the back of the room, and as their eyes met Lucius smiled and nodded, his face lit with pride and some other emotion that Justin could not interpret.

Hours later, when the sun sank low over the valley of the Sacramento to the west and sent long slanting shafts of light through the foothill forest, Lucius and Justin walked up a path behind the house to the top of a wooded hillside. At the summit was a grassy clearing, and a flat-topped rock that seemed almost to have been set there for the purpose of providing a convenient viewpoint.

Justin, having led the way up the path, stopped to wait. In a moment Lucius reached him.

"Well! It's nice here," he said, looking around.

"Yes," Justin said.

Lucius pointed to the rock. "That looks like a good spot. How about sitting up there?"

"All right." Justin led the way.

They sat on top of the flat rock, their faces awash with the golden light of sunset. Below them were folds of hillside and valley, and velvety-green billows of pine foliage slowly turning to dark blue in the lengthening shadows.

"Beautiful view," Lucius remarked.

Justin pointed down the slope at their feet. "Look down there, Papa. You can see the top of our house."

"Yes. It's a nice little house, isn't it?"

"It's the best house I ever saw," Justin said emphatically. "Except maybe Mama Sarah's house."

"You remember her house, do you?"

"A little. Not very well. I want to go back and see Mama Sarah someday."

"Of course. And you will, I'm sure." Lucius moved a little closer to the boy. "Speaking of houses . . . I wanted to tell you about the one we're going to have pretty soon. It'll be up in a canyon that goes for several miles back into some hills. There's a stream down through there, and a lot of big cottonwood trees along the way, and at one place there's a little waterfall where the creek drops over a rock ledge and forms a pool down below. Prettiest thing you ever saw. And the house is going to be in a kind of meadow not far from there, so at night when you're in your bed you can hear the waterfall. Don't you think that'll be nice?"

Justin was quiet for a moment, solemnly thoughtful. "Is that why you wanted to go for a walk with me, Papa? To tell me about the waterfall?"

"Uh, well . . . no. There are some other things." Lucius took a deep breath. "Justin, I, uh . . . I really must beg your forgiveness, my boy. It's a hard life you've had, shunted about from one place to the next, in the care of one person after another, with never a place to call home. It's a bad thing, and . . . I'm sorry."

"Oh, that's all right, Papa. Uncle Isaac and Aunt Catherine are so good to me, it's just like—"

"Yes, but you see, the thing is . . . we're going to have a home of our own now, and our little family can all be together at last, as it should be. You and I and Dolores, and your little sister Elena, and the new brother or sister who'll soon be here. Justin, do you realize Elena is seven months old, and you've never even seen her? She needs a big brother, you know? I was hoping you'd have a nice Shoshone name all picked out for her."

Justin looked off down the hill. "I don't do that so much anymore."

"Dolores needs you too. She loves you dearly, and it grieves her that we're not all together."

Justin was unresponsive. He had begun to watch a big dark-crested jay in a nearby tree.

"And *I* need you, Justin," Lucius said softly.

There was silence between them, taut with the strain of clashing wills.

"I want to stay here," Justin said then. He kept his eyes away from Lucius.

"But, Justin, I'm your father, and where *I* am is where you belong."

"I belong here. This is where I want to stay till I'm a grownup man."

"Justin, son . . . don't you remember the promise we made to each other? Way back at Fort Hall, where Uncle Baptiste and Aunt Mali live? We promised to stick together always, you and me. Don't you remember?"

"We will, Papa. You can come and visit me lots of times, and I'll come and visit you, and—"

"Justin, this is ridiculous!" Exasperation had begun to creep into Lucius's manner. "Look here, now. Day after

444

tomorrow we'll be starting back to Rancho Las Sombras, and I want you to begin right now getting used to the idea of coming with us. I'll be needing you to help me plan the new house. You can decide just where you want your room to be, and..."

Justin was steadfastly observing the antics of the big noisy jay.

"Look at me, Justin," Lucius commanded. "Pay attention."

The boy looked briefly, then turned his eyes downward and stared at his hands clasped tightly together in front of him.

"If you take me I'll run away," he said.

It was a strange utterance—words of defiance spoken in quiet timidity—and it brought the conversation to an end.

The sun was down. The jay had flown off into the darkening forest, and all was still. Soon Lucius got to his feet and stood looking down at Justin's bowed head.

"It's getting dark," he said in a gentle voice. "We'd better go."

Halfway back to the house they encountered Catherine, coming up the path to meet them. Justin was again leading the way, twenty yards ahead of Lucius. Catherine greeted him with a playful tousling of his hair.

"Hurry along and get washed up, Justin. Supper's almost ready."

He went flying on down the path as if exuberant with some blessed relief.

Lucius came down to her then, and they walked along more slowly, side by side.

"You two had a nice long visit," she remarked carefully.

"That we did. A good heart-to-heart talk. Father and son, and all that."

"I had a nice talk with Dolores too," Catherine said.

"Did you?"

"I like her more and more all the time, Lucius. She's really a very sensible young woman."

"Well, of course. Did you think I'd marry a ninny?"

"She always seemed to me so...I don't know...so melancholy, somehow. But when I talk to her I can see she's really quite happy. She seems to love you very, very much."

"We have a perfect marriage," Lucius declared.

"Well, I'm glad to hear it." Catherine became thoughtful as they strolled down the path. "You know, it's strange, Lucius. In all the time Justin's been with us I've never heard him mention his mother. How much does he really know about her?"

"Very little. He was awfully small when we—" Lucius pulled up short, and laughed. "Oh, I see what you're thinking. You're wondering how long I can keep up the fiction of being a widower. Well, my dear, it may interest you to learn that Dolores knows all about my first marriage. *And* my divorce."

"Really?!"

"Yes, indeed. You see—" he gave her a sly sidelong look—"I don't believe it's practical to live a perpetual lie. A small temporary untruth now and then might be justifiable, but—"

"What are you suggesting, Lucius?" Catherine had stopped, and her cheeks burned with an angry color.

"Nothing, my dear, nothing at all. Only that you're hardly qualified to look at other people's lives with an air of moral superiority." He smiled.

"I'm sorry," she said in a tight voice. "If I have ever done that, I'm sorry. And if you ever see me doing it, please correct me at once."

"With pleasure."

They walked on. After a moment Catherine spoke again. "May I tell you about my conversation with Dolores?"

"If you like."

"As I said, she's a very sensible person. She told me she hadn't realized how it is with Justin here. She says now she thinks you ought to leave him with us for a while longer."

This time it was Lucius who stopped abruptly, and Catherine paused a few steps farther along and looked back at him, apprehension shining in her eyes.

"It's entirely meaningless for you to discuss the subject with Dolores," he said coldly. "I will make the decision myself."

"Yes, I know, Lucius, of course you will." She hastened to sound conciliatory. "But now that you've really seen how it is, surely you'll..." Her hands twisted themselves together, revealing her nervousness.

"I'll what? Give up what is rightfully mine?"

"I was going to say...surely you'll do what's best for Justin."

"Which in your view means keeping him separated from his father."

"Lucius, it...it means recognizing that your child is not

446

your *possession*, like a horse or a wagon. He is a human being who's going to walk a long path in this world, and he's going to walk most of it on his own, without any help from parents. What's best for him is that you do all you can to set his feet firmly on the path, and encourage him to make a good start."

For a long moment he stood looking at her while the shadows of nightfall gathered around them. Then when he spoke again his voice had become bleakly empty, reflecting a rapidly crumbling resolve.

"I can't compete with you, can I, Catherine? You're much too strong. Your weapons are too formidable. You've enchanted the boy with books and learning. You've rung the town crier's bell, and plied him with stories about elephants and lions and tigers and strange beasts from foreign countries. How can I compete with that?"

Her hand went out as if to touch him with tenderness. "Lucius . . . someday, when he's all grown up, he'll understand what you did for him. And he'll love you for it."

Lucius turned away a little, and his eyes wandered aimlessly in the gloaming beneath the trees. "Isaac, dear old chum," he murmured. "My good brother Isaac, whom I have defended with my very life . . . is a thief."

Catherine touched him on the arm. "Lucius, what—"

"He has stolen from me all my precious possessions. My son. My daughter. And my true heart's wife—"

"Lucius!" she hissed at him fiercely. "Stop that, do you hear? You are breaking the pact we made!"

He whirled on her and grasped her arms, his eyes piercing her with a ferocious light. "Just tell me one thing, Catherine. Answer yes, and I'll be satisfied. Do you ever think of those two days we spent together in the wilderness? Do you ever think of them with *longing*?"

She pulled against him, turning her head away. "Let me go, Lucius—"

"Answer me, Catherine!" His grip tightened. "Answer me!"

The answer came trembling but defiant. "I will not. I will *not*! Let me go!"

She broke away and, with a little choking gasp, ran like a wild creature down the path toward home.

He stood for several minutes alone in the forest, feeling the slow silent closing-in of darkness. Then he went on the last hundred yards to the house, from which the yellow glow of

447

lamplight radiated a stream of warmth and comfort.

By the time he got to the door he was whistling a jaunty tune.

(14)

FROM THE JOURNAL of Lucius Hargrave:

I have never been able to get a firm grip on Time. It is an element much too elusive for my grasp; like the waters of a rushing stream it slides between my fingers and goes gurgling away, and will not tarry to be felt, experienced, or savored. My early life in California seemed but a flicker of a moment, yet before I had time to draw a leisurely breath almost four years had passed!

On the wide stage of politics and war, pages were being written for future history books that would make liberal use of fantasy and romance, and the fictional gilding of shabby facts. Fremont's move toward Oregon in 1846 was but a feint, of course. He returned, and proceeded with his despicable plan of trying to get the American settlers and the *Californios* shooting at each other, whereupon he would seize California in the name of "restoring order," present it to the United States, and be celebrated ever after as one of America's great men. It did not quite work out the way he intended. After placing himself at the head of a rebellious rabble he marched on the Presidio of San Francisco, an almost deserted fort near Yerba Buena, spiked a pair of rusty Spanish cannon that had not been fired in forty years, and pronounced California conquered—only to find that U.S. naval forces had already taken the capital city of Monterey and run up the American flag. War between the United States and Mexico over the annexation of Texas was just beginning, and the occupation of California ports by the navy was one of the first American acts of hostility.

No doubt Fremont was greatly chagrined; his thunder had been stolen right out from under his nose, and his hoped-for glory crumbled into ridiculous farce. (I believe his one worthy contribution to California was the occasion when, looking out from the Presidio over the beautiful strait that connects San Francisco Bay with the ocean, he gave it a fittingly poetic name: *Chrysopylae*—the Golden Gate.) Nevertheless he had done his dirty work well; harmony between the Americans and the Spanish-Mexican natives was gone forever, replaced by mutual distrust and bitterness.

The California phase of the war with Mexico lasted for a year or so, and was conducted in the best local revolutionary tradition—with marvelously little bloodshed. Its outcome was predictable, and came with the total surrender of the *Californio* forces at a place called Cahuenga, near Los Angeles, in January of 1847. A great empire had been neatly stolen, and the thieves wore the gorgeous cloaks of heroes. Such was the Conquest of California.

I drew back from all this, simultaneously revolted by my countrymen's rapacious behavior and preoccupied with private troubles.

To begin with, further stresses and strains had developed in my marriage to Dolores. A gentle creature, unreal as a woodland nymph, she had been born and bred to a life of quiet seclusion, and found incomprehensible the dynamic forces that urged me to my constant endeavors. She liked to spend her days dispensing good deeds and charity to the workers at Las Sombras, and grieved over what she perceived as a lack of philanthropic instincts in her husband. She complained bitterly that I made insufficient efforts to be friends with her beloved Spanish cousins, and stubbornly refused to notice the thousand subtle ways in which those cousins rejected me. I was unappreciative of their customs; I was slow in learning their language; I was less than properly ardent about their Catholic faith. The criticisms were discreet, but endless.

Meanwhile I chafed at living in another man's house, especially now that my family was growing. (At the end of our first year of marriage Dolores had presented me with a beautiful baby daughter whom we named Elena, and a year later was expecting again—this time, I prayed it would be a son.) But she would not understand how I could fail to be overwhelmed with gratitude at her uncle's generosity in allowing us to live on at Las Sombras—was it not one of the most beautiful houses in California? She was shocked when, patience finally exhausted, I forcefully insisted that Don Lorenzo make good his promise of a parcel of land as our wedding gift. At last he yielded—reluctantly—and gave us not a piece of choice Las Sombras land as we had expected, but some property of lesser quality on the opposite side of the valley, which he had acquired from his son-in-law, Ricardo Cortina. Fortunately the property did include a fine home site, and I plunged immediately into work, hoping that a home of our own would provide my little family with the privacy we needed, and my relationship with Dolores would improve.

Then there was Justin. It had been like a dagger thrust in my heart to leave the boy with Isaac and his family, but it was a decision blessed with wisdom; under Catherine's inspired teaching skills his intellect grew like a sapling, reaching out toward all corners of Man's knowledge. Like a good son he wanted most of all to be with me, of course, and earnestly I assured him that soon there would be a new house in a beautiful wooded canyon, and that within its sturdy walls our little family would be together at last.

But all these domestic matters were petty trifles, and the rolling of the drums of war but a feeble murmur in the distance. The supreme adventure of my life, the quest for my lost father, was again creeping forward. I had finally found a man who had sailed on the *Bold Venture*. Only a lowly cabin boy was old Ned Holloway, his dim intelligence nearly extinguished by old age and senility—but from his halting recollections I managed to extract some priceless information.

The *Bold Venture*'s original owner-master had operated the ship between Atlantic, Caribbean and Gulf Coast ports for some years, then had sold the vessel in 1842, at which time Ned, too, had left the crew. A stinging disappointment here: Ned's time of service failed by just one year to coincide with the period in which I was interested—the spring of 1843. But a minor mystery was cleared up. My letters of inquiry to maritime companies had produced no results, and here was the reason: the *Bold Venture* was a privately owned vessel. Yet another vexing puzzle remained. If the second owner had put the ship into service to the Pacific Coast after 1842, as was obviously the case, why could no one in California ports recall ever having seen it? A cold fear gripped the pit of my stomach—but was resolutely suppressed. The *Californios*

450

paid remarkably little attention to the comings and goings of ships; even the customs officials at Monterey incredibly kept no records.

But there was more from Ned Holloway. After much hemming and hawing he succeeded in calling to mind the name of the man who had become the *Bold Venture*'s second owner—one Captain Lionel Roberson—and the fact that Captain Roberson had lived when ashore at a certain boardinghouse catering to seafaring men, in Gloucester, Massachusetts. I had a start now, something to work on at last. I sat down immediately and wrote to Captain Roberson.

In the summer of 1847, after more than a year of the agonizing torture of waiting, came a reply—not from the good captain, but from the proprietress of the house in Gloucester. She informed me that Captain Roberson had not lived there for several years, having removed himself to Panama and taken up residence there at a place called the Mariners' Union. I clutched this letter to my bosom and breathed a prayer of thanks to a helpful lady in Massachusetts whom I would never see, but who would live affectionately in my heart forever.

Then I took up my pen once more.

Dear Captain Roberson (I wrote): My name is Lucius Hargrave, and I desperately seek information concerning a ship called the Bold Venture...

My hand trembled so that I could barely form the letters.

(15)

ON JANUARY 30, 1847, an item of passing interest appeared in the *California Star*, the first newspaper in the little bayside village of Yerba Buena and only the second of two in the vast new U.S. possession. After a brief *Whereas*, which explained that Yerba Buena was a local name unknown beyond the bay district, the proclamation concluded:

> *Therefore, to prevent confusion and mistakes in public documents, and that the town may have the advantage of the name given on the public map,*
> *It is hereby ordained that the name of San Francisco shall hereafter be used in all official communications and public documents or records appertaining to the town.*

> *Washington A. Bartlett*
> *Chief Magistrate*

Thus did a young naval officer who had been appointed temporary civilian governor of a remote colonial outpost place his stamp on history.

And in the summer Jasper Hawkes, in keeping with the spirit of new beginnings and awash in the wave of optimism that flooded the community, added a few more improvements to his inn, threw away the old Hawk's Nest sign, and renamed his establishment the New American Hotel.

The world took little notice of this development, and still less of the fact that in September of that year, on a day of sparkling sunshine and crisp sea breeze, Jasper Hawkes and Delia Walsh were married. Something had been decided between them, which was that in this day of rising hope and expectations of an undefined greatness hovering on the horizon, a hitherto neglected flower must be to some small degree cultivated: respectability.

Then on a drizzly day in December the proprietor of the New American, sitting at ease at his own bar—he had a hired bartender now—glanced up at someone who had just come in, and grinned as he recognized an old friend. He jumped up and bounded toward the newcomer, hand extended.

"Good Lord, Lucius 'Argrave! Ain't seen you since before the war!"

Lucius shook hands casually. "Hello, Jasper. How are you?"

"My, my, Delia's goin' to be tickled pink to see ya! How are things, buddy-boy? How's the missus?"

"Fine, fine, couldn't be better."

"Me and Delia are married now too, y'know."

"Yes, so I heard. From Ricardo Cortina. I got the feeling Ricardo wasn't absolutely overjoyed with that development."

"Yes, well . . . things change, y'know?"

"That they do."

Jasper grabbed Lucius by the elbow. "So come sit down, Lucius, 'ave a drink on the house. I'll fetch Delia."

Lucius allowed himself to be led to his old table in the corner, and took his usual chair. "Just passing by—can't stay but a minute. Want to talk a little business with you."

"Oh, all right." Jasper took a seat across the table. "What's on yer mind?"

"What's on my mind is the five hundred dollars you owe me."

Jasper was taken aback. "Oh." He rubbed his chin musingly. "Well, uh, this is kind o' sudden, Lucius. You need it right now?"

"It was a short-term loan. That was two years ago."

"Yes, well . . ." Jasper grinned. "Time sure does fly by, don't it?"

"Understand, Japser, it's not that I don't trust you. But I've been building my new house, and I'm a bit hard up all of a sudden."

"Hmmm. Wouldn't think you'd 'ave that problem, bein' married into one o' the wealthiest families in California."

"The Valadez wealth is in land and cattle. You'd be surprised how short of cash we can be."

"Hmmm." Jasper pondered a moment longer. "Tell you what, Lucius, let me think on it a bit. I'll just run upstairs and tell Delia now—she'd wring my neck if she knew you were 'ere and I 'adn't let 'er know." He was up and hurrying away.

Lucius was busy working on a meal of steak, eggs, and potatoes when Delia came floating toward him, beaming, arms outstretched in welcome.

"Lucius, love! What a thrill to see you!" She was wearing a long silken dress and trailing yards of lace shawl over her shoulders.

"Hello, Delia." Lucius stood up, accepted a huge hug, and, with his hand resting in easy familiarity on her waist, glanced boldly up and down the curvaceous body. "You're looking great. A little heavier. Just a little—not too much."

She giggled. "Careful, Lucius. I'm a respectable married

lady now." She sat down opposite him, smiling and leaning forward so that her opulent breasts were resplendently visible. "But now, tell me, what brings you here?"

"Got business down at the harbor."

"What kind o' business?"

He gave her a mischievous wink. "Harbor business."

She made a face at him. "All right, smarty. How long you goin' to be in town?"

"Depends. Might be a day. Might be a week or more."

"Good. You'll stay here, naturally. I'll get your old room ready for you."

"Well, I don't know ..." The impish glint was still in his eye. "In view of the fact that you're a respectable married lady now, why ..."

This time Delia's laugh was low, sensuous, and seductive. "You know how I feel about you, Lucius, honey. Say the word, and I'll find a way. Jasper's easy to fool."

Lucius took a big mouthful of food and winked at her again.

Jasper was back in a few minutes, beaming. "Well, well, you two talkin' about old times?" He pulled out a chair and sat down.

"No, we're talkin' about things to come," Delia said dryly.

"Good!" Jasper said with enthusiasm. "Always look ahead. That's the ticket."

Delia's eyes were fixed on the visitor. "So how are things at home, Lucius? How's the little wifey?"

"She's fine. Eager to move into our new home. Beautiful place it is too, up against the mountains on the west side of the valley. And it's practically all done. We can move in anytime."

"What's holding you up?"

"Dolores. She's about to produce another baby."

"Oh, that's nice! Congratulations!"

"This time it'll be a son." Lucius's eyes went dreamy. "To have *two* sons ... *that'll* be something."

"And how's the little girl? What's her name?"

"Elena. Fourteen months old and jabbers a blue streak. Mostly Spanish and Indian, picked up from the servants. Can't understand a word she says. But she's an angel, one of the two most beautiful girl-children in California."

"Who's the other one?"

"My brother Isaac's little girl, Martha."

Delia studied Lucius's face. "You're gettin' to be quite the family man, aren't you?"

"Always have been. Family means everything to me."

Lucius had finished his meal, and Jasper took this as a cue to turn the conversation back to business.

"About that little matter we were discussin', Lucius . . . I'm sorry it's been so long. We ain't seen much of you lately, and . . . time sort o' slips by . . ." He had taken some papers out of his pocket. "Then, too, I 'ave a lot o' the same problems you 'ave—short o' cash most o' the time. So I was wonderin' . . ."

Jasper unfolded his papers and laid them out on the table. "I was wonderin' if you'd be willin' to accept some property deeds as settlement on my debt."

"What kind of property?" Lucius's tone indicated a distinct lack of enthusiasm.

"City lots. Down near the waterfront."

"City lots?" Lucius scowled. "What the hell city you talking about, Jasper?"

"San Francisco. It's goin' to be a big place one o' these days, Lucius. They've 'ad a survey and laid out streets, and—"

"Streets?! I haven't seen any streets."

"Well, not out 'ere yet. But down by the waterfront they got Montgomery Street, and Clay, and Washington, and—"

"Good God!" Lucius leaned back and rolled his eyes toward the ceiling. "I need *money*, Jasper, not goddamn empty patches of sand dunes—"

"Look 'ere, Lucius, just look 'ere . . ." Jasper thrust the papers toward Lucius for inspection. "I'm offerin' you eight lots. Three on Montgomery, three on Clay, and two on Kearney. Bought 'em last summer, paid fifty dollars apiece—"

"You're a damn fool, Jasper. You got money to throw around like that, you ought to pay your debts. Anyway, that's only four hundred dollars' worth."

"But they'll be worth two or three times that much some day, you mark my words. Look 'ere, I've written your name in, transferrin' ownership to you. Now, you 'ang onto 'em, and one o' these days you'll be glad you did."

Lucius sighed, and gave Delia a long-suffering look. She gave him back a sympathetic smile.

"Might as well take 'em, Lucius, honey. Better to have sand dunes than nothin' a-tall."

Lucius picked up the papers and stuffed them carelessly in his pocket. "Oh, all right. Put the meal on my bill, will you? I'll be back tonight."

"Where you goin'?" Jasper wanted to know.

"Down to the harbor. Got to meet a ship."

"What ship? What for?"

"Don't ask, Jasper, he don't want to tell," Delia said.

Lucius was on his feet. "A certain ship that ought to be bringing me a certain letter. Just might be the most important letter of my life."

"You *see*?" Delia said knowingly to Jasper.

Lucius chuckled, gave Jasper a playful slap on the shoulder, went around the table and bestowed an antiseptic kiss on Delia's forehead.

"Thanks for the hospitality, friends. See you later." With a smile and a quick wave of his hand he departed.

After he was gone Jasper and Delia sat for a few moments in pensive silence.

"Wonder what the devil 'e's up to," Jasper murmured.

"We'll probably never know," Delia said wistfully. "He's a mystery, that one."

(16)

JUSTIN HARGRAVE was eight years old on Tuesday the twenty-eighth of December, and festivities were planned at the house at Ponderosa Hill—a fancy dinner, a big birthday cake, and presents. Homemade gifts had been lovingly prepared for him by Abby and Byron and Martha; there was a special package full of little treasures from Mama Sarah in far-off Indiana, which had been received a month before and saved for the occasion; and from Isaac and Catherine came something that had been a year in the planning and acquiring—a set of books, all his own.

The day was dark and glowering with the threat of a winter storm, but the house glowed in the warmth of a blazing fire in the big stone fireplace, and the children's animated voices shut out the moan of cold wind that swept through the pine forests and climbed toward the snow-covered peaks of the Sierras far to the east.

In observance of the special occasion Isaac had promised to come home from the mill early in the afternoon. He arrived a little past two o'clock, and when he came in Catherine started toward him, smiling a greeting. Then she stopped short, surprised by the strange look on his face and the realization that someone was with him. The other man was a Spaniard with a heavy black mustache. He stood just inside the door gripping his hat, his dark eyes darting.

"You remember Dolores's cousin, Ricardo Cortina, don't you, Catherine?" Isaac said to her.

"Oh, of course!" She smiled and held out her hand to him—then the smile died suddenly as she was struck by a frightening thought. "Is anything wrong, Ricardo? Is it Dolores?"

"No, no, Dolores is all right, *señora*. That is, as far as I know." Then Ricardo became hesitant. "It is, uh...Lucio. Something strange seems to be—"

The children had clustered around in curiosity. Justin, recognizing the stranger as someone vaguely connected with Lucius, gazed expectantly up at him.

"Sir? Did you bring me a birthday present from my papa?"

Ricardo became acutely uncomfortable. "Well, you see, your father, he is, uh...he is away on business right now, and uh..."

"Excuse us, children," Catherine said crisply. "I'm going to show Señor Cortina to the guest room. I'm sure he's tired from a long journey. Will you come this way, Ricardo?"

She led him to a room at the back of the house, then turned to confront him. "What is it? What's happened?"

Isaac, having followed them in, closed the door softly behind him. Ricardo licked his lips and began.

"It is a difficult thing to tell, *señora*. I do not know what has come over Lucio. He is...well, to start at the beginning...last week I brought my family to Las Sombras to spend the Christmas season with Don Lorenzo and Dolores. I found them in a state of deep anxiety. It seems Lucio had gone to San Francisco on some sort of business the week before, intending to be away a short time only. He had not returned. Dolores is expecting at any moment, you know, and she was most distressed that Lucio was not with her. I left immediately to go and see if I could determine what was the matter. I went

457

to some mutual friends we have in San Francisco—a Señor Hawkes and his wife—they operate a small hotel there. They are nice people, and run a very respectable—"

"Yes, yes, I understand," Catherine said, her voice tight with impatience. "And what did you find?"

"I found...a puzzle. The Hawkeses said that Lucio had been there several nights, spending his days at the harbor waiting for a certain ship. He was expecting a letter. What ship...a letter from whom...nobody knew. Then one night he did not return. The Hawkeses had assumed he had finished his business and gone back home. They were most alarmed when they learned he had not. So was I, of course. I could not comprehend—"

"So what did you do, Ricardo?" Catherine urged him on.

"The Hawkeses and I began a search. Well, I will not keep you in suspense—we found him. He had taken up residence in the back room of a filthy hovel of a saloon on the waterfront. He had been there for days. He was in a state of extreme drunkenness, barricaded in his room, taking almost no food, refusing to come out or to talk to anyone except the saloonkeeper. We tried to speak to him through the door, to reason with him. He shouted at us in great anger, telling us to leave him alone. Señora Hawkes tried to talk to him. He insulted her shamefully, called her a...an obscene name which I will not repeat. It is a strange and painful thing to report. The poor man seems to have taken leave of his senses."

Ricardo paused. Pale and tight-lipped, Catherine waited for him to continue.

"It was Christmas night when we found him. I was desperate to know what to do. I went back to the hotel with the Hawkeses, and we sat for hours discussing the problem. At last we concluded that I must seek your assistance. The next morning I sent my servant galloping back to Las Sombras to tell them not to worry, we would bring Lucio home as soon as possible. Then I left to come here. Meanwhile the Hawkeses will continue to watch Lucio as best they can."

Ricardo suddenly became apologetic, looking pleadingly at Catherine and twisting his hat in his hands. "I am sorry to burden you with this, *señora*. But I thought you or Señor Isaac might know what is wrong, and perhaps...what we can do about it..." His voice trailed off.

"Well, we don't," Isaac said grimly. "But it was good of you to come, anyway."

"I was afraid I could not find you. But some people at the

458

fort of Señor Sutter gave me good directions. Fortunately you are well known."

Catherine and Isaac were staring at each other.

"What can it mean?" she said in a trembling voice.

He shook his head in bleak helplessness. "God knows."

"You'll go, of course?" she asked him.

"Sure I will. Ricardo and I have already talked about it. We'll leave early in the morning." He hesitated. "Wish you could come with us."

Her response was instantaneous. "I *will* come with you."

Ricardo shot her a surprised look. "But, *señora*, what about your children?"

"We have friends living near Sutter's Fort. We can leave them there."

Isaac nodded in quick eagerness. "Yes, the Kendrickses. They'll be happy to keep 'em a few days. Or . . . however long it takes."

Ricardo was frowning. "This place where Lucio is, *señora* . . . it is not a very pleasant place for ladies—"

"You don't understand, Ricardo," Isaac said. "Y'see, Catherine has a strong influence on Lucius, maybe more than anybody else in the world. He, uh . . ." Isaac groped in his mind for an explanation. "Well . . . he respects her."

Ricardo nodded solemnly. "Ah. I see."

Through the house sounded the shrill voices of children, and a burst of laughter. Catherine took a deep breath and smoothed her hair.

"So, we leave first thing in the morning," she said. "In the meantime we'll be happy and cheerful. It's Justin's birthday."

The two men nodded assent, and stepped aside for her as she moved across the room to the door, and went out smiling.

(17)

DON LORENZO VALADEZ sat dreaming of his boyhood days in Spain.

It was dusk, and the light was a blend of pale amber on the

western horizon and darkening shades of blue above. From somewhere came the peaceful sound of a strummed guitar. Up there against the sky a young shepherd cupped his hands to his mouth and flung a long echoing call across the brown hills. Don Lorenzo jerked spasmodically and shouted back.

"*Aiee-yee-ee!*"

Someone put a gentle hand on his shoulder. "Wake up, Papa. You are dreaming."

Don Lorenzo opened his eyes and found his daughter Margarita bending over him, her face pale and drawn. It was night, and he was in his small bedroom in his big house in California, and the light came not from the sky but from a lamp standing on a polished tabletop. The shepherd had vanished, the music faded and gone. They belonged to Old Spain, ten thousand miles and half a century away.

"Yes, I was dreaming," Don Lorenzo said peevishly. "I am an old, old man. What is there for me but dreaming?"

"They have come, Papa," Margarita said, "Ricardo is here."

He glanced sharply up at her. "He has brought Lucio?"

Then Ricardo was there, taking Margarita's place before the patriarch. "Yes, Don Lorenzo, I have brought Lucio. With us also are Señor Isaac and Señora Catherine."

"*Dios mío!* Doña Catherine, too?!"

"I am ashamed to say it, Don Lorenzo. It was she who put an end to the difficulty that was confounding us all." Ricardo sank wearily into a chair.

"Well then, tell me what has happened," Don Lorenzo commanded. "The reports I have received have been most baffling. Why has it taken so long?"

Ricardo took a deep breath and began. "First, bad weather. Terrible storms kept us stranded for two days at Señor Sutter's fort. When we finally arrived back in San Francisco we found Lucio still withdrawn from human society, barricaded in his hovel of a room in the tavern. Again we knocked on the door and pleaded with him. First I, then Señor Isaac. In vain. He shouted at us to go away. We appealed to the proprietor. He was no help. He said, 'That man has paid his rent, leave him be.' The scoundrel was interested in nothing but his money. We told him we would break down the door. He said he would take a gun and shoot us if we damaged his property. Then we brought in Señora Catherine. She spoke to Lucio through the door for a minute or two, very quiet, very calm, told him we had come not to reprove but to comfort. She asked him please to open the door. He did so, meek as a lamb. He was in terrible condition. Very weak, barely able to stand. We took him to the Hawkeses' hotel for a night of rest. The next morning, he was no better, so we thought we had better bring him right home. Señor Isaac rode behind him on the horse all the way, holding him upright."

"Where is he now?" Don Lorenzo asked.

"Put to bed. He is a sick man. Señor Isaac and Señora Catherine are resting also. They are very tired. So am I." Ricardo sighed, and slumped in his chair. "It is a strange thing..."

"Tell me, Ricardo..." Don Lorenzo leaned forward and fixed piercing eyes on the other man. "Do we yet know the reason for it?"

"We have asked Lucio this again and again. He gives us no answer. He only keeps mumbling to himself. 'It is over,' he says. 'All this way, all this time, for nothing.' We do not know what it means."

Don Lorenzo was scowling. "That is all?"

"Well, there was one clue. Maybe it was a clue, I do not know. I picked up a piece of paper lying on the floor of the room. It was a letter, addressed to Lucio. I suppose it must have been the letter he had been waiting for. I handed it to Señor Isaac, and he showed it to Lucio and asked if it was something important. Lucio flew into a rage, snatched the letter away and shouted at us, saying we had no right to read his mail."

"*Had* you read it? Either of you?"

Ricardo shrugged apologetically. "I only wish we had been as ill-mannered as Lucio accused us of being."

Don Lorenzo was silent for a moment. "Ricardo... have you heard what happened here today?"

Ricardo's face went dark. "Yes. Alfredo informed me."

"Does Lucio know?"

"No. He was in no condition..."

Don Lorenzo grasped the arms of his chair and began to rise. "Well, I will go and convey my thanks and greetings to Señor Isaac and Señora Catherine. Then I will go and have a talk with Lucio."

"Oh no, not tonight, Don Lorenzo. He is a sick man, he—"

"He must know what has happened," Don Lorenzo said

461

sternly. "If he chooses to be secretive with us, that is his affair, but we will not be secretive with him." Something in the old man's tone made it clear that the conversation was closed.

There were flickering shadows on the ceiling, almost invisible in near-darkness.

Lucius opened his eyes, blinked several times, and listened. Was someone there? Had someone spoken to him, or was it another one of the phantom voices that had whispered like cold wind in his ear for days and nights incalculable?

He licked his lips, swallowed painfully, and said, "Where am I?" It was a feeble croak.

"You are at Las Sombras," Don Lorenzo said quietly. "The place that has been your home for more than two years. Have you forgotten it?"

Lucius touched his chin and found an unaccustomed stubble of beard there. "What time is it? What day?"

"Very late. Near midnight. When the sun comes up again it will be Wednesday, the fifth of January, 1848."

Lucius's bloodshot eyes had wandered until they found the speaker. The old man was sitting in a chair by the bed, watching him.

"Where's Dolores?" Lucius asked.

"She is not here."

"I want to see Dolores. Where is she?"

"She has been taken to the home of my eldest daughter, Teresa de la Rio. She will receive good care there. She needs rest and quiet."

"Good God, isn't it quiet enough in *this* tomb?!" Lucius growled. Then his eyes narrowed suddenly in wariness. "What is it, Don Lorenzo? Has something happened to her?"

"Yes, indeed, something has. Be still, and I will tell you." Don Lorenzo pulled his chair a little closer.

"Your child was born on Saturday, the first day of the new year."

Lucius waited, hardly breathing.

"Your wish was granted. It was a boy."

Lucius reached out and grasped the older man's arm. "Something's wrong, isn't it? Badly wrong. Tell me."

Don Lorenzo nodded. "He is dead, Lucio. He lived three days only."

Lucius stared, the muscles of his jaw working soundlessly. Then he put his hand over his forehead and gripped hard, covering his eyes.

"We tried," Don Lorenzo said gently. "We did what we could. Someone was by his side morning, noon and night. We kept watching and waiting, hoping we were mistaken, and that somehow he'd win the fight. Once he opened his little eyes wide and seemed to look at me, and they were so bright and clear, I thought, oh, *Dios mío*, a miracle, a miracle . . . but it was not to be. He was . . . how you say? . . . not well-formed. There was no chance."

Lucius uncovered his eyes and hastily wiped at them with his fingers as he turned his head to face the wall.

"Three days . . ." He could barely choke out the words. "How can three days contain a life? A wonderful . . . miraculous creation . . . gone in three days . . ."

"All things are for cause, Lucio," Don Lorenzo said solemnly. "God presides over the world. He watches, He observes all, and He rules with justice and wis—"

"That is not true," Lucius snapped. "There is no observing, no ruling, and no justice."

"Are you denying God, Lucio?"

"What God finds it amusing to play games with helpless creatures? Why does He give some of us more life than we need or deserve, and others so pitifully little? Justice would have been better served if He had taken the rest of the time allotted to me and given it to the child. That little fellow could have used it to good advantage, but I have no further need of it, no need at all—"

"Lucio! You must not speak this way, I forbid it! It is as sinful to damn life as it is to damn God—"

"Life! God!" Lucius cried out in a voice grown powerful with a passion of fury. "You are frauds, and I damn you both! Only death is true!"

"Silence!" Don Lorenzo roared. He was on his feet and towering despite his diminutive stature. "You are wallowing in self-pity, Lucio. You have sinned, and when God pronounces punishment upon you, you react like a spoiled child, seeing it as unjust cruelty—"

"Oh, that is beautiful, Don Lorenzo!" Lucius shrieked with wild laughter. "I have sinned, so the just and merciful God punishes me by killing an infant. Or maybe he was a sinner too. A fellow can get into a lot of mischief in three days, eh? And how about Dolores? Is *she* a sinner?"

He stopped, suddenly aware of a wider audience. The door of the room had been opened and faces were clustered there, wide eyes bright with alarm.

463

"Come in, come in!" Lucius struggled up on an elbow and waved an arm in cheery greeting. "We were just having a little theological discussion here. I was pointing out to Don Lorenzo some of the flaws of the religious dogma he holds so dear. And of course he's beginning to take offense, because in this polite Old World society one doesn't challenge the views of one's elders, does one? Let alone the views of the Church..." He lay back, panting and exhausted.

"Blasphemy in my house!" Don Lorenzo said, his voice shaking. "I will not endure it!"

The others had come into the room now, the tense and rigid faces gathered round, staring down at Lucius.

He beamed at them. "Come on, folks, don't be bashful, join the discussion." He examined the faces, searching. "Alfredo, come. Are you there, Alfredo?"

"I am here, Lucio." The big man stepped forward.

"Do not talk to him, Alfredo," Don Lorenzo commanded.

"Ah, come, Alfredo, talk to me," Lucius pleaded teasingly. "You are my children's godfather, I trust in you. I hang on your every word."

Alfredo leaned over the bed. "Lucio, you are in bad condition. You must not talk now, you must rest—"

"No, no, Alfredo, we will talk now, because there are things I have to know, and only you can tell me." Lucius was up on an elbow again, clutching Alfredo's sleeve. "Did you discharge your duties to my little son?"

"To the very best of my ability, Lucio."

"Good, good. More than that I couldn't ask. Now tell me... was he baptized?"

"He was, Lucio. Praise be to God, who was merciful in that respect. Little Juan was baptized before he died. His soul is safe in heaven."

"Ah! I *knew* I could depend on you, Alfredo." There was something in Lucius's voice that sounded like mockery.

Alfredo chose to ignore it. He made a move to settle Lucius back into bed. "Rest now. We will talk further tomorrow."

"Wait, Alfredo, one more question." Lucius held onto the other man's arm. "Did you bring the priest here, or did you take the baby to the priest?"

Alfredo hesitated. "We will talk about it tomor—"

"Answer me, Alfredo!" Lucius barked. "The child was too weak to be taken out, wasn't he? So naturally you brought the priest here."

Alfredo took a long time to answer. "You are looking for

464

someone to blame, aren't you, Lucio?"

"You took him out," Lucius said grimly. "A weak helpless infant, clinging to life by a thread—you took him out in the raw winter weather, miles and miles on horseback—"

"You are being unreasonable, Lucio." Anger had begun to creep into Alfredo's voice. "Padre Mendoza is himself clinging to life by a thread. He is bedridden, cannot go out anymore. We had no choice."

"Is there no other priest, for God's sake?!"

"There is Padre Raimundo, but he was away, making the rounds of Indian villages. We were forced to make a decision. We could take the baby to Padre Mendoza, or we could wait, and risk seeing the little one die unbaptized—"

"And is *that* such a tragedy?!" Lucius scoffed. "What is that, damnation?"

"Well, not exactly. The soul would be in limbo, it would—"

"Damnation, my friend, *damnation*! That will be *your* reward!"

With a swift movement Alfredo wrenched himself free of Lucius's grasp and stepped back.

"We made the decision as best we could," he said in a hard voice. "I think we made the right one—the child was dying. But, right or wrong, we did the best we could, and we did it with no help from the father. *He* had chosen to abandon his family in time of trial, and had gone off to wallow in filth and—"

"You know nothing about it, nothing!" Lucius was sitting up, the veins in his temples throbbing with fury. "You know nothing about anything! You were born in ignorance and you will die in ignorance!"

"I know all I need to know about *you*, *señor*!" Alfredo shouted. "I know you are a liar and a cheat, and an infidel who pretended to accept our church but has all the time despised it. You married my cousin Dolores for wealth, but you despise her as well. You despise all of us, everything we believe—"

"Murderer!" Lucius bellowed. "For the sake of your damnable religious rituals you have killed my child—"

"Yes, Lucio, you are looking for someone to blame. Point the accusing finger at someone else, and maybe it will make you seem innocent, eh?" Alfredo leaned down and thrust his face close to Lucius's. "But if you are really looking for guilt, look to yourself."

Lucius clutched at him. Alfredo stepped back, eluding the grasping hands.

"You bastard . . ." Lucius was quivering with rage, his voice a hoarse whisper. "You bastard, I'll *kill* you!"

He was up out of bed and hurling himself at Alfredo. The big man moved with surprising quickness, stepping deftly aside. The others in the room moved back in instinctive horror at the emergence of fury and violence. Lucius swung at Alfredo and missed, staggered, turned and prepared to lunge again. Alfredo waited, crouched in a fighting stance, ready now to abandon evasive tactics and meet his adversary head-on.

Then Isaac stepped between them, grasping Lucius by the arms and holding on tenaciously. "You stop that, Lucius, just stop it, right now—"

"You!" Lucius raged. "Will I never be done with you, you *thief*?" With a groaning effort he broke away from Isaac's grasp. "I saved you from a life of stagnation and led you out into the world, and what thanks do I get for it? You steal from me everything I've ever—"

"Lucius, be still." It was Catherine's voice, low, calm, and full of authority, and it brought instant quiet to the room.

Lucius hung his head. He was panting heavily, swaying in exhaustion, and trembling. "What am I to do?" he mumbled. His bleary eyes, restless as a caged animal's, searched the room. "I've got to get out of here . . ."

Catherine turned to the others. "Leave us, please. All of you. I want to talk to Lucius alone, if you don't mind."

Obediently and in odd silence they all filed out. Isaac, the last to go, paused in the doorway and looked back at Catherine.

"See if you can find out why he called me a thief," he said, and closed the door.

Lucius sat on the edge of the bed while Catherine stood in the center of the room and looked at him. No one spoke for a long moment.

"Why don't you scold me?" he said finally. "Isn't that what schoolteachers usually do when people misbehave?"

She went on studying him, her eyes distant and pensive. "Sometimes I find it hard to believe that you and Isaac are related. He's so solid, so reliable. You're like the will-o'-the-wisp, fluttering in every little breeze. Nobody can get a grip on you."

"That's a good beginning," he said sullenly. "Go on."

She complied. "Alfredo was right about the baby, you

466

know. I've heard how it was. They were cautious and prudent, they weren't reckless. They waited until the very last minute, when it was plain to see he couldn't last through another night, before they finally decided to take him."

Lucius sat stolidly silent, eyes down. Catherine went on relentlessly.

"That's not all Alfredo's right about, Lucius. He's right about you. These good people offered you their friendship. A daughter of this house consented to be your wife, and has never asked for anything more than a chance to love you devotedly. And you accepted everything, all the benefits of being a member of one of the most distinguished families in California. But it was all nothing more than a maneuver on your part, wasn't it? Such a deep commitment, involving so much from so many people—and for no better reason than personal advantage. Alfredo's right, isn't he? You're a liar and a cheat."

Lucius sighed. "Yes, Alfredo's right. Don Lorenzo's right. They're all right. I stand revealed in my utter magnificent *wrongness*. I am alone, surrounded by enemies."

"No you're not. Because in spite of it all, there are people who love you. And most of all, Dolores. She loves you fiercely, I know it. The only enemy you have is yourself."

Lucius stared at a dark corner of the room and remained silent. Catherine came and sat beside him.

"What has happened to you, Lucius?" she said gently. "Won't you tell me?"

"I've thrown my life away," he said. "It's all wasted, all useless, and I'm a miserable fool."

"You keep talking like that. Is that *all* you can say?"

"I gave up everything and came to California in search of...some phantom or other...but it's not here. There's nothing here for me. Nothing anywhere."

She gave it up. "All right. I'm tired of begging you to tell me what's in your mind, I'll never ask again. If you're content to have us all think you're just a capricious lunatic, fine, we'll think it. But you owe Dolores something better than that."

"They've taken her away from me. And rightly so—I was never any good for her, anyway—"

"That's nonsense, Lucius. She's your wife, and if you'll just *look* at her you'll discover something rare and wonderful, something few men ever find in a lifetime of searching. She'd be so *good* for you, if you'd only *let* her."

467

Lucius had turned toward Catherine and was staring at her with a wild look in his eye.

"Write her a letter, Lucius," she went on. "Beg her forgiveness, and ask her to come to you, to the new house that's all built and ready. It's not too late, it's never too late as long as you're—"

She stopped with a little shock of surprise. Lucius had caught up both her hands in his.

"Catherine . . . let's go back."

"What?!"

"Back to that little valley way over yonder somewhere in the Rocky Mountains."

"Why, you're out of your mi—"

"Just us, Catherine, nobody else." He pulled her closer and the words came rushing out as if beyond thought or control. "I'll build us a little house, and we'll live in that beautiful valley where we spent the only two days of our lives that ever meant anything for either of us—"

"Stop it, Lucius, I refuse to listen to any more of this—"

"Please, Catherine. It'll be like dwelling in paradise—"

"No!"

The cold word stabbed him. He fell silent. She wrenched free of his grasp and was on her feet.

"You're a married man, and I'm a married woman, and we both have responsibilities to our families—but there's no point in my standing here telling you things you already know. So I'll tell you something that maybe you *don't* know."

He waited, balanced between despair and some irrational hope.

"I'm not just a married woman, Lucius. I'm deeply in love with my husband."

Lucius shook his head as if unable to comprehend her words.

"Oh, I know what you think," she said. "You think I married Isaac out of sheer decency, because I couldn't bear to hurt him. Well, that's true in a way; I did. In fact I was terribly noble about it. I was a heroine out of a book. But all my lovely nobility was wasted, Lucius, because, you know what? Love came. Slowly, almost without my realizing it, it crept up on me. And it's better than anything I've ever known."

Lucius stared, caught up in a trance. "It can't be," he breathed. "He's so . . . so . . ."

"*Weak* is the word you're looking for." She permitted herself a small smile. "You think he's weak. But what you

468

mistake for weakness is something else altogether. It's kindness, gentleness, it's what you thought *I* had too much of—decency. But it's not weakness. He's as strong and sturdy as a California oak. He'll outlive you, because it'll take a lot more to do him in than it'll take to do you in." She took a step back, and finished in a soft voice that did not quite conceal a hard edge.

"He's a better man than you, Lucius."

There was a time of frozen silence in which neither moved. Then with a long breath Lucius let his eyes fall away from hers. His shoulders sagged. With his forearms on his knees he leaned far forward and fixed his gaze on the floor.

Catherine sat down in a chair. "I'm sorry." Her voice was drained of strength. "I think you deserved that, but . . . I'm sorry, I truly am."

"That's all right," he said evenly. "You're the schoolteacher, you did your job. I thought I was going to get a scolding, and I got a good blistering instead. That's fine. It hurt plenty. It'll do me good."

She spoke to him like a patient mother to a wayward child. "Will you behave yourself now?"

"Oh yes. I won't ever dare misbehave again." There was a little banter in his voice, but it was strained, feeble, halfhearted.

"I hope I can depend on that. Because I've got a family to take care of, and I haven't time for such insane carryings-on as this."

"Right. Absolutely not."

She got up and moved across the room to the door. His eyes followed her. With her hand on the doorknob she looked back at him.

"Are you all right, Lucius?"

"My son, my daughter, and my true heart's wife," he murmured dreamily. "All those precious things he has, and besides . . . he's a better man than I."

"Lucius, I am going to settle that account with you, and I'm going to do it as fairly as it can possibly be done. That's a promise."

He went on looking at her in a curiously absent way.

"Are you all right now?" she asked.

He nodded. "I'm all right. I'll try to get some sleep. In the morning I'll come out and apologize to everybody for everything."

Her eyes lay mistily upon him for a moment longer.

"I love you, Lucius," she whispered, and smiled. "Like a sister I love you."

She blew him a kiss and went out, and he sat for a long time staring at the door she had closed softly behind her.

(18)

FROM THE JOURNAL of Lucius Hargrave:

I have sought the nadir of my existence, and found it. I have cornered the dragon of despair, grasped him by the throat, felt his claws tearing my flesh, and fought with the desperation of one caught in a struggle to the death. My recollections of it all are mercifully dim. I recall being dismayed at the power of the monster, and thinking: I am vanquished at last. I felt the icy touch of doom chilling my blood, and the curious sense of tranquility that comes with the thought that there is after all no great difference between surviving and perishing, victory and defeat.

The ordeal began on the San Francisco waterfront in the closing days of 1847. When I came to my senses again—at Las Sombras, exhausted and bleeding and barely alive—it was well into January of the following year. Several weeks of my life had been submerged in a nightmarish black void in which my soul had been rent by horrid cruelties. I cannot dwell on these injuries now. I can only list them with the emotionless detachment of a clerk itemizing an inventory.

Item: the little son for whom Dolores and I had waited so long was born, lived out his life in three days, and left us. I was fighting the demon in San Francisco, and could not reach him. We never saw each other.

Item: Dolores they took away, and my little daughter Elena. I had suffered hideous misfortune, and it was evidently

a sin in the eyes of my rigid Span...
Now they would punish me. Wiu...
admitted no trace of compassion they pr...
upon my luckless head—banishment. I was ...
entourage consisting of the young Indian, Pabi...
servant, three or four *vaqueros*, and a few horses and ...
and was sent off across the valley to live in lordly loneliness n.
the big new house that had been lovingly built for a bride who
would apparently never set foot in it.

Item: the greatest loss I mention last, the terrible stroke of
the dragon's claws that had left me temporarily insensible to
all else. From Panama had come a letter from Captain Lionel
Roberson. Yes, he was the former master of a brig called the
Bold Venture. Yes, he distinctly remembered a passenger
who was known as Father Xavier, and his black manservant,
Camus. They had boarded the ship at New Orleans in the
spring of 1843, bound for Monterey, California. It was a
voyage never completed. The final port of call was Panama,
from which the *Bold Venture* departed in late summer. On the
night of the 28th of August it foundered in a storm one
hundred miles off the southern coast of Mexico. Throughout a
horror that lasted five hours Father Xavier had behaved with
magnificent courage, staving off panic among the other
passengers with his calm and comforting words. All in vain. At
dawn on the 29th the *Bold Venture* went down. Captain
Roberson and two of his sailors managed to cling to a bit of
wreckage for three days before being pulled out of the sea by
another ship. In a distinct tone of embarrassment—as if he
were all too well aware that his story made a mockery of the
noble tradition of self-sacrifice expected of sea captains—he
concluded his sorry tale with the information that, besides the
two sailors and himself, there were no other survivors.

So there it was. My long quest was ended by a scrawled
letter from a confessed coward, and my life had lost its central
purpose.

Things prospered at the new *rancho* without any help from
me. The house was a fine one indeed, a nice mixture of
Spanish and Southern plantation. Its low front veranda looked
out past great twisted sycamores growing along a little
rock-strewn creek to sunny pasturelands dotted with oaks,
beyond. Pablo would have surprised and delighted me had I
been capable of either surprise or delight. Always sullen and
withdrawn in Don Lorenzo's house, he became energetic and

en almost cheerful, preparing a garden plot, small orchard, and laying out the beginnings of a planting. He kept me well-fed with his expert cooking, and looked after me with solicitous care. My *vaqueros* came, reporting progress. Calves were born, the herd was growing; soon we might begin the production of hides and tallow.

I nodded and smiled at everything, and took pleasure in nothing. I had not even given the place a name. For a time I busied myself writing to Dolores, assuring her of my love, pleading with her to forgive what she could not understand, and come to me. There were no replies. I was certain my missives were all being intercepted by hostile Valadez hands. No mercy would there be to soften my punishment. I became a hollow man, vacant-eyed and lifeless. Day after endless day I sat on my veranda and gazed out over beautiful tawny hills lying warm under a golden sun, and thought: It is all for naught. Soon I will die.

Three months after the ordeal began it drew to a quiet close. The dragon lay mortally wounded, its life-blood draining away—and I had survived.

On a bright day in March a group of people on horseback came up the trail from the valley and brought their mounts to rest under the sycamores beside the stream. Several *vaqueros* there were, escorting two women. From my chair on the veranda I studied them dully, with little interest, and— oddly—recognized first Dolores's old Indian servant, Rosalia. Perched on a sleepy donkey, she held in her lap my little Elena.

I leaped up, my heart pounding. The other woman had dismounted and was coming toward me—a vision shining like an angel in a dress of pure white, the color Dolores always wore, the only color that came close to matching her character. I rushed toward her and, with a sob catching in my throat, enfolded my wife in my arms.

"You got my letters," I breathed into her ear. "You listened to my heart speaking to you, and you believed. You forgave."

"It is not quite like that, *amado*," she said. "It was Señora Catherine who did it. Señor Isaac brought her to see me. She told me that you have wandered for a long time in some dark wasteland, and must be taken by the hand and led into the light again. And it was I who must lead you. She said you loved me and needed me, and you would die if left alone." She looked at me with that childlike earnestness that so often

472

... see the little stream del Agua Mansa. ... Two miles ... the hills. Follow it, and you will come ... There is a trail along the ... That is what ... not, the travelers dies." "The ... he had ... buenos dias

... see that
... swept away.
... her because she
... believe her was to

... ok from her our beautiful
... rare radiant smiles, gave the

"... ," she said.

How st...e—one moment capriciously cruel, the next kind bey... all deserving. But cruel or kind, it is always, always mysterious.

Through that first night of our reunion, a night of starry silence when the world was stirring beneath the surface with lovemaking and new ardor, I held my young wife in my arms. Her soft yielding body trembled in tender joy under my caress, and over and over she moaned and murmured in my ear, "Oh, Lucio, my Lucio, my golden man, I love you." Heavenly words, drugging the senses.

But the pledge I gave to her was deeper than words, deeper than the act of love itself:

My Lady of Sorrows, you will sorrow no more.

(19)

THE MEXICAN brought his horse to a halt at the top of a little rise and waited for the others to catch up. Then he raised himself in his saddle and pointed toward the wooded mountains.

473

we call Arroy⋯
stream, leading up in⋯
to the house of Don Lucio. ⋯

"I appreciate your help, sir," one ⋯

"It is a pleasure to be of service, *señor. D*⋯ Mexican turned his horse around to go back the way ⋯ come.

The traveler turned to his young companion and smiled. "Almost there," he said.

Lucius was returning to the house from the vineyard when he glanced ahead and saw his brother Isaac coming toward him. He hurried on, his face alight with astonishment.

"Isaac, old chum! What brings you here?!"

Isaac was upon him, pumping his hand and grinning. "Surprise, Lucius! Just passing by, thought I'd drop in and see your new place. And it's a beauty!"

"Passing by? Where from? Where to?"

"Been down to San Francisco to take delivery on some machinery parts I ordered from the East. Tools, boiler plates, saw blades, a cast-iron crank that weighs six hundred pounds—" Isaac chuckled. "It'll cost me a hundred dollars just to get the whole mess hauled up to Ponderosa Hill."

"Good Lord! You're in a building phase again."

"I'll say I am. Goin' to have me a steam-powered sawmill, Lucius. One o' the first in California. And the best."

They walked on toward the house.

"So things are going well with you, then," Lucius said.

"Things are fine with me, Lucius. Things are fine with you too. I can tell."

"Can you?"

"I sure can. We stopped at the house first, of course. I've been talking to Dolores. I've never seen her look so happy, so cheerful. She tells me you and Pablo have quite a little vineyard going."

"Thought we'd try a little winemaking," Lucius said smilingly. "If we run out of food, at least we'll have plenty to drink."

"Well, that's great, Lucius. To be interested in somethin', and to get *on* with it—that's what you've been needin'."

"Is, uh...Catherine with you?" There was wariness in Lucius's question.

"Nope. Justin is."

Lucius paled, and stopped on the path. "*Justin?*"

"Sure. Took him to San Francisco with me. He loved it. Eyes big as saucers, lookin' at everything and everybody, askin' a million questions that I couldn't begin to answer. We stayed at the New American Hotel with your friends the Hawkeses. You should'a' seen Justin sittin' there askin' Mr. Hawkes all about the operation of the hotel. And Mrs. Hawkes—she couldn't keep her eyes off him. Or her hands, either."

"I'll bet," Lucius said dryly. His eyes were searching the house, fifty yards away.

"He's inside, talkin' to Dolores," Isaac said. "He was sittin' there with little Elena on his lap just like a grown-up man, havin' a discussion with Dolores about the meaning of various Spanish words. I tell you, Lucius, at eight that young fella knows more than I did at—"

Lucius put a hand on Isaac's arm and brought them both to a stop. He had caught sight of Justin, who had come out of the house and was standing there gazing at them across the intervening distance.

"Excuse me," Lucius said, and went forward.

For a moment man and boy stood in awkward silence eyeing each other.

"Hello, Justin," Lucius said. "It's really good to see you."

"H'lo, Papa."

"How've you been?"

"Fine."

Lucius's fingers twitched nervously. "Well, uh . . . shall we have a little hug, or . . . would you rather just shake hands?"

Justin thought about it. "I guess we can just shake hands."

"All right."

They shook hands in stiff and solemn dignity. Then, Isaac having come up to them, the three walked on into the house.

Pablo served an afternoon meal in the patio, which, like the one at Las Sombras, was a spacious island of paving and greenery, though enclosed only on three sides by the horseshoe-shaped house.

Isaac fingered the surface of a great oaken table, examining it with sharp professional interest. "Beautiful table," he pronounced. "Beautiful wood."

"It was a present from Uncle Lorenzo," Dolores explained. "I believe it was intended as a—" she shot a hesitant glance at her husband—"a sort of peace-offering to Lucio."

Lucius smiled absently. He had his chin propped on his hands and was watching Justin demolish a plate of beans and rice.

Isaac was still admiring the table. "One o' these days, soon's I get my power mill set up, I'll be cuttin' hardwood too, instead o' just pine and cedar."

"But you've accomplished so much already," Dolores said warmly. "Catherine must be proud."

Isaac shrugged the compliment away. "Whatever I've accomplished is as much her doin' as mine. She encourages me every step o' the way. She says California's growin', movin' ahead. We've got to do the same."

"Yes, I'm sure," Dolores said. She sounded faintly troubled.

Isaac waxed enthusiastic. "Yes, it's growin', all right. So many settlers around Sutter's Fort, they'll have a regular town there pretty soon. And San Francisco too. Every time I go there I see new buildings and more people. Jasper Hawkes figures it'll be a big city someday."

"That is amazing," Dolores said. "Is it not, Lucio?"

With difficulty Lucius pulled his attention away from watching Justin. "Oh, well, Jasper's a dreamer. Always has been."

"And you know what's happened, Lucius?" Isaac said. He had taken a small piece of paper out of his pocket, unfolded it, and handed it to his brother. "Look at this little item out of the San Francisco *Californian*, from the fifteenth of March."

Lucius looked at the clipping with idle interest, and read aloud:

> "*Gold mine found. In the newly made raceway of the sawmill recently erected by Captain Sutter, on the American Fork, gold has been found in considerable quantities. One person brought thirty dollars' worth to New Helvetia, gathered there in a short time. California, no doubt, is rich in mineral wealth...*"

With a disdainful chuckle Lucius stopped reading and handed the clipping back. "Oh, that's just another one of Sutter's harebrained concoctions."

"No, it's true, Lucius. You remember I told you about this fella named John Marshall that Sutter hired? Well, he built this mill up on the American River, and one day he noticed these

476

strange-lookin' bits of yellow in the water—"

Lucius was laughing. "Old chum, Don Lorenzo can name you half a dozen men who've claimed to have found gold in the mountains at one time or another. It's an old California myth."

"Well, maybe." Isaac put the clipping away. "But I got a feelin' this is the real thing."

"Gullibility, old chum," Lucius said with a knowing smile. "That's always been one of your failings."

Justin had finished eating and was sitting quietly waiting for a lull in the conversation. Now it had come.

"Papa?"

"Yes, son?" Lucius leaned eagerly toward the boy.

"How far is it to the waterfall?"

"Just a little ways. Want to go and see it?"

Justin suddenly became shy and hesitant. "Can it be just you and me?"

Lucius blinked. He glanced quickly at Isaac and Dolores. They were silent, watching him.

"Of course it can," he said. "Just the two of us."

Isaac and Dolores exchanged a secret look.

They followed a little path that wandered through fragrant spring-fresh foliage, thickets of willow and alder and birch that lined the banks of the little stream. The boy went first, darting far ahead with the agility of a deer, then waiting for the man to catch up.

Once he paused to announce approvingly, "These are good woods, Papa."

Lucius smiled and started to say, "Glad you like 'em." But Justin had scampered away again.

The waterfall was not much of a fall. At a certain point the stream quickened its pace in response to an invisible pull and then tumbled six feet down a steep moss-slickened granite slope. In the pool below, the water achieved its greatest depth—three feet—took on a blue green tint, and displayed a disposition to linger there awhile before going on. It was a gentle place, and the afternoon air was made drowsy by the soft sounds of water murmuring and tree leaves rustling and the occasional piping of a songbird.

Lucius and Justin sat on a rock at the edge of the pool and watched little bubbles of foam trace aimless patterns on the surface of the water.

"I like it here," Justin decided.

477

"That's good. Glad you do." Lucius watched the boy out of the corner of his eye.

"What's the name of your house, Papa?"

"Uh...don't know. Haven't really thought much about a name."

"I had an idea for a name. There was a Mexican man who helped us find the way here. He said this place is called Arroyo del Agua Mansa. I asked Tía Dolores what that meant, and she said it meant Little Stream of Quiet Waters, or Still Waters—something like that. So I thought maybe we could call it Rancho del Agua Mansa. Don't you think that'd be a good name for our house?"

Lucius swallowed hard as he studied the boy's earnest face. "You say *we*, Justin. You say *our* house. What does that mean?"

Justin locked his arms around his knees and gazed intently at the surface of the pool. "I've come to live with you, Papa. If you still want me to."

"*Want* you to?! Of course I want you to, Justin, I...I've always wanted us to be...to be..." Lucius searched in vain for the right words.

"I know, Papa."

There was a short silence.

"Whose idea was it?" Lucius asked.

"It was my idea. Well...maybe it was partly Aunt Catherine's idea, and Uncle Isaac's too, I guess. One time Uncle Isaac took Abby and Byron and Martha off someplace, and Aunt Catherine and I were by ourselves. And Aunt Catherine said, 'Let's go for a nice long walk.' So we walked up to that big rock at the top of the hill, and she told me all about everything."

"About...everything?"

"About you. She told me how people don't know you very well. How you always seem so strong and so sure about things, but all the time you have a lot of pain hurting you down inside, because you've had a lot of strange things happen to you, and some of them you have to keep secret, and some of them you just *want* to keep secret, and that makes the hurting worse, and...and you're really not sure of anything much."

"Oh. She said that, did she?"

"Yes. And she said you needed me. And I said I didn't know about that, but she said oh yes, you did, and she thought if I went and lived with you now maybe I could help you get over all that hurting and everything. But she wasn't telling me I *had*

478

to, she said. It was up to me."

"I see. Up to you."

"And then I figured out that Uncle Isaac had taken the others away so Aunt Catherine could talk to me about all that. So I guess it was pretty important."

For the first time in the conversation the boy turned his eyes directly on Lucius. "Is it true, Papa? What she told me?"

Lucius hesitated for a moment before replying, "I expect it is, Justin. I have never heard your Aunt Catherine utter an untruthful word. But I can tell you this. That part about my needing you—*that* was most certainly the truth."

"Well then . . ." Justin chose his words carefully. "I guess I need you too, Papa. I guess we need each other."

"Yes, I, Uh . . ." Lucius's voice cracked. He cleared his throat hurriedly and went on, "I think that's the perfect way to put it." He looked away, brushing at the corner of his eye with a fingertip.

On the way back they walked hand in hand.

"Do you have any writing paper at home, Papa?" Justin asked.

"Sure I do. Need some?"

"I want to write a letter to Mama Sarah, and tell her I'll be living with you and Tía Dolores and Elena now."

"All right. Good."

"I got a letter from her not long ago. 'Master Justin Hargrave,' it said on the outside. A whole long letter, all my own."

"That was nice."

"You know what she said, Papa? First she said how glad she was to hear I was getting along so well and everything. Then at the end she said, 'When you see your father, please give him my love and tell him I wish we could forget all about the past and just be friends again.' Papa, did she do something bad to you?"

"No, no. Just a misunderstanding."

"Don't you write to her, Papa?"

"Oh sure, I, uh . . . well, I guess I have been a bit neglectful lately. So busy, you know? But, tell you what. When you write your letter I'll write one too, and we'll send 'em off together. How's that?"

"That's a good idea. Mama Sarah'll like that."

"I hope she will." Lucius smiled down at the boy, and squeezed his hand.

479

Isaac departed early in the morning. Lucius left the house first, went out to the stable, and in a little while brought his brother's horse and packmule around to the road in front of the house. Isaac was there waiting, alone.

"Goodbyes all said?" Lucius asked.

"Yep. Gave Dolores a little kiss, and Elena several of 'em, and, uh...well, Justin and I, we just shook hands real quick and let it go at that. No use draggin' it out. We both figure we're too old to cry, y'know?"

They walked slowly down the road together, leading the animals, avoiding each other's eyes.

"Soon's I get home I'll send a couple o' my men back over here with the rest of Justin's things," Isaac said. "It'll take two mules to haul it all, I expect. You know, that boy's got a whole darn library of books, all his own. Reads 'em, too. It'll take one mule just to haul those books." He chuckled.

They came to a gate where the *rancho* road joined the trail that led down to the Santa Clara Valley. Here they stopped. It was the place of parting.

"Wish you didn't have to rush off so fast," Lucius said.

"Got to get back. This is all pretty tough on Catherine, y'know. Tough on the children too. Bad enough for the older ones, but for Martha...she's not four yet, and she doesn't understand about Justin goin' away."

Lucius compressed his lips and stared at the ground. "Thanks for all you've done, old chum. Tell Catherine too...I'm sorry I've caused you so much pain."

"It's all right, Lucius. Everything's fine." Isaac held out his hand. "Well...be seein' you."

The handshake was intense but brief, then Isaac swung into his saddle.

"Why do you have to live so damned far away?" Lucius said peevishly.

Isaac gave a little shrug. "Oh, if we had it to do over again maybe we'd do it different, but..." He gazed off down toward the valley, and a distant look came into his eyes.

"I don't know. Sometimes Catherine and I sit together in the quiet of late evening and talk about the things we've been through. Our past, our early years...mine in Indiana, hers in Pennsylvania...our first marriages...the terrible journey west...it's all so far away now, it just seems like a long dream or somethin'. Sure, we miss things. And people. I'll never get over missin' Mama Sarah, you know that. But the dream's over now, we're awake and livin', and this is our real life."

He looked at Lucius again, and his face was lit with a comforting certainty. "We've found home at last, Lucius. It's Ponderosa Hill, California."

Lucius nodded. "G'bye, old chum. I'd wish you good luck, but it's no use saying *that*. You've got an angel of good fortune hovering over your head. It's always been there, and it always will be."

With a chuckle and a cheery wave Isaac moved off, and Lucius leaned against the gate and watched him until he was out of sight.

When he was halfway home Lucius found his family coming down the little road to meet him—Dolores and Justin on either side of Elena, holding the toddler by the hands. Dolores's face was in quiet repose, reflecting a mixture of sadness and contentment. Justin was red-eyed, trying hard to look cheerful.

Lucius came up to them and stopped, and studied their faces one by one. "Hey!" he said abruptly, and his eyes sparkled. "Let's play a game."

The others stared at him.

"What kind of a game, Papa?" Justin asked.

"Well, let's see. How about a skipping contest? That's always fun."

Dolores and Justin exchanged quick looks of astonishment.

"Skipping?" Dolores asked. "What is that . . . 'skipping'?"

"You mean like this?" Justin said, and gave an expert demonstration.

Dolores laughed, and little Elena squealed baby delight.

"That's it," Lucius said. "Used to do that quite a lot when I was a boy. Good for the digestion." He winked.

Holding hands and taking small steps so Elena could keep up, they skipped toward home.

(20)

A WEEK LATER Justin's things were brought from Ponderosa Hill. Two men came on horseback, each leading a heavily laden packmule, for, as Isaac had predicted, the worldly possessions of that eight-year-old—his clothes, a few trinkets and toys, the desk and chair that his Uncle Isaac had made for him, and, most prominent of all, his considerable collection of books—were far too great a load for one animal.

It was late afternoon when they arrived, and Lucius was supervising the work of Pablo and one of the *vaqueros*, who were putting up a fence around a grassy cattle range near the entrance to the *rancho*. He saw the small caravan coming up the road from the valley, recognized the lead rider as Ygnacio, a grizzled half-breed who was Isaac's sawmill foreman, and went hurriedly to meet him with a genial smile of welcome.

Ygnacio touched a finger to his sweat-stained hat. "*Buenas tardes* señor, I bring Señor Justin's things."

"Good Lord, he'll be glad to see you!" Lucius exclaimed, and indulged in a fond fatherly chuckle. "That boy's been driving us all crazy with his fretting, afraid you'd forget to come, or wouldn't find the way, or *some*thing."

The weathered features of the foreman crinkled with a kindly fondness of his own. "Leetle *señor*, he ees fine boy. He loves hees books."

"*That* he does," Lucius agreed emphatically. "That's why I insisted he stay at Ponderosa Hill so long—so he could get a good start on his education."

"*Sí, sí*," Ygnacio said, and this was followed by an awkward pause.

"Well, come on up to the house and have something to eat," Lucius said.

He started off at a brisk pace and the little pack train followed, and before they were halfway to the house Justin came running down the road to meet them, his face flushed with excitement.

Early the next morning Isaac's men said goodbye, mumbled their thanks to their young hostess Señora Dolores, who had so graciously seen to their comfort, and mounted their horses for the return trip home. Almost as an afterthought Ygnacio requested that Lucius accompany them as far as the *rancho* gate. Mildly puzzled, Lucius walked along with them.

At the gate Ygnacio pulled his horse to a stop and sent his companion on with the packmules, saying he would catch up in a minute. Then he drew from an inside jacket pocket a small piece of paper, tightly folded and sealed.

"Letter from Señora Cat'erine," he said as he handed the paper to Lucius. "She ask me to geeve it to you. Een private."

Lucius blinked at the neat, firmly disciplined handwriting on the outside of the letter, and studied his own name with a look of blank wonder as if he had never seen it before.

"Thanks," he murmured automatically. After a moment he glanced up to find himself held in Ygnacio's penetrating gaze.

"Uh . . . probably some instructions about Justin's things." Lucius seemed to be offering an answer to a difficult question.

Ygnacio smilingly shook his head. "I am not curious, *señor*. That ees why Señora Cat'erine send eet by me. I am a man who can be trusted."

Without waiting for further response he nodded and touched his hatbrim again. "*Buenos días, señor.*"

He was well on his way before Lucius recovered his presence of mind and called hastily after him, "Yes, uh . . . g'bye, Ygnacio. And thank you."

He waited until he was completely alone before he tore the letter open. It was a short note, and he read it through eagerly.

Dear Lucius,

Three precious things you claimed—a son, a daughter, and your true heart's wife.

I tear a part of myself away to give you back the first. The second, which is rightfully mine, I keep. The third is fantasy, a half-imagined remnant of another time that must have existed briefly once (because evidence remains, like Cinderella's slipper), but is gone.

There may be, somewhere in remote mountains, the heavenly little valley you have dreamed of, but it could never be found again. Never, never, never.

May our account be closed now?

Catherine.

Lucius leaned against a gate post and read the letter over and over again, his eyes lingering hungrily on each word. Then he looked up and saw Pablo coming toward him from the house. By the time the young Indian servant arrived, his master was squatting by the side of the gurgling little stream a short distance from the road, and was placidly watching the last of a handful of tiny paper fragments go spinning on the current down toward the lowlands miles away.

"Want to go on with that fence this morning, *señor*?" Pablo called.

Lucius was up and coming toward him, smiling brightly. "Right, Pablo." His voice rang with enthusiasm. "Let's get cracking."

He slapped the young man on the shoulder, and together they went off to start another day's work.

(21)

FROM THE JOURNAL of Lucius Hargrave:

They have brought my son to me. Justin is here, my family is complete, and I am a whole man again—or as whole a man as I can ever be.

He came in quiet reserve, wrapped in a dignity that was wondrous to behold in a child of eight. In a few short weeks his being here has wrought a cluster of small miracles. Our days are filled with busy-ness now; our Ranch of Quiet Waters is anything but quiet. We are hard at work with our crops, our cattle, our orchard, and our vineyard, and what I hope are the rudimentary beginnings of vigorous agricultural industry. And Justin is right in the middle of all of it, his inquiring mind darting tirelessly from one subject to the next, seeking knowledge with the constant demand of a plant seeking sunlight. He has given Dolores a comforting presence with which the painful emptiness left by the loss of her own boy-child is at least partially filled; he has given little Elena companionship and a big brother to adore; and he has given me back that which I first felt on a winter's day in far-off Louisiana eight years ago and lost somewhere in my wanderings since—an unshakable conviction that my son and I can hew the common path together, and together prevail over all the obstacles of the world.

Not long ago he made the first major responsible decision of his life. He left the comfortable home he had grown so used to with Isaac's family and came to me, and he did it because by some miraculous coalescing of universal truths he and I realized at the same moment that our need for each other was greater than all other considerations. But we both know that the impetus for that decision was given to us by someone else—by a woman to whom I am indebted for more than I can speak of, and whom Justin could not love more dearly if she were his natural mother. With wise and skillful patience our gentle teacher led us on a path of self-discovery, and let us find for ourselves the things she knew must be.

Soon after Justin arrived here two of Isaac's employees came from Ponderosa Hill, bringing the boy's belongings, and when he saw those familiar things in this strange new place his eyes brimmed with tears. It was not regret he felt—merely the normal welling of sadness a person feels at the sudden realization that a part of his life has ended. An hour later it was forgotten, and he was happily bustling about arranging his room.

My days have become tranquil at last, then, and for the second time in my life I feel impelled to put my journal away. It is a backward-looking thing, and I am suddenly too busy living in the present and preparing for the future to have time for looking back. The forlorn old leather satchel that contains it is woefully tattered, weary with age and long travels, and deserves a rest. It must be preserved with love and care, for in a certain special sense it is a kind of Cinderella's slipper—a shred of corporeal evidence remaining of something that once was and can never be again. It is all that is left of my father.

There was once a passionate man who lived and breathed and suffered in a distant time that is fading from my mind and will soon be past recall. He had battled demons of his own, and he was weary and heartsick, and he longed to leave the sordid world of sinners and dwell in fields of shining cleanliness.

Beloved phantom, may it be granted that you have found your clean fields at last.

So I will put this chronicle away, and take it up again perhaps soon, perhaps in future years still undreamed of, possibly never. But first let me disclaim all valor for myself, and set down gratitude in its place.

It is not I who slew the dragon in my breast. It was the kindness and wisdom of one virtuous woman, the infinite loving forgiveness of another, and the great hearts of both. Between them Catherine and Dolores have shamed me unto the darkness of death, and from that darkness have brought me forth to a new life.

If there be a God, cruel as He may be, let His Name be praised at least for the one everlasting blessing He has bestowed upon this world of vainglorious men. Good women.

Lucius Hargrave

At Rancho del Agua Mansa, California
One month into my thirty-third year
April 30th, 1848